"You have been broached," Lexander declared thought-fully. "Why such girlish modesty? Your first lesson, Marja, is that blushes can be appealing on occasion, but a steady diet of them is tiresome. Who did this to you?"

I was hardly able to speak. My hands clenched against the padded top of the bench. "Boys of the village."

"Oh, none were special to you?"

It was difficult to think, but one man sprang to mind. "There was a trader who came to Jarnby. He said he helped the chieftain launch a great *knarr*, and the big man tossed him a copper. He gave it to me." I didn't add that I had given the copper to the *olfs* because they were jealous of their gifts.

"And you fell in love with him," Lexander finished.

I shook my head as he pulled away. "No."

Lexander's brows rose. "That is the first you've said that interests me."

His sharp tone couldn't be mistaken, but why did he chastise me? Surely I didn't know my place, but it wasn't my fault. Yet I couldn't seem to form my lips around a protest. I submitted to Lexander, not because he had earned or deserved it, but because something inside of me surrendered to him. It was my first taste of life in his hands. . . .

To Serve and Submit

Susan Wright

A ROC BOOK

ROC

Published by New American Library, a division of
Penguin Group (USA) Inc., 375 Hudson Street,
New York, New York 10014, USA
Penguin Group (Canada), 90 Eglinton Avenue East, Suite 700, Toronto,
Ontario M4P 2Y3, Canada (a division of Pearson Penguin Canada Inc.)
Penguin Books Ltd., 80 Strand, London WC2R 0RL, England
Penguin Ireland, 25 St. Stephen's Green, Dublin 2,
Ireland (a division of Penguin Books Ltd.)
Penguin Group (Australia), 250 Camberwell Road, Camberwell, Victoria 3124,
Australia (a division of Pearson Australia Group Pty. Ltd.)
Penguin Books India Pvt. Ltd., 11 Community Centre, Panchsheel Park,
New Delhi - 110 017, India
Penguin Group (NZ), cnr Airborne and Rosedale Roads, Albany,
Auckland 1310, New Zealand (a division of Pearson New Zealand Ltd.)
Penguin Books (South Africa) (Pty.) Ltd., 24 Sturdee Avenue,
Rosebank, Johannesburg 2196, South Africa

Penguin Books Ltd., Registered Offices:
80 Strand, London WC2R 0RL, England

Published by Roc, an imprint of New American Library, a division of Penguin
Group (USA) Inc. Previously published in a Roc trade paperback edition.

First Roc Mass Market Printing, February 2007
10 9 8 7 6 5 4 3 2 1

One

Do not suppose that I should be discounted because I was born a wild child of the fens. Even before I knew my true nature, I served my gods well. I lived with moss in my hair and mud between my fingers, ever at home in the land that resides in water. I suppose the lesson of yielding, of one thing giving way to the next, flowing ever back and forth, was in my blood. My da's Noromenn family had lived in the village Jarnby between the fens and the Klaro Strait for four generations, while my mother's Beothuk ancestors had roamed Nauga Sea for longer than memory serves.

At birth, my mam heard my name called in the wind and knew that I had been touched by the Otherworld. Indeed, my kin said Marja was a fanciful name, more fit for a sprite than a girl. As soon as I began to walk, my da declared that I had the *vanderlust,* while my mam taught me how to hear the will of the land embodied by the *olfs*.

So I danced and sang for the *olfs* until the ones who favored me showed me where the bog iron nestled. I was one of many who searched for iron, but I had a true knack because I understood the spirits that dwelled in the land. There were places that could swallow a grown man without a trace, but I knew where the water had been banished. Yet there were many times, I must confess, when I returned with my sling-carry empty because I had been beguiled by the *olfs* into wasting away my day. Then my da would growl fiercely at me, for the smiths needed the iron to make their goods.

It was Lexander of Vidaris who showed me my true path. I was little more than a girl when Lexander appeared. His arrival was heralded by the beat of oars against the river and the low chanting that kept the rowers in time. I daresay I didn't hear the boat until it was nigh because of the heavy mist that shrouded the evening. But as I emerged from the fens with my sling-carry over my shoulder, I met my brother as he was driving the sheep back to our home pasturage. He skipped in front of our ragged herd, pointing his staff toward the river. "Marja, look!"

There, a vision emerged from the low-lying fog. The square, red-striped sail hung empty of wind as the swooping oars propelled the longship forward. The river was glassy flat, marred only by the ripples spreading from the boat. The towering prow was carved into a bird of prey with a fierce hooked beak and eyes that seemed to penetrate me even from afar.

Lexander stood with one hand resting on the sweepback wing of the mighty bird as if taming it with a touch. He called out a word and the oars broke their rhythm, splashing as the longship turned toward the shore. I had never seen a seagoing boat so far upriver before.

"Could it be a Hun?" my brother blurted out.

"Hush," I murmured. *Olfs* appeared around me, curious as always. I opened myself to them, and suddenly felt as if I were being swept away. I was lifted up like the wind, above my brother and the green bank of the river. It was so unexpected—and at odds with the nearly silent longship gliding toward us—that I abruptly broke my communion with the land.

The boat ran aground on the sloped bank near us with a solid scraping sound, belying the fantastical vision I had seen.

The sheep milled around us, clipping the rich grass along the river, while the *olfs* danced on the bank, showing off their chubby bodies and merry eyes in their excitement. My brother claimed he could see only the rainbow sparks that they emitted, but the *olfs* often revealed themselves to me, from their round red cheeks and curly hair to their tiny bare toes. When I was a small child I had often confused my kin by calling to the "babies" floating in the air, until I learned not to speak of the *olfs* to those who couldn't see them.

Now even the *olfs* couldn't distract me from the sight of Lexander. I didn't know his name, but I could feel his power. In truth, Lexander looked like a Hun chieftain, with the fierce, hawklike face of those from the land of the rising sun. My da often sang the saga of a battle with the brutal Hun who lived in the Auldland. They were said to have hair as black as midnight, but Lexander's head and face were as smooth as my palm. His fine wool cloak was bordered with blue and gold tabards, marking him as a wealthy man.

Lexander jumped down from the boat, landing lightly despite the height of the deck. "To be sure, I can hardly see them beneath the mud," he declared in amusement. He strode through the sheep to gaze down at us, two skinny marsh rats. All I saw were Lexander's tawny eyes, strangely bright with flickering depths.

My brother's mouth hung open, and his face and legs were streaked with dirt. His gray homespun tunic was fringed at the hem and hiked up by a rope around his waist. I surely looked no different.

"You, the tall one, be you a girl or a boy?" Lexander asked me.

I felt my first strange thrill of yielding to command. "I'm a woman grown," I said, though I had only just matured.

"Do you live in the village?" he asked.

"Our da works the smithy," my brother replied proudly. With a final, lingering gaze, Lexander returned to his longship. A few of his crew pushed them from shore as the others manned the oars. The graceful boat turned and headed back to our village on the bay.

It could have been a minor thing, a chance encounter far up the river. Traders and travelers often made their way to Jarnby to acquire iron tools and gear. Yet everything around me stilled. The incessant humming of the guardian spirits and the *olfs* grew hushed, a warning of distance to come between me and my beloved watery world. The oars of the boat beat in a compelling rhythm, beckoning me forward. But my brother shattered my trance by calling after the straying sheep.

When my da returned home that evening, he said that a great man from Fjardemano, a prosperous island in the commonwealth of Viinland, had come to bargain for me. Lexander of Vidaris was known throughout Nauga Sea for producing finely trained slaves in the art of personal service and pleasure. It was said that his slaves lived in the courts of rulers in the Auldland and beyond, growing powerful themselves through their talents.

Lexander had pledged to my da that he would return next year, after the ice broke, to tender his final offer for me. He had agreed to give me fine clothes and costly ornaments, and sworn that I would be well cared for. In exchange, he would give our family two strong cows.

My poor mam, long separated from her own Skraeling people because of her love for my da, knew many stories of the ancient Norogods as well as those of the Otherworld. But this tale clearly troubled her. Nothing was ever exactly as it seemed, and Lexander of Vidaris was not a man to be easily deciphered. I knew what she had taught us—that the *inua,* life force, of the dead lived on in newborns who were named for their ancestors. That certain signs in the sky and water could reveal when the guardian spirits were angered about taboos that had been broken. And that Arnaaluk, the sea-mother, provides food from her generous depths, protecting her people. My da's stories were all about the Norogods, recounting deeds of daring and jealous sparring. The brash exploits of these gods seemed much like my fair uncles and aunts who sported and fought in our cold village.

My eldest brother, who worked in the smithy, said that Lexander had described me as "the girl with the faraway look." My mam, her body worn with childbearing and endless hard days, pulled me to her side at the loom as if loath to let me go. In truth I felt more eagerness than fear to hear about Vidaris, a wealthy estate that basked in the sun off the southern waters of the Nauga Sea. Though it was only a day's sail away, to me it sounded as mysterious and far away as the Auldworld itself. But by evening's end, my da grew ill-tempered at the thought of a man owning me. He swore that I would not be sold as a thrall and that I would marry as my older sister had. He decreed there would be no more talk of the stranger.

Yet everything was disturbed after Lexander came to us, and word of his offer spread quickly through our iron-making village and outlying homesteads. I looked at everyone with new eyes, changed by my vivid impression of Lexander. He was different from the people I knew. His jaw was perfectly smooth like the Skraelings, but their faces were flattened and round while he had the prominent nose and cheekbones of my da's people. He was neither fair nor dark, his skin, like his eyes, shimmered gold as if lit within by the sun.

I wondered if he was a half-breed like me and my siblings. We were different, too. We spoke Skraeling among ourselves, and our hair was bronzed on top and dark beneath, like the peat I dug in to find the iron nuggets. From my da, I got my long limbs, while my mam gave me her almond eyes with the ability to see what others couldn't. She would sit sometimes and chew her thumb in the deepest twilight, staring as my younger sister bobbed the spindle up and down, teasing out a long cord of wool. Sometimes she told me of her visions—that my older sister would marry and go south to live, and that my baby brother would fall into feverish fits that would dull his mind.

I didn't share with my mam the dream that took hold of me after Lexander came. I remembered his few words to me and the tone of command in his voice, feeling light-headed as if it were happening anew. I can hardly say why the restlessness moved me when so many others were content to live and die on the same patch of ground. Too often I was lured into climbing to the highlands overlooking the fens, and I never felt so alive as when I could endlessly trace the layers of folding hillocks spreading before me. Whenever I stumbled into a dell that I had never seen before, it nearly made me burst with pleasure. My fingers would sink into the earthy muck as I became one with the water, trickling and dripping through the hollow. I wallowed in the joy of discovery, communing with the spirits and *olfs* that inhabited each place.

In this way, Lexander laid a trap for me. My da would never have sold me on first sight, and even if he had, my wild nature would have resisted the training. But thinking on it for a full turn of seasons, working it over in my mind, I made myself ready for him. As Lexander told me later, the waiting period served to weed out those who couldn't accept the duties of a pleasure slave. He often returned to promising prospects only to discover the young man or woman had found a mate and refused servitude. The ones who were adrift, alone, or eager for something new—like I was—fell into his hands like ripe cloudberries.

The winter was cold and wet, as it always was. Long after Lexander was no longer talked about in Jarnby, after the snows and darkness sealed the strait with ice, I still thought of him. The day the *olfs* whispered that our harbor would soon be free of towering bergs and would become a glassy smooth sea again, I wondered with a sinking heart if Lexander had forgotten me.

One morning soon after, I left the village and was heading out to forage for iron. My brother caught up to me on the edge of the fens with news that a ship had been sighted. The sail sported red and white stripes, like Lexander's longship.

By the time we returned, the boat was close to Jarnby. The mast dipped as the waves rocked it, while the oars lifted and fell with the rowing of the crew. The villagers gathered, leaving their work as word rapidly spread that Lexander had returned. My mam appeared in the doorway of our longhouse holding the youngest in her arms.

When the boat reached the shore, Lexander jumped out and strode through the spring mud, soiling his knee-high leather boots. Our village suddenly seemed smaller under his gaze. He smiled, his eyes unerringly seeking me out. "I've come for Marja."

My name sounded exotic with the rolling caress that he gave it. I should have been frightened of this stranger, but I felt only the exhilaration of being chosen. He had returned for me!

My da arrived from the smithy, his great belly swathed in a dirty apron, as Lexander's men lowered two cows on slings from the ship. To my practiced eye, the brown and white cattle were in milk and well fleshed, unlike our poor bony animals. It would double our herd. My da seemed fair taken with them, licking his lips at the sight.

"What assurance do you give me of her safety?" my da bargained, and in those words I heard the end of my life on the fens. I looked at the younger children who needed the milk. It would mean more food for all in this lean time until the sea hunts. There were too many babes born in our home, and it was unlikely I would marry. My love for wandering the fens had marked me long before Lexander came.

Lexander promised reports on my progress and offered to bring me back next spring for a visit. The bargain was concluded when my brothers were called to take the cows. I was a slave. Foreboding began to grow inside of me. It had been a stirring fancy, but now I would have to leave in truth. Perhaps my kin were right and my desire to roam was leading me too far astray. It might be best for me to stay on the fens, where I belonged . . .

I glanced at my da, but the decision had been made. I had made it myself when day after day I went into the fens like an errant child rather than staying at home like my younger sister to do a woman's work beside my mam. It was made in the fibers that formed me, in the blood of my da's grandda who had set sail across the endless waves of the ocean to come to this fertile land. How could I be content to stay? And what reason did they have to keep me?

Lexander saw my uncertainty. "I must know now, Marja. Will you serve and submit to me?"

I felt no urge to deny him. "Yes," I whispered.

"Then come with me." His tone was more kindly than not.

The dogs began barking, breaking the hush, and my brothers called out to one another as they pastured the cows. My da's elder sister hurried up to say, "I will put her things together." I thought of my childish treasures secreted in a leather bag under the moss of our sleeping ledge, but Lexander put an end to that.

"She needs nothing that I cannot give her," Lexander said firmly.

My mam passed the babe away, and I went to stand before her on the paving stones at the entrance to our home. Her hands gathered the damp folds of my cloak, as if to feel me there in front of her. She looked into my eyes and saw my need to fly. She had felt it herself long ago when she left her own people and followed my da from Helluland to live in Jarnby. She accepted what her vision showed her, as always.

"I will see you as I spin," she assured me, "and I will know if you do well." With a narrow look at Lexander, she added, "Think on me if you wish to depart, and your father will come to redeem you."

"I will think of you always," I promised, though I knew my own lack. Often I forgot my family when I went into the fens.

Lexander smiled coldly at my mam, perhaps reading me better than she did. "You shall see; she will prosper in Vidaris."

With that, my mam reluctantly released me. Lexander silently held out a gloved hand to me. I couldn't help but contrast my world with Lexander's—his healthy well-muscled oarsmen, and magnificent longship piled with boxes and barrels of goods. Painted rattles of iron rings hung from the mast, making a merry jangle to ward off evil spirits. Perhaps because my mind was savage and unformed, I followed the shiny lure, willingly going with him.

Lexander led me down to the waterfront as his crew readied the longship to launch. He lifted me up in one strong arm and deposited me on the deck. It felt as if I were standing on the curved, grassy roof of our longhouse. The green pastures spread along the river, with the darker hillocks of the fens beyond.

"May the blessings of Arnaaluk be on my daughter!" my mother cried out.

The crew lifted the sail and tightened the ropes as it filled with wind. The longship pulled away from shore, and my kin called farewell. I raised my hand until I caught a last glimpse of my brother, closest to me in age, standing next to our sister on the shore. Our longhouse was a low green mound among the others, with only the wooden doorway and a line of smoke to indicate it was my home. The nearby longhouses were all alike, with brown tracks and low palisades for the animals between them. Too soon, Jarnby melded into the fens, while the highlands were a formidable ridge beyond.

We sailed into the Klaro Strait, its waters tinted a deep, icy blue. Fog hung thickly in the folds of the land, revealing an inlet or a strand of black spruce in the clefts. I held on to the smooth wooden side of the boat, swaying with the up and down of the waves. Listening to the creaking of the ropes that held the sail taut, I could hear the sea spirits speaking to me. Unlike *olfs,* spirits were disembodied and could reveal themselves only through visions. The sea spirits evoked endless depths and the creatures that flowed through their waters, dangerous predators and beasts that looked strangely like clouds or rocks.

A light but steady rain fell as we sailed south into the Nauga Sea, leaving Markland behind. Lexander tried to give me *skyr,* thick, milky whey, which he said would sit easy on my stomach. But I couldn't eat. He did insist that I drink some watered mead. I crumpled my day-meal of fried porridge my mam had given me into the sea to appease the spirits for my passage. I usually would give a sacrifice to the *olfs* on the fens, eating some myself as well.

It wasn't long before the rocking motion began to make me feel ill. The oarsmen passed comments about my condition among themselves, wagering on my ability to hold my stomach. I did, though I didn't know how long I would have to endure.

But none of that mattered. The sail bellied full, lifting me from the moorings of my life. In spite of my illness, I went to the bow to look ever ahead. Lexander smiled indulgently, reclining on a padded bench in the stern. It was as if my body underwent a paroxysm of grief, clenching and convulsing at leaving behind the land and *olfs* that I loved, while my spirit soared in front of the great vessel urging me ever onward.

The journey across the sea seemed endless as the sun crossed the sky between the banks of clouds. I was groggy with nausea and fatigue when a shout went up. A light had been sighted. As we neared the island of Fjardemano, a great bonfire pierced the fog shrouding the banks, leading Lexander home. By then the day began to die, and we were in the gloaming.

The shore was backed by a red sandstone bluff, with the fluted sides starkly bare of plants. The sand of the narrow beach was the same distinctive red. At the top, a woven palisade stretched among the trees, blocking my view beyond. The fence was very tall, made of saplings that were bent around sturdy posts. I wondered uneasily who Lexander could possibly fear. A palisade such as this could defend against a Skraeling attack, not that there had been any in recent memory. The chieftains, under the direction of the overlord of Viinland, had made peace or pushed back any Skraelings who were inclined to raid. My mam had told me stories of those dark times when many of the Beothuk had been killed, mistaken for the vicious Skraeling tribes who lived farther inland.

The longship was moored with a flurry of shouts as the oarsmen tied down the sail. I stumbled as I stepped onto the wooden dock, feeling as if the world were still moving around me. Lexander noticed my lack of balance and casually supported my arm, the first time he touched me since we had left Jarnby. I hardly noticed the useful dock, which allowed us to walk from the boat to the beach without wetting our feet.

Lexander and I climbed a tall flight of wooden steps to reach the top of the bluff. The evergreens in Fjardemano were dense cones of bright emerald, unlike the spruce of my homeland, which spread dark scraggly arms against the sky. As we climbed higher, I could see the shoreline receding into the distance, with the bluff rising to form the dramatic line of vermilion cliffs. A mass of green conifers crowded the top.

When we passed through a wide gate in the palisade, the sky was still bright enough for me to see a number of structures amid the clearings. Lexander took me up the gravel path to the largest structure, much longer than my old home. Sheer walls rose as if a god had chiseled them from the ground. The roof didn't have grass growing on it, and the pitch seemed impossibly steep.

It was so unlike the low, turf-covered duns of Jarnby that I gaped in surprise. I couldn't accept what lay before me. I thought that my own confusion was interfering in my ability to sense the spirits of the place. It would have been easier if some *olfs* had appeared to lend me their aid, but there were none.

We skirted the huge structure; then the gravel path began to curve back down. For a moment I was high enough to see the woven palisade encircling a series of low hills, scattered with wooden buildings and a few familiar sod longhouses. Leafy trees were swaying over small ponds in the clefts. Spreading far beyond the palisade were plowed fields, as red as the cliffs, while in the distance lay the shadowy forest.

Since I could not commune with the land directly, I had to ask, "What is this?"

Lexander gestured broadly. "This is Vidaris, your new home, Marja. Five dozen slaves and freemen live here, working the fields and running the *haushold*."

It was nothing like Jarnby, which blended into the green banks of the river. Yet despite its differences, Vidaris smelled the same—burning wood, cooked meat, human waste, and too many animals crowded together. There were more cattle than sheep, another indicator of wealth. As the dusk deepened, I was heartened to see that children ran about in the distance. Their playful shouts were almost drowned out by the mournful braying of hounds.

The gravel path led back down to the stream. Lexander guided me up the steps into a small building next to it. The room was long and narrow. A light burned on the near wall, a tiny flame fed by the whale oil within a bubbled glass sphere. A glow also came from coals slowly burning out in the hearth in the opposite wall. Under my feet were rectangular slabs laid a finger's width apart. They were exactly the same size, slightly longer and wider than my hand, and laid together to form a flat, hard floor. My eyes followed the straight, crisscrossing grooves endlessly like a spell. I had never seen a room without a dirt floor before.

"Master!" a young man called out as he ran up the steps. He was as clean and as white as a new-bloomed flower, with long curling brown hair. His tunic was belted with gold cord like the lacings that held his elegant, fitted shoes. I could feel how much warmer it was here in Viinland, but his scanty attire startled me. His face was without a beard, making him appear younger than he was.

Lexander briefly caressed the young man's hair. "See to my things, Bjorn. The men left my boxes by the *haushold*." His tone indicated he expected to be obeyed without question. The young man spared only a brief glance at me as he left.

"Is he really a slave?" I asked when he was gone.

"Yes. Bjorn is one of my treasures. You should look to him as your guide for how to behave. He is ever ready to please."

I stared after the beautiful slave as he ran back up the gravel path to the large structure. If my mother could see Bjorn, she would think him a godling, he was so fine. It seemed as if I had been granted a rare gift the day Lexander had chosen to sail up our river. But I knew there had to be a price for all that I would gain. It must be that way, as air gave way to water, as did water to earth, and earth to wind in an endless cycle.

Lexander stepped close to me, and I looked up to his face. I was used to being taller than most people—a long-limbed, lanky girl. My softer, rounder cousins were always favored over me.

He removed his gloves with practiced motions. "I should sluice you down proper before the bath." He examined me, his full lips twisting in distaste. "Well, nothing left but to do it. Off with your clothes, girl. Put them over there by the door. The house servants may be able to use them as rags."

I squirmed at the thought of disrobing in front of him. "Here?"

"'Tis time to rid yourself of false modesty, Marja. I own you now, and you will do as you're told. Or you'll do it with tears in your eyes."

My da had switched my brothers on occasion when they ran off without doing their duties. The switch left red slashes across the backs of their legs and stung like a hundred bees, they claimed. But da had never done it to me. My mam told him it was beyond my power that the *olfs* called me so.

But Lexander did not look at me with indulgence, and he surely owned me as much as my da ever did. I slowly untied my cloak, hesitating until Lexander impatiently urged me to be quick. He went to pour a bucket of water as I dropped the scrap of wool that served as my cloak. Uneasily, I glanced behind me, but Bjorn was not in sight. I slipped my arms out of the loose sleeves of my tunic and pulled it over my head. Both were wet through from the generous spray of the sea. I tossed the soggy bundle down near the door, left in only my skin.

"Stand still," Lexander ordered as he dashed water from a bucket against my face and chest. I cringed, but the water was as warm as if it had lain in the sun. Lexander walked around and threw the rest on my rear. It poured off me onto the floor, running through the cracks and out a clever hole in the wall. I could hear the stream splashing on the other side.

"Get into the smaller bath." Lexander sat on the bench and pulled off his own splattered knee-high boots.

Muscles aching from the rocking motion of the longship,

I slid into the square pool, grateful for the water that covered me. It was warm and so clear I could see the mosaic tiles embedded in the sides and bottom, each a slightly different shade of blue. The pattern formed a sinuous wave in the floor and sides. It was cleaner and larger than the pools in the fens that I normally bathed in, and it was much warmer than the sea. Yet it felt empty. I couldn't understand why there were no sprites delighting in the water. Sprites might be tiny invisible creatures, but they were able to touch this world much like *olfs* could.

Lexander stood up, and with a mocking glint in his eyes, undid the cord of his pants and slid them off, leaving only his long belted shirt. I drew back. "You don't mean to—"

"I would take you if I wanted to," Lexander interrupted. He went to gather a basket and brought it to the pool. "But as you are now, you hold no interest for me."

Stung, I crossed my arms over my chest as he stepped into the pool. The water reached just above his knees, well below the hem of his shirt.

"Let's get on with it." Lexander sighed as he picked up his first implement.

The brush was made of musk-ox bristles, cut to uniform length. It scraped my flesh unmercifully. The skin verily peeled from my body and burned from the foam he rubbed into the bristles. He scrubbed me down in broad swaths, muttering to himself about "years of filth." Then he forced me under the water to rinse. If I had known what he had in mind for me, I would surely have chosen a simple rutting.

As I righted myself in the pool, Bjorn returned to the baths. His face was a cool white oval in the dimness. His features were truly distinguished, particularly his aquiline nose. Lexander called, "Bjorn, come help me with this rat's nest of hair. I only hope that there's something salvageable within."

Bjorn obeyed instantly, his hands joining Lexander's on my head. I crouched in the tub, shivering despite the warmth of the water. Darts of pain shot through my skull as they tugged and pulled at the small braids that held the waving mass away from my face. Throughout they exclaimed at the things they found—bits of cord and string, dried stems from flowers woven into the braids, and tufts of white and black wool. They amassed a motley pile next to the bath, and the more they stared down at me in disfavor, the smaller I felt.

Lastly they brushed, each taking a side, snagging the snarls and making the pain flash through my tender scalp. But I closed my lips tight, refusing to let them know how they hurt me. It was like the invisible hands that plucked at me in the fens, pinching and tweaking the very lashes from my eyes. I had learned that you don't show weakness or evil spirits will take more than they need, just to delight in your torment. So I sat as straight as I could, bracing myself.

When they were done, Lexander lathered my hair, soothing the fierce burning of my scalp with creamy lotion. Bjorn made me lean over and poured buckets of water on my head, rinsing again and again until they judged my head free of vermin and grime. Bjorn took the brackish pile pulled from my hair with an expression of frank disgust, his fine nose turned away. He tossed it far beyond the stable yard and carefully washed his hands when he returned.

Lexander concentrated on pinning my hair to the top of my head with two bone combs. "Tell Sigrid to bring my meal to table. She will serve me tonight."

A flicker of resentment passed over Bjorn's face, and I learned later that he competed with Sigrid as a favorite of Lexander's. He inclined his head gracefully. "As you wish, Master." He withdrew with a measured gait that was the height of grace.

Lexander turned and caught my wide-eyed stare. "As I said, Bjorn is perfectly trained. You will learn soon enough. You, too, will draw all eyes when you stroll through a room, and be able to please a patron with the slightest touch."

I held my breath, remembering the days on the fens that I had dreamed away, thinking of what it would mean to be a pleasure slave. All I knew of pleasure was the artless rutting I had enjoyed with some boys in Jarnby. But the way

Bjorn moved held a deeper promise of what I could become.

I thought we were finished, but Lexander emptied the dirty water in the bath through a plug in the bottom. I realized that was why no sprites could settle in the tub. Then Lexander filled the bath again by tilting an enormous vat that swung out from the fire, pouring in a stream of freshly warmed water.

The second brush he used was softer, but the burning foam was more copious. He moved the brush in firm swirls across my neck, down my back, and under my arms. Every finger was scrubbed from my knuckles to nails. As he moved downward, briskly rubbing between my legs, I felt a sudden rush of heat. Bracing myself against him for a heady moment, I longed for a more sensual touch. The feeling persisted even as he continued to treat me like a root he had pulled from the ground, to be scraped clean before being pounded for mash. Then he clipped the nails on my feet and hands and let my hair down to trim it evenly above my waist. Several ragged handfuls were thrown aside, and I was glad Bjorn had been sent away so he wouldn't see me shorn like a sheep.

The cleansing left me shiny pink and throbbing. My nipples stood erect, having received far too much attention. Even my toes felt distinct, aching like new-grown buds. He smeared salve on the chilblains on my hands and feet, soothing the sores that always burned raw in the winter.

Then Lexander examined me, bending me over the bench and bringing the small, round lamp close. His fingers prodded my crotch, pulling at the nether lips and questing inside me. At first he was gentle; then I gasped as he slid his finger in fully deep.

"You've been broached," Lexander declared thoughtfully. "Why such girlish modesty? Your first lesson, Marja, is that blushes can be appealing on occasion, but a steady diet of them is tiresome." I tensed, feeling his finger still deep inside me. It wiggled in emphasis. "Who did this to you?"

I was hardly able to speak in such a position. My hands

clenched against the padded top of the bench. "Boys of the village."

"Oh? Were none special to you?"

It was difficult to think, but one memory sprang to mind. "There was a trader who came to Jarnby. He was from Tillfallvik. He said he helped the chieftain launch a great *knaar,* and the big man tossed him a copper. He gave it to me." I didn't add that I had given the copper to the *olfs* because they were jealous of their gifts.

"And you fell in love with him," Lexander finished.

I shook my head as he pulled away. "No."

Lexander's brows rose. "That is the first you've said that interests me."

His sharp tone couldn't be mistaken, but why did he chastise me? Surely I didn't know my place, but that wasn't my fault. Yet I couldn't seem to form my lips around a protest. I submitted to Lexander, not because he had earned it or deserved it, but because something inside of me surrendered to him. It was my first taste of life in his hands.

Two

I woke the next morning in a narrow room with a remarkable peaked ceiling. It was filled with a dozen slaves, each sleeping on a moss-filled mat, which were laid end to end along the walls. My fuzzy wool blanket was made of a much finer thread and weave than I was accustomed to. After sleeping my whole life on an earthen ledge in a pile among my sisters, it was luxury indeed.

The *haushold* was a remarkable structure. I learned later that the rectangular blocks were bricks made from clay deposits molded by hand along with the red earth of Vidaris. The slaves slept in one of four halls that formed a huge rectangle with a courtyard in the center. The fire hall was the longest, with the dining table at one end. The kitchen hall had rows of storerooms and a scullery. I noticed several round baking ovens in the kitchen yard when Lexander had brought me up from the baths. He informed me that the fourth hall had chambers for guests, himself, and his consort, Helanas. It was the first I had heard mention of Helanas, though it was to be expected that a man such as Lexander had a wife. He warned me their hall was not to be entered unless we were given express permission.

I shyly imitated the other slaves as they straightened their bedding, then dressed in my new woolen tunic and sandals. My legs felt strangely bare with such a short skirt, but it was warm enough to be comfortable. The shoes would take more getting used to, and I scuffed clumsily over the brick floor.

As they filed into the fire hall, I followed a frightened young man my own age. He had cried in the night, and his face was still streaked by traces of tears as we sat down at the long dining table. Niels had arrived at Vidaris a few days before me, all the way from Hop on the southern mainland of Viinland. I was envious of his experiences, but he seemed childish despite his advantages.

Several of our fellow slaves served us generous bowls of hot oat porridge. I sat on a bench next to two Skraeling girls, watching them sadly fumble with a flat wooden utensil. When I tried to use my fingers to eat my porridge, my hand was sharply rapped.

I dropped the bowl and turned in shock to find Lexander's consort, Helanas, glaring down at me. A red silk veil was wrapped over her head and around her neck, trailing down to her waist, where it was belted with her pleated dress. With her tawny skin and full lips, Helanas resembled Lexander. But her dark eyes were cruel.

My knuckles throbbed, as Helanas ordered, "You will use your spoon or your food will be removed!" She caressed the heavy leather flap at the end of the rod.

Bjorn smirked from across the table, his patrician nose crinkling with distaste. From the other slaves' expressions, I could tell they, too, thought I was a barbarian. Only the two Skraeling girls next to me stared into their porridge tremulously. It showed me how alone I was.

If I was lost in my new role, the tension among the elder slaves made things worse. After the meal, when I tried to step outside to see the clouds, I discovered that they were ordered to make sure we didn't run away. I wanted only to get in touch with the spirits of Vidaris, but it seemed they thought I would try to go home. The slaves barred me from the outer doors, claiming we would all be punished if any of us left.

Rosarin, a girl with striking golden hair, took pity on me and led me into the section of the courtyard used by the pleasure slaves. The enclosed yard had benches and gravel pathways, but the greenery was more restrained than the abundant garden I could see through an open archway.

That part of the courtyard was a veritable paradise in spring with exotic broad-leafed bushes and miniature trees in bloom. Braziers released scented smoke, warming the air.

I felt an otherworldly summons from within, but when I went to the archway, Bjorn blocked my way. "The inner courtyard is not for us."

"It calls to me," I tried to explain. But Bjorn shook his head firmly. It was the first time I had felt the presence of spirits in Vidaris, and my longing to commune with other-worldly creatures pressed on me like a sore. But Sigrid, the oldest slave, joined Bjorn to guard the archway. The spirits cast a craving inside of me to enter until I was almost determined to defy them.

Helanas arrived and my infant rebellion shriveled under her glare. Then my training began in earnest. Helanas ordered, "*Gesig!*" and the slaves all knelt in surrender. I tried to emulate the others, going down on my knees on a woven grass mat with my hands held behind my back.

Helanas circled, correcting our poses with harsh smacks of her crop. She adjusted me with skilled hands, prodding my lower back and pulling the hair on the very top of my head until I sat straight and tall, resting my buttocks on my heels, with my eyes downcast. After a few minutes of sustaining the pose, my body began to feel strained in places I had never felt before. But the older slaves held perfectly still and at ease.

Helanas ordered us to release, then slowly proceeded through a series of poses starting with the kneeling ones. Many of them made me blush at the way I presented myself, nether parts raised and offered for viewing or access. Thankfully Niels and the two Skraeling sisters were as awkward as I during the drill, so Helanas concentrated her attention between the four of us. I was sweating and shaking by the third pose.

Helanas frightened me in a way I hadn't felt with Lexander. He had watched my every reaction, adjusting his response to my own. He had sent Bjorn away from the baths just when I was feeling most pitiful, so he could concentrate on me. Helanas, on the other hand, randomly swiped her crop at us as if bored and impatient, growing more harsh as the session continued. I doubted she even knew my name because she only addressed me as "girl."

The older slaves were limber and stretched into graceful curves. They led each other on a drill of more advanced poses while the four novices watched. I doubted I would ever be able to balance and extend in a like manner.

After the long session, I was relieved when Helanas sent us off. The house servants assigned tasks to each of us. Some were also slaves, but they ordered us to do everything from refilling the braziers and water vats to brushing the brick floors and walls. A matronly freewoman named Hallgerd was in charge, and she used a long wooden spoon to smack heads and buttocks whenever we moved too slowly. Hallgerd was imposing, with wide copper broaches pinning a white apron to her pleated dress. There was a helping of her mistress's ferocity in Hallgerd, so I did exactly as she ordered and received no undue attention.

At one point I stumbled across Lexander training the older slaves in the hall where we slept. It was the first time I had seen him that day. The slaves were all naked, and Sigrid was kneeling in front of our master. Lexander's tunic was raised, and he firmly held the back of Sigrid's head. Her hands were helplessly clasped at the small of her back.

I hastily retreated, but Lexander's head turned. He took in my shock, then gazed down with approval at Sigrid, his hips pumping languorously.

I returned to my duties with a new understanding of how the poses would eventually be put to use. It unnerved me to imagine myself kneeling in front of Lexander like Sigrid had done. But part of me wished I could.

Late that afternoon, the pleasure slaves returned to the baths for our grooming. Lexander was waiting for us. I was grateful that he had a full dozen slaves to deal with so that I didn't receive another prolonged scrubbing. But he seemed to delight in cleansing the tender parts of my body, as if to prove that he owned every part of me. The older slaves bathed each other, and by the firelight I could see they stared with envy whenever Lexander touched me.

From the talk I had overheard among the servants, our master and mistress came from faraway Stanbulin, the gateway to the Orient. My brother had nearly been right when he had called Lexander a Hun. Helanas was as fine as Lexander, formed near as perfectly as a woman could be—tall, curvaceous, with powerful limbs and refined features. Her only flaw was her muddy-blond hair, which was very thin and lay close to her skull. The rest of her body was perfectly smooth, like Lexander's. They rubbed lotion onto us to remove most of our hair as well.

Each of the slaves had their own special beauty, though we were all tall and slender, with lean limbs and lithe bodies. Rosarin appeared to be as haughty as Bjorn, but she was kind to me, trimming the front of my wavy hair so it flowed neatly like her own thick tresses. The two Skraeling sisters were like twin shadows, with dusky skin and the narrow black eyes typical of the icy north. The male that caught my attention was not the dramatic redheaded Sverker, but Ansgar, who had a calm reserve that was pleasant compared to the constant orders of Bjorn and Sigrid. Those two relished taking control whenever Lexander was busy elsewhere. I could tell the other slaves didn't like it, but in spite of myself I couldn't help but obey, refilling the baths and stoking the fire as ordered, all the while admiring their elegance.

Under their tutelage, a new Marja appeared. My hair, which Lexander had despaired of, was commented on most favorably. The bronzed layer on top shifted and glistened gold at the slightest movement, accenting the waves that grew tighter near my face. My almond eyes were green with brown flecks, much like ordinary moss, but they were framed by startlingly dark brows and long lashes. The misty light of the fens had given my skin a fairer glow than Rosarin's, even though she was blond. How could I not admire this new Marja who appeared in the silver mirrors of Vidaris?

*   *   *

As the days wore on, the stringent physical and mental discipline of training was difficult, but I was warm and well fed for the first time in my life. I missed my mam, but sometimes as I went about my duties, I felt as if she were near. Then I knew she was thinking about me, and I willed myself to reach her across the distance. Our *inua* was too weak to truly commune, but the spirits of the land, air, and water lent us their aid so our minds could touch.

She must have felt my anxiety born of confinement in the *haushold*. I went outside only during our daily trip to the baths. And that wasn't enough to make me stop missing the wind and the rising scents of the warming season on this beautiful island. I did everything I was told with one eye on the sky, watching for the sudden rain squalls that poured into the courtyard. The fields outside were greening with new growth, and the trees budded with flowers that Ansgar said would give way to fruit, ripened by the full-bodied sun. I longed to go into the woods or kneel to sing to the tiny sprouts that appeared in the grass alongside the gravel path. But I never escaped the watching eyes of my fellow slaves.

I was like one of the brightly colored birds in the inner courtyard, kept in a fanciful cage and singing with frantic hope that I would be released. I soon realized that was why the spirits of the garden kept calling me, to right the wrong that Helanas had done by caging those pretty creatures for her amusement. Early one morning before the dawn mist lifted, I woke before the others and managed to sneak into the courtyard. I lifted the tiny latch and felt a burst of gratitude from the red bird as it flashed out. Carefully I relatched the cage, fearing there would be terrible repercussions. Yet I also freed the other two birds, blue with orange throats, before sounds from the kitchen hall forced me to flee. As I returned to our hall, I sensed the spirits within the courtyard were finally appeased.

Later that day, an *olf* revealed itself to me. I was fetching a cask of pressed-seed oil in the storeroom for Hallgerd when I heard faint, bell-like laughter. It was up high, near the thick slanted beams of the ceiling, so I knew it couldn't be one of the other slaves. It was like the sound I heard on the fens whenever the *olfs* beckoned me. This time it circled the room, seemingly delighted with my eager interest. Then a whisper dropped into my ear. *"Cheerful wayfarer, cheerful giver, cheerful worker doth gain all!"*

It disappeared in a puff of scent that was so rich and earthy that I breathed in deeply. As it faded, I was alone again and knew why. The otherworldly creature was taunting me for my discontent. I had forgotten my earliest lesson—a happy heart was the way to peace. I resolved to freely accept my confinement and no longer pine. When the missing birds were never mentioned within hearing of the slaves, I knew the *olf* had somehow deflected suspicion from me.

After that, I brought the *olf* the remnants of my bowl of milk every morning, which it licked clean sometimes as I sat nearby. As the days passed, I began to see through the shimmer in the air the shape of the little creature of the land. It was neither male nor female, as all *olfs* were, and its smile showed small pointed teeth. Many times I found the floors of the hall were cleaned in the night. Then I would sit in the storeroom and sing songs to entertain the *olf*. It cheered me to know there were otherworldly creatures here that I simply couldn't see, but once I had proven myself to them, perhaps they would acknowledge me.

Then one night, only eight slaves were sent to bed. The four eldest, including Bjorn, remained in the baths with Lexander and Helanas. It was not uncommon for us to be trained in small groups, so no mention was made of it as redheaded Sverker led us back to our hall. I laid my head down near Niels' feet, as always. But as the others fell into soft snores, I heard the soft laughter again. It was the first time the *olf* had reached for me outside the storeroom.

I could not resist the lure. The *olf* laughed again, making a mockery of my obedience as if knowing at heart that I was as mischievous as it was.

I was dressed only in my sleep shift, and my bare feet

didn't make a sound. By now I had scrubbed every brick and knew exactly where to step. Naturally, the laughter led me through the fire hall into the kitchen. As I stepped into the kitchen yard, the gravel path beckoned to me.

I knew Bjorn could return to our hall and raise the alarm that I was gone. It was not to be taken lightly—I had seen Helanas punish a slave several days earlier. She had hung Sverker's wrists from a rope and forced him to balance on a narrow rod. He'd stubbornly held out as we were ordered to watch. Niels had broken down long before Sverker, crying for him. But eventually Sverker began to beg forgiveness and pleaded for his torment to end. Helanas watched with her arms crossed and a smile on her face until he sobbed with pain. I wanted to turn away but was disturbingly captivated by the sight. That night, I had thrashed on my bedding unable to sleep, feeling frustrated and feverish, as if I were battling an evil spirit.

As I stepped foot outside the kitchen yard, the *olf*'s laughter disappeared over the curve of the hill, following the path to the palisade above the beach. The muffled rush of the ocean and the rich scent of the flowering trees lured me forward. Even with the specter of Helanas hanging over my head, I couldn't retreat.

When I reached the gate, I could see the source of smoke beyond. A bonfire was burning on the beach with a roaring rush of sea wind.

I scurried along the top of the crescent bluff, keeping within the shadow of the palisade. That's when I saw people standing near the bonfire. One looked up, and I ducked down among the hillocks of grass, realizing it was Lexander. I froze, expecting him to come seize me.

But Lexander was speaking to the four eldest slaves, his voice carrying up to me. ". . . and now you understand what your fate will be. You have completed your training; I bid you farewell."

As he finished speaking, a marvelous sight appeared on the water. A giant bird was skimming across the ocean with its wings slanting up toward the moon. I forgot my shivering as it swiftly approached the beach. It was as if a god himself had taken the form of a fantastic eagle and flown down from the heavens.

As the bird drew near, into the light cast by the bonfire, I realized the two wings were the triangular sails of a mighty ship larger than any I'd ever seen before. The moonlight made the white sails glow. I had never seen a ship with two masts before, or with cross posts that slanted down toward the bow and thrust high into the sky in the stern. The hull of the ship was flattened, unlike the sweeping curve of the boats I knew, and there was a high platform in the rear.

The four elder slaves were illuminated by the fire, their expressions rapt. Earlier in the baths Bjorn had been as jealous as always, but now he had eyes only for the mysterious ship. It drew up, dwarfing the dock, silent except for the splashing of the water against the hull. I wanted to touch the side, to see if it were truly made of smoked glass, as it appeared to be.

Silhouettes of men working on the ship moved against the white sails. I didn't hear a sound, but a rope ladder was let down to touch the dock.

Lexander gestured to the ship. "Go now and give glory unto Vidaris."

Bjorn didn't even spare a glance for Lexander as he jostled to be the first to reach the dock. He climbed quickly and disappeared over the side. Sigrid was more hesitant, but she and the other two slaves went up as well.

Lexander followed them, climbing as if he had done so a thousand times. For a moment I thought he was departing with the slaves. I almost rose to follow, but Lexander soon dropped back down onto the dock. As he approached the fire, a rare satisfaction lit his face and his full lips softened into a smile.

The sails shifted, and the ship slowly began to turn away from the dock. There were no oarsmen, so its silent motion seemed magical, as if the hand of a god reached down to guide the craft. A rush of excitement filled me as it sailed away. I desperately longed to go with it. If this was my destiny, then I could endure anything Helanas did to me. Oh, what joy to be carried away by a great bird! To see magnificent places far away from these isles. It was a reward I could scarce hope for as I followed the white sails with my fervent eyes.

But I should have been watching Lexander, because by the time the ship disappeared into the darkness he was standing at the gate.

"You will come with me, Marja," Lexander ordered.

Trembling, I knelt before Lexander in the large fire hall. My sleep shift was muddy at the hem, and my palms were smeared with grass. I expected Lexander to summon Helanas, but he lounged on the padded bench looking down at me. I was spoiling the pristine floor. I was sure I would have to pay for the mess I was making as well as for my transgression in leaving the *haushold*.

Indeed, fury etched his deep voice. "What did you hear, Marja?"

I almost denied everything. But I couldn't lie to him. "You told the other slaves to bring glory unto Vidaris, Master."

His eyes narrowed. "What else?"

"I saw them go inside the magical ship and it sailed away." The awe in my voice couldn't be hidden.

Lexander sat forward, elbows on his knees, to glare into my face. I wanted to pull back, but that would displease him. "You will tell me everything you heard!"

"There was nothing else, I swear it." My dirty palms ground together. "I am sorry I have angered you. The *olf* woke me and I was compelled to follow it . . ."

"I see." Lexander quirked one brow. "An *olf* did it."

"The *olf* called to me, so I went."

For some reason, that seemed to amuse him. "I'd say it was a wicked imp to put you there at that time. So you saw the ship arrive. What am I to do with you now?"

I answered, "Whatever you desire, Master," as I had been taught by Helanas.

"True, you are obedient enough for a new slave, unusually so. This is the first time you've left the *haushold*, isn't it?"

I nodded, thinking of the long hard days I'd spent inside.

"And you a girl of the fens. I wonder that you haven't sneaked out before this. I've seen how you've suffered." He smiled almost wistfully. "And I've seen how hard you have tried to be content in Vidaris."

I felt a rush of warmth in my face. He had seen the quivering tension in my heart. I longed to be free while I also yearned to be quiescent under his touch. I squirmed on the hard floor, loosing my pose for an instant.

Lexander considered me while I resumed kneeling in the pose of obedience—*lydnad*—straight from shoulders to knees, toes pointed and touching, gazing downward. After days of practice, I could hold the pose for quite some time. It was familiar now and did serve to calm me. But fear fluttered deep inside. Helanas' punishment pole seemed paltry compared to what Lexander could inflict. What if he sent me away? What would my life be then?

Lexander held my gaze. "Will you promise not to speak of what you saw, Marja? Not a word?"

"Of a surety! I will never speak of it."

"You won't brag to the others? Would you not be tempted to tell your friends of what you saw this night?"

"Nobody talks to me," I blurted out, "except sometimes Niels. And he's so good he wouldn't want to hear it."

Lexander reclined back on the bench. "Perhaps it is best to keep yourself alone among the slaves. Helanas breeds competition, and to survive this intact you must learn to please her."

I nodded, grateful for his advice.

"If you ever speak of this night, Marja, you will be punished severely. For now, you may return to bed. Tomorrow, you will pay the penance of my choosing. Then you will be forgiven."

My mouth opened, struck by his possessive tone. It made me want to please him, to be forgiven now. I couldn't bear his displeasure when I could atone. I almost begged for it.

"Go," he ordered.

I slowly stood up and left the hall. For a long time after I slid back onto my pallet, I could not sleep. It was not an evil spirit I fought this time, but a longing I was unsure I could ever fulfill.

The next morning, Bjorn, Sigrid, and the two older slaves were gone. It wasn't unusual for slaves to spend the night with Lexander or Helanas, even a group of four together. But when they didn't join us at the day-meal, Sverker said knowingly, "Their training was complete. They've been sent to serve."

"Does it always happen without warning?" Niels asked in a quavering voice. If Helanas had been present, we wouldn't have spoken.

"Yes, this is the second time I've seen it happen," Sverker replied. "The first was after harvest."

"Will new slaves be joining us?" I asked.

"It depends on where they are found and when Lexander returns to fetch them." He nodded to the Skraeling sisters, who had their arms around each other, though as usual they didn't say anything. "Those two came at the end of winter."

"Where did the others go?" Niels had to ask.

Ansgar lifted his hands. "We aren't told and are forbidden to ask. All I know is that we are destined to serve emperors and kings."

"Each to our own best ability," Rosarin murmured in agreement.

I closed my mouth tightly against any desire to confide what I had seen. It was not for me to tell them their fate.

That day, the kitchens were busy preparing traveling food for Lexander and his crew. He was leaving on another one of his periodic searches for new slaves. I wondered if he would forget about my penance. I hoped so, for it meant he had forgotten my transgression.

But that afternoon, Rosarin summoned me to bring my bucket and brush to clean the floor of the fire hall. With a flinch of distaste, I recalled the muddy streaks left by my feet on the bricks.

When I arrived, Lexander was seated at a grand marble table near the hearth. Nearby were a handful of benches. One low table had a grid painted on it, with carved ivory and hardwood figures standing in the colored squares. Niels had explained that they represented Thorr and the other Norogods, and were used to play *hneftaf*. Bjorn had been Lexander's favorite opponent, and I wondered if Niels would take his place now.

On both sides of the closed door leading to the courtyard, the windows were shuttered against the chill spring air. Slanted beams of light with tiny sparkling motes shone through the chinks. I knew that the *olfs* and spirits could see images caught in such beams. Perhaps they were on the fens right now watching me in this place. What did they think of my choice to leave them? I wondered if they missed me or if they could feel my presence even far away.

Lexander's table was lit by the fire and a shining glass lamp hanging from a pole. I approached and bobbed down in deference as Helanas had taught me, my back straight and head held high with eyes downcast. I noticed the double doors to outside were unbarred today, with the iron-bound crossbar leaning against the wall.

"You will clean the floor, Marja," Lexander ordered without glancing up. He held a quill and was writing on yellow parchment before him. I didn't recognize the runes he made.

I went to the spot where I had knelt the night before. The cushions on the bench were still impressed with marks where his body had reclined. I quickly washed the red mud from the bricks, letting the water flow into the cracks before polishing them with the long cloth tucked at my waist. There were a few footprints leading up the steps and into the main hall, so I washed those as well.

When I finished, I tried to escape quietly, but Lexander raised his head. "You will put the bucket away and come here."

The penance! I tucked the bucket and cloth out of sight beside the steps, a trick of neatness I had learned from the other slaves. Then I returned and began to kneel.

"You will take the pedestal." Lexander gestured to the closest window. In front was a low, round pedestal, barely two hands high.

I stepped up and turned around. Pedestals were scattered about in the halls and gardens, looking very much like the bases of the marble columns in the courtyard. Helanas often ordered us to pose on the pedestals when we had nothing to do.

"You will remove your tunic." Lexander stared at me briefly, as if I should have remembered, before resuming his writing.

I unbuckled the enameled bronze clasp on my red leather belt and let it fall behind the pedestal. In the warmth of the *haushold* it wasn't needful to wear anything more than my short tunic. It was white with long, tapered sleeves. The wool was woven with a narrow gold tabard around the edges at my neck, wrists, and the hem at my thighs. As I had seen the other slaves do, I pulled the scarlet silk tie from my hair, letting it fall unbound. I wore only the bronze twisted neck ring at the base of my throat and the wide metal bracelet I had chosen that morning from the cask of jewelry shared by the slaves. I had seen how the ornaments made the other slaves appear more naked.

For a moment I stood there awkwardly, until I remembered one of Helanas' poses—*bojakna*. I bent one knee to the front and held my arms curving downward to graze my thighs in front and back. It was one of the more demure poses and called for a slightly tilted head, gazing off and down to one side. The narrow sunbeams passed around me and hit the floor, casting an elongated shadow of my form. Any *olf* or spirit who cared to look would surely see me now.

The scratch of the *stilo* was all that I heard. I settled into the pose thinking it was a pleasant penance. The fire kept me from shivering, yet my nipples tightened at being displayed before my master. More than ever before, I felt what it meant to belong to Lexander.

Then came a knock on the outer doors, which pushed open at Lexander's summons. I startled in surprise and briefly lost my pose. Lexander said, *"Marja!"* with quiet re-proach. I remembered my actions would reflect on Vidaris.

Through the doors strode two men shrouded in sea cloaks. At first I thought they were freemen from Vi-daris, but as they unwrapped they both hailed Lexander as equals. My master went forward to greet them. Sverker and Ansgar arrived at the bell to fetch their boxes. I could tell by the rich cut of their clothes that they must be magnates, leaders of a village or a tract of homesteads.

I resumed my pose, and they turned to gaze at me as if I were a living statue. "A new one?" one of the men asked with a laugh. More sly comments were passed, but Lexan-der actually smiled and encouraged their speculation.

I trembled and blushed till my skin fair burned with it. Every low laugh, every knowing remark only half heard, made it near impossible for me to hold the pose. And Lexander knew it. He had devised this penance because my weakness was modesty. As I struggled to obey him, he didn't even deign to glance my way.

A small bag of coins passed from Lexander to the elder man with white hair and a deeply lined face. The younger magnate made a crude comment that I couldn't under-stand, but I nevertheless knew it was about me.

Lexander laughed out loud, and I almost broke my pose at the unfamiliar sound. "Your favorite, Rosarin, is still here, if you want her. This one may be too shy for your tastes."

I was suddenly afraid that I would be sold for my dis-obedience. The younger magnate approached me, thick in chest with bowed-out legs that seemed too short for his stout body. His beard was black, as was the hair straggling over his skull and on his chest.

Lexander called after him, "Feel free to touch her. She has lovely skin. Would that all of them were so fine."

"Fair little one, aren't you?" the magnate asked as he leered at me. I felt his rough hands on my breasts and grab-bing my waist. His fingers pinched my nipple as if he de-lighted in seeing me tremble and start under his hands. I tried to hold still, as I tried not to flinch under the crop when Helanas trained us every morning.

His hands slid down to my legs, and his fingers pressed into the soft hair at my groin. My legs were tightly locked together. Even so, my muscles eased under his touch. But he was impatient and his hands slid around my buttocks to assail me from the rear. I knew in that moment—I wanted to please him. My lustful tension had been building since coming to Vidaris, and for a moment I could imagine taking my pleasure with this crude magnate. Anything to slake my desire, to let me shudder in release . . .

Then the older man impatiently called him away. "Do your sporting in your own chamber, *svin*!"

The young magnate lingered to give me a sharp smack on my buttocks. I let out a yelp. He left a fierce burning brand of his hand that I knew would leave a red mark for the rest of the day. He guffawed as he returned to Lexander, loudly complimenting him on his stock.

I could hardly see as they followed Sverker into the courtyard to the guest chamber. They would be staying at the *haushold*. I wondered if the greasy magnate would touch me again, and a rush of emotions overwhelmed me—shame, excitement, outrage, weakness, desire . . .

Lexander barred the outer door, then crossed the hall to the inner courtyard. My anxiety eased at his casual words, "Well done, Marja. You pleased him."

I longed to break my pose to rub my smarting buttock, but didn't dare. "I tried to please *you,*" I admitted hoarsely.

Lexander paused, hearing more in my words than I had intended to say. He came closer, examining me. I swayed in the pose. His palm gently smoothed my hip, watching me gasp at the sensation that ripped through me.

"Is it true?" Lexander murmured to himself. His hand quested between my legs, and at his gentle pressure, my thighs eased open. He felt the moisture that flowed from me. With a brush of his finger, I gasped again.

"You're a true submissive," Lexander whispered. There was a yearning note I had not heard before. "You'll do anything for me if only I play your body and emotions."

I breathed a sigh of acceptance, finally leaning into him. I had never felt such a response before. But then I had always had sex as a bird does—a quick tumble on the grass that left both of us chattering and flying off on our own. I had never felt a touch like Lexander's.

"I can use you as you deserve," he whispered into my hair. With urgent hands he pulled me from the pedestal and pushed me over the marble table. His boots spread my feet apart, and quickly he took me. It was not too soon to suit me. I remembered Helanas' drills as I lifted my hips for him. I wanted his passion. I wanted him to lose control and clutch me closer . . . as I writhed in ecstasy beneath him—

"Well, well," Helanas drawled from across the hall. "Toying with the new girl, are you, Lexander?"

Lexander didn't pause in his thrusting. If anything, he moved more slowly and deliberately, looking at Helanas the entire time. I felt a blush of humiliation pierce my heart, but as Lexander discovered, I also felt a corresponding rise in excitement.

"You want it," he muttered loud enough for Helanas to hear. "Admit it."

"Yes!" I gasped.

He finally strained and spent himself inside of me to Helanas' slow applause. "Nicely done! Aren't you glad I was here so you had an audience? It would have been so much more boring alone."

Lexander seemed unconcerned by her teasing, but I couldn't bear to raise my eyes. I was limp across the table, but when he released me, I rushed to my tunic and pulled it on. My hands fumbled at the belt before it hooked. Then I knelt with my head bent, back on my heels in abject surrender—*gesig*—awaiting an order to go.

Helanas was laughing meanly. "My stars . . . what a pretty picture. I see you're going to dote on this one."

"You could never truly appreciate her, Helanas. Stick to what you know—sulky peasants you can break. I'll make her sing at a touch."

"I will do what I wish with her!" His taunt seemed to inflame Helanas. She stamped her boot against the floor in irritation. "I won't allow you to spoil every slave that enters Vidaris. This one will be disciplined until she is nothing but dirt beneath my feet."

Helanas swept away while I held myself in the pose by force of will. With my juices still smearing my legs, throbbing with desire for more, I knew it was true. I wanted what Lexander did to me.

Lexander left without looking at me. It was a long time before I gathered myself together to fetch the bucket and continue with my duties.

Three

Barely a moon had passed when Vidaris was invited to the annual midsummer celebration by the chieftain of Markland. We were finishing the morning's drill in the slave hall, sheltering from a squall, when Helanas made the announcement. We were now a group of eight, but I believe we were all more comfortable with fewer numbers. I had made my first tentative overtures to Ansgar and Rosarin, but was hesitant to truly befriend them after Lexander's advice to remain aloof.

"We will depart for Markland in two days." Helanas looked down her nose. "We will be taking four pleasure slaves to spread the fame of Vidaris. Sverker, Ansgar, Rosarin, and . . . Marja." Her mouth twitched in reluctance. I caught it only because I was watching her through my lashes, never expecting she would name me.

Niels' eyes went round with awe, while the two sisters moved together slightly. Kinirniq looked relieved. The scrawny male Skraeling didn't take to the training as the rest of us did. There were whispered stories, only half told, of how Kinirniq had tried to run away from Vidaris twice last summer. The second time, Helanas hadn't merely punished him; she had broken his spirit. It was evident in his plodding steps and his perpetually downcast eyes. It was one of the cruelest things I had seen in Vidaris, a place where not much kindness was to be found.

Helanas strolled over and slapped my face hard. I bowed my head, realizing I had been gaping at her openmouthed.

I held the proper pose for surrender until Helanas swept from the hall, the heels of her boots thumping in irritation. I was learning to tell my mistress's mood by her feet, restless when agitated and whisper-quiet when she was content.

"A feast at midsummer is a great display of extravagance," Niels hissed enviously behind me. He would have known how to act in the company of a chieftain. "Fortune smiles on you."

"Mayhap," Sverker retorted direly. "We will be at everyone's whim."

Serious Rosarin agreed. "We must excel. Woe to those who cast a shadow on the name of Vidaris."

I quailed at her pronouncement of *geasa*. A god or guardian spirit could take offense if a *geasa* was broken, and could lash out at us. I feared drawing the attention of Issitoq, the punisher of taboo breakers. People sickened and even died for crossing a taboo. I would have to watch carefully to see the signs that would show me safe passage. I, who was so secure on the fens, felt as if I were standing on shifting ground.

Yet I didn't envy my peers—Niels and the Skraeling sisters—because they would be safe in Vidaris. I danced with delight at the prospect of leaving as I helped the servants prepare. Our finest garments were folded and packed, along with plenty of blankets, linens, and tableware for our use. The hold of the longship was stacked with the chests and casks of good Viinland wine, pressed from grapes grown and aged on the estate. There was also a copper-bound coffer that contained costly ornaments to decorate ourselves.

I couldn't restrain my glee until Helanas sharply rapped my head in rebuke. "She will be unmanageable!" she snapped at Lexander. "Better to take only three slaves."

"You don't know our Marja," he retorted. "She will do all we ask and more."

His praise made me swell with pride. Yet whenever I was near Helanas, I turned away my face to hide my true feelings. My exuberance seemed only to amuse Lexander, and

several times I grinned outright at him. I had noticed that
the other slaves were too afraid of Helanas to even smile.
Once, Lexander responded by clasping a beautiful new
broach onto my travel cloak. I admired the green enameled vines, certain that I would not fail my master and violate the *geasa*.

The morning I climbed into the longship after Ansgar, I
gave a few twirls in praise of the sea spirits, hoping to gain
their favor for this voyage. Lexander and Helanas reclined
on padded benches under a yellow canopy in the prow. I
stayed with Rosarin, Ansgar, and Sverker near the hold in
the center, warm and comfortable in my suede tunic and
leggings.

Soon the red-striped sail filled with the wind and the
ship sailed forth. I stood and swayed with the motion of the
longship, allowing the rhythmic cadence to penetrate my
flesh. It wasn't long until the sea spirits were whispering to
me, only this time I was able to respond through the
chaotic tumbling of the water as it swelled and rolled. The
spirits heard me with much joy, and I knew I wouldn't
sicken on this journey. I could add only a simple note to the
vast cacophony of water life, but the sea spirits seemed
pleased by my efforts.

We sailed along the red cliffs toward the rising sun.
Fjardemano was aptly named for its curved, quarter-moon
shape. Each inlet and series of fields that appeared in the
valleys was like a rare wine that went straight to my head.
I laughed out loud at the straight plow lines marching in
precision over the crests and the muddy cart roads running
past farms and linking wealthy estates like Vidaris. Or-
chards gave way to fields, and everywhere flowers of all
colors and shapes sprang up in the long grass. I have never
known such a profusion of blooms growing wild.

I ignored the stares of the other slaves, who had grown
accustomed to my quiet, subservient ways. How could I
explain my delight in what to them was a simple voyage?
To me, every twitter of a bird I'd never heard before or the

shape of a new flower seemed like a god's blessing to savor.

Eventually we turned away from Fjardemano and headed north into Nauga Sea. The wind picked up, skimming us across the small swells. The oarsmen seemed in fine spirits, reveling in the good seas. As they sang their songs, I communed with the sea and the sky, riding the waves while I flowed with the clouds overhead. It filled me up after the barrenness of Vidaris, like rain falling on parched, cracked ground.

The trip to the southern coast of Markland was not as long as my first sea voyage, but the sun was in the west before land appeared ahead. Sparse woods fringed the hillsides. Here there were no fruit trees or endless manicured fields. Instead, there were grassy hills with sheep grazing in the folds and familiar sod longhouses with windblown roofs.

I felt the singing welcome of *olfs* as I returned to my homeland and reached out with my senses to respond in kind. The boat turned and sailed into a narrow channel between the hills, some forming islands off the shore, until I could not tell where we had entered the bay. The grand bank protected the harbor and chieftain's settlement of Tillfallvik. Boats thickly dotted the calm waters, fishing and transporting people or goods from one side to the other. Dozens of the larger ocean-going *knaar* with deep hulls were anchored with their square sails bound tightly to the masts. Slender longships like our own sailed in with guests who had been invited by Chieftain Ejegod to celebrate the longest day of the year.

The shoreline undulated as we sailed by, the hills plunging into the calm waters forming small coves and inlets within the bay. My breath quickened at the number of homesteads and pastures. Then we rounded a promontory and there was Tillfallvik. Buildings crowded the steep sides of the hills, spreading along the shore and disappearing into the crumpled land.

"Takes little to impress you," Sverker muttered as I gawked. "Go to Viinland or Kjalarnes if you really want to see a city. Sigrid came from this pathetic backwater, and she never excelled like Bjorn." He sneered at me. "But you're from a paltry mud hole north of here, aren't you?"

"Hold your tongue," Ansgar said under his breath. "Do you want to be noticed by our mistress?"

Sverker uneasily glanced toward Helanas and Lexander. He couldn't do much more than taunt me, a habit he had picked up from Bjorn. I lifted my chin, remembering that Lexander thought me good enough to please the chieftain's guests. I would trust my master rather than Sverker.

We docked at one of the many timber piers jutting into the bay. Shipbuilding was underway. Workers were cleaving the great logs of the woods and bending the planks around the keels. Tillfallvik was known for its fine boats, and I was sure that some of my da's nails were being used in those hulls, perhaps made from ore that I had unearthed in the fens. I had always imagined floating away on one of the longships that visited our village and had dreamed of coming here to the premier town of our misty land.

Our oarsmen carried our belongings, and each slave had to hoist a bag or coffer onto our backs as we followed Lexander and Helanas. An open marketplace of frame and sod booths sprawled on a flat shelf of land beyond the docks. The sound was deafening as the merchants shouted, trying to get our attention, calling Lexander "magnate" in recognition of his powerful bearing. Unpleasant odors assaulted my nose—overly ripened fruit, soured meat, the tang of unwashed bodies, and hot seal tar. In small pockets where we were enclosed by walls on every side, the worst smells were masked by spicy incense burning in pots. But I loved the dizzying whirl of color and movement— something strange and different everywhere I looked.

From the market we trudged up the hills, through narrow passageways between the buildings. Some were sod covered while others were capped by high-peaked roofs made of overlapping planks. There were animals everywhere: pigs in pens beside the doors, cattle shifting restlessly, and chickens roosting in the eaves. Soot from the hearth fires rained down, blackening my cloak and the dirt road, which had a ditch running down the center, full of unspeakable things. I even saw a dead rat with staring white eyes that had been half gnawed by its kin.

We eventually reached the chieftain's estate. It covered a broad hillside far back from the waterfront. At the gate, there was a sweeping view of the surrounding hills and most of the bay, including the grand bank beyond. But the terrain was so rugged that I could see only the mast tops of the boats moored at the docks.

Lexander and Helanas gave commands to the porters, and I rushed to catch up. I could have easily gotten lost, unable to tell one structure from another.

I could sense the power of the spirits of the estate, protecting everything within. The enormous fire hall sat on the crest of the hill, bristling with the horned skulls of cattle Ejegod and his ancestors had sacrificed to gain the gods' protection. The *olfs* and spirits were clearly happy here, and I wondered if they were linked to those I used to play with on the fens. They gave me a glimpse of Jarnby, the smoke coming from the forge and my brother slogging through the mud with the sheep; then it was gone.

We were lodged in a sod longhouse. It was dark inside, dug deep into the ground. Yet it was paved by quarried stones and was wide enough to form a row of rooms along a narrow hall. We were given our own space with a sleeping ledge. Sverker told us it was a measure of the chieftain's respect for Vidaris that we were lodged with members of his own retinue.

With Helanas lolling on the bedding we had brought, Lexander ordered us to kneel in a row. "You will submit to everyone who requests it," he ordered. "If you disobey, you will besmirch the glory of Vidaris."

I murmured acknowledgment, not daring to look at the others. It was the *geasa,* spoken by my master himself. It was a sober reminder that I must be ever vigilant in this place. I only hoped I was not given conflicting orders by the guests. I did not trust my own ability to see through the tangle to choose the right path.

Then it was back to our normal routine with Lexander overseeing our grooming while Helanas was tended to by

Sverker. She favored the slender redhead despite his sulky behavior, which I could not fathom. She punished me at the slightest mistake or imagined offense. Perhaps it was because Sverker was graceful and refined, suiting our mistress's taste, while I picked up streaks of dirt and mussed my clothing during my dancing. I do know she never praised my constant obedience.

Helanas had no cause to blame me as we prepared for the night's festivities. I didn't murmur as my hair was gathered tightly to the top of my head and tiny braids were formed into loops, interlaced with gold beads and tinkling bells. Then I was stripped and suspended naked from a pole by one leg. Lexander bound me so that my other leg curved back to my secured wrists. It was an advanced inverted pose, but I breathed deeply as I had been taught and relaxed as the intricate knotting supported my weight.

I swung from side to side as the pole was lifted. The bells dangling from my head rang out as I was carried from the room by Sverker and Ansgar. Their naked bodies were bound around and around with tiny, gold-linked chains. Everything was upside down, and my face was suffused with blood. Then I caught sight of Rosarin, bound in a standing pose with silk rope. Her arms were woven together over her head and her body was crisscrossed by knotted rope down to her ankles. Her legs were trussed together to her knees, barely allowing her to walk. Yet she moved as gracefully as always, her back perfectly straight.

I was carried into the shock of the evening air, across the estate and up to the fire hall for the pleasure of the chieftain's guests. *Olfs* played among the tables, stealing sips of wine and teasing the dogs, though I alone seemed to see them. My head spun, and I wasn't sure if it was a daze induced by the pose or my agony at being immodestly displayed. Hands reached out to touch me as I was carried by, but the welcome dark kept me from seeing their faces.

I think it was then that I truly understood my place. I had been a freewoman until my da sold me, but as a slave I had little more worth than those cows my family now owned. I was fondled and pinched, sometimes painfully, because my master willed it so. Yet even as these strangers probed me, I hummed with desire. It mattered not how long I might hang for them. When I felt Lexander's hands checking the knots, tweaking my body to stimulate me even more, I almost passed out from the waves of pure pleasure.

Through it all, a booming deep voice laughed and brayed, dominating the hall. Birgir Barfoot had led a hundred warriors and displaced families from Danelaw to our land. He was being feasted that night by the gathered *jarls* of Markland and Viinland. I saw only the guest of honor's huge, hairy feet, bare of any covering, as it was said the warlord went into battle. I heard Bigir's approving bellow as I swung near him, and I knew that he had surely seen me.

An elaborate midsummer celebration was held the following night. Huge bonfires flamed throughout Tillfallvik, sending their smoke into the heavens on the longest day of the year to honor the Norogods. I danced in abandon around the fire, pleased to honor my da's gods, until hunger drove everyone inside. The guests crowded around the tables filled with a sumptuous feast.

Helanas dispatched the other slaves to serve various chieftains whom they wished to woo, but Lexander kept me by his side, perhaps because of my inexperience. I was responsible for the fine serving utensils brought from Vidaris—bowls, platters, horn cups, and flat spoons. Many of my fellow Noromenn used only their knives and fingers to eat, much like my family. Lexander and Helanas were more fastidious.

They both were wearing fine linen and rich golden jewels, making me proud to belong to Vidaris. I particularly admired the ropes of embossed gold coins that hung on my master's bared chest. I wore ivory ornaments: strings of carved beads, chunky bracelets depicting wild beasts, and a carved diadem that held my hair away from my face, letting it fall down my back in rich waves. My gold tunic was my best, and it was belted by a silk cord with cunning tassels.

We were entertained by great saga tellers, who wove pictures in the air with words of daring deeds both past and present. The *olfs* delighted in the rousing tales and likely came from far away every summer to enjoy this fete. My favorite of the night was a story I'd never heard about the fire god Loji. My da had told me how Loji had married a giantess and fathered three children, one of whom ruled over a dreaded part of the Otherworld where evildoers suffered. But this story told of Loji's intimate dealings with a giant stallion, which resulted in him giving birth to the most wonderful of all horses—an eight-legged steed ridden by the king of the gods. I listened in wonder with my mouth open until Helanas snapped that I gaped like an idiot.

Servants circled with an astonishing number of dishes—live oysters, mounds of shiny fish eggs, slimy squid, baked mussels, and even an enormous smoked redfish that draped over one long table. Niels would have adored the lavishness of the roasted fowls stuffed with their own eggs and decorated with real feathers. I loved the honey-soaked cakes that were passed on large platters, and took as many as Helanas allowed me.

At the great table, elevated on a dais, Chieftain Ejegod sat next to his wife, Silveta. The chieftain was much older than his bride, his third, according to gossip, but said to be beloved nonetheless. The ruling couple received a constant stream of gifts brought by the guests, and the chieftain loudly bestowed his own gifts on loyal Markland magnates.

Earlier in the evening, Silveta had represented the goddess Freya in the midsummer fertility ritual. She had deftly used her knife to sacrifice the white birds and snowy sheep that were then burned on the square altar in the *vi*. This fire had been used to light bonfires throughout Tillfallvik. The ritual was mostly obscured within the standing poles defining the sacred space, but I had been impressed by Silveta's righteous dignity. Now at the feast, her elegant hands moved deliberately when they weren't demurely folded in her lap. Her beauty was half hidden behind a filmy sky-blue veil.

Sitting at the table on the other side of the chieftain was Birgir Barfoot, a big man rivaling Lexander's height. He wore a thick silver chain around his neck, with a medallion in the shape of a knotted cross bigger than my fist. His florid red cheeks and white-blond hair were striking but not attractive to my eyes. I had already become accustomed to the clean, sleek lines of my master's face. I must confess that I hoped Birgir would not notice me. His meaty fist pounded the table in front of him, and I feared it would split asunder. The frail woman who was seated as his dining companion wilted with trembling.

So passed my first midsummer celebration among the elite *jarls*. Late that night, I was captured by some guests and taken back to their room. There were two men and one young woman from Kjalarnes, far to the south. Their drawling accents were entrancing, and their languid gestures unlike any I had seen before. The men wished to see two women kiss and make love. I had recently begun my training in female arousal with Rosarin and the two Skraeling sisters, so I had some familiarity with the arts of pleasing a woman. They were much kinder to me than Helanas, so I relaxed as I kissed and licked the soft *freya* all over her body. It had not been my intention to become a lover of women, but I found I responded to her. The men began having sex with us before I had finished all I wanted to do, but lying next to her as we received them was enough to drive me into raptures.

When they finally fell asleep, I escaped back to our room. Lexander used me to warm his pallet, but he barely touched me. With the blood still coursing through my body, I knew I could not lie quiescent. He was annoyed by my modesty, so I decided to entertain him by abandoning all inhibition and pleasuring myself. I began to stroke and rub my groin, building slowly, my hips lifting and muscles tensing, as my breath came faster.

Lexander didn't order me to stop, so I knew he was intrigued. Gradually I let go of all restraint, writhing against him, gasping out loud. That's when he reached for me, his *tarse* eager and ready. I didn't care if everyone heard our passion, but his hand went over my mouth to keep me from disturbing Ejegod's bondsmen on either side of the wall.

Helanas scoffed at us, but then she allowed Sverker to enter her as well. Their muffled, rhythmic cries spurred me to a higher peak. It was far more satisfying than the hours I had spent with the Kjalarnes guests because I was with Lexander. Afterwards, falling asleep in his arms was the fulfillment of a dream I had longed for since I had arrived in Vidaris. With the tickling of the *olfs* at the edges of my mind, I wondered if they had helped spur Lexander into joining with me.

During the day, Lexander instructed us not to be seen about the estate—even a priceless gift can be tarnished by too ready access. We slaves were to mingle with the guests only after sunset. So we were forced to confine ourselves in our room. The other slaves didn't mind, but for me it was a torment I couldn't endure. For once, I was too restless to obey, knowing there were so many new things out there to see.

So I took to climbing up the grooved wainscoting until I could slip beneath the canopy tied over our room. I sat on the crossbeams that supported the pitched ceiling. From the network of beams, I watched the guests passing below in the hallway. I could hear if Lexander or Helanas entered the longhouse and was able to climb back down before they saw me. Even Sverker kept my secret. We had nothing as slaves except for what little we gave each other.

Sitting in the rafters, I mostly saw Ejegod's cousins and bondsmen. The highest-ranking guests, including one of the overlord's sons sent to represent Hop, were housed in new buildings made of stacked logs, while the dozens of Markland magnates with their retinues were staying in common longhouses, some of which looked older than those of my village. My da's uncle was the magnate of Jarnby, a position I had once thought quite lofty, but our village was so poor that he had visited Tillfallvik only twice in all his years.

The conversations I overheard among Ejegod's retinue mainly concerned the new immigrants who had come for the *landnam*, land-taking. The chieftains and magnates who ruled the western islands and vast tracts of forest were all descended from land-takers. Their ancestors had packed children, home goods, and livestock into their enormous *knaar* and ventured across the ocean. Yet Ejegod's men spoke with disdain of these new fighting men in their heavy chain mail and helms. Some had brought along their women and children, rejected from settlements in Danelaw. Most were relegated to a rough-hewn encampment across the bay from Tillfallvik. Yet they had arrived in their own fleet instead of the merchant ferries, so they could in truth take the land of their choosing at any time. With so many warriors, they could surely protect their own settlements like true *vikingr*.

On the third day, it was nearly sunset as I crawled along the rafters of our longhouse. That's when I heard the call of an *olf*. I'd rarely heard such a plaintive cry, barely at the edge of hearing. I felt a tug, and a single hair was pulled from my head. In exchange for the gift, it left a whispered word floating behind my head.

"Come!"

It had been years since I heard an order so clear from the gods' favorite creatures, not since I had been led to a ring of trees in the deep fens as a child. I had found gifts there for me, a few glass beads and a bronze disc. I had given what little I possessed—a broken buckle and a bit of a mirror I'd found on the shore. I never went inside the ring of trees, fearing I would be drawn unwittingly into the Otherworld, but sometimes presents were left there to tempt me. I would do much for the *olfs*, but I would not leave my own world at their behest. It was the one *geasa* my mam laid on me when she first explained the sight.

But now, I couldn't resist following the tinkling call. I crawled down the center beams to the other end of the longhouse where I had never ventured. There was a storage platform there, so I was less exposed. With a final trill, the *olf*'s voice disappeared, to be replaced by ordinary voices.

Quietly at first, but quickly growing louder, a woman demanded, "Who do you think you are? Unhand me, you lout!"

Edging through the shadows in the vaulted ceiling, I tried to stay hidden as I looked down into the hallway. There was no mistaking the giant Birgir wrestling with the woman. She wore an embroidered green dress without a cloak. He locked his arm around her and clamped his hand over her mouth before she could scream. "You belong to me, Silveta! I will show you."

With that, he dragged her across the hallway. Her feet kicked the air in desperation. In a flash I saw the heavy wooden door and knew that Birgir intended to take the chieftain's wife inside. The leer on his face and the way his tongue licked her cheek made his intentions clear.

I acted quickly, shoving a cask from the storage platform, sending it shattering against the hard floor. The vat held a dark red wine, which splashed over both of them.

It startled Birgir, who loosed Silveta enough for her to let out a piercing scream. The outer door banged open as people came running to investigate. Birgir whirled to look up, but I ducked behind the other casks and barrels on the platform. Silveta sagged to the ground, crying out for help. Birgir cursed as he pushed past the house slaves.

Silveta explained that the cask of wine had fallen. She sent the two women to get water and rags to clean up.

I started to withdraw along the beam as quietly as I could, but Silveta called out softly, "You, up there, who saved me! Who are you?"

I remembered Lexander's order to obey, so I climbed down the ladder of the storage platform to face her. "I am Marja of Vidaris."

"Oh, one of those pleasure slaves." Silveta slumped back against the wall. I dared to look at her, marveling at the ropes of tiny amber and glass beads around her neck and entwined in her hair. Her skin was like rose petals and fresh cream. It was frightening to see such a great *freya* brought so low.

Then Silveta looked up at me again. "You're supposed to obey above all else, aren't you?"

"Yes, *freya*."

"Then don't speak of what you saw here, Marja."

That was what Lexander had ordered after I had seen the winged ship. "Surely it will be so. I give you my pledge!"

The two slaves returned and began clucking over the spreading red stain across the stones. I went to help Silveta to her feet. She was looking more composed, but her seafoam veil had pulled loose, revealing most of her coiled honey-blond hair. Her wrists still had red marks on them. Because Birgir had been between her and the cask, her skirt had only a few dark splashes, like blood.

"Help me," Silveta murmured, and I supported her weight on my arm as I assisted her through the wooden door. Inside, the ceiling was enclosed by wood panels, offering complete privacy. I took note of several elaborately carved chests and two bronze coffers with enameled plaques and concluded this was Silveta's sleeping closet.

Silveta slumped onto the platform that held the bed linen, putting her hands over her face. "What shall I do? If I feign illness and refuse to take the night-meal, then he's sure to come for me. I should have left once the ritual was done!" Her icy blue eyes focused shrewdly on me. "You swear you'll not speak of this? I don't need everyone to know that the chieftain's honored guest intends to rape me."

Her scornful words shocked me. Silveta was too refined to say such base things, but I had seen it with my own eyes. Birgir acted like a bull in rut, oblivious to anything but the cow beneath him. "But your husband must defend you!" I exclaimed in dismay.

"Ah, yes, that's what most would say," Silveta replied.

I waited, but she merely shook her head in agony. "Can you not ask for your own guard? 'Tis only to be expected."

"No, any bondsman would tell my husband about Birgir.

And then Ejegod's life as well as my honor would be forfeit. That is why you *cannot* speak of this."

I nodded, mesmerized by her frantic eyes. But I didn't understand.

"Ejegod would lose face," Silveta explained in despair. "He would have to fight Birgir, but he could not best him in a duel. Even if my husband were only injured, that would spark a feud between our *bondi* and Birgir's warband that we cannot hope to win."

I was stunned. Our chieftain protected Markland and stood as final judge for disputes between the local magnates. I felt such deep respect for my own great-uncle—he maintained the peace and was responsible for the rituals that kept Jarnby safe. I had imagined our chieftain's powers were near to those of a god. And now, to hear that Ejegod was so weak . . .

"Surely there must be a guardian spirit you can call on?" I protested.

Silveta waved off my suggestion. "I will get no help from the Otherworld in this matter."

I thought she was too quick to deny the power that had summoned me to her aid. But if the *olfs* had not revealed themselves to her, then it was not my place to tell her. I wished that I knew more about the path the *olfs* had set me on so I could better advise the chieftain's wife.

"I have held him off for a week," Silveta continued, "but it seems that Birgir Barfoot would do anything to gain his purpose. I never expected to be attacked outside my very room. He has watched Ejegod drink himself senseless every night and has timed it well indeed. He will not wait another day to take what he wants." She glanced at her closed door. "I don't doubt it would be easy for him to come through those boards in spite of the iron bolt."

"I almost believe he would," I agreed.

Silveta raised her head, brushing the loosened strands of hair from her face. "If I had my own loyal *bondi,* then I would be protected without involving Ejegod . . . someone who would fight unto death against Birgir for my honor alone. I must escape tonight. I'll tell the chieftain I've re-

ceived a missive urging me to return to Hop. I can ask my
father for men who can protect me without betraying my
secret to the chieftain."

I nodded, understanding the complex ties of kinship. If
the men came from her father and swore themselves to Silveta, then they would adhere to her orders alone.

But the hope fled from her face. "What if Birgir follows
me? There is little time until the night-meal when he will
find that I am gone. He could send his warriors to catch me.
His ships are very fast. After today, I could believe he
would be so bold."

She was so despairing that I offered, "I can ask my master for help."

Silveta turned to me as if she was considering it. She
slowly stood up and reached for my shoulders, examining
me closely. Her perfume smelled like an armful of flowers
warmed by the sun. So close to her, I could see the delicate
stitches of vines and leaf embroidery on the long panels of
her dress. She came close to rivaling Helanas in her form,
yet Silveta was nearly as young as I.

"Praise be the gods," Silveta breathed. "*You* can take my
place here tonight. If Birgir attempts nothing, you can go
back to your people in the morning. But if Birgir does
come, surely in the darkness there is little to tell between
us. Your hair is as long and nearly as bright as mine."

Shocked, I blurted out, "You want me to deceive
Birgir?"

"Yes, you must!" Her expression was resolute. "This is
my only hope to escape. I would rather kill myself than
spawn his get."

I had heard enough to know the old chieftain's lack of
issue was a delicate matter. His children did not long survive, and his wives had died in childbirth. Ejegod's loyal
subjects were pinning their hopes for an heir on young,
healthy Silveta. We pleasure slaves never conceived; Helanas had given me a mug of foul-tasting tea that would keep
me from quickening for the next turn of seasons.

"You must help me," Silveta insisted.

I thought of the *geasa* and agreed. "Yes, I must obey you.

But my master is surely missing me by now. May I go tell him what you've asked of me?"

"No, you'll stay here. It's better that nobody knows." Her air of command was complete. I think she despised me a little for my obedience, but that was no matter as long as she got what she needed. "I'll leave immediately. I'll ask my husband to not speak of my departure. He can do that much for me. Lock the door and don't let anyone in here, no matter what they say. Will you do it?"

I had to fulfill my duty, no matter how difficult it would be. If I disobeyed, I would suffer untold consequences. Vidaris itself could be destroyed by my actions.

I whispered, "Yes, my *freya*."

Perhaps Silveta peered into the future as my mam often did, because it happened exactly as she predicted. Birgir returned to Silveta's door when she didn't appear at night-meal and pounded on it with his fist, demanding that she join them at the table.

I stayed against the wall, terrified of the shaggy giant, and called out, "I am unwell and cannot leave my bed!"

Birgir raged at my denial, but I repeated myself, growing fainter all the while. Soon enough he gave up and returned to the fire hall.

I worried about Lexander and Helanas. Would they search for me? Had the other slaves confessed that I had climbed out of our room? If so, perhaps Lexander would simply assume I had been caught by a guest and was entertaining him. Rosarin had been gone until midday every day since we arrived.

I tried to call the *olf* to come cheer me, but the inexplicable creature merely giggled at me from a distance, refusing to enter Silveta's closet. I finally lay down in her bed, stroking the fine fur cover until I drifted off warm and drowsy.

A loud bang woke me. It was the door flung back with the clash of a key removed from the lock. I came awake knowing Birgir was inside. I didn't think it could happen, but Silveta had known it would. I clutched the fur to my chest.

"I have the key, my sweetmeat!" Birgir exclaimed, slurring drunkenly. But he was sober enough to bolt the door behind him. "I'll swear you sent it to me through that pretty maid. She would lie for me, indeed. Then all of Tillfallvik will know you for the doxy you are. But I'll protect you from your husband. I will, my lovely! Even if I must kill him, eh?"

In the utter blackness, Birgir stumbled into the chest at the foot of the bed. I whimpered, "Please, no . . ."

"So you're there," Birgir chuckled. "Waiting for me in your nest. You knew I would come for you. I've seen how you watched me and longed for a virile man. No girl such as you should be clutched to the breast of a dried-up old cod!"

His hand clutched my ankle in a tight grip, hurting me. I kicked, but I couldn't get away. Remembering how the servants had come running to help Silveta, I opened my mouth to scream.

I was cut off midshriek by his hand. "They'll not help you tonight, my lovely! You're all mine, and come morning, I'll deal with the chieftain and we'll prepare for a wedding. The magnates of Markland may squawk, but I'll gain the *jarls* of Viinland on my side with one of their own as my wife."

I choked in outrage. I resisted as much as I could because every touch caused pain. But there was nothing I could do to dislodge his massive bulk. Birgir pressed down so heavily on me that soon he removed his hand, content that I could hardly breathe as he spread my legs and pummeled into me. This was not pleasure, and there was nothing that could make it so. Even his silver pendant bit cruelly into my chest.

I desperately clung to only one comforting thought—I had kept my chieftain's wife from going through such hell. Silveta and I had outwitted him, though he knew it not.

Four

I lay awake, trying to ease myself from under Birgir's arm and leg, but the warrior slept light and clenched me more tightly to him every time I shifted. All night, I called for the *olfs* to help me. But I heard nothing in return for my sacrifice. When the *olfs* had called me to save Silveta from Birgir, they little knew it could end in my rape.

By morning, I was muzzy-headed from fatigue, thinking only of the door that lay between me and release, when Birgir finally grunted and awoke. As always, I could feel the dawn breaking even though we were in darkness. As Birgir sat up, I tried to roll out of bed away from him.

He grabbed my arm and held me in place. "Not yet, my pretty. I want to see your face this time. 'Twill make it all the more rousing."

His threat and the way he pushed me to the bed made it all flash before me again: his sour breath in my face, his nasty tongue probing my mouth, sweat dripping onto my chest. I felt scoured by his rough, hairy body. There was a deep ache in my groin that shot sharper pains into my gut every time I moved. He had torn into me last night, not caring how I cried in protest. Only my submissive nature had saved me so that the damage was not worse.

Birgir expertly struck a spark against the floor and lit the taper. He turned to me, the light casting shadows against the paneled walls of the closet.

Terrified, I stared up at him. He smirked through his blond wooly beard. He had planned his betrayal well—

with the maid's testimony that Silveta had intended for
Birgir to come to her closet, the chieftain's wife would appear to be complicit in this deed. Ejegod would be forced
to fight Birgir for his honor. Birgir was gloating as if his victory over the chieftain was assured, and he was envisioning
the power and influence he would gain by taking Silveta as
his wife.

It took a few moments before he truly saw me.

I braced myself for a roar at his indrawn breath. Birgir's
hands closed hard on my bare arms. "*Who* are you?" he
breathed through gritted teeth.

"Marja," I gasped.

Birgir hauled me up, shaking me soundly. "Who put you
here?"

I knew I must speak carefully or I would violate the
geasa laid on me. But it mattered not because his next
words were, "It was that fox bitch, Silveta, was it not? If she
thinks that she will get away with her petty tricks, she will
learn another lesson."

He dragged me out of bed, his hands clenching as if to
snap my neck. Spittle flecked his beard as he snarled, "Tell
me where she is hiding or I will kill you now! That would
be a surprise for her, would it not? That would teach her
not to leave another to take her proper place."

I believed him; his bloodshot eyes were wild with anger.
He might kill me even if I told him. But Silveta had not ordered me to keep her destination a secret. Soon enough
she would return with her new bondsmen and all would
know she had gone to Hop. It was far too late for Birgir to
follow her there, where she would be protected by her father's kin. Clearly the *geasa* required I tell him the truth,
even if he took his anger out on me. "*Freya* Silveta has
gone to her father's house in Viinland."

"No!" Birgir growled as he shook me hard. I saw stars
and thought I was facing death. My last thought was not of
Vidaris, but of the fens of my youth. I wished I had died
there instead, to become one with the watery land. Perhaps
Lexander would take my body back to my family and my
brother would insist on laying me near the *olf* ring I had

discovered. The *olfs* I loved so well would carry me to the Otherworld . . .

But instead of the darkness I expected, Birgir threw me aside to the floor. The hard stones scraped my knees and palms. I lay naked in the chill air, fearing to move in front of him. He paced around the closet, muttering and grunting with anger as he covered his well-muscled legs and chest beneath layers of wool and buckled on an everyday breastplate made of reindeer hide. There was no other sound outside the walls, which meant the exalted guests were still sleeping off the merriment of the night before. A massive bearskin with a winter ruff served as his cloak, but he left that aside to glare down at me.

My legs curled in and my arms protected my bare chest, knowing how vulnerable I was lying by his stiffened leather boots. "Who else aided Silveta in this?" he demanded.

"It was me alone," I whispered.

He grabbed my hair and lifted me from the floor. I screeched, but his big hand clasped over my mouth. "Not a sound or you will die before it leaves your throat. Now, answer me—who are you?"

"I'm a pleasure slave," I gasped, twisting as I dangled. I grabbed hold of his wrist with both hands to lessen the pressure.

"Who owns you?"

"Vidaris," I managed to say.

"A Viinland estate, no doubt." Birgir shook me. I bit my lip to keep from screaming. "Did they help Silveta escape?"

"No one knows I'm here! I escaped our room while my master was gone."

"Somehow I doubt that, little pawn. Silveta has laid her plans deep." Yet he released me and I dropped back to the floor. For a moment, I had a giddy feeling that I might survive.

Then there was a snap of leather as he folded his wide belt in one meaty hand. "I think you lie to me, girl." The belt landed on my hip with a searing blow.

I choked on my scream, jamming my fist into my mouth. I could never get used to being struck, even though Helanas made a habit of it with me, administering sharp, sudden blows during training drills or whenever she happened across me.

But this was even worse because it didn't stop. Birgir seemed infected by an evil spirit. He hit me again and again as I curled into a ball to protect my face and stomach. I writhed with the effort of biting my tongue on my cries. But I remembered the *geasa* and I was silent, as he ordered, even though it was far worse than anything Helanas had done to me.

"Tell me the truth," Birgir ordered. "Who helped you do this?"

"It was me," I cried, "me alone!"

Birgir lashed out with the belt, striking my legs and sensitive feet. A strangled moan burst from my throat. "Lay still!" he ordered.

It seemed impossible, but I did it. I let him shove me around with his feet, positioning me where as he wanted. I thought only of Lexander as he pronounced his *geasa*. I couldn't fail.

Pushed to my limit, I somehow found the will to surrender to his blows. The moments when I wasn't struck almost felt good. I relaxed, accepting the sharp pain, which made me float above everything. I could hear him grunting with the effort as he moved around me. The belt as it landed reverberated deep into my ears and down into my bones.

When I was a limp, sweating rag, stinging in every part of my body and throbbing where he had bruised me, Birgir was still not through. He dragged me up by my hair and unbolted the door.

I could hardly feel the stones beneath my feet. There was the slickness of blood on my skin, but most of my attention was on my hair where he pulled unmercifully. The shock of cold as he took me outside served to jolt me into awareness. There were servants moving around the estate, preparing for the day-meal, transporting water, and tending to the animals. My head was twisted up to one side as I stumbled along next to him.

We entered the fire hall, where some of the guests were beginning to gather, fatigued from their long night's festivities. Birgir threw me down in front of the chieftain's dais. The table and chairs were empty.

Birgir put his hands on his hips and bellowed to the rafters, "I summon Ejegod Oddason for reckoning!"

I was left to lie on the dirty stone floor, the straw and worse sticking to my bare skin. It reeked of sour ale and rotting food. A few of the mangy curs that roamed the estate sniffed at my blood and growled, nipping at each other until Birgir kicked them away.

People were arriving, their feet shuffling and voices rising in speculation at the sight of me. It crushed me to be so exposed. I couldn't hide myself or my pain. For a moment I thought that I might die of it.

When Chieftain Ejegod arrived, loudly berating the men who had pulled him from his warm bed, Birgir dragged me up. "On your knees, girl!" he hissed.

The chieftain settled into his chair of bound walrus tusks, cushioned by snowy lynx fur. His eyes were bleary and down-turned, with deep lines beside his fretful mouth. Silveta's husband was an old drunkard, with the swelling belly of one who loses himself in strong wine. His noticeably stiffened fingers shook until he clasped them on his belt. I understood Silveta's reluctance to trust to her husband to protect her. He was nothing like the great chieftain I had always imagined.

Yet Ejegod did radiate power, and his word was law. I had been called for judgment before him. He mumbled the traditional invocation of his sovereignty, then formally requested Birgir's sworn fealty.

When Birgir Barfoot knelt before him, agreeing to obey Ejegod as his liege lord, the murmuring of the guests rose sharply. It was the first time Birgir had surrendered authority to his host.

Then Birgir stood and began his case against me. In my confused state, I thought he would accuse me of impersonating Silveta. I was resolved to conceal the reason for her departure.

But to my dismay, Birgir declared, "I awoke this dawning in the clutches of an evil spell! This slave was weaving a golden fog around me, attempting to unman me after a night's dalliance. I felt this sorceress draw the breath from my mouth and heard the urging of demons for her to do their bidding. But no mortal, not even in the service of the Otherworld, could best me! I called on the mighty power of Kristna, the one true god, and was given strength to seize my tormentor by the hair." He shook my head hard to emphasize his point, and I had to stifle a scream. "Then I cleaved the fog with my sword, releasing myself from her bondage."

He finally let me go, and I fell forward. There were too many eyes on me, as more guests crowded in to see the sport.

The chieftain leaned over to stare down at me. "Did you cast a spell on this man, slave? Speak up for all to hear! For I will know the truth of what you say."

"N-no . . . ," I stammered uselessly.

"What say you? Or I will pass judgment on ye now."

"No, Chieftain," I managed. "Never would I do that. I am but a pleasure slave."

"Someone here lies." Ejegod pointed down at me. "My sworn man tells me you talk with otherworldly creatures. He speaks the truth, I think. Answer me!"

I hesitated, but I must not violate the *geasa*. "Yes, the *olfs* do speak to me."

Ejegod's rummy eyes narrowed. "Here, on my own land?"

I remembered the *olf* who had beckoned me to "*come!*" The creature had led me to save Silveta, of that I was sure. "Yes," I acknowledged.

Ejegod sat back, satisfied. I glanced up at Birgir, who growled and kicked me. I cringed again, knowing even in my muddled state that I couldn't speak the truth. Silveta had sworn me to secrecy under the *geasa*. She would not allow me to pit Birgir against her husband. I understood why—I could spark a feud that could rage for generations. Birgir was from the Auldland, where wars were constantly fought. I could not let him do that here. I could not tell Ejegod that I had saved his own wife from Birgir.

The chieftain waved one hand at Birgir. "I grant your claim against this slave. She will be exiled from Markland, from sea to strait, forever."

I sagged to the floor, shattered to hear that I could never return home. But the straw rustled and a familiar scent wafted over me. Helanas strode forward, her voice ingratiating as she made her appeal. "Chieftain Ejegod, surely you must see this girl is daft! She is not a sorceress. She has no power. She is simply one who chatters to flowers and trees, as heedless as a child—"

"Silence!" Ejegod thundered. "Vidaris has offended my hospitality. Your house is henceforth cast out from this land. Leave here at once."

Helanas was outraged. "Vidaris has served you well, Chieftain! Is this how we're to be repaid?"

Ejegod gestured curtly to his *bondi*. "Escort them from my estate."

I felt Lexander's hands on my shoulders. In that moment, I knew I was safe. I would not die while he could protect me. I looked up into his face and whispered, "I obeyed . . ."

"I know," he murmured. "Can you stand?"

"Yes." I managed to get to my feet, but my knees weakened beneath me. I would give anything to Lexander, but my body had been pushed too far.

He wrapped his cloak around me and lifted me, cradling me against his chest. Turning to Ejegod, Lexander responded with deference, "Vidaris will comply with your commands as always, Chieftain."

When Helanas seemed ready to protest, Lexander quelled her with a look. I leaned my head on his shoulder, closing my eyes so I wouldn't have to see the haughty gazes of the guests as Lexander marched through the hall and out the door. The rumble in his chest was soothing as he quietly told the other slaves to gather our belongings.

Even covered by Lexander's cloak, I was shivering. The

town was a blur of harsh noises and smoke, but I fell asleep in his comforting arms.

When we reached the harbor, the fresh sea air stirred me, reminding me of Jarnby. For a moment, I felt as if I were a young girl again, held by my da with hands that were always blackened by the forge. I wondered if my mam could see me now in her spinning, and what she thought of me.

I peeked from the shelter of the cloak at the bustle of activity on the shorefront. Arnaaluk, the giving god of the sea, had bequeathed two giant gray whales to the townsfolk of Tillfallvik and Ejegod's guests. They lay on the sand beside small boats and nets that had been used to drive the pod in to shore. The proud hunters were slicing the flesh and packing it into barrels as women boiled the fat, rendering it into oil. Bags of grain were being offloaded from the longships moored around us, while fresh butchered whale meat and jars of oil were packed into the holds. I didn't need to see our own empty hold to know why Helanas was seething mad at me.

Lexander stepped easily from the dock into the longship while still carrying me. But Helanas blocked his way. "Throw the worthless creature overboard to drown! That is sure to appease Ejegod."

"You are shortsighted, as always," Lexander countered, quietly enough for only the two of us to hear. "Ejegod does not care about this slave. He merely used her to seal his bond with Birgir. I'm sure Birgir would not have bargained away so much over our little Marja unless he had very good reason to."

"Perhaps." Helanas frowned at me. "I will get it out of her, if that is so."

"Don't interfere," Lexander warned. "You've shown you're unfit to play this game, Helanas."

She gave a scornful laugh. "Don't forget it was I who made sure Vidaris benefited from that old man's marriage to a mere child! The slaves we've gotten from Hop in return for convincing Ejegod are our best stock."

"You will go too far one day, Helanas. The chieftain has ears throughout Tillfallvik."

"Stanbulin will be displeased about this," she warned.

"Get out of my way," Lexander ordered.

I shuddered at his cold indifference, as if nothing his consort said mattered to him. When I had first come to Vidaris, I thought that Helanas was the perfect mate for Lexander. But now I could see how viciously they clashed.

Lexander laid me on one of the benches as the oarsmen unfurled the yellow canopy to grant us shade. Helanas remained in the bow, giving shrill orders as the other slaves settled our gear into a corner of the hold. The paltry pile of crates taunted me, and I remembered Hallgerd had gloated about the goods our master received in Tillfallvik in return for Vidaris' gifts, including the entertainment provided by the pleasure slaves.

The longship cast off from the dock and the oarsmen sliced into the waves. The rocking settled me, allowing the sea spirits to weave tendrils of comfort through my body. In the sea's embrace, I knew the otherworldly creatures were satisfied by my service, though they had not lingered to tell me so. I little wondered why the *olfs* had fled in the face of Birgir's rage—the creatures were repulsed by violent emotions. And I was glad that I had not denied knowledge of them to the chieftain. Never would I disavow them as long as I lived!

"I didn't bespell Birgir, I swear," I murmured as Lexander settled me in.

He sat down on the bench beside me, his face close to mine. "You must tell me everything that happened. Leave nothing out! It could mean everything for Vidaris." His eyes crinkled at the corners and his expression softened. "No matter what you've done, you've already been punished enough, my brave girl."

I laid my head on the velvet pillow, yielding to him. "I climbed the wall into the rafters so I could see the people passing through the longhouse." He nodded, unsurprised. That meant one of the other slaves had already told him. I wondered if it had been Sverker. Just the thought of how he would torment me over my public shaming made me briefly close my eyes.

"Go on," Lexander urged, his hand cupping my shoulder to comfort me.

"Then I heard the *olf* calling me." I told him what had happened, leaving out no detail; how I had saved Silveta from Birgir, staying in her bed while she fled to get help from her father's house. "The *olfs* placed me there to help her."

Lexander nodded throughout. "Indeed, I understand. Did Birgir bed you?"

"Yes, last night, after using the key to enter Silveta's closet. Birgir was enraged when he discovered this morning that I was not Silveta."

"She knew she could trust no one here." Lexander thoughtfully watched the oarsmen stroke us away from Tillfallvik before turning back to me. "I believe you obeyed my orders, Marja. And for your service to Silveta, you've gained Vidaris a valuable ally."

His expression was full of pride and affection for me. I knew then that I had succeeded in following the *geasa*. The torment of fear and doubt, more oppressive than any physical pain, ebbed away.

Lexander smiled to see my relief. "You surely saved Ejegod from facing a duel, one he would have lost. It seems to me you have done a fine deed for your first time in society."

My eyes shifted uneasily to Helanas. "But what about . . ."

"That is none of your concern. I can deal with our superiors." His clipped words were chastisement enough.

I nodded as a drowsy feeling stole over me from the gentle motion of the waves. Now that I was safe and warm, I wanted nothing more than to fall asleep and escape the pain.

After a moment, Lexander asked, "Did you cry?"

It took me a moment to remember. "No, I did not."

"Did you beg for mercy?"

I shook my head. "Birgir ordered me not to speak, so I was silent. He told me not to move, so I was still."

Lexander smoothed my hair from my forehead. "An ig-

norant bully. He didn't even know what he had in his
hands. A waste of all the good that is in you."

It felt divine to be touched so sweetly. I closed my eyes
and let myself slip away. The last thing I heard was Lexander murmuring, "Never fear, my wild child. I will make you
cry exquisitely."

Five

When I returned to Vidaris, the *olf* in the storeroom was gone. I knew that I had been used by the *olfs* for their own grander purpose. Yet as inscrutable as their ways were, I must confess, I thought only of what my master had promised.

My skin was a mass of bruises and welts, with cuts where the hard edge of the belt had dug into me. I was allowed to remain in my snug pallet for a few days before rejoining my fellow slaves in training. Helanas was just as cruel to me as ever, perhaps more so. The other slaves picked up on her disdain and avoided me. But there was no punishment for my actions that had resulted in the banishment of Vidaris from Markland.

After I had recovered enough to resume my duties, I was fetching water from the cistern in the kitchen yard when I overhead Hallgerd tell the cook, "And here's another visit canceled! If it goes on this way, they'll not be invited to any of the great estates this summer. You know what that will mean—we'll be eating only what Vidaris can grow."

"No more coco?" the young scullery maid cried.

"No, so you won't be licking the pot, as you like!" There was the sound of a spoon smacking against her buttocks. "And none of those nice orange melons or cinnamon or that good date wine, neither."

My foot was on the stoop, but I couldn't move. The full water buckets balanced at my sides from the shoulder pole as birds flitted overhead in the sunlight. Usually my heart would have been filled with the beauty of the day, but their words made it all clear. I had seen the resentment from the other slaves and servants. They blamed me for the dishonor to Vidaris, but I didn't realize that hardship would come because of me. I felt a burning shame spread throughout my body.

I stepped inside the kitchen. Hallgerd harrumphed and closed her mouth. They knew from my blush that I had overheard.

"I did only as I was ordered," I declared, facing them all. "Would you have me defy our master and bring ruin on us all?"

Hallgerd put her hands on her hips. "That's not the tale I heard, missy. You've disgraced us with your otherworldly ways! Don't deny it to me, for I have ears to hear you speaking to the tricky beasties that live in the walls."

Out of respect to the *olfs*, I would not defend my love of them to anyone. "If you would have disobeyed our master, say it now. I did only as I was ordered and *he* is satisfied with me."

Hallgerd raised her hands in disbelief, and even the scullery maid frowned, angry no doubt about the sweets she would miss. None of them believed me, and why should they when Birgir's claim went unchallenged?

So I said nothing more. I walked through the gauntlet, knowing that I didn't deserve their condemnation. Yet as soon as I entered the scullery to pour the water in the cistern, they began complaining of me again. I let the splashing cover their words, grateful that my duty allowed me to ignore them. My forehead rested on my hand as I poured, knowing this was only the beginning.

I waited for a moon for Lexander to fulfill his promise, but my master rarely touched me. At first I thought that he was giving me time to heal. He administered the oils and unguents that soothed my skin after every bath. There was a new look in his eyes as he gazed at me, appraising and curious, as if I was not at all what he had expected me to be.

It made me feel warm inside, and I eagerly wished he would pursue his budding interest in me.

But many days passed after I was perfectly recovered, and still nothing happened. Lexander usually took Rosarin or Ansgar to his bed at night, and occasionally the sisters joined him. Helanas favored Sverker and Niels because they were refined, and dispirited Kinirniq. I was the only one who slept on my pallet alone every night.

Everyone took that as a subtle but effective sign of their disapproval, especially as the season warmed and not once was our longship launched to carry Vidaris to another estate. Even mild-mannered Niels grumbled about not being able to return to Hop for the annual Landfall celebration. Things got so bad that none of the others sat next to me at meals or spoke to me when we were at leisure.

I was even lonelier without the friendly *olf* who had lived in the storeroom. In spite of the danger the *olfs* had put me in, I continued to leave the remnants of my bowl of milk there in vain, hoping to lure back the little creature. I was afraid that I had displeased the *olfs* in Tillfallvik somehow. Perhaps I could have done better.

Then one morning as usual, Hallgerd ordered me to gather the washbasins. I was accustomed to doing the menial work because no one cared if my skin was chapped from the water or my palms were raw from scrubbing.

I tried to be very quiet as I went into Helanas' chamber, prepared for anything. The brick walls were covered in fine tapestries woven with patterns of birds and flowers unlike any I'd ever seen before. The bed was draped in gauzy white silk that shrouded the linens and embroidered pillows. It was empty, the cover twisted and trailing off. Kinirniq had spent the night with our mistress and was curled in one corner on the cold floor. I knew what that felt like. The young man rejected sympathy from the other slaves, but I had felt compelled to help him from time to time. One evening when Helanas was starving him to get some kind of emotion from him, I had given him my meal. Kinirniq had shoved the meat into his mouth with shaking fingers as I watched. It was only after he was done that I realized Lexander was watching us from the doorway. He seemed pained, a deep line between his eyes, and I thought I had angered him. But he left without a word to either of us, and I knew as if an *olf* had told me that he was pleased.

Now I could do nothing for Kinirniq while he was in our mistress's chamber. I went straight to the porcelain bowl that held the water Helanas had used to wash herself. It was the custom of my master and mistress to wash both morning and night, and I had seen how it greatly enhanced their beauty.

As I lifted the blue bowl, Helanas emerged from behind a folding screen. Instantly I bobbed down deeply, knees bent and back straight, holding the *vordna* pose of deference. With my gaze resting on her feet, I could see when she turned away from me. That was my signal to continue with my duties. As I started toward the door, she smacked my head from behind. Perhaps she was testing me to see if I would spill the water. But there was also frustration in her blow, as if she knew she could not tame me despite my obedience. The restless fire that burned inside of me could never be quenched.

With my head bowed, I waited, still holding the bowl. Naturally I didn't speak—that would be grounds for real punishment.

"Get out of here at once!" Helanas snapped. I bobbed deeper, then was on my way before she could change her mind.

After dumping the water into the runoff trench in the kitchen yard, I returned the blue bowl to the scullery to be washed and replaced in her room. Then I went to Lexander's chamber. I preferred his room even though there were no brightly colored tapestries. The brick walls were hung with weapons instead—swords and knives with jewels in the hilts and intricate handles. One had a massive curved blade.

Lexander's bed was very wide and low, covered by luxurious brown fur. I had once reached up to stroke it while washing the floors, and I longed to sink into it next to him.

I wanted him to hold me as he had on the longship—tenderly, as if he truly cared about me.

Lexander was seated in the window, a remarkable construct with small diamond panes of glass embedded in lead. Through it I could see the corn and oats waving in the fields, with the stream passing along the bottom of the hill. A window was a vast improvement over a smoke hole, which let in the weather along with light. Yet the other slaves said Lexander's room was much colder in the winter than Helanas' because of the glass.

I bobbed down in the pose of deference, but when Lexander ignored me for the scroll in his hands, I went to the table. His basin was pure white, showing the cloudy water he had used to wash in. I bent down to pick it up with both hands, and I couldn't help myself—I sniffed deeply because it smelled so like my master. I remembered his arms around me as he spent himself inside me. My eyes closed in pleasure.

"Marja," Lexander said.

Guilty, I straightened up. "Yes, Master?"

"Pick up the basin."

My hands slid under the curved base. I turned to leave, but he added, "You will stand in the center of the room and hold your arms straight out."

I wasn't at my most graceful as I tried to determine the exact center of his chamber.

He seemed amused. "Your only fault, Marja, is that you are sometimes too literal in your desire to obey."

I immediately faced the window where he was seated and lifted my arms out so the bowl was level with my shoulders. My stomach tensed and I felt the strain in my arms and back.

"Good, keep holding it up like that." Lexander looked back down at his scroll as I tried to adjust my grip on the basin. It was made of fine porcelain and would shatter into a hundred pieces if I dropped it. I was always very careful when I carried the basins because one stumble and they would be destroyed.

Lexander didn't look at me as my arms gradually began

to shake and every part of my body clenched, holding up the basin. But I had always been strong, and since coming to Vidaris, I had worked my body in many new ways.

I wanted desperately to please Lexander, to have him praise me again and touch me with desire. My breath came sharp and fast as I called on everything inside of myself to withstand the burning across my shoulders. It felt like a vise was squeezing my chest, like I was drowning.

Still I held the basin, repeating my mantra in my mind. "*Obey, obey, obey . . .*"

My vision blurred as sweat began to flow down my forehead and spine. I forced strength into my arms to hold the basin; I couldn't fail!

Finally Lexander came to stand in front of me, and that made me even more determined. Tears streamed from my eyes, and my head felt as if it were going to burst. I couldn't even count my heartbeats, they were going so fast. My hands slipped on the basin, and for a moment I thought I was going to drop it.

As it slid away from me, I collapsed beneath it, catching the basin and somehow bringing it safely down to my lap. Water sloshed over the edge and onto the stones.

I sprawled out, letting the basin carefully down to the floor. I never imagined something so ordinary could cause such torment.

Lexander reached down and touched my cheek, showing me the wetness on his fingertips. "See, Marja. It's not so difficult to make you cry. If one only knows how."

I struggled to sit up, my arms shaking. I had failed, but he wasn't annoyed with me. With a flush of excitement, I leaned toward him. Our eyes connected, and I knew he wanted me.

He hesitated for only a moment. Then he lifted me and put me onto the bed. Tugging off my tunic, he pressed me down into the fur. I wanted him to lie with me, but he drew the edge of the fur over me, wrapping me entirely in the softness. His hands pressed the fur against my body, stroking me through the supple hide. I could feel every finger as he rubbed me from my face to my toes. The fur felt cool on my bare, sweaty skin.

Then he kissed the tears on my face, kissing my closed eyes as I relaxed under him. His lips caressed my neck, then my arms, which still trembled from trying so hard to please him. He held me in the fur, not letting me touch him. I felt like I was being buried in silk when he finally took me.

He pressed his face in my hair as we rocked, murmuring my name over and over again. I squirmed and fought the enveloping folds, wanting to touch him, to hold him as he held me. But I was forced to take it as he wanted, unresisting and compliant, until he shuddered inside of me.

When he finally pulled away, I was still wrapped tight within the fur. I felt safer than I'd ever felt before.

With a final stroke of my hair, Lexander stood up. His voice was rough, but he was composed once again as he ordered, "From this day forth, you will not speak, Marja. Not to anyone, not even to answer a question. Not until I give you permission. Do you understand?"

I looked up at him, astonished at his request.

"Say it," he commanded. "It will be the last words you speak for many a day."

My fingers dug into the dampened fur. "Yes, Master," I whispered.

The other slaves tormented me for my silence. Even gentle Rosarin thought I was trying to gain their sympathy and attract attention with my ploys. I was slapped and scolded, but still I didn't speak. If anything, my silence only increased their dislike for me.

Lexander paid little attention to me, so I had nothing to ease my ordeal except for the memory of the winged ship that had taken the other slaves away. Now that I couldn't speak, I was free to think of that glorious vision without fearing I would inadvertently reveal what I had seen. Anytime I wanted to, I could recall its gleaming shape receding into the darkness and feel the anticipation of knowing that the greatest adventure lay before me. My only bitter regret was that I would have to leave Lexander. I knew that my desire to submit would be sorely tested when I was torn from him. Sometimes just the thought of our inevitable parting almost rendered me in half, even though his command of silence hurt me so.

But sitting in the courtyard one day, my arms around my legs and the brilliant sun on my face, I realized that Lexander had given me a gift, a way to escape the confining walls of the *haushold* and everyone in it. Unable to reach out, I dove into myself and found a deep well of stillness that allowed me to accept even the most excruciating lessons. As much as I longed to venture into the world, I began to slip into trances. During our training, I held the poses and breathed until I was one with each form. Even while cleaning, my usual humming was stilled. My thoughts that had once flowed into the sky to flit among the clouds and tree-tops now shrank down to each brick, as I lovingly examined its fine surface cracks, listening to every scratch of the brush, every drop of water, every distant footfall.

Though I had been outwardly submissive before, in silence I learned to sink to the very depths of my inner nature. There I found a place inside of myself that could never be tarnished or breached. This restless fire that fueled me would not die, but would return to the Otherworld with great glory when my earthly life was ended.

Time was suspended, and I lost my grip on the day-to-day. Everything eased into one single flow of obedience. The only thing that stirred within me was a constant yearning for my master's touch. I flamed into life whenever Lexander was in the room. Even as I obeyed Helanas and endured her punishments, I watched Lexander. Sometimes when she hit me the crease appeared between his brows, as if he would like to intervene. But he never did, and I soon believed it was a half-imagined fancy.

My thirst was quenched only when the slaves were taught the art of pleasure, learning how to stimulate every part of the body. I came to know my fellow slaves in a way I had never imagined. Rosarin had a languid yet deep response that shook the room when she peaked. The softness of her flesh and the sweet scent of her skin were enticing.

Now I knew why so many men loved to bed Rosarin. The two Skraeling girls were taught as a team to titillate us, and they took that to mean they would not be separated, which cheered them. They dove into their training with a lustiness I had not seen before, and I was never unhappy when I was ordered to stimulate them or receive their attentions for myself.

To my surprise, Sverker was my favorite partner. I truly admired Ansgar more for his kind nature, but he was too tentative a lover to suit me. Kinirniq was so dispirited that he seldom could respond, though Helanas seemed to revel in forcing us to try to revive him. But there was too much darkness woven into the fiber of Kinirniq. Sverker, on the other hand, burned hot and fast with an engrossing frenzy that was magnificent. He preferred me to the others, perhaps because he could be selfish with his desires, with plenty of encouragement from Helanas. They knew that I loved to be overwhelmed during sex, but that didn't stop his enjoyment. Sometimes Sverker caught me when I was going about my duties, and without a word, took me there and then. Sometimes he pressed my head to his groin so I could lick and suck him to satisfaction. Slaves were not supposed to touch each other outside of our training sessions, but I kept his secret. It bonded us together despite my silence, a precious closeness in the midst of my silent isolation.

I shared passion with my fellow slaves whenever I could, and in those moments I truly lived. With Lexander, I could only watch as he took his satisfaction from the other slaves, for their enlightenment or his own enjoyment. He never chose me to serve him. I longed to be the one who pleased him with every indrawn breath or groan. Helanas didn't choose me to touch her either, but that was from disdain, while Lexander had more exalted motives. I couldn't understand why, but I knew I must bow to his plan.

So I was astonished when one day Niels, Rosarin, and Ansgar brought in to decorate the hall boughs that were covered in red, orange, and yellow leaves bigger than my hands. It didn't seem possible that the summer had slipped away so seamlessly, almost without my notice, when I had always been attuned to the seasons, watching them come and go like a jealous lover.

I touched the waxy leaves, feeling like a young child again in my wonderment. Had I been silent for so long?

The others didn't notice, and it seemed as if they had stopped seeing me. I moved through Vidaris doing as I was told, always compliant, always ready to please, never a thought for my own desires . . . except for Lexander. I glanced over at my master, who was seated at his desk. He was writing a letter on a thin piece of birch bark, scratching it with a bone *stilo*.

When the slaves finally left, I carried the stool to the next oil lamp hanging on the wall. My pitcher had just enough oil to fill the rest of the lamps in the fire hall. My attention was on Lexander as usual. Yet there was intensity in my gaze, a tension in my body that had not been there before. Why, I wondered, had he done this to me?

I neatly filled the reservoir of the lamp, standing on my toes to see through the glass. It made an oily mess if it overflowed, so I was very careful. As I settled the wick and climbed back down to move to the next lamp, Lexander didn't look up. But he must have sensed something, because he abruptly ordered, "You will take off your tunic, Marja. Then finish your work."

It was as if he knew I had awakened. With a shiver, I slid my tunic over my head and dropped it at my bare feet. He watched me climb the stool and stretch to fill the lamp.

Lexander put down the *stilo* and began to pleasure himself, leaning back in his chair. I felt a growing anticipation. He was indulging himself in me, finally. I almost gasped as I stepped down from the stool, my thighs rubbing against each other.

Again and again, I went through the ritual, bending and lifting the stool, moving it to the next lamp, climbing, straining to reach, the careful slow pour, then climbing back down again. I grew moist knowing what would happen next. He was obviously waiting so he could finish with me. I wanted to show him how much I had learned this summer, how much I desired him.

I slowly placed the empty pitcher on the stool under the last filled lamp. I was ready for him.

Lexander stood up, straightening his loose pants. As he came closer, I thought that he would take me. But his expression was remote, as if he was already thinking of the next thing he needed to do. I was stunned, left dangling over a precipice.

"You may have one word, Marja."

I didn't even have to think. *"Why?"*

Lexander smiled. His hand slid up my thigh, trailing to my waist and curving around my breast. I drew in my breath, every fiber of my being alive to his touch. Then his finger barely brushed my stomach, dropping down between my legs.

"For this," he murmured.

I shuddered in the grip of a shattering release that caught me unawares. He was so close, watching the waves of climax overtake me, that I could feel his breath on my face.

Then he was gone, and I was left alone again, sagging down next to the stool. He had tuned me to his slightest touch. Perhaps it was the long silence or simply my nature, but Lexander had revealed the sensual power I possessed.

With my new awareness, I helped prepare Vidaris for winter. The storerooms were packed with bales of sun-dried fish, barrels of salted mutton, and smelly bladders of sea-mammal oil and sheep tallow. The stacks of firewood under the kitchen sheds grew to momentous size, while the silos were filled with grain and hay to feed the livestock through winter. When Skraeling traders came, Lexander bartered sacks of grain for whole hides of walrus, casks of ivory tusks, and sealskin sacks filled with fetid tar for waterproofing the roof of the *haushold* and the barns.

As the cold settled on the land, our exile by Ejegod had long repercussions. No new slaves arrived in Vidaris. Lexander was forbidden from returning to Markland, and the people of Viinland didn't want to be associated with Vidaris while we were denounced by a regional chieftain.

The only break in our routine was when we woke one morning to find Helanas had sent Kinirniq away with a passing Kebec trader, as a gift to the inland nobility in an effort to curry their favor. It reminded us of the consequences of failure. Kebec was a rustic place, more Skraeling than not, and it wasn't the grand fate the slaves dreamed of. They talked sometimes of the lives they would lead as companions to emperors and queens in exotic climes. Yet none of them seemed overeager to venture into the unknown. I sometimes wondered whether they would be more ardent if I could tell them of the marvelous winged ship, or if it would simply frighten them.

When I was finally released by Lexander to begin speaking again, it hardly sent a ripple through the *haushold*. In truth, it was the happiest winter of my life, especially since Lexander began to regularly call me to his bed. I was able to savor his strong body and feel him delight in me during the night. Under cover of darkness, he stroked me and murmured words of tenderness that I had never heard from him. I knew that when he entered me, moving together with me like the sea I had come to understand, we were both fulfilled. He reveled in my shameless response, pitched to great heights because of the silent seasons. I was glad my modesty had been burned out so that I could serve him in the way he liked best. When we awoke, I enjoyed his suffused expression in the light slanting through the window. The mornings that he did not make love to me were a disappointment, but were rare for all that.

Because of Lexander's attentions, Helanas treated me more harshly. When one of the Skraeling sisters spilled a full bucket of water, Helanas descended on the poor girl in wrath. She was the weaker of the two and I feared her spirit would break as Kinirniq's had, so I claimed it was my fault, though both Helanas and Lexander knew that it wasn't.

Helanas eagerly dragged me to the fire hall, where there was a ring mounted high in the wall. It was intended for lifting up barrels and crates to the storage platform. But it was also Helanas' favorite form of punishment. She tightened the ropes around my wrists and hauled me up into the air. My feet couldn't get purchase against the bricks, so I dangled. It grew harder to breathe and my arms felt as if they were being pulled from my shoulders. Helanas poked at me, laughing as I cried out from the pain of twisting away.

She toyed with me for a long time, and when she finally let me down, none of the other slaves returned to help me. So I lay there on the floor trying to summon the strength to crawl back to the slave hall.

But Lexander found me. Kneeling beside me, he asked, "Did you want to be hurt, Marja?"

"No." I winced as I tried to sit up. "But better me than the Skraeling girl. I can accept it."

His eyes were shining in the darkness as he put his arms around me, lifting me up. He carried me through the courtyard to his chamber, murmuring, "I saw your selflessness first in Tillfallvik, when you helped Silveta at the cost of your own flesh. I knew then you were special, that you give everything of yourself."

It nearly made me swoon with pleasure to hear his praise.

Yet as close as we grew, I didn't feel that he cared for me more than the other slaves until one cold winter morning. We had slept late, and it was peaceful on the estate, with everyone avoiding the lightly falling snow. I couldn't even hear the sounds of dogs barking or the freemen feeding the cattle in the snug barn. I lay in bed watching the fat white flakes float down past the window, thinking it was magical to be able to see the snow from our snug nest.

Lexander slid out from under the warm furs and padded softly across the room. I could tell he thought I was asleep. He went to the window and sat on the cushioned seat, gazing out at the snow-covered hills. Though he was naked, he didn't seem to notice the chill air.

I watched him in the pearly light for a long time, wondering what he was thinking, staring out on his estate. He had everything a man could desire, yet he seemed dissatisfied. His hand kept clenching into a fist, as if he longed to fight, but he could not bring himself to do it.

Finally I got up and went to him, putting my arms around him from behind. When we were alone he encouraged me to be assertive. The other slaves were conditioned by Helanas to be always timid and meek. She tried to break me as well. But after I learned that Lexander enjoyed my boldness, I expressed my affection for him whenever I could.

Standing behind him, I caressed his neck and shoulders, feeling his muscles beneath his skin. It seemed I could never get enough of him. As I leaned forward, I saw the mirror on the table. It was angled in such a way that it caught his reflection. His expression, normally so reserved, shifted before my eyes. As I kissed him lightly, letting my lips tell him of my love, his face seemed to crumple as a tear slipped down his cheek. The hardened mask he always wore fell away and his *inua* shone through. I saw his deep misery and confusion, and it pierced my heart. But before I could speak, his tension eased and his eyes shone brighter. My simple touch was soothing him, as if he felt an immense relief just from being in my arms.

He grasped my hand, and without turning, kissed it. Tears rose in my eyes. *He needed me.* I had never imagined such a thing before. This great man with everything in the world lacked the one thing I alone could give him—true and pure devotion from a fervent heart.

When he finally turned, his face was back to normal. But now I could see his pain, and it made me ache inside to know my love was in torment.

He took me in his arms and kissed me deep, as if clinging to a rope in a stormy sea. We made love, and it was something beyond passion. It was soft yet urgent, wordless. I knew it was the first time we had come together as equals rather than master and slave.

We had many such mornings, treasures I stashed away to examine in the privacy of my own thoughts. I never told the other slaves.

*　　*　　*

With the simplicity of youth, I didn't question my prosperous life until early spring when I returned home to my village for a visit. Lexander had promised my da that I would see my family when the ice broke, and as soon as Nauga Sea was open, Lexander was true to his word. I thought it was an innocent indulgence, a fulfillment of his agreement with my da. Then I remembered that Vidaris used slaves as bait, letting us testify to the luxury of the estate and the sophistication of our lives. Our stories undoubtedly spread to inspire other young people to leave their homes in his care. Whatever his reason, Lexander announced that his word to my da held prior claim over Ejegod's proclamation of exile.

As we sailed across the Nauga Sea, I communed with the sea spirits the entire way, telling them everything that had happened to me in Vidaris. When I finally saw the familiar purple line of the highlands beyond Jarnby, my heart leaped in joy. The fens were a shade of green that I remembered best, as were the hummocks of the longhouses.

I saw my mam from far way, as she stood on the shore waving her shawl. She was usually so reserved and serene that I wept when I saw the tears streaming from the outer corners of her eyes.

I was one of the first to leap from the boat, forgetting even Lexander in my haste to reach my mam. Her arms enfolded me, but I was surprised to find I had grown while I was away, and now towered over her. But she smelled the same: of sinew and peat smoke and moss.

"I'm home, Mam," I murmured brokenly.

"I never knew," she whispered, her arms tight around me. "My own mam must have felt this way when I left her. I never knew it was this difficult or I would not have done it . . ."

My tears near blinded me as Lexander called to my da, and my master was openly smiling and proud of me. He tossed my bag over the side and lifted down a basket full of gifts for my family. "I'll return five days hence. How is the passage through the strait?"

"Open to Helluland," my da replied. "An early warming, praise be the gods."

Lexander gestured down to his feet. "You notice I do not set foot on your land. But you would do well to not speak of our visit here."

My da growled, startling me. "You'll not find us blathering to those sons of death! We know how to protect our own." With that he clasped a hand on my shoulder, telling me, "You've turned fair as a flower, my girl. I never thought it of ye."

"Is there trouble?" I asked, finally looking around at my siblings, cousins, and aunts. They were a dirty, draggle-haired lot, and I realized with a start that this was how Bjorn had viewed me when I first arrived at Vidaris. It was a wonder that Lexander had picked me out from amongst them.

"Aye, there's enough heartache to spare," my da agreed. But my mam ended the discussion by pulling me away from the longship, glancing back uneasily at Lexander. I waved to my master, but he was already ordering his oarsmen to launch the ship.

In reality, I was unnerved by my return. I was back in my familiar home, every face and every sod-house worn like a groove in my mind. But they watched me with an eagerness I couldn't understand. My kin kept touching me, stroking my cheeks and hands, which glowed with a vitality missing from their own wan, tired faces. I was used to thinking of home as a place where I belonged, but now that had changed.

I hardly recognized my brother with his gawky limbs and fuzz on his chin, teetering on the edge of manhood. He stayed far away, while my younger sister walked close beside me, stroking the embroidery on the edge of my cloak. I was glad Lexander had packed gifts for everyone. What I now regarded as an ordinary suede tunic and leggings, along with my spring cloak, were considered splendid by my kin. I knew that the other pretty clothes in my bag would never be worn here. Tonight I would sleep among my sisters on the mossy mound covering the ledge.

My da set the basket on the chopping block, and I dug into it. There were jars of exotic food—date preserves and spices from the southern lands, along with grains to make thick, nourishing porridges. Their excitement grew for we were in the lean season, and I remembered well the feeling of ribs hard beneath my skin. My mam and aunts opened and sniffed everything, while I distributed silk ribbons, hand mirrors, and clasps among my siblings and cousins.

"Where is Deidre?" I asked, holding up a green ribbon that would match her eyes. "This one is for her."

The silence and downcast gazes told me there was a tragedy. The men looked ready to kill, their hands going to the axes on their belts. Even my brother seemed fierce and older than his years when he put his hand to his knife.

"What has happened?" I asked softly. Deidre had been one of my playmates when I was younger.

My mam hushed me and helped me take the last of the gifts from the basket to hand out. I knew better than to dwell on sadness while my family was creating a celebration to welcome me home.

The next day, before I went into the fens, I asked my brother about Deidre.

"She was killed," my brother said shortly. "Killed by the men who follow that berserker Birgir Barfoot."

"Birgir? He was here?" I asked, horrified.

"Aye, you must have heard of him. His warriors came, but they scorned our land. Some settled on the long lake south of here. They've taken women to be their wives, Skraeling and Noromenn both, but Deidre was killed because she fought them. Right there on the shore. We found her body, but the *knaar* was already out to sea. You should have seen our uncle. He was furious and claimed he would go to seek justice, but the word is they claim land with the blessing of our *chieftain*."

My brother spat at the word, and I could not blame him. My own opinion of Ejegod was less than good, and I wondered not for the first time how Silveta had avoided Birgir's bed through a full turn of seasons. Perhaps she had triumphed with her own *bondi,* fetched at the cost of Vidaris' good name. But it was not my place to speak of what had happened in Tillfallvik. I was grateful that my own name had not been linked to the tale of the exile of Vidaris.

"Deidre was promised to Gorm," my brother ventured. "I saw him watching when you arrived."

I hadn't noticed Gorm, a big blond man who was destined for the forge like my da. But I remembered him well. He was one of the boys I had innocently rutted with in the fens. I had enjoyed his simple lust and allowed him to take me anytime he followed me away from the village. But he had never spoken of it to anyone, and he left me without a word when we were done. That was how all the boys were, ashamed of dallying with a maid who was known to be half addled by the *olfs*.

"He might consider you for his wife," my brother added. "Then you could stay here where you belong."

Startled, I protested. "I belong to Lexander. I can't marry Gorm."

"But you're here now," my brother pointed out. "We could hide you when he returns. Vidaris can't protest or they would risk the wrath of Ejegod. You don't have to go away."

"But . . . I want to go." It seemed as if I were being sucked under by sticky mud when I tried to imagine myself as Gorm's wife.

"You made a mistake," my brother insisted. "You belong here on the fens. I know how you are and how you must feel to lose everything you love."

I was so accustomed to subservience that I almost agreed. But my heart knew better. I could no sooner return to Jarnby than I could return to being a babe in my mam's arms. I shook my head wordlessly.

"Faraway eyes . . ." my brother murmured. That was how Lexander had described me the first day he met me. Then my brother went back to his work in the fields, the care of the sheep now given to our younger sibling.

I spent most of my days on the fens, as I always did. I could once again hear the *olfs*. Their voices had been silent for so long, and I had almost thought that part of my life was over. But now I heard their singing, drawing me from place to place, gleefully showing me a black pool where I could bathe or a dry hillock to nap on. I danced again in their praise, my feet hardly touching the ground. The *olfs* were the purest embodiment of the land, and their lure went deep in me.

It was during my time on the fens that I finally realized the *olfs* avoided Vidaris because of Helanas' viciousness, which was powerful enough to keep all good things at bay. It was not a failure of mine that kept me from sensing the otherworldly creatures in Vidaris, but the presence of oppressive spirits smothering the land.

I also thought long on my kin in Jarnby, seeing all the more clearly now that I had gone away. There were too many children inside the narrow, cramped duns, and no privacy for contemplation or pleasure. Only hard work and more work to survive. After my mam's first burst of emotion, she retreated to silent movement at her loom, forever spinning, weaving, and sewing to keep her brood in clothes. She was never one to tell me what she thought unless she was in the grip of a seeing. It seemed she already knew my future, one far away from her, and had accepted it as I did. My poor da drank himself into a stupor at night, until his great body lay snoring on the sleeping ledge. It was something I barely remembered from before, but now I felt a great sorrow for him and my mam, forced to labor so hard.

I missed Lexander desperately as the days passed. I felt adrift despite the love that poured from the *olfs*. It was only in part because Lexander had trained me so exquisitely to respond to his every mood. He had devoted himself to me over the winter, and I missed waking up beside him and feeling him touch me. Part of me wished I had sailed with him to the northern straits, past the great bergs and icy land. Everything here in Jarnby was constrained, as familiar as an old moldering sack. At times I broke out in song or chattered on about Vidaris until my family's eyes glazed over with incomprehension, and I knew I no longer fit into their world.

So I was ready when the red-striped sail came into view. I ran to meet the longship in my haste to greet my master.

Lexander stood in the prow, exactly as I had seen him that first day. I smiled and waved to him. But when the boat reached the shore I noticed there was a woman close by him. She was Skraeling, with long dark hair and black eyes. She seemed defiantly proud, holding her head high, and was wearing sumptuous white furs.

"Marja! Come aboard quickly," Lexander called. "We must catch the turning tide."

I remembered to hug my mam and my da pulled on my braids that held my hair neatly. My brother scowled with his arms crossed defiantly, but I shook my head at him. I couldn't stay. Indeed, the envy in my sister's eyes reassured me.

But when I was lifted into the boat, my throat closed. The Skraeling was beautiful. Her expression was haughty, reminding me of Bjorn although she was as dark as he was fair. I covertly tried to brush away the mud of the fens that stained my leggings. I had forgotten until this moment that I had braided some wool into my hair, and her eyes were scornful as she stroked her own glossy hair that fell below her hips.

Lexander gestured to the young woman. "Marja, this is Qamaniq, my new slave."

Six

When we returned to Vidaris, everything was different. Not long after my visit home, I found myself kneeling in the fire hall watching Lexander teach the four new slaves the art of *fotternoje*. The two newest slaves, blond brothers from Fylkeran in Hop, were mesmerized. I don't think any of us had ever eroticized feet until our master taught us how. The new Skraeling male, Torngasoak licked Helanas' toes while Qamaniq bent her shapely body over Lexander.

Jealousy burned inside of me. I hated every moment that Lexander spent with Qamaniq and the other new slaves. It had ruined our increasingly complex rapport, so subtle that the others hadn't noticed, but as challenging as the daily games of *hneftaf* I played with Lexander. But now it was gone, the constant interchange of feints and parries, and my ultimate release. Now he was busy and had no time for me.

He glanced up and knew exactly what I was thinking. There was no resentment on my face, only perfect obedience. But he knew nonetheless. We were so in tune with each other that I had only to stand before him for him to know how I felt.

I chastised myself for my own jealousy of Qamaniq. Had I learned nothing of acceptance at my master's knee? I sank into myself again and again to find the peace in submission, only to have it vanish at her next coquettish laugh or when Lexander tenderly stroked her head. It was my most trying test to date and I sometimes raged at the fates that had made me fall in love with Lexander.

Qamaniq's striking figure, made for passion, and her bold, expressive face were far more beautiful than I could ever be. I had an earthy presence, while Qamaniq was a goddess incarnate. Everyone watched her, lingering on the curve of her bosom and the poised tilt of her head. I wanted to be the Skraeling beauty so I could compel the same admiration I saw in Lexander's eyes.

Suddenly Helanas pushed Torngasoak aside. "You encourage her infatuation!" She took two strides to grab me by the shoulders to shake me. "You will stop acting like a lovesick girl!"

"Whatever you desire, Mistress," I responded as I had been taught. I went limp under her hands because to resist would provoke her even more.

"If you can't control yourself, I'll do it for you." Helanas dragged me over to the wall. I huddled down, making sure I didn't glance back at Lexander. Helanas was ever ready to find me at fault. Lately, looking at Lexander had become my most serious infraction.

Helanas flung open a chest and tore the cushions and blankets from it. "Get in!"

I climbed into the small space, lying on my side and bending my knees so I could fit. The last thing I saw was Helanas, her face twisted in an ugly, helpless expression. As the lid fell and darkness engulfed me, I realized it was jealousy. I had never seen any sign of tenderness between Helanas and Lexander, but from my new vantage point, it appeared as if she felt the same about me as I did about Qamaniq. It was very strange because I thought Helanas hated Lexander. But I couldn't doubt my own eyes.

I took a few deep breaths, my fingers seeking out the cracks where cool air poured in. There were distant murmurs as the training continued. Lexander hadn't protested my punishment. He never did. He was probably engrossed in the satisfaction Qamaniq was giving him. He wouldn't miss me when the winged ship came to take me away.

I tensed as sharp pains shot through my legs and back. I wanted nothing more than to turn and stretch hard in relief. But I was trapped, for how long was anyone's guess. I had been bound all night before, but never had I been shut inside a chest.

Breathing slowly and deeply, I relaxed every muscle, starting from my toes all the way up to my neck. It took concentration to keep from clenching back up, especially when someone banged on the lid of the chest a few times. It must have been Helanas. I ignored her as I focused on releasing every trace of resistance, falling into that deep pool inside of me that was never ruffled, never emptied. Lexander had trained me to know my body so thoroughly that eventually I was able to drift into a doze, feeling quite comfortable. It probably wasn't what Helanas expected, but that was the triumph I gained from submission.

The creak of the latch woke me. I started to rise, but was trapped by the sides of the chest. For a moment, I panicked and almost started thrashing and kicking to try to free myself. Then I remembered Helanas wanted me to lose control. I willed myself to relax to the inevitable.

The lid opened to darkness. I had been in the chest for a long time.

Hands reached into the glow of the lamp set on the floor. It was Lexander. He gently lifted me from my confinement. I could feel how strong he was, he did it with such ease. Even I could not stand after such an ordeal, confined for half a day or more. Lexander had shown me scrolls with images of the body and explained that inside us were rivers and streams that watered our flesh like the earth. Now it felt as if my limbs were clogged and sluggish, rendering them numb.

Lexander's arms went around me, holding me up. He bent over me, pressing his cheek against my hair. The feel of his body against mine made me nearly swoon with delight. "She'll tell them that I am too weak with the slaves. But I care not. I could not forget you, Marja."

His voice caressed my name, and I closed my eyes, savoring the moment.

"Tell me," Lexander whispered, holding me so close, "would you have resented me if I had left you there?"

"No!" I was shocked at the question. "Never would I resent you."

He pulled back to look into my face. His eyes were shadowed by the dim light. "But you do begrudge me my new slaves."

Slowly I shook my head. "I belong to you even when you don't touch me. Yet . . . I cannot help myself. I always long to be by your side."

"What if I never saw you again, Marja? Would you still be mine in your heart?"

"In heart, body, and mind." I felt the truth of my words in the core of my being. "Always, I will be yours."

"You will serve other masters. It is in your nature to give yourself to those who command it." His head turned, and for a moment there was a struggle on his face. Could it be that he was also jealous of me? It didn't seem possible, but I had already seen it in Helanas. Lexander surely felt more for me than he wanted to reveal.

"Go to bed, Marja. You will need your strength for tomorrow."

The others were still asleep when I awoke to the sound of *olf* laughter very early in the morning. The *olf* had braved the evil spirits that infested Vidaris to come whisper in my ear, *"A journey begun is a journey ended."* The *olf* showed me the winged ship plying the waters off Viinland. They knew I had been expecting the ship to return to take me from Vidaris. The *olfs* avoided Vidaris because of the evil that dwelled here, so they were delighted I was finally leaving.

As for Lexander, perhaps he had been forewarned of the ship's arrival. Last night he had bid me good-bye in his own way, confirming our bond before I was taken away by the winged ship forever.

I couldn't bear to think of leaving Lexander, even though I yearned to quit the estate and venture to new places. I passed the chest in the fire hall, with the bedding returned and the lid closed. There was nothing to indicate that something momentous had happened in that spot. My brief talk in the dark with Lexander almost seemed like a dream.

I never questioned that the great winged ship would arrive this night to take the slaves away and that I would be going with them. In truth, now that I had returned to Jarnby and fulfilled Lexander's promise to my da, there was no reason for me to stay in Vidaris. Helanas would be glad to see the last of me. And I was as trained as I would ever be.

There were signs among the older slaves that they were also ready to depart; in their boredom at the routine, the unthinking perfection of their movements, and a restlessness I had not seen before. I waited for them to realize what lay ahead, but it wasn't until our evening bath that they began to sense something. Lexander and Helanas cleaned the four of us—Rosarin, Sverker, Ansgar, and me—with a thoroughness usually reserved for new arrivals. We were clipped, polished, and scrubbed inside and out.

Then the new slaves were sent to bed along with Niels and the sisters. Only Niels had seen Bjorn and the other slaves depart Vidaris and recognized as we did that our time had come. His face crumpled as he left the baths. Qamaniq slinked away, casting an envious look over her shoulder at me. With a burst of agony, I realized that my rival would have Lexander's undivided attention from now on.

When we were done, Helanas gave us brief tunics to wear. Mine hung by two silver cords from my shoulders and was open on the sides, with a small catch at the waist. The spring weather was not mild, so the steamy warmth of the bathhouse was welcome.

"Kneel," Helanas ordered.

We formed a straight line in front of her, our knees on the wet bricks.

"Your training is complete," Helanas told us. "You are now fit to serve."

"Where will we go, Mistress?" Sverker asked. He was the bravest with her, though she had beaten him for it in the past.

Helanas actually smiled this time. "We've prepared you specially to serve our own people. You'll sail to Stanbulin, many days away. From there, you'll be sent to our native island. You will find that we are a much more advanced society than you are accustomed to. You will have luxuries you've never dreamed of."

Anything that pleased Helanas was usually something to fear. Yet it could only be good for me to get far away from the evil she wove within Vidaris.

"Do not be afraid of the many strange things you shall see," Lexander told us.

"It is not meant for you to understand your betters," Helanas put in.

"Remember your training," Lexander finished, giving me an intent look. "It will serve you well."

I nodded briefly, choking at the thought of seeing him no more. I couldn't bear it! I had always known this day would come. But I couldn't hide my distress, and Helanas was gloating over it. But the others had the same stricken, reverent expression that I had seen on Bjorn's face. They were thrilled at the promise of living among superior people like our master and mistress. But I was not so fickle. I belonged to Lexander. It suddenly didn't seem possible to live without him.

"You will follow me," Lexander ordered. And I had to obey.

I knew what I would see when we reached the open gate. The sun had set and the last light was leaving the sky. I shivered in the chill air and was the only one who looked back at the *haushold*. Helanas had gone inside, leaving Lexander to take us down to the bay. A great bonfire blazed in the middle of the beach, illuminating the dock. Often Vidaris had a bonfire at night to lure in traders at sea. The longship's sail was tied down and it rocked gently in the waves, the empty mast swinging from side to side.

There was no one else in sight as Lexander started down the long flight of wooden steps. None of the freemen or servants could see the beach because of the palisade along the top of the bluff.

When we stood in a group near the fire, Lexander announced, "This is to be your fate, to serve my people to the best of your ability. Go and give glory unto Vidaris."

I looked out to sea, expecting the winged ship to appear. As if a vision descended, the giant white swan sailed toward us out of the darkness. The other slaves were overawed by the sight.

Lexander knew by their expressions that I had never broken my promise. At his slow nod of acknowledgment, I felt a flush of pride. I also wanted to cry, knowing this was my last service for him.

We were all trembling now, not from the cold but at the sight of the miraculous ship as it rapidly approached. Rosarin gasped out loud and clutched my arm.

Lexander moved behind us as it lightly drew up to the dock. The flames of the bonfire reflected in the curved hull.

I felt Lexander's hands fall on my shoulders. His fingers held me tightly, as if he didn't want to let me go. I moaned, knowing I couldn't bear to leave him.

A rope ladder fell to touch the dock. "Go now," Lexander ordered.

Ansgar was the first to step forward, and like a sleepwalker Sverker followed. Rosarin was right on his heels. But Lexander held me back.

He whispered in my ear, "Quick, Marja! Slip away and hide among the rocks. Wait there until I come for you."

He stepped past me, leaving me staggering in the soft sand. I almost thought I had imagined it, but his piercing look convinced me I had heard correctly. As always I obeyed, backing into the shadows of the cliff, my eyes still fastened on the winged ship. None of the other slaves seemed to notice I was not with them. Lexander followed Rosarin up the ladder.

I felt the rocks under my feet and climbed over them in the darkness under the bluff. My bare knees got muddy, reminding me of the first time I had seen the winged ship and how I had served my penance. I never did learn the name of the magnate who had touched me so roughly. He had avoided Vidaris along with everyone else since Ejegod's proclamation of exile.

Then Lexander reappeared and returned to the fire. I was watching him so closely that I missed the first moment when the ship turned to depart. The sails caught the wind and it moved away swiftly.

I was gasping, whether it was in disappointment or relief, I did not know. The winged ship sped away like the wind, dwindling to a white blur.

Lexander glanced toward me, one hand motioning for me to stay. Instantly, my doubts were gone. I had not misunderstood him. Lexander started up the steps to the gate of the estate. I watched him as long as I could, then settled down to wait. It could be a long time, like last night in the chest, but I was doing as he wished and that was enough to satisfy me.

Lexander soon returned carrying a bundle under one arm. As he neared the base of the cliff, he peered into the darkness. "Marja, you can come out now."

I extricated myself from the rocks, scraping my feet and legs. The silk tunic was sodden and stained nearly to my waist. I crossed my arms in front of my stomach as I trembled.

"Take that off and put on these." Lexander held out the bundle.

I opened it and knew from the scent that the clothes had belonged to Rosarin. I shrugged off the flimsy tunic and pulled on the brown suede leggings and knee-length tunic. The boots were my own, the ones I used when I helped unload goods from longships or fetched firewood. When I finished, I slung the long cloak over my shoulders. It was Ansgar's spring cloak, but it felt heavier than mine.

Then I stood facing Lexander expectantly. "No questions?" he asked. "Of course you haven't any. You are the perfect slave, ever willing, ever compliant."

I wasn't sure if he was pleased or not. "I am what you made me."

"No, you are what nature made you. And I won't have you wasted by those like Helanas who would scorn your gift. I've saved you from that fate, Marja."

"I won't be sent to your people?" I had to ask.

"Never, as long as I live. You are too precious to me."

He kissed me, his lips taking possession of me. I felt myself falling into him, held in his arms, protected and cherished. I had dreamed of this—Lexander declaring that he desired me above everything else. He had always felt it, now I was sure. He would not let me go because he felt the same as I did.

"Marja," he finally said, still holding me tightly. "We'll be together. I cannot endure it any longer. I will not heed their insatiable demand."

I had seen enough to know that he was dissatisfied, but I hadn't realized his unhappiness ran so deep. It was shocking that a man so powerful could be brought so low. "I will help you," I pledged. "I would die without you."

"Marja!" He shook me slightly. "I fear I've been too thorough. You must take care of yourself, as you did in Jarnby. I can't come with you now. Soon enough I will be able to excuse my departure without raising Helanas' suspicions."

"What am I to do?" I asked, bewildered.

"Go to Markland to stay with Silveta. She will have to help you." He pressed a square packet of parchment into my hand. "Here are coins for your passage. Tell Silveta that my price for silence about Birgir is that she protect you until I come."

"But I've been exiled!" I protested. "I can't go to Tillfallvik."

"You must. The slaves who left may inquire about you, and the ship could return. Then Helanas would discover that you didn't depart with them." One corner of his mouth raised. "Tillfallvik is the only place she will not think to look for you. She would never expect you, of all people, to defy Ejegod in his own estate. Will you do it if I ask you to?"

It was the first time he had requested something rather than simply ordering me to do it. Nonetheless, I felt the same compulsion to agree. "Yes, I will do as you say."

"Then come. I'll show you the road to Brianda, the port in southern Fjardemano. It's two days' walk. You can get passage from there to Tillfallvik."

My eyes widened. I had never been so far alone before.

"You know what to do, Marja. Go to Silveta. Don't tell anyone you are a pleasure slave. I will come for you in Tillfallvik and we shall be reunited." He kissed me once more, clutching me tight.

The darkness spread around us as we proceeded along the shore, my hand held tightly in his. We walked in silence, everything said and everything left to do before me. When we reached the mouth of the river, a dirt path wound through the bushes, leading to a bridge. A wagon lane with two ruts disappeared into the darkness on either side.

Here Lexander hugged me close, murmuring, "I should have left long before, but I needed you to inspire me. You are all I want in this world." I could have stayed in his arms forever. But too soon he released me. "Go now, and do me proud, Marja."

He headed down the lane to Vidaris. I was left alone, clutching my cloak around me.

Everything in my life had led to this moment. I knew I could do as he asked, what the other slaves could never hope to accomplish. I could strike out across this unknown land and commune with the *olfs* to safely pass, with my own spirit singing in pleasure because I was free to roam.

With a shiver of anticipation, I stepped into the night and was off.

Seven

Yet as I crossed the bridge and ventured down the lane, I faltered. The trees arching overhead shadowed the wan light of the half-moon. I could hardly see to put one foot in front of the other. I was used to playing in the night with the *olfs,* using their uncanny glow to light my way. But no *olfs* appeared despite my plaintive summons.

So I calmed myself, putting aside Lexander's revelation. I could hardly believe he had openly declared his love for me; I wanted to dance with abandon, giddy with release after such endless longing. But I had to reach Tillfallvik. My hand still clutched the parchment with the weight of coins inside, and I carefully stowed it in the deep pockets of Ansgar's cloak. I looked out at the ocean as if to glimpse the winged ship through the trees, carrying my slave-mates away to a life I had long envisioned . . .

When my breathing grew steady, I relaxed and reached out with my senses. The pounding of the ocean beat like the heart of the earth while the night breeze flowed over me. But the land was empty, draining my strength where I should have felt invigorated.

Instinctively I followed the lane like a lifeline out of the ravenous muck that sought to swallow me whole. I stumbled at first over rocks and fallen branches, but let nothing slacken my pace. Despite the cold air, nervous sweat beaded my skin. I rushed onward, hardly seeing with my eyes, but feeling with the fibers of my being the way to safety, becoming more surefooted the farther I went from Vidaris.

I know not how long I followed the curving lane through the woods, crossing streams and climbing hills. I heard no sounds of men, only the haunting cries of night birds, the rising and falling drone of insects, and choruses of croaking toads. I might have charged through blind to all but my goal if I hadn't reached the torrent of a river, swollen by melted snow. The water picked up the glow of the moon and revealed a wide sparkling expanse that I had to cross.

So I retreated back into the woods, seeking a pile of dead leaves in the midst of a grove of slender birch trees. Curling up in the cloak, I breathed deep of the mingled scents of Ansgar and Rosarin in the clothing. Finally I was still enough to let the night sounds wash over me.

But it was Lexander in my thoughts. He was in the *haushold*, perhaps looking through the diamond panes of glass and wondering how I fared. He loved me.

I slept little that night, alert to the sounds of the rising wind or the animals that crackled through the underbrush. I drowsed in a deep communion with the land, settling into the rocks and plants that the spirits enlivened. My fragmented dreams were frightening in their intensity, with Helanas emerging time and again. Sometimes I saw only her eyes, angry and malevolent. Or her hand, rising to strike me.

When I awoke, a miasma hung over the woods behind me. The evil spirits that infested Vidaris sent tendrils of hatred in my direction as if trying to draw me back in. I had escaped intact, not realizing until now the danger I had endured in their midst without succumbing to despair. Lexander had said his people were all like Helanas, a terrible thought indeed. What would happen to gentle Rosarin and brave Ansgar among them?

I shook myself, realizing that the demons were reaching ever closer. I gathered my cloak around me, heading up-river to find a ford I could cross. As I began to move about, the wisps of evil dissipated, and I could feel the land awakening under the rising sun.

A spirited *olf,* more bold than his fellows, appeared between my feet, tripping me again and again. Its white hair formed a halo around its head, and its dimpled legs and buttocks looked so rosy and fresh that I was heartened. Surely I was safe from the evil seeking me in this creature's company.

I laughed at the *olf,* knowing that it was only testing me to see if I would become annoyed by its antics. Then I danced a bit, echoing its hop-skip rhythm. In delight, the *olf* led me to a downed tree that I could use to cross the river. It was high up between the banks as the water rushed through a gully, pounding against the submerged boulders. I wanted to crawl across for safety's sake, but I knew the *olf* wouldn't like my trepidation. The *olf* flickered in and out of sight as it scampered across, then back, jumping high before landing lightly on the peeling bark.

Once I reached the other side, nearly a score of *olfs* were darting through the air and skimming around me, glowing with light that sparkled with color. I was thrilled to have them near me, and I skipped down the lane, singing every song I could remember. I felt as if I could travel forever with them bounding along beside me. They showed me caches of nuts made by busy squirrels and forgotten over the winter. I recognized the tender greens I could eat from the bushes and plants that grew at the water's edge.

In most places the lane was crowded with bushes and thick clumps of grass overgrowing the rutted wagon tracks. Birdsong filled the air, and the sun slanted cheerfully through the trees, drawing out the first buds of flowers in the meadows. The morning sun pulled the mist from the ground, and every hollow was filled with a fine white blanket of down.

I would like to think I sang and danced to honor the spirits and the gods, but Lexander was constantly in my thoughts. When I remembered him saying, "You are too precious to me," it filled me to overflowing.

As the sun drew overhead, the lane curved over the top of a bluff, offering a view down into a small cove with a narrow valley beyond. It was another great estate, but unlike Vidaris, there was no protecting palisade to mark its borders. The ocean seemed impossibly blue, my eyes having become accustomed to the vegetation. Two longships were tethered at the dock, with people busy working on the beach and plowing the ruddy fields.

Neither of the longships had a red-striped sail, so they weren't from Vidaris. I feared I would be stopped and questioned, but no one so much as turned to look as I passed through. The *olfs* cavorting around me must have blocked me from their sight. It happened that way with people who were willfully blind to the otherworldly creatures. One young child chortled gleefully, reaching out with a tiny hand as I went by with my merry band. Dogs barked and tried to chase me, but the *olfs* addled their brains and sent them off in the wrong direction.

I applauded the *olfs'* antics, and more of them began showing themselves to me through the light, their merry grins and small legs upturned as they cartwheeled over the ground. Some wore flowers woven in their hair as I used to, while others decorated their chubby bodies with cords of woven grass, tied with bows like presents waiting to be opened.

When the sun began to sink, turning the clouds to deepest purple and flaming orange, the *olfs* lured me to the base of an enormous tree. I nestled down between two broad roots that rose higher than my prone body. The *olfs* slowly dispersed, attracted to the dreams of sleeping people. But I could sense a few that remained up in the top of the oak, swaying with the wind in the branches.

I finally fell into a real sleep. But I was awoken in the night by the *qiqirn,* a pack of wild dog imps that ran through the woods. They were yipping their high-pitched keen that froze their prey. I shook in fear as the *qiqirn* grew louder, whipping closer through the trees. A rabbit screamed as it was snapped up. I could only imagine what they would do to *me.*

The *olfs* in the treetops stilled to wait out the passage of the *qiqirn.* They were in no danger from the beasts' razor-sharp teeth, but I was at risk because I was alone. The *qiqirn* fed only on solitary prey.

I covered my face within my hood and pressed against the oak, willing my mind to become wooden and treelike. I thought only of the shape of the leaves, of the warmth of sunlight on my limbs, and of sweet sap rising in the trunk and flowing into the smallest branches. I felt the flow as if it were part of my own body.

As the *qiqirn* descended in a deafening roar, the pack split to flow around the mighty oak. *I am the oak,* I silently willed myself. *Rooted in the earth, reaching to the sky . . .*

Then the *qiqirn* were past, and their eerie noise began to recede. My heart was beating too fast. Lexander would never have known what happened to me if I had been caught and devoured. I was very lucky they had not found me during my first night in the woods, when the birch grove would not have protected me as the powerful oak had.

Gratefully, I snuggled closer to the tree roots, falling into a deep sleep. If I could lie safely within the oak's embrace while *qiqirn* roamed the woods, then I had nothing to fear.

Indeed, I'd little thought of the dangers when Lexander had asked me to travel alone. The next morning, sensing my fear, the *olfs* led me around the places where evil lurked, avoiding the shadowy mouth of a cave and a smelly sulfurous swamp. Though I was hungry, I wasn't tempted to stop at the occasional farm we passed to ask for food. I wanted only to reach Brianda.

The *olfs* began to leave me by late afternoon as the estates and farms grew more numerous, with only patches of woods and fields between the clusters of houses. These were woodsy *olfs*, unaccustomed to people. I was sorry to see them go, but I understood and was grateful they had helped me through their land.

The third night, I crawled into a meadow where sheep had gathered. A pile of straw made a comfortable bed, and I was protected from the *qiqirn* by the sheep's warm, furry bodies.

I gazed up at the cloudless sky with brilliant stars shining on the fields, and it all seemed so peaceful that I was lulled to sleep. But in the darkest night before the dawn, I felt a chill pass over me and awoke to see an *adlet* settling on a sheep. The poor ewe bucked and tried to get out from under it, but was quickly lulled by the poison in the adlet's fangs. I heard the sucking noise as the *adlet* fed on the sheep's blood.

Shuddering, I couldn't go to help the ewe, knowing the *adlet* would turn on me instead. Once it drank its fill, it drifted up and across the fields, a blue-black shadow of shapeless form. The ewe settled down onto the grass, dazed by the loss of life force. I went over and gathered her close, giving her warmth so she could survive until morning.

The rain was falling and a heavy mist blanketed the land when I opened my eyes. I was heartened to see the ewe tottering away, weak but alive. In Jarnby, we locked our livestock into byres at night to keep the *adlets* from sucking them dry. But that was the first *adlet* I had seen in Fjardemano.

I trudged through the cold spring rain, my boots soaked in the thick mud. Two curious farm *olfs* followed me for a while, dressed in colorful rags filched from a quilting bag. But I could not summon the spirit to dance for them. I hummed and sang when I could, but was too busy concentrating on the slippery mud. It wasn't long before the last *olf* bade me good-bye and returned to its beloved home.

More people appeared on the road as the day wore on, with carts pulled by donkeys and horses ridden by freemen wearing brightly dyed cloaks. My own was well crafted and kept me dry, but my boots were sodden, squelching with every step. People talked around me, calling out to one another or giving short, angry commands to their animals. I spoke only to ask the way to Brianda whenever the road forked or crossed another path, letting nothing divert me from my task.

I was surprised out of my dreary slogging at the sight of the ocean. I had crossed Fjardemano and arrived on the leeward side of the island. As the sun struggled to pierce the low-hanging clouds that were gathering, I saw Brianda ahead of me.

A river emptied into the ocean, cutting through the slight rise. Within the river valley was the town. The buildings huddled close to one another, some sharing common walls. The busy harbor bristled with docks, and moored boats of all sizes rocked on the gentle sea. I could feel the mainland in the distance, just out of sight on the horizon.

My goal was to find a ship that could sail me to Tillfallvik. It was only midday, so I could reach Markland by night. Surely Silveta would take me in because of the service I did her last midsummer. Hopefully I wouldn't have to wait long for Lexander to arrive.

I plunged down into the town. The warren of buildings and twisting streets confused me. I seemed to never get closer to the harbor. The echo of noise—shouts, horses clopping, rattling wheels, chisels falling on stone—rang in my head, making me long for the subtle sounds of the woods.

I stopped for a drink from a round rain barrel and was entranced by the tiny sprite living there. I bent over the dark pool crooning as the tiny fishlike sprite whispered back, until a woman chased me away, brandishing her broom after me. Her hair was tangled and hung around her lined face, but for all that, the sprite had said she was not old. Her red dress looked festive, but her apron was so soiled that Hallgerd would have beaten any slave who dared to wear it.

After that, I wandered around until I came upon a handcart piled with meat pastries. The man selling them had hands and a face that were gray with ground-in soot. The rich aroma of spices and mutton made my mouth water. I had gone too long without food.

Pulling out the packet of coins Lexander had given me, I found several slender silvers that looked much like the ones the people were handing the man. Holding one out gingerly, I waited until no one else was around before approaching him.

"What you want, girl?" he growled, looking me up and down.

I pointed wordlessly at the large meat pastries. He took

the coin and tried to bend it. Grunting, he handed over two of the pastries into my greedy hands. I bit into the top one and let the juice spill down my chin. I filled my mouth gratefully, hardly chewing before swallowing.

"Get along with ye!" the man snapped, swiping at me with a large hand.

He missed me, deliberately perhaps, as I darted away. But I didn't go far. The food absorbed all of my attention as I wolfed down the final bite of the first pastry.

Then I realized there were others watching me, mostly young boys and girls who gathered under the eaves of the nearby houses out of the rain, watching the cart as I had done. I took a bite of the second pastry, thinking some of them looked nearly as hungry as I was. The gleam in their eyes made me wonder if they would try to snatch the food from my hand.

A boy not three paces from where I stood edged closer to me. He was skinny and the rough clouts on his feet and short cloak were as gray as the stone walls around us, or I would have noticed him earlier. He was the same age as my brother.

I broke the pastry in half, holding out one end in my hand. "Take me to the longships in the harbor and you can have this." It was the same sort of bargain I usually struck with the *olfs*.

He darted forward, snatching the pastry from my hand. I had hardly swallowed another bite before his half was gone, he ate so fast. His eyes shifted from side to side, watching as the others gawked at him enviously.

"Come on then, girlie," he ordered, pulling his cloak closer around his waist as he set off. I hurried after him, noticing that his knobby knees were wider than his shins.

I could hardly keep up as he turned into alleyways I hadn't noticed, and scampered up and across a roof and down a slippery ladder leaning against the wall. With the boy's help, I reached the harbor in no time. When we appeared at the docks, he gave me a wave of his hand and left, much like an *olf*.

The docks were full of activity despite the falling rain,

with people pushing cartloads and barrels of goods into the warehouses that lined the shore. Boxes and crates were piled everywhere, either waiting to be loaded or ready to be taken away. Bags of apples were stacked together in a pile under a canvas, the smell of them bearable only because I had stuffed myself with the savory meat pastries.

I went to the first dock and began asking the men working on the longships if they were traveling to Tillfallvik. Some were kind, but many yelled at me to get out of the way. I went to the next dock, ducking to avoid a group of oarsmen who were swearing loudly at having to return to work before nightfall.

At the third dock, an older woman directed me to a group of longships with painted hulls. "Theys go to the north, deary."

Several of the large seagoing boats were packed for a journey, and in one oarsmen were napping under the canopy in the stern. A grizzled man lounged on the dock, leaning against the first mooring post with his legs stretched out. The drops of rain ran off the brim of his round leather hat.

"Are you going to Tillfallvik?" I asked.

He looked me up and down, smoothing the brown beard covering his face. "Mayhap. Who wants to know?"

"My name is Marja," I explained. "I have to go to Tillfallvik. Tonight."

"Ye running away?"

Startled, I replied, "No. I have to . . . see someone there."

His brown hands were as weathered and dark as the oars as he chafed them together, looking me up and down. I realized I was dressed much better than he. "A trip like that will cost ye, girl."

"I have coins." I pulled out the parchment and jingled the coins together.

The man stood up, suddenly interested. He peered into the folded parchment, his finger stirring the half-dozen coins. "This would be enough to take you there," he said, fishing out the larger pieces and leaving me the two remaining silvers.

I tried to take the coins from him, but he shook his head. "Ye be careful, *freya*. There's people here who would as soon shove you off the dock for your pains. If you've got coins, I can help ye, I can. Me name's Finn, and I can make sure ye get to Markland, yes I can."

Uneasily I glanced around, wondering which of the men were the ones he warned me about. "Where is your boat?" I asked.

"Here she be," Finn replied, smacking his hand against the first longship. Its bright yellow hull was peeling and scraped, but it looked strong and ready for travel. The hold was packed with a mound of goods covered by a dirty canvas to keep the rain off. There was nobody inside. "Wait here for me, girl. I'll round up me oarsmen."

He held my hand as I stepped inside the great boat. The rain was falling hard, and I was glad to get under the canopy. I sat down wearily on one of the hard benches that crossed the deck. I hadn't thought to ask Finn how long he would be. Slumping down, I hardly cared now that I had accomplished my goal. When I reached Tillfallvik, it should be easy to get to Silveta.

Finn disappeared into the bustle of the docks.

It was some time before I roused myself, hearing a low giggle coming from under the dock. I was surprised to see an *olf* hiding there. It jumped out and hopped onto the mooring post, then onto a nearby crate. Unlike the innocent woodsy *olfs*, this one seemed as hardened as the sailors I had seen, with a knowing squint to its eyes. Nobody else noticed it, of course. But I watched its antics from my place in the longship. The *olf* was pleased to have an audience, and it made two sailors stumble as they approached. They muttered irritably, and I had to put my hand over my mouth to hide my smile. I knew I shouldn't encourage the *olf*'s mischief, but it was curiosity not malice that drove the creatures.

"Hey, you!" one of the men shouted, pointing at me. "Get out of there!"

They rushed toward me and I stood up, trying to assure them. "Finn told me wait here. He's gone to look for you and the other oarsmen. I'm going to Tillfallvik with you."

The taller man with a close-cropped blond beard jumped into the boat with me and took hold of my arm in a tight grip. "None of your tricks, now, girlie!"

The other checked the knots on the rope. "Nothing's been bothered, mate. Looks like she was just taking a rest out of the rain."

"Finn told me to wait here," I explained again, thinking they hadn't heard me. "I'm going to Tillfallvik with you."

The man shook me, angry despite the other's reassurance. "We're not going to Tillfallvik. We sail for Hop this night. Now get out before I call the guards."

I couldn't believe my ears. "But I paid Finn! He took my coins and told me to wait for him."

The younger man gave a harsh laugh. "He was supposed to be watching our cargo. You paid him well for his trouble, I'm sure!"

I was pushed to the edge of the boat, and I stepped onto the dock back into the rain.

"Be gone from here!" the blond man shouted at me.

I backed away, unwilling to risk his wrath. But I didn't go far. I waited, crouching next to several barrels where I could watch the yellow boat. More than a dozen men arrived, but none of them were Finn. As my cloak grew sodden, they readied the longship to depart. Until they cast off the mooring rope and the oars lifted, I kept expecting Finn to appear. The yellow longship slid slowly away, the oars rising and dipping together until the ship was swallowed by the mist.

My hand went to the parchment in my pocket, knowing there were only two silvers left. I had done only as Finn told me to, but it had cost me everything.

Eight

I huddled in the midst of the barrels, unable to move for fear that something worse would happen to me. I had no more coins, no way to get to Tillfallvik. And if I didn't reach Tillfallvik, I couldn't find Lexander. It was too terrible to contemplate.

I kept staring at the empty slip where the yellow long-ship had been, as if willing it to reappear, ready to take me to Tillfallvik.

I was a fool. I should never have trusted Finn with my coins. He was no friend of mine like the *olfs* were. Lexander had told me I would need to take care of myself, but I had let my training in obedience interfere with my true duty. I swore to myself that I would never let it happen again, that I would be unwavering in my efforts to reach Tillfallvik, but my resolution did little to help me.

I wished I could flee as fast as I could into the woods, back to Vidaris. Back to Lexander's protecting arms. I knew I could do it, despite the dangers I would face on the journey.

But everything inside of me protested at the thought of entering that miasma of evil that blanketed Vidaris. My eyes had been opened, and now I could not ignore it. I would be even more vulnerable having acknowledged its presence and power. I also had no doubt that it would tell Helanas that I was near. Then her fury would be unleashed on me. What if she called back the winged ship to take me away from Lexander forever? No, I could not return to Vidaris.

Drenched and hungry, I was at a loss for what to do.

"Ho, you there!" a deep voice rang out near me.

I raised my head, seeing only the gray murky twilight, thick with rain.

Something jabbed into my shoulder, a jolting pain that barely pierced my shock. "Move it along," ordered a muffled-up man. "You can't sleep here."

"But . . ." I stammered. "I'm waiting for a boat . . ."

"Do your waiting elsewhere." He batted me with his long ebony stick.

Struggling to my feet, I pleaded, "I don't have anywhere to go. What should I do?"

His stick smacked the back of my legs. "Get off the docks! Move along now."

I did as he ordered, just as I did when Helanas hit me with her crop. I trudged wearily to the nearest archway with the man following to be sure I left.

In the waning light, I made my way past the houses and shops. I stopped when I could, crouched down next to a wall or under some stairs, then moved on whenever someone yelled at me. Eventually it got dark, and I shivered unseen under the narrow eave of an outbuilding.

I didn't feel any otherworldly presence. All the stone walls blocked me from sensing anything beyond. I was more alone than I had ever been before. I dozed off and on, always more exhausted with no relief in sight. It was the longest night of my life.

My two silvers didn't last long in Brianda. My cloak and boots weren't stolen off my body only because I fought to keep them, flailing my arms and scratching with my fingers whenever someone tried to wrest them from me. I often awoke to find people—men, women, and youths—digging into my pockets as I lay in an alleyway or on a stoop behind a shop. When I was back in the fens dreaming of what the world would hold, I had never imagined this would happen. I realized that Helanas was not the worst I had to fear.

Then I stumbled across a lane on the upriver side of Brianda, lined with cottages and a few imposing stone buildings. Every wall was covered in vines growing thick with leaves and flowers. Feathery ferns lined the street, which was packed with gravel and was well drained.

People lolled in windows and doors, calling out to passersby. I felt as if I had stumbled onto a training session in full swing, and with a rising excitement knew exactly what was going on behind these walls. The pleasure doxies were of all ages, from matrons and wiry elders to maidens barely out of childhood. They wore rich fabrics and scanty clothing, some Oriental in cut. Jewels highlighted their best features, hanging around their bare chests and exposed hips.

I was elated at my find. I had been trained to perform any service the mind or body could possibly desire. Whatever these cheerful pleasure tarts could give, so could I. And more. Did they know the place to massage just before climax that made a man's entire body spasm in delight? Did they know the hidden core of delight that could drive a woman mad? I did, and I could earn coins with that knowledge—enough coins to take me to Tillfallvik.

This would be my salvation. I drifted along with the stream of visitors. Many were men, but there were also women, single and in couples. They appraised each other, and even I came into scrutiny though I was hardly an attractive sight. My hair was tangled and my face and clothes were fouled. But I could fix that.

I retreated to a roof that I had found earlier with a cistern on top to catch the rain. It was capped now that the sun was out, but I shifted the lid aside to reach the water. It was not a very satisfactory washing without brushes or soap, but it was enough to make my cheeks shine and my hair wave tightly at my face. I raked my fingers through the rest, leaving it long and, with luck, looking alluringly tousled as if fresh from bed. I even washed my boots and tried to clean off my pants and stained cloak.

When I returned to the pleasure quarter, I folded my cloak back over my shoulders, showing the lining of dark green, which still looked fairly decent. I undid the lacings over my chest, exposing a deep V-shape swath of creamy skin and the cleft between my breasts.

Almost immediately I was accosted by a man. He wordlessly considered me from head to foot, as I lifted my face and moved closer to let him smell my eagerness. The others flowed around us. He was older, with a sagging belly and narrow, shrewd eyes. His white, straggling beard was stained yellow by tobacco juice.

"You, for how much?" he asked abruptly.

I hadn't considered it. "The usual."

He let out a short bark. "What's that? Two silvers?"

"Yes," I agreed, not knowing how much that was. Anything would be good.

"Where's your house?"

"I . . . don't have a house." Seeing him lose interest, I quickly added, "Surely you live near here—"

"And bring the pleasure masters down on me? Not for a rouge like you."

Then he was gone. It wasn't long before I found out who the pleasure masters were. I was yelled at and shoved whenever I tried to negotiate with a patron. Burly men burst out of the larger houses to pummel me away with their fists. One grabbed me and tried to drag me back inside with him, but I fought him, bursting out in a frenzy of punches and kicks. I drove him off, baring my teeth like an animal, and soon enough he retreated, shaking his head in disgust. I didn't care what they thought of me as long as I kept my freedom. If I was taken by one of these pleasure masters, I would have trouble getting away.

After that, I hung around the edges of the pleasure quarter rather than risk going inside. But the shopkeepers and matrons also yelled at me, trying to shove me back in, calling me everything from "daughter of delight" to "filthy *kunta*." It confused me because I had come to think highly of my services. Certainly the guests at Ejegod's estate last midsummer had honored us. But these people twisted their faces in disgust, shoving me with brooms and brandishing pokers. It was worse than when

I merely tried to sleep in their neglected crevices and corners.

But I managed to attract a potential patron even as I scurried from spot to spot. He was not much older than I, an attractive young man with close-cropped, silky chestnut hair on his chin and cheeks. His square and sturdy hands made me nearly swoon in delight.

He responded to the honest interest in my eyes. Yet he glanced down the street where the other pleasurefolk were waiting, as if intending to see what dainties were being offered before choosing amongst us.

I moved closer, loath to lose this one. "I can do anything you desire, *freyr*. Just tell me what you long for, and I will give it to you." My hands slid up his strong arms, savoring the hardness of his lean chest beneath his shirt. My hip brushed his thigh, promising much more to come. I was ready to fall to my knees and press my face against his groin to entice him into taking me.

"Yes, yes!" he agreed eagerly. "Show me to your place."

I jerked my head to the alley behind me. It was dank and smelled from the offal flung out the windows. "We can go there . . ."

His eyes widened at the unappealing sight. Then he looked back down at me, seeing the desperation in my face. "Please, kind *freyr*—"

"Oh, you poor girl," he murmured, disengaging himself from me. I fell to my knees, reaching out after him as he strode into the pleasure quarter. Tears of frustration spilled from my eyes, but I didn't have time to mourn. I was chased from the street by yet another shouting shopkeeper.

When I finally found a patron who would put up with a quick suck in an alley, I should have known it would be horrid. From his brown weathered face and hands, and his salt-smelling clothes, he was clearly an oarsman from the dock. He was nearly as dirty as I, so perhaps he didn't care what I looked like or that we did it in a nook in the wall. With a few mumbled words, he set the price at one silver.

An *olf* appeared behind him as I breathlessly agreed.

The *olf* bobbed back and forth, agitated. Its eyes were wide, showing too much white around its silver pupils. It wouldn't come closer, probably because the man was infected with noxious spirits. But I was starving and the sight of the coin sent all reason flying from my head. I went into the alley with the oarsman and let him do what he wanted with me. His hands were rough and when I tried to pull away from his stout *tarse* to breathe, he smacked my face hard several times, bringing tears to my eyes. He shoved himself into my mouth and down my throat over and over again, leaving me limp and my face wet. I had to reach to that deepest place inside of myself that could not be overwhelmed no matter what I endured. He seemed to take much longer than he needed, but finally he spent himself inside me.

With the silver I was able to get food to fill my flat belly. Then I curled up again in the street for another long, miserable night. My cheek throbbed as a reminder of the pain my patrons would bring to me.

And so it went, as I tried to live by selling my body to any who would take it. I eventually moved down near the docks where there were a few other street doxies, since only oarsmen were willing to take us. We were all hard-beaten by the wind and rain, and were filthy to varying degrees. Some men used me, then stole back what they had given me, despite my screams of anguish and frenzied pursuit. Others were kind enough to give me an extra silver when they saw how wretched I was. Sometimes the *olfs* warned me against a man, and after the bruises left on my face by my first horrible patron, I listened and fled. I was barely surviving, coughing from the chill air and constantly hungry.

Once an oarsman was kind enough to let me sleep in the room he rented for the night, hardly bigger than the narrow bed and resounding with the noise of snores and arguments in the berths around us. But it was divine to sleep warm beneath a blanket, and my boots dried for the first time since I had left Vidaris. After that, I began to bargain for a place to sleep along with a silver, realizing I was selling myself cheaper than anyone else in Brianda. Surely I was worth more than that!

After too many dismal days of this, I finally met Gudren of Sigurdssons. I was down on the docks, having become adept at finding places to hide, usually with help from the playful *olfs*. So I saw the beautiful longship sail in. The long sweeping planks of the hull were polished to a high gloss, and the carving of a mermaid on the prow and stern was of the most superior kind. There was a sudden interest on the docks at its arrival.

It moored with a flourish of the oars in unison. The blue sail was folded down on a vast crossbar. The boat was lean with a shallow draft.

Gudren was not the first to leap off, but he was the one who caught my eye. He stood back and watched, his bare hands on his hips, as the captain shouted orders to the oarsmen to secure the longship. Gudren's cloak was lined with sky-blue silk, and his thick boots were made of shiny black beaver. His flaxen hair curled at his shoulders, held back from his face by a wide leather band around his forehead.

What caught my eye was that he was clean-shaven, like my master. His generous mouth and square jaw were exposed for all to see. I had been scraped raw by the hair on men's faces, and I disliked how it hid their most pleasing features. I was captivated by Gudren. So were several *olfs*, who tumbled out of warehouses and from under the docks, gathering to cavort around the tall man. He didn't notice them, but they wanted to be near him.

When Gudren left his men unloading the goods packed into the longship, I hurried over, intercepting him at the archway to town. I was staring frankly, the admiration clear in my eyes. As he strolled by me, his lip quirked in a smile.

Encouraged, I clasped my hands to my breast and called out, "I will do anything to please you, Master. Take me into your bed and I will not leave you unsatisfied."

The honorific slipped out without thought because his bearing reminded me so much of Lexander.

Gudren lifted his brows in wonder, breaking his stride. Like so many of the other men, he looked me up and down as if unsure whether I was a doxy. The ones on the pleasure lane were beautiful in sheer silks and skirts that were split to show their legs. By rights I looked as if I should be mucking out a byre.

"Truly," I murmured, not daring to touch him as I had with the others. "I can give you anything you desire."

"A tempting offer, my dear," Gudren acknowledged, but his eyes slid toward the road. "But it will have to be another time."

He went on, leaving me standing there. His cloak flipped up, showing the blue underside, like a bright summer's sky. I don't know what came over me, but I couldn't let him disappear into the crowd. I followed him. An *olf* came along, as drawn to Gudren as I was.

Gudren strode through the shops, greeted with waves and shouted offers to sell him everything from fresh fried eels to waxed sail thread. I trailed along after him, remembering with a sharp pang how the shopkeepers in Tillfallvik had similarly hailed Lexander as befitting his high status.

As I watched him, I knew this man would be a patron worthy of my talents. I could not let him elude me. This was no time to let my submissive tendencies run free. I would have to win Gudren's attention.

Gudren disappeared into a building with a round stone tower at one corner and a snug, timbered roof over the rest. It was several stories high, with bow windows on every floor. It could have easily been the home of a magnate, even a prince. I thought it was Gudren's estate, but then I noticed the small signboard near the double doors. The *olf* followed him inside as people entered and left. I squatted at the base of the steps and no one paid any attention to me. I waited a long time while Gudren was inside, but I felt no urge to give up. I was as focused as a hawk on its prey.

When Gudren emerged, I smiled up at him, letting my eyes light up with joy. He seemed preoccupied, but when he noticed me his lip quirked again in spite of himself. He ran down the steps and up the road.

I followed him as he turned into a market street. He glanced over the goods displayed on open carts, disdaining to examine anything until he saw a pile of pelts. The white ice-bear hide interested him the most. The merchant knew it and dickered hard on the price. Gudren seemed irritated at one point, shaking his head and putting down the pelt to leave, but the merchant called him back and quickly settled. The large hide was folded and rolled to protect the fur, and the merchant tied it with two thongs. It made a bulky bundle that Gudren slung over his shoulder.

I ran forward. "May I carry that for you, *freyr*?" I offered, using the correct honorific this time. "No need for you to labor."

He had to shift the bundle to see me. "Is that you again?"

"I am here to serve you," I said honestly.

"I'm sure I would see the last of you if I gave you this fur," he retorted.

I didn't understand his meaning at first. Then I vehemently denied it. "Never would I steal from you! I have suffered much from thievery."

He looked at me closely for the first time. "Where's your master, girl?"

My mouth opened, ready to confess everything. But I remembered Lexander had ordered, *"Don't tell anyone you are a pleasure slave."* I couldn't disobey.

"Come, come," Gudren urged. "Surely you're a slave. I won't be dealing with a runaway, if that's what you think."

"I haven't run away!" I denied. "Believe me when I tell you, I've done nothing wrong. I want only to help you as I know I can so well."

He assessed me again with his eyes, and as I learned later, Gudren was a savvy businessman who could judge a man's character in one glance. I had not that skill, and relied on the otherworldly creatures to help guide me through the maze of people's hearts. The *olf* that hovered at Gudren's shoulder told me that this man was true.

"I'll not take it kindly if you try to run away," Gudren warned me. "You see I have friends in Brianda, and I'll have you hunted down and punished if you try."

"I would never do that," I swore, looking him straight in

the eyes. I couldn't understand how such a perceptive man couldn't see the *olf* at his shoulder, giggling at me.

After that, I trailed behind Gudren carrying all the bundles he passed to me. Nobody noticed me when I was by his side and following his orders.

After he was done shopping, Gudren took me to a large inn on one end of the harbor, a place I had seen before but never imagined I would enter. He fed me a rich stew in a terra-cotta bowl and offered to let me wash in the basin in his room. I quickly cleansed myself, expecting him to return at any moment.

I purposely did not dress again, to show him my readiness. I would do anything to please him.

But when Gudren entered and we were finally alone, he merely smiled to see me in the flesh. He didn't take me as my master would have. Instead, Gudren sat on the large bed draped in red curtains, his arms crossed expectantly, more amused than not by his smile. "I can see you have something in mind."

For a moment, I was unsure. Then I remembered my training, which Lexander had always said would carry me through. I sank down into *gesig,* with my head bowed in surrender. Then I moved slowly through the poses Helanas had taught us. Rosarin and I had learned how to make a dance of our poses, echoing each other's bending and pointing, raising our nethersides to be viewed. It was not as pretty when I was alone, but I threw my heart into it, making each movement graceful and alluring.

In the end, I remained in a standing pose, one leg bent, my hip thrusting to one side, emphasizing the curves of my body and my arms reaching out to him. There was a long moment, then Gudren languidly applauded. He didn't take his eyes off me, but he remained where he was.

So I went over and knelt at his feet. I untied the laces of his boots and pulled them off. I knew he was looking down at my bare back, gleaming in the candlelight. Then I untied his shirt and pulled it over his head.

He reclined back on the bed, putting one hand behind his head. He still made no effort to touch me though I was leaning over him. So I let my breasts graze his chest as I moved down to his pants. They were tied front and back, standard sailing gear. My hands moved slower as I pulled the tie loose. He was breathing hard now, watching my every move.

I tugged on the heavy leather pants, and he lifted his hips so I could take them down. His body was nearly as smooth as Lexander's, with fine silky hair in the hollow of his chest and dusting his groin. Still he didn't try to touch me.

So I leaned over him, barely letting my nipples graze his skin. His eyes closed briefly as his *tarse* stirred, growing turgid.

Moving languidly, I skimmed his body with light fingertips from his head down his chest and stomach, then along each leg to the base of his feet. I kept stroking him, slowly and delicately, letting my nails scrape him only when he became flushed and his body began to twist. I tantalized him, setting his entire body alight with sensation.

When I finally neared his *tarse,* blowing gently as I rubbed my cheek against him, he let out a moan. As I continued brushing against him, his hands clenched in the bedclothes as his hips bucked, as if he longed to grab hold of me but didn't want me to stop. I was breathing faster now, too, caught up in his response.

When I thought we would both explode from this simple touch, he couldn't restrain himself any longer. He growled, "Mount me, now!" as his hands pulled my hips to his, my legs straddling either side.

I sank onto him and I finally let go. His hands moved me up and down. I rocked hard until I fell forward, resting on his chest as he thrust into me. My mouth was on his neck, breathing the manly scent of him, as he moaned in release.

I lay on top of him as he held me there, luxuriating in satisfaction. He stroked me absently, smoothing the moisture on my skin. Then he rolled me over so I was tucked under the blanket with him. I fell asleep contented.

I never took money from Gudren. Not that night or the two that followed as I stayed with him at the inn, following him during the day as he went about his business. He fed me well and even purchased my first long dress for me to wear when he tired of seeing my suede pants. He told me about his family, the Sigurdssons, who owned a trading fleet that operated out of Djarney. He traveled up and down the coast as far south as the citrus fields and all the way back to the kingdoms of the Auldland. I asked many questions and delighted in his adventurous tales.

The day he told me he was returning to his estate in Djarney, the northernmost island of Viinland, I cried. I couldn't help it. Tears coursed down my cheeks at the thought of being alone again, starving and chased from one filthy hole to another.

"You'll come with me," Gudren declared. I flung my arms around him, knowing I had accomplished what I had set out to do. Gudren was a good man, I knew that now even without the *olfs'* approval. He treated me well, and though I was supposed to go to Tillfallvik, I had failed to reach it from Brianda. I could very well die here if Gudren deserted me. My only way out of Brianda was with Gudren.

So as I boarded Gudren's longship for the journey, I stared at the town that had nearly defeated me. Gudren allowed me to sit with him under the fringed canopy on a cushioned bench. His men covertly examined me, sitting so demurely in my full cotton skirt that was dyed lavender like my favorite flower in the fens.

Then once again I was on the open sea, leaving Fjardemano behind. I concentrated on the rolling waves and soon I was linked with the sea spirits, wallowing in their neverending motion, twisting and turning. Gudren didn't expect much from me, so he let me sit there in a daze, telling the spirits of my escape from Vidaris and suffering in Brianda. In turn they showed me Lexander on the dock; I was not sure if he had just returned from a voyage or was readying to depart Vidaris.

In this way, the day passed quickly. I had mead to drink when I was thirsty, plenty to eat, and Gudren's warmth to lean against when the wind picked up.

But the sight of land ahead broke me from my trance. It was a gentle rise of tree-covered hills with a flat shoreline. The boat sailed into a deep bay with knolls on either side and a channel of water ahead. It went on for some time, and I was surprised when the channel opened up into the ocean again.

The oarsmen rowed into a perfectly calm bay within the channel, surrounded on every side by gentle hills reflecting in the waters. Trees flowed along the inclines and dotted the broad lawns. White-painted buildings perched here and there, taking advantage of the beautiful views.

We sailed around a wooded headland, and there were busy docks with *knaars* and longships moored. More boats were anchored out in the bay. Warehouses waited to receive goods, reminding me of Brianda. But there was no town, only a scattering of serviceable buildings and paddocks.

"This is the Sigurdssons estate," Gudren proudly declared.

" 'Tis beautiful," I said honestly. I knew there would be *olfs* on this land.

When we docked, Gudren lifted me from the boat though I could have leaped out on my own. "Carry that," he ordered, thrusting the ice-bear fur into my arms. Except for his traveling case, he left everything else in the longship for his men to deal with.

He led me through the warehouses and sheds, up a road to the estate proper. Each building we passed was much larger than it looked from the water. The walls were made of clapboards laid one on top of the other, and the peaked roofs were covered in overlapping shingles.

When Gudren finally led me inside one, I discovered the floors were also wooden. Brass lamps hung from the rafters of the large open room. A good fire burned in the hearth, but there was no kitchen to speak of, merely a kettle for water and a basket of red apples on a table. A rack along one wall was hung with wool that had been dyed bright shades of green, yellow, and blue. I went to touch the soft strands in admiration. A long table was littered with objects, to which Gudren added his cloak and pigskin traveling case.

Gudren urged me to be silent as we climbed up the steps to a loft. It was completely enclosed for privacy. A busty woman turned from tying on her cap at the mirror. "Is that you, Gudren?" she exclaimed, rushing to hug him. "They didn't ring the bell! When did you return?"

"I wanted to surprise you, my darling," Gudren exclaimed. "Did you think I wouldn't come to see you first?"

I smiled at the joy in their reunion. Obviously this was Gudren's wife. She beamed at him, her round cheeks and dimpled chin making her look younger than her years.

Gudren laid a passionate kiss on her lips, and I was heartened to see how aggressive he could be. When he bedded me, he was always quiescent, expecting me to please him. It little mattered to him if I took pleasure myself.

"I've some gifts for you, Alga," Gudren assured her, holding her tight. He gestured toward me.

Alga's eyes went round. "What have you done, you beastly man?"

"Show her," Gudren urged me.

I remembered the ice-bear fur in my arms, and I struggled to untie it under their amused eyes. I flung it out on the ground, letting the white fur glow in the lamplight. My fingers sank into it to show how deep it was.

"Ohh . . ." Alga moaned.

Gudren helped her sit down on the plush fur. She stroked it, lying down luxuriantly. "Gorgeous!" She looked up at me slyly. "And her?"

"For you, as well, my lovely." Gudren kneeled down on the fur, his hands at her waist. "Do you approve?"

She examined me from her recumbent pose. "*You* must approve," she teased, "or you would never have brought her here."

Gudren laughed again. He ordered me, "Marja, give pleasure to my wife as you have with me."

I was surprised, though I shouldn't have been. I smiled shyly down at Alga. "I do as I'm told, *freya*."

She stretched her arms out, rolling slightly toward me. "Then I suppose you should get on with it."

I knelt down beside Alga and leaned over to give her a soft kiss. Lexander had taught us that the lips were the gateway to pleasure. I suspected it was so with her. Alga responded with warmth tinged with a pleasant wonder at her husband's gift. I could tell I was not the first woman he had brought home to his bride.

I lightly pulled the satin tie that held her robe closed. It opened and her abundant breasts spilled out. I undid the one at her waist and the robe parted over her curved belly. Her waist was small and her hips widely flaring, with thighs like pillows. I was used to my slave-mates, who were tall and lean; even Helanas had no extra flesh on her strong body. But touching Alga was like sinking into a feather bed. She was so white and soft that I hardly knew where she ended and the silky bear fur began.

Gudren undressed, then came over to remove my clothes. I let him strip me while I concentrated on Alga, stroking and kissing her from her forehead down to her toes. She responded quite differently than Gudren—wiggling, gasping, and moving under every feather touch. I teased her, knowing exactly what she needed from the way she moved. It was an effortless joy to stroke her to ecstasy.

The house *olfs* joined us, whirling around in pleasure. They apparently enjoyed a lot of vicarious delight here. Gudren and Alga had no inhibitions or hesitation in being intimate with me. Gudren lay on his side, watching me touch his wife, pleased at her rapid breath and arcing back. His own passion was clear as he stroked himself.

Then Alga let out a guttural cry. "I can't stand it anymore!" With that, she grabbed Gudren and rolled on top of him. "I must have you now."

It was my turn to lie beside them, my arousal building as Alga rode Gudren. She took him fiercely, and I saw that was the way Gudren liked it. He kissed her breasts, his hands at her hips, stroking her generous thighs. She moved like a woman possessed, drawing him deep inside of her.

I touched myself, feeling the dampness between my legs.

They climaxed together, Gudren allowing himself release only when Alga began to cry out.

When they collapsed, I lay back and smiled at them both. I had not climaxed, but that was not unusual when I bedded Gudren.

But Alga turned to me while she was still breathing hard. "Now for you."

"I am very happy," I told her honestly.

"Yes, but *I'm* not satisfied yet," she retorted.

Alga straddled my hips much as she had done with Gudren. I was a tall, well-made girl, but Alga held me down easily. She rubbed her groin into mine, slowly bumping me. Her fingers pulled on my nipples, twisting and turning them until the rush of blood made me gasp out loud. Gudren grabbed my wrists and held them over my head, a sly grin on his face.

As Alga humped me, she panted into my face, "You'll come when I tell you to."

I almost swooned right there. The tugging on my breasts, Gudren's hands holding me down, the rhythmic grinding, her breathy order . . .

But Alga was not done, so I struggled to hold back. I wanted to please her . . .

When she felt me slip and start to tense my body, peaking despite my best intentions, she bent down and whispered, "Now."

I needed nothing more than that. I let everything float away as I wallowed in ecstasy. Gudren kissed Alga over me, his tongue deep in her mouth. All I knew was that it felt better than anything had in a very long while.

The three of us dozed off lying on the bear fur, with Alga cradled in the middle.

Nine

I soon learned that Gudren and Alga were not a solitary couple like Lexander and Helanas. The Sigurdssons were an extensive family, with cousins, second cousins, great-aunts, babies of all sizes, and a matriarch who ruled over everyone with an iron fist. This grandmother was statuesque though she was at least six decades old. Her bright yellow hair rivaled that of her daughters and granddaughters. The clan intermarried, as I discovered when Alga laughingly referred to Gudren as *kusin*.

Every meal in the communal hall was like a fete, with laughter and noise at its highest pitch. They gathered twice a day to feast together. The family houses and servants' halls were scattered through the hills, connected by well-maintained roads. The barracks for the oarsmen were down by the commercial port, out of sight from the rest of the estate. As I explored farther afield, enjoying the freedom Alga gave me, I was surprised to find there were barely enough gardens and groves to provide fresh vegetables and fruit for the family, servants, and slaves. In truth, nearly all of their food came from trade.

I became Alga's companion, more a pet than a maid. I slept on a mat in their room, and I helped Alga dress and bathe. I was not truly a slave, but I was not paid a wage like a servant. I watched how the others treated me to learn my status, yet it remained unclear. Servants did as I asked only if I was passing on orders from Gudren or Alga, yet I was free to call them both by their first names while the others used *freyr* and *freya*.

Their kin mostly ignored me except when I was pleasuring them. I was passed among them, and sometimes when I was caught running an errand for Alga, they indulged themselves with me right there, taking advantage of bushes and lean-tos where we were partially hidden. It was exciting, their heightened sense of urgency and the chance that someone would catch us in the act.

I continued to please Alga and Gudren together and separately. Gudren was usually passive, allowing me to explore his body to discover the means to tantalize him. Sometimes Alga joined me in stroking him, quickly picking up on my trained techniques, such as *fotternoje,* the art of tantalizing the feet with both mouth and hands. He moaned as we each sucked his toes, his entire body tensing in passion.

I most enjoyed pleasuring Alga. Her soft, curvy body was extraordinary. I could sink into her milky white breasts or cushion my head on her belly, breathing her lush womanly scent. Usually she was the aggressor with me, making me climax again and again as if I were a new toy to be endlessly played with. She never said a harsh word to me, so I relaxed under her hand and trusted her.

As for my other duties, Alga quickly found I was useless when it came to helping her sew, knit, or weave, so I was mostly relegated to fetching and carrying things. No one expected me to scrub the floor or tend the garden. I had nothing to do many days but watch the *olfs* play. They were everywhere, going about their games unseen by everyone in the family except the youngest. I played with the children on the estate a great deal, I must confess, enjoying their purity of sight. I understood why the *olfs* in Brianda could sense Gudren's rich heritage. It made me realize what Vidaris could have been, a hum of activity and amusement for the *olfs,* if only Helanas had not blighted the land with her malevolence, allowing evil spirits to gather.

It was easy and pleasant living in the Sigurdssons' estate,

but I was always thinking of Lexander. One morning, as Alga embroidered yellow daisies on a pretty round collar, I tried to explain to her. "I was on my way to Tillfallvik that day when Gudren found me."

She looked down at me, sitting on the floor brushing her favorite dog to remove its heavy winter coat. "Gudren thinks you've run away from your master."

There it was again—I couldn't tell them I was a pleasure slave, so how could I explain about Lexander? I could hardly form my words around a lie, I felt such trust and affection for them.

Seeing me hesitate, Alga leaned closer, lowering her voice. "Don't think I blame you, Marja. I know about men. I'm sure if you of all people suffered enough to rebel, it must have been severe indeed. You can confide in me."

"I've always been obedient" was all I could say about that. She pursed her lips in disappointment when I didn't spill out a gory tale of my slavery. But I had an idea of how to explain. " 'Tis love that calls me to Tillfallvik. I must go there or I'll miss my beloved. He gave me the coins to sail there, but I was robbed most cruelly or I would be with him now."

Alga considered me anew. Her round, red-cheeked face was serious. "You are so young to know anything of love, Marja."

"Many girls my age marry."

"Yes, but love takes time. Has your father countenanced this marriage?"

Again, I would have to be evasive. "My da gave me to him."

Her brows went up very high. "So you are married already?"

"No."

She shook her head at that, uneasy at the gaps in my story. What father would give his daughter to a man yet let her remain unmarried? What man would leave his naïve lover in the rough port town of Brianda, expecting her to follow him across the sea? I sat there, awkwardly silent with too much to tell. One thing I had learned was that these Sigurdssons were shrewd at obtaining what they wanted. If my desire conflicted with theirs, I knew who would win. My only real safety lay in concealment, a lesson well learned from the *olfs*.

"I will speak to Gudren about this," Alga assured me.

That night, I was sent to service one of Alga's brothers. He was my own age, and he spent himself far too quickly. I should have prolonged his delight, but my mind was with Alga and Gudren. They were discussing my request, and in my preoccupation with that, I could not attend properly to her brother. But he was too young to know any better and was pleased with his prowess. He boasted of it a bit as he took me again the next morning.

When I returned to their house, I waited for Alga to broach the subject. In this case, a show of subservience would serve me well.

Gudren was preparing his gear to travel south on a business trip to Hop. I thought they had forgotten about my tale of love. But before he left, Gudren bade me good-bye, grasping me by the chin. "Alga tells me of this silly passion you have, Marja. But that man isn't worthy of you. If your father only knew the state you were in when I found you, he would agree. You are much better off here with us. So let's have no more talk of leaving."

My mouth opened in a protest. "But I belong with him."

"You belong with us now," Alga insisted soothingly. "What do you expect us to do? Send you to Tillfallvik and drop you at the marketplace to look for this brute? Surely you can see how impossible it is."

"Why he abandoned you in Brianda, I may never know," Gudren added with a shake of his head. "But he does not deserve your love, Marja."

He turned away from me to kiss Alga farewell. He would be gone for a handful of days, and I knew he had brought me to the estate to help keep his wife from pining for him. Of all the men in the Sigurdsson family, he was the one who most often traveled to their trade destinations, perhaps because they were the only couple who didn't have children. They were kindly folks, and I had relied on that in telling them my story, only to have it turn against me in the end. They truly thought they were doing what was best for me.

But I was no longer the gullible girl who had given Finn my coins. I kept my churning feelings hidden from Alga as we went with Gudren to wave from the dock. It must have worked because she never mentioned it again during the days that followed. Sometimes I ran down the road to the docks to look longingly at the boats, wondering which ones were sailing north to Markland. The oarsmen were too busy to pay attention to me, but I could never sneak aboard one of those open ships without being detected.

One day, I even ventured into the woods around the compound, finding that they were much the same as those on Fjardemano. I longed to set off, ready to strike out on my own and walk all the way to Tillfallvik, but the Nauga Sea lay between me and my destination. It would be impossible to swim that far.

So I settled into my place in the Sigurdssons' estate. Gudren returned from his trip, and everything went on as usual. Soon it seemed that I had known nothing other than this soft way of life with plenty of pretty clothes and a respected place in their home.

Then I got a friendly hint from one of my favorite *olfs*. I was leaving the communal hall in the gloaming when I saw the moon hanging just over the treetops. Its pregnant shape was waxing, looking much larger than usual, tinted a rich yellow color.

As I gaped at it, wondering what the moon god sought to be so low, the *olf* appeared beside my head. This one often let me see its tiny hands as it tangled the yarn Alga dyed, leaving her scolding the cat as the *olf* laughed. This time it spoke to me. *"Midsummer summons!"*

In that instant, I remembered how I had danced around the huge bonfire in celebration of the Norogods in Tillfallvik. I could almost see Silveta in the role of Freya, slicing the snowy dove's neck and spilling crimson blood on the altar.

"Midsummer," I murmured. I had forgotten it was nigh, and now the moon said it was only a few days away. It had been a year ago that Silveta had asked me to help her and I had been raped and beaten by Birgir.

With that vivid memory on my mind, I wasn't surprised when Gudren brought up Tillfallvik when we three were alone by their fire. "Now, Marja, you've given up this wild idea of finding your paramour, have you not? Tillfallvik is no place for you to be alone. Why, it's far more savage than Brianda!"

"She never speaks of it," Alga assured him.

"I am happy here with you," I admitted honestly if not fully.

"The Sigurdssons have been invited this year to Markland's midsummer feast." Gudren paused, gauging my reaction.

I silently blessed the *olf* for its warning, or I'm sure my eagerness would have been clear. Now I simply gazed back at him as if it mattered little to me.

"The chieftain is ready to expand their trade and has asked me to come negotiate terms with him," Gudren explained to Alga. "I think you would enjoy it very much. And I'm loath to leave our Marja here alone for that many days."

"Let's take her with us," Alga agreed. "She will be a great help to me."

They both looked at me expectantly. "I would be glad to go with you."

Satisfied, they began to make their plans to leave. I had to tamp down on my excitement to keep them from suspecting. Instead, I feigned interest in the dresses Alga chose for us to wear during the festivities and which gifts would be best to take to the chieftain.

But deep inside, all I could think about was Lexander. I only hoped it was not too late. I had spent nearly a moon with the Sigurdssons, and half that long in Brianda. What if my master had already gone to Tillfallvik and had given up hope of finding me?

*   *   *

When we finally set sail, it was a relief to allow myself to become entranced by the sea spirits. Gudren remembered I had been similarly enthralled on my way from Brianda, with glazed eyes and a faint smile on my lips, replying to no one's inquiries. He assured Alga that I was merely beguiled by the rhythm of the waves and would return to myself once we landed.

Indeed, when we passed the islands that speckled the mouth of the narrow bay of Tillfallvik, I broke away from the spirits. The town looked small and drab after all I had seen in Viinland. The buildings were low, and most were sunk underground with sod walls and dirt floors. The town covered the hills near the waterfront, and the woods on the taller hills beyond looked barren compared to the lushness of Djarney. But I never could agree with Sverker that it was a place of little importance because it was the living heart of Markland.

From the moment I set foot off the boat, Gudren clasped one hand around my arm, keeping me close by his side. Our boxes were carried by the oarsmen through the open marketplace that lined the waterfront. It nearly rivaled Brianda for the energetic bustle of its merchants. But this town was dirtier, with trash left to rot where it was flung and livestock living in rooms beside the townsfolk.

I had no urge to try to get away from Gudren and Alga. My goal was the same as theirs—Ejegod's estate. But they didn't suspect that. Once we were through the gates, which closed behind us, Gudren relaxed and finally released me. I felt a deep pang of guilt, knowing that I was not telling these good people the truth. It wasn't right, but my goal was to reach Lexander despite all obstacles, even the most loving ones.

As we walked through the estate, I was nearly bowled over by *olfs*. Gudren and Alga were busy with their porters and finding our lodgings, so I waved my hands at the *olfs*, grinning at their welcome. They were such a merry crew and had entertained me mightily during the last midsummer celebration. One of these *olfs* had used me to save Silveta, though she knew it not. I had not felt betrayed when it lured me into trouble. But I had been sorely hurt when the *olfs* hadn't appeared to comfort me while Birgir beat me, or when I had to face the chieftain. I had hoped that they approved of my service, and now by their joyous flips and flourishes, I was sure of it.

We were taken to a different longhouse than the one in which I had stayed the first time. We were quite a distance from Silveta's closet, and under Alga and Gudren's watchful eye, I realized it would not be easy for me to reach her.

I didn't see Silveta until that night, seated at the table raised on the dais. In the center was Chieftain Ejegod, somewhat shrunken in his imposing chair made of walrus tusks and cushioned by snow-lynx fur. I did not remember his legs and arms being so slight, though his belly swelled just as grandly. He was fretful, picking at his food, his hand shaking as he downed cup after cup of wine. His bleary eyes stared out into the hall, but seemed to recognize no one.

Silveta sat erect beside him, never looking at her husband though they ate from the same trencher. Her garments were lovely, as always, but the sheer white veil couldn't hide the stiffness of her shoulders. The last time I had seen her thus, she had radiated a graceful reserve. Now she seemed ready to bolt at the slightest noise. Her fingers were clenched tightly around her mother-of-pearl knife.

The *olfs* tugged at her gold-embroidered skirt and plucked at the cord that held her purse to her belt. But they couldn't rouse her interest. I wondered at that because the *olfs* had claimed her for their own. Yet there were not as many otherworldly creatures frolicking in the hall compared to last midsummer. I saw only a few among the colorful banners decorated with bulls that hung from the rafters.

There was no one from Vidaris in the hall. Likely the exile still held, and they had received no invitation this year. Until that moment, I had hoped peace had been made and Lexander would be seated here waiting for me.

Even if Helanas was by his side, I would have been over-joyed. But I had no such luck.

I sat with Gudren and Alga, unafraid that I would be recognized as the slave accused of sorcery by Birgir last mid-summer. Who would associate that wanton, naked girl with me in my long plaid skirt and demure braid? The only one I feared would see through my guise was—Birgir.

Birgir strode into the hall as if he owned the place, his long ax hanging at his waist. Men called out to him from every table, and the dogs came running at his whistle. Everyone watched Birgir as if the chieftain himself were arriving. It made me cringe in shame to see him claim the chair of honor next to Ejegod as if it were his right. His wool shirt was finer than I remembered, but the large links of the silver chain and the fat, knotted cross were the same. He was paler, having lost the windblown redness he had gained from fighting in Danelaw with his warriors. In comparison to Gudren, Birgir was as coarse as a burly peasant while the Sigurdssons looked like the true *jarls*.

I cowered down behind Alga, letting her plush body hide me. How could I go up there to speak to Silveta when Birgir was near?

So I endured the feast, listening to the talk that swirled around us. Gudren was ever eager for the news because it could give him an edge in his trade negotiations. From what was said at the table that night and discussed later in their bed, Birgir Barfoot was now the power behind the chieftain. His warriors had settled all over Markland, giving him a foothold in every thriving settlement. There were even rumbles that Birgir would make a better chieftain, stronger and more able than Ejegod. Gudren acknowledged that Birgir had conducted their trade discussions while Ejegod simply sat nearby. He thought it a smart tactic at the time, but now he doubted whether the chieftain truly held the reins of Markland.

I thought of Silveta's guarded eyes and wondered if she had managed to keep Birgir from her bed all these seasons. It seemed impossible, yet the balance of power was un-changed. A bondsman stood behind her, watching everything with suspicious eyes, so likely that was the source of her safety.

I tried to catch Silveta's attention, but she hardly glanced down the hall. She was an island of stillness in the midst of the merriment. When Silveta left early, while the wine was still being poured, I gave up hope of reaching her that first night.

The next evening, Silveta played her role as Freya in the ritual sacrifice to the Norogod of fertility. She still seemed unusually withdrawn. I saw her speak to no one, though one of her bondsmen always stayed close. It was reassuring to see the two strong men who cleaved to her. I was more convinced that all was not well with her, but at least she appeared to be protected from Birgir.

I was growing frantic, afraid that the celebration would end and Gudren would take me back to the Sigurdssons' estate. I couldn't leave now that I was so close! Yet Silveta seemed as far away as when I was in Djarney, with the sea separating us.

After the blood was spilled, Silveta stood at the altar and watched expressionlessly as torches were lit from the fire to start bonfires all over Tillfallvik. Her green robes flowed around her, pooling at her feet, a symbol of her fertility though there were numerous comments this night about her lack of child.

I danced among the others around the bonfire, desperately trying to reach out to Silveta, trying to penetrate her head-blindness. The *olfs* skipped beside me, agitated at my frustration.

Silveta gathered up her skirts to leave the hilltop, undoubtedly to retreat to the fire hall, where she would sit in silence throughout the meal. I knew we would be seated at the opposite end, while the Markland magnates and Viinland *jarls* were closer to the dais.

Panic shot through me. If I didn't reach her now, I would lose my chance.

Two of the *olfs* darted away as if propelled by my anguish. They both leaped between Silveta's feet, causing her to stumble. Her bondsman was there to make sure she didn't fall, as I left the crowd and started toward her, hoping to catch her attention. One *olf* clung to her skirt until she turned to pull it free.

As she straightened up, she noticed me. Her blue eyes widened in shock. I was almost relieved to see her face lose its stony reserve. Now she no longer looked like a polished marble statue.

Instantly she was by my side, watching for Birgir all the while. "You! What are you doing here?"

"Help me, Silveta, as I helped you," I begged. "Lexander told me to come to you. I'm to wait for him here."

"Do you know the danger you court?" she insisted.

"Yes, but it is of no matter! Gudren wouldn't let me go, and I can't speak of Lexander to them—"

At that moment, Alga arrived breathlessly by my side. "My apologies, *freya*! Our girl is simple and unschooled in etiquette. Come, Marja . . ."

Her fingers dug into my arm, but I frantically beseeched Silveta with a look. It took far too long, as Silveta judged the situation. She did not want to speak of the service I had performed for her, and there was Birgir himself to consider. Alga had dragged me a few steps away when Silveta finally declared, "No, stop. Marja must stay with me."

Alga was astonished. "But . . . she belongs to us."

"That's not true," Silveta said more firmly as I silently encouraged her. "She belongs here, not with you."

Alga still didn't let me go, but she looked over her shoulder for Gudren. "You must talk to my husband, *freya*."

"Go find him, if you must. But Marja stays with me."

Reluctantly, Alga finally released me. She must have realized that I was not going far under Silveta's protection.

As soon as Alga was gone, Silveta asked, "Why aren't you in Vidaris? Do you know what Birgir would do to you—to me!—if he found you here?"

"Lexander sent me. I told Gudren and Alga that I needed to come to Tillfallvik to meet my lover, but they wouldn't let me. Am I too late? Has Lexander come for me?"

"He sent a message, asking about you. I told him that you had best avoid Tillfallvik if you valued your life."

I gasped. "Send word to him, please, *freya*! He must know I am here."

"Come, this is no place to talk." Silveta kept a sharp eye out for Birgir as she took me to her longhouse, the one I remembered so well. One of her bondsmen was left behind to escort Gudren and Alga to her.

I began to tremble when I went through the door of her closet and saw the bed where Birgir had attacked me.

Silveta saw how it upset me. "I heard about the exile of Vidaris when I returned. What did he do to you?"

"Rape," I gasped. "Then he beat me. I could not even stand on my feet."

She nodded grimly, as if making up her mind. She went to a nearby casket and unlocked it with a key from around her waist. I stood awkwardly to one side, afraid to sit on the bed in her presence, but weak at the knees with fear. I kept staring at the stone floor, remembering how I had lain there as Birgir struck me with his belt. I had never thought I would have to return here.

Gudren and Alga arrived quickly, brought by Silveta's bondsman, who waited outside the door. The couple was anxious, I could tell, and Alga immediately joined me, taking my hand. I realized then how much she truly cared about me. I felt my throat tighten.

Gudren introduced himself, his elegant politeness strained. "My wife tells me you've laid claim on Marja. Can this be true, *freya*?"

Silveta turned, the candlelight sparkling on the garnets entwined in her crown of braids. She was all golden and shining, like the low-hanging moon, and just as distant and powerful. "I will pay you handsomely," she said firmly, clinking a purple silken bag in her hand. It had a twisted cord and was filigreed with embroidery. "Please name your price."

Gudren's forehead creased as he glanced back at Alga. They were likely thinking of their important trade agreement with Ejegod, for they debated every issue of note with an eye to the consequences it would have on their business. The Sigurdssons were merchant princes indeed, with their wealth and life of luxury, but they were still merchants at the heart of it.

Finally Gudren ventured, " 'Tis not a thing to be taken lightly, *freya*. We care for Marja, and would be loath to let her leave us."

"You have no right to keep her." Impatiently, Silveta gestured to me. "Tell them, Marja. You must stay here."

Gudren looked at me as I swallowed hard. "You are both very kind, truly. But I must stay with the *freya*."

Alga still clasped my hand, looking into my eyes as if she couldn't believe what I'd said. But Gudren went into bargaining mode, seeing a way to finally pierce the mysteries I offered. "We are concerned that Marja is well cared for. After all, *freya,* why should you be interested in a doxy I found on the streets of Brianda?"

Silveta drew herself up, her expression icy. "If you care about Marja, as you claim, you will leave her with me and mention this to no one. I *will* have my way. If you cause problems, then Marja is the one who will suffer."

There was silence as they considered this. Then Alga patted my hand, releasing me. They could ill afford to anger a chieftain's wife.

Gudren named a high price for me, but Silveta refused to bargain. She passed over the gold coins without a word. I wondered if despite their genuine feelings for me, Gudren and Alga simply considered me as one of their possessions.

Then Alga kissed me, reminding me of the pleasure we'd had together. Gudren gruffly ordered, "Send word by our boats if you fall into trouble again, Marja. We will always be ready to help you." His hug was not that of an owner. I wondered then whether he hadn't demanded a high price to test Silveta's desire for me. Regardless, they left me with fond, worried looks that I would never forget.

Ten

Silveta disguised me as her new maid, giving me a gray homespun dress and a white apron pinned at my shoulders with small bronze broaches. I kept my hair slicked down tightly and coiled against the back of my head. With the cap on top, I looked much like the other servants. For the first couple of days, I stayed locked in Silveta's sleeping closet, even during meals, eating whatever she could bring back to me.

Several days after the midsummer festival, when all of the guests had returned home, Silveta entered, looking disturbed. "The courier has returned." She had secretly sent a messenger to Vidaris. "Lexander is no longer there."

"No . . ." I breathed, sitting back on my heels. Everything I had feared was true. I had delayed too long in reaching Tillfallvik.

"Helanas questioned my courier. She doesn't know where Lexander is. The courier didn't leave my letter because I instructed him to put it only in Lexander's hands."

Despite the anguish I felt, I was glad Silveta was handling everything. If the courier had given Helanas the letter, she would have discovered that I was in Tillfallvik. I had no doubt that my mistress would come to get me.

"Where could he be?" I asked plaintively.

"He might be here in town. But I can't risk telling Ejegod's men to look for him because of the exile. He will have to come to me. The problem is," she said, considering me on my blanket on the floor, "what am I going to do with you?"

I was gaining more understanding of the threat Birgir posed. The crafty warrior had bided his time, influencing Ejegod in many ways until the chieftain had come to rely on him. It was a masterful move that allowed him to use his influence on behalf of certain supplicants, becoming a welcome presence within the chieftain's retinue.

Every day I pressed my ear to the chinks in the boards, listening as the estate folk passed in the hallway. They were all Ejegod's *bondi* with their women and children. Silveta told me that her husband's most loyal bondsmen had aged along with him, and a handful had retired this winter to their well-earned estates, leaving their lusty sons to serve. These young men were Ejegod's *bondi*, but they cleaved more naturally to Birgir, who was a seasoned warrior and natural leader. Birgir had kept a dozen of his best fighters and they were housed in a newer longhouse, while the others had left to claim land. These men were treated with the same respect as Ejegod's *bondi*.

"Birgir is too strong," Silveta said, wringing her hands. "I watched him this midsummer, sealing alliances with as many of the magnates as he could. Even making deals with Viinland *jarls*."

Our chieftain was frail; anyone could see it. "I don't understand why your husband allows Birgir to gain such power over him."

"Ah, that is the shame in this! Birgir plays with Ejegod, acting the loyal son." She grimaced at her own failure to give Ejegod a child. "To an old man whose line ends with him, it is a strong lure. Birgir credits Ejegod with saving his people by giving them land for their names, and claims he considers the chieftain his true forebearer. Birgir swears that he will burn sacrifices to Ejegod's family forever in praise of his spirit."

Considering the chieftain's befuddled state, I wondered if Birgir had done more than simply talk. Perhaps he, like Helanas, had drawn evil spirits here to help diminish the old man's vigor. In truth, the *olfs* avoided both Birgir and

Ejegod, even on the occasions when they danced on the high table itself. I did not sense anything specific, yet I could not forget that I had not felt the miasma at Vidaris until I escaped. As I had discovered, evil was much harder to detect than good, insinuating itself into people in devious ways. But the presence of evil spirits would explain why there were decidedly fewer otherworldly creatures in the estate than there used to be.

"I cannot let you continue to skulk about in here," Silveta decided. "The servants are already talking, wondering if your illness is serious. If they inquire too closely, they may realize you're the Vidaris slave."

"What should I do?" I cried.

"Do you never think for yourself?" she countered irritably. "No wonder the Sigurdssons wouldn't let you go, the way you were clinging to them. As you are now, Marja, you're a risk to *me*."

Chastised, I remembered Finn and how he had stolen from me because I had been too gullible. I had assumed that when I finally reached Silveta my task would be accomplished. But I would have to continue to fight for myself, even if I was not sure in which direction my path led. "Lexander told me to stay with you."

Silveta shook her head, closing her eyes briefly. I knew better than to speak. I had seen that look on Helanas' face too many times.

"Well, we must take the risk," Silveta decided. "You don't look like a pleasure slave now. Don't start showing your legs or letting your hair go wild. You'll have to act as my maid in truth. I've not had one since the last wench stole my key to give to Birgir."

"I remember," I said quietly.

Silveta considered me, recalling the service I had done for her. Then, having no other option, she began to explain what being her maid entailed.

The masquerade began as I hid in plain sight. I soon realized that most people simply believed what was set be-

fore them, with few questions asked. I claimed I was
from Kebek, with Ansgar's tales of his home still fresh in
my ears. My almond eyes, my most distinctive feature,
were not uncommon in Kebek, where Noromenn were
known to wed Skraeling.

Silveta declared to anyone who inquired that she had
purchased my bond from the Sigurdssons. But serving Silveta was nothing like my life with Alga and Gudren. Silveta expected me to sew and help the bondsmen's wives
keep her costly garments in good repair. Most were gifts
from faithful magnates, elaborately embroidered by their
womenfolk for the chieftain's wife. I also fetched her wash
water and dressed her hair, familiar chores from Vidaris.

First thing each morning, I accompanied Silveta to the
kitchens, where she doled out the food supplies, unlock-
ing the tiny room that contained precious Auldland spices
and the cellar for the wine and mead. She also directed
the senior servants in the cleaning and laundry. She was
truly the chatelaine of Ejegod's estate with more serious
responsibilities than Alga, who had plenty of time for
leisure and play while her indomitable grandmother gave
the orders.

It appeared Silveta was safe from Birgir as long as her
bondsmen were present to vouch for her virtue. Birgir
could not simply force himself on her—common law decreed that any man who violated a *jarl* would be drawn and
quartered. His bid for the chieftaincy would not survive
such a crime. So Birgir needed to make it appear that Silveta had encouraged his advances, and she did everything
she could to counter this claim by publicly snubbing him
and his *bondi*.

The first time I ran into Birgir, I was caught unawares. I
had Silveta's bedclothes over my arms as I took them to
the washtubs. There was a friendly *olf* jaunting along beside me, as usual. I couldn't understand why it suddenly
leaped in front of me, holding its frail arms wide as if to
stop me.

Birgir was walking toward me with one of his bondsmen,
speaking too loudly as usual. "If he wants the fishing rights,

he must come here to win them. I will not give them for naught."

I missed a step, but it was too late to turn aside. I didn't want to draw more attention to myself. So I continued on, my head bent and my eyes on the path, silently imploring the *olf* to help me.

But Birgir saw me. He blocked me with one thick arm, bared in the summer warmth. "You're the new maid for our *freya*, are you not?"

I bobbed a curtsy, pitching my voice higher than usual. "Yes, *freyr*."

I couldn't look up, but I felt the *olf* move between us, floating right in front of me to stop Birgir from recognizing me.

To his companion, Birgir boasted, "So the haughty lady provides me with another pretty face. 'Tis generous of her, I must say."

Still hiding behind the *olf,* I scurried around them.

"Don't be so quick, sweet *fitte!*" Birgir called after me. "Every maiden should have some pleasure, and I'm the man to give it to you." The two men brayed with laughter, entertained by my fright. Little did they know that I had already felt the full extent of Birgir's lust.

I blessed the *olf* over and over, promising all of my milk the next morning for its service. Surely Birgir would have seen who I was, staring directly at my face as he did, if not for the intervention of the *olf*.

After that, the otherworldly creatures kept me informed of Birgir's whereabouts. When he walked the paths, I stayed inside. If he came near the kitchens, I slipped outside. For meals, I ate with the other servants at one of the distant tables, keeping my back to the dais at all times.

Mostly I stayed near Silveta, because she always had a bondsman with her. It was seen as a mark of honor to have her father's *bondi* in her retinue, reminding everyone of her status in Viinland. From Perus, the more loquacious of the two bondsmen, I discovered that Silveta's father was a chieftain, controlling a series of rich valleys along the coast of Hop. Perus had known Silveta since she was a child, and they had a way of speaking shortly, conveying much to each other but little to others. Perus was a man in his prime, a widower who ignored every woman on the estate. But I heard the malicious comments of Birgir's men, made to besmirch Silveta's good name. On seeing them in private, as I did at times, I knew that Perus showed no softer feelings toward her. He was intent only on surviving his post. Both of Silveta's bondsmen were cold, distant warriors who never asked questions of me, merely accepting my presence and reserving judgment about my trustworthiness.

One morning, I accompanied Silveta and Perus to the loft in the fire hall where Ejegod spent most of his time. It was both his bed and receiving chamber. I had never been inside, but I caught a glimpse of him in a great chair, wrapped in furs despite the warmth.

I waited with Perus on the landing, high above servants who were cleaning the tables after the meal. A handful of men lolled on the benches near the open doors. Since it was full summer, the fire in the enormous hearth had been allowed to go out.

Perus went down to relieve himself. I felt exposed on my perch above the others. With the double doors propped open, the interior of the hall was far more illuminated than usual. I could see the *olfs* jumping along the rafters that crisscrossed between the walls, swinging from the banners. The corners of the hall were filthy, piled with soggy rushes and debris. They had been fouled by the large number of guests at midsummer. This morning, Silveta had ordered the servants to gather the rakes so the mess could be mucked out.

Suddenly the *olfs* ceased their spirited hopping, pausing to stare at the doors. A few of them faded away in front of my eyes.

Birgir's voice boomed outside.

I ran quickly down the stairs and slipped into the shadows below. I barely made it in time.

Birgir entered, calling that a pod of whales had been sighted in the bay. The place boiled over as men rushed in all directions, some up the stairs to tell Ejegod and others past me to the kitchens for supplies. I pressed against the wall within the striped shadows cast by the steps.

Birgir set off for the docks, followed by most of the men. I breathed a sigh of relief, knowing he would be gone for some time.

Then the last man returned from the storerooms, carrying a sack of wine over his shoulder. Niall was one of Birgir's most loyal bondsmen. It was said Niall was bedding a wash girl, and he came right into the servant's longhouse and took her in front of everyone.

Niall stopped at the sight of me. "Ah, the shy maid who scurries about staring at the ground! Are you lying in wait for me, dearling?"

I bowed my head, hiding my face, as I was wont to do now. "Silveta is . . ." I faltered, gesturing upward.

Niall lowered his voice as he stepped closer. "If your *freya* doesn't need your services at the moment, I can think of one who does."

I thought he meant Birgir, and my breath caught. "*No.*"

"Yet your eyes plead so lovely," Niall declared, stepping under the stairs with me. "I think you mean otherwise."

I tried to look away. But he was too close. I could see only his broad chest and stained leather belt. The wine sack sloshed as he set it down.

"I think you agree." One finger lifted my chin, and his arm went around my back to hold me against him. It was fairly masterful without being hurtful. I went very still. He brought his mouth down on mine, tasting me, feeling my lips. His black beard and mustache were clipped short, and his lips were full and firm. My body responded in spite of myself. Niall was everything that Gudren was not— dominating and passionate. He became wildly aroused merely by kissing me.

His hand dropped to my breast. I gasped into his mouth, and that inflamed him more. His palm cupped my breast, squeezing—

"What are you doing with my maid!" Silveta demanded.

Niall pulled away slowly, as my hands scrabbled on him,

trying to push him faster. His black eyes were amused as he licked his lips at me. "Delicious! Just as we thought."

Silveta stood there with her arms crossed. Behind her was Perus, sneering slightly. Any hope I had of gaining his trust vanished.

Niall resettled his wine sack on his shoulder. "Very tempting, my dear, but I've got a whale to slaughter. I shall redeem your pledge later."

With a laugh, he went past Silveta and gave a mocking salute to Perus. I blushed at the contempt in Silveta's eyes. When Niall was far enough away, she hissed, "How stupid must you be? Now Birgir will never rest till he has taken what Niall has tasted."

"I was hiding and he caught me."

"You didn't even try to stop him." Her voice lowered so Perus wouldn't hear. "I know what you *are*. But can't you have some dignity while you're in my hands? Have you no self-control?"

"My apologies, *freya*." I didn't know what else to say.

Silveta sighed heavily. "I think you must go stay in town. Perhaps Torgils would take you in. But I fear he would recognize you as the Vidaris slave, and he would doubtless tell the chieftain."

"You're sending me away?" I was torn between wanting to stay so Lexander could find me, and eagerness to get away from Birgir and his men.

"Yes, until . . . you are claimed." She wouldn't risk naming my master. "You're a danger to me here."

Chastised, though I didn't know what I could have done differently, I followed Silveta as she organized the servants in cleaning the fire hall. Some stayed behind to rake the floor and pile the mess in a cart that pulled up to the doors. I went with Silveta and the others to gather bundles of new rushes and wildflowers. They laughed and sang as if it were a holiday from their normal chores, and the *olfs* danced along with us. But I couldn't be merry. With Lexander gone, and Silveta casting me away in disgust, I would soon be alone again.

*   *   *

That night, Silveta slept in Ejegod's chamber, as she did from time to time. The couple still tried to conceive an heir, but I could tell by the way Silveta girded herself that it was not a pleasant duty. Ejegod got drunk as usual during the night-meal.

I stayed in Silveta's closet. Only she had the key to the new lock, which had been installed since last midsummer. She entrusted no one with it, not even her bondsmen, for fear someone would take it from them. She escorted me there with Perus, and neither bothered to speak to me.

But by late morning, no one had returned for me. Silveta must have simply gone from Ejegod's chamber to the morning meal, then to work. All of the *olfs* had left for the fire hall as soon as the meal was served, anxious to pilfer bits from the plates of unwary diners.

Earlier I had heard deep, rumbling voices in the hallway, but it had been quiet for some time. I would be lucky to get the browned remnants of porridge from the bottom of the pot if I went to the kitchen now. So I unlocked the door. The sound of the metal scraping seemed very loud. I pulled it open a crack to peer down the longhouse.

A hand smacked the door, pushing it against me. Birgir's face appeared, framed by yellow-white hair. "So you finally emerge, pretty little maid! I've heard you're eager for some rutting."

I tried to close the door, but it was no use. Birgir pushed me back as if I were a babe. Then he slammed the door shut behind him.

It was like a terrible nightmare. I put my hands to my face, desperately hoping to keep him from realizing who I was.

Birgir grabbed me and pulled me against his sweating body. His touch was cruel, making me cry out. His teeth scraped against my mouth, drawing blood, as his fingers dug into me. Before I knew it, my apron had been pulled off and the buttons ripped on my kirtle, exposing my breasts. He bit my neck, then the white flesh of my breasts.

I screamed. "Stop it! No!"

His hand went over my mouth, cutting off my breath. I

struggled for air. He was looking into my eyes, enjoying the panic he saw there.

That's when he recognized me. He grabbed my chin, taking in my face. "It can't be! You're the slave that Silveta used to trick me. Why did I not see it . . . You *are* a sorceress, aren't you?"

I tried frantically to breathe. Birgir would use me against Silveta. He could question her loyalty to Ejegod because she defied his edict of exile.

But Birgir was not thinking of that now. His groin ground into my hip as his arm tightened around me. His other hand grasped my hair and pulled my head back until my neck was exposed. He bit down on my throat again, like he was going to rip it out. The pain lanced through me.

"I never got to take you the way you deserve, pleasure slave." He loosened his pants with quick jerks. Then he shoved me flat on the ground.

His bulk pressing down on me brought it all back in a horrible rush . . . his sweaty, hairy stink . . . the sharp jab of his pendant . . . the sour stench of his mouth. With his weight on me, I couldn't make much more than helpless squeaks as he pummeled into me. Like the first time, I was not ready. But my submissive nature kept me from panicking and blacking out as some might do under such an assault. Indeed, he noticed how I shifted under him to give my hips a better angle so my flesh wouldn't tear.

"You slut," he growled. "Trained to be a filthy doxy . . ."

Birgir could not sustain his pleasure. Like the first time, he had barely begun before it was over. Mercifully brief. Yet the beating that followed last time had been protracted. He rolled off me, finally allowing me to breathe.

Then I heard his belt buckle clank on the floor. I couldn't let him strike me. Not again! I was no longer under the *geasa* that demanded absolute obedience to Ejegod's guests.

I rolled to my feet, surprising him. His hands were on his pants, pulling them up.

Before Birgir could turn to me, I grabbed the jewel cask

from one of the carved chests. I swung it against the back of his head with all my might. He shifted to defend himself, but I was too quick. The cask cracked against his head, sending him reeling.

As Birgir fell, I darted through the door.

Eleven

y attempt at escape ended abruptly when I reached the door of the longhouse. Niall and another bondsman were lolling there lazily, waiting for Birgir. Niall caught me with one hand. "Hold hard, there, missy. What are you running from?"

They marched me back down the hallway, Niall's hand biting into my shoulder. Then they saw Birgir, sitting muzzy-headed from my blow. The cask was overturned on the floor.

Niall slipped one arm tightly around my neck. "Should I kill her?"

"No!" Birgir grimaced at the blood on his fingers. "She's that pleasure slave—the one who cast a spell last summer to unman me."

"Silveta's maid?" Niall asked, craning his head to look down at me. "No, this is too rich!"

The other bondsman helped Birgir get to his feet. The big man stood none too steady, and his gaze was unfocused. "I had my fill of her again, though I must say the price for this thin shank is too high."

One of the servants paused in the open doorway, gaping at the sight of us. "You there," Niall called out. "You serve as witness. This girl lured Birgir into Silveta's closet, then tried to kill him."

The woman stared at me openmouthed. I couldn't deny it because Niall choked me into compliance.

They marched me into the fire hall, my hands clenching at Niall's arm. My kirtle swung open, revealing my breasts for all to see. This time it was much worse when I was dragged into the hall. These were not strangers. Their faces were familiar even as they gawked at me.

Birgir kept rubbing his head and groaning, as if my blow had been a lucky one. He left it to the others to summon Ejegod for reckoning. In the uproar, the *olfs* scattered away, avoiding the rising anger.

The chieftain emerged from his chamber, bent and moving stiffly. He paused at the rail, as if reluctant to come down when he saw Birgir surrounded by his men. Silveta appeared on the landing behind him, hardly distinguishable in the dim light except for her crimson gown and the bright sheen of her hair.

The men in the hall began to shout for Ejegod to appear for reckoning. I knew it was over. There was nothing more Silveta could do to help me.

But I was not Birgir's target. He stepped in front of Ejegod, refusing to let the old man mount the dais. "Your wife's maid attacked me! Is this how you return my loyalty, Ejegod? You conspire to slay me?"

A growl arose from Birgir's bondsmen. Even Ejegod's men stared as if taken aback.

Silveta's lips were compressed in agony. She stayed on the landing, watching over the heads of the men who were gathering. Perus stood grimly behind her.

I managed a breath as Niall's arm eased. "Birgir raped me!" I gasped out. All eyes went to my hanging kirtle, ripped asunder.

Birgir pointed at me, seizing the moment. "Has she bespelled you all? This woman was exiled for conspiring with demons. Do you not recall midsummer last, when reckoning was pronounced on this very floor? You yourself, Ejegod, cast her out after she attacked me."

To varying degrees, most of them did recognize me. Ejegod's eyes widened as he peered closer. "No, this cannot be," the chieftain murmured.

Niall tightened his arm again, keeping me from defending myself. But he refrained from choking me into unconsciousness.

Silveta cried out, "I know nothing of this!"

"She attacked me at your behest," Birgir countered, pointing up at her. "You and your husband have conspired with this sorceress to slay me. If I had not been stronger than her dark arts, she would have succeeded."

"That is false," Silveta denied. "I bought her bond from a Djarney merchant. I have proof of it. You have mistaken her."

"Do not deny your hatred," Birgir declared. "All have seen how you scorn me. You wanted me dead, *freya*. And your maid did your will for you."

"I wanted you to leave Tillfallvik," Silveta said desperately. "That is all."

Birgir touched his head gingerly, still trying to shake off the effects of my blow. He confronted the old chieftain. "You cannot claim ignorance in this matter, Chieftain. Your own wife's maid is a sorceress, declared so by you yourself. I call you out, Ejegod of Markland, to face me, man to man, to settle this now."

Silveta's chest rose and fell as her lovely face contorted. "You've always craved my husband's status, Birgir Barfoot! You contrive at this ugly reason to fight."

Birgir bared his teeth at Ejegod, ignoring Silveta. "I have sworn to you and been your loyal man. No one here can claim otherwise. Now that you've made a cowardly attempt on my life, I must defend myself."

Ejegod looked very old, standing before them uncertainly. But the faces around us were hard. Birgir brought a legitimate claim to duel. Anyone who heard his tale would accept that Ejegod must defend his honor.

Silveta turned away in anguish, while Ejegod drew himself up. I could see what manner of a man he used to be in the sure way he pulled his knife and ax from his belt, hefting them in his hands.

"No man accuses me of using a woman to best him," the chieftain swore stoutly. "I defend my honor as I am called to do."

Everyone drew back. Niall still held me tightly, but I had no desire to protest now. I was sickened at how Birgir had used me to manipulate Ejegod into a fight.

Birgir pulled out his huge ax, half again as long as Ejegod's. The chieftain's weapon looked merely ceremonial, while the edge of Birgir's blade was stained dark from the blood he had drawn in battles in Danelaw.

Birgir faced Ejegod, taking the measure of the old chieftain. Ejegod's expression was strained, as if he felt betrayed by a man he had thought was a friend, nay, more than that—the son for which he had always longed. He had indeed been mesmerized into trusting Birgir.

Ejegod took the first swipe with his ax, slicing the air in front of Birgir's stomach. I wondered wildly if perhaps the chieftain could beat the warrior, but Birgir blocked the swing with his own ax. Birgir snapped up his knife, going for Ejegod's arm, but the old man dodged away just in time.

The two men separated and circled each other, their feet scuffing through the rushes. Ejegod's men shouted out encouragement to their chieftain while Birgir's men seemed driven to fair drown out the calls with their own. Niall's taunts near shattered my ears.

Then Birgir leaped high at Ejegod. The old man's legs were too slow and he was forced to fall back into the crowd. He was supported for a moment by his own men, who helped him regain his feet.

I glanced up at Silveta, whose hand was over her mouth. She had little love for her husband, but I knew the horror she faced if he fell.

The clash of metal echoed into the rafters as the men met again. Ejegod's parries and attacks held a semblance of expertise. I could almost see him as a young man warding off challenges to his rule over Markland. Yet now his limbs were stiffened with age and his eyes were bleary from overindulgence.

The watching men shifted as the fight did, keeping their distance from the battle. They parted around a table as the men came closer. Ejegod parried Birgir's ax, then pinned it against the edge of the table. His arm drew back to swipe his knife across the warrior's neck.

It looked as if the chieftain would succeed. But Birgir sneered into the old man's face. With a hard thrust, he drove his own knife into Ejegod's belly. Ejegod's hand opened and his own knife clattered to the floor.

Grunting with the effort, Birgir slashed his knife downward, gutting Ejegod. As the old man staggered under the impact, Birgir spun, unloosing his ax and bringing it around to bite into Ejegod's exposed side.

A spray of blood burst out and a cry went up. Ejegod sprawled on the fresh rushes, red flowing out from his wounds in a great gush.

Silveta ran forward to her husband along with his *bondi*. But it was too late. Blood stained his mouth, frothing with every pained breath. He couldn't speak, though he tried.

Birgir knelt down on one knee, his forehead on the hilt of his ax, praying aloud to the Kristna god to forgive Ejegod's sins and grant him peace in heaven. I couldn't bear to listen, but Niall murmured the words into my ear along with Birgir.

The fire hall was hushed and tense as Ejegod's body was born away by his *bondi*. Silveta went with them to prepare the chieftain for his journey to the Otherworld. Niall refused to let me leave his side. He looped a leather thong over my wrist and kept me tethered to him like a horse. Silveta would have to abandon me in order to save her own life.

Casks and fine tapestries were carried down from the loft and out of the fire hall. Ejegod's bondsmen kept uneasily away from the thick clutch of Birgir's warriors and busied themselves with the preparations for the funeral. Birgir and his men stayed by the empty hearth, speaking in low voices. But their somber mood crackled with excitement.

I was in the midst of Birgir's men and heard their muttered words of preparation. They expected retaliation from

Ejegod's *bondi,* but for now the servants and estate folk accepted the duel as warranted. I could do nothing but crouch down beside Niall, dismally awaiting my fate. The sun moved slowly that day as I wondered if my death would be the next to come.

I didn't see Silveta until late that evening, shortly before sunset, on the point of land at the mouth of the bay. Amber beads were woven through her yellow crown of braids, dangling down like a crystal mourning veil. Her gown was deep red, the color of Ejegod's spilled blood. Her face was pale and drawn. She let everyone see the terrible anger that burned in her eyes at what Birgir had done.

An enormous crowd had gathered, everyone in Tillfall-vik. The children were subdued, as their parents looked fearfully at the warriors led by Birgir. The chieftain was laid out in the middle of a longship with a black sail. All around his pallet were casks of mead, food, weapons, shields, tapestries, furs, and other goods that Ejegod would need on his journey to the Otherworld.

The pitched wood piles inside the boat were set afire by Ejegod's bondsmen, and the boat was pushed away from shore. Silveta stood at the water's edge, her face glowing with the reflection of the flames. Soon, when the sail caught fire, it grew brighter than the orange sun sinking below the water. The wind carried the burning boat past the small islands at the mouth of the bay, out to sea.

We stood in silence long after it grew dark, watching the flames dart up, until Ejegod was gone.

Silveta turned, her eyes hollow. I was glad to see Perus beside her, supporting her arm. I couldn't go to her because of the tether around my wrist, but Perus picked me out among Birgir's men. I wanted to explain to him that I had not betrayed Silveta and Ejegod, but his contempt was clear.

When we returned to the fire hall for the traditional feast to celebrate Ejegod's life, it was even worse. Ejegod's chair, with its snow-lynx cushions, was left empty in the center of the table. Silveta sat stone-faced next to it, not touching her food, while Birgir glared from the other side.

The burly man had complained to his men throughout the day of an aching head. He was in a foul mood despite his victory. I sat on the floor, next to Niall at the end of the table. Silveta studiously ignored me, but Birgir shot me a sour glance every once in a while, letting me know he was not through with me yet. I cringed when I remembered the beating he'd given me. Now he intended even worse. Some of his men had openly speculated that he would allow all of them to use me. He cared not if I survived.

Yet, even so, I was concerned about Silveta. Surely Birgir would not hesitate to take her now.

Indeed, as the cups were filled one last time at the end of the meal, Birgir stood up. "It pained me to challenge my old friend, Ejegod Oddason, on this day. I regret that he saw fit to succor a sorceress in his household, one who has attacked me repeatedly."

Silveta's knuckles were white on her cup, and she spilled the mead as she set it down. But she didn't speak.

"By right of conquest," Birgir thundered, "I hereby claim the chieftaincy of Markland. Ejegod's goods and chattel are forfeited to me." Birgir smiled down at Silveta. "Including his wife."

Silveta leaped to her feet. "Never! I would rather die than let you put your hands on me."

"Be grateful I let you live after your treachery," Birgir hissed.

"This estate is mine by right of my marriage contract with Ejegod!" Silveta retorted.

Ejegod's *bondi* were starting to shout as well, having expected no doubt to compete for Silveta's hand and estate themselves. The man who held both would be the favored candidate for chieftain. Several men called, "You claim too much!" and "The magnates choose their chieftain!"

A cousin of Ejegod's, a tall man who was not smart, but who had by way of his kinship the better claim to become chieftain, came forward to defy Birgir. But Birgir pushed over the table and abruptly ran the cousin through with his knife without even responding to his challenge. Birgir's men suddenly leaped onto the dais from the floor, swinging their mighty war axes at Ejegod's older *bondi*.

Servants screamed and scattered as pockets of fierce fighting broke out. Birgir grabbed Silveta, who screamed in shock and outrage. Perus tried to block him, but was cut down by an ax to the back of his head.

I cried out, but Niall dragged me to the rear of the dais, watching the fighting with his ax hefted in his hand. Tethered to me, he couldn't attack Ejegod's *bondi*. Birgir's warriors clearly had the advantage in both weapons and ferocity. Those they didn't cut down were forced from the fire hall.

Birgir slung Silveta over his shoulder amid her screams. He carried her up the stairs and into Ejegod's solar. The door slammed shut behind them. Abruptly, Silveta's screams broke off.

I ran to the end of my tether, but Niall jerked me to a stop. "There's nothing you can do for her, my sweeting. She has gone to the fate that Kristna decreed the day we arrived in this fine land."

Perus lay crumpled half under a table. His eyes were wide open, but there was no life in them. Too many other loyal men lay dead or dying. Silveta was being raped by Birgir. I was alone and would soon be at the mercy of a dozen bloodthirsty men.

"Please," I begged Niall, "take me away. I will do whatever you wish, please you in a thousand ways, only don't give me to these men this night." He laughed, but I added, "You'll barely get your fill of me with all of them to have their turn. Surely tomorrow is soon enough for that. Spare me this one night, and you will be pleased as you've never been before . . ."

A greedy light came into his eyes. With Birgir gone and satisfying his own base needs, who was to say what Niall deserved? "Come," he ordered, taking me by the arm.

We circled the downed men, escaping under the loft into the kitchens. Frightened servants and cooks screamed and ran when they saw Niall, his ax held ready. He slipped into the cheese room, where pans of milk were covered by cloths and the cheese rounds were stacked on shelves. The narrow room was cool and smelled of curdled milk. I knew the *olfs* must come here often to filch crumbled bits of cheese. But there were none to be seen now. They must have fled when the fight began.

Niall dragged the heavy table against the door to block it. With his tether still binding my wrist, he declared, "You had better be true to your word, or I'll let my friends have a turn when I'm done."

I went down on my knees, thrilled that I had managed to avert certain disaster, even if I had only delayed the inevitable. I swiftly untied Niall's trousers. Silveta would likely say I was shameless for servicing Niall, but I knew no other way. I licked and sucked his thick *tarse* with abandon. His bemused moans said he had never felt a woman's lips on him before. I remembered all I had done to rouse Gudren, and the sensations that Lexander taught me that he liked best. I pleased Niall as I knew how, drawing it out, not letting him spill too quickly, urging him higher and higher into ecstasy. He had a fortitude that was admirable, giving me plenty to work with.

Eventually, I dragged him down to the ground and straddled him as Gudren liked. Only now I could make it last, having watched Alga perform her magic. My hips rocked slightly as his panting grew faster, while my nails dug into his chest and arms, peeling his clothing away. The sharp scratching blunted his need to spend, allowing him to plateau and rise again.

Even Helanas would have been proud of me. I pleased Niall knowing my life depended on it. After he spewed into me with cries of delight, I barely let him drift away before rousing him again. As he thrashed wildly beneath me, I knew I had succeeded.

Within a few dozen heartbeats, Niall was snoring with me held tightly under his arm. I waited, forcing my tension to ease, knowing that a warrior such as Niall would be quick to rise from sleep. He had to be lured into deep dreams by the *olfs* before I could make my move. It felt like eternity, but an *olf* finally arrived to help me and began expertly spinning out Niall's nocturnal fancies.

I concentrated on the tether. I couldn't risk taking his knife to cut it, so I painstakingly undid the knots that held me. I eased carefully away from him, then shifted from under his arm a tiny bit at a time to keep from waking him. Finally he snorted and rolled over, releasing me.

I squatted there, waiting to be sure he was sound asleep. The *olf* continued to wallow in his dream. My skirt was bunched underneath Niall, so I untied the waist to slide out of it. Birgir had ripped off my apron earlier. My chemise was short, covering me less than my slave tunics used to. But modesty was the least of my concerns.

I listened at the door, but there were no sounds in the hallway. I couldn't move the heavy table without waking Niall, but I could climb the wall easily enough. I would have to watch out for Birgir's men visiting the privy or cavorting with a kitchen maid.

Then another *olf* appeared. It was nothing more than a shimmering blob that whispered in my ear, *"Without Silveta, we are lost."*

That plaintive plea was enough to stop me in my flight. The *olf*'s thoughts mingled with my own. There was a terrible evil infesting Birgir, and it had grown more powerful since he had killed Ejegod. The strong pillar of the family's rule had toppled with the chieftain's death. The evil in Birgir was spreading even now, taking over the estate. Soon it would lap over Tillfallvik, then extend through Markland, destroying my homeland. Birgir would bring darkness to my people in the same way Helanas had blighted Vidaris.

The *olfs* had chosen Silveta as their champion. They had such freedom themselves, they could little understand the constraints on ours. They knew only that she longed to quit the solar but must have someone's help to do it. How, would be up to me.

I tugged on the shelves holding the cheese rounds to find they were bolted to the wall. Stepping from one shelf to the other, I carefully climbed up to the top. The next storeroom over held sacks of grain and bins of beans and vegetables.

From the top of the wall I could see the crossbeams that held up the roof. I pulled myself up and straddled the beam, glad I wasn't wearing my entangling skirts.

Delighted, the *olfs* darted ahead of me, lighting the easiest way along the rafters of the storerooms. Some were enclosed to secure their contents, with boards fastened over the top, forming storage platforms that were piled with boxes of goods.

The old building was very dirty, and soon I was covered in soot and worse. I passed over the main kitchen, but no one tended the banked fire. All the women had fled. There had been loud shouts and screams as I pleasured Niall, but I had shut my ears and tried not to think about what was happening to my fellow servants.

I shimmied carefully across the beams, pausing to listen before I swung out and around the slanted posts that supported the low-pitched ceiling.

I was afraid I would have to descend in order to enter the fire hall, but narrow triangles of wood led to the sides of the loft. I climbed up and peered into the gloom that gathered in the hall. I clung to the slanted post with my knees, trying to ignore the splinters that dug into me. I didn't dare go out onto the landing of the loft where Birgir's men might see me. Instead, I climbed higher into the peaked roof of the hall. My thighs ached from clutching the beam so tightly.

When I topped the wall around the solar, there was devastation within. Ejegod's chamber had been ransacked, first by the chieftain's *bondi* gathering goods that would go with him into the Otherworld, then by Birgir examining all that was left.

Silveta lay on the wide bed clutching her torn clothing about her. Mercifully Birgir was gone, perhaps fearing that Silveta would try to kill him if he slept. She was crying hopelessly. The *olfs* watched her dejectedly.

I swung over to climb down the wall, using the tiny chinks and uneven boards to get purchase. Silveta didn't hear me until I landed on the floor of the loft. Her head went up sharply. Her cheek bore a bright red mark, and her mouth had been scratched raw. I put my hand to my own lips, feeling how Birgir had scraped the skin from me with his beard when he raped me.

" 'Tis only me, *freya*," I whispered. "Do not be afraid."

"You traitor!" Her hands clenched in anger as she slid painfully out of bed. "You've done this to me! Helped kill my husband and my *bondi*. Brought that butcher's son down on me—"

I interrupted her raving. "*Freya*, I've come to rescue you. Please don't let them hear you."

"Rescue me?" she demanded, albeit in a lower voice. "What can you do?"

"I was able to get in," I pointed out. "The *olfs* showed me how. And I can get back out with you."

She finally realized that I had indeed snuck into her cell. "How? Show me how!"

I checked her torn underskirt. The overdress was gone completely. "You'll need to take that off or it will get caught between your legs."

Looking at my own lean, bare legs, Silveta grimaced. But her hands went to the waist, untying the band. That left only her chemise. Her braids were hanging loose, so I rummaged among the furs on the bed to find the pins, fastening them tight to her head along with the tangle of amber beads. I could see the shadow of fine blond hair at her groin whenever she moved.

"This way." I showed her where I put my toes and my fingers. She shook her head in disbelief. " 'Tis not hard," I whispered insistently.

I climbed up, and then quietly guided her as she scaled the wall. Once her toes slipped out of a crack, making her squeal. She froze, expecting the door to crash open. But the guards suspected nothing. The *olfs* began to prance with glee when she reached the top.

Silveta was almost too afraid to straddle the slanted beam that went down into the darkness. But I went first and stayed an arm's length below to support her as she swung out. She kept her lips pressed together firmly to keep from making another sound. The landing was just on the other side of the wall.

Taking it very slowly, as I whispered advice every step of the way, we withdrew back along the beams into the storage rooms. I climbed down into the scullery, avoiding the cheese room where the *olfs* told me Niall still lay sleeping. As soon as he awoke, he would raise the alarm.

The entire estate seemed to be asleep, including the hounds. It felt very late. I wondered how long I had held Niall in thrall, and hoped it would keep him snoring far into the morning.

Slipping out the side door of the scullery, Silveta and I started down the path. The *olfs* led us away from the main gate where Ejegod's *bondi* must have taken a stand. I kept expecting Birgir to rise up in front of us brandishing his ax, still shining red from Ejegod's blood. We waded into the deep grass of the meadow where we had gathered the rushes yesterday. Though it was dark after the moonset, I remembered what it had looked like under the sun, as the grasses bent in the breeze and clouds scudded across the deep blue sky. One day could make such a world of difference.

Then we had only the palisade to surmount to reach freedom. It was not very high, reaching barely to my chin. "This way," I told Silveta, and we boosted ourselves over.

Twelve

Shouts went up as Silveta and I crested the top of the palisade. Silveta slipped getting down. It looked to me as if the *olfs* supported her, letting her sink gently to her feet. I grabbed her hand and tore through the bushes into the scattering of trees on the hillside.

Silveta gasped from the unaccustomed exertion. I was ready to flee, but she stopped as she bent over to catch her breath.

"They're coming," I insisted, trying to see along the palisade toward the gate at the rear.

"One . . . moment," Silveta wheezed.

"There's no time." I reached out with my senses and wasn't surprised to find a handful of *olfs* nearby. Some had followed us from the fire hall. When they saw my need, they glowed softly so I was no longer in darkness. Silveta held her hand out blindly, as if she couldn't see a thing.

"Relax," I urged under my breath. "Sink into yourself. Reach out . . . then you'll be able to see."

She gave me a look as if I had gone dotty, but I was spared her retort as she struggled along beside me. I guided her over fallen logs and through the sparse woods, practically dragging her along. I could have darted over the rough ground like a frightened deer, but she stumbled as branches scraped her legs and her bare feet twisted on the rocks.

I started describing what lay ahead so Silveta could more easily maneuver. She did better after that, but protested at my uncanny vision. "'Tis pitch-black! How can you see?"

"The *olfs* show me." I headed uphill, knowing the men would be naturally more inclined to go downward. Likely they thought we were servants escaping from the estate and wouldn't put too much effort into chasing us.

Silveta didn't complain, though her breathing was harsh and uneven. We crossed a barren ridge, then descended through the thick scrub and briers. I tore heedlessly—the thorns were nothing next to my fear of Birgir.

Near the bottom of the ravine was a stream. Silveta fell down to her knees, scooping up water to drink. I knelt nearby, also slaking my thirst. The number of *olfs* had increased. They were very happy, not realizing that we could be recaptured by Birgir's *bondi* at any time. *Olfs* were creatures of the moment, so our escape was enough to please them.

"I can't . . . believe . . ." Silveta finally stammered.

I waited, but she didn't finish. "That we got away?"

"Everything!" She glared at me, reminding me with one look that I had set off this terrible chain of events. "Why didn't you *kill* Birgir, you idiot!"

I let out my breath in a rush. Could I have killed Birgir? Yes, I could have beat him on the head with the cask, splitting his skull open. "I don't think I *could*," I breathed. Just the thought of doing it nauseated me, yet I wondered if I should have tried. The *olfs* started to pull away from me as I considered it, so I pushed the repulsive image from my mind.

Silveta angrily turned away. "I must get to Tillfallvik. There are loyal men there who can help me."

"We can go down this ravine. It will take us to the bay."

"How can you be sure? It feels like we're going in circles."

I shook my head though she couldn't see me. "The town is that way. I can smell it."

"Of course you can." Silveta grimly got to her feet. "Let's go. We haven't much time."

* * *

When we reached the outskirts of Tillfallvik, it was still dark, but I could feel sunrise was near. Silveta futilely tried dabbing at the blood on her scratched-up legs. She was miserable wearing nothing but her short chemise, but only the animals saw us slink through the muddy lanes.

We arrived at a snug wooden home and, with a knock on the door, we were quickly drawn into a kitchen lit by the coals in the hearth. A gnarled old man spoke with Silveta while two women sobbed on a bench. They were so overcome that they barely spared a glance at our scanty clothes.

"My son was killed in the fighting. His body is still on the estate." The old man spat on the dirt floor in fury. "It's said that Birgir holds you hostage and that he will marry you in the morn."

"I will never wed Birgir Barfoot," Silveta swore. "He cannot become chieftain."

"There's plenty who agree with you." With a sour glance at the two mourning women, the old man said, "You'll need to go to Torgils' house. They've gathered there."

Silveta didn't like it, but we had another dash through town as the old man took us along the narrow alleyways down to a house near the waterfront.

Torgils' longhouse was large and filled with men lounging and sleeping in various positions on the ledges along the walls. Some of those still awake were heatedly discussing their plans for the morrow. The *olfs* followed us right inside. They hovered near the sod ceiling, one drifting down to tease the baby that lay in a basket by the fire. A woman was hunched over the hearth in the center of the hall, trying to warm herself.

Silveta was greeted with glad cries, and her embarrassment was banished when the woman quickly fetched her a skirt to wear. I squatted down near the baby, watching it bat its hands through the *olf*. Young children always liked to do that.

"So this is the Vidaris lass," Torgils declared. "We heard she tried to kill Birgir at your behest."

I was taken aback when all the folk turned to stare at me.

"Not at my behest, though I wish she *had* killed him," Silveta grumbled. "Then we would not be faced with this mess. Does Birgir hold the estate?"

"Yes, and we have the waterfront." Torgils sat on the table made of rough-hewn planks. "Boats have been sent to summon the magnates who are loyal to Ejegod. Birgir's warriors will hear of what happened and return. The merchants have already started boarding up their storerooms, expecting looting and fighting."

"I can't stay here," Silveta decided.

"If Birgir marries you, then his claim will be hard to dispute."

"I seek blood vengeance against Birgir Barfoot," Silveta declared. "I must get to my father in Hop. He can convince the overlord to help me."

"We need good fighting men to wrest Birgir from your estate. A dead man can't claim the chieftaincy. And what about her?" Torgils asked, gesturing to me.

Silveta considered me. "Birgir would tear her from limb to limb if she's discovered. So I suppose I must bring her. Can you get her some clothes as well?"

Torgils' wife reluctantly went to fetch a homespun gray skirt. It was a narrow sheath of substandard weave, with a ragged hem. I put it on, thanking her but getting nothing in return. She picked up the fat baby and put him to her breast, sitting down on the little stool near the fire.

I felt as if I were a harbinger of evil. Silveta wanted nothing to do with me. Yet I trailed in the wake of her ragged retinue as we trooped down to the docks. The sky was still mercifully dark.

Torgils pointed to a longship anchored in the bay. "You can take that one. I'll send for oarsmen, though they'll be boys too young to fight. We need every man we have to keep Birgir from taking the waterfront."

Silveta went under a lean-to near the dock to wait. The waves slapped against the side of a rowboat moored nearby, ready to ferry us out to the longship. Two of the men gathered casks of water and supplies for our trip.

Silveta anxiously watched as the sky brightened with the

coming dawn. "Surely Birgir knows I am gone by now. We must leave."

"Perhaps they think we're in the hills," I suggested.

Silveta frowned but refused to speak to me. Rather than upset her further, I backed out of the lean-to and sat down against the slanted side. The grass was wet with dew, but that didn't bother me. I was exhausted, having not slept all night.

As I drowsed in the chill air, I heard a voice calling my name. "*Marja . . . Marja . . .*"

At first I thought it was my da summoning me from the fens as he had done since I was a little girl. But it grew more insistent, and I opened my eyes.

"Marja!" It was my master's voice.

"Lexander," I breathed.

It couldn't be true, but I got to my feet, looking wildly around. There were a dozen men guarding the waterfront, pacing back and forth along the docks and staring at the crests of the inland hills. A man stood in the doorway of a nearby shed, beckoning to me. He wore rough brown pants and a jacket belted with common leather and a brass buckle. His cap went down around his ears and was slightly pointed.

But I knew it was Lexander by the way he moved. I ran straight into his arms.

"Marja, where have you been?" He pulled me back into the shed, where no one could see us.

"Is it really you?" I exclaimed, even as he clasped me close to him. His sublime scent engulfed me, and every plane and curve of his body felt so right under my hands. "You came for me!"

"I've waited for you for nearly a moon," he said, with his face pressing into my hair. "I thought I had killed you, sending you off on your own. But you made it here, as I knew you would."

I didn't care about anything at that moment, not the mistakes I had made nor the terror I had felt. None of that mattered now that I was in Lexander's arms.

"I thought I knew how much I loved you," he murmured. "But it's much stronger than I imagined. I was desperate to find you again. I couldn't leave. I couldn't stop hoping I would hold you again."

Since leaving Vidaris, I had wondered sometimes if I had dreamed his outpouring of devotion. Now I knew I hadn't. "You can't ever send me away again," I pleaded.

"Never."

He began kissing my face as if treasuring every part of me— eyes, cheeks, brow, lips . . . I forgot where we were and lost myself in the wonder of his touch.

There was a hitch in his voice as he repeated my name. "Marja." His hands held my face like a precious gift.

Even this closeness was not enough. Impulsively I opened myself up to him, diving into the flow of the spirits to reach out to him. I had never thought to reveal myself in that way to him. But now a barrier inside of me was gone. I could feel as he felt—overwhelmed by passion and relief that we had found each other. I knew without words that he had lurked about the estate and watched for my arrival on the waterfront. But I had landed unseen in the midst of the midsummer guests, concealed within Gudren's retinue. Afterwards, I had hidden myself too well while avoiding Birgir and his men.

I could feel his blood running hot, burning with the need to join with me. He lifted me to the top of a barrel of whale oil, and I helped to pull up my skirt with an eager sound of assent. *Olfs* appeared and twirled around us in the small space. They were in a frenzy at the way I reached out to the otherworldly currents while I shared my love with Lexander. It seemed miraculous that no one else saw their explosion of light and glistening motion inside the shed.

Lexander wrapped my legs around his hips, holding me with a firm hand under each thigh. I steadied against him, lowering myself as he penetrated me. My head arched back as I let out a cry, grasping him around the neck. The tension between us, balancing each other while we joined together, went on forever. I opened myself up until I could feel his very heart beating. The *olfs* whirled in the sparks we radiated.

He submerged himself inside of me, filling me, feeling each wave of our ecstasy together. His emotions, then mine, echoed between us. He went to his knees, taking me with him.

I collapsed, lost within him and the swirling maelstrom we had created. Our bodies had merged and I was lit on fire, blazing . . .

"Marja!" Silveta called from outside the shed. "We're leaving now."

I struggled to lift my head as she repeated her call. She sounded impatient, but I could also hear her fear. There were more voices outside the shed. That brought me to my senses.

" 'Tis Silveta," I gasped. "Birgir is after us. He discovered me posing as her maid."

"Silveta kept you on the estate?" he demanded. "Is she mad?"

"We were desperate," I explained. "Birgir killed Ejegod when he discovered me."

Lexander untangled himself, helping me to my feet. He was seriously troubled, but I smiled with complete love into his face, giddy from our joining. I was as glowing and dewy as a new bloomed flower. I had escaped Birgir and was with Lexander now. Surely the worst was over.

I had only to stay at Lexander's side, overcome by the fact that he was here and that he loved me so very much, as he dealt with Silveta and Torgils. Lexander agreed to take charge of the motley crew of boys sailing Silveta to Hop.

I was eager to quit Tillfallvik and was the first to board the small boat with Silveta. Her disdain for me was clear, but she admitted to Lexander, "Marja helped me escape from the estate. I would never have found my way through the hills without her."

His hand caressed my hair. "Yes, she is a wonder at finding her way."

My heart was singing, but I couldn't help but feel sorry for the *olfs,* left melancholy on the shore. They wanted Silveta to be safe, but they felt as if they were being abandoned.

The boys Torgils had rounded up for us could barely control the boat as we rowed through the bay. The water was much darker than the sky, which finally began to brighten. Thankfully the summer waves were not high, and Lexander went among the boys, helping them row. He set course with the rudder, then gave it to me to hold. Silveta stared behind us, watching for Birgir's men to break through the line of townsfolk protecting the waterfront and skillfully man a boat to come after us. But we left the bay and threaded through the small islands at the mouth.

Striking out into open water, the shore disappeared behind with no sail following us. Soon after, her face lined with weariness, Silveta retreated to the bow to lie down on a rough pallet.

Then I finally remembered the sea spirits. I relaxed, letting my fingers sense the currents in the water through the rudder. I conveyed my need through my story, starting when the Sigurdssons had brought me to Tillfallvik for the midsummer celebration. The sea spirits drank in my long and convoluted tale, giving me encouragement to remember every detail.

"The wind is rising!" Lexander called. "Pull up the sail, lads!"

My hair blew around my face as I hung on the tiller, showing the spirits how I had run from Birgir and his men, taking Silveta with me. They, unlike the *olfs*, had little concern with Silveta and her battle to save our land. But they appreciated our valiant struggle.

Lexander eventually came to sit beside me, taking the tiller from my hand to steer himself. I was jolted out of my communion with the spirits. The longship was scudding along briskly, with the boys resting, curled up on their benches. Our blue-green sail, much like the sea itself, bellied out full of wind. It had taken Gudren a full day to reach Tillfallvik from Djarney. It would take twice that for us to reach Hop.

"How long have you been with Silveta?" Lexander asked me.

"Since the midsummer celebration."

His expression was concerned. "Why did it take so long to reach Tillfallvik, Marja?" When I looked away, his hand grasped mine. "What happened to you? I must know."

"The coins you gave me were stolen by an oarsman in Brianda. After that I struggled mightily."

"Were you hurt?" He didn't realize his grip was too tight on my hand, revealing his torment.

I thought of the sailor in the alley, the one who had hit me until I was bruised in the face. "Yes. I was lucky to reach Tillfallvik. Silveta gave me protection, though she knew it was a risk."

"Silveta claims Birgir struck down her husband in a duel."

" 'Twas a true betrayal," I agreed. "The chieftain thought of Birgir as a son."

"Poor old man. Silveta intends to go straight to the overlord to claim his protection."

"And will you help her? As she helped me?"

"I have some allies that may be useful, but that would alert Helanas that we were in Viinland. Silveta's family has influence with the overlord, and likely she will do well for herself without having to call on the name of Vidaris."

"Silveta says that Helanas is looking for you."

Lexander shrugged slightly. "I have until the return of the Stanbulin ship in the fall, when Helanas must report my absence to our superiors. Helanas would most likely try to force me to return to Vidaris before then. Their wrath will fall on her when they discover I have gone to ground."

I could feel there was so much more behind his words. "You're in danger, are you not?"

"Yes. And now that you are with me, you are also in grave peril." He kept one arm on the tiller, maintaining our course. "I know you will not divulge what I have to say to anyone."

I nodded, staring into the flickering depths of his golden eyes. "Of a surety, I shall keep silent."

"Marja, the ship you saw takes the slaves from their training houses to Stanbulin. From there, your slave-mates are sent to live among my people on an island that few of your world ever see."

"My world?" I repeated in confusion. "Is it not yours as well?"

"No. I am different than other men, as you may have sensed. My people came here a long time ago and we have lived among you, though we are not men. I have been at Vidaris for nearly two decades. Before that, I was in Veneto for two decades and before that it was the Orient."

So many years! A man with that many decades should be old, older even than Ejegod, who had been ancient indeed. Yet Lexander was still in his prime . . .

Suddenly I understood. Lexander was a god. It explained so much that had eluded me—his strength, his fast reflexes, his uncannily smooth skin as golden as his eyes. And Helanas, with her perfect beauty and callous disregard for people, just like the tales of the Norogods my da often recounted.

My mam had taught me that disaster strikes whenever folk consort with gods. They could pull you into the Otherworld without warning. I shifted away from Lexander, remembering how I had almost lost myself when we had joined together. What if Silveta had not called out, breaking our union? Would I have been transported to the Otherworld?

The pain in his eyes at my reaction was terrible to see. But I feared him as I never had before.

"Yes, I understand your fear," he said sadly. "My people have used you most foully. I would swear never to hurt you, but your life is at risk being with me."

I believed him. The gods had terrifying power. They could strike and kill with a look. Surely that was why the *olfs* had been so ecstatic during our passion—they could feel the Otherworld uniting with this one.

"I don't . . ." I started to say, but could not finish. I couldn't reject my love for Lexander, but every instinct told me that it was dangerous for me to touch him.

"I understand," Lexander murmured. "It is much to absorb."

I shook my head, tears welling up in spite of myself. I had thought the obstacles between us had fallen, but now

I knew my own barriers had protected me while I was in his training. I loved him and would follow him anywhere, yet I could not go to the Otherworld while I was alive. For the living, the Otherworld was a torment, a place where they watched their wasted existence play endlessly out, unable to touch others or feel anything. Only the dead or creatures such as the *olfs* or sprites who were created there could prosper in the Otherworld.

"Go, Marja," he ordered. "I would never force myself on you or make you submit as Helanas did. I saved you from that, and I will protect you."

I could hardly meet his eyes, I was so afraid of giving in to my longing for him. But my mam's terrified expression flashed in my mind. She would walk through fire to fetch me home if she knew what I faced.

I went to the prow to lie down next to Silveta. She murmured anxiously but did not awaken. The relief I had sought for so long had been ripped away from me again, and I was glad to see her despite her dislike of me. We curled up together to sleep.

Thirteen

I knew that I risked everything by loving Lexander. I had seen through his eyes and felt his every sensation as when we made love. I had almost lost myself in him. Surely that was why he had warned me. He didn't want to harm me, but his very nature could be deadly to me.

For so long whenever I had been afraid, I had imagined how Lexander would protect me when we were reunited. But that was a childish fancy. I had not been safe in Vidaris, where the evil infesting Helanas was always near. And my dreams of being taken away by the winged ship had been foolish, without regard for the ruthlessness of Lexander's people. Now I couldn't go to Lexander and hold him as I longed to. I couldn't rely on him when he posed such a tempting danger himself. My conflicting desires chewed me up inside.

When I awoke, Lexander was once more the master I had known in Vidaris—cool and reserved. And I returned to watching him, always watching. I understood now, why Lexander was the best of men with his superior confidence and understanding. Despite our dire circumstances, he was in absolute control. His otherworldly power gave us wings as our narrow boat skipped through the towering ocean waves. The boys did as he ordered without question. Even Silveta ate and drank at his command.

By evening, Silveta no longer returned to the stern to watch for Birgir. Instead she hung on the prow, drenched in spray, staring ever forward as if willing us to go faster. In spite of her rough skirt and the dirty shawl tied over her head, her regal bearing was not diminished.

As the sun lowered over the western horizon, Lexander sent one of the boys up the mast to look for a sail following us. The boy called down that there were none to be seen.

Silveta let out an audible sigh of relief, but her eyes were haunted, as if she couldn't truly believe she had escaped from Birgir.

"We'll arrive at the bastion by morning," Lexander assured her.

"It would take another half day to reach my family," Silveta said, as if to herself.

"You can't risk it," Lexander replied. "You must speak with the overlord first. Birgir will not ignore the most powerful man in the region. He'll send his best men to plead his case."

Reluctantly, Silveta nodded agreement. Without saying a word or even looking at me, Lexander returned to the stern to hold the tiller.

I settled in for the night, wondering who Birgir would send to the overlord. It was not likely to be Niall since he had been responsible for letting me escape. I shuddered to think what Birgir would do to him. Niall had no evil spirit dwelling within him, but he was selfish and did whatever suited him best. I was thankful for that, because his flaws had saved me from a terrible fate.

In the first morning light, we reached the expansive Straumsey Bay, which was dotted with wooded islands. The sparkling water was light blue, indicating a mighty river must empty into the ocean here. The mass of trees along every shore revealed only glimpses of log houses on the waterfront. There were a great many sailing ships everywhere as fishermen worked the outgoing tide. High on the wind, I could smell ripening grain and fruit trees growing farther inland.

One island stood out from the others because it had no

blanket of trees, only bare stone cliffs. But as we drew closer, I realized what I had taken for natural rock were walls that enclosed the entire island. Narrow arched windows pierced the levels, and those with their shutters thrown back revealed dozens of diamond panes of glass.

It was a fortress to withstand anyone who challenged the overlord of Viinland. There was only one place where we could dock, on the narrow hooked end of the island. As we sailed closer, I marveled at the slender towers marking the corners where lookouts sheltered.

An official-looking man in a short cape met us on the dock. Lexander pled Silveta's case, citing her *jarl* status as her right to see the overlord. The man gestured for two guards wearing broad short-swords. The guards refused to allow the boys off the boat, so they settled in to raid our meager stores while they waited.

Lexander and Silveta started out with the guards. Neither of them asked me to come, but I went along anyway. We looked quite the humble group in our peasant garb.

I had never felt more overwhelmed by a place. The bastion was entirely enclosed, a city fortress made of stone. There were colonnades of arches and covered walks, while the buildings shared common walls with a continuous line of windows rising three and four stories above our heads. Even the street was paved with flat stones fit together like puzzle pieces. Puddles pooled in the cracks, and shopkeepers were busy sweeping outside their doors.

We slipped unseen through the narrow streets. At the other end, we were taken through a massive iron gate into the bastion proper. We went down long corridors and up stairs, then through an open courtyard lined with columns and round arches. I looked around in frank astonishment at the tapestries and carved furniture in the large chambers we passed. Every surface was paneled in wood, with parquet floors forming cunning patterns. I had never seen anything near as grand as this place.

Children ran about everywhere among the servants and folk who gathered in the bastion for business or for pleasure. Guards were posted here and there, blocking doors and overlooking the enormous chambers. It felt like the Sigurdssons' household, but on a much larger scale, large enough for a dozen families to live within.

Inside one hall, folk milled near long tables as the morning meal was served. I was heartened to see that *olfs* gathered in droves for the pickings. They were cheerful and much more plentiful than on Ejegod's estate. Truly, Birgir was a blight on my homeland.

We were shown into a small antechamber where there were several benches and a window looking out on the sparkling blue sea. One of the guards stood with his back to the base of the archway, while the other retreated.

"When will we see the overlord?" Silveta asked the guard.

He made a noncommittal answer, glancing at Lexander, who settled onto a bench. Silveta twitched at her poor skirt and tried to smooth her hair. I went to help her, undoing the bedraggled braids and combing the golden strands with my fingers. I untwined the string of amber beads she had woven through her hair. They wound a dozen times around her throat. It was sad to see the vivid scratches near her mouth and the purpling bruise of her cheek where Birgir had hit her. I braided small strands of her hair away from her face, but had no time to do the rest before boots were heard through the open archway.

Silveta handed me her shawl. "Put this over your head. Even in rags you look like a doxy from the streets."

I put the cloth over my head, tying down my unruly locks. The guard stiffened as several men returned. Silveta slowly stood up, as did Lexander.

"Silveta, it is indeed you." A ring of *olfs* floated around the burly man in the center, drawn like moths to a flame. He stood with his fists on his hips, as if he were more comfortable on the deck of a longship than on land. His mane of grizzled auburn hair swept back from his weathered face. Yet his garments were rich, with his cape lined in ermine and his shoes embroidered in silver thread.

"Greetings from Markland, Overlord Jedvard," Silveta replied, dipping down in a respectful curtsy.

Jedvard took in her tattered clothing. "What is this, Silveta? What brings you to my home in this sad state?"

"My husband was murdered most foul, Overlord, by Birgir Barfoot. Even my bondsmen were killed. I've come to ask for your help."

Jedvard drew back, his bright interest growing more serious. "Surely your own magnates must administer justice in your land, Silveta."

"The magnates support me, yet Birgir has taken my estate by force and now fights with the townsfolk of Tillfallvik. I must put down his insurrection so the magnates can gather in peace to choose their next chieftain."

Jedvard laced his fingers together, as if considering her plea.

"With fifty men I can end this insurrection tomorrow," Silveta insisted. "Birgir's loyalists are scattered far and wide. Ejegod granted them estates so they would disperse. We little expected Birgir would kill Ejegod on his own hearth!"

I held my breath at Jedvard's silence. But the young man next to him couldn't contain himself. He had been staring indignantly at the bruises on Silveta's face. "I say it's barbaric! Birgir was your father's honored guest, wasn't he? Artur just returned from your midsummer celebration and he told me there was unrest in Markland over this *vikingr*."

Jedvard smiled indulgently at the young man. "My son Jens will escort you to a guest chamber, *freya*. I must consult with my council on a matter such as this. I will summon you soon."

Silveta clasped his hand in gratitude. "Your generosity will be well rewarded, Overlord."

He turned and marched out with the rest of the men, leaving only Jens behind. Several of the *olfs* lingered with the son, obviously fascinated by him. Jens was tall but wiry, with a dusting of peach fuzz on his chin. I liked his dewy freshness; it reminded me of my fellow slaves.

Silveta was barely two summers older than we, but she replied to Jens' innocent queries as if he were one of the children that littered the place. From their familiar tone, I could tell they had known each other for along time. Silveta had grown up not far away, and was likely accustomed to regularly visiting the bastion.

Indeed, Silveta instructed Lexander on where to go to send word of her plight to her father and call him to her side. Meanwhile Jens showed us up a spiral staircase into a round room with a low, peaked ceiling. There was a richly draped bed and the air smelled fresh like the ocean breeze that wafted through the window.

Then as casually as she ordered her own servants around, Silveta requested water to bathe and some proper clothes. Jens left, looking somewhat daunted but determined to find something that would suit Silveta's nobility.

When he was gone, I blurted out, "Why are you treating him that way?"

Silveta turned away from the window in surprise. "What are you talking about?"

"He's the overlord's son."

"Jens is a child!" She laughed.

"He could marry tomorrow, if he wished. And he certainly has his father's fond eye. You could do worse than to cultivate his goodwill."

Silveta blinked a few times, sitting down on the bench. "Jens was always a silly boy, getting under everyone's feet. But I suppose he's not so young anymore. I feel I have grown so old . . . a widow after a few scant years of marriage."

"You are too forbidding, Silveta. I know 'tis due to need. But you can be softer to him."

Silveta jerked her chin. "You want me to tempt that poor boy? I'm not like you, throwing myself at everyone I see. I have my dignity."

"You're running for your life, *freya*. I say bed him if you can."

She blushed rosy red. "Never! I would not buy freedom with my body."

Jens came back before I could ask why not. I traded what others valued in order to survive. Surely Silveta had done the same when she became the wife of the aged chieftain.

I was pleased to see that Silveta was much kinder to Jens when he returned, thanking him for the clothing he brought, even holding out her hand in gratitude as she had done with his father. Her obvious emotion, since it was so rare, was all the more touching. I remembered how she had begged me to take her place in bed to deceive Birgir. Even if I hadn't been under Lexander's *geasa*, I likely would have done as she requested.

I slipped outside to stand on the stairs, closing the door to a crack to give them privacy. Silveta narrowed her eyes after me, but I trusted in the *olfs*. They did not venture near those who were wicked, and they clearly adored Jens. He absently brushed them away from his head, like errant flies, as if sensing how close they were.

Silveta seemed torn, having become accustomed to holding all men at arm's length to protect herself, and now traumatized from being raped. However, Jens was not a full-grown man, but a youth, and her early association with him must have been comforting. She gazed at Jens as if she had never really seen him before. He was a handsome lad, with his father's auburn hair curling at his shoulders and round blue eyes.

He still held her hand. "I know my father will help you, Silveta. How could he not counter such brutality?"

"I can only hope the overlord will see how much he has to gain by supporting me."

"He'll meet with his council this afternoon. I just heard word has gone out to summon those who are not in the bastion."

"It's not likely my father will make it here in time," Silveta said, biting her lip. "I have no one to speak for me."

"You can speak for yourself. Surely you'll be allowed. I'll come to escort you to the council, myself."

Her expression softened. "You've been more than kind, Jens."

Something clearly bothered him. Hesitantly, his fingers touched the bruise on her cheek. "Is it painful?"

"Yes." She hesitated, unused to revealing any weakness. "I fear I will be forced to endure more at that butcher's hand."

He gazed into her eyes, and she too seemed caught up in the moment. He bowed down to kiss her hand, and she drew in her breath. Jens kept his lips to her hand for a long time, and she did not try to pull away.

I felt a touch on my shoulder and started in surprise. It was Lexander. He looked through the crack to see Jens reverently kissing Silveta's hand. "Good instinct," he murmured, "but wrong man. Jedvard is not likely to send his youngest son into battle against Birgir, however toothsome a prize Markland would be."

Lexander pushed open the door. Silveta pulled away from Jens, mortified at being caught in even this innocent act. She was flushed and breathing faster. Jens was grinning as if he would never stop. He assured Silveta several times that he would return for her. Then he finally left.

"I'll go with him," Lexander told Silveta. "Perhaps I can learn more to your advantage in the negotiations. They will expect trade rights in return for their support."

"I'll consider what concessions you can convey to the overlord," Silveta agreed, retreating behind her dignified mask.

I slipped out after Lexander, but he waved for me to stay behind. When I tried to return, Silveta shut the door in my face.

I had nothing to do but to sit in the wooden staircase that spiraled down several floors, waiting until I was needed again.

I had plenty of time to consider my plight. I did not want to go back to Tillfallvik while Birgir was there. But surely Silveta intended to return with the overlord's men to fight for her estate.

Lexander reappeared twice to confer privately with Silveta, then left to pass on her concessions to the overlord. He didn't speak to me. Though I listened through the door to their discussions of trade rights, I couldn't tell if Lexander intended to return to Tillfallvik with Silveta. Lexander owned me, and I would do whatever he ordered. The only thing I would not do was surrender myself to him. I had too great a fear of the Otherworld to risk being subsumed.

Olfs came and went all day, no doubt curious about us. They popped into the stairwell to examine me, then disappeared into the round room where Silveta bathed and prepared herself. In the mystical way of otherworldly creatures, it seemed they knew of Silveta and her importance to the northern *olfs*. They mocked my somber mood, and soon convinced me that our presence in the bastion was cause for celebration.

By the time Jens returned, Silveta was her elegant self once more—perfectly coiffed and wearing a dress of yellow silk that Jens had given her. Jens was stricken into awed silence at the sight of her. I watched from my hiding place on the steps huddled in the shadows.

Jens led her reverently down to the landing on the second floor. I had explored as far as I dared during the day. I could tell they were heading to the northernmost end of the bastion, where the tallest towers were gathered. I trailed after them.

After a short walk, we met up with Lexander outside a stout door. It was constructed of heavy beams bound with iron, as if meant to hold off the wind and snow even though we were deep inside the bastion. Two guards watched us from either side as we gathered in the wide hallway. A few servants loitered about, waiting to be given orders.

Half a dozen women were seated on benches at the end of the hallway, doing needlework by the sunlight slanting through two high windows. They were dressed as finely as Silveta, and their muted conversation grew more animated as they examined us.

Jens opened the door at a nod from the guard. The narrow room beyond was so long that the flat beamed ceiling seemed low. But Lexander could not have touched it with his hand. A row of chairs ran along each wall, and at the end sat Jedvard. His massive wooden chair had an elaborate carved canopy projecting over his head. The big man rested one elbow on the polished arm.

I paused near the door, wary of all the eyes that turned

to us. The dozen men who made up the overlord's council were seated in high-backed carved chairs. Then I saw an *olf* sitting on the top of Jedvard's chair, kicking its feet playfully over the edge. Surely that was a good sign.

Silveta went through the hall to stand directly in front of Jedvard. Lexander was one step behind at her right, acting as her *bondi* though I had not heard him give her a vow. I stayed behind them both, with my shawl tied firmly in place. I held the standing pose of submission with my head bowed and my hands clasped together, trying as hard as I could to disappear. I did not want to be a pawn in this game played by great men.

Jedvard sounded much more eager than he had earlier. "I have explained to my councilors your need, *freya*. And the terms your man has conveyed. But it is a weighty matter involving ourselves in civil war."

"Though I am a daughter of Viinland," Silveta proclaimed, "my right to Ejegod's estate is confirmed in my marriage contract. There will be no civil war, only a battle against a brigand who murdered my husband. I am quite sure that years of cooperation between our nations are worth far more than the little help I am asking for."

Lexander nodded slightly.

An old man seated to our right spoke up. "What if Birgir Barfoot does not surrender? If I am correct, he arrived with a hundred warriors. Surely he could prove to be the victor and remain the chieftain of Markland."

"My people have not and never will accept Birgir as chieftain," Silveta swore, looking straight at Jedvard. "Without their support, he has no hope of success. I can guarantee our trade agreements will be honored, and surely that is advantageous to you."

Jens had gone to stand beside his father's chair. His eyes were shining as he watched Silveta passionately defend her rights. But he was merely a boy in rut. I wished he had been more of a man.

The overlord considered his councilors, who had no further protests. "We accept your proposal, Silveta. Fifty of my best men will go with you to Tillfallvik and stay until your new chieftain is named. If that man is not your choice for husband, perhaps you would consider one who has direct links to the overlord?"

Silveta bowed slightly. "I am pleased to honor the overlord in any way I can. I cannot thank you enough for assisting me in my time of need . . ."

She trailed off as the door swung open and a guard hurried in. He went straight to the overlord's chair, asking a question in a low voice. Jens looked urgently at Silveta as if silently trying to warn her.

Jedvard straightened. "It seems Birgir Barfoot has sent his own emissary. Send him in so he can speak to my council."

A chill went through me. My hands clutched at Lexander's cloak as several of Birgir's *bondi* entered the chamber. Niall was among them. His black pointed beard made him stand out among the blond warriors.

Niall spied me immediately, and his dark eyes snapped with anger. Lexander looked down at me as I tried to hide behind him. "What did you do to this man, Marja?" he murmured.

"I escaped from him," I admitted, "after I pleased him into oblivion."

Niall was clearly in disfavor because one of the other men addressed the overlord. "Greetings, Overlord Jedvard! We bring a missive from Birgir, Chieftain of Markland," he announced, holding the parchment up for all the councilors to see. "As Chieftain of Markland by right of conquest and forfeit, Birgir will swear fealty to the Overlord of the commonwealth of Viinland if Silveta, his bride-to-be, is returned to him."

"No!" Silveta exclaimed. "That is not true! Birgir has not been confirmed as chieftain by the magnates."

Niall stepped forward. "The magnates support Birgir. Already they are flocking to him. Markland needs a strong hand to rule."

Silveta gasped. "Birgir slew my husband, stole my estate, and raped me! 'Tis against every common law."

Niall sneered at her. "Your rights are forfeit because of

your crimes, Silveta. You succor a sorceress, named so by Ejegod himself, who attempted twice to kill Birgir at your behest. You lie, as all women lie!"

Jens started forward, his hand on his knife as if to attack Niall.

Jedvard stopped him with one hand. He silenced the rising questions from the councilors. "There will be no brawling in my chambers!" He gestured to his son. "Take Silveta back to the tower. My councilors must consider how to deal with this matter."

I was only too glad to get away from Niall. But Silveta dragged her feet, staring anxiously at Jedvard. "I beg you support my people, Overlord. A man who begins with treachery could not be loyal to you. You cannot trust Birgir as you can trust me. I have given you my allegiance my entire life."

Jedvard gestured to the guards to go with us, while Birgir's *bondi* smirked as they watched us leave. Lexander's brows furrowed as two more guards joined us.

When the door closed behind us, Jens assured Silveta, "My father must deal with Birgir's men wisely. Who knows where their sights may land next?"

I realized that Birgir's warband could be as much a threat to Viinland as to Markland.

Silveta wrung her hands and cried, "Oh, where is my father?"

The three of us filed up the spiral stairs and into the chamber at the top of the tower. The guards would not let Jens enter with us. He called out, "I'll return shortly! I must hear their negotiations. Never fear, Silveta."

Lexander stood beside the door as it closed, listening. At a scraping sound, he tried to lift the latch. "They've locked us in. A guard is outside."

I was shocked. "The overlord would not betray us!"

"I wish I were as confident as you," he retorted.

"But . . . he couldn't be evil," I finally said, thinking of all the *olfs* who flocked to him. "How could he harm us?"

Silveta was pacing back and forth by the windows. "Jedvard would do whatever it took to protect the commonwealth. He would even congratulate himself on gaining the wealth of Markland for his people."

Lexander agreed. "Birgir offers far more than Silveta, with no risk for the overlord's bondsmen. Even if you offered to become a province of Viinland, Silveta, fighting to win your estate back would still be the greater risk for him."

"I could never offer that," she insisted. "I could not break the vow I made when I married Ejegod, to uphold Markland's independence."

"Birgir is willing to give that much," Lexander reminded her.

"No, there's still my father," Silveta declared. "He would never let Birgir get away with this."

"Then that is our last hope," Lexander said.

Silveta stared at him, no doubt thinking as I did—Jedvard could turn us over to Birgir's men and gain another province for Viinland. A wealthy gift, indeed, for very little effort. Then Silveta would be forced to wed Birgir and be subjected to his sadistic ways, while I would be devoured by his *bondi*. And the *olfs* . . . they would take flight from Tillfallvik as they had fled from Vidaris, while Birgir's evil spread unfettered throughout the land.

Fourteen

"We must flee," I whispered. I went to Lexander, grasping him by the arm. "Please, Master! We must get to our boat."

"You think I can escape from the bastion?" he retorted in disbelief. "This place is impregnable. We will stay here until Jedvard decides what to do with us."

I couldn't believe it, but the resignation in his eyes was unfeigned. Yet surely a god could do whatever he willed . . . perhaps I had misunderstood him after all.

Silveta collapsed on a bench, her hands clenched against her face. Yet she seemed convinced that her father would rise to her aid.

With the specter of Birgir and his men before me, I could not be so sanguine. I went to the window and opened the glass panels. The window was high in the wall, so I dragged a bench underneath to stand on. I pulled the shawl from my head so I could lean out. The wall curved away from me in both directions. The roof came down at a sharp angle above us.

My hands caressed the stones. They were round and slippery from the moisture of the sea. Most were the size of my head or larger. Mortar was packed tightly between them. I would never be able to scale this wall as I had the timber buildings on Ejegod's estate.

I pulled back inside and considered Lexander, who was listening at the door. It seemed impossible that he could suffer. Slowly, I sat down on the bench to watch him. I sank into myself, instinctively sending out a call for the *olfs* to come to me. I wondered why none were here.

As the long day wore on, the beam of sunlight moved up the wall. Still Lexander did nothing but listen at the door. Silveta got up to pace time and again, murmuring to herself.

When the sky shaded to twilight, an *olf* finally appeared. It hovered at the ceiling near the door, watching us and staying unusually still. I had hoped it would flit around happily to show me that all was well, but its wretched expression told me we had much to fear.

I went to stand directly beneath the *olf,* trying to calm my agitation and radiating soothing thoughts. I couldn't think about Niall or Birgir because my dread could frighten the *olf* off. I breathed slowly and deeply, touching the flow of spirits in this place.

The feeling in the bastion was one of alarm. We had brought the troubles of Markland into the very heart of Viinland. The council feared what Birgir would do to their land, while the folk in the bastion thought it a neat resolution to marry Silveta to Birgir. Few people took seriously her refusal to marry him. After all, her first husband had been an old man who could seed no child. A lusty warrior was seen as a much better alternative, even if he had the presumption to bed her before he wed her.

Through the *olf,* I could even sense the overlord's secret elation. He had a deeper reason for sealing an alliance with Birgir—his grandfather had dreamed of gaining sovereignty over all of the western maritime lands, but Ejegod's family had ruled with far too strong a hand. Jedvard had bribed Silveta's father to marry her to Ejegod, but had not imagined it would bring him this boon. Silveta's father was still a thorn to be dealt with, but the magnificent bride price that Birgir would be forced to pay would solve her family's current financial problems.

"Jedvard intends to accept Birgir's oath," I murmured, as it became clear in my mind. Lexander turned to look at me.

"No! My father will not allow it," Silveta snapped, her eyes wild.

I shook off the last trace of my communion with the *olfs*. "Your father is here now."

"My father!" Silveta stood up, as if ready to run to him. "How do you know?"

"The *olfs* told me."

Silveta let out a disbelieving laugh. "You *are* daft! Do you think I'll believe some mythical creatures informed you that my own father would betray me?"

The *olf* above my head vanished. They hated to be denied.

"The *olfs* are watching over you," I said seriously. "They've saved you time and again."

Silveta dismissed me with a wave, sitting back down. "They do a poor job, if this is the result."

Stung, I remembered how often the *olfs* had prevented harm from falling on her. "Would you have me prove their devotion to you? The *olfs* are the ones who led us through the woods when we escaped. They told me to save you."

She remembered how I had guided her in the dark, though she hadn't believed it was possible. I found that people often refused to see what was right before their eyes. But I could not let Silveta deny the *olfs*. They depended on her.

Lexander was listening closely. He did not see the *olfs*, but he had never questioned my understanding of them. My da's kin treated *olfs* as a mere superstition. They had laughed and thought me half addled. But Lexander had always been respectful of them though he couldn't see them himself.

"Hush!" Lexander whispered, leaning closer to the door. Voices echoed up the stairwell.

"My father!" Silveta exclaimed, leaping to her feet. "He's come for me."

I hoped for the best. Jens had promised faithfully to return. But faint tendrils of evil seeped into the room, and my skin grew cold.

The latch on the door lifted, and it swung open. Two guards came in first, their short-swords in their hands. They stepped to either side of the door as another man climbed the stairs, carrying a basket.

Niall looked directly at me as he entered, smiling slyly. "That kindhearted boy insisted that you get some food. No candles, of course, or you might burn the place down."

He thrust the basket into Lexander's hands. Then Niall came so close to me that I backed against the wall, feeling the wood paneling beneath my desperate fingers.

"Yes, you would do well to run from me," Niall murmured, never taking his eyes off mine. His hand twitched at his side. I thought he was going to hit me.

Lexander dropped the basket to step up to Niall.

"Stay out of this," Niall told him. "Birgir cares not that you've helped this wildcat." He gestured over his shoulder to Silveta. "You can leave now. The guards will let you go. Return to Tillfallvik and tell them that the overlord supports Birgir's rule of Markland, in the name of the one true god of Kristna."

Silveta cried out, "But my father!"

"He cares not who you're wed to," Niall retorted. "So go, man, be loyal to your chieftain. You have much to gain from cooperating with us."

Niall clearly thought Lexander was a simple man from Tillfallvik, loyal to Ejegod. Fear washed over me at the thought of my master leaving us. But he must go; Lexander could get help from his allies for us.

Silveta's voice was harsh as she spoke to Lexander. "Go, man! You did your duty to bring me here. I release you now."

"Yes," I murmured. "Go." It was our only hope of rescue.

"The girl wants it," Niall taunted. "But then, you were exceedingly eager last night. This time you will not bespell me, sorceress." He ordered the guards, "Take him away. His crew of boys awaits him. And lock the door after you."

Lexander's amber eyes narrowed. His hand went to the short knife at his waist.

"Go," I repeated through gritted teeth. Surely I could survive what Niall did to me until Lexander returned to save us. I would do whatever I could to keep Niall from attacking Silveta. But if she could endure Birgir, Niall could hardly be worse.

Lexander pulled his knife. "Not while I stand."

Both the guards lifted their swords, crying out, "Halt!"

Niall's eyes widened. "She has suborned you, too? Quick work, girl," he drawled. "Did you bed him on the journey here in front of all of those lusty boys?"

"You'll not taste her charms," Lexander declared. "I'll kill you first."

Niall's hand went to his ax. "No man lives who makes such a boast!"

"Stand down," one of the guards ordered. The big one stood in the doorway. "There'll be no fighting here. You"— he pointed at Niall—"you've delivered the food. Now get out. If the bondsman wants to stay with his *freya*, then 'tis his right."

Lexander held his knife ready as Niall hesitated.

Then Niall grinned, letting his hand fall from his ax. "I'll have her soon enough. We depart at dawn to speed Silveta to her loving husband. Then this slave shall be mine."

Niall laughed at my shock, then gave Lexander a mocking salute as he withdrew. The two guards followed him, and the latch fell with a solid clank as it was locked shut.

"Why didn't you go, Lexander?" Silveta cried. "You could have gotten help for us."

He resheathed his knife. "I couldn't leave you here with that man."

"Better that than to condemn me to Birgir's mercies!" Silveta tore at her hair and threw herself on the bed, the drapes billowing out around her.

I felt much the same, but I couldn't protest when I saw how his decision tormented him. Lexander knew I understood, and he put his arms around me. I melted into him in my need for solace.

"I couldn't let him harm you," he whispered.

If only I could have stayed that way forever. I leaned my face against his chest and heard his steady heartbeat. But instead of being flushed and warm from his confrontation with Niall, his skin was cool to the touch as always, reminding me that he was not a man.

He felt me stiffen, and released me. I almost protested,

willing to give anything to be one with him again. But my mam's warnings were too true. I couldn't let myself surrender to him. I must go to the Otherworld only when I was safely dead. At this moment, it looked as if it would be at Niall's hand.

With a sigh, Lexander returned to his post by the door. I sank down on the hard wooden floor. Silveta was crying helplessly on the bed.

When Silveta finally slept from sheer exhaustion, the curtains drawn tight around her, I approached Lexander.

By the light of the crescent moon, I went to kneel before him. My pose was *lydnad*, obedience, kneeling straight from shoulders to knees with my eyes down. "I beg of you to help us, Master."

He sat, leaning against the door. "Marja . . . I am not as powerful as you think."

I swallowed. "Do you require a sacrifice? I would give anything of myself to escape."

"I saw that." His hand reached out to caress my hair.

"Then why won't you save us? Surely a god could keep us all from harm."

His hand dropped away from me, and he stared off into the darkness. "It's true that some of my people, the oldest among us, are considered gods. With only a thought, they could smite Birgir where he stands. But I haven't their powers, not yet. I can control only my own flesh, not the elements around me. I could not fly from here, nor carry you with me, much as I long to."

"So you can suffer, too?"

"Yes. I will fight these men who try to harm you, but you must know that even with my great strength, I can be struck down."

"Can't you ask your people for help?"

His voice was soft but resolute. "I abandoned Vidaris, Marja. They would sooner kill me themselves. But I could not endure it another moment longer. I could not see you broken as a toy for their amusement."

I was stunned. "Is there no hope then?"

"It seems to me that you have powerful friends, Marja. You escaped from Birgir once before and saved Silveta. Look to yourself for your deliverance."

It was too dark for me to see him well, but he was in earnest. He was my master, a godling in his own right, yet he needed my help.

I knew what I must do.

I went to the basket and rummaged through it by touch. There were ripe cranberries along with a heavy loaf of bread and two joints of a large bird. A water jug held mead. I drank deeply and gave it to Lexander to do the same. Then I set it on the hearth uncorked. The coals were long dead, merely ash. I glanced up the flue, but it was a tube too small for me to pass through. *Olfs* leaped into the draft of a flue to be sucked outside, enjoying the rush of air and the ride.

I sat down to concentrate, calling the *olfs* to me. I could feel them out there, milling about in the bastion. But none of them responded. After trying over and over, I knew that Silveta's denouncement was keeping them at bay. *Olfs* were very sensitive. It did not seem likely that any would be tempted to come back for the mead when they could get all they wanted elsewhere in the bastion.

The longer I sat on the floor, the more I heard the booming of the ocean waves against the base of the cliffs. The sea spirits were trying to answer my call.

I fetched the loaf of bread from the basket, hefting it in my hand. It smelled like ground barley and rye mixed with whey and honey. My belly was empty and I longed to taste it, but my sacrifice would mean more if I was hungry. I climbed onto the bench under the window and leaned out, tearing off a chunk of the bread and tossing it far into the air. The bread arced away from the wall of the bastion, tumbling down to bounce off the rocks below and into the boiling waves.

I threw out chunks of bread again and again, giving it all before they were satisfied. I could not touch the water, so my only hope lay in reaching them through sacrifice. I received scattered, faint images from the sea spirits as if I were looking through layers of silk—our longship had departed with the boys, taking a message from the overlord in support of Birgir as chieftain. There was fighting in Tillfallvik, with Ejegod's *bondi* still holding the waterfront, waiting for Silveta to return with reinforcements. I even saw Helanas standing at the gate of Vidaris, looking out to sea and wondering where Lexander was.

I tried to ask the sea spirits for guidance, but they were like the *olfs*. The creatures thought only of what was happening now—the future was of no consequence to them. They could not predict what Birgir would do, or what would become of us. Only gods and humans considered the coming days and manipulated events to suit their desires.

When the bread was gone, the sea spirits had nothing more to show me. I could not jump out far enough to dive into the water. The rocks would take me first to my death.

I slowly turned away and sat down on the bench under the window. Lexander was still leaning against the door, watching me. He was in the shadows, while I was bathed in the faintest glow from the sliver of moon.

Was there nowhere else to turn? From the overlord's reaction, I could tell the Norogods were supporting Birgir, though he claimed to have only Kristna at his side. I was not surprised my da's gods would choose Birgir since he had won at arms. They thrived on conflict. As for the bastion, I did not know the spirits who claimed it and would have no right to call on them.

Then my mam's face appeared before my eyes, answering my anguished cry for help. She was woken from her sleep by my need. The roaring of the ocean here echoed the waves in far-off Jarnby, linking us together. I praised the wisdom of the sea spirits for bringing us together.

She prayed to her Skraeling gods to answer my call for help. Issitoq, the punisher of taboos, replied to her, acknowledging that betrayal was at the heart of my pain.

We joined together in our call, seeking retribution for the overlord's duplicity. He had agreed to support Silveta and had spoken his pledge aloud before his own councilors. Then he had sacrificed her for his own greed. I pleaded with Issitoq to claim vengeance by saving us.

In my mind's eye, my mam sat staring into the fire in our modest longhouse, chanting under her breath so as to not awaken the others. She pulled a small knife from her belt, letting the glow of the coals glint off the blade.

I went over to Lexander. "I need your knife."

He handed it to me, not knowing what I intended. I returned to the bench where I could hear the sea beneath me. My lips began to move in the same chant as my mam, the Skraeling words coming to me with her thoughts. I let the plea for help roll through me as we both pressed the point of the knives into our palms.

"Marja," Lexander protested.

I let the sharp blade slice into my skin. I dragged it to form a red line to the base of my hand. Blood welled up, running down my uplifted arm. I could see my mam's hand covered in blood. We let it drip onto the floor, chanting to give our *inua* wings to fly to Issitoq, to satiate him with our sacrifice.

Then I could hold it back no longer; the pain flashed through me, severing my connection with my mam. I gasped out loud, holding my wrist to let the blood drip free. I forced my lips to continue the Skraeling chant, over and over again. With each shining drop, I gave of myself to Issitoq. I knew that in Jarnby, my mam was doing the same.

I was still chanting dully when the moon set. I felt the chill that comes with the approaching morn but did not dare pause in my pleas to Issitoq. I, who had honored the gods always, begged to be heard.

It seemed like a dream when Lexander moved away from the entrance at the sound of the latch lifting. The door swung open. A candle lit the stairwell, revealing a guard. My lips faltered on the chant and finally stopped. The blood had congealed on my skin and left a shiny splotch on the floor.

Then Jens appeared. "Silveta! I've come to get you out of here."

The curtains of the bed flung back, and Silveta came flying from her nest. "Jens! Can it be true?"

Lexander gestured to the guard. "What about him?"

"Gris has guarded me since I was a child—he's my *bondi*." The guard went back down a few steps to hold watch.

Jens held out both of his hands to Silveta. "Gris relieved the other guard early, but we must hurry for the real guard will arrive soon. No one must know you're gone until Birgir's men come to fetch you in the morn."

Silveta hugged Jens in her eagerness. "You are truly a gift from the gods, Jens!"

Lexander started down the steps, calling, "Marja, come quickly!"

Fifteen

I was jolted out of the last vestiges of my trance. Cradling my hand, I hurried through the door. Jens latched it behind us, and Gris took up a stance in front of it. Then Jens led us down the spiral stairs, checking at each archway before gesturing us to pass. On the lowest floor, he led us to another set of stairs, this one more rickety and dark than the others. At the bottom, he gestured to the corridors with low stone ceilings that branched off in several directions. Lexander had to stoop so as not to brush his head.

"Through here," Jens whispered. "There should be no one about right now. This will take us to the docks. You must get away quickly, before it's discovered you're missing." Then he glanced at me. "Birgir's men claim that she's a sorceress, and they'll likely think she flew you over the ocean."

Lexander grinned at me. In spite of the danger I suddenly wanted to laugh.

Had Issitoq induced Jens to help us? Or had Silveta truly won his heart?

But I had no time for such musings as we hurried through the dark passageway. In some sections, it tunneled through rock and changed levels, but Jens dashed along as if he knew the way. I could imagine him as a boy with his brothers, racing along these passageways to the far parts of the sprawling bastion.

Olfs popped up occasionally, but mostly they stayed at a distance. I was so drained from my long chant that I could barely acknowledge them. Most of them were preoccupied with spinning in the trailing cobwebs of dreams.

Then Jens led us into an alleyway that opened up above us. It took a moment for me to realize we were in the streets. The crash of the waves lay not far beyond these walls. The buildings were several stories high, with living quarters above shops and services for the townsfolk.

It was still dark, and Jens held his candle high for a moment. "It's down this street all the way to the docks. If someone stops us, you go on and I'll distract them."

With that, we dashed down the narrow, twisting street, stumbling and slipping on the cobblestones. Once Silveta fell down on both knees, soiling the golden dress Jens had given her. He took her arm and supported her, holding the candle with his other hand.

Even at that late hour, a few people were on the streets. Several guards passed by, but they hardly glanced at us. A couple hurried down a cross lane, and I knew they were going somewhere to rut.

Then we reached the wide plaza that backed the gate to the docks. We stayed in the shadows, hiding behind the colonnade. There was a trio of guards on duty at the gate, but they were sitting aimlessly on a pile of empty crates. One was carving while another slept. There was no port official on duty. Likely they would alert their superior, who was sleeping in the gate tower, if they sighted a ship coming in.

"There's the docks. Your oarsmen are still onboard your longship," Jens assured Silveta.

"No, they're gone." I realized I had not told them. "The boys were sent back to Tillfallvik with a message that the overlord supports Birgir as chieftain and that Silveta will marry him when she returns."

"How do you know that?" Jens asked incredulously.

"Don't ask," Silveta retorted. "But she's been right so far."

Jens gave us both a sharp look, then moved a few columns to one side so he could see through the gate. "There're too many crafts between us and your longship to see."

"How can we get another boat?" Lexander asked, impatiently. "Even a small one would do."

"You'll have to take mine," Jens decided. "I use it on the flats to dig for clams."

Silveta put her hands on his arm. "But then your father will know you helped us escape."

"They may not realize it's gone," Jens countered. "And it matters little if they do. I think it's wrong to force you to marry that brigand."

"What will your father do to you?" Silveta exclaimed.

"It won't be nearly as bad as what would happen to you."

Silveta looked at him wordlessly. I could tell she was worried about him. But Jens was looking more manly by the moment in my eyes.

"What will you do?" Jens asked her.

"I'll raise a warband," Silveta said tightly. "I've sworn blood vengeance on Birgir. He will not take Markland. Not while I live."

Jens straightened his shoulders, echoing her pose. "I'll help you, Silveta. I can't sit by and watch this happen."

"No!" Silveta protested. "You can't go with us."

Lexander added, "Your father would search for us as fiercely as Birgir. He would think we kidnapped you."

Jens looked deflated. "I don't want to bring you more trouble."

Silveta squeezed his arm. "You've saved us, Jens. I'll never forget that."

"We're not safe yet," Lexander pointed out. "Let's get on with this."

Silveta and I prepared to act the role of doxies, snuggling in close to them. I felt a rush of pleasure as Lexander's strong arm went around me. As we passed between the guards, I realized that they were far more concerned with those entering the bastion rather than leaving. Indeed, the most attention we got was an appraising glance from the guard who was carving. Likely doxies had to pleasure the guards to get back inside.

Jens took us down the main dock. There were many

oarsmen in the boats, sleeping or waiting for orders to depart. Jens turned off into one of the side jetties. His boat was pulled onto a ramp along with others of a similar size. The three of us would be crowded in it, but there was a short sail mast that could be raised. With only two oars, one man could handle the boat.

Lexander helped him slide the flat-bottomed boat into the water. Jens held the stern while Lexander and I climbed in. Silveta gave Jens a brief hug, murmuring something to him that I couldn't hear. But it made Jens straighten his shoulders and nod firmly as he pushed us away. I hoped he would not suffer too much if it was discovered he had helped us. Niall would be enraged when he found out I was gone.

Lexander dipped the oars in quietly, and we pulled away from the island. Soon, there was blackness all around except for the sheen of the waves. I dipped my wounded hand into the salt water and hissed in pain. The direct contact with the sea spirits pulsed through my body. They applauded my sacrifice and our escape and took the dried remnants of blood for themselves.

"Go south," Silveta ordered. "I must convince my family to help me."

Lexander pulled hard as we bobbed on the water like a cork. The sea felt very different in such a small boat. Even in the bay, the waves rose higher than our heads. The moon had set, but regardless I knew we were not heading south.

"You can return to your family if you insist," Lexander told her. "But I will not set foot on their land. They have colluded with Birgir."

She put her hands to her face and her shoulders began to shake. I knew how helpless I would feel if my da had done such a thing. He had sold me, but only with my consent.

My mam must also be suffering from the sacrifice she had made with me. I let myself flow into the sea spirits, and conveyed my satisfaction in seeing the lights on the towers of the bastion disappear into the distance. The sea spirits let my mam hear me, and her own relief flowed back. I would never know if we had worked a miracle together, but she had indeed stood beside me in my darkest hour. It was no wonder Silveta cried, knowing her family had abandoned her.

I reached out and touched Silveta's shoulder to offer comfort. When she finally managed to look up, I knew that she would survive even this.

The rowing seemed not to wind Lexander at all. "None of Viinland's chieftains or magnates will aid you now that the overlord has declared himself for Birgir. Do you have allies in Kebec?"

"No," Silveta admitted with a sniff. "And their envoy seemed fair taken with Birgir at midsummer. Perhaps I could buy the bonds of fighting men in one of the larger cities . . ."

Likely she would need a large bag of coins to do that. I glanced back at Lexander. What did he intend to do?

"For now," he said, as if reading my mind, "we need to get far away from Hop. Perhaps to the upper reaches of Viinland—Furdustrand or Djarney. You may be able to negotiate a trade there."

"Djarney!" I exclaimed. "We could go to the Sigurdssons. Remember, Silveta? Gudren told me to contact him if I ever needed help."

Lexander broke his rhythm. "You mean the merchants?" At my nod, he asked, "How do you know the Sigurdssons, Marja?"

I turned to face him. "Gudren saved me in Brianda, after my coins were stolen. He took me to live in Djarney for nearly a moon until we came to Tillfallvik for the midsummer celebration."

"So that's where you were. Basking in luxury with a trade prince."

I could tell he was amused. "I had trouble getting away from them. They're kind people."

"The Sigurdssons are very attached to Marja," Silveta agreed thoughtfully.

Lexander continued rowing. "This boat is too small to handle the ocean. We'll have to take the back way through the Straumsey Bay."

"What about narrows?" Silveta asked.

"I'm sure we'll manage. It will be safer than the ocean because it's the most unlikely direction for us to take."

It began to rain shortly before sunrise. But with the morning breeze, the sail of our little boat skimmed us past the woody islands in the bay. I slept deeply, depleted from my sacrifice. My hand throbbed dreadfully whenever I awoke, heating my body and making me feel dazed.

Silveta and Lexander were always talking, trying to plan how she could pay for armed men and boats. They also strategized on how best to attack the estate and its weaknesses. Mostly I heard Silveta's growing desperation and Lexander's distrust of every idea she proposed. Surely he would not risk us falling into Birgir's hands again.

We reached the innermost end of Straumsey Bay when the squalls were finally breaking off. Despite the cloud cover, I knew the sun was directly overhead. It took only a few coins for Lexander to buy the use of a cart and donkey to haul the small boat across the narrows, the neck of Furdustrand. On the other side was the Nauga Sea. When we stood on the northern shore, we were directly across the strait from Fjardemano. The island was a flat smear in the distance. Vidaris was at the northern tip.

I felt as if I had come full circle. Indeed, we soon were sailing briskly past Brianda. The busy port town filling the river valley looked so peaceful from our boat. But I knew what it was really like to be alone on those streets.

Lexander rowed without ceasing even when the wind blew hard. I was used to seeing my da work the forge, so I knew it was a remarkable display of strength. Even seasoned oarsmen rotated in rest. But despite his efforts, it was full dark before we passed through the channel that separated the peninsula of Furdustrand from the island of Djarney. In the sheltered harbor between the two lands, the familiar manicured lawns of the Sigurdssons' estate appeared.

The warehouses were closed down for the night and most of the oarsmen had gone away. Only a few loitered in ships or lay on the dock. Nobody paid attention as Lexander moored our small boat. Likely they thought we were independent traders, come to dicker with the merchants.

An *olf* appeared as soon I stepped onto shore. It was spinning with excitement. Apparently Silveta was big news among the *olfs*. It wasn't long before we were surrounded by them.

I led Lexander and Silveta through the estate to Gudren and Alga's house. I was ready to walk boldly inside, but Silveta and Lexander both urged caution. They believed it possible that Gudren could betray us to the overlord if he thought it profitable enough. I wanted to dismiss the suggestion, but then again, I had been fooled into thinking Jedvard would treat us fairly because of the *olfs'* approbation.

So we waited near the house, hidden behind a woodpile, to catch Gudren as he returned from the night-meal. Alga was with him, of course. I met them at the door and greeted them both quietly.

It took only a moment for them to recognize me. Gudren hugged me so tightly that my ribs creaked. Alga seemed near bursting with her smile, refusing to let go of my arm. "We heard what happened in Tillfallvik. The chieftain dead! Where have you been?"

"In Hop." They were so genuinely glad to see me that I knew I could trust them. I called out Silveta and Lexander.

Gudren was instantly wary. He had not been that way with me. He gave a respectful bow to Silveta. "We heard that you were to marry Birgir, *freya*. Tillfallvik is under siege, but my last boat got away with most of the goods we were due."

"I will never marry that beast," Silveta insisted, as if she was tired of having to tell everyone. "Can you help me hire the warriors I need to oust him from my estate?"

Alga shrewdly pointed out, "You won't find many men

prepared to defy the overlord. It's said that Markland has petitioned to join the commonwealth of Viinland."

"Surely your trade agreements with Markland would suffer in that case," Silveta countered. "Birgir gives too much to the overlord."

"Goodwill with the leader of Viinland is far more valuable to us," Gudren said flatly.

"Then you can't help me find the men I need to fight?" Silveta cried.

"I am not a warlord, *freya*. Such men are not at my disposal. And I cannot risk the wrath of the overlord to finance such a scheme. It is too much to ask."

Alga nodded righteously next to him, obviously concerned for her family. "Who would back you against the overlord?"

"Then I must go elsewhere," Silveta said faintly. "To the Auldland, if no one here will lift a finger to support my rights."

Gudren nodded. "I've a *knaar* leaving tomorrow for Gronland with a load of spars. You are welcome to journey with them."

Silveta blinked a few times, as if she hadn't thought it through. "Could I find warriors in Gronland?"

"Birgir and his men were not the only ones to be ousted by the conqueror," Gudren reminded her. "Surely there are other warriors who fled Danelaw and have settled on the northern islands. They could be eager for new ventures."

There was silence for a moment as Silveta considered the possibility of finding hardened warriors who were dissatisfied with the icy islands of the north.

Lexander quietly reminded her, "If there are no warriors there, Silveta, you may find a better life far away from this war that has started in Markland. I do not think Birgir will be so easily defeated now that the overlord has a vested interest in seeing him become chieftain."

Silveta shook her head impatiently. "I have declared a blood vengeance against him. I will not rest until he is destroyed."

Gudren and Alga saw there was little more they could say to her. Despite their best interests, they were very generous to us. They brought us into their home and gave us plenty of hot food, which Alga fetched herself. They even dismissed their servant for the evening so there would be no idle talk of our arrival.

When Alga saw my wounded hand, she bustled around me, cleaning and bandaging it. I knew it could endanger them if it was known they had helped Silveta, so I said, "I'm sorry if my coming here brings you trouble. I didn't know where else to go."

Alga shrugged it off and gave me a hug. "I have thought of you often and wondered how you fared. Now you must stay here where you belong! Let Silveta fight this hopeless battle. You are foolish to take such a risk with her."

I gave her a kiss. "I am too deeply involved, Alga. The overlord will be looking for me as well as Silveta, I've no doubt."

I explained how I had helped Silveta escape, and the personal stake that Niall had in retrieving me. Alga was even more concerned. I could tell she longed to keep me safe in their estate.

Then I realized that Lexander was watching us. He noticed every time Gudren or Alga touched me or spoke to me. He saw how familiar I was with their ways.

When Alga asked me to come up to their loft, I obeyed. It didn't occur to me to decline anything she or Gudren asked of me. As I followed her up the stairs, Lexander stood up.

I hesitated, glancing back down at him. I belonged to Lexander. It was ultimately his choice whether or not I was intimate with Gudren and Alga.

His mouth opened as if to speak, his brow drawn in concern. Then he gained control of himself, and his remote mask fell into place. It was familiar from my training, when he had watched me pleasure one of the other slaves. I never knew whether he got enjoyment from it or not.

Lexander turned back to the fire.

Alga was waiting at the door. She was watching Silveta to

see if she would protest, believing I belonged to the chieftain's wife rather than Lexander. But Silveta didn't even notice where I was going, much less care.

When I entered the room, Gudren was waiting for us. They both hugged me close as if they had thought they would never see me again. It took my breath away.

"Stay with us," Gudren urged, holding each of us in his massive arms. "Alga says you worry about the danger you bring us. But surely 'tis only Silveta that the overlord cares about."

Once again they were prepared to keep me here. The gilded cage was pleasant, but I had to confess, "Lexander is my master. I was going to meet him when I was stranded in Brianda. He told me to stay with Silveta until he returned for me."

They were astonished. Alga exclaimed, "Why didn't you tell us before?"

"He ordered me not to reveal that I was a pleasure slave."

Gudren laughed. "It was clear to me from the moment I met you. So this man is your master . . . I believe I've heard of him. Of a place called Vidaris."

"Yes, but it must not be spoken of," I begged them. "We are both in grave peril if it is known."

Alga pressed her body against mine, hugging me close. "We would not say a word, my darling. And do not be afraid. We will take care of you."

I took pleasure from them that night, caressing and kissing them until we weren't sure where one left off and another began. It had never been so good between us, and it seemed their desire had sharpened from missing me. Gudren had not been aggressive before, but now he was enthralled. His goal was to please me, as I had pleased him so many times before.

Alga was equally passionate, but that was her charm. Her soft, insistent body was everything I had longed for in Helanas—powerful yet tender, self-assured and true. She had always reminded me of Lexander, and never more so than now, when she took me as she wanted.

I realized that night how much I cared about them both. It drove my fear of Birgir and even my pain about Lexander away, until I finally slept nestled in the soft blankets in their bed.

Sixteen

The next morning when Gudren had left us, Alga announced, "Once the other two have sailed, I'll take you around to see everyone. They will be thrilled that you've returned to us."

I was surprised and could not speak to contradict her. But Alga was so confident of herself that she didn't notice. Instead she clucked disapprovingly at the rough rags I had been wearing. She opened an iron-bound chest and pulled out a pretty dress of light wool dyed deep green to match my eyes. The bodice would fit my waist perfectly when she tightened the laces.

"I dipped the wool for you right before we left for Tillfallvik," she confided.

Alga then helped me bathe and dressed my hair in a crown of braids like her own. She chattered on about everything that had happened on the Sigurdssons' estate since I had left. "The blueberries will soon be ready to be picked. You'll like that, I know."

"But Lexander—" I tried to say.

Alga made a face and waved her hand as if that were unimportant. "He is busy helping Silveta. I'm sure Gudren will be able to work something out with him so you can stay. He would pay anything your master demands."

I wondered if her prediction were true, especially when Lexander didn't so much as look at me when I came down. I was disappointed because he had never seen me dressed so well, but he seemed preoccupied by other matters. Perhaps Silveta *was* his main concern now.

Gudren called Lexander to their loft before the morning meal. Silveta was eager to get to the docks and on our way. But I was in a panic wondering what Lexander would do. He had promised to never send me away from him again, but the gods were unpredictable.

Alga finally came down in tears. "He refuses to sell you to us!"

My heart leaped. I was so relieved that Lexander would not let me go. Alga saw it, and she was hurt. "He is cold and beastly," she declared. "Gudren swore he would not let him sail on our ships because of it."

"You have already been more than generous," I assured her.

Alga pouted. "Why don't you want to stay? Don't you care about us?"

"You know I do." I put my arms around her. "You have both been magnificent. But I'm not meant to live in one place, Alga. I was born to flit around like a bird. Can't you feel that in me?"

Mollified somewhat, she had to nod. "You're like Gudren in that way. We could work something out, Marja. You could travel with Gudren if you need that. I would miss you both, but I would prefer that than to lose you altogether."

I was touched by how much she truly cared about me. "I enjoy being here with you, Alga. I adore you both. But I must go. Silveta needs my help. And I love my master."

Alga sighed, finally accepting the truth. "You tried to tell me before and I wouldn't listen. I know better now. I'll talk to Gudren." She gave me one last, long hug, wetting my cheek with her tears. "I can't even ask you to promise to return because you belong to that awful man!"

I had to smile at that. "I will *try* to come see you, Alga. I promise you that."

When I joined Lexander and Silveta outside, I didn't tell them that Gudren wanted to deny us the use of his ship. I would leave that to Alga. Lexander didn't say a word about the Sigurdssons' offer to buy me. He waited with an absent gaze over the water, leaning against a fence. When Gudren emerged, I followed them down to the docks as if nothing had happened.

Gudren made a great display of his affection as he bade me good-bye. I could tell he did not want to let me go. The shipmaster noticed, as did the oarsmen waiting on the oceangoing *knaar*. It truly pained Gudren to let me sail away from him. He had lost me once to Silveta and had obviously decided to keep me this time. But Alga had the final word, as she always did.

My parting with these good people was eased by the prospect of our journey. Though we were running for our lives, I felt safe enough on the Sigurdssons' estate to begin to enjoy the adventure of it all. I could tell Silveta did not feel the same way, so I didn't speak out loud about my delight in setting off.

I had never been on a *knaar* before. The ship had a large open space in the center that was filled with towering stacks of wooden logs stripped of their bark. There were also supplies for the twenty men for the journey. I didn't realize how long it would take us to travel to Gronland until much later.

I stood in the stern waving to Gudren as the *knaar* pulled away from the dock. I cared very much for them, but I knew in my heart that I would not be happy there for long. Their estate was too confining, their lives too monotonous for one such as me. It made me sad that I could not give them what they wanted—just as I could not give Lexander what he wanted.

My desire to roam had conflicted with my submissive ways before, but never so sharply. The turmoil of my own emotions prevented me from losing myself in the sea spirits, so I had only my own thoughts to dwell in. If Lexander had wanted to stay in Vidaris forever, keeping me with him, could I have been content? Nay, I was certain my longing for what lay beyond would have tormented me more and more as time went by. Likely that would have created a crack inside of me, allowing Helanas' evil to penetrate.

I was also defying my submissive desires by refusing Lexander my intimacy. But I was certain I was right in resisting his lure. I wanted to touch him, to give him my love and affection without restraint, but I was afraid to lose myself in him. I couldn't leave him, yet I feared that I would weaken the longer we were together. That was the otherworldly way, to tempt us with our hearts' desires into giving up our lives.

The great *knaar* sailed across the Nauga Sea to Markland. By the time we reached its easternmost tip, the buttes of my homeland were enshrouded in shadows as the sun slowly sank behind the trees. I finally removed the bandage Alga had put on my hand and dipped my wounded palm into a bucket of seawater.

The sea spirits showed me fierce fighting, not only in Tillfallvik, but in some of the settlements where Birgir's men had seized the best lands and violated the womenfolk. Birgir's warriors were abandoning their homesteads and retreating to Tillfallvik, where the decisive battle would be fought. Magnates in every settlement were also preparing to depart for Tillfallvik, where they intended to choose the next chieftain of Markland.

Birgir's specter darkened all our prospects. I should have been exultant to have escaped. Yet I was plagued by an unreasoning fear that Birgir might still catch us, that his own *knaars* would unerringly hunt us down.

As we were passing an outcropping of rock that curved into the ocean like a fleshy paw trying to bat our ship, an *olf* suddenly appeared onboard. Its face as round as the moon with merry eyes, it was comforting to see. The *olf* floated over my head, assuring me that it was the means by which the Markland *olfs* would keep vigil with us on our journey. I could not hide from it what had happened with the overlord and Lexander's dire prediction that Birgir would be harder to beat with the powerful Jedvard on his side. But the *olf* cared only that we were sailing now to get help.

Silveta couldn't hear the spirits, but she seemed to understand the turmoil that was happening in her land. She sat in utter silence, staring at the shore until Markland disappeared into the dank mist behind us. Alga had given her a man-sized cloak to cover her festive silk dress on the voyage. She huddled in it like a child, sheltered somewhat from the fierce ocean spray in the stern.

As darkness fell, Silveta and I crept under the canvas that stretched over the center of the ship, protecting the logs. The cargo was much valued in the northern islands where trees were scarce. We lay down on the bumpy surface to try to sleep with the rocking of the ship. I was not sure whether I truly slept or merely swam in the thrall of the sea spirits.

The next morning, I awoke to find Lexander speaking quietly with the shipmaster. When I climbed over the benches to get closer to him, he absently ordered, "Stay in the stern, Marja, where you'll be safe."

I glanced at the oarsmen who were watching us closely. I did not think they would harm us, but mayhap Lexander was more concerned about me getting in their way. So I retreated to the stern to sit beside Silveta, watching as the oarsmen went about their duties. Lexander treated both of us the same—with distant courtesy. I felt as if our moment of connection inside the bastion had not happened at all. He knew the risk I faced in loving him and was truly trying to help me avoid him. The shipmaster never spoke to us at all, dealing only with Lexander.

As we sailed north along the coast of Helluland, stunted spruce and evergreens lined the shore, looking much the same as my homeland. Soon enough we reached what the Skraelings called flat-stone land. The endless rocks started at the shore and continued into the distance, stopping only where great mounds of ice began. It was so different that I was astonished, but it was generally regarded by the Noromenn as having no good qualities.

For days thereafter, we saw nothing but water, ice, and naked rock. The ice came in all shades and consistencies—crumbling brown at the edge of vast fields, and deep, clear blue ice at the heart of floes. The water grew frigid, but I could not touch it even when I leaned far out. It made Silveta too nervous when I tried, so I refrained. But the oarsmen drew up buckets of water to dash on their heads, letting out loud, satisfied cries at the shock of it.

The sunlight lasted longer every day, yet it was weakened and diffused the farther north we went. It reflected off the water, the ice, and the tiny crystals that hung in the air or blew with the force of sand that scraped my face. Fat brown seals and walruses covered the rocky islands, and the noise of their barking filled our ears as we sailed by. Seabirds flew overhead, craning their necks to see if we carried a whale carcass or piles of long silvery cod.

I loved it all. It was so different from the green land that I knew. I could feel there were Skraeling out there, though we saw few of their small, round boats. I even enjoyed the constant diet of salty, dried fish and hard biscuits that had to be soaked to soften them for chewing. Silveta refused to eat the oily bars of fat that the oarsmen ate by the handful, but I found the strong taste satisfying.

Then we left land behind and were surrounded by only the ocean and icebergs. The bergs grew bigger, like floating mountains, with bases that went far down out of sight. When the waves grew still, the surface of the water turned into a mirror, reflecting the tops of the bergs. The ice shone white in the sun and sky blue in the shadows. I marveled at the shapes, some like spires or large slabs with holes piercing through, showing the sky beyond. They crested in frozen waves, with swoops and divots along their irregular knifelike edges. I could stare at a shifting ice field forever, it seemed.

Occasionally a fountain of spray marked a whale surfacing, and I grew adept at guessing where the next one would appear. The oarsmen paid little attention, though these giant water beasts were much larger than our *knaar*. Their great tail fins spanned a huge distance, and the explosion as they hit the water reverberated far and wide.

I saw it all because the sun never set. The round silvery disc swung around in the sky low to the horizon. The constant rocking of the ship linked me with the sea spirits, and without a daily rhythm to pull me from their clutches, their presence flooded my mind. I saw sea creatures going about their inscrutable ways far from these icy waters, in places filled with brightly colored plants and fish. I discovered more through the sea spirits than I had ever seen in my travels.

My dreams were also disturbed. I slept not knowing if it was day or night. After a while, I gave up going under the canvas with Silveta. Instead, I lay curled up on the bench under the open sky, impervious to mist or rain in the thick cloak Alga had given me.

Then somehow I found myself entwined in Lexander's arms. It seemed inevitable, yet the shock of it as his lips nuzzled my neck was almost more than I could bear. We were floating naked, skin against skin, with the milky green light filtering down from above. Bubbles rose from our mouths, tickling as we laughed. Lazily, we turned together underwater end over end. Perhaps I had jumped overboard with him in a fit of madness, giving in to his otherworldly power. An eternity of torment awaited me, but somehow that was a very distant concern.

He rubbed effortlessly against me, like we were part of the water, moving as the currents tugged and lifted us. My hair flared out, undulating in a nimbus around me. He tangled his fingers in it, snagging some strands close to his face. We rocked together so gently that it nearly maddened me. But everything was sinuous underwater, in gentle motion with no resistance, no struggle. I surrendered to it, relaxing into him, and felt ripples of release overtake me though we merely brushed against each other. He let out a long sigh as his seed spilled into the water. It seemed to go on forever, and satisfied me like no other lovemaking had.

We broke to the surface with a surprising burst of air and water. Breathing deeply, the waves lifted us up high, showing me cresting water in every direction. With a rush, we were carried back down into the vast trough. As we lifted again, we kissed, melting into each other as we had underwater.

When I opened my eyes, my body was humming on the hard bench. I had to touch my hair to be sure it wasn't wet. It had felt so real, a vision mayhap, rather than a dream. I was breathing fast, unable to catch my balance, wondering if it had really happened. The *olf* was perched on the mast, grinning as if it knew something I did not. Likely it had dabbled in my dream.

When Lexander emerged from under the canvas, our gazes met. The intensity in his animal eyes, too golden for a man, made me wonder if he had seen the vision, too. Whether it had been sent by the sea spirits or was something of his own making, I did not know. Yet he did not approach me, and I knew he would not press me. But he wanted me, of that I was certain.

By the time land was sighted ahead, Silveta roused herself. At first I could see only the field ice of polished, melting bergs. Then greenish brown hillsides rose beyond. The green was too radiant to be grass, and as we approached a great fjord, I realized it was a film of lichen covering the bare rock. The water rippled, reflecting the cloud-pocked sky and the bergs silently floating by.

There were scores of longhouses dotting the steep hillsides. Most were made of sod, and some were covered with yellow plants rather than grass. The more imposing buildings were made of stone or logs, though these were relatively few.

I could feel the *olfs* sending out joyous greetings as we approached. The *olf* on our ship responded as if it was familiar to them.

The oarsmen were in high spirits, and from their comments, they hoped to sell their cargo here in Erisstadir. A system of low docks floated directly on the water so they could be pulled out if need be, away from the invasive ice and bergs. When I jumped down from the *knaar,* the dock felt more unsteady than the great boat. Silveta needed Lexander's help to get down. I noticed she also had trouble standing on shore and relied on the support of his arm.

She had become accustomed to the motion of the sea. Lexander was at ease, as always, and I tuned in to the land, listening to the *olfs* and sensing the flow of spirits to quickly adjust.

Lexander's tone of command carried Silveta along, securing us a place to stay at an inn. She asked Lexander to help her negotiate for warriors and boats to fight Birgir, and he quietly agreed. As Silveta readied herself to meet with the leaders in this town, I was far too restless to wait, as usual.

Without a backward look, I left the inn and started up a path deeper into the fjord. All of my senses were open, savoring the rocky land that was frozen yet vibrant with life. From the *olfs,* I knew there were hundreds of homesteads and small farms with sparse gardens and fields lying in velvety clefts between the outcroppings. But I didn't see a single tree anywhere. It seemed unreal, as if the ground had shed its fur coat and lay naked under the sky.

The *olfs* danced along beside me as I climbed and ran far up the fjord. They enjoyed my astonishment at everything I saw, delighting in my sense of discovery at the sight of a glacier curving over a pass. The blunt end was roughened with chunks of snow and ice littering the ground at its base. It looked like water had frozen in midflow, as if time had somehow stopped.

I sensed sprites living inside the glacier, staying always within the ice. It was not a hard mass as I had thought, but was riddled with crevices and caves that glowed blue and green. The ice sprites slid from place to place, floating over the black depths and dodging dripping water. They beckoned to me, whispering that they knew secrets they must share with me. But I was already shivering and knew that my flesh would soon freeze if I joined the ice sprites.

As I wandered through the scattered settlement, I wondered if we had somehow accidentally sailed into the land of Malina, where the sun god resides. It seemed enchanted, as only the home of a god could be.

Then I found a strange building. It was made of logs and

was in good repair, but no one lived there. It was a single room with several benches and an empty hearth, but I couldn't step inside. The *olfs* also stayed at a distance. Yet it didn't feel like an evil spirit inhabited the place. It felt like nothing.

As I finally withdrew, latching the door, the *olfs* helpfully whispered, *"Sanctuary of Kristna."*

So this was a haven for Birgir's "one true god." I had never seen a room dedicated to a god before. Perhaps only Kristna worshippers could enter his abode.

I walked for far longer than I intended without the promise of a sunset to send me back. The sun merely swung around low in the sky, and for once I lost my sense of direction. Only my utter weariness finally prompted me to return down the fjord to the shore.

The inn was a huge sod longhouse sectioned off into rooms for privacy. The walls were covered in cracked plaster, and the floor was paved with blue-gray stone.

I heard familiar voices in the common room. When I entered, Silveta was seated on a rough bench with Lexander standing to one side. The Markland *olf* followed me right inside.

A large bear of a man stood facing them. His muddy blond hair covered his head and face, leaving only his small eyes peering out. Even his bulbous nose had hairs sprouting from the tip. He was shaking his head even as Silveta spoke.

" . . . and I could provide what arms you require," she was saying urgently. "Your men would be returned as quickly as we could secure Tillfallvik, and in reward I could give you as many spars and wood products as your community needs."

I knew even before the man replied what his answer would be. "We are farmers here, *freya,* not warriors. Our young men with hot blood return to the Auldworld to find their victories. We have none here to spare, especially not in midsummer when our fields need tending."

Silveta seemed to be desperately holding on to hope. "Surely you could put the word out and let your people decide for themselves. I offer a rich return for those who accompany me."

"We have no use for western squabbles here," the bearish man said definitively. "But you and your folk are welcome to stay. There are homesteads open up the fjord."

The man didn't even wait to hear her answer, but turned and stomped heavily from the small room. Lexander motioned for Silveta to wait and quickly followed him. He gave me a curious look as he passed, making me wonder how long I had been gone. It was impossible to tell in these endless days.

Silveta slumped back, putting her hands to her face. "They won't give me the men I need. They say they have no warriors in Gronland."

I nodded. "I sense only peace here."

Irritably, she snapped, "Where have you been? Lexander was afraid you'd lost your wits and would never come back."

"I was seeing the land."

"Not much here," Silveta said bitterly. "Barren, ugly place!"

My brow rose. "I think it's stunning."

Silveta shook her head, a frown line between her eyes. "What would I do here, marry a farmer? Live like a peasant for the rest of my life, buried in snow and darkness half the year?"

"Does it get dark?" I asked eagerly. I could hardly imagine it. One of the *olfs* obligingly gave me a glimpse of midwinter in Gronland. The world was blanketed in white, with nothing but moonlit snow and starry skies. I was dazzled for a moment.

Silveta stood up and began to pace, wringing her hands. Her hair hung down her back in a neat braid. "What am I going to do?"

"What about the other Gronland settlements? Perhaps they will be more receptive."

"I've spoken to several men already, but they claim the season is wrong for them to leave, even if they wanted to. Lexander thinks it's hopeless, but he is loath to tell me that."

"You can't give up," I replied. "The *olfs* . . . your people are depending on you."

"Nothing I do is ever enough." Silveta dropped to the bench again, burying her face in her hands. After a moment, I realized she was crying. "Every time he . . . caught me was worse than before. His foul words, his brutality, his love of pain . . ."

I drew my breath. "Birgir? He raped you? I thought the first time was the day he killed Ejegod."

"No, to my everlasting shame, no . . . He took me several times since you saved me last midsummer. Once he broke through the ceiling of my closet to do it. Perus knew he would be forced to fight Birgir one day. I prayed the good man would not be slain, but he paid even that price for me. Oh, it is too terrible! In that hell, my only hope was that Birgir would get me with child." Her expression was bleak. "It seemed unlikely that Ejegod could ever become a father."

"*Are* you with child?" I had to ask.

"I pray not! If I am, then there are enough witnesses that night who saw Birgir take me to the loft. I was able to hide what he had done before, and he could not reveal his conquest or I would cry rape. But now a child would simply confirm Birgir's claim on me."

I felt very sorry for her, but she did not seem to want my sympathy.

Tears streaked her face, yet there was still an uncanny determination in her eyes. "I could slay Birgir with my own hand for what he's done! His men I could pardon, if they have not done rape themselves. If they have, then death for them, as well."

I thought of Deidre, struck down by Birgir's warriors because she had refused them. Her fate would have been mine if Jens had not saved us in the bastion. My homeland's fate was the same. The evil in Birgir would infest the land, as surely as the sun spread light.

Silveta looked up at me. "I could slay my father, as well, if he stood before me now. Yes, my own father, who sold me to that butcher's son! He is no father to me now. I am alone. Completely alone."

I went to her, sitting down next to her on the bench. She let me take her hand. My own fingers were dirty, of course, from picking up rocks and climbing the steep hillsides. But for a wonder, Silveta didn't flinch away from me. She clung tighter to my hand.

"I won't abandon you," I swore. "I'll help you destroy Birgir."

The *olf* began spinning around the room. Soon others appeared as well. They were happy with my pledge. I felt much better knowing I was serving them as I should. They had clearly been waiting for me to declare my intention to help Silveta oust Birgir from my homeland.

Then Lexander returned, ducking his head to get through the low doorway. "Silveta, it's no use trying to get men here in Gronland. But the *knaar* leaves for Issland tomorrow. There may be warriors there."

Her fingers tightened on mine. "I thought the ship would return to Viinland."

"They can't get their price for the spars, so it's onward for them."

"Issland!" Silveta's expression was suddenly rapt. "Birgir was turned away from there. They're a civilized people. And I have distant cousins in Issland. I can appeal to them." She held out her other hand to Lexander, still holding on to mine. "Will you help me, Lexander of Vidaris? I will reward you handsomely—"

He held up his hand to stop her. "That is not my concern. I've abandoned a fine estate and all that I could want. No, this is Marja's decision to make."

"Me?" I asked in surprise.

"Yes." He glanced down briefly. "If you want to return to Gudren and Alga, I will take you there myself. But I refuse to sell you to them. You'll go to them as a freewoman or not at all."

"You would send me away?" A bolt of pain shot through me.

"I saw how it saddened you to leave them," Lexander replied, his mouth set firmly. "If you want to return, I will take you there myself."

Silveta turned to me. "No, Marja, you promised you would help me. You'll come with me to Issland. You and Lexander both. You can always go to the Sigurdssons after our return."

The *olfs* wanted me to help Silveta, so I simply agreed. "I shall help you, Silveta, as I pledged."

Seventeen

When we reached the harbor, Lexander prepared to pay our passage. The shipmaster refused, saying, "I was ordered to take this woman"—he pointed at me—"anywhere she chooses, along with any friends of hers."

My eyes widened at the news. I was pleased and touched by Gudren's gesture.

"The Sigurdssons are generous, indeed," Lexander replied quietly, his trust in them confirmed. I knew Lexander was trying to protect me from himself when he offered to take me back to them.

The sea spirits assured me as soon as I boarded the *knaar* that they would watch over us on the way to Issland. Silveta was apprehensive, I could tell. Indeed the voyage called for close reckoning to cross a vast stretch of ocean to reach the tiny island. The oarsmen were dejected at the news that their spars would not fetch what they needed in Gronland. The shipmaster was also in a nasty temper when we set out, and a glum spirit permeated the voyage.

Lexander continued to shun me. But I still had dreams of us joining together, floating in the air cushioned by the clouds or deep underwater mingling with the sea spirits. It seemed that whenever I closed my eyes, we were together. And he was always watching me as I came out of my trances, as much as I used to watch him.

One evening, the sun finally sank below the horizon for the first time in ages as we sailed ever southward. I was thankful for night's familiar cloak. Perhaps Lexander thought I could not see him, but the *olf* showed me everything. There was naked desire in his eyes. Despite my rebuff, he wanted me still. But he would not come to me. He would not seduce me. I would have to surrender willingly to him. But if I did that, I would lose everything. My whole life I had managed my relations with the otherworldly creatures carefully, ensuring my safety. There was much more I wanted to see. I faced a terrible choice with Lexander.

I wanted his love, but I could not make myself reach out to him. He stood tall despite the rocking of the ship, with the golden tone of his skin grown brighter from the constant sun. His shoulders were broader even than the oarsmen. I think if he had summoned me then, I would have rushed into his arms. But the few times he spoke, it was to Silveta, who gazed at him as if he were her last hope for salvation.

I grew jealous, I admit, to see their rapport. Silveta was so elegant, even subsisting on the deck of a ship in the middle of the ocean. The way she gestured, decisive yet graceful, and the carriage of her head, so proud despite her anguish, was beguiling. How could Lexander resist her? He had been so fascinated with Qamaniq, the noble Skraeling, and had enjoyed teasing out her submissive response, overcoming her intuitive sense of authority. I saw him do the same with Silveta. She, who had not bent her head to anyone, began to serve Lexander in small ways—filling his cup with water, attentive and agreeable when he spoke, touching his arm in quiet emphasis to her words. Lexander seemed to call it from her naturally, as if he would always be a slave master despite his abandonment of Vidaris and his people.

So I existed side by side with them, jealousy flaming in my chest, while fear kept me from kneeling at his feet and begging for his touch. Only when I slept did I release my desire, giving it wings to fly to Lexander. There seemed no end to the ways we made love, sometimes only kissing as if we were drowning in each other, everlasting caressing of my lips and face until I trembled in joy. He had trained me to climax with a touch, and now it took only a dream to make me shudder over and over again. I woke with a heated body, flushed and gleaming from our phantom love. Even the oarsmen eyed me like a plump peach dangling before them, ripe and juicy. Only the threat of Lexander kept them at bay.

After too many days, we sighted the glacier-capped island by the towering plumes of ash and smoke that rose from a fiery volcano. I did not think we could have found the tiny island without the smoke, but the oarsmen took it as a matter of course, having made this journey many times before.

There was talk of how favorable the winds were for summer. I attributed it to the *olf* onboard, and to the cooperation of the sea spirits who slipped us into the southward currents. It seemed the Otherworld conspired to help Silveta, confirming I had done well to join her quest.

As we neared the shore, I was intrigued by the broad plains leading to woods at the base of distant mountains. But I felt an odd emptiness. Only in Vidaris had I sensed such a lack of welcome from the land. The *olf* onboard was also subdued, crouching on the mast.

The wind suddenly died. The shipmaster blamed it on the lowering sun. But I knew it was something more. The sea spirits were already pulling away from me, though we weren't yet close to the shore.

With the *knaar* stalled, the oarsmen began to row to take us into a narrow bay. There were some stands of trees—unlike on Gronland—and the emerald-green mantle was grass and moss instead of lichen. Everywhere on the plains were hundreds of sheep, horses, and cattle grazing on the bounty. The mountains in the distance were dark and foreboding, a sharp contrast to the rich plains close to the ocean. Even in full summer, clouds gathered around the summits that were capped with ice and snow. I couldn't tell exactly where the ash and smoke emerged, but the plume stained a huge swath of the sky.

Our *knaar* set down anchor within the sheltered bay

among dozens of other ships. Rowboats were busy plying the waters, and the shipmaster soon hailed one to take us to shore. I had been expecting a great city, much like the bastion, or even a seaport like Brianda. But instead there were only a few dozen houses and outbuildings dotting the flat coastline. More buildings were sprinkled in the distance among the meadows and hills. Most were sod houses, more square than long. Some were made of porous stone blocks with perfectly straight sides.

There was a well-trodden road that cut through the emerald meadows, leading inland. The shipmaster arranged with a wagon master for the four of us to travel to Pingvellr. Our bedrolls were loaded into the back of an open wagon. The oarsmen would wait near the ship to prevent the valuable spars from being taken.

My last sight of our ship out in the bay revealed the *olf* still crouching on the mast. In Gronland, it had rushed out to enjoy the new sights along with me. Its behavior now was exceedingly odd.

Silveta asked the wagon master about finding the lawspeaker, the man who ran the proceedings of the assembly. He promised to set us down within reach of the man. I had heard Silveta and Lexander discussing their plans on the journey but had not been able to contribute. I certainly did not know we would travel for half the day in a wagon that jolted through the ruts, heading toward the base of the mountains.

I chose to walk most of the way rather than endure the rough ride. As I lifted my face to the breeze, I kept reaching out, wanting to feel the dazzling, crystal awareness that I had enjoyed in Gronland. But there was no response from any *olfs*, only a faint glimmer in the distance of an otherworldly presence. Even the spirits of the place felt weak and diffused, as if they had not rested there long.

I was not tempted to stray as I had in Gronland. I stayed near the wagon as it traveled ever higher inland, up successive levels of plateaus, passing sparse strands of trees along the watercourses. We met few people on the road, which made the place seem even more deserted.

Then we topped the final plain stretching between three mountain ranges. A black, craggy outcropping formed the upper end of the plain. A waterfall fell in churning white foam to a short river along the base of the cliffs. The river spilled onto the plain as if the ground had cracked open and water rushed to fill it up.

There were no *olfs* within reach, so I was unable to consult with them. It reminded me of my first sight of Vidaris, and I shuddered to think that Issland could be as empty. "What is this place?" I asked.

"Pingvellr," Silveta replied. "The chieftains assemble here every year."

The land near the lake was occupied by temporary camps, with sod lean-tos and shelters to protect the travelers. There were almost as many horses as people on this edge of the plains.

Beside the river, between the waterfall and the lake, there were several low buildings. The cliffs that towered over everything were rough and blacker than any rock I had ever seen.

When I went forward and thrust my hands into the river, the water spirits showed me a boiling heat within the earth and red-hot rocks moving in a molten flow, dazzling my mind's eye. I saw how the island had been built from this liquid rock, spreading to form the plain I stood on now.

When I withdrew my hand, I once again saw what my eyes showed me. Truly only the water and molten rock were alive in Issland.

I caught up to Lexander and Silveta near a low sod building. Despite the covering of green, there was a sterile echo inside. I recognized it as another sanctuary of Kristna. I lingered to try to sense the god's spirit, but even without the distracting call of the *olfs* in Gronland, I felt nothing.

Silveta stood with a rail-thin man who never met her eyes. "But we must be able to do something," Silveta was pleading. "We've traveled all the way from Viinland to appeal to the assembly."

"The chieftains have closed the session," the man explained. "Nothing can be done."

"Where are the chieftains now?" Silveta asked.

The thin man gestured to the camps along the lake. "Most will leave on the morrow." He departed without a glance, as if strangers were a common occurrence in these parts.

Silveta put her hand on Lexander's arm as if in need of support. "I must speak to the chieftains now. Perhaps I can bargain for warriors and boats."

Lexander nodded, frowning slightly. Silveta turned and started back to the camps, the great cloak wrapped around her and her yellow skirts lifted high above the muddy road.

"You are disturbed," I said quietly as I took my bedroll from him. He carried Silveta's as well as his own slung across his shoulder. The shipmaster of the *knaar* was nowhere in sight.

"It's not likely any chieftain will risk crossing the ocean to fight on foreign soils," Lexander explained. "There is a law here against making war on other countries, and only the assembly can vote to put that law aside. With the assembly over, there is no hope."

"But Silveta is asking for their help. They won't be making war on us."

"Why should they believe us? The fortunes of the western lands matter little here, I assure you. All they know is that a warband makes war wherever it goes."

"But Silveta must get help. Markland depends on her."

Lexander started after Silveta's retreating form. "Markland may well have to manage with Birgir instead."

Nearly a thousand Isslandirs were gathered on the plains under the lowering sun. I had never seen so many people in one place at a time. Many milled around the merchant stalls, taking heaping platters back to their camps. They feasted through the long evening on smoked and salted lamb, singed sheep heads, and pickled salmon and shark. One man fried bread in a vat of oil, producing wafer-thin rounds. Ale makers brewed potent drinks for the chieftains, while farmers and craftsmen displayed their wares for sale. I heard the loud voices of entertainers telling stories and saw jugglers performing miraculous feats. There were itinerant farmhands looking for work and vagrants begging everywhere. Pingvellr reminded me of a carcass lying under the sun, being picked clean by scavengers.

There was no central figure, no place of honor for their leader. I soon realized that the lawspeaker held only ceremonial functions. Everyone here was equal, and even servants sat down to eat with the families they waited on.

I would have enjoyed myself mightily, but for one thing. There was not an *olf* to be seen despite the free-flowing food.

Throughout the evening, Silveta searched the crowd to find the chieftains. They were usually surrounded by a retinue that included bondsmen, women, servants, and children who screamed and chased each other in circles. Everyone discussed the cases that had been brought this year to the assembly, including the petitioners who still argued their sides with their friends and foes.

After listening to Silveta make her plea to a handful of chieftains, I feared for my homeland. They listened courteously, as if they were accustomed to receiving petitioners. But their faces were closed. None was willing to risk a single man on her distant blood feud.

Even Ketil Grimsson, the chieftain who was related to Silveta through common ancestors, was barely interested. Ketil was a giant man, with masses of black hair and a long, bushy beard. "My advice to you, little coz, is to go to your family in Hop," Ketil declared flatly.

Silveta didn't try to explain that her own father had abandoned her. " 'Tis impossible to bargain with Viinland when the overlord would annex my land."

"But you yourself are of Viinland," the chieftain retorted.

"I pledged myself to Markland when I married. And I will not rest until Birgir Barfoot is dead. It is a great prize he has sought, for my land is prosperous enough to reward you as you deserve."

Ketil waved a meaty hand at that, returning to his meal. Silveta watched him carefully, gauging her next words. I could feel that she was desperate, but her distant expression, honed under Birgir's constant assaults, served to hide her distress.

While Silveta cajoled her cousin, Lexander surprised me by taking my hand and drawing me away. I went quiescent under his touch, unsure of what he intended. The moon was rising, lighting our way through the thick grass.

Finally, he turned to face me. "You realize that Silveta doesn't have a chance."

"But she must get help," I insisted.

"The risk of returning to Markland is too great, Marja. Think of what Birgir would do to you! I would fain keep you far away from that benighted land forever."

I wrung my hands at this terrible impasse. I could not help feeling that it was my own fault. "If only I had killed Birgir when he discovered me."

Lexander looked more sharply at me. "Did you have the chance?"

"Yes, after he raped me. I hit him in the head, but it was enough only to pain him."

Lexander's hands clenched into fists. "To think I could have spared you that fate! Truly, I did wrong when I sent you away from Vidaris. I should have gone with you though I had not decided to leave until that moment. It was a poor decision, made hastily."

I could not bear the pain in his extraordinary eyes. "Do you regret abandoning Vidaris?"

"Never! I left because I had to. I regret only the things you've been forced to endure."

"None of that mattered once I found you again."

He reached out as if to take me in his arms, his fingers tensing as he stopped himself. I could not make myself move forward, to give the slightest sign of desire. I wanted him so deeply. I was heady just from being near him. I could lose myself in him, falling headlong into the Otherworld.

"Marja, why do you shun me?" he demanded.

"I love you! I do." I dropped my eyes. "But I'm afraid . . ."

His head turned as if I had slapped him. Then he took a step away. "You are right to fear," he murmured. "When my people come to find me, as they surely will, there is nothing I can do to protect you. I must find another way to keep you safe."

Before I could protest, he headed back into Ketil's camp. The set of his shoulders was determined. I raced after him, catching up as he pushed his way through.

Silveta had a tear trickling down her face, but Ketil looked bored and resolute in his refusal. The rest of his retinue were curious but unaffected by her pleas.

Lexander addressed Silveta. "*Freya*, has this man acknowledged kinship with you?"

"Yes," she answered, covertly swiping at the tear.

"Then as your bondsman, let me challenge Ketil to win his rightful protection for you."

I stifled my gasp. Lexander had never sworn himself to Silveta . . . or had he? They had talked endlessly on the ship, and often I was lost in the sea spirits rather than listening.

Ketil pointed his knife at Lexander, a chunk of salmon speared on the tip. But it was a long knife, making his meaning clear. "You can't force me to hire a warband."

"No," Lexander agreed with a slight smile. "But Silveta can demand that you recall the assembly."

"Yes!" Silveta exclaimed. "Ketil, let me plead my case before the chieftains. They could authorize our venture, and it would matter little to the coffers of Issland to give me the warriors I need."

Ketil was affronted, as well he should be at Lexander's challenge. He drew himself up to his full height, as tall as Lexander and more massive in thigh and arm. "I will not recall the assembly by threat of a duel! If your bondsman wants to fight, then I shall give him that."

The people around us erupted into cheers.

I grabbed Lexander's arm. "You've forced him to fight!"

"It's the only way. If I can beat him, he will support Silveta. Now stay back and don't interfere."

Lexander pulled away from me, joining Ketil as they sought a wide-open space. The revelers flocked to watch, bringing torches that lit the ground like day. Some shouted encouragement to Ketil, while others made bets on the outcome. I was gasping at how fast it had happened.

"Let this westerner see what kind of flesh is born of fire and ice!" Ketil shouted as he pulled off his shirt, revealing a broad, hairy expanse. His knee-length kilt freed his legs, which were protected by well-wrapped boots. He unhooked his huge ax from his belt.

Lexander had only his knife, shorter than the one Ketil brandished in his left hand. Lexander's rough clothing and cap made him look more like an oarsman than the magnate of Vidaris. But there was something special about Lexander that even this crowd could see. He stood eye to eye with their largest man, a match for Ketil in every way. And he was eerily calm.

"Will no one lend him an ax?" Silveta cried out. "Would you go against an unarmed man, Ketil?"

"He has his pig sticker," Ketil laughed. "It will teach you to better arm your bondsmen, Silveta."

With that, Ketil lunged at Lexander, swiping his ax in a quick arc. Lexander didn't flinch though it came within a hand's breadth of his chest. Instead, he outwaited the swing of Ketil's arm and moved forward to jab him with his knife. Ketil parried with his knife, taking another futile swing with his ax.

When they parted and faced each other again, there was more respect in Ketil's eyes. He measured Lexander carefully before he resumed his attack. Without an ax, Lexander could hardly defend himself, much less pose a threat. Yet he kept whirling away at every strike.

It went on much longer than Birgir's brief fight with Ejegod. Ketil had murderous intent in the force of his swings, especially as he grew more frustrated at missing Lexander. I expected a spray of blood to burst from his flesh at any moment. I wanted nothing more than to rush between them, to stop this madness. But Silveta was clutching my arm, holding me back. The fear in her face was not only for Lexander.

Then Lexander dodged in as Ketil lifted his ax. His knife glanced off Ketil's belly, leaving a curving line of blood. From where I stood, it seemed Lexander could have sliced it much deeper, gutting his opponent.

Ketil roared in fury. His attack became more vigorous, driving Lexander back. The crowd scattered around them, shifting and moving as they did. I dragged Silveta along, though she would have stayed frozen where she was.

Then Ketil's ax sliced through Lexander's shirt, tearing the sleeve from shoulder to elbow. I cried out at the flow of blood, as red as mine. Somehow I had expected a god's *inua* to look different. I almost prayed to Lexander's people to help their own, but I feared they would descend on us in retribution. There wasn't a single spirit at hand to call on, not even an *olf* to trip Ketil's feet.

Lexander saw no one else, nor heard their taunts and rude cries. He focused on Ketil, as the heavy man grew winded from his exertion. Though Lexander was wounded badly, with blood dripping down his side, he was still light on his feet. He darted forward, then back, throwing Ketil off balance.

In a blur of motion, Lexander was suddenly inside Ketil's reach. But this time his goal was not the belly. His knife slashed sharply upward, cutting into Ketil's forearm.

The ax flew from his opponent's hand. Lexander could have followed with a swipe at Ketil's throat, but he stepped away instead. Ketil went down to his knees, still holding his knife. By rights, Lexander could have finished him off then. But he backed up another step, lowering his own knife.

Ketil's bondsmen leaped forward to protect their chieftain. Though Ketil had not capitulated, there seemed to be no thought of continuing the fight. I feared what the bondsmen would do to Lexander now.

But in the silence, Lexander declared, "I call on you, Ketil, to honor your cousin's request to recall the assembly."

Everyone gathered around heard and knew why the

duel had been fought. Though Ketil did not reply, from the crowd of men surrounding him, several of the bondsmen nodded acknowledgment to Silveta.

"Yes," Silveta breathed, sagging in relief. "Now they must hear me."

The revelers dispersed in a noisy throng as if the duel had been but a momentary diversion. Lexander was surrounded by well-wishers, hidden from my view. Meanwhile Silveta was taken in hand by Ketil's serving women. She held on to me as if afraid of what would happen to her now that her declared bondsman had injured their chieftain.

From the way the senior woman behaved, I suspected she was Ketil's concubine. His wife had remained on their estate, watching over their interests, and his daughters were not yet of marriageable age. The mistress was clearly furious with Silveta, but apparently it was expected that the defeated Ketil would take us into his entourage.

But when I looked around, Lexander had disappeared. I feared for his life, and my heart leaped into my throat.

One of Ketil's servants finally directed me to the lake. I was thankful for the moon, without which I would have been in complete darkness. I followed the flat shore toward the cliffs. To one side a veil of steam drifted up, forming low-hanging clouds over the water. The plains looked much flatter from up here, spreading to the ocean, but I knew we stood on the shoulder of the mountains.

Then I saw the flicker of torches. Men were standing next to a round pool near the lake. It was Ketil's bondsmen, tending the big man as he reclined in the blue-white water. It looked like ice, but heat radiated from the surface.

Lexander was also lying naked in the water. Nobody was tending him, and his eyes were closed. For a dreadful moment, I thought he was dead.

"Lexander!" I cried, rushing to him. I put my arms around his shoulders, bending to touch my face to his.

His good arm raised to hold me tight. But the other hung

limply in the water. "Do not fear, Marja. I am healing. They claim these waters have restorative powers."

I plunged my hand into the milky water. It glowed like the sky at dawn. The smell was very strong, as were the spirits who responded from deep inside the earth, where the everlasting furnace burned. They were healing spirits indeed, active from the heat and minerals that filled the water.

"Yes, this is good for you," I agreed.

I checked his shoulder, lifting his arm as he grimaced. There was a nasty, jagged cut down the curved outer muscle below his shoulder. It gaped open at every movement, making me wince in sympathy. Blood welled up, staining the water pink.

"That must be cleaned and tied up," I told him. He couldn't move his arm at all. "It is very deep."

"No, the water alone will help."

The bondsmen were removing Ketil from the hot spring and were binding his wounds. From the drunken slurring of his speech, I could tell Ketil was not in mortal danger. He was drinking to relieve the pain of embarrassment. Surely he had done worse to Lexander.

The bondsmen carried Ketil away, taking all but one torch with them. One of them stared back at us as he left. I sensed more curiosity than animosity.

"This cut should be bound closed. You could bleed to death." I wondered if I should ask the bondsmen to return to help me.

Lexander seemed wistful. "You forget that I am different from you. The wound will heal on its own. Already I feel it closing. There is nothing you need to do, Marja."

My hands were on his arm. His skin felt the same as mine.

I pulled away, and he sighed in regret. But I unlaced my bodice and slipped off my dress, dropping them next to his clothes. Naked, I slid in beside him.

He clasped me close with one arm, and we bumped into each other, floating just above the smooth black rock on the bottom of the spring. It reminded me of my dreams.

Perhaps I had envisioned this moment, when we would truly join together.

I molded my body against his. "I can't live without you, Lexander."

"I can't put you at risk any longer," Lexander swore, kissing my hair. "I was selfish to want to take you with me. You will be safe with Gudren and Alga, and that is all that matters."

"No, I belong to you."

He started to protest, but I wouldn't let him. I kissed his cheek, then his lips. I pulled myself on top of him, floating with him even as his arm dangled uselessly. He tried to restrain himself but couldn't.

"I want only you," I murmured.

With the water spirits tickling my senses, I opened myself up to them, reaching out to Lexander at the same time. I knew I risked everything, the loss of my very self. But I couldn't deny my desire any longer.

And in a breathless rush, I felt his emotions—the pain of avoiding me, of trying not to touch me, of knowing that I was afraid to be intimate with him. But his own longing raged, barely contained throughout our journey, when he wanted nothing more than to throw me down before the oarsmen and take me for his own.

No longer was he closed off from me. It was as if he poured himself into me, and I emptied myself into him. I could feel the throbbing pain in his arm like it was my own. I could also feel his arousal overwhelming everything else. For once he lay supine and I mounted him, swaying against him. All the while, I was feeling him as he felt my response. We rolled in the water, joined as one, as if in a dream.

The darkening sky overhead suddenly ripped in two. A curtain of blue light shone above us. Beyond it was another ribbon, rippling green. Everything was splitting apart and I was falling into the Otherworld.

I fought it for one brief moment, then held Lexander tighter, refusing to let go. I lost myself in him, surrendering completely.

*   *   *

When I finally came back into myself, the sky was still rippling with colored fire. But I was whole again.

"Am I in the Otherworld?" I had to ask.

"You're with me," Lexander whispered.

We were still floating in the warm waters of the spring. I could sense the pleased water spirits that had satiated themselves on our passion. In the distance was the sound of revelers in the camps, singing and shouting as their fete continued.

Eighteen

I woke at sunrise, curled in Lexander's generous cloak. The clarity of the rising sun was very different from misty mornings in my homeland. The shadows were sharply defined, making the looming cliffs seem even more rough and jagged.

Lexander was floating in the spring again, its milky blue waters brighter than the silver sheen of the lake beyond. I relaxed, watching him. He slept little, from what I had seen on our journey. But his eyes were closed as he let the water support him.

Lexander had kept me safe last night. Though I had surrendered willingly, he had refused to let me pass into the Otherworld.

I stretched in perfect luxury. I was free to touch him now, to kiss him, to serve him in every way. I could let my passion shine in my eyes for all to see.

Lexander rose slowly from the water. Then I noticed his arm. The deep gash was now merely a dark line that marked his skin.

I sat up from my warm cocoon as he walked out of the spring. It was hard to believe my eyes. I had seen the badly torn flesh just last night.

My fingers touched his arm as he sat down next to me. It was nearly smooth, with only an amber ridge to mar it. His muscle felt hard as he moved his arm, showing me he was perfectly healed.

"Miraculous," I whispered. "You are a god, indeed."

Lexander laughed. "Closer to a man than a god, as surely you've seen by now. I must use my wits and my strong arms to get what I desire."

His fingers twined in mine, drawing me closer. He took my lips, savoring our kiss. I melted into him again, wanting more, always more.

But voices grew louder as people approached. Lexander slipped into his weathered oarsman clothes and wrapped the rags of his shirt around his arm to hide it. "It's best if no one else sees this. Don't speak of it to Silveta."

I nodded solemnly. Fear would drive their response if they knew a godling was in their midst.

I quickly donned the green dress that Alga had given me. Now there was no thought of me returning to live with the Sigurdssons. Everything between us had changed last night. Lexander would not let me go, despite his fears, and I no longer feared his touch.

As we started back down to the camps to find Silveta, I had to ask Lexander the question that had bothered me for moons. "My slave-mates who were sent away in the winged ship—are they with your people?"

"Yes."

"Are they being hurt?" I dreaded the answer, but I had to know the fate of Rosarin, Sverker, and Ansgar.

Lexander put an arm around my shoulders as we walked. "I wish it were not so . . . but you deserve to know the truth. They've been separated by now, and are being handed from one master to another, treated as objects, without even the value our training house gives you. They are likely unhappy, though if they take pleasure in serving, their burden will be lighter. If they are lucky, they will find a loving master who will keep them. But few are lucky."

"You saved me." I tightened my grip on his arm. "You gave up everything for me."

"I could not harm your people any longer. Your mates were the last slaves I sent to that fate."

*   *   *

It took until midmorning for the assembly to be called to order. The chieftains had celebrated until the wee hours and did not take kindly to having to assemble rather than depart for home. Silveta complained of having to go from camp to camp to coax nearly every chieftain to come hear her plea.

It seemed Lexander and I were avoiding everyone when we crossed the river, jumping from rock to rock. We passed through the meadow and climbed the grassy slope to the base of the cliffs. The rock appeared to have been torn with one side pushed high into the sky.

Lexander and I waited, looking over the peaceful plains. From the base of the cliff, I could no longer see the mountains or the plume of smoke that pierced the white clouds. Yet in the night, I had felt the ground rumbling as if in discontent. All was not well here despite the stark beauty of the place.

From our vantage point, we could see hundreds of people slowly making their way from the camps beside the lake, crossing the river to mill about in the meadow below us, between the river and the cliffs. Now I understood why the plants there had been trampled. Beyond the camps, the plains spread in undulating waves down to the ocean.

Still, I was surprised when the lawspeaker climbed up to join us, stepping forward as far as he could on the slope to address the crowd. Apparently the Isslandirs did everything outside, including their lawmaking.

Then Ketil appeared with his retinue. They climbed up the slope to join us and provided a stool for him as far back against the cliff as he could get. Ketil sat down, his elbows jutting out and his hands on his knees. He seemed unbothered by the scratch to his stomach, but the bandage on his arm was thick, though it showed no seeping blood. His eyes were clear and alert, and I doubted there was any putrefaction in the wound.

Lexander was treated with wary respect. Ketil ignored him, and he was not overwarm toward Silveta in his greeting. Apparently his entourage tolerated her presence rather than welcomed her.

When the lawspeaker finished his recitation of the law that allowed a chieftain to reconvene the assembly, he called on Ketil Grimsson. Ketil rose, his reluctance clear. But he stomped forward, as if to show everyone that he had not been weakened by his injury.

With a growl deep in his throat, Ketil declared in a ringing voice, "By debt of honor, I must recall the assembly to hear the plea of Silveta of Markland, my kinswoman."

He retreated back to his stool, refusing to stand by her side or give weight to her plea by speaking of it himself. Silveta blushed high on her cheeks as she stepped to the fore, aided by a hand from the lawspeaker. Lexander ground his teeth at the insult, but he didn't dare move closer to her. Because he had bested one of their strongest men, he would become the focus instead of Silveta.

She settled her stained yellow skirts, much bedraggled by our long journey. But I was proud of her splendid bearing. She appeared perfectly at ease, though it must have been odd to address hundreds of people milling about in the bright sunlight. I could not tell which men were the chieftains.

"My request is simple," she declared, raising her voice high so everyone could hear her above the muted roar of the waterfall. "By right of marriage contract, my estate and my hand are mine to give now that the chieftain is dead. Yet Birgir Barfoot, a brigand who lately passed through Issland, has seized my estate and taken me by force. I have come to you for help, for a warband to put down this butcher."

The faces turned up to us looked bored at best, skeptical at worst. Loud grumbles rose from the crowd. "What is this babble?" "We've missed the tide." "Give her the boot, Ketil!"

Silveta held up the amber beads that had been twined in her hair that long-ago day for Ejegod's funeral. The facets sparkled in her fingers. "Markland will pledge tribute to Issland every year in amber such as this! Yes, and fine woods and ivory. Trade will flow freely between our nations."

" 'Tis against the law to trade with heathens," a queru-
lous voice countered.

Similar protests rose. Lexander was right—the western
maritime lands held little interest for these people. I kept
expecting someone to rise up to quell the riot of sound, but
none did. There was no overlord here in this assembly of
equals. Even the lawspeaker did not try to stifle the free
flow of opinions.

Silveta glanced back at Lexander. He was in front of me
so I couldn't see his face, but he gave a slight shake of his
head. He had not believed she could convince the assembly to help her. But Silveta had hoped.

It seemed her plea would be rejected out of hand. A few
moments' work after we had come such a long way, only to
accomplish nothing. My worst fears were realized.

But the thin man we had encountered by the Kristna
temple climbed up the slope toward us. A hush fell over the
crowd at the sight of him. His black garments enshrouded
his body, but nothing could mask his long, wattled neck and
bony hands.

When he stood next to Silveta, his voice was reedy, caught
by the wind over the plain. But everyone listened well. "My
fellow Isslandirs, we should consider boons other than
worldly gain when we hear this request."

"What say you, Bishop?" a burly man called out.

"If this woman will take Kristna into her heart and carry
his message to the western lands, then I believe it is worth
granting her a warband."

A chieftain I recognized from last night shouted, "A high
price to pay for matters of the spirit."

"Do you so lightly prize the salvation of your immortal
souls?" the bishop called. In the silence, he turned to Silveta. "Would you agree to take clerics with you to Markland, to give them land for sanctuaries so they can
address your people? If you offer protection, as lady of
the land, surely they could spread the word of Kristna in
peace."

I was unnerved by the idea. But Silveta smiled at the
bishop. "It is certainly something we could negotiate. As

long as the assembly agrees in principle that I will get the warriors I need."

Ketil finally rose from his stool. "The bishop and I can work out the details with you. Your tithe will be split among the chieftains who send men."

The lawspeaker called out in a basso voice, "All in favor?"

A chorus of ayes arose.

The lawspeaker chanted a ritual closure to the assembly, but everyone was already milling about discussing their immediate departure. Only a few seemed interested in our venture. Silveta climbed down the steep slope, helped by Lexander.

The bishop joined Silveta and Ketil. "You must come to worship with us, *freya*. Surely if you let Kristna into your heart, you will understand our purpose. You will be saved for all eternity."

Silveta was gracious, and as they talked, her pretty laughter lifted over the din. It was the first time I had heard her so happy. She was obviously heartened to have won their support.

But I was afraid. I did not understand the lure of this Kristna worship.

It was arranged for us to stay in Pingvellr to gather supplies and assemble the men. Ketil's retinue delayed their departure, and he took charge of the arrangements. I was glad to see that he warmed to Silveta immediately after the assembly supported her petition. He kept recounting his amazement at her audacity, seeming to take pleasure in it now. He had never formally ceded the fight, so he made a point of telling Lexander that they should "finish what we started." It made me quail to hear his challenge, but Lexander refused to take offense at Ketil's taunting.

Lexander did tell me later, "We must leave soon. I cannot fight him again."

I, too, feared another battle between the two men. Ketil had underestimated Lexander the first time. He was not likely to do so again. Lexander took the precaution of purchasing a fine ax and broadsword, which he wore on his belt conspicuously. He found a sword sharpener among the merchants and sat patiently while the edges were honed to razor sharpness. I noticed some of Ketil's bondsmen among the crowd. They were always within sight.

Silveta made it clear she was willing to give whatever the Isslandirs required to obtain her warband. To seal their agreement, Silveta joined Ketil at the evening's service in the Kristna sanctuary. Lexander insisted we attend, but I needed no coaxing, anxious to find out more about this god.

The sanctuary was bare as we approached. It baffled me that there was no trace of the god in the place that was dedicated to him.

Inside, the narrow room had an uneven black rock floor. It quickly filled with people, who sat on benches and three-legged stools facing the bishop. He stood next to a tall table, holding an open book, with an altar behind him that was clean of any trace of blood. Pale clouds of incense seeped through perforated brass lanterns. The bishop spoke, but I could not understand his words. Since there was no kindly *olf* around to tell me what he meant, I sat uncomprehending.

Glancing around, I saw that the others held small books in their hands. It was a communal rite with chanting and strange words that they spoke together. I wanted to clasp Lexander's hand, but I saw no one else touching and feared it might offend their god.

And still I felt no otherworldly spirit. Instead, there was a subtle commingling of the worshipers' *inua*. The bishop's *inua* led, weaving among the others, but they contributed by focusing solely on him. The spirits of Silveta, Lexander, and I were not drawn in because we did not truly participate in the ritual.

When the words finally ceased and the people left the sanctuary, it was empty again. There was nothing left of the spirits they had woven together. Each person took away a part of it.

That's when I understood. The Kristna god lived inside of these people instead of maintaining its otherworldly presence. Kristna followers had a desire to share the god inside of them, to give it to another, thus making their worship stronger.

The bishop asked Silveta, "Can you accept Kristna as your savior?"

She smiled uncertainly. "I did not understand much of your worship."

He included me in his nod. "It will come to you in time. I will speak to you every day about the love of our lord and savior and the salvation that lies in accepting Kristna into your heart. Soon enough you will be saved."

"Never," I breathed, stumbling away in revulsion.

Gods weren't supposed to dwell inside of people. The only spirits I knew that infested folks were evil ones that encouraged harmful deeds. Though I didn't feel evil in Kristna, it still seemed wrong to take a god inside myself. Surely the god changed his followers. What vital part of myself would I have to give up in order to accommodate this god? It was a risk too great to take.

Silveta seemed to have escaped unscathed, yet I could tell by the welcoming of the others that she would not long be able to withstand the lure of this communal worship.

After the ritual, I was overcome by my discovery and wandered aimlessly along the river. Everyone else returned to their camps by the lake, so I went the opposite direction, toward the waterfall. The thundering of the water grew louder, echoing off the cliff face. Lexander could see that I was distressed and he followed me silently.

I desperately tried to sense an otherworldly presence, but there was nothing. Not an *olf* or sprite responded. I had only felt water spirits since coming to this glorious yet benighted land. Now it felt as if the plume of ash and smoke coming from the mountains was an ominous sign.

I went as close as I could to the base of the waterfall. The air was charged and felt more alive here than anywhere else. I knelt on a tumbled square rock, blasted by the spray of mist, plunging my hand into the white stream that poured between the boulders.

The turbulence overpowered everything else as the water tumbled down. But the water spirits were there, connecting this foaming fall with the deep river above, flowing through a long gorge, over gravel flats between grassy banks and into the fiery mountains towering over us.

These water spirits saw few Isslandirs until they emerged on this assembly plain. But they responded to my need to see some *olfs*. There were several *olfs* not far away, in the gorge above, dodging around a giant rock that had fallen into the water.

It was such a relief to reach out to touch them. Though we were not close, the water spirits helped carry my call to them.

In a few moments, the *olfs* appeared at the top of the waterfall. I laughed out loud, beckoning to them. "Yes, come!"

They darted down to circle our heads. Lexander stood very still. "What is it?"

"Finally, some *olfs* are here." I gave him a curious look. "I know you don't see them, but I don't understand why not with the powers you possess."

"I'm not of your world," he reminded me. "Your spirits are tied to this earth in ways I cannot fathom."

"They are glad to see us," I explained. "It must be lonely for them here, without others of their kind."

"Is it so very barren?"

"Their god stifles the worship of other spirits. Kristna fills people, pushing the Otherworld away. This land is in pain."

He clasped my hand in both of his. "I can hardly believe it, Marja. The meadows are rich and fertile. I've heard it said the number of farms continues to grow."

I took a deep breath, closing my eyes. "Now I can feel it through these *olfs*. In truth, this land is being rent in two, split down to the very depths where we stand. The few trees that are left are being cut for houses and ships. The dirt crumbles under the roots as plants try to grow."

Lexander bent down and touched the soil. It sifted, sandy and poor, through his fingers. "Not like home, to be sure."

"The *olfs* are warning me. The same could happen in Markland if Silveta brings Kristna there." I stared at Lexander in horror. "Surely the *olfs* did not save Silveta merely to replace Birgir with Kristna. Is Markland's spirit to be blighted forever?"

Lexander looked into the air, as if wishing he could see the *olfs*. The shy creatures were overjoyed to be so openly acknowledged. They lived in the fringes somehow, despite the pervading presence of Kristna. Though their numbers were depleted, some of the hearty creatures had survived on the generous gifts of Isslandirs who remembered them. I could not imagine a similar fate for my homeland.

"I must tell Silveta," I declared, "before it's too late."

Silveta gave us an appraising look when we returned to Ketil's camp. "So you two have mended your quarrel." She looked at Lexander. "I suppose you'll go back to ordering her around all the time."

Her wild expression belied her bitterness. She had not looked so desperate since Ejegod died.

"What's wrong?" Lexander asked, going to her side. I felt a pang of jealousy, remembering how close they had grown on the voyage.

"The bishop expects me to take clerics as my advisers." Her voice quavered slightly as she added, "Ketil says I must leave you both here on Issland to guarantee my tithe."

It was too awful to be true. "No, I can't bear this place!" I cried. "And Ketil will not let Lexander sleep many nights before fighting him again." I turned to Lexander. "He wants to kill you for besting him. What will happen if you are forced to slay him?"

"It can't be borne!" Silveta wailed, her hands at her temples. "It's too dangerous. Why should I abandon my only friends to satisfy Ketil? But the bishop says that you're heathens and can't be trusted."

I went to Silveta, taking her hands. "You can't let the Kristna god inside of you. His worship is sucking the life out of Issland. This land is suffering."

"Am I to let Birgir destroy Markland instead?" she countered.

"You can't lose the very thing you are fighting for," I said. "There must be something else we can do."

Silveta pulled her hands away. "We've tried everything! This is my last hope. Would you have me sail all the way to the Auldland on a fool's quest?"

I shook my head. "We've gone too far already." I could feel it in my bones. The salvation of Markland had never seemed so near as when I was with the ice sprites. Those special imps had tried to tell me something, though I had kept the knowledge at bay.

"Helluland," I declared. "We can ask the Skraelings for help."

"Skraelings!" Silveta repeated in disbelief. "A bunch of screaming savages?"

Lexander put in quietly, "Those 'savages' wreaked havoc on Markland and Viinland for generations. They are serious warriors indeed."

"You must jest," Silveta protested. "I can't even speak to them."

"My mother is Skraeling, so I know their ways," I declared. "I can convince them to help you, to retake Tillfallvik from Birgir and his men."

"How can you be so sure?" Silveta retorted. "I already have the warband I need here. Why should I take the risk?"

I knew she might not believe me, but I had to try. "The otherworldly creatures told me you should seek help from the Skraelings."

Lexander and Silveta exchanged a look. "You said yourself that she's been right so far," Lexander pointed out.

"So I'm to take Skraelings into Tillfallvik, where they've not been seen in living memory?" Silveta asked.

"Skraelings honor the spirits around them," I pointed out. "They will not blight your land. The *olfs* will ensure we conquer Birgir, who honors the Kristna god himself."

Silveta put her hands to her face. "I must think. It is too much to ask that I turn away the help I am offered."

"But at what price?" Lexander asked. "Marja and I cannot stay here."

She was terribly upset. "Maybe I can convince him to let you go ... But no, Ketil is determined to keep you here. He would challenge you the moment I left!"

"Think on it deeply," I told her. "Your decision means life or death for Markland."

"If only there were some other way," she cried. "But I can't betray you. Not as my father betrayed me. You've both been steadfast." Silveta turned away, her voice hopeless. "How can I deny you?"

Nineteen

1n the end, after many tears and much doubt, Silveta agreed to reject the Isslandirs' offer. Ketil was enraged when she made one last attempt to reach a compromise and take us with her. He was too eager to fight Lexander again, and the bishop insisted that Kristna clerics alone must accompany her. He was confident that Silveta would accept Kristna under their influence during the long journey together.

Silveta never did tell Ketil that she had changed her mind. Lexander thought it best to avoid a confrontation. We left Ketil in Pingvellr still preparing for the venture, sneaking away at first light with the shipmaster of the Sigurdssons' *knaar*. He had sold the spars for a good price and intended to return to Viinland.

The shipmaster was incredulous when Lexander requested our passage back to the western lands. In truth, the man believed we were mad. He had heard of Silveta's agreement with the assembly, and he thought it was a fair offer. But he allowed us to board his *knaar* as Gudren had ordered.

Silveta was pensive, as if some part of her had given up hope. Agreeing to appeal to the Skraelings had taken a leap of faith, and she was simply worn out from her efforts. Her eyes were far away, and she often frowned as if mulling over her plight.

Where Silveta was uncertain, I was finally on my true path. I was glad when the plume of smoke from the moun-

tains disappeared over the horizon. I was united with
Lexander in every way, and the *olf* onboard was clearly delighted with our plan to go to Helluland.

Is it little wonder I cared not for the dangers of the sea?
The ocean spirits sang through me, and I opened myself up
to Lexander so he could feel them as well. Finally united in
mind and body with him, I curled in his arms, sheltered by
his cloak and snug in his warmth. We were never apart, and
I grew to know his body as well as my own. I felt protected,
even when we were whipped by gales that sent waves towering over our *knaar*.

Though I didn't have to dream of intimacy with Lexander, a true joining was difficult. Silveta and the oarsmen
were always within arm's reach. I became adept at sitting
on his lap, facing him, my arms around his chest. Our
groins rubbed against each other, and when he grew firm,
he slipped inside of me. Silveta could not help but notice,
but she mostly tried to ignore us. He wrapped his cloak
around me to hide my trembling as we moved to the motion of the ship, sometimes for hours, as pleasure flashed
back and forth through us. I opened myself to him, as always, letting him feel as I did.

Once he lifted a strand of my hair and kissed it. "It's as
if you've become translucent, and all that exists is
pleasure."

We could not conceal the passion that permeated the
ship and drove the *olf* to a gibbering frenzy. Often it snuggled up to us at night, tangled together under the cloak. I
had never seen an *olf* so satiated with delight.

The oarsmen, on the other hand, grew more surly and
tense, unable to release their own desires. They gave me
and Silveta sidelong looks, licking their lips and appraising
our charms. If Lexander had not made a name for himself
as a strong warrior in Pingvellr, they would have tried to
take what they wanted. He regularly sent me under the
canvas with Silveta to sit on the bags of linen cloth that
were part of the payment for the spars. He wanted us out
of sight so the men's lust could cool. He made sure to
sharpen his ax and knife every day. His point was clear.

They had seen how fast he moved and how great was his reach. Alone, they had no chance. But Lexander could have been overwhelmed by their sheer numbers. Only the shipmaster, fearing for his post with the Sigurdssons, kept the simmering crew under control.

We didn't pass near Gronland, far to the north, so the days grew long but never endless. Our *knaar* was lightly loaded, making us skip across the wave tops. Thankfully there were fewer icebergs to be avoided in the rough, open ocean. By the time Helluland was sighted due west, I was one with the water spirits.

Silveta stood by the prow, searching the forbidding rocky land. "How shall we ever find the Skraelings?"

"When I traded with them," Lexander told her, "I always went to their winter settlements farther south. In the summer, they move inland. They'll come back together in a few moons."

"Birgir will surely be chieftain by then," she retorted. "If he's not already. We must have help now."

The *olfs* of Helluland were putting out a fine welcome for us. I was relieved to feel it after the dearth of other-worldly creatures in Issland. Though the coast looked desolate, there was life here that went far deeper than in more populated lands.

They were both looking at me expectantly. I didn't need to consult with the sea spirits. The *olfs* were already showing me walrus-hide boats bobbing in the mouth of a river. A gush of blood stained the rocks on the shore where fat salmon were being gutted.

"There," I said, pointing to an inlet south of the *knaar*.

The gray rocky hills of the inlet were no different than the others we had sailed past, but I knew this was the right spot. We were north of the tree line in the tundra. Ferns, mosses, liverworts, and crucifers spread across the ground wherever the bedrock didn't poke through. A heavy coastal fog was hugging the thawing land. It felt like a colder version of my beloved fens.

The shipmaster claimed the tide was wrong and refused to beach the *knaar*. Lexander argued with him as the oarsmen grumbled at the delay. I asked our faithful *olf* to let the Skraelings know we had need of them.

Two round boats emerged from the low-lying mist that clung to the shoreline. There were six people in each of the *umiaks,* which bristled with harpoons and long sinew-backed bows that the Thule were renowned for. This was the fiercest of all the Skraeling tribes.

Silveta was frightened of them, drawing back as the *umiaks* glided silently up to our *knaar*. I saw my mam's face in theirs—the narrow black eyes and dark complexion, creased by the everlasting sun. The blood of salmon washing their sealskin boots attested to their work that day. The hoods of their formfitting parkas were thrown back, showing their top-knotted hair. The boats were rowed by strong young men, but my eyes went unerringly to the two elders amongst them.

"Greetings!" I called out in my mam's language. "I see the blessings of Arnaaluk are upon you."

Their surprise was evident. One of the elders, with white-frosted hair, asked, "Are you a daughter of the true people?"

"My mam is Beothuk." The language came easily, the first I had heard whispered to me as a babe. The guttural sounds came from the back of my throat, an emphatic way of speaking.

The elder nodded slowly, glancing up at the *olf* that now hovered over his *umiak*. I gestured, and it flashed back to us. It began to bob and weave about Silveta, though she could not see it. That truly interested the elder.

Silveta could restrain herself no longer. "What are you saying? Are they going to attack us?"

I wasn't sure about that myself. Lexander spoke in Skraeling to the elder I had addressed. "We need safe escort to speak to your leaders."

I had heard him speak to the Skraeling slaves in their own tongue, so I was not surprised. But Silveta was. Not many Noromenn knew Skraeling—my siblings and I were the only ones in Jarnby who could talk with their traders. But Lexander had bargained for decades with them to acquire slaves.

The elders spoke low amongst themselves. Silveta was shaking in fear. "Are you sure about this?" she asked.

I closed my eyes, reaching out. We were in harmony with the flow of the spirits of the land and the sea. These fierce men with their weapons were a sign of more help to come.

"Yes." I smiled at the elders, knowing they must feel this, too. They did not understand how our fates were intertwined, but in the Skraeling way, they were content to let the path guide them.

"Come with us then," the elder declared.

I hiked up my skirt and swung one leg over the side. Lexander caught me with one hand before I could slide over. I gave him a reassuring nod, and he let me go. I dropped from the *knaar*. The Skraelings made sure I came down safely.

I held on to the flexible side of the boat, feeling it shift beneath me. I motioned to Lexander and Silveta. "They'll take us to shore."

The *olf* who had accompanied us jumped into the midst of the Helluland *olfs*. But Silveta hesitated. "What if we're stranded here?"

"It's a little late to question our course." Lexander also swung over the side of the *knaar*, landing in the other boat very lightly for such a big man. He reached up for Silveta. "Don't worry. I won't let you fall."

With evident reluctance, Silveta leaned over the side of the ship. But she was afraid to swing her legs over. Lexander was much taller than the Skraelings, and he plucked her off the ship, setting her down next to him. I saw the way she clenched him so hard and how protective his arm was around her. But his expression when he looked at me was full of pride, and that was enough.

The Lootega clan consisted of an extended family. The eldest were two withered sisters, with interlocking cousins and siblings descending to a tiny babe strapped to a board on a young mother's back. The middle-aged matrons ordered everyone around as they smoked the fresh fish to preserve it, feasting well that night.

For the first time, I saw how my mam had lived before coming to Jarnby. They slept in two long tents, narrower than a longhouse, supported by arced staves of antlers. I had to duck my head to walk inside. We slept in the midst of the family, with less privacy than we had on the *knaar*. But here, there were couplings throughout the short night, the moans and groans casually ignored by everyone.

Silveta was lost, unable to speak to anyone or understand their customs. The Thule, from the children on up, stared in fascination at her yellow hair, more golden than the sun in their sky. I insisted we trade our dresses for warm parkas and caribou leggings. Hers was much desired for its brilliant color even though it was stained. Silveta hated wearing pants, but she finally stopped complaining of the cold. I adored the waterproof boots and leggings, cozy with fur lining.

Whenever I could, I tramped far from camp, communing with the *olfs*, who skipped over the rocks and dived in the ponds of water that laced the undulating ground. There were tiny ice sprites living underground, where the frost reached nearly to the surface. In winter, they were freed to dance over the drifts of snow and crystalline air. They sent joyous sparks through the ground in their excitement that I had heeded their summons to Helluland. I could feel the much slower, deeper agreement of the very old spirits that inhabited the rocks, older than any I had sensed before. In truth, I was surrounded by an abundance of otherworldly creatures.

The clan appreciated the *olfs* and spoke with them as a matter of course, placating and bribing them to ensure good luck. Many times I couldn't distinguish the Markland *olf* from its northern cousins. When I wasn't roaming the tundra, I stayed among the women, asking them about everything from the fish they were drying to the intricate signs they painted on their caribou clothing. They were preparing for the big hunt, when they would acquire the hides they would need for the coming year. It was important to respect the great spirit of the caribou so that many animals would be given to them.

"We have to hurry," Silveta insisted every day. "The longer we delay the more entrenched Birgir will become."

"The elders say they will leave soon for the caribou hunt. 'Tis where we'll find enough people to get your warband."

"Can't you urge them to hasten?" she pleaded.

"They will go when the signs tell them to. Why should they risk delay or sickness when following the portents will ensure their safe arrival?"

Silveta rolled her eyes. "Why aren't you talking to them about Markland, to get them on our side?"

" 'Tis not the time."

Silveta tried to appeal to Lexander again. "You speak Skraeling. Why don't you do something?"

He still wore his cloak and oarsman garb because he was much too large for Thule clothing. But he never noticed the cold. "My trades were all simple—so many ax blades for a boy, sacks of grain for a girl. You have no goods in hand to give them. The only way they will help you is if you gain their trust."

"The *olfs* will make sure they give us aid," I assured her.

Silveta covered her face, shaking her head as if she couldn't take it anymore. But at least she left me alone after that so I could enjoy my mam's people. The Beothuk roamed the southern coastline of Helluland, where the trees grew thick, but they were Skraeling just like the Thule.

When the shaman finally decreed the spirits were with us, the family transformed their tents into boats and packed their furs into surprisingly small bundles. Their entire camp was mobile, with bags to hold their whetstones, tools, fishing gear, and carved soapstone pots and lamps. The shaman had his own special waterproof sack that contained the wooden masks he wore during trances to speak to the guardian spirits and gods. I was allowed to watch the ritual he had performed to ensure favorable travel, dancing and singing in the mask of a walrus, the totem of the Lootega clan. I could hear faint echoes of the animal spirit speaking to the shaman, and it made me long to see more.

We paddled up the vast inlet for three days. I was surprised when the water remained salty as the inlet undulated deep into the interior. The farther we got from the coast, stands of conifers appeared in the creases between the barren hills. The low, rocky shoreline passed by, covered in purple and umber plants that hugged the ground. From what the clan told me, it was difficult to wrest life from this cold world. They usually moved south during the winter season despite having to compete with the Beothuk and Micmaq tribes who lived there.

When we finally reached the hooked end of the inlet, the Lootega clan packed up their boats and dragged them on sleds over the surrounding hills.

Topping the rise, I suddenly felt as if I could see forever. Hundreds of Thule tents hardly made a notch on the edge of a great bowl of tundra. It stretched into the distance farther than I could see. Here and there were lines of brown specks as caribou passed through on their annual migration. The feeble sunlight glinted off thousands of tiny puddles and pockets of water smearing the landscape.

Silveta cheered up at the sight of so many people. "Surely there are a hundred stout men here who can fight," she declared. "What would they take in trade?"

Lexander shook his head. "It must be something they need enough to make them risk their lives. Marja, do you know what they desire most?"

I looked around at the Skraelings, busy setting up their snug tents. The enormous encampment smelled cleaner than any Norotown I had seen. Their smiles told their own story as they greeted friends and kin. We were included in the welcome simply because we were with Lootega clan.

"It seems they lack for nothing," I had to admit.

Silveta pushed her hood back, causing a sensation with her blond hair. "Tell them what I need, Marja. Let them set their own price."

But I was distracted by the sight of someone who looked familiar. A young man stood next to one of the tents. He was alone and had one elbow slightly raised as if to ward off a blow.

I went closer to be sure. It was Kinirniq, my former slave-mate from Vidaris, just as scrawny as before. He was trembling all over.

"Kinirniq!" I exclaimed. "Can it be true? What are you doing here?"

He looked at me blankly, too exhausted to acknowledge my presence.

As Silveta joined me, I turned to Lexander. "Don't you see? It's Kinirniq."

Lexander was looking at him intently as if he, too, couldn't believe it was he. "What happened to you?" he asked, concerned by the young man's lack of response. Kinirniq's eyes were reddened and watery, and he was mumbling something to himself.

"Kinirniq, are you unwell?" Lexander asked, reaching out to touch his bared shoulder.

The Skraeling youth reacted as if he had been struck. His hands went to his face and he began to scream. He collapsed to the ground, shrieking in pure terror as he warded Lexander off.

Twenty

"**K**inirniq!" I cried. But he flinched away violently from me and bellowed like an animal in pain. His arms shielded his head.

Thule began to gather. An elder I had not seen before gestured to some youngsters to go to Kinirniq. The poor young man could not bear to have us near him. I was touched by the way the little children surrounded him, cooing in sympathy, calming his cries.

"My cousin's son was returned to us this way," the elder told us. "Two summers ago, he strayed from our winter camp and was not seen again. How do you know him?"

Lexander was impassive, as usual, and Silveta looked at me in bewilderment.

"I knew Kinirniq in Viinland," I replied cautiously.

The elder was a powerful man in his prime, with silver-dusted black hair and brows that met in a deep crease between his dark eyes. His complexion was burnt near black. "Kinirniq was sent to us from Kebec. The traders claimed him as a slave, but his past is locked in the depths of his mind. He does not speak. He rarely sleeps, and is frightened even then. Do you know what caused this malady in him?"

The *olfs* were watching us curiously, coming from all around. They also wanted to know what evil spirit had blighted this poor young man. Kinirniq was a cipher to them. Now he sat on the muddy ground, breathing heavily as if he had run very far. The little girls and boys were patting him and sitting by his legs. Their energy soothed him.

"It was Helanas," I blurted out. "Our mistress tortured him. She summoned a deadening miasma of despair that enveloped Vidaris and drove away all the good spirits."

The elder's gaze was unnaturally compelling, as if he was reading the truth from my essence as well as my words. "We have not been able to expel that evil spirit. Kinirniq breaks into rages when he is touched. He is cared for only by the young ones."

I thought of the abuse Helanas had inflicted on Kinirniq, the endless restraints, the unwanted penetration and forced ecstasy. She had abused me as well, but I had enjoyed everything far too much for her taste. Even her worst torture was merely a prelude to Lexander's touch. But evil had seeped into the cracks made in Kinirniq before I ever came to Vidaris.

I turned to Lexander with pain in my eyes. How could he have taken a boy so unsuited to be a pleasure slave? But I could not ask it out loud. My stomach twisted in fear at the thought of how these righteous Thule would react if they knew what Lexander had done to Kinirniq.

He saw my revulsion, and it hurt him deeply. There was self-loathing in his own eyes. "It was wrong," he told me quietly. "This is exactly the reason why I had to leave Vidaris."

"I know that name well!" another man called out, pushing his way to the fore. "This man is Vidaris, Amaruq. He lured my granddaughter away with tales of fame and riches in Viinland."

Amaruq, the elder, was watching me, clearly concerned by my reaction. "Nerriviq is the elder of the Tomalik clan."

I was silent, afraid of implicating Lexander.

But the enraged grandfather was already focused on Lexander. "Where is she now, our Qamaniq, our precious girl?"

So Qamaniq was Thule, as well. I had not guessed it before, though I knew the stately Skraeling was exceptional. Indeed, Kinirniq and Qamaniq had the same high cheekbones and prominent nose ridge, instead of the flatter,

rounder faces of the Beothuk like my mam and the Skraeling sisters. But Kinirniq had been sent to Kebec before Qamaniq arrived, so I had never considered their similarities.

"Qamaniq is in Vidaris," Lexander said quietly.

"The very place that stole this boy's *inua*?" Nerriviq demanded angrily, pointing at Kinirniq. "Is that the fate of
our girl?"

I knew Qamaniq was strong-willed, but Helanas would
probably enjoy tormenting her stubborn streak. Helanas
was capable of anything, especially if her anger at Lexander's abandonment was turned against the defenseless
slaves. The best Qamaniq could hope for was to be taken by
the winged ship, to suffer as Rosarin and Ansgar did now.
Perhaps Kinirniq was the lucky one, to be returned home,
even in such a terrible state.

Again, Amaruq seemed to know my feelings, as if he had
gained a great understanding in his life. The thoughtful
elder did not interfere as Qamaniq's grandfather summoned his kin to confront Lexander. My master had little
to say.

Silveta couldn't understand, so she tugged on my parka.
"What is it? Why are they mad at Lexander?"

"Kinirniq used to be a pleasure slave," I explained
hastily, trying to follow the argument that was going on
among Nerriviq's kin. The elders of the Lootega clan lingered, but they didn't seem eager to get involved.

"*You* did that to him, Lexander?" Silveta appraised the
pathetic Kinirniq sitting on the ground, his head bowed. "It
looks more like Birgir's men got to him."

I shuddered, and looked away. I couldn't bear to meet
Lexander's eyes.

"Tell them why I'm here, Marja," Silveta insisted. "This
looks like it's not going well."

I gestured to the *freya*, hoping to distract the Thule from
Lexander. "This great woman has come from Markland, all
this way to trade with you. We wish to work with the Thule."

"Compensation must be given," Amaruq abruptly declared. The elder was clearly a big man among the Thule.

Others began nodding, including Nerriviq, the aggrieved

grandfather. He sneered at Lexander. "Have *you* anything of value to give us?"

Lexander hesitated, accustomed to having wealth to rely on. "No, I have nothing."

"You have strong arms and back," Nerriviq countered. "You will work for me, and after the hunt we will take back my granddaughter."

"And what compensation will there be for Kinirniq?" Amaruq asked mildly.

"You can have the women." Nerriviq shrugged.

"You can't trade us like livestock!" I protested. "Silveta is the widow of the chieftain of Markland. She possesses a great estate."

Amaruq noted Silveta's commanding bearing. She nodded at him to show respect, since she couldn't speak to him directly.

"The women will stay as guests with the Tulugaq clan," Amaruq announced.

The others accepted that as final. The Lootega clan moved on, dragging their sleds to set up their tent on the outskirts of the sprawling encampment. Nerriviq and his kin approached Lexander.

I clutched his arm as he murmured, "I'm sorry, Marja. I can't involve you in this."

He gave my hand a reassuring squeeze. I was forced to watch him walk away without revealing how it frightened me.

When Lexander disappeared among the tents, Silveta reached out and took my hand silently. We'd had my master's protection ever since leaving Tillfallvik, even through the darkest times of our imprisonment in the bastion. He was our guardian, keeping anything bad from happening to us. And now he was gone.

Amaruq urged Silveta and me to sit with him before his tent. The Tulugaq clan had two long tents, set up at right angles to each other. We scraped the mud from our boots and sat cross-legged in a row on a pile of furs. Amaruq threw back his sealskin cloak, revealing he was a fine,

He was likely the same age as my da's father
d passed away, but whereas my grandda had
n and gray, Amaruq was straight-backed with a
oulders.

A shaman appeared wearing a wooden mask with slits
for eyes and a mouth that was sewn shut. Dried grass was
tied in bunches around his elbows and knees, and his face
and chest were streaked with red ocher.

Silveta drew back, frightened by his odd appearance, but I
whispered, "He's making sure we carry no evil with us that
will drive the caribou away."

The shaman muttered over us, shaking his carved staff in
front and over our heads. I knew we carried no evil, but the
shaman made a great show of cleansing us. As Thule from
the rest of the encampment passed through the open
square in a steady stream, examining us, I realized it was
done more for their assurance than to ward off true evil.
Confidence was important during the hunt.

"Where have they taken Lexander?" Silveta whispered
back to me.

"I don't know," I confessed.

The shaman continued his ritual with us, then turned
to Kinirniq. The young man was listless, sitting in the
mud at the end of the tent. I was anguished at the sight,
yet I also wanted to believe in Lexander's innate goodness. The shaman was energetic in trying to drive out the
evil that clung to the poor boy's *inua*, but it did no good
that I could see.

Silveta had her own pressing needs. "Did you tell them
why I'm here? Why aren't they talking to us? We have to
get back to Markland as soon as we can."

I did as she ordered, explaining to Amaruq, "Silveta is
the *freya* of Markland. The *olfs* have championed her
cause to remove an evil warlord from her land. She
needs warriors to aid her own men who are fighting him
in Tillfallvik."

Amaruq considered me for a long time. Silveta grew impatient. "Is that all you've got to say, Marja? Convince him!
You said you could."

Now I was not so sure. With Lexander gone, everything seemed to have gone terribly awry. But I tried again. "Respected elder, this woman has great wealth and can give your people all the riches they desire. She is prepared to generously reward those who help her right this great wrong that has been done to her."

"And who are you, little one?" Amaruq asked. "You who plead for others but not yourself."

"Me?" I asked in surprise. "I'm Marja."

"What is your relation to this woman?"

I glanced at Silveta. "We are not kin. She asked for my help to free our homeland from a tyrant."

"What about the Vidaris man?" he pressed.

I did not even consider lying to this elder. "I belong to Lexander. I am his pleasure slave."

"I saw there was a deep attachment between you." He sat back, considering all that I had said.

The parade of Thule began to slow as they returned to their duties. There were large racks with skins spread between the poles filling one end of the Tulugaq camp. Women and youths were busy scraping the flesh from the skin to cure the caribou fur. The men were tending to their weapons, sharpening the points of their arrows and spears.

"What does he say?" Silveta asked impatiently. "Will he help us?"

Amaruq was amused by Silveta's questions. Though he couldn't understand her words, he heard her impatience. "Tell your sun-haired friend that the Thule now hunt. When the hunt is over, her request will be considered."

I knew Silveta wouldn't like that. "When shall the hunt end?"

"When it ends," Amaruq replied evenly.

I took a deep breath, then turned to Silveta. "They have to hunt now while the caribou are migrating. The fur is very important to them." I touched her parka. " 'Tis what they make their clothes from. So they have to stay here for a while, but when their hunt is over, they'll consider your request."

"How long will that take?" she demanded.

"Less than a moon, I'm sure."

"A *moon*?" Silveta glared at me, struggling to regain her composure. "I can't wait that long. Every supporter I have will be killed or suborned by then. They'll think I've abandoned them."

"This hunt is very important to the Thule. There's nothing you could give them that could replace the furs they'll take here."

"If only I could speak to him," Silveta muttered, glancing at Amaruq.

I felt as if I had failed Silveta and Lexander by insisting we come to Helluland. But the *olfs* had shown me this path. The ice sprites had confirmed it when I arrived. I couldn't understand why it was not going well. Then I remembered how happy the *olfs* had been in the bastion, yet we had been betrayed by the overlord there. I subsided into watchfulness, hoping Lexander would return soon.

We were not the only ones who were distressed. Amaruq's wife, Keelat, had a sour, set expression on her face as she strolled about the camp. Keelat was a round woman with fleshy jowls from age. She muttered to herself as she tended the evening roast of caribou haunch, watching everything that happened in her camp.

It was clear that Amaruq was well respected by the other clans. Even while we ate, sitting in our place of honor before the main tent, men came by and consulted with Amaruq about the morrow's hunt. The shaman emerged, wearing a different mask this time, one with great antlers on the brow, and he spoke over the array of clan weapons that had been laid out. The shaman called on Tekkeitsertok, the god of hunting, to bless them with success.

Silveta yawned and fidgeted. When it came time to crawl inside the tent, despite the languid sunshine that continued well into the night, she was so exhausted that she didn't protest the smelly furs or the night sounds around us. I knew that sleeping among the Skraeling was trying for her. Likely she longed for the privacy of her closet at home.

I had slept my whole life huddled against my siblings

and had quickly gotten accustomed to curling up in Lexander's arms on the *knaar*. I sorely missed that. But even separated from him, our uneasy dreams mingled. Nightmarish images of Birgir raping me and Lexander's helpless fury as he could only watch, restrained against his will. I had not seen it at the time, he had hidden it well, but Lexander had truly wanted to kill Birgir last midsummer. I could feel his rage knowing that Birgir had raped me again while he was not far away . . . I kept swimming awake in a wash of unfettered fury. Every time I slipped back down, there was more waiting for me, heightened by Lexander's fear that someone was hurting me now and that he could do nothing to stop it.

I finally gave up trying to sleep when the Thule rose early to prepare for the hunt. Silveta was still curled in her furs and refused to budge. Kinirniq wandered aimlessly through the camp, lost to himself. His shouts when he woke from a nightmare were shattering. But his kin had the utmost patience with him.

Once the bustle of the hunters' departure was over and Keelat led the women to fetch water, I slipped away. I searched through the tents, trying to find Lexander. There were mostly women and children about, as well as some older and injured men. The *olfs* wanted to be helpful, but there were so many here who acknowledged them, while Lexander could not. That distracted them.

Eventually it was the Markland *olf* that showed me where to find him. Lexander was near some tents on the outer edge of the encampment. He was carrying stones in a leather sack, with his cape thrown back over his shoulders. Overjoyed, I ran up to him, but then stopped short.

There was a metal collar around his neck, and a copper chain swung from the front down to his wrist. He dumped the sack of stones at an order from an older woman who was directing her kin in building a smoker.

When Lexander saw me, his expression was unreadable. I think he wanted to reach for me, to hold me close, but his hand was stopped short by the chain. He could not stretch his arm out all the way.

I went to hug him, leaning my face on his chest. "What is this?" I breathed, frightened.

"Nerriviq won't risk me leaving," he explained, "or fighting with his men."

I grasped his arm, looking at the copper band around his wrist. The end of the chain was welded to the band. "They treat you like a slave! How can you let them do this to you?"

"Nerriviq doubts they will be able to get Qamaniq back. They believe she is like Kinirniq now. If she is, then I am to blame for that."

I glanced at the women and elders who were working on the smoker, warily watching us. "Lexander, why did you take Kinirniq? He was not fit for training. Surely you must have seen that."

He winced. "It is a terrible thing. I had a quota to fill. My superiors in Stanbulin were always complaining that we didn't send them enough slaves. I came to despise it, that pressure to always bring more and more youths into service, then send them away with only the most rudimentary preparation. The demand among my people exceeds the supply."

I was confused and must have shown it, for he added, "I always needed more slaves, Marja. When the traders offered Kinirniq to me, I saw how miserable he was with them. I thought . . . it would be no worse for him as a pleasure slave."

"You didn't give him a waiting period?"

"No." His chain clinked softly as he shifted. "Most houses don't. It is something that only a few masters do to ensure we train slaves who are willing."

"Kinirniq was not willing." Helanas may have broken Kinirniq, but Lexander had slain his *inua*. It was even worse than I had thought.

"It was a waste from beginning to end," Lexander said through clenched teeth. "Kinirniq was so far gone by the time Helanas was done with him that we couldn't even send him to Stanbulin. I can never forgive myself for what I did to him."

I wondered if Helanas' evil had somehow affected Lexander. Surely he had done right to escape. For me, it was enough that he now walked a better path than the one that destroyed Kinirniq. "I'll help you get away. 'Tis a long journey on foot to the coast, but we can—"

"No, Marja. This is no more than I deserve. I've no qualms about helping Nerriviq get his granddaughter back. These Thule can help me do it."

"But what about Helanas?" In truth, I wondered how much he cared about Qamaniq.

"I should have released all of the slaves before I left. I put them in Helanas' hand, and I'll do whatever it takes to free them."

The pain in his eyes when he had faced Kinirniq's forlorn body was still there. In truth he was atoning for the evil he had aided.

I had to relent. It was not my place to intervene in matters such as these.

Silveta was sorely disheartened when I informed her that Lexander was in chains. She returned to her sleeping furs and stayed there for the rest of the day. The hunters eventually came back to camp bloody and exhausted. Amaruq was surrounded by his admiring kin, and they talked excitedly about the two caribou that had been killed by their clan.

As the men rested the next day, I tried to help the clan, scraping skins and carrying water. It was mainly to appease Keelat, whose mutterings had grown loud enough for me to overhear. She disliked treating us as guests when we had no ties to familiar clans. Keelat had a very narrow view of what was good for her family, and she kept her daughters and the wives of her sons under her thumb.

That night, I noticed that Keelat didn't retire to their sleeping furs with Amaruq. From the whispers I overheard the next day, Keelat shared nights with an elder from another clan during the hunting season. This elder was now a widower, so his wife no longer came to sleep with Amaruq.

I thought Amaruq's gaze when his wife returned the next morning was sweet and sad, as if he was thinking of pleasures in the past. She briefly touched his hand, a rare sign of Thule affection, her own expression momentarily contented.

Then it was back to the concerns of the day as the hunters departed. I took that as my chance to go see Lexander again. I knew the way now, so I darted quickly through the tents. But when I arrived, I couldn't believe my eyes.

The tent was gone. A trampled space on the ground and the half-built smoker showed where it had once stood. Several other camps around it were also gone.

I ran to the nearest tent and asked a young man, "Where did Nerriviq's clan go?"

"They are gone to the southern bay."

"Why?" I asked.

The youth shrugged. "The hunting is good there, they say."

I let him go, sensing he knew nothing more. I was afraid Nerriviq's departure had something to do with Lexander. For the rest of the day, I asked the Thule about the southern bay. The *olfs* showed me what they knew as well. It was much larger than the narrow waterway we had traveled to reach the northern encampment, and the southern bay was surrounded by trees rather than tundra. Most of the Thule avoided it because swarms of flies were biting, but there were clans who preferred the hunting there.

Lexander was gone. I was on my own again.

Perhaps I was mistaken, but I did not rush to tell Silveta that Lexander had been taken away. She was already so depressed in spirits that I feared for her sanity. She could speak to no one but me, and her helplessness seemed to wear on her like nothing else had during our journey. Always before she had been our driving force, carrying us ever onward. But now she was idle and she suffered because of it.

As I waited for Silveta to emerge from the tent, Amaruq returned to camp. He paused to wave away some flies from a prime haunch of caribou that had been carefully hung between two carved posts. Ravens ate from the fresh offerings after every hunt. The crafty bird was the clan totem. The children picked up the shiny feathers that the birds dropped, decorating the camp and their clothes with them. Amaruq usually wore an iridescent black feather tied to a small braid in his hair.

Amaruq went to sit before the tent. His older sister was not far away, chewing on a square of leather to soften it. Others were moving about the camp, but I didn't return to my usual duties. Instead, I went to sit near Amaruq. I knew better than to address an elder first, and left it to Amaruq to decide if we would converse. I hoped he would.

It wasn't long before Amaruq gestured over his shoulder at the tent. "Has the sun-haired woman sickened?"

"Silveta is heartsick," I replied truthfully, adding, "Her husband was cut down before her eyes and her home was stolen from her. Many people were killed, her loyal bondsmen included."

"You were there?"

I squirmed a bit, remembering I was the ostensible cause of the duel. "Yes. But it is Silveta's story."

"I want your story," he countered. "I have never before seen a pleasure slave."

I felt no wanton attraction from Amaruq like I had with Gudren. The Thule concealed their passions well by day, while at night there was no hiding the sounds of pleasure. It was considered taboo to cross generational lines, but among peers it mattered not who coupled with whom. Since I was younger than his own children, Amaruq might consider me taboo.

"It is simple, really," I explained. "I have been trained to give pleasure to people."

"Does that give you pleasure?"

"Yes, it satisfies me. I am suited to this life by my nature."

Amaruq watched the *olfs* that were rolling across the ground near me. "They sense no evil in you, as there is in

Kinirniq. Our shaman agrees, though he is puzzled. How did you escape Vidaris unscathed?"

I knew it was not merely my love for Lexander that had carried me through. "Perhaps it is because I chose my fate as a pleasure slave. I was satisfied by my training."

"Kinirniq was taken against his will," Amaruq agreed. "He would have fought against his fate."

I glanced over at Kinirniq, who was accompanied as always by the children. "Innocence may heal him. Helanas hurt him and made him live in fear. She broke his spirit, allowing the evil to get inside of him."

Amaruq smiled. "Even when you tell your story, you turn it to others. Have you nothing of your own?"

He was sincere, so I answered honestly, "Everything in my life is tied to others—my kin, my master, and my friends in this world and the other."

"Perhaps that is why you are so often merely a reflection of other people's desires."

I thought it a likely conjecture. Here I was alone again, and my first impulse was to gain the help of the most powerful person in the camp. It was comforting to know that Amaruq was interested in me. But Keelat kept narrowing her eyes in our direction the longer we spoke. The others didn't seem to notice anything, while Amaruq's wife had already sniffed out my intentions.

I had brought Silveta and Lexander to Helluland, so I had to fulfill my promise. The way through this turmoil was the path I had first chosen, and I only hoped it would lead me back to Lexander as well. But I could not think of my master now, or my longing for him would disrupt the spell I was weaving with Amaruq.

I lowered my voice. "I would be honored to reflect *your* desires, respected elder."

He understood instantly. His interest began heating in a more familiar way. But Thule were subtle people. I did not dare overdo my advances.

I sat beside him in a charged silence, waiting for him to make the next move. I kept my eyes down, thinking only of him, feeling his presence beside me.

It went on for a long time as the shadows slowly moved across the ground. As I radiated my desire for him, he simply accepted it. How could I not be attracted to Amaruq? He was strong, commanding, and wise. He held my fate in his hands.

Finally Amaruq glanced over at me. "You are relentless."

A smile played on my lips, as I met his eyes. "You would like to know me. Let me show you more . . ."

His breath caught as he watched my mouth. Among the reserved Thule, his reaction was as blatant as a kiss.

Suddenly Keelat was standing before us. I drew back at her trembling rage, wondering if I had overstepped myself.

"Will you mate so openly?" she demanded. "Where all the children can see?"

Amaruq actually smiled, unconcerned with her outburst. "Will you be with our friend tonight, wife?"

Her face twisted. "Yes, you need not ask."

"Then our guest will share my furs." With that Amaruq stood up. He clasped Keelat's arm lightly, and that instantly appeased her. They exchanged a nod; then he left, heading deeper into the encampment.

He had not touched me, nor had he asked for my agreement. It left me heady with anticipation.

Nothing more was said between us. Amaruq paid no attention to me during our night-meal. Keelat was not as self-controlled, and her expression slipped to bitter irritation at times. But once the last morsel was swallowed, she set off for the widower's tent. I had to assume she accepted Amaruq's declaration or she would have stayed.

Only after Keelat left did Amaruq let his eyes linger on me. I flushed with excitement. Finally, here was a man worthy of Lexander's gifts to me.

Amaruq waited as his kin began to sleepily enter the tent, reverently touching a thick bunch of black feathers hanging over the door. I realized he did not wish to make a show of our rutting, so I quietly slipped in after he did. It was darker inside the tent.

By courtesy, Amaruq and Keelat shared furs at one end, where it was warmer and they didn't have people brushing past their feet to go outside. Silveta was near the other end, where we had been placed. I wasn't sure if she slept or not, but she had barely touched her meal before crawling back inside. I had never seen anyone dream away so many days without ceasing, and feared it boded ill for her. I was glad to see our Markland *olf* stayed nearby, protecting her.

The *olfs* knew what I was doing, naturally. Their chubby curves gleamed as they swung across the curved roof of the tent. I was thankful the shaman, the most observant of the clan, did not sleep in this tent. The others were tired from the ceaseless work of the hunt, and hurried into their furs with babes snuggled in and children lying between couples. We were a full two dozen in all.

Despite the darkness, I knew it would be a very public coupling. There was no privacy in the tent, and every rasping breath could be heard. Indeed, as I slipped off my parka and leggings, I heard similar movements that heralded the night games.

I slipped naked between the furs, more silky than the ones I usually slept in. Amaruq and Keelat were given the best the clan possessed. The daughter-in-law who lay down not an arm's length away noticed I was there, and she whispered to her husband, Amaruq's eldest son.

I felt an old tinge of modesty and had to smile, remembering how innocent I had been when I had first arrived in Vidaris. I had been embarrassed to take off my clothes in front of Lexander. Now it merely heightened my arousal to know others were avidly listening to us.

Amaruq's hands touched my face. Then his fingers began lightly tracing down my neck to the swell of my breasts and the curve of my waist. I sighed as his palm slid to my hip. He grasped my thighs, feeling their strength. Then his fingers tangled in the short, soft hair of my groin.

I bit my lip to keep from moaning. His touch was tantalizing as he traced the contours of my body.

But when Amaruq had taken the measure of me, it was

clear he wanted more than that. "Tell me how you learned to be a pleasure slave," he urged, as his fingers stroked me.

"I was taught poses and discipline," I said with difficulty. "We slaves practiced sensual techniques on each other, and sometimes with our master and mistress."

"No, don't tell me in that way. Describe it to me." His voice was urgent. "Tell me something that happened to you in Vidaris, a time when you were surprised at yourself."

It was not easy to think while he stimulated me so, but I understood what he wanted. Instantly I thought of my penance and how Lexander had ordered me to pose naked on a pedestal. It was embarrassing to reveal it, but I knew that honesty was what he needed in order to trust me. So I told Amaruq, sparing no detail of my initial pleasure at being displayed, then my shock when the magnates arrived.

"The younger was so greasy and nasty," I murmured, "I was repulsed at the very sight of him. Yet when he touched me, I was aroused." My body moved as I recalled the magnate's rough touch and my conflicting emotions. "I was ashamed for wanting him. Yet I discovered it is my nature to respond when someone wants to make use of me. He merely touched me, and I was ready to bed him right then and there. But the magnate chose Rosarin that night, and I must admit, I was envious of her."

As I spoke, Amaruq's hands still moved over me. It was almost mesmerizing, his constant touch as I flushed at the memory of my penance.

I braced myself against his chest, feeling his smoothness. With his hard muscles and creamy skin, I was reminded of Lexander as I ran my hands along his body. His *tarse* was full and heated, yet Amaruq made no attempt to take me.

"So it was not merely the man's hand on you," Amaruq said thoughtfully. "You responded to his desire for you. But this man did not take you to fruition. Was there any time that you felt strongly satisfied, both in body and emotion, by being used in this way?"

I did not want to speak of how Lexander took me after the greasy magnate had left. That was too intimate a confidence.

So instead, I told Amaruq of one time when Sverker had taken me on the sly. He had been denied by Helanas for many days, and when he caught me in the storeroom, I thought he wanted only a quick suck. But that time, he was angry about something, most likely because Helanas had hurt him. He took me from the rear, slipping into my tightest hole. Just describing how he had done it made me wildly aroused. Amaruq whispered encouragement, making me tell every part of my shame and delight.

"It hurt terribly at first," I confessed, "but I felt an incredible rush at being used solely for his pleasure. It mattered not what I felt . . . yet I was able to make him lose control so that he had to take me."

"And were you satisfied?"

"Yes, very much so. I was limp and so relaxed afterwards. I kept smiling, and Sverker thought that was strange, I could see. I never told anyone about it, not even my master."

I could feel the heat in Amaruq's groin. Unable to restrain myself any longer, I bent forward to lick his chest. He tasted of smoke and sweat, a fine manly scent.

Gradually I moved lower, breathing on his skin, stroking him with my fingertips and kissing every part. He hissed as I gently blew on his *tarse,* then took him inside my mouth. Lexander had taught us every technique to pleasure a man's organ, from stroking to licking. I swear I tried them all on Amaruq, hoping to make him lose himself.

But the man was more resilient than I expected. Ultimately, his hands held my head as his hips pumped into me. He strained, and I knew he wanted to release his seed into my mouth.

Instead, he abruptly pulled me up. As my head emerged from the furs, I could hear the silence in the tent. They all listened to us.

As Amaruq took me, I cried out softly, knowing it inflamed the others. Men were reaching for their wives to satisfy the lust that whipped through the tent. The *olfs* were wheeling as if they were drunk.

I lost myself in the rhythm, my body tightening around

Amaruq again and again. He was a potent man and gave me much pleasure. Yet I felt no urge to reach out with my senses and open my emotions to Amaruq. Our joining was purely physical, nothing otherworldly.

Finally he spent himself because he could not withstand it any longer. I joined with him, reveling in the endless moment. Afterwards, Amaruq did not hold me close like Lexander did. But I was comforted by his warm body lying next to me.

Twenty-one

"How could you rut around with that old man?" Silveta exclaimed the next morning. She had gotten out of her furs to drag me into the boggy tundra where we could speak freely. "I thought you were in love with Lexander! He's been magnificent to you. How could you give yourself to another man?"

The *olfs* were listening, of course. There was nothing I could do about them carrying tales. But likely Amaruq knew my ultimate goal as well as I. "Amaruq won't help us fight Birgir unless he trusts us."

Silveta looked frankly skeptical. "That's not how you negotiate to get a warband, Marja."

I met her eye squarely. "I sell myself to survive, Silveta. It's what I am. Gudren helped me escape Brianda. And Niall enabled me to escape from Birgir—that's how I was able to rescue *you*."

She frowned. "So Lexander told you to do this? I wasn't surprised when you threw yourself at the Sigurdssons—they have some kind of hold over you. But this is going too far."

"Lexander doesn't know." I realized I would have to tell her. "He's gone. Nerriviq's clan went to the southern bay to hunt."

There was silence for a few moments. "Oh," she said softly. She looked as alone as I felt.

"Don't worry," I assured her. "I'll make sure Amaruq helps us."

But Silveta was despondent as we walked through the encampment back to the Tulugaq. I expected her to retreat in despair to her furs again, but instead she seated herself outside the tent and watched everything. The last hunt had been very successful, so the men were helping to cure the hides. I did whatever was requested of me and usually took on the messy job of hauling bones over the ridge to a gully for disposal.

After my night with Amaruq, there was a marked difference in how the others treated me. Now they weren't sure what to think of my status. Since I was a guest, that implied my stay was temporary. Yet shared intimacy among the Thule usually meant there would be a longer association. Keelat and Amaruq had bedded the widower and his wife for decades.

The *olfs* were elated by the clan's curiosity. They always liked to feed off a mystery. The children picked up on the *olfs'* excitement and ran around the camp laughing and screaming in unusually exuberant games.

Amaruq paid no attention to me or Silveta. Yet I could see that he was quicker to smile. I carefully hid my interest in Amaruq, knowing that it would disturb his kin, especially Keelat. From time to time his wife assured me, "You are a guest. There's no need for you to assist us." To which I always proclaimed my desire to work. She kept assigning me tasks to keep me under her control and away from her mate.

I was busy dumping baskets of bloody bones onto a hide to be dragged to the gully when Silveta approached. "How can you do this?" she exclaimed, waving at the flies that swarmed up. "Have you no dignity?"

"I don't judge what the spirits bring me," I demurred. "I simply perform my duties to the best of my ability. As you do."

Silveta hesitated, but the blood that coated my hands made her shudder in revulsion. I realized she was remembering Ejegod's gory death. Before I could say anything to reassure her, she turned away.

As Silveta passed the hanging haunch of meat, she absently flapped her hand at a raven that had just settled and begun to pull at the flesh. The bird startled and flew up.

Keelat was instantly there, grabbing Silveta roughly by the arm and throwing her up against one of the posts. It happened too quickly for me to intervene. The next moment, Keelat's curved knife was at Silveta's throat.

Silveta froze, her eyes glazing with terror. I had no doubt that Birgir had raped her at knifepoint.

I didn't dare touch Keelat's arm. "Silveta meant no harm! She didn't know the raven was an honored guest."

"She has disrespected our totem!" Keelat raged.

I knew that Silveta had broken a taboo that could lead to sickness or injury for members of the clan. It was especially dangerous because of the hunt. If the raven was offended, it could influence the caribou spirit to resist the hunters.

But Keelat's anger was over much more than Silveta's thoughtless action. She resented the whispered comments about my lengthy coupling with Amaruq. I knew it would take only a slight pressure from the knife and Silveta would be dead to spite me.

"If you kill her," I warned Keelat, "I will stay here *forever*. Nothing will take me away."

Amaruq's wife heard my threat. She glared at me. "Take care that you don't suffer the same fate she does, halfbreed."

I knew Keelat would not risk breaking the taboo of harming a guest unless she had a very good reason. So I kept my voice light. "I could be very happy here. Right now I am under obligation to this woman, but if that ends I have nowhere else to go . . . and I have been shown how welcome I am here."

Keelat growled, baring her worn teeth, ground down from chewing hide. Her cheeks hung laxly and wrinkles radiated from her eyes and around her mouth. But she began to finally ease back.

Silveta sniffled like she was about to go into hysterics. I grabbed her arm hard. "Be silent," I said to her. To Keelat,

I explained, "I want nothing more than to leave here with Silveta; tomorrow would not be too soon. You can make that happen for us."

Suspicious, Keelat still held her knife between us. "How?"

"Silveta needs a hundred warriors to retake her estate in Markland. We'll go with them, never to return here."

Keelat actually bit off a laugh. "Why would we risk our sons to fight your battle?"

I knew I had her. "Silveta can give you winter settlements on Markland. The land is fine with tall trees and whales swimming close to shore. You would no longer have to take the worst of the lands in the south, and risk having your children stolen as Kinirniq was."

Keelat's eyes widened. "The sun-haired woman can give us settlements? If she has such power, why does she beg here?"

"Her estate has been seized by a fiendish man. She can reclaim it with the help of one hundred warriors."

Silveta murmured faintly, "What is happening?"

"I told her that you would give them winter settlement lands in Markland." I glanced at her. "Don't make that face! You have to convince Keelat now, or you'll never get the help you need. Birgir is willing to grant the overlord far more. Do you want to best him or not?"

Slowly Silveta nodded, warily regarding Keelat. "I can guarantee the next chieftain will honor a grant of tracts of land on the northern coast. It's empty because it's too exposed for good farming. The Micmaq used to live there, but many left or died of disease."

I relayed this to Keelat, leaving out the last part. Thule were much less likely to interact with the Noromenn, and that would preserve them. "You see, Silveta agrees," I added. "Your men can win her rights, then take possession of the lands for yourselves."

"And you?" Keelat asked. "What do you gain from this?"

"I will fulfill my pledge to Silveta and my homeland, and

the *olfs* will be pleased with me. Then I will be free to go to my master. He is the man I love and long to be reunited with."

Keelat sheathed her knife. Her kin were watching our heated argument from around camp, but did not dare to come closer out of respect for the elder. "This woman will live for now. I must consult with Amaruq."

Silveta was impatient to hear their decision, but I tried to explain that Skraelings had their own way of deliberating. That evening, after Keelat conferred with Amaruq, the shaman emerged wearing an elaborate winged mask with a raven's beak. The black feathers had an iridescent shimmer. He began to dance and chant to the beating of the drum. I was glad to see them consult the animal spirits, but Silveta was frightened and unconvinced.

I could not rest if there was something more I could do to help sway the Thule. So I turned to the *olfs*, as always. I walked far beyond the encampment, into the rolling ground pocked by puddles and blossomed into full flower. I felt the *olfs* more strongly here, much like the fens. I could also sense ice sprites dancing among the crystals underground.

I lost track of time in this light-filled world, listening to the ice sprites' tales of the long dark winter of snow. No wonder the Thule sought to escape by going south for half the year. I knelt on the tender moss and closed my eyes, letting the surroundings sink into me. My anxiety kept interfering, snapping me back into myself. But I persisted and finally was accepted by the spirits of the place. It was soothing. My concerns melted away amidst the greater rhythms of life.

Then for some reason, my cousin Deidre came to mind. Her bright green eyes were much like the tiny-leafed plant that spread across the ground. But now she was dead, after being raped by Birgir's men.

My eyes opened wide. I understood what the spirits were

telling me. I had given the Skraelings a reason to help Silveta, but they must be inspired by passion to fight.

As I returned through the encampment, I pulled aside one of the younger men of Tulugaq. He had taken an interest in me before, but now that I had bedded Amaruq, he was truly fascinated. I flattered him about how comfortable I felt among them, my true people. Then I confessed how frightened I had been in Markland because Birgir encouraged his men to rape and kill, like they had done to my cousin Deidre.

The young man was appalled, yet he could not hear enough about the warlord's terrible ways. There were one or two other youths I could confide in, so I kept back some details for their ears. That would get the talk flowing. Then I trusted the spirits would move them.

When I returned to the Tulugaq camp, Silveta had a circle of six elders, including Amaruq, seated on mats before her. A piece of old leather lay in the center, marked with black lines. Lexander had consulted maps regularly in Vidaris, planning his next voyage and keeping track of his finds. I had not understood them at first, but Lexander had shown me where Jarnby and Vidaris were, with the Nauga Sea between them. I had seen enough to know at a glance that this map was a rough outline of Helluland with the huge triangular island of Markland off the southern coast.

There were X marks along the northern shore of Markland, freshly made with a charcoal stick.

Silveta was frowning in concentration as an elder asked a question, pointing to the map, trying to pantomime the number of moons they could stay in their winter settlements. "Oh, Marja, thank the gods you've finally returned. You have to tell me what I've just agreed to."

I knew from Amaruq's satisfied expression that he had purposely negotiated with Silveta while I was not present. He wanted to observe Silveta without me around to instruct her.

"It looks from the map like you've agreed to give them ten winter settlements," I said.

"Yes, for as long as needed for two generations," she said.

I translated that to the Thule. A couple of elders sat back, clearly wishing the grant had been perpetual. But they had enough familiarity with Noromenn customs to understand that their contracts usually had limits.

Amaruq waited for any other questions. Most looked satisfied, but one elder complained, "It may be tempting, but can it be worth the lives of our men?"

"You can but ask them," I said simply.

Another day passed as I continued to spread the tales of women who had been stolen from their families by Birgir's men. When Silveta learned of my plan, she recounted all of the harrowing stories she had heard in Tillfallvik. Deidre's fate had been shared by many others. I did not tell anyone that both Silveta and I had been raped by Birgir lest they think we simply sought revenge. We wanted more than that. We wanted to bring peace back to Markland.

Keelat set her jaw and left that evening to bed the widower. I thought there was something of pride in her behavior, to keep others from supposing that she stayed in Amaruq's furs simply to prevent me from taking them. I followed Amaruq inside the tent at a glance from him. As soon as we were lying together, he pulled the supple snowcat fur over our heads so we could whisper without being heard.

"You inflame the men with your talk of rape and slaughter," he murmured. "Is not the *freya*'s promise of winter land enough to tempt us?"

"The Thule people care about justice and harmony," I insisted. "Your men must know what they fight—an evil spirit as venomous as the one that stole Kinirniq's soul."

Amaruq considered my words. "You are passionate in all ways, pleasure slave. The spirits say you can be trusted."

"Does that mean you'll help us?"

"Perhaps." He paused, and I knew he was not yet convinced. "Perhaps you desire more than to fulfill your pledge to the sun-haired woman."

My hands clasped together tightly. Of course Amaruq knew me. I had opened myself to him, speaking with complete honesty to gain his trust. " 'Tis true, I would like to have Lexander help us in this fight. He will understand how best to beat Birgir. And he can speak to you as Silveta cannot."

"Ah, you seek your master."

It was a delicate moment. "As you would seek Keelat if you were separated, would you not?"

"I would not make her presence a condition of our agreement."

"Neither do I. Regardless of whether Lexander comes with us, Silveta will give you settlements for fighting for her. You asked what I desire, and I think it wise if Lexander assists us."

In the charged silence, I ventured to stroke Amaruq's chest lightly. Words were not enough. If he trusted me body to body, it could be sufficient to sway his decision.

But Amaruq would not relent. "Does your master love you?"

"Yes," I said firmly. "We seem made for each other."

Amaruq pulled me closer. "Tell me why you are so sure of that. What is special between you?"

I knew what Amaruq wanted—the details of our intimacy. That was the treasure I had to offer him. If he didn't get it, he might not join with me. Without that, he would be much less likely to trust me.

"Lexander holds an infinite appeal for me," I admitted. "Even this summer, when I met a couple who were truly kind and generous, I could not forget him. If I hadn't longed for Lexander, I would have stayed with Gudren and Alga, for a while at least."

"You bedded the man?" he guessed.

"Both of them, together and apart." He was surprised at that, and I was glad to see that I had distracted him from Lexander. "I adored Alga. She was very dominant with me, but never was she mean or angry. Once I broke her favorite comb while I was dressing her hair. I felt awful about it, inconsolable, but she was as sweet as honey to me. Though it seems odd to think of it that way."

"Tell me," Amaruq urged.

I smiled at the memory. "Alga was laughing at my torment of guilt. I felt so clumsy and stupid. Then finally she said she had to punish me in order to make me feel better. She bent me over the table and pulled my skirts up to my waist. I was completely exposed. Then she struck my buttocks with her palm over and over again." I wiggled remembering it. "She held me down at my waist, leaning on me. The smacks were hard enough to sting, but not truly hurt. The longer she went, the harder I could take it. The rhythm, the impact, felt so much like rutting, I was shocked!"

"Did she satisfy you?" he asked.

"Oh, yes, when I thought I could take it no more, she began kissing my tender, reddened skin. At first it stung even more, but soon it made the throbbing feel better. She spread my legs wide so she could lick me, holding my wrists against my thighs so I could not squirm away."

Even now, I blushed to tell Amaruq. But my words inflamed him. He slid down under the furs, kissing my stomach down to my groin. He pleasured me as I had done him the first time. He already found me wet with desire, but he toyed with me for a long time, making me hiss with suppressed cries.

Amaruq kissed and stroked me until I was in a frenzy. He was a virile man, as he proved again that night. He seemed intent on pleasing me. I had heard Keelat's muffled exclamations at night, and knew she appreciated his newfound enthusiasm.

When we were through and Amaruq dozed off, I lay there wondering if he would agree to help us. I dreaded returning to Markland without Lexander's protection. But I had to fulfill my promise to Silveta to help cast Birgir from my homeland.

The next day, word spread that the warriors would depart for the southern bay in two days and from there leave for Markland to fight for new winter lands.

Silveta could not believe it was true until the Thule lashed ten *umiaks* into shape and launched them in the narrow inlet. The boats bristled with weapons, more than I had seen even during the hunt. There were eighty men and a handful of youths. The clans remained in the encampment so the women and elders could finish curing the caribou hides.

Keelat was unhappy when Amaruq left with me. The elder had been chosen to lead the warriors. But she knew it was the first step to ridding herself of me completely. The nod of farewell we gave each other was respectful, befitting our understanding.

The narrow fork of the inlet flowed south in a steady silver line, wider than a river but much longer and narrower than a typical bay. The Thule expertly paddled their boats and we were swiftly sped away. Our faithful Markland *olf* who had followed us so far on our journey clung to the shafts of the spears, riding along merrily.

Silveta was uncomfortable as always in the Skraeling boats with their curved, wet bottoms. But I liked the small craft with the low sides that allowed me to trail my hand in the water. It gave me a stronger link with the sea spirits. The water was a mixture of fresh and salt, which gave a unique taste to their images. But in none of them could I see Lexander.

At first, we were surrounded by tundra, but as the inlet gradually opened up, the land around us began to change. Shrubs crowded the banks, then scraggly evergreens appeared. When we reached the southern bay, I could hardly see across the vast inland sea.

I was heartened despite the never-ending flies that swarmed into our faces, biting us mercilessly. My only fear was that Nerriviq had already departed with Lexander for Vidaris. It was late though still light when we finally arrived at the mouth of a great river that flowed into the southern bay.

As soon as my feet hit the ground, I wanted to set out in search of my master. We had to scramble up a steep incline to reach the encampment. It was much smaller, set on the top of a bluff to catch the wind and away from the dense undergrowth along the water where the flies swarmed. Silveta was also looking around, clearly doubting our purpose here.

Amaruq prevented me from leaving. "The man you seek will be brought here."

The boats were soon converted into tents. Amaruq told Silveta and me to sit beside him, to wait for Nerriviq to appear. It was beginning to seem as if the elder would not come, and I worried myself into fidgeting. Amaruq noticed.

When Nerriviq finally appeared, his expression was set in annoyance. He must have been roused from his furs.

Lexander followed behind. I sat forward, drinking in the sight. He was worn and haggard, as I had never seen him before. The chain still ran from his collar to his wrist, forcing him to keep his arm bent. As he drew closer, I could see inflamed skin where the metal had rubbed against his flesh. Considering how quickly he healed, it was bad indeed.

I almost protested out loud, but Amaruq quelled me with a motion of his hand. I realized more than ever how necessary it was to please Amaruq.

Lexander was glad to see me, I could tell. But he didn't try to speak to us. He sat to one side and slightly behind Nerriviq, just as we did with Amaruq. The elder explained Silveta's offer to exchange winter settlements for a warband to quash Birgir. Lexander nodded thoughtfully at that, his eyes meeting mine in a flash of approval.

"The Vidaris man is necessary for our success," Amaruq added. "He knows the weaknesses of our enemy."

"He is our only hope of retrieving my granddaughter," Nerriviq countered. "I care not for your quest for settlements."

"The goal you seek is not far from ours. We will prosper in numbers."

"What if he is killed in this battle of yours?" Nerriviq demanded.

Amaruq gestured to me. "Then this woman will take us to Vidaris. She was lately in the same evil place."

Nerriviq examined me doubtfully. "She is not tainted?" he had to ask.

"Marja is sound, as you can see."

Nerriviq kept looking at me, and I tried to act like I was in full possession of my wits. "We intended to leave soon for Viinland," Nerriviq protested.

"Come with us to Markland first. You can win a winter settlement for your clan. Then we shall find your granddaughter and bring her back."

Nerriviq nodded shortly. "We will consider your offer. But this man will stay with me. He owes my clan a debt of honor."

I must have looked unhappy because Lexander gave me a slight shake of his head. I wanted nothing more than to rush into his arms and tend to him. But that was not to be.

Nerriviq stood up, tugging at Lexander's chain. "You hear that? Do you agree to help us win this battle? Then we'll fetch my granddaughter."

"As you say," Lexander responded, much as he had taught his slaves to reply. It saddened me to hear him so subdued.

Amaruq again put out his hand as if to stop me, this time touching me on the knee. It was a possessive gesture, and an intimate one for the Thule. No man would touch a woman's leg unless he was bedding her.

Lexander saw it, and a flash of anger lit his eyes. Suddenly he looked much bigger, as if he were ready to explode. He clearly thought that I had been coerced. I sat there helplessly, unable to explain what had happened between me and Amaruq.

But I had to assure him somehow. I mouthed, " 'Tis fine."

Lexander hesitated, but at my nod, he managed to restrain himself and turned away. He must have been think-

ing of Niall and how I had urged him to leave, willing to
take the abuse that would have surely followed.

As Lexander walked away with Nerriviq, my tears
threatened to spill. We were so close to our goal, yet it felt
as far away as ever.

Twenty-two

Silveta and I hardly fit inside the small tent that night with Amaruq and his men. The flies were so bad that we would have been eaten alive if we slept outside. Because of our close quarters, I didn't share furs with the elder. I was glad of that, preoccupied as I was by the heartrending sight of Lexander.

In the wan light when we awoke, the other Thule clans shared their meal with us. When Nerriviq finally joined us, he brought nine men, the most warriors sent by any clan. Amaruq had brought only four of his kin, including his middle son, who was full grown.

Lexander, Silveta, and I were placed in different boats for our journey through the long inlet to the ocean. We traveled much faster than our journey inland, sailing past low stony hills that were draped with patches of evergreen cover. With eight men in each boat, they took turns sleeping, leaning against each other's backs as they paddled late into the night.

I could only exchange glances with my master. I smiled in reassurance whenever I could. It was nearly impossible because the very sight of him pained me. It was not simply his strength that had been taxed, but his spirit as well. The demands of being a slave were wearing on him in countless ways, though he tried to conceal it.

On one of the few stops along the way, I managed to get close to Lexander. He put his unchained arm around me briefly. "I don't want them to know how close we are," he murmured. "They might take revenge on you."

I grimaced. "I've told Amaruq that you're my master."

He shook his head. "No more. I would not own a slave after this to save my life. You are a freewoman, Marja."

"But I belong to you," I protested.

"I thought I could protect you by being your master. I was afraid people would take advantage of you otherwise. But I see that is wrong. You are free to make your own choices, however you will."

He hugged me openly, the chain wrapping around my shoulder. I lifted my face to kiss him. His lips were so warm and tender. I could hardly believe I now kissed him as a freewoman. It was a little frightening. Part of me wanted to beg him to remain my master. What were we now if not master and slave?

"Did they hurt you?" he whispered.

"No," I assured him, hugging him tightly. "These people have treated me righteously, Lexander. They remind me of my mam."

"Even a merciful slavery is heinous," he retorted darkly.

Nerriviq appeared and ordered Lexander to return to their boat. He distrusted Lexander completely. Perhaps the Thule sensed his difference and felt the danger of having a godling in their midst. If Lexander did not have sympathy with their cause, he would not have remained bound. I had to be content knowing this was his choice of atonement, however difficult it was for both of us.

I smelled the open ocean long before we reached it; the salty breeze and smell of seabird colonies was unmistakable. The Thule stayed close to the coastline, paddling south just outside the breaking waves. The sun sank earlier every day. When it grew dark, the Thule returned to familiar coves where they could haul the *umiaks* out of the water. Without the terrible flies to bother us, we slept under the stars rolled in our furs, on ground that was finally firm. I was glad we didn't have to squeeze into the small tent anymore.

The next evening, when we reached our final stop in Helluland, the fog shrouded the northern peninsula of Markland across the strait. But with one sight of the smudge of land, I heard the *olfs* beckoning. They had been waiting for us. Our faithful witness sped away to join them, ecstatic at having returned home at last.

The Thule made camp among the thick patches of ground cover, while I once again tried to wander near Lexander. But Amaruq kept a wary eye on me. I was afraid that if I angered Amaruq, he might abandon our quest. He still doubted my motives, fearing he was leading his kin into some fearsome trap.

I was not surprised when Amaruq motioned for me to follow him over a slight rise into a protected cleft of the hills. He had his furs under one arm, ready to settle in for the night. At the top, I turned to see Lexander among the other men. He seemed alarmed, but I nodded and motioned to him that I was safe.

Sheltered by the rocky hillsides, Amaruq spread his furs on a mat of thick moss. It looked like it would be comfortable.

"Does your master allow you to share my furs?" Amaruq asked quietly.

I was instantly on guard. He believed I had been ordered to seduce him in order to gain the assistance of the Thule. Silveta had suspected the same.

"I do as I will," I declared. "Lexander has freed me."

Amaruq considered me, the crease deepening between his eyes. "Was your freedom a reward for accomplishing your task?"

I smiled. "No. Lexander has not given me an order since he sent me away from Vidaris. He cannot bear to enslave another while he endures it himself. I can see how it makes him heartsick. He wants only to free Qamaniq and the other slaves."

"Does Lexander have a stake in Markland?" Amaruq

demanded. "Will he marry Silveta? Or gain lands himself?"

That startled me. "No! The house of Vidaris was exiled from Markland by Silveta's husband. Lexander cannot show his face there. He assists Silveta only because I wish it. He would fain keep me from returning to that dangerous place, but I gave Silveta my pledge."

Amaruq slowly nodded. Several of the floating *olfs* were curious about our conversation, hovering intently. They reflected the absolute truth of my words to him.

"Do you wish to share his furs tonight?" Amaruq asked.

"Yes," I readily admitted, "but Nerriviq will not allow it."

"I would sleep with Keelat this night if she were here."

Since Amaruq was Thule, I had to consider that a proposition. "You know I would be delighted to please you, Amaruq."

He smiled slightly, sitting down on the furs. He gestured, and I sat down next to him. "I've noticed that you avoid speaking of your master. Do you not share intimacy with him as well?"

"Yes, whenever we can." I thought of the *knaar* and how we rutted in plain sight of the oarsmen and Silveta.

"I want to hear about that," Amaruq said. "When did you first know you loved him?"

"I'm not sure. It happened so gradually," I hedged.

Amaruq looked hard at me, waiting. I realized he would never be satisfied until he understood my connection to Lexander. He would accept no less. If I didn't meet this crucial test, he could abandon us here, while Nerriviq would take Lexander to Vidaris to fight for Qamaniq.

I drew a deep breath. How could I explain how tenderly Lexander had cared for me after Birgir beat me? Or how he had saved me from the fate of my slave-mates? "I can't say exactly when I began to love him. But something special happened between us last winter, before the new slaves arrived. He was taking me to his bed regularly, spending time with me alone during the day, and talking to me about things he read in his scrolls."

"Was he treating you differently than the other slaves?" Amaruq asked.

I had to admit, "Not really. It was actually the first season he began treating me the same as the others. Before then, he had mostly ignored me, setting for me impossible tasks that I tried to fulfill."

Amaruq furrowed his brow in confusion. "And this made you love him?"

"It called out my submissive tendencies. I didn't truly love him until we began sharing tenderness." I glanced down at my hands, thinking about those nights of passion during the cold season. "We used to stay in his room long into the morning sometimes, hiding away from everyone else. I know now that he was unhappy with his life as a slave master. But I didn't understand it then. He had everything any man could desire. But his consort was evil, and it must have sorely tried him in ways I never saw."

"When he hid away with you, was he satisfied?"

"I pleased him again and again," I said slowly. "I thought he was satisfied, but now, I think not. I remember one time we had slept very late, but it was unearthly quiet on the estate. I could see a fresh layer of snow coating the hills. He was sitting there, gazing outside. I went to him to put my arms around him from behind. I had learned he liked me taking liberties like that when we were alone."

I looked down at my hands again, remembering how I had caressed his neck and shoulders. "Unbeknownst to Lexander, I could see his face in the mirror propped by the washbasin. It had been angled slightly, just catching his reflection. You have to understand that my master's expression is always so controlled, as if he observes from a great distance. But as I touched him, kissing him lightly, thinking that he was everything in the world to me . . . his face seemed to crumple. He didn't move under my hands, but it was as if his *inua* peered out, revealing his misery and confusion in the tear that fell. Then I could tell he felt an immense relief at my touch. He grasped my hand, and without turning, kissed it." My throat caught. "He needed me, and I comforted him by being near. But he never knew that I saw it. When he finally did turn to me, he was back to his usual self."

"Did you bed him then?"

I nodded, feeling thoroughly exposed, feeling as if I had violated Lexander's trust by telling Amaruq. "We made love without words. It was the first time we truly came together as equals rather than master and slave."

Amaruq's hand stroked my cheek, his eyes seeing it all. Even my fear that I had betrayed Lexander by telling him.

I thought of nothing but Lexander, yet when Amaruq touched me, my body responded. Amaruq was my savior, bringing his family and friends to fight our battle and free my homeland. He had brought Lexander back to me. How could I not feel strongly for him?

Amaruq's fingers gently questioned my desire for him. I briefly closed my eyes, savoring the sensation. His touch transported me into that heady submissive state that was so enthralling. There was nothing I could do to fight it. Indeed, it was one of the most pure physical sensations I'd ever felt.

Amaruq was very dominant that night, as if responding instinctively to my need. I had only been a freewoman for a day, but I wanted to be taken by a virile man and claimed as his own. He clutched my hair in one hand, holding me still as he stared into my eyes.

At first I tried to stifle my sounds of excitement, hoping the others couldn't hear. Then I lost myself in the sensation. Undoubtedly the *olfs* relayed everything that we did to the rest of the Thule. I wished Lexander could know how good it felt so he would not worry about me. Then that thought was gone with all the others, and only pleasure remained.

Our rutting was fast and hard, most unlike Amaruq. He entered me in one long thrust, then could hardly contain himself to the finish. He seemed surprised himself at his powerful response, but was pleased nonetheless.

Afterwards I relaxed back into the fur nest he had made, breathless and heated. Contented. I sent out my farewell to the ice sprites, giving them praise for their assistance and promising to return to them someday.

I hardly spoke to Silveta before we climbed back into the boats. I expected her to disapprove of my rutting with Amaruq, but she merely smiled at me and reached out to touch my arm. Oddly enough, I think she was grateful. But my passion with Amaruq had less to do with obtaining his help for our quest and more to do with my own desires.

On the other hand, in order to gain Amaruq's trust I had revealed something about Lexander that even he wasn't aware I knew. I felt uneasy, certain that I had betrayed Lexander.

Lexander was truly upset. He must have sensed my guilt and my desire to confess. I had never seen him show his feelings so openly. It was as if he couldn't control himself. In every glance, every frown, I saw his anger.

We didn't have a chance to speak all day as the boats entered the Klaro Strait. The clamoring of the Markland *olfs* grew more triumphant as we sailed southward. I concentrated on the sea spirits, asking for their help to make our small boats pass swiftly without being seen. The spirits responded to my pleas by sending a strong current to carry us rapidly down the Markland coast. I wasn't certain when we passed by Jarnby, but I could feel the presence of my mam somewhere nearby. I refrained from trying to reach her through the sea spirits, knowing that she would only feel my turmoil if I did.

The spirits did tell me of other boats on the waters, filled with men who carried shields and long spears. Some were Birgir's warriors coming back to stand by his side to hold Tillfallvik and proclaim him chieftain. Others held local magnates and their *bondi*. And there were others I sensed farther to the south. I wondered if Birgir had indeed brought his war to Viinland after we had disappeared.

With the generous aid of the sea spirits, we reached southern Markland that night. The Thule used the light of the *olfs* to find a series of rocky islands off the coast not far from the mouth of Tillfallvik Bay. The shores were covered with tall black-and-white seabirds. My mam said they were part seal and part bird so they could swim through the water like it was air. The sea god of the tides, Alanerk, was said to have created them as the epitome of his realm. Since the birds were a symbol of joy, I took the sound of their harsh barking calls as good luck.

The Thule beached in a deserted cove protected between several islands from sight of both the ocean and the shoreline of Markland. The Thule did not try to build fires with the sparse foliage. These barren knobs were deserted except for us and Alanerk's creatures. I enjoyed seeing the craggy hills rising around us after the endless flat vistas of Helluland and the ocean.

Silveta stayed near my side, as usual. "I know these islands. Tillfallvik is just west of here. Why are we stopping now?"

The Thule were subdued, preparing mentally for the coming battle. "They're planning to attack tomorrow."

Silveta's expression was wry. "They've already made their plans? Without consulting me?"

Disregarding Nerriviq's attempt to stop her, Silveta marched past him and his men to confront Lexander. "Tell me, what are they planning to do?"

Nerriviq glowered at Silveta, shouting at her though she couldn't understand. "You'll not conspire to free this man! My granddaughter must be returned to our clan."

I assured him, "Silveta wants only to know how you intend to attack Tillfallvik. She may have insight that can help you."

Amaruq joined us, clearly seeing a need to mediate. "We will rest here for a short while, then sail to Tillfallvik before dawn. We'll attack the estate at first light."

I translated for Silveta, as Lexander added, "They'll need you and Marja to make contact with the townsfolk while I'm taking them to the estate. You must tell everyone that the Thule are fighting on your side."

Silveta nodded eagerly. "Let me and Marja go tonight. I

can rally the loyal *bondi* and get information about Birgir's strength and position within the estate."

When I passed along her request, Amaruq did not like it. He shook his head curtly. "No one must be forewarned."

I explained to Silveta, "He thinks you might set a trap for his men. He doesn't completely trust us."

"Then how are we to get help for them in time?" she asked despairingly. "They don't know what they'll face."

Lexander spoke again, this time in Skraeling to appease Nerriviq. "That is the way of battle. We will adjust our strategy to what we find. You should concentrate on how to keep the townsfolk from attacking the Skraeling. If that happens, these men are ready to withdraw with all haste. We will be abandoned."

I nodded slowly, considering that terrible possibility. When I explained it to Silveta, she suggested, "We could make several banners with Ejegod's signet, the great horned bull, and mount them on long poles. The Skraelings could carry them."

"That might slow down the Noromenn, at least," Lexander agreed.

I explained to Amaruq. "Silveta's totem will protect you if you carry its image."

None of the Skraeling had any affiliation with the spirit of the bull, but they understood the need to appease the spirits in the place where they sought victory. Leather was quickly gathered and cut to Silveta's specifications under the flickering light of a few torches.

Nerriviq was appeased by Silveta's offer of protection. He stayed nearby watching, but he didn't interfere anymore. Lexander spoke to us only about constructing the banners. But his resentment was clear.

That worried Silveta. "Do you think we'll fail?" she finally asked him. "Tell me if I have brought all these good men into certain death."

I knew she was remembering Perus and her other bondsmen. Silveta was headstrong and stubborn, but blessed with an admirably acute conscience.

"No, your plan is sound," Lexander assured her. "This is

a stronger warband than I had hoped for. As long as the townsfolk help us, we have a chance of success."

"Then why do you look so . . . so bleak?"

He refused to look at me. "I question your tactics." At Silveta's confusion, he added, "Did you have to thrust Marja into that man's bed to seal your agreement with him?"

My eyes opened wide. Silveta protested. "If you think that was my doing, you're daft, man! Marja arranged everything herself."

Now he looked at me. "You've been so conflicted, I can tell, Marja. Do not deny it. This morning when you returned, I could see how tormented you were."

"I've been worried about *you*," I protested. "I know that slavery is wearing on you sorely."

He shook his head. "There is more to it than that, Marja."

I couldn't confess my betrayal in front of Silveta, for that would unfairly expose him to her. "The Thule would never abuse me," I insisted. "I truly desired Amaruq, or he could not have responded. I had to be completely honest with him to win his trust."

Lexander was not convinced, sensing that I was withholding the truth. For once our wordless understanding was not enough.

Silveta turned her head aside irritably at being unjustly accused. "I left Marja in my bed last midsummer, full knowing what Birgir would do if he found her. For that, you can be angry at me, Lexander. But I've spoken my mind ever since for her to stand up for herself and stop using her body as common coin."

"I would have died in Brianda if I hadn't relied on my talents," I pointed out.

Silveta ignored me, shaking her finger at Lexander. "It's your fault in the first place for tossing her out of Vidaris to make her own way to me. What did you think she was going to do after all your *training*?"

"You cannot conceive how difficult that was," Lexander

retorted through gritted teeth. "The alternative was worse. If I had not prepared a plausible excuse, Helanas would have immediately pursued us with all vengeance."

"I'm glad you sent me away," I put in. "I would never have seen so much if you hadn't."

Silveta still glared at him. "You left us stuck with these Skraelings, Lexander, in that terrible, desolate place. We had to fend for ourselves. Marja did everything! She made an even better agreement than the one I had with Issland. If she had to bed their leader to do it, then that's fine by me."

"But you were upset about it," I pointed out.

"I'm not anymore." Finally Silveta looked at me. "If I regain my estate, it's because of you. Who am I to question your methods? Talking to *olfs*—after all of this, I can respect that." She smiled. "I actually like the idea that there are some little creatures who watch out for me. Apparently I need all the help I can get."

The *olfs* were so happy to be acknowledged that they began spinning. I knew it would give them strength for the morrow.

But Silveta wasn't finished. "Marja, you've been more loyal to me than my own family. Whatever you need, I'll not forget what you've done for me. You'll never be a slave as long as you're in Markland."

I took Silveta's hands, choked with emotion.

But Lexander declared, "Marja is already free. She can choose for herself. I would not presume to command her."

He walked away, carrying the banners over to the Thule to be tied on the long poles. Silveta glanced after him, her tone sad. "He is upset about your intimacy with Amaruq. I would not have thought it of him. He of all people should not be possessive of you. But he truly loves you."

Soon after, we laid out our furs directly on the granite for our short rest. I curled up next to Silveta but didn't sleep. All I could think about was the impending battle. Any of these men could die. Lexander would be in danger. And I shuddered to think of our fate in Birgir's hands if Silveta and I were captured. I did not want to return!

While I dreaded Tillfallvik, the *olfs* were quite cheerful simply because we had returned. They continued gathering from far and wide. Only their luminous light gave me the strength to wait for the signal to arise.

When it came, the men prepared for battle in full dark. I could see well enough by the light of the *olfs,* as could the Skraelings. Only Silveta stumbled and struggled, as always, unaware that she was the only blind one among us. I was sorry that Lexander made no effort to speak to me alone before we set off. I felt it boded ill for us.

As our boats silently slipped into the mouth of the bay, heading for Tillfallvik, I sensed something new through the water. The sea spirits were notoriously lax about events that happened on land, so I had received no clearer picture of the town except that there had been fighting.

But now I realized the warriors who guarded the docks were wearing the heavy leather armor and the metal helms marking them as Birgir's men. It seemed that the magnates had responded too slowly, though they had been alerted by Ejegod's quick messengers. Birgir must have planned well with his warriors, for they held the Tillfallvik waterfront in strength as the magnates had arrived one by one. Most of the magnates loyal to Ejegod had turned back at the sight of the warriors rather than face a massacre. Those who were loyal to Birgir had landed and paid homage to their new chieftain.

I saw it in a flash, in all its horrid misery for the townsfolk. "Birgir's men are guarding the docks," I said aloud. "They have control of Tillfallvik."

Amaruq shifted next to me. "You can see this?"

"Yes, through the water. They have shields on their chests that will deflect your arrows."

Amaruq gestured to his son, who gave a low owl cry through his cupped hands. The boats gathered close together as he explained the situation to his men. *Olfs* hovered over nearly every man, prepared to light their way.

The Thule decided to split into two groups, intending to land on either side of the town, where they would be concealed from the docks. They would approach the docks by land.

Silveta and I were taken to the leeward side of Tillfallvik, close to the river, where we had emerged from the hills the night we escaped. I wished the Thule could simply retrace our steps and attack the estate from its vulnerable rear, but Amaruq said it was better to deal with Birgir's men in two smaller groups rather than all at once. Attacking the estate first would leave the Thule exposed from behind.

When we landed, Silveta took my hand tightly in a nervous grip. Lexander was with the other group of Thule. I wished I'd had the chance to tell him I loved him before he went into danger. What if he paid the ultimate price for Markland's freedom? I would never forgive myself for insisting that Amaruq bring him with us.

Several of the youngest Thule, mere boys, were sent with us to alert the townsfolk. Silveta led us in a scrambling run in the dark, up a familiar lane toward Torgils' house. But now the town was empty without all the animals and carts that used to crowd the muddy roads. There was a barren look to the place with many of the buildings boarded up.

A loud groaning sound echoed through the town, and I knew it was the Skraeling gods. "Do you hear that?" I demanded, stopping Silveta. "Foretelling many deaths . . ."

" 'Tis but the wind in the eaves," she protested. But the Skraeling boys held their knives more firmly, as if prepared to face the worst. They and the *olfs* knew I spoke the truth.

Silveta's hasty knock was answered by a man I didn't recognize. Apparently, neither did Silveta. She backed away.

In the small circle of light cast by the candle, the man's eyes widened. I thought for a moment that we had stumbled onto a nest of Birgir's bondsmen as he mouthed Silveta's name in disbelief. "We thought you dead, *freya*! It is said you leaped to your death from the bastion. . . ."

"I escaped from the overlord," Silveta told him. "I've brought warriors."

He ushered us inside, where Silveta was greeted with even more amazement by Torgils. The Skraeling boys were eyed suspiciously, but when Silveta hastily explained the battle plan, Torgils called for his weapons. There were only a few men with him, and I remembered with a pang how many had filled the longhouse the last time we were here.

"Gather the loyalists," Torgils ordered them. "We'll meet at the marketplace to keep the warriors from retreating to the estate. By the gods, *this* is what I longed to do all these days! Well done, *freya*."

As we impatiently waited in Torgils' home for the other men to gather, I realized the Skraelings were already at work. The *olfs* showed me their shadowed forms creeping along the waterfront, approaching the docks. Birgir's warriors seemed unaware of the danger, with most sleeping. A handful were on guard, but several were playing at dice, huddled together and ignoring the darkness over the water.

My eyes glazed as everything else disappeared except for the impending fight. Skraelings notched their arrows, sending *olfs* dashing ahead to light their targets. Nearly three-score warriors were lying on mats on the ground, prepared to leap into action at the first alert. Their weapons lay beside them, reflecting the dim light of the *olfs*.

Amaruq gestured to his men to take their positions. They crouched tensely in the night with only the lapping of the waves to tell them they were close to the water. A soft hoot from Amaruq was echoed by other Skraelings, carrying the sound to the men who had approached from the other side of the docks.

The Skraelings notched their arrows, pointing them high so they would arch down into the mass of warriors. I held my breath as the signal went out. Arrows were loosed and a rain of death fell on Birgir's men.

Screams pierced the night. Many of the arrows fell harmlessly, but others found their mark. Men writhed on the ground, clutching their bellies and legs. Some lay still with shafts protruding from their prone bodies. Though death was a fearsome sight, I felt my heart racing with excitement.

The rest of the warriors leaped into action, snatching up their weapons and frantically trying to find their attackers in the darkness. The savvy ones shouted, "Cover your heads with your shields, men!"

They were just in time to stop another rain of arrows that fell among them. More shrill cries shattered the night. But the warriors were now forewarned and they gathered in a defensive line to fend off the Skraelings.

Then the *olfs* showed me something that almost made me swoon—Lexander knelt at the back of the line of Skraelings, far away from Amaruq. Nerriviq stood over him, a heavy knife raised high. He brought the knife slashing down toward Lexander's throat.

I screamed out loud, thinking Nerriviq had betrayed Lexander and was taking his life. But Lexander didn't flinch as the knife arched down in front of him and hit the chain that lay against a rock. Sparks flew as the links broke and the chain was severed from the metal band around his arm. Lexander stood up, meeting Nerriviq's eyes squarely as he took the knife as his weapon. He intended to join the fight!

Silveta shook my shoulder hard. "Marja! What ails you?"

I lost my link with the *olfs* and was back inside Torgils' home. The men were staring at me. "The Skraelings have attacked the docks!" I exclaimed. "We must hurry to help them."

Torgils frowned at my proclamation, but he shouted for the men who had arrived to follow him. Silveta was urged to stay where it was safe, but she shook them off unheeding. With Lexander in danger on the docks, nothing could stop me from accompanying them there.

We rushed down the steep street as the sky was beginning to lighten. Sounds of the high-pitched Thule war cry rose as we neared the marketplace. *Olfs* skimmed along above us, but they were increasingly subdued by the death that was being dealt.

"Stand back!" Torgils roared to Silveta.

The townsfolk rushed past us into battle, brandishing their axes and swords. More were arriving every minute, and I grabbed Silveta's arm. "This way," I urged, knowing where there was a vantage point from the images I received from the *olfs*. Birgir's warriors were being slowly driven away from the water by the Skraelings.

We ran around a row of buildings, and suddenly the sounds of fighting grew louder. At the end of the lane, where it opened into the marketplace, a clump of townsfolk closed in on the warriors wearing breastplates and helms. Then another flurry of arrows appeared, arching down into the mass of Birgir's warriors. At least five went down screaming and clutching their necks or arms.

The remaining warriors turned and ran straight into the townsfolk, who were armed and ready. Their weapons clashed with the high-pitched ringing of metal. I saw Torgils raise his sword and bring it down on someone; then he was gone in the shifting bodies.

I clasped my hands together, pleading with the *olfs*, "Don't let them shoot!" I was afraid the Skraelings would massacre the townsfolk who were trying to help them. Somehow my plea must have gotten through because no more arrows fell from the sky.

Silveta started forward as the townsfolk drove the warriors back toward the docks. I cringed at the sight of *adlets* hovering over the wounded. The shadowy creatures were sinking down to drink in the blood and agony. The wounded were all Noromenn, no Skraeling that I could see. The *olfs* were fleeing from the marketplace, driven by the pain that drenched the area.

By the time we crossed the open marketplace, the battle on the waterfront was over. All of Birgir's men were down, dead or wounded. Skraelings were kneeling beside each body, jerking their arrows from their wounds. Blood and worse spilled onto the dirt.

I looked anxiously for Lexander, and found him near Amaruq. He had acquired an ax and a long sword, and both were bloody. The chain dangled from the metal collar and swung at his waist, freeing him to fight. His cloak was gone, but the leather cap still concealed his smooth head.

The townsfolk gathered uneasily in front of the Skraelings, eyeing the threatening bristle of spears and long bows. But the crude banners that the Thule carried, displaying the shape of a bull, were unmistakable signs of their support for Silveta.

Lexander began translating between Amaruq and Torgils, so Silveta and I quickly joined them.

"Birgir has nearly seventy men inside the estate," Torgils explained.

"The sentries must have alerted Birgir by now," Lexander said. "A frontal assault on the estate could be disastrous."

I nervously eyed the hilltop that hid the estate from view. Surely Birgir had placed sentries up there to watch what happened on the docks. A warlord such as he would not dare be caught by surprise.

"Take the Skraelings to the rear," Torgils decided. "We'll attack the estate from two places. You go first, and we'll wait until men are drawn from the front gate; then we'll move in. Make some noise so we can hear."

Lexander looked doubtful, but every second they delayed gave Birgir more time to prepare. He quickly explained to Amaruq, who gestured to the Skraelings. They melted away, heading inland.

Lexander glanced at me as he left, and I put my fingertips to my mouth, wanting to kiss him. But he turned away. Dozens of *olfs* appeared and darted after them, leaving only a few behind to protect the Thule wounded. As for the Noromenn, those who were not dead yet would soon be struggling under the *adlets'* otherworldly assault.

I wanted to go with the Skraelings, but Silveta could not

manage the rough terrain in the darkness. And I couldn't leave her alone. The sounds of the crying, cursing wounded echoed after us as we followed the growing crowd of townsfolk, men and women alike. Many carried ordinary tools—pitchforks or long wood axes. They looked grimly ready to strike a blow against the tyrant who had killed so many of their kin. From their lean, haggard faces, it appeared that Birgir's war had cost them more than anyone else in Markland.

We ran up the sloping streets to the chieftain's estate. It was on the top of a tall hill, giving Birgir the advantage. A blackened ring of exposed ground surrounded the palisade. Under Ejegod's rule, it had been overgrown with evergreens and shrubs, but Birgir's men had burned everything back in a wide swath to better defend the estate. It looked formidable.

The men conferred, then crept closer, taking cover behind the fences and buildings of Tillfallvik. Silveta and I were too far back to see anything but the townsfolk ahead of us. They were carrying ladders, which they expected to use to breach the walls. There was no sound from behind the palisade. The *olfs* drifted up and over the top.

"Warriors are there, waiting for us to attack," I whispered to Silveta.

Her eyes shifted. "It was too much to hope we could catch him unawares."

I had no doubt who she meant. Birgir was inside those walls. I shivered at the thought of facing him. I had done everything I could to bring this about, but now it was beyond my control. The only thing I could do was pray to Ignirtoq, the god of light and truth, to right this terrible wrong that Birgir had done.

In the distance rose the sound of unearthly wailing. It roared louder and higher than I thought possible, going on and on. Fear clutched my heart as I imagined the vengeance of a god descending on the Skraelings. Perhaps this was the sound the Kristna god made as he smote Birgir's enemies . . .

But the *olfs* showed me the truth. A few Skraelings were

swinging long cords in circles over their heads, making the horrid wailing sound. Birgir's men inside the palisade trembled in fear, shrinking back from their posts. The Skraelings sent scores of arrows over the palisade, guided by the *olfs* to hit their targets. Many of the arrows bounced harmlessly off the warriors' metal helms. They crouched beneath their round shields to outwait the deadly rain.

The Skraelings took advantage of this and raced toward the palisade. They began nimbly climbing the logs, cresting the top with their spears held ready. Birgir's warriors met them with cries of encouragement to their fellows as they tried to stem the tide of Skraelings spilling over the top.

"What's happening?" Silveta demanded, shaking me from my trance.

"They're going over the palisade," I told her.

The townsfolk froze around us, waiting for the signal to attack.

The familiar screams of battle rose in the distance. *"Lexander,"* I breathed. How could he escape this maelstrom unharmed? I pleaded with the *olfs* to show me Lexander, but they were so disturbed by the violence that they sent me no vision in return. I shook in fear, silently pleading with the Skraeling gods to protect him.

The warriors behind the front gate began moving toward the rear of the estate to fight off the incursion. *Olfs* floated deeper inside, spinning to urge us forward. Silveta and I clutched each other tighter.

At a signal from Torgils, the townsfolk erupted from their hiding places, running to the gate with their weapons. Silveta and I hurried to the last protecting wall where we could see. The townsfolk propped their ladders against the palisade and began climbing up. It was so smoothly done that I felt a spurt of hope.

Then a few of Birgir's men appeared at the top. They threw down large rocks, hitting several of the men who were halfway up. Others shoved the ladders to one side or toppled them over on their back. Cries burst out and men fell limply to the ground.

"They're killing them!" Silveta said.

I kept her from rising. "Don't let them see you!" Doubt-less Birgir would order his men out in force if he knew Silveta was here. She was the ultimate prize that all now fought over.

Frightened by a rain of hefty rocks, the townsfolk had no choice but to flee back to the safety of the buildings. Some dragged their wounded neighbors out of danger. Even the *olfs* retreated, no longer joyous. There was too much blood on the ground for that. I felt much the same way.

"Maybe the Skraelings are beating them . . ." Silveta started, then cocked her head.

"I don't hear anything," I agreed.

"Are they inside?" Silveta asked.

It wasn't long before we learned the truth. Lexander returned with several dozen Skraelings. Silveta and I ran to join Torgils to listen to their deliberations.

"They've raised the palisade in the rear," Lexander was saying quietly. "We can't get in that way. The Skraelings are gathering logs to make ramps to get over, but the estate is well defended."

Torgils frowned as he nodded. "Have them bring around a couple of stout logs. We need battering rams to get through the gate."

Lexander passed on the request. "The Skraelings aren't going to be much help in such close quarters."

"Tell them to hang back and pick off any warriors who poke their heads above the palisade. We could also use a phalanx of Skraeling with spears to clear a path through them once the gate is open."

Silveta had her hands clasped together tightly, flinching at the cries of the wounded around us. "We've lost so many people! How can we possibly win?"

"We need help," Lexander agreed. "Can't you rally more townsfolk?"

Torgils glanced from side to side. "Shall we sacrifice our children, too? Any who are able-bodied are already here."

"This is dreadful," Silveta cried.

"You wanted war," Lexander pointed out.

"No," I countered, "she wanted to save our land."

Torgils grunted. "Then it looks as if we are the ones to try." His fond gaze rested on Silveta. "It gives me heart that you returned, *freya*. With a warband of Skraelings, no less! You are truly fit to rule Markland. I only wish we could give you what you deserve."

Shouts went up, and for a moment I thought Birgir was attacking. But everyone pointed in the opposite direction. The misty morning light glinted off the waves of the bay down below.

"Ships!" Silveta exclaimed.

We retreated to a street where we could see the waterfront. Two *knaars* moved swiftly for such deep hulls because there were many men rowing them.

"That's the overlord's crest," said sharp-eyed Lexander.

"Oh, no . . ." I moaned. I doubted the overlord would be content to shut us in a tower this time. But I would rather risk my life in his hands than in Birgir's.

"Why has the overlord come here?" Torgils demanded.

"To seal his bargain with Birgir, no doubt," Lexander replied grimly. "But Jedvard rarely leaves the bastion . . ."

"What are we to do?" Silveta asked.

Lexander considered it. "To be sure, Birgir has already seen them sailing into the bay. Torgils, keep the warriors bottled up inside while I go down to the docks."

I wasn't about to be left behind. Silveta and I held on to each other for balance as we dashed down the muddy roads after him.

A dozen Skraelings were concealed near the waterfront, their arrows notched and ready to fly. As we ran up to the docks, Silveta gasped and cried out. Tears flowed down her cheeks and her knees gave way.

I thought she was overcome. I helped her sit down on the wooden planks. "Are you ill, Silveta?"

"Don't you see! It's *Jens*," she exclaimed, pointing out to the *knaars*.

"It *is* Jens!" I agreed. Not the overlord, but the overlord's generous young son.

I pulled Silveta to her feet, and she waved and called out

to Jens. He stood on the side of the ship, holding on to the prow. In spite of her Skraeling parka and pants, he recognized Silveta. Perhaps it was the spill of her golden hair, or it could have been something more.

"Thank the gods, it is *him*," Silveta exclaimed. In her voice I heard the wonder she felt.

Twenty-three

When the boat landed, Silveta's first words were, "You've come to save me yet again, Jens?"

I understood why she was overwhelmed by the sight of him. None of her own family had helped her, but this young man had come to her rescue, looking so proud. From his gauntlets to his plumed helm, he was magnificent. He wore a silver chest plate with links of chain mail sheathing his arms and thighs. His sword and shield looked as if they had seen some wear, even if it had been only in training sessions.

"*Freya* Silveta, you were promised a warband by my father, the overlord," Jens said formally, yet with a glint in his eye. "I am here to deliver it to your service."

"But your father denied me."

"I am fulfilling the promise he made you," Jens assured her. "These men are in my employ."

Silveta's eyes shone. "You've proven yourself truer than any man in Viinland."

"I've been waiting for your return," Jens assured her. "I've kept my men encamped in the islands. When my sentries reported there was fighting on the waterfront, I knew it must be your doing."

Lexander nodded to Jens, vastly relieved. "Birgir and his men are holed up in the estate. We've attacked with the townsfolk and a warband of Skraeling, but we can't get inside."

Jens' hired men had disembarked and were lining up for the march through the town to the estate. I counted eighty men, all in good condition and wearing strong breastplates and helms. Their axes looked very sharp, and they grunted to each other, posturing in preparation for battle. These mercenaries seemed rather cheerful over the prospect. The docks couldn't be spied from the estate because of the hills that lay between, but Birgir must have seen the ships sailing in and knew a mighty warband had landed.

"We were just about to ram down the front gate to get inside," Lexander added.

"But Birgir's men are dropping stones to drive everyone away," Silveta protested.

Lexander was not concerned. "The Skraelings can shoot anyone who shows his head."

Silveta was clearly worried about Jens, just as I feared that Lexander wouldn't survive the fighting. "Can't Jens claim he's an emissary from the overlord?" Silveta asked. "Perhaps Birgir would let them inside."

Lexander considered it, but the *olfs* showed me that was a massacre in the waiting. "No," I protested. "Birgir is under siege. He won't let down his guard for anyone."

Jens agreed. "No fighting man would. We will make a frontal assault, and I've brought the men to do it."

Silveta wrung her hands but didn't gainsay her savior. I added, "We must warn the townsfolk or they may try to fight you off."

"And the Skraelings," Silveta added. But I knew the *olfs* had already told them help was on the way.

Jens grinned. "You go first to tell them reinforcements have arrived. They can follow my warband inside the estate."

Silveta was standing so close to him that they could have kissed. But she was too shy in front of all the mercenaries. Lexander and I exchanged a glance, knowing that that wouldn't have stopped us. Suddenly, we were in accord again. I slipped my hand into his and felt him squeeze mine tightly.

"Take care of her," Jens told Lexander, his eyes only for Silveta.

"I will," Lexander swore.

We alerted Torgils and the townsfolk, who let out glad cries at the news. Amaruq nodded shortly when his part in the attack was described. The *olfs* had shown me that some Skraelings had died when they tried to breach the palisade in the rear. They would be in danger again, but they were sorely needed. The townsfolk separated to take their places, awaiting the arrival of Jens and his warband.

Lexander remained with me and Silveta, which was a relief to both of us. We watched from a low roof where he had lifted us for safety. We could see the main street leading to the estate, and from one corner was a view of the gate.

Jens came striding up the road, looking like a true conqueror. A boy ran along next to him, carrying the banner with the overlord's crest quartered with Jen's seabird signet.

Torgils had left the two stout logs in the lane for the Viinland mercenaries. They were tied around with rope, with long lines for the men to hold. A full dozen men picked up each log, standing side by side. The Skraelings stayed hidden out of sight.

Jens formed his men behind those with the battering rams, then called out, "Forward!"

As his warband crossed the open space around the palisade, Birgir's warriors peered over the top. There were more of them now than before. One large rock was thrown down, striking against the helm of a Viinland mercenary.

The Skraelings took that as a signal and began to fire their arrows. Cries came from behind the palisade, and soon no heads lifted above the protecting wood. But Birgir's men continued to throw rocks over, aiming them to land in front of the gate.

Jens shouted a command and other mercenaries rushed forward, protecting the men with the battering rams by holding their shields overhead. The rain of rocks sounded like an avalanche.

But Jens' men moved forward steadily despite the assault. Every time one fell, another quickly took his place.

Silveta's eyes were wide. "Oh, Jens! Stay back," she murmured.

But the valiant young man was in the thick of things, directing his men. The early-morning sun shone off his helm, polished to a mirror.

The battering rams were quickly positioned and soon the rhythmic pounding drowned out the sound of rocks hitting their metal armor. Each log was aimed against one half of the gate. The mercenaries let the logs swing far back, then drove them forward into the stout fortress.

"It's bowing," I exclaimed. Indeed, light could be seen between the two halves of the gate.

Jens urged his men on, and their shouts rose. A splintering sound shattered the morning as the great timbers of the gate strained under the beating.

As if in response, more rocks showered down from above. The Skraelings let loose their arrows in a constant stream, sending them arching over the palisade and down behind. The screams within told their own story. Some of the arrows stuck into the top where they didn't quite surmount the palisade. The *olfs* told me the Thule would soon be out of arrows and then Birgir's men would be free to give their missiles deadly aim.

"It's not working," Silveta cried, trying to see Jens in the midst of the milling mercenaries.

"No, they're breaking through," Lexander insisted.

With a mighty heave of the ram, one half of the gate broke at its hinges, sagging drunkenly. Another few strokes and it broke completely, swiveling on its remaining hinge and the heavy crossbar that locked it from within.

Jens shouted, "That's it, men! Break it down!"

They rammed against the gate harder now that success was assured. Suddenly the fall of rocks ceased. The *olfs* told me there was confusion within, but Birgir was likely rally-

ing his men into defensive positions. The warlord would
not give up so easily.

With a terrible ripping sound, as if a huge tree were top-
pling over, the mercenaries smashed the gate down.

"They're through!" Silveta exclaimed. "No, Jens, don't—"

Jens was one of the first over the splintered remnants as
his men poured inside the estate in a rush. A fresh rain of
rocks fell down, and the mercenaries held their shields
over their heads to protect themselves. But the Skraelings
also rushed forward, and aimed their last arrows through
the open gate directly into the mass of men on the scaffolding at the top of the palisade.

Shouts filled the air as Birgir's men fell back under the
onslaught. It was a complete melee, with axes clashing
against shields and men falling from the scaffolding.

We watched breathlessly as Jens' mercenaries pushed
Birgir's warriors ever deeper into the estate. Torgils and
the townsfolk rushed through the gate when it was clear.
Their shouts and brandished pitchforks seemed all the
more fearsome.

"Are they winning?" Silveta gasped.

"The first battle, yes," Lexander agreed. "But there are
many warriors inside that estate."

Sometime during the struggle, Lexander's arm had gone
around my shoulders, and he didn't let go. I snuggled in
close, knowing how much he had feared for me while we
were separated. Though he had been the one in battle, he
had worried about *me*.

He silently kissed the top of my head, pressing his face
into my hair. I felt the copper collar around his wrist digging into my arm.

Silveta was engrossed in trying to see through the gate,
but the fighting had moved deeper behind the wall. The
only sight left was the forlorn forms of men lying in their
own blood. "What is happening?" Silveta cried impatiently.
"I can't bear this."

She moved as if to jump down and run into the estate,
but Lexander held her back. " 'Tis too dangerous for you.
With you as hostage, Birgir could still win this battle."

Silveta was in agony, holding her hands to her mouth in shock. I took a deep breath and humbly asked the *olfs* for a glimpse of the fighting inside. They responded, though many had been driven away from the estate by the ferocious killing.

Birgir had retreated with his closest bondsmen to the fire hall to make his last stand. Through my communion with the *olfs*, I watched as the great doors were soon battered open. They were fighting in such close quarters I couldn't tell the mercenaries from Birgir's warriors.

Then I saw Niall being backed into the fire hall. He fought beside Birgir, a wild grin on his face. The evil had taken him completely, and he laughed as he dealt death to the mercenaries with his ax.

I gasped as Torgils rose before Niall, afraid the good bondsman would be struck down. But Torgils parried Niall's strikes, ignoring his berserker rage. I silently begged the *olfs* not to flee the fray but to help Silveta's bondsman. She would loathe losing another loyal man to Birgir's madness.

One *olf*, smaller than the rest, heeded my pleas. It darted in and tangled itself in Niall's feet. As the dark-haired man went down, disbelief in his face, Torgils moved in. With a swipe of his ax, he split Niall nearly in two. Torgils' expression was grim, as if he disliked his duty but knew it must be done.

"They're in the fire hall!" I could see Niall's death spasms, his teeth bared in agony. "Niall has been killed by Torgils."

Silveta grabbed my arm hard. "Jens! Where is Jens?"

I stared into the sky, seeing only what lay within the fire hall. Torgils joined Jens, who was facing down Birgir himself. One of their mercenaries protected Jens' other side. Together the three of them pressed their advantage.

Birgir seemed to grow larger by the moment, swelling from the power of the evil within him. His weapons sparked fire as they landed against his attackers' swords. The man seemed to have no thought of defeat. Nay, he shouted his defiance in their face. "I am Chieftain of Markland! I will take your wives and daughters for my own pleasure!"

For a moment, I thought the evil that possessed him was too strong. Birgir leaped to the dais, swinging his ax in broad swaths, striking the mercenary and taking him down.

I almost could not recognize Jens—he was no longer a boy. Birgir's ax glanced off the strong chain mail on his arm, bruising but not cutting through. Jens didn't let that stop him. He risked certain death by leaping within Birgir's reach, slashing the big man's legs with his sword. Torgils shoved Jens aside at the last moment, preventing Birgir's ax from splitting his head in two.

Birgir roared in pain as his legs buckled underneath him. Torgils caught his ax on his own, hooking the blade to keep the warlord from swinging it against Jens. Jens righted himself and brought his own ax down on Birgir's bowed shoulders. The blade bit deeply into Birgir's neck.

The blood seemed to fill my own eyes, as Birgir slowly toppled. He rolled as he landed, looking up at the youth who had beaten him. His tongue protruded, and I could see the evil light in his eyes long after his *inua* began to fade. The spark of Kristna embraced his *inua* and carried it away. So the god had truly dwelled in Birgir, yet it had not been powerful enough to resist the evil that had infested him. As terrible as the sight was, at least it would replace that indelible image of Birgir's gloating face as he raped me.

"Birgir's dead!" I gasped.

The *olfs* couldn't stand such noxious matters and my vision of the fire hall vanished. I could still see Birgir's eyes, though, and knew I always would. The evil that had infested him had been strong enough to bring a nation to its knees. But we had prevailed.

"Is it true?" Silveta cried. "Oh, by the mercy of all the gods, say it is true!"

I sagged against Lexander, ravaged from my contact with the *olfs* under such a terrible onslaught. He held me tenderly, murmuring words of love that soothed my sore spirit.

*   *   *

When Jens finally returned, his grim expression made him look more like his father. Silveta cried out, clutching my arm in fear. I also trembled, wondering if somehow worse was yet to come.

But Jens brightened when he saw Silveta. "It is done," he quietly declared.

Apparently the violence had changed Jens. The *olfs* stayed at a distance. They could feel the difference in him. Jens had been their favored child, but he had dealt death today and that left a taint in his spirit. I knew it would take time for him to be truly cleansed from his deeds this day.

Silveta jumped from the roof into Jens' arms. She clung to him as Lexander lightly dropped down, lifting me off himself. His hands around my waist made me feel safe.

"Birgir is truly dead?" Silveta asked.

"Yes, though it's not a fair sight for your eyes. I've ordered a mass grave dug for the warlord and his men in the hillside beyond. They don't deserve an honorable burning."

"I need to see him," Silveta declared.

I nodded agreement, too choked to speak.

Jens protested, but Lexander took one look at us and declared, "They must see him, Jens. Take us there."

Puffed up in his newfound manliness, Jens would have tried to protect us. But he couldn't withstand Lexander. " 'Tis on your head," he warned Lexander.

Jens led us into the estate. I gasped on seeing the dead and writhing wounded littering the ground. Birgir's warriors were left slaughtered where they lay, while Skraelings and the mercenaries tended their own.

I didn't see Amaruq, but I ran up to his son. "How many did we lose?"

"Eight of our own have departed for the Otherworld."

"Amaruq?" I cried, wishing I had thought to ask the *olfs* to help the generous elder. How could I have forgotten him?

"He lives." My relief was so profound I couldn't speak.

Amaruq's son shuffled away with a Thule I barely recognized. His leg was bloody.

"I lost nearly two score men," Jens added. "And more are wounded. They fought superbly."

"I shall reward them," Silveta offered breathlessly. The carnage was difficult to bear. "I'll need good bondsmen by my side."

Indeed, she seemed dazed to have her dream finally come true. She was back in her own estate. Though it now looked very different from the peaceful prosperity we both remembered. Women and children who had belonged to Birgir's men were being herded into a longhouse, crying out their pleas to be forgiven for matters they had no part in. I saw Silveta grimace and knew she would not harm the truly innocent.

"Here." Jens pointed.

We entered the great fire hall that bristled with the horns of the bulls Ejegod's family had sacrificed to the gods. The site of my first appearance in Tillfallvik—tied upside down and hung naked from a pole—was very different now. The straw that Birgir had pushed me into when he denounced me to Ejegod was filthy and sodden with blood. Tables were overturned and the colorful banners that had hung from the rafters had been torn down.

On the ground in front of the dais lay Birgir, just as I had seen him fall in my vision. He still wore his hammered silver helm with the nose and cheek guards surrounding his wide-open eyes. His chest armor had been unbuckled and thrown back to reveal his unmoving torso covered by mail. A great gash opened his neck and one cheek. I could see the pink bone underneath and the flesh torn in half. He seemed to leer at me even when dead. I shuddered as I looked at his hands, still massive but now curled like a baby's. They were as bare as his great hairy feet.

"My blood oath has come to fruition," Silveta proclaimed, a fierce light in her eyes. She kicked his body, but he was so heavy and stiff that he hardly moved.

There was no life in Birgir, evidenced by the *olfs* who came close, curiously floating over the man whose malevolence had driven them out of Tillfallvik and threatened all of Markland. There was nothing inside of him now. The darkness that he had wrapped around him like a cloak was finally dissipating, as were the *inua* of his slain men.

"Who did it?" Silveta declared. "I want to kiss the hand that slew this beast."

Jens blushed and looked gratified. "In the end there were three of us against him, your man Torgils included. But it was my ax that caught him in the neck."

Silveta dropped to her knees and took his hand in both of hers. Her eyes were shining. "I owe you everything." She pressed her lips to his hand.

Jens insisted on pulling her to her feet. "No, 'tis only what the overlord promised you. Now I've redeemed his pledge."

"Not him," Silveta denied. "Never him. It was you."

Torgils agreed, standing respectfully to one side. "Jens Jedvardsson has a claim of conquest on Markland. We could not have stormed the estate without his men."

"That was Birgir's claim!" Jens protested.

Silveta tilted her head. "Would the magnates agree to a chieftain and wife who are both of Viinland?"

"You've risked your lives for Markland," Lexander countered. "How could they protest?"

"You've saved us all from Birgir Barfoot, Silveta," Torgils agreed. "None would gainsay you now. The man you marry will become chieftain."

Twenty-four

We left Silveta with Jens and Torgils, newly sworn as her bondsman. Lexander and I returned to the waterfront, where the Skraeling were regrouping. On the way through Tillfallvik, I realized I must confess all to Lexander.

"I am sorry I betrayed you," I admitted. At his confused expression, I explained, "I told Amaruq of some ... intimate moments between us, so that he would understand and trust me. I spoke of things I've not even confessed to you."

He looked at me sharply. "Is that what made you suffer, Marja?"

"By rights, I shouldn't have done it."

"Never fear." He stopped me and put both hands on my shoulders so he could look into my eyes. "I want you so much that I long to own you, but I must let you go. You have no responsibility to me, Marja."

"But I shared our intimacy with another."

"I understand the need that drove you to it. I also see that there is something that binds you to Amaruq and these Thule. You've finally found your own people. I know you could live out the rest of your life among them."

I thought of how the *olfs* were happily acknowledged every day by the Thule. It was true that I felt comfortable in the icy north, more so than on the fens. "I will always love Helluland and its folk," I agreed. "But there is more to see in this world, and I shan't ever tire of crossing the next wave or climbing the next ridge. That is who I am."

The relief that eased through him was palpable. "I thought you had found what you were searching for."

"Yes, I found a way to help my homeland. Just as you now seek to help those you enslaved and left under Helanas' care."

Lexander's eyes narrowed. "I should have released them before I left, but I could not see it as I do now." He glanced down at the manacle on his wrist, then lifted the end of the hanging chain.

There was a rawness in his voice, an emotion that was no longer hidden. Lexander was proud, a godling in his own right. I couldn't imagine what he had endured as a slave. But I thought he was wise to choose to help others when he was so vulnerable himself. Surely that way led to healing.

With his arm around me, we went to find the Skraelings. They refused to stay inside the estate and were wary of the Noromenn who were still in the throes of bloodlust. All I had to do was look for the *olfs,* many of whom had followed the Thule down to the shore near the river. Their *umiaks* were beached upright, ready to be pushed into the water at a moment's notice, revealing their distrust of the Noromenn. Two of the boats were out in the bay, netting fresh fish. The Thule seemed as subdued as the *olfs* by the bloody battle.

We didn't spend long in their camp. Amaruq and a few of the Thule leaders returned to the estate with us. Amaruq had suffered a wound on his arm, but he was striding along as if he were unhurt. Lexander stayed back to keep from interfering in Amaruq's consultation with me. It was a gesture of respect that I appreciated.

One of Silveta's first orders was to sacrifice the finest bull in Tillfallvik, spilling its blood into the fire to honor all of the gods who had supported her quest. It also provided much-needed food for those who had fought for her. We saw the bonfire from the Skraeling camp, as the smoke and sparks flew into the heavens. Provisions were lacking, but somehow the overjoyed servants on the estate were pulling together a feast fit for midsummer as the bull roasted on an outdoor spit.

The guards at the broken gate addressed me by name, though I didn't recall meeting them. It seemed as if all of the townsfolk and mercenaries knew who I was. We were ushered into the fire hall without a single challenge.

Silveta was seated in the lynx-fur chair on the dais. The place looked very different with the fouled straw swept out and fresh grass hastily spread over the bloodstains. The doors were open, letting in the last of the sun's rays. Silveta had changed from her Skraeling furs into a lovely silk dress. The pale blue overdress echoed her eyes, while the yellow skirt couldn't rival her rich golden hair. She was even more regal and dignified than when she had been Ejegod's wife.

"Good, you're finally returned," Silveta said when she saw us enter with the Skraelings. "These are the letters for your Thule, granting them land on the northern coast. I've included a map with each one showing where they can place their settlements. Please make sure they don't try to settle on my people's estates. If there are any problems, they're to bring them directly to me and I will send my bondsmen to assist them."

Lexander distributed the packets among the Thule while I explained everything to them.

Amaruq stepped up on the dais, even though that made some of the Noromenn nervous. "You've honored your word, sun-haired lady," he acknowledged. "We will be pleased to make your home our own."

I translated for Silveta. To her credit, she didn't flinch as some of the other Noromenn did at the thought of Skraelings living cheek to cheek with them again. "I welcome you," she declared. "And I'm sure the *olfs* do as well."

I knew the Thule would help cleanse the land through their rapport with the spirits. Silveta's acknowledgment of both them and the *olfs* made the otherworldly creatures leap about in ecstasy. The Thule would get the winter settlements they deserved, while the *olfs* finally had a ruler who respected them.

The Thule did not choose to stay for the feast. Word had rapidly spread through Tillfallvik that these Skraeling were being honored for their part in ousting Birgir. But I noticed that no one ventured near them. They would return to their camp, intending to leave at first light.

I didn't know if I would ever see Amaruq again, but much like the *olfs* it was not the Skraeling way to think about the future. Now was the only important thing. "You have my everlasting gratitude, Amaruq," I declared.

Lexander was silent in the face of the connection I felt with the elder Thule. Surely he understood that he would feel the same resonance with a fellow godling. These people knew me like no other except my mam. I did feel at home with them, though I could not stay in Helluland.

Amaruq saw my sadness at saying good-bye, yet he was serene in the knowledge that it was my path. "Go with the spirits, Marja."

"I am blessed to have your friendship," I murmured to him.

In a rare gesture of open affection, Amaruq leaned in to kiss my forehead. If neither of us loved another, we could have been happy together roaming Helluland. Amaruq was wise enough to appreciate my differences.

With my eyes still wet from unshed tears, I watched them leave. Silveta was not so moved, though surely she appreciated all the Thule had done for her. "Perhaps I can let them stay in their settlements for longer than two generations," she mused. "Without them, I could not have returned home, and Jens would not have come to help me."

"The Thule are ever honorable allies," I said quietly.

Silveta shrugged as if that was something to consider another time. "Go get ready for the feast, Marja! You're both to have the place of honor beside me. I've ordered you a bath in my old closet. I've taken the solar for my own."

I must admit the thought of a good wash was appealing. I had little prejudice about dirt, but living in Vidaris had taught me the luxury of bathing. I stepped up onto the dais so no one else could hear. "What about the rest of Lexander's chains? We must strike them off."

Lexander joined us. "That can wait until morning. And

it's best if you don't honor me this night, Silveta. Word may reach Helanas before we do."

"So you'll pose as Marja's slave?" Silveta asked with a smile. "I like that idea."

I didn't want to leave the metal bands locked on him, but that was Lexander's choice.

Silveta met my eyes, reaching out her hands to me. "I plan on saying this more fully tonight, to proclaim to everyone that you were beyond faithful, always giving more than the gods could ask. I . . . and Markland, are more grateful than you will ever know. You'll always have a place here with me and in my heart, Marja."

"I am glad I am welcome in my homeland again. And that you are safe," I assured Silveta.

Lexander agreed. "You've found a worthy man in Jens to help you rule. That is more than I had hoped for."

Silveta lifted her chin slightly. "Oh, I think I could have done well enough alone. But I am fortunate to have Jens at my side."

I felt such a relief that I could not express. I treasured Silveta, but she required much from those around her. Now my pledge was finally fulfilled and redeemed. It was the most significant service I had ever done. Jens could take care of her from now on.

Lexander followed me out to the longhouse. I hesitated at the door to the closet, and he knew immediately what was wrong. I had been raped twice by Birgir in this room, but as I stepped inside holding my breath, the cozy space no longer held his shade. *Olfs* were playing in a great tub of water that steamed slightly, but they disappeared at the sight of Lexander. Candles had been distributed liberally on every surface, illuminating the mirror and one of Silveta's dresses that had been carefully laid out on a chest. A gold cord was looped in several rich strands, dangling gold teardrops along its length.

I fingered the crimson silk. "Is this for me to wear? It is far too fine!"

"You will outshine everyone," Lexander assured me. "While I hide my head under a cap."

I turned to him. "There's little chance Helanas would hear of your presence in Tillfallvik. Why did you tell Silveta that?"

"Word could spread and my superiors might hear of it. I would not bring danger on Silveta for the world. It's bad enough that you are at risk."

"'Tis nothing to me," I swore. "I would endure far more to be with you, Lexander."

"Can it be true, even knowing what I have done? Kinirniq is not the only one I've harmed."

"Surely you cannot doubt me now? Must I go to the very ends of the earth to prove my love?"

Lexander was serious. "It's not your love I doubt, but my own lack."

"Lack? I know you've given up everything you were. Perhaps you don't know what you will become. But I am content with my love."

Lexander looked at me a long moment. One hand touched the metal collar around his neck; then he began to pull off his homespun clothes, baring his strong chest. When I sat down to untie my boots, he said, "Wait."

There was something in his voice I had not heard in some time—a command. It sent a tingle of expectation through me.

He removed his boots and pants, leaving him naked. I had not seen his body thus since leaving the milky hot spring in Issland. Every proportion was perfect, his muscles well defined like a statue made of gold. It made me draw my breath in wonder.

"Don't move," he told me, coming to kneel down at my feet. His collar and the hanging chain gleamed in the light. He had never knelt to me before.

Lexander unlaced my boot and gently pulled it off. With sure hands, he undressed me from toe to head. I lifted my arms and moved as he requested, compliant under his touch.

When he stood again, I wanted to hug him close. I

wanted him to take me as I was. But he warded me off with his eyes, amused at my eagerness. "When are you ever unready, Marja?"

"I'm always ready for you, my love."

His face came very close to mine. It was almost unbearable, my need to touch him. But he backed away, and I managed to restrain myself.

He held out one hand to help me into the bath. I lowered myself gratefully into the warm water. It had been scented with rose oil.

Taking up the brush, Lexander stood behind me, combing out my hair. It reminded me of my first evening in Vidaris, when he had cleansed me so roughly. This time his hands were tender, teasing out every long strand, stroking my head and neck. "I'll dress your hair myself," he murmured. "You'll rival Silveta this night, if I'm not mistaken."

My eyes closed as he washed my hair. He had never taken such time, had never leaned over me so temptingly. In Vidaris he'd had to split his attention among the slaves, and we jealously watched if he lingered with his favorites. But this night was different. He was making love to me through every touch.

By the time he began to lather my neck and shoulders and down each arm, I could hardly contain myself. I wanted to feel his body against me. I grew more aroused from his hands on my breasts, pinching and pulling at my nipples. Then he made foamy circles down my waist to the cleft between my legs. His fingers sought to inflame me. I gasped and held on to the sides of the tub to keep from touching him. He had ordered me not to . . .

There was nothing I could do but writhe underwater at his mercy, as he deftly rubbed me to ecstasy.

"Please, please, please . . ." I begged.

His lips curled in a grin. "You want more?"

"You!" I exclaimed. "I want you now—"

He lifted me from the tub and put me right on the stone floor with a rush of water. I had a flash of Birgir leaning over me, taking me, but this was Lexander. Everything I loved and trusted was in his face. I opened myself to him, diving into him as he did to me. We entwined our arms and legs. He let out a growl as if he couldn't restrain himself, taking me for his own. It had been too long in coming. My release was complete.

Afterwards we lay together, satiated and unable to rise. My arms and legs intertwined with his. The stone floor felt like heaven and I didn't ever want to let him go. I couldn't imagine being without him for one moment.

As if reading my mind, he murmured, "I will be gone for only two days. Then my duty will be done and the slaves will be freed."

I raised my head to look at him. "I will not let you return alone to Vidaris. You helped me in my quest, and now I must help you."

"Marja . . ."

I would not let him protest. I sat up to make sure he understood my seriousness. "You enslaved me, Lexander. You gave me to Helanas to torture as she would."

His face was pained. "Are you trying to hurt me, Marja? I atoned all I could for that, freeing you as you deserved."

"If I am truly free, then you'll not stop me from helping my slave-mates. Don't they deserve the same freedom I have? Am I not the one who truly understands their need? You cannot deny me this, Lexander, not if I am free."

Lexander struggled with this. "Marja, you may see things that you . . . would not like. I must put an end to Helanas' inequity once and for all."

I swallowed hard. "You intend to kill her."

It wasn't a question, but he replied, "Yes, I must. Or she will take her revenge on other innocents for my deeds. I cannot allow that to happen."

"Then I will help you." I knew I might lose my rapport with the *olfs* for good if I assisted him. But even if that terrible price must be paid, it was worth it to ensure Helanas would not hurt another slave. "Righting this wrong means everything to me, Lexander. Everything. I can't face knowing that others could be tortured until they become like Kinirniq."

The mention of that poor boy was enough to break

Lexander's resistance. "I cannot withstand you," he
fessed. "I would give you anything, Marja. Even if it
me your love."

I hugged him tightly, feeling his cool skin beneath
cheek. "Never! You could never lose my love."

He wrapped his arms around me, and I felt his doubt an
fear. I knew his face would never appear to be a mask to
me again. I would always be able to see his *inua* and know
his heart.

And in that moment, I knew that it mattered little that
he had freed me. I would always belong to Lexander. We
would overcome the evil in Vidaris; then we would roam
the world together. No one—neither man nor god—would
stop us.

con-
cost

my

d

With my first step onto the ruddy sand of the beach, the evil spirits infesting Vidaris pressed in on me. Clinging wisps of foul air snaked along the ground. My instincts cried out for me to flee before they found a way to seep inside.

The native Thule who had brought me and Lexander back to Vidaris also sensed the demons. The dark-skinned warriors gathered close, silently supporting one another's *inua*. They left everything in the round-bottomed *umiaks* except for their spears and bows. Even the two wounded men readied their weapons, making the warband a full score strong. They had come to free Qamaniq, the granddaughter of Nerriviq, who had been lured away by Lexander to become a pleasure slave.

There would be no rest—Lexander planned to attack Vidaris at once.

The sliver of moon cast barely enough light through the clouds to reveal the sheer red cliffs of Fjardemano island. On top of the cliff, there was something new; a rough wooden tower rose next to the gate in the palisade, over-looking the ocean. I urged the *olfs* to rise up the cliff face to illuminate the tower. There was no sentry in sight.

Lexander could see through the darkness even without the *olfs'* light. "I hear one freeman on watch." He tilted his head. "He's snoring."

I didn't doubt Lexander's uncanny ability, though the crashing of the waves nearly drowned out the howling of the wind through the forest trees above. "Helanas built it?" I asked.

His golden eyes shone much brighter than those of the Thule. "She intended to be forewarned of my return."

I shivered at his tone. "What do you intend to do?"

"That is my concern." Lexander turned away so I couldn't see his face.

Nerriviq approached, his distrust for Lexander evident in his watchful eyes. "My granddaughter waits."

Lexander gave Nerriviq a curt nod. "Stay with me, Marja," he told me.

He led the Thule to the mouth of the river that followed a crevice in the line of cliffs. Vidaris had been Lexander's estate for nearly two decades, and he knew every step up the winding path along the river.

As we climbed inland, twisty little demons, mere puffs of smoke, whipped branches into my face, seeking to tear out my eyes. The Thule chanted in low voices, begging the *olfs* to aid us. Those faithful creatures gathered around us, sur-rounding us in a warm glow and warding off the malevo-lent spirits.

Some *olfs* flew ahead to light our way, while others dab-bled in the dreams of those sleeping in Vidaris. A fussing baby was lulled by the gentle singing of a pair of *olfs*. Even the animals sighed and drowsed.

We ducked under the bridge for the wagons and not far beyond was a ravine. One by one we pushed through the brush that filled the bottom of the gully, then climbed the crumbling sides into the fields. The oats were near ready for harvest, with the heads of the stalks glowing golden in the moonlight. The rich sound of insects buzzed around us.

The *olfs* spun multicolored balls of light, floating everywhere. It showed me what Vidaris could have been if Helanas had not blighted the estate with her cruelty.

When we finally reached the *haushold*, I was panting from withstanding the malicious pressure that was building around me. I feared one of the demons would wake Helanas and warn her about us.

The servants had gone home to their own cots, so the kitchen was empty. Lexander lit a handful of candles from the rack, and conferred briefly with Nerriviq. The Thule split up, going in opposite directions to block any possibility of Helanas' escape.

I followed Lexander into the fire hall. Everything was achingly familiar, from the red brick walls to the padded benches set before the hearth. Nerriviq and his son followed us, stepping cautiously over the cool bricks and warily watched the towering ceiling far above them.

Lexander motioned for the Thule to wait while he entered the smaller slave hall. Sleeping ledges lined both walls, but there were only six slaves now where once there had been a dozen.

"Wake up," Lexander called out softly, "but don't be frightened. I've come to take you away."

I lifted my candle higher to see Niels sitting up, rubbing his eyes. It reminded me of my first morning in Vidaris when his face had been streaked with tears. The two Skraeling sisters huddled together, their long, dark hair tousled and their narrow eyes fearful at the reappearance of Lexander. Torngasoak was brave enough to put an arm around each of them. The two blond brothers from Fylkeran were confused, but in the scant few moons they had been in Vidaris, they had learned not to ask questions.

Lexander went to check the other door. Niels stood hunched over as if expecting to be hit, whispering, "Marja, is that really you? Where are Sverker and Rosarin?"

I was pained by the thought of what my slavemates suffered now in the hands of Lexander's people. He had saved me from that fate, but my slavemates had not been so fortunate.

Lexander returned. "Quiet, or you'll wake Helanas."

The slaves went very still at her name. At our gentle urging, they followed us into the fire hall, scurrying in fear when they saw the Skraelings waiting for us. They clung to one another, including the Skraeling slaves who surely recognized the Thule as a northern clan.

"Where's Qamaniq?" Lexander asked.

"She was summoned to Helanas' chamber," Niels offered.

Lexander gestured to me. "Take them to the bath house, Marja. Stay there until I come for you."

He sounded much like the master of Vidaris that I remembered, though he had freed me himself a few days ago, before the battle of Tillfallvik.

Lexander took Nerriviq through the courtyard. He meant to face down Helanas.

I paused in the doorway to the kitchen, the slaves close behind me. "Niels," I ordered, "take the others and go to the bathhouse."

"What about you?"

"I'll be there soon. Now *go*."

He gasped, shocked that I would defy our master. But he was accustomed to obedience and left without another word of protest. The baths were familiar. The slaves would be safe there.

I went through the courtyard, and was surprised to see Lexander's chamber was open. He appeared holding a long sword. It had an ornate guard on the handle, yet he held it lightly as if its weight were no burden.

He glared when he saw me. "Go away!" he insisted under his breath.

I set my lips and shook my head.

He hesitated but could not take time to argue. The Thule blocked the hallway on either side of us, their spears pointing inward.

Lexander handed the heavy casket to me, opening the top to pull out a key. With a motion of his hand to stay back, he threw open the door to Helanas' chamber, rushing inside with the Thule warriors behind him. As I followed, my candle shook, casting wild shadows on the flow-ered tapestries that hung on the walls.

Someone screeched in protest. I wasn't sure if it was Helanas or Qamaniq. Then I saw the Skraeling woman on the floor, her dark hair a tangled mess and her body limp. I knew that Qamaniq was beyond suffering right now.

Nerriviq's kin picked up Qamaniq, exclaiming over her naked form. But I only had eyes for Helanas. My mistress was on her feet, a knife in her hand.

Lexander caught her with the point of his sword against her throat. Her shapely body was bare. Many times had I caressed those generous curves and stroked my mistress until she writhed in pleasure. Yet Helanas had never smiled when she took her satisfaction, preferring to glower and furiously taunt the slave who served her even as she cli-maxed.

With two steps, Lexander drove Helanas back against the tapestry until she could go no farther. "Drop your knife!"

Helanas hesitated, her eyes taking in the Skraelings in the room. She sneered when she saw me. "That sly bitch! She's seduced you from your duty, Lexander. You will live to rue the day you found her—"

"Silence!" Lexander demanded.

There was an edge to his voice that I had never heard. Perhaps Helanas was right that he would someday regret the choice he had made to leave Vidaris and abandon the ways of his own people. Perhaps he feared that fate more than anything else.

"You drove him to it," I told Helanas. "If only you had not been so cruel—"

"You will *not* look at me, slave." Her hand tightened on the knife. "*Gesig!*"

My knees buckled in an unreasoning compulsion to obey. But I fought my trained reflexes and stayed on my feet, clutching the heavy casket tighter. The brass studs dug into my flesh, piercing the demon-roiled cloud that threat-ened to overcome me.

Disgust twisted Helanas' face, marring her satiny skin

and perfect features. "Think of what you've done, Lexander! You can still rectify this terrible mistake. Stay here in Vidaris. I won't tell Saaladet—"

Helanas hardly shifted, but suddenly her knife slashed up.

"I'm

"It's not just about yo
"Ellen needs a mothe

"I can't mother her. I w

"I think you will. You're
strong." He hesitated. This was not the way he ever
imagined proposing to someone. For that matter,
he hadn't really imagined proposing to anyone. His
solitary life had suited him just fine. "But you're also
gentle. She needs a woman's hand."

"I can't think why you'd do this for me." Lily bit her
bottom lip.

"It's like the verse." He pointed to her needlework.
"We're taking care of the needs of others. Ellen
needs us both."

Lily's face turned pink, and she met his gaze. "What
kind of relationship do you expect the two of us to
have?"

He could tell it cost her a great deal to form the
words. Then he felt the same heat rushing into his
face. "Miss Warren, I'd expect for you to care for
Ellen as a mother. This arrangement will be strictly
for the sake of my niece."

Edward watched her as the breath she'd been
holding seeped out of her to be replaced by relief.

"For the sake of Ellen?"

"Yes. And you."

Angel Moore fell in love with romance in elementary school when she read the story of Robin Hood and Maid Marian. Who doesn't want to escape to a happily-ever-after world? When not writing, you can find her reading or spending time with her family. Married to her best friend, she has two wonderful sons, a lovely daughter-in-law and three grands. She loves sharing her faith and the hope she knows is real because of God's goodness to her. Find her at angelmoorebooks.com.

Books by Angel Moore

Love Inspired Historical

Conveniently Wed
The Marriage Bargain

Visit the Author Profile page at Harlequin.com.

ANGEL MOORE

The Marriage Bargain

HARLEQUIN® LOVE INSPIRED® HISTORICAL

Recycling programs
for this product may
not exist in your area.

 LOVE INSPIRED BOOKS

ISBN-13: 978-0-373-28352-1

The Marriage Bargain

Copyright © 2016 by Angelissa J. Moore

www.Harlequin.com

Printed in U.S.A.

Let nothing be done through strife or vainglory;
but in lowliness of mind let each esteem
other better than themselves.
Look not every man on his own things,
but every man also on the things of others.
— *Philippians* 2:3–4

To my editor, Emily Krupin.
Your encouragement makes me work harder.

To my mother, Mary Ellen, for sharing her love of reading. Thank you for celebrating with me at every step along the way and for teaching me to be brave.

To Lisa, for the love only true sisters know.

To Austin, my first editor and reader.
Your insight and knowledge are priceless.

To Jason, for understanding when Mama has to work.

To Bob, who taught me everything I know about Happily-Ever-After.

And, as always, to God, Who makes it all possible.

Chapter One

Pine Haven, Texas
January 1881

The sound of shattering glass snatched Lily Warren awake. She bolted upright in bed with a gasp, only to feel her lungs fill with acrid smoke. Coughing uncontrollably, she threw the quilt back and tugged on her dressing gown.

Unfamiliar with her surroundings, she fumbled about in the darkness, searching for the doorway to the stairs that led to her new shop.

Heavy footsteps pounded on the staircase outside her room. Lily turned toward the sound, desperate for fresh air. The coughing racked her chest, and she was getting dizzy.

She cried out between coughs. "Help!"

The door burst open, and the orange glow of flames gave her enough light to stumble toward her rescuer.

Her landlord, Edward Stone, came into the room with an arm across his face in an apparent effort to keep from breathing in the smoke. "Do you have something to wrap up in? A blanket?" His voice was intense.

She reached for her mother's quilt on the bed, though the coughing hindered her movements.

He snatched it up and, before she knew what he was going to do, wrapped it around her shoulders and picked her up like a child.

She stiffened and argued, "I can walk."

"Try to keep your mouth closed until I get you outside." He kicked the doorway open wider and started down the stairs.

"What?" Pressed against his chest, she couldn't hear over the roar of the growing fire.

"Quiet! The smoke." He reached the bottom of the stairs and turned toward the back door.

She could see the flames licking up the side of the back wall and climbing across her workbench. All the beautiful hats she'd made for her shop were being consumed by the hungry fire.

Kicking and squirming against Edward, she screamed, "My stock!"

He tightened his hold on her and reversed his direction to take her out the front door. He turned back to face the building and lowered her to stand in front of him.

The church bell rang from the opposite end of the street.

She tried to move away from him, but her hair was tangled in the buckle on his suspenders. She cried out in pain as it pulled.

"Hold still." He spoke close to her ear. "I'll try not to hurt you, but I've got to put the fire out." He tugged at the knotted curls.

A voice barked behind them. "Stone! Is anyone still inside?" The sheriff came running up the street.

With a final and painful pull, Lily was free of him. She turned to see what must be most of the town's population coming from every direction.

Edward shot around her and hollered his answer to the sheriff as he went back through the front door of her shop. "No one else was here. I think it's contained in the workroom in the back. There's a rain barrel in the alley behind the back door." The sheriff ran toward the rear of the shop.

Lily stumbled on the ends of her mother's quilt when she started up the steps. A man she hadn't met in the two days since her arrival in Pine Haven restrained her. "You can't go in there, miss," he said.

"My stock is inside!" She turned to plead with him to let her go. He wasn't tall or large, but was strong for his size, and she couldn't break free. "Everything I own is in there."

The lady from the general store came up beside them. "Miss Warren, you mustn't resist. The men need to put out the fire so it doesn't spread to the rest of town." Mrs. Croft put an arm around her shoulders. "Doc Willis, I've got her. Help them! Please!"

Smoke boiled through the open front door now. Lily could see Edward's shape through the haze as he swung his coat to beat back the flames. Every available man and woman scurried to form a line and pass buckets filled from the water troughs and barrels near the surrounding buildings.

Lily shrugged off Mrs. Croft's confining arm. "I've got to help at least." She let the quilt drop to the dirt and ran to fill a wide place in the line of townsfolk fighting to help their newest resident.

. It had only been minutes, but seemed like hours, when Edward appeared in the front doorway with his charred coat lifted high in one hand. "It's out! We did it!"

Cheers went up from the crowd, and the line fell away. Everyone gathered near the steps of her shop.

Lily pushed her way through the people and stopped at the open front door. Water covered the floors she'd polished on her first day. Mud tracked through to the workroom. She leaned against the jamb.

She turned to look at Edward. "How bad is it?" Water ran in tiny rivulets through the soot on his face.

"I'm afraid your stock is ruined. What didn't burn will be damaged by the smoke and water." He dragged an arm across his forehead and smeared the soot away from his eyes.

Mrs. Croft came through the crowd at the bottom of the steps. "Miss Warren, please." The woman held Lily's quilt up by the corners. She lowered her voice to a conspiratorial whisper, and her eyes darted toward the people gathered behind her. "You need to cover yourself."

Lily gasped and looked down at herself. The tie to her dressing gown had loosened while she passed one bucket of water after another. The lace of her nightgown peeked out where the robe gaped open. She snatched the quilt from Mrs. Croft and wrapped it around her shoulders, clenching it tight, high against her neck. The heat climbing up her throat let her know she was turning as pink as the nightgown everyone in town had just seen.

"Thank you, Mrs. Croft." The mortification she experienced at the woman's condemning stare almost dwarfed the loss of her belongings. Almost.

She turned back to Edward. "Thank you for saving me." She remembered the feel of his arms around her as he carried her from the building. Strong, determined, protecting.

"You don't owe me any thanks. I'm just sorry we couldn't save your merchandise." As her landlord, he'd want Lily's Millinery and Finery to be a success. How could it be now, with nothing to sell?

Mrs. Croft's tinny voice broke into their conversation. "How did you see the fire, Mr. Stone?" Her lips were pinched tight, and her eyes narrowed.

"I was on my porch and saw the glow through the shop windows." He seemed at ease explaining what happened, but Lily's stomach sank and pressure built behind her eyes when she looked at Mrs. Croft and knew the woman was making an accusation.

The busybody confirmed Lily's suspicions with her next words. "But your porch faces in the opposite direction." A hum of low conversations ran through the people who'd only just put out the fire. Now the woman from the general store was trying to start another one. The kind that could destroy Lily's reputation. The potential damage could forever ruin her business before it opened.

Several of the people gathered looked over their shoulders in the direction of the blacksmith's shop and home. His porch faced a lane that ran perpendicular to Main Street. Lily held her breath.

Edward's tone was clipped. "I was leaning on the corner post and watching the night sky. The view of the moon is best from there."

"I see." Doubt hung on each syllable from Mrs. Croft. "It's just that when we came out to help, you were holding Miss Warren in your arms."

Mr. Croft interrupted. "Liza, he just pulled the woman from a burning building." He put a hand on his wife's shoulder. "Let's go home and get some rest. The whole town will be tired tomorrow after the excitement of tonight."

People murmured around them. Some were in agreement with Mr. Croft, but Lily knew in her soul that others were siding with Mrs. Croft. Only two days in her new town and something beyond her control had drawn her character into question. She couldn't let them all disperse without an attempt to protect herself.

"Mrs. Croft, I assure you nothing improper went on here tonight. Mr. Stone was merely rescuing me. If he hadn't come, I'd never have found my way out of my bedroom."

A light gasp escaped some of the ladies.

"I see." Mrs. Croft's eyes swept across Lily from top to bottom and then landed on Edward. "I guess it's okay where you come from to entertain gentlemen in your home after dark, but you'll soon learn that in Pine Haven we hold to a higher standard of propriety."

Edward took a step closer to the edge of the porch. "Miss Warren has told you there was no impropriety here." He looked at Mr. Croft and then the others standing in the street. "Thank you all for your help. By saving my building, you very likely saved many others from certain disaster."

Dr. Willis spoke up then. "And at least one life."

Lily let her gaze move over the crowd then. "Thank you all so much." She turned to Edward. "Especially you, Mr. Stone."

People began to walk away a few at a time, the rumble of voices fading into the night.

She pulled up the bottom of the quilt so she wouldn't stumble and stepped inside the shop.

"Miss Warren, I don't think you should stay here tonight." Edward's voice was kind.

Lily stilled for a moment. "Is the building sound?"

"Yes. And tonight when I say my prayers, I will thank God that the fire didn't spread to your private rooms. But the smoke and water damage are serious." He gestured toward the floor and the workroom.

She stepped inside and took in the magnitude of the destruction. There was a trail of muddy water from the front door to the workroom where water had sloshed from the buckets as they were passed from the porch and through the shop to put out the fire in the back room. She picked her way slowly to keep from slipping and stood in the entry to the workroom. Water dripped from the workbench. The stench of the smoke hung thick in the air. And everywhere she looked, the remains of all her hard work lay soaked and covered in soot. Now she had to begin anew. Not from the beginning, but from a new beginning much further behind any point she'd imagined.

She squared her tired shoulders and spoke. "All the more reason for me to stay and get to work." She nodded in dismissal. "Thank you again for all you've done. I'm certain it would have been a lot worse if you hadn't seen the fire." She looked down at the quilt her mother had made. "I'm grateful you saved my mother's quilt. I don't have many of her things. This one is important to me." As much as she'd tried to keep her emotions in check, she couldn't stop the tears from spilling over her lashes now. With a sniff she stood straight and moved to the front door.

Edward followed her and stepped onto the porch. His hand came up to keep her from closing the door on him. "Cleanup can wait until morning. It's only a few hours."

She shook her head. "The water will damage the floors if I don't mop it up now."

"Then let me stay and help you."

She'd come to Pine Haven for independence. Her recent failed engagement had driven her to create a new life for herself. The first two days now seemed like a distant dream. Making hats and polishing the furniture her father had sent with her to use in her new shop had filled her hours. The memory of humming while she cleaned the floors and set up the private rooms to suit her needs faded behind a cloud of dense smoke.

This was a major setback, but she wouldn't become dependent on her landlord. Now. Or ever. "No. You best get home to your niece. I'll be fine." She'd met his young charge on the first day and knew the child would be home alone.

He chuckled a bit. "Ellen can sleep through anything. That child wouldn't hear the church bell or commotion unless it was in the room with her."

"It's good she has such peace. Sound sleep is often a sign of contentment."

Edward looked over his shoulder toward his house. "In all her seven years, I've never known her sleep to be disturbed. Not since she was a baby. For her, it's more about how she wears herself out when she's awake. The child has more worries than a body ought."

"All the more reason for you to go home now. In case she awakens and you aren't there." When Lily was five, her mother had died. Being young and frightened was something Lily had experienced firsthand.

He dipped his head in agreement. "Please get some rest. I'll be back in the morning so we can assess the damage and begin repairs."

Lily stood in the doorway to her workroom after he left. The hats she'd made yesterday were scorched and ruined. What wasn't blackened by fire was covered in ash or wilted from the water that had doused the flames. She thought about crying, until her bare feet reminded her of the floors and all the work she needed to do.

She shrugged off the quilt, bundled it into a ball and tossed it onto a crate in the corner of the front shop. Lighting a lantern, she went through the workroom into the alley behind her shop and retrieved the mop she'd used to clean the floors. Bucket in hand, she determined to prevent as much damage as possible. Repairing the building would take more skill than she possessed, but she could clean up the mess. Then Edward could get started as soon as he arrived in the morning.

Could she undo the damage done by Mrs. Croft's words in the aftermath of the fire? Why had the woman so blatantly accused her and Mr. Stone of poor behavior?

Losing a night's sleep did not compare to what she stood to lose if she didn't get her shop open before her father arrived in a few weeks' time. Now she not only needed to get Lily's Millinery and Finery open for business, she also had to repair the damage done to her reputation in front of the townsfolk by Mrs. Croft's words. Her own lapse in decorum when she was unaware of her appearance in her dressing gown in front of the entire town added to her problems.

The water on the floor was the least of her worries, but it was the only thing she could control at the moment.

* * *

Edward urged Ellen out of the front door the next morning.

"I want to see what happened." Ellen protested by dragging her feet.

"You can't go inside the building until I make sure it's safe for you to be there." He stooped to be eye level with her. "Promise me you won't try to sneak in."

Her reluctant nod came after a long pause. "What did she do to set Momma's shop on fire?" This was the reaction Edward had been afraid of. He knew his niece might blame Lily for the fire and use it as an excuse to spew the frustration and fear she was warring with against his tenant. "I said it was bad to let someone in Momma's shop." Her face turned into a pout.

"I'm not sure what caused the fire. That's one of the things I need to find out today." He pulled her into a quick hug. "Now you need to head off to school so I can get to work."

"I don't see why I got to hurry 'cause you got to work." He reminded himself to be patient. She was at the age where she often wanted an explanation for things. Knowing that was how she learned, he complied.

He put a hand on top of her head and pointed her in the direction of the school. "Because you are one of the reasons I work, ma'am."

Ellen went a few steps, swinging her lunch pail in one hand and holding her slate close to her chest in the other. Then she pivoted and looked at the shop across the street from their cabin. He watched her study the building, which showed no outward signs of the fire last night except for the film of smoke on the windows. She bolted back to wrap her arms around his middle. "I know you can fix it like new, Uncle Edward. You're the best uncle a girl could have."

"I'm going to do my best, Ellen." He kissed the top of her head. "You know you're my favorite niece."

She leaned back and scrunched her face at him. "I'm your only niece."

Edward peeled her arms from around him. "Just like I'm your only uncle." He chuckled and turned her toward the school again. "Now get to school, or I'll be the only uncle at school today being scolded by the teacher for letting you be late."

The school bell rang, announcing the time, and she kicked up the dust around the hem of her skirt as she ran. "Bye, Uncle Edward," she hollered over her shoulder.

He laughed as she stumbled and caught herself. The child was fun and loving. He wished he could make her as happy as she deserved to be.

When he'd come back home after the fire, just as he expected, she was curled up in the middle of her bed. The quilt had slid to the floor, so he'd pulled it back over her. He'd marveled that the commotion in the street hadn't awakened her. Oh, to be so carefree.

Only she wasn't carefree. She waited every day with him for news from her mother. When his sister had insisted on leaving town with her husband to start a new business in Santa Fe, he'd begged her to reconsider. Ellen needed her mother. Jane and Wesley had wanted to get their business started and come back for Ellen in a few weeks. Edward wished they'd been contented with running the local hotel, but Wesley had lost interest in Pine Haven when he'd heard of the growing economy in Santa Fe. Edward had purchased the building he now leased to Lily in hopes that Jane could convince Wesley to stay and let her open a bakery to add to their business interests in Pine Haven.

In the end, nothing Edward said had changed their minds. And now the weeks had turned to months. No word from them for the past several weeks was causing him to worry. He tried to dampen the fear that pulled at his heart and caused him to wonder if something dreadful had happened. Ellen's future was his responsibility. He'd have to give her a proper home if his sister didn't return soon. He said another prayer for Jane and Wesley and went into his blacksmith shop to gather some tools.

He needed to start the cleanup and repairs on his building. Having Lily's father lease the shop from him had eased the strain to make the mortgage payments. But he couldn't in all good conscience take money from her while the building was damaged.

He'd stop in at the post office first and see if there was a letter from Jane.

"Quite a night we had, Stone," Jerry Winters, the postmaster, greeted him. "Glad you saw the flames. Hate to think what could have happened to my family, it being right next door and all."

Winston Ledford walked into the post office as Jerry was speaking. "It's a good thing for all of us that you had your eye on Miss Warren. I'll admit she's worthy of a second look." A smirk Edward didn't like crept across the saloon owner's face.

Edward's gut roiled. This was exactly the kind of gossip he worried about after Liza Croft made such a scene in front of most of the town. He refused to rise to Ledford's goading.

Instead, he nodded at Jerry Winters. "I think we were all blessed by God's mercy."

Mrs. Winters came from the private quarters behind the post office and joined her husband. "We all owe you a debt of gratitude, Mr. Stone."

"I doubt he'll be missing much of what goes on at the new hat shop, Mrs. Winters." Winston Ledford came to stand beside Edward at the counter. "Do you have any mail for me?"

The disapproval on Mrs. Winter's face almost made Edward chuckle. If it wasn't such a serious subject, he'd laugh at how soundly Ledford's comments were dismissed. She turned to search the cubbyholes behind her and handed several letters to the man.

Winston shuffled through the small stack, tipped his hat and said, "Good morning to you all." He opened the door to leave. "I think I'll stop by and see how our newest resident is this morning. Must have been quite a shock to her."

Edward's back tightened, and he drew a deep breath. "That won't be necessary, Ledford. I'm on my way there now to begin the repairs."

A cantankerous laugh burst from Winston. "As I suspected. You've already staked a claim on our new merchant." He stepped onto the sidewalk and turned to close the door. "Don't be surprised if you find yourself engaged in some friendly competition over the likes of Miss Warren." The door closed, and his grinning face filled the pane of glass before he turned in the direction of the building next door.

Edward followed him at a brisk pace.

"Stone, don't you want to know if you have any mail?" Mr. Winters called.

"I'll check back later." He was through the front door.

"It's not fitting for Miss Warren to be subjected to the likes of Mr. Ledford without warning."

It was one thing for Mrs. Croft to make unfounded accusations, but for Winston Ledford to think that a fine, upstanding lady like Miss Lily Warren was open to his attentions was another matter. Edward wouldn't leave her unprotected from the saloon owner's lack of good manners.

Serving as an unsolicited chaperone was the only right thing to do. It was more about protecting Lily's reputation in the community, and thus his income from her rental, than anything else.

Edward opened the door to Lily's shop and found Winston Ledford leaning on the glass display case Lily had brought with her when she'd arrived only two days earlier. She caught sight of him over Ledford's shoulder. Was that relief in her gaze?

"Thank you for checking on me, Mr. Ledford, but I assure you it isn't necessary. I'm quite all right." She stepped from behind the case and walked toward Edward.

Once again he was struck by her beauty. When she'd first come to Pine Haven and stepped from the train, he couldn't help but notice her. Everyone noticed her. But within moments, her independence had become clear to him. She was lovely, but she wasn't the kind of woman who wanted to settle down and care for a home and family. Not the kind of woman he'd begun to think he might need for Ellen. After a childhood of being neglected and mistreated by his stepmother, he'd replaced any yearning for love with a mistrust of women years ago. If he did marry for Ellen's sake, he'd choose carefully.

"Good morning, Miss Warren." Edward set the

wooden box he'd filled with tools on a crate near the front door and removed his hat. "I've come to get started on the repairs."

She lifted a handkerchief to her face and coughed. "That's very good of you."

Winston Ledford turned to face them. "If you're certain there's nothing I can do for you, Miss Warren, I'll leave you in the care of Mr. Stone." He sauntered toward the door. "He seems determined to watch over you." He tipped his hat at Lily and walked through the door Edward held open for him.

Edward closed the door with a snap. "I hope you aren't taken in by the likes of Mr. Ledford." He picked up his toolbox.

"I'm a big girl, Mr. Stone. You don't have to worry about me." Lily went back toward the workroom behind the shop. Perhaps the relief he'd seen in her face earlier was imagined. Nothing she'd done since he'd met her upon her arrival in town Monday had suggested she was anything other than a woman determined to make her own way in the world. Her single-minded focus might be the very thing that protected her from people like the saloon owner.

"That's good to know. Some women are swayed by fancy talk and refined appearances."

"I assure you, I appreciate fine things. I also look for quality. In people and things."

She directed him toward the workroom. "Thank you for coming so early. I've done what I could about getting everything dry and removing the rubbish."

Her movements were swift and fluid, like a bird on air. She'd brushed her hair into a loose bun and changed her clothes, but the fatigue of her ordeal showed in eyes. Another coughing spell wrenched her breath.

"You didn't need to do all that by yourself, Miss Warren. I assured you I'd be here this morning."

She lifted a hand and waved it in dismissal of his words. "I couldn't sleep anyway. My schedule was tight before the fire. Now I'll need to work at a quicker pace than I'd planned."

He entered the workroom behind her. The back door stood open, and he could see the pile of rubble she'd created in the alley beyond. "You stayed up all night?"

"It's a matter of no consequence." She indicated the shelving on the left of the storeroom. "Do you think any of this can be salvaged?"

Obviously she'd moved beyond the fire and had set her mind on repairs. Most women would be wallowing in a pool of pity, bemoaning their misfortune. Her determination was admirable.

"First things first," he said. "I need to discover how the fire started, so we can make certain we don't have another incident." He turned to see her blush and lift a hand to her forehead. She rubbed her fingers across her brow in a smoothing motion.

"We won't have to worry about it again." A deep breath caused more coughing. "Please forgive me." She tucked the handkerchief back in the pocket of her apron.

"How are you feeling?"

"I'm fine. Just frustrated with the amount of work I've caused us both."

"You caused?"

Could Ellen be right? Had his tenant been the reason for the fire? The last thing he needed was for his niece to discover Lily had put the building in jeopardy. The child already resented her presence in the shop. Edward didn't have the energy to deal with more trouble in their lives—especially not from a woman he'd just met.

Chapter Two

Edward prayed he'd misunderstood Lily. "What do you mean, 'you caused'?"

"It seems the fire was my fault." Lily pointed to the wall near the back door where the most damage appeared to be. "I was working late, trying to make a few extra hats. I had set a lantern on this workbench."

She didn't seem the irresponsible type. "Surely you didn't leave a lantern burning when you went to bed. You'd have noticed the light."

"No." She jerked her head to stare at him. "Of course not! I took the lantern with me."

She pointed to a small stack of charred kindling near the stove. It was considerably smaller than the amount he'd cut and placed there before her arrival. Normal circumstances wouldn't have caused her to use so much kindling.

"Right before I went upstairs, I swept up the trimmings from around the workbench. Bits of ribbon and feathers. Things like that. I swept them into a pile near the door, intending to dispose of it this morning. Then I checked the stove. Some embers must have blown out and landed among the trash. It must have smoldered and caught when it got near the kindling. I don't know how else it could have started. I'm so sorry." Another cough stopped her from speaking. "I'll pay for the damages."

Edward stirred the kindling with the toe of his boot and studied the scorched wood and the wall in the corner of the room between the stove and the door.

"It's possible a gust of wind blew under the door and carried the embers back to the kindling." He turned to Lily, who was coughing again. "No one was hurt. That's the most important thing."

"Please forgive me. I never meant to start the fire." She covered her mouth again to cough.

"You took in a lot of smoke. Have you been to see the doc?"

"No. I'm fine. There's too much work to do to stop for a minor cough."

He knew how much smoke had been in her rooms. The stairwell had acted like a chimney and drawn the smoke upward. No doubt a draft around the windows had pulled the dangerous fumes under the door at the top of the landing.

"I'm taking you to see Doc Willis." He headed for the front of the shop. "Where's your coat?"

When she didn't follow, he turned and waited.

"You are not taking me—" a cough interrupted her words "—anywhere."

He raised his eyebrows. Would she be so stubborn as to refuse medical treatment? "Then I'll have to ask Doc Willis to come here." He opened the door and stepped onto the sidewalk. "We need to get this place ready for you to open your business. The sooner you get that cough taken care of, the sooner that will happen."

"Wait, please." She coughed again. "If it will set your mind at ease so we can get to work on the repairs, I'll go." She shrugged her arms into the sleeves of her coat and turned up the collar.

The January wind whipped around him, and he rubbed his arms against the cold. They walked briskly in the direction of the doctor's office. "I'll feel better knowing you aren't making yourself worse by not resting."

Lily turned to look at him. "You must be freezing."

"I'm fine." He dropped his hands to his sides.

"Your coat was ruined when you put out the fire."

"It was time for a new coat anyway. I'll go by the general store after lunch and get one." She walked beside him across the main intersection in town. He hoped she didn't notice the curious glances being sent their way. It was obvious to him that the events of the night before were on everyone's mind this morning.

"You must allow me to pay for it." She seemed too focused to notice the people who turned their heads to whisper when they passed. He wasn't sure that was a good thing. It might be better if she were more aware of what went on around her. If she were, they wouldn't be the object of town gossip. He knew it wasn't fair to blame her, but he didn't like the idea of anyone gossiping about him. Ellen would be harmed if he was cast in a poor light. And it wouldn't do Lily's new business any favors to open the shop in the midst of swirling lies smearing her name.

"I'll pay for my coat. And the repairs." He opened the door to the doctor's office.

She opened her mouth as she entered the building, most likely to argue the point with him, but quickly succumbed to another coughing spell.

* * *

Lily continued to cough while Edward called out, "Doc. I brought you a new patient."

Lily sank unceremoniously into a chair near the door. The smell of camphor and dust assaulted her senses. A curtain rustled and parted. The man who'd kept her from running back into her shop during the fire came into the room.

"Hello, Edward. Finally find yourself a wife?" The short man with spectacles looked from the blacksmith to Lily.

"A wife?" What was this man thinking?

"No, Doc. She's my new tenant. You probably saw her last night. I went by to start the repairs this morning." He pointed to Lily as she interrupted them with a cough. "This is how I found her. I think the smoke got to her. She's been hacking away."

"I saw her. Actually had to restrain her to keep her from following you into the burning building." The doctor motioned for her to have a seat on the table in the center of the room.

"I'm not injured, Dr. Willis." She moved to the table and sat stiff with her hands in her lap.

He seemed to ignore her. "Are you light-headed?" He peered into her eyes and checked the pulse at the base of her neck.

"I am not." She glared at Edward, who had retreated to stand near the door. "I told Mr. Stone this trip was unnecessary, but he insisted." She slid toward the edge of the table, but the doctor prevented her from getting up.

"Just the coughing?" He assembled his stethoscope and pressed the bell against her back. "Take a deep breath."

She drew in a breath, and the coughing began again.

He moved to the opposite side of her back. "Again." The results were the same.

"I don't think you've done any major damage to your lungs, but it's probably going to take a few days for you to recover from taking in so much smoke." He paused to look at her. "Your color is good. I think it's just a matter of getting some rest."

"I don't have time to rest. I've got a business to open." She coughed into her handkerchief again, hating that her body was betraying her so. She needed to work. There would be time for rest later.

"A hard worker, are you?" The doctor tilted his head to one side and studied her.

Lily straightened her shoulders. "I am. It's how I was raised. We Warrens don't cotton to laziness or excuses."

He turned to Edward and nodded his head in Lily's direction. "She looks as good as any other lady around here. You oughta think about this one."

"I don't think so, Doc." Edward seemed to be laughing at her from his place in the corner of the room. First he'd insisted on bringing her here, and now he was a party to her ridicule. She wouldn't stand for it.

"I don't need a doctor." Anger gave her fresh strength, and she turned her eyes to the blacksmith. "Or a husband."

"As you wish." Dr. Willis backed away from the table. He turned toward the curtains where he'd made his entrance.

Another coughing spell overtook her. Between coughs Lily said, "Wait a minute, Doctor."

The doctor stopped with a hand on the curtain and raised an eyebrow. "Don't got all day, missy."

"I'm sorry. Can you give me something for the cough?" She hated to submit to the man but had no time for set-backs. Her father and sister would arrive in a few short weeks. She needed to have her shop open and bringing in business before then.

The doctor went to a glass cabinet against the back wall. Lily caught Edward looking at her with a grin of satisfaction. He was enjoying having been right about insisting she see the doctor.

"I want you to use this flaxseed to make a tea." The doctor handed her a bottle. "You can do it several times a day. It will help with the cough and clearing your lungs."

She took the bottle reluctantly. "Thank you."

Dr. Willis nodded. "Sensible, too, Edward. You need to reconsider this one."

Lily might submit to his ministrations but not to his attitude. "Really, Doctor, I don't think it's appropriate for you to discuss me as if I'm a prize horse."

"I didn't say you were a prize. Just worth a second consideration." He looked at Edward standing with his back to the door. "But only if she's given to moments of quiet."

The blacksmith laughed then. "I haven't seen one yet, Doc."

Lily scowled. "If you'll tell me your fee, Doctor, we'll be on our way." She hoped this ordeal was drawing to an end. How was it possible for her to be at the mercy of not one, but two belligerent men?

Edward waited while Lily paid the doctor, then held the door open for her to walk through before him.

"I'm coming back to the shop to get started on the repairs."

"Thank you for being so eager. I'm going to have to work harder than ever to get ready to open."

"Just don't try burning the candle at both ends."

"Very funny." She gave a tiny giggle. Then, in a fashion he could only imagine a cactus flower able to perform, her prickly expression transformed into beauty with a smile like none he'd ever seen. Golden hair framed her face. Vibrant blue eyes sought him out. His heart jolted. Nothing could lessen the power of her grace.

He shook his head. What was he thinking? She was beautiful all right. A rare beauty. But gentle and graceful? Not with the sharp tongue and feisty resistance he'd witnessed in the short time he'd known her.

Lily Warren might be named after a gentle spring flower, but her cactus-like thorns could prove dangerous, if not deadly, to a man not on his guard.

And Edward Stone was a man who would not let his guard down. Ever again.

"Possum run over your grave?"

"What?" He had to pay better attention.

"You're shaking your head and shivering." Lily's expression teased him, but he wouldn't tease back.

"No. Just a bad thought." He turned away from her and continued down the sidewalk. "Nothing to worry about." He'd make certain of that.

Lily picked up her pace and left him to follow. When they arrived at the shop, she opened the door, and the bell announcing their arrival clanged to the floor and bounced.

She sighed. "Great. Something else to be fixed."

"Be careful not to break anything else."

Her eyes widened in question. "Oh, so that's my fault? I see. Looks like our relationship will be one of blame and accusation." The smile was there again, but Edward was determined to thwart its power.

"Our relationship will be landlord and tenant." He stooped to retrieve the broken bell from just inside the doorway. "And the fault of this was mine, so I'll be responsible for the repair."

"You think it can be fixed?" Her uncertain gaze met his.

"Sure. It's a simple repair." He turned the bell over in his hand. "I should have made it stronger in the first place."

Blond brows lifted. "You made it?" Disbelief crossed her face.

"Don't look so surprised. I am a blacksmith."

"I'm sorry. The blacksmith in East River made horseshoes and wagon wheels. Not art."

Was she complimenting him? Did she realize it?

"I make horseshoes and wagon wheels, too. And iron gates, and farm tools…"

"I understand. Sort of a jack-of-all-trades, are you?"

"Are you suggesting I'm master of none?"

"Well, the bell did break…" Her smile was the only clue she was teasing him. Tormenting might be a better word, given the tightening of his gut when she looked at him.

"I wouldn't call myself an artisan. But I do enjoy creating unique things." He drifted into the past looking at the bell. It had been a gift for his sister, Jane. One she'd never taken the time to enjoy.

A swift movement had the bell in his pocket. Hidden with the memories it evoked.

When he raised his eyes, he found Lily staring with open curiosity.

"I best get to work, Miss Warren." He stepped into the center of the room. The late-morning sun lit the street beyond the deep windows. Windows Jane had dreamed of filling with pastries and cakes.

Lily breezed through the opening, which led from the large front room into a work area, with a lightness he'd never seen in any woman. If he'd had to describe it, he'd say her steps floated across the floor.

He followed her, and together they came up with a plan for the repairs. He would tear out anything damaged beyond repair. She proved a strong helper by toting all the charred boards out to the alley behind the shop.

They stopped at midday, and he made a list of the supplies he'd need to get the shop back in good shape.

He prepared to leave. "I'll stop by the lumber mill and order what I need before I go to the general store. I'll get a quick bite of lunch and come back."

"What about your coat?" she asked.

"That's why I'm going to the general store."

"Let me come with you so I can pay for it. You wouldn't need a coat if there hadn't been a fire."

He shook his head. "No."

"I insist."

Edward turned to look her full in the face. "Miss Warren, what do you think Mrs. Croft would think of that? After all she insinuated last night?"

Lily's cheeks went pink.

He looked over his shoulder out the front window. "I'll bring my wagon when I come back. We can use it to haul away the debris."

"I can help with that." She was unlike any other woman of her type, and Edward was impressed by how determined she was to help. At first glance, she gave the appearance of a lady accustomed to fine things. But she hadn't shied away from any of the work brought on by the damage from the fire.

"No, ma'am." He still wouldn't let her help load the rubble piled in the alley.

Lily smiled. "You must be as strong as an ox." Shock covered her face almost before the words left her mouth.

"I can haul my share of a load." He couldn't resist teasing her. As hard as he tried, his reserve kept slipping. "Most people don't call me an ox."

"Maybe not to your face, Mr. Stone." At least she had the decency to blush when she said it.

Edward heard the rumble of laughter in his chest. It had been a long time since he'd laughed out loud. "I'll be back after lunch." He tipped his hat and escaped through the front door.

He sobered immediately on seeing Mrs. Croft exit the post office next door. Her scowl spoke louder than anything she could have said before she turned and walked in the direction of her store.

Dust stirred in the street as his boots beat a path away from Lily Warren and her shop. He'd only rented it to her father out of desperation. The mortgage on the shop needed to be paid, not to mention the cost of providing for Ellen. He couldn't afford to let the shop stand empty any longer. When Jane came back, they'd make new arrangements. Until—or unless—she did, he needed the money.

He had to protect Lily's reputation, because if her shop failed, he could lose the building to the bank. He turned the corner and headed to the general store. His hands were shoved deep into his pockets, but the cold of the day was biting at him. Or maybe it wasn't the cold of the day, but the cold realizations storming his thoughts.

Life was complicated now. More than he'd ever wanted it to be.

In the back of his mind was a growing dread crying out for his attention. As a single man, if something tragic had happened to his sister and her husband, he'd need to marry. A young girl shouldn't be raised by her lone uncle. Ellen would need a woman's hand. Someone who was strong and gentle at the same time.

Someone like Lily.

Lily opened the door and wrapped her older sister in a hug. Could it be eleven years since Daisy had married and moved away from East River, their childhood home? When they'd reunited on her arrival in Pine Haven, Lily understood why their father had come home after his recent visit to Daisy's family wanting to sell everything in East River and move here. When he and Jasmine arrived in the spring, he'd have all his daughters together again. They'd been apart too long.

One look at Daisy's face and Lily prepared herself to be scolded. Even at twenty-four years old, her sisters still treated her like the baby of the family.

"What happened?" Daisy shifted baby Rose onto her shoulder and looked around at the destruction left by the fire.

"It was an accident." Lily knew Daisy wouldn't be satisfied without some explanation.

"How did it happen?"

She pointed to the chair she'd set up in front of the hall tree so her customers could view their hat selections in the mirror. "Have a seat, and I'll explain." She pulled up a stool and told her sister all that had happened.

"So Edward Stone saved you?" Daisy pushed Rose's bonnet away from her face and handed the child to Lily. "Handsome, isn't he?"

Lily lifted the baby and took in the sight of her chubby face. "She's so like Momma. I'm glad you named her after her." She pulled Rose close and breathed in the sweet baby smell. Rose twined her fingers into Lily's hair and gave a firm yank.

"Ow… She's a strong one, too." Lily loosed the tiny hand and nestled the babe in the crook of her arm.

"That she is." Daisy's face shone with love for her daughter. "You didn't answer my question about Edward Stone."

"Did you ask a question?" She hoped to avoid this kind of question about any man, let alone one who was already being accused of paying her too much attention. She couldn't risk feeding those rumors. Not even to her sister, who obviously hadn't heard them yet.

She jostled the baby. "Where are the twins?"

"They're in school."

"I can't believe they're nine years old. Seems life has begun to move at such a rapid pace."

"It comes from growing older, I suppose." Daisy looked her square in the face. "Lily, what do you think of your landlord?"

Lily stilled and answered. "He's my landlord. Yes, he saved me, but he also saved his building. That's all there was to it."

Daisy turned first one way then another and surveyed the shop. "If you say so."

"I do." Lily swept her free arm toward the open space.

"I wanted to have it in better shape, but I wasn't planning on a fire. What do you think?"

Daisy reached for Rose as the child started to whimper. "Don't worry. I'm sure Edward will have the repairs done in no time."

"I hope so. I've got to make this place work, or Papa will insist I live with him and Jasmine when they come." Lily fought back the fear of being isolated again. She'd spent too many years taking care of her sick father at home while all her friends had married and started families.

Daisy paced the floor, gently rocking the baby. "That wouldn't be so bad, would it? You've always lived with Papa. Why is this shop so important to you now?"

"It just is. You wouldn't understand. You have your life. A family. A farm. I didn't have anything." Anxiety sent her voice up a notch. "Until now."

She put a hand on Daisy's arm and stopped her motion. "Daisy, you have to pray for me. Papa isn't convinced a woman my age should be on her own. But I've just got to do this. I can't live in the shadows anymore. I want my own life."

"You talk as if you've been locked away as a slave. I know that isn't true. I lived there, too, you remember."

"It's not that at all. It's just…well." Lily wasn't certain she could articulate her thoughts. "I love Papa, and I'm so pleased he's well now. We weren't sure for so long that he'd ever get better. I'd do it all again in a heartbeat." She willed Daisy to understand. "But I need this for me."

"Of course, I'll pray for you, sweetie. I'll even make sure all my friends come see you as soon as you open."

That was encouraging. She could almost see the unknown ladies milling around the shop, fingering the lace on a handkerchief or smiling at their reflection wearing a new hat. "Are the ladies of Pine Haven ready for fancy hats and parasols?"

Daisy chuckled. "What ladies aren't?"

Lily was grateful for the support she saw in Daisy's expression. "Thank you. I promise I'll make you proud. Papa, too."

"The thought of having all of you here in Pine Haven is more than I ever dreamed. Your shop is like an extra blessing on top of that."

"I've got a lot of work to do to replace the things that were ruined. Thankfully, I hadn't opened all of the crates I brought." She indicated the crates stacked around the front of the shop. "These things are undamaged."

After lunch she'd gone over everything in her mind. Hopefully a couple of days would see the shop repaired. Maybe two more days after that and she'd be back on schedule for her new life.

She prayed the insinuations made by Mrs. Croft had been forgotten by those who heard them last night. That was the one detail she hadn't told her sister. If God answered as Lily wanted, she'd never hear of those accusations again.

She shook off the doubts that threatened from the recesses of her soul. A new life full of promise. She would do everything in her power to make it happen.

Chapter Three

Edward pulled his wagon behind the building and loaded the debris. He came to the front of the shop to enter, so anyone watching from the nearby businesses would see him. He was determined to do his part to squelch the rumors. Going in the back way would only feed the gossipers.

Lily was kneeling in front of an open crate rummaging through its contents and didn't hear the door when he opened it.

"Think I'll have to stop by Doc Willis's office and let him know how you're taking it easy."

Startled, Lily jerked up straight. "I'm perfectly fine."

He watched her frustration as the coughing overtook her again. "As long as—" she coughed "—no one tries to scare the breath out of me."

He closed the door. "Have you rested at all?" Everywhere he turned he saw evidence that she'd been busy.

"I stopped working and visited with Daisy. She came by to check on me."

Did he dare bring up the subject that he'd heard being discussed everywhere he'd gone in the two hours since he'd left her? "I saw her when I was leaving the lumber mill."

"Were you able to get the lumber ordered?" She didn't seem the least bit curious about anything other than the progress of the repairs.

"I did. Will Thomas said he'll have the order ready for me after I haul off the debris behind the shop."

She stood and brushed her hands together. "Let me help you load it."

"It's done." Knowing she'd be stubborn, he hadn't let her know he had returned until after he loaded the rubble into the wagon.

"I told you I would help."

"Doc Willis said you need to rest. I only came inside to see if you have anything else that needs to go."

"No." She rubbed her hands down the front of her skirt to smooth it. "At least let me go with you to unload it." She stepped toward the workroom. "Where are you taking it?"

"I've got a small burn pit behind my shop. What can't be salvaged, I'll burn later."

She came back into the front of the shop tugging on work gloves. "Are you ready?"

"Miss Warren, you can't come with me."

"Why ever not? The sooner you unload, the sooner you can get the lumber order and start on the repairs."

He cast a glance out the front window. "Have you been anywhere today? Besides the doctor's office?"

Her brow furrowed. She was cute with her face scrunched in confusion. "No. There's been too much to do here to go visiting."

Was it possible she had no clue? "Did your sister go anywhere before she came to see you?"

"No. She stopped by on her way into town." She looked at him. "Why?"

He didn't know the best way to tell her, so he just said it straight out. "We seem to be the topic of conversation all over town today."

"We? You mean about the fire?"

"No," he said. Her face had relaxed, and he didn't think she understood what he was trying to tell her. "I mean you and me."

Her shoulders lifted, and she gave a small snort. "That's silly." With one hand she gestured between the two of them. "There is no 'we.'"

"I know that." He paused. "But..."

She rose up a bit taller now and drew in a slow breath. "But what?" She angled her head away from him as if it would prevent the full onslaught of something she didn't want to hear.

"It seems that Mrs. Croft's assumptions from last evening have captured the fancy of some of the townsfolk."

Her eyes closed, and she drew her pretty lips inward. He watched her sigh as the implications sank in.

"Everywhere I went, someone brought it up."

Lily dropped onto a crate and wrung her hands together. "Oh, my. I hoped it would be forgotten in the light of day. No one knows me here. Why would they think I'd be so bold as to entertain a man in my home—unchaperoned—late at night?" Her gaze snapped to his. "Unless...what kind of reputation do you have, Mr. Stone?"

How dare she imply that his name in town was without respect! "Me?"

"Yes, you! In East River no one would ever suspect me of any behavior other than that of a Christian lady."

"I had hoped because you're Daisy's sister these rumors would not take hold." He shrugged his shoulders. "But they have."

The front door opened, and Daisy entered the shop. "Oh, Lily! I've just come from the general store." She put a hand on Lily's arm. "Why didn't you tell me what happened?"

Lily must not have expected it to be a problem, or surely she would have told her sister what had been said the night before.

Edward could see the panic filling her eyes when she answered. "Nothing happened! Except a fire!" She lowered her voice and asked, "What are they saying?"

Daisy hesitated. "I'm embarrassed to say." She glanced at Edward, then took Lily by the hand. "Mrs. Croft has given details about you being held in Mr. Stone's arms." She seemed to choose her words with great care. "In your dressing gown."

He needed Daisy to understand the truth. "I pulled her from a burning building. Her hair caught in my suspenders. There was no embrace. I carried her outside because she was overcome by the smoke."

Daisy shook her head. "That's not how Mrs. Croft portrayed it." She looked at Lily. "And because so many people were coming to see what was happening, they witnessed just enough to lend a hint of truth to her tale."

Lily stiffened her arms at her side and clinched her fists. "Truth? We'll tell them the truth! You tell them, Daisy. They'll believe you."

Daisy's husband, Tucker Barlow, came into the shop. Edward knew from his expression that this situation was not going to fade away.

Tucker removed his hat. "I see the news has made its way to all of you."

Lily almost begged for an answer from them. "What am I going to do?"

Edward didn't know what she was going to do. All he knew for sure was that his situation had become more desperate after he'd left Lily just before noon. He'd stopped in at the post office, and there was still no word from his sister, Jane.

He'd gone by the telegraph office and discovered the query he'd sent to the sheriff in Santa Fe had been answered. An outbreak of influenza had hit the community where Jane and Wesley lived, and they'd become gravely ill. The local doctor had sent them to a hospital in another community. No word on the name of the community or their condition.

If Jane and Wesley had passed, he was Ellen's only living relative. He'd do anything necessary to take care of her. He wouldn't risk losing this building. Talking of opening a bakery here would be one of the last things Ellen had shared with her mother. He'd keep the shop for Ellen to have when she was grown. A legacy in Jane's memory.

He cringed when the answer entered his mind, but he knew it was for the best. "What are *we* going to do?" He had to protect Ellen from the gossip that would surely swirl around the shop—and Lily if they didn't act quickly.

"We?" Lily countered.

They were standing in the workroom. The ravages of the fire all around them.

Edward pointed to a small frame Lily had hung on the wall over the workbench. "Are these the verses you live by?" The edges of the frame were scorched, but the intricate needlepoint was intact.

Lily followed his gaze. "Yes. Philippians is one of my favorite books in the Bible."

He read the words aloud. "'Let nothing be done through strife or vainglory; but in lowliness of mind let each esteem other better than themselves. Look not every man on his own things, but every man also on the things of others.'" He looked at her, hoping she'd agree. "That's what we need to do now."

"What do you mean? I'm not at strife with anyone in Pine Haven. I'm not out for vanity. But I do need a good name to run a successful business. What man will want his wife to patronize my shop if he thinks poorly of my character?"

"I'm afraid that's already happened. People assumed the worst when they saw us together last night."

"But we weren't together."

He shook his head. "That's not what they saw. I don't think we'll be able to convince them otherwise."

Lily put her hands to her face and closed her eyes. After a moment she opened them and held her hands out, palms up. "I came here to be independent. How can I do that without the goodwill of the townsfolk? You've ruined everything!"

"Would you rather I'd let you die in the fire? I couldn't stand by and watch the building burn to the ground, knowing you were inside."

Her shoulders slumped. "You're right, of course. But what are we going to do?"

Daisy and Tucker stood quietly while he and Lily tried to sort out this conundrum.

What he had to say next was private. He didn't know

Lily well, but he was most certain no lady would want witnesses for what he was about to say. "Will you excuse us, please?"

Daisy looked at Lily. Sisterly sympathy emanated from her.

Tucker took his wife by the arm. "We'll go for a slice of pie at the hotel and come back after you've had time to talk."

When the door closed behind them, Edward turned to Lily. "You know you're going to have to marry me now."

Lily's jaw dropped. To his surprise, words seemed to fail her.

"There is more to consider here than just you and me. I received word today that it's very possible my sister and her husband may have died of influenza."

She closed her mouth. "I'm so sorry. Poor Ellen." She'd gone from incredulous when he spoke of marriage to compassion for his niece in an instant. He hoped it would help her understand why he was making this proposition.

"I won't allow gossip to cause an innocent little girl to lose the only family she may have left. If my name is smeared with yours, I could lose her. A judge could say I'm not fit to be a guardian as an unmarried man—especially if I'm purported to have committed unseemly behavior."

"But we're innocent."

"I know that, and you know that." He put a hand on her sleeve and turned her so she could see through the entry of the workroom to the windows in the front of the shop. Two women had stopped to peer in the glass. When they caught sight of Edward and Lily, they frowned and hurried away. "But we'll never convince them. Or the people who are like them."

"Did the doctor put this notion in your head?"

He shook his head. Never would he have imagined himself offering marriage to someone he'd just met. If it weren't for Ellen, he might not have offered.

Then he looked into those blue eyes, churning to violet with emotion, and knew he was doing this for Lily and himself, too. No one deserved to be destroyed by gossip and rumors. "Believe me, I was just as resistant as you. Until I spent part of the day trying to convince people that nothing happened. Now it looks like we don't have a choice."

He willed her to understand. "If you don't open your shop, I don't know how I can pay the mortgage. I can't lose this building. I need to be able to give it to Ellen when she's grown. Maybe it will help her remember her mother."

"But why would you want to marry me? I'm not your responsibility."

"It's not just about you." He drew in a breath. "Ellen needs a mother. It's something I started pondering lately, and this must be God's way of answering."

"I can't mother her. My own mother passed when I was younger than Ellen. I won't know what to do."

"I think you will. You're strong. She'll need to be strong." He hesitated. This was not the way he ever imagined proposing to someone. For that matter, he hadn't really imagined proposing to anyone. His solitary life had suited him just fine before Jane left Ellen in his care. "But you're also gentle. She needs a woman's hand."

"How did this ever happen?" Lily's head sank into her hands.

"It seems that it was out of our control from the beginning."

She looked up at him. "Do you think we can do it? Raise Ellen and protect my reputation so the shop will be successful?"

"From what I've seen of you, I don't think the shop's success is in question, as long as we take care of your honor." He prayed he was doing the right thing. "As for Ellen, it looks like the good Lord left her in my care. I don't think He orchestrated your problems, but I'd say as His children, He's giving us a way to make the best of it."

"I can't think why you'd do this for me." Lily bit her bottom lip.

"It's like the verse." He pointed to her needlework. "We're taking care of the needs of others. Ellen needs us both."

Lily's face turned pink, and she met his gaze. "What kind of relationship do you expect the two of us to have?"

He could tell it cost her a great deal to form the words. Then he felt the same heat rushing into his face. "Miss Warren, I'd expect for you to care for Ellen as a mother. This arrangement will be strictly for the sake of my niece."

Edward watched her as the breath she'd been holding seeped out of her to be replaced by relief.

"For the sake of Ellen?"

"Yes. And you."

"I didn't come to Pine Haven to find a husband. I'll never forget what you've done here today, Mr. Stone. You're giving up an awful lot to take on a wife you didn't want."

"I want Ellen to have a mother."

"In that case, I accept." She offered her hand for him to shake. Did she really see this as a business arrangement like the one he had with her father for the lease on his building?

It was a relief she seemed to accept his reasons so quickly, but the reality of how much his life was about to change threatened to overwhelm him at any moment.

"I do." Lily stood in front of Reverend Dismuke and repeated the marriage vows.

Daisy and Tucker had agreed with Edward, and it had only been a matter of hours before they'd arrived at the church. Long enough for Lily to change to her best dress. The lingering hint of smoke in its fibers reminded her of the reason she was doing this. When she'd prepared for bed the night before, she'd never have dreamed today would be her wedding day.

Edward took her hand and slid a small gold band onto her finger. She'd told him she didn't need a ring, but he'd insisted, saying it was another way to reinforce their union in the eyes of the community. He'd escorted her into the general store and asked her to choose from the tray of rings. She'd been relieved when he'd asked Mr. Croft to assist them, leaving Mrs. Croft sputtering and mumbling as she'd moved on to help another customer.

Lily looked at the delicate, plain ring. Edward didn't release her hand for the rest of the short ceremony. His hands were large but gentle. And strangely comforting, as if he was trying to reassure her they were doing the right thing.

"You may kiss the bride." Reverend Dismuke's words rang out in the nearly empty church. Only Daisy and Tucker, with their twin sons and baby daughter, sat on the bench opposite the reverend's wife, who kept an arm around the shoulders of Edward's niece. Lily wasn't sure if it was an effort on the woman's part to comfort Ellen or an attempt to keep the child from fleeing. The young girl had refused to attend until Edward told her she had no choice.

Edward took his other hand and turned Lily's chin to face him. A small smile played on his lips. He'd said they'd have an easier time overcoming the gossip if everyone was convinced their marriage was born of affection and not shame. But did he honestly intend to kiss her?

"Relax," he whispered. Then he grazed her cheek with the briefest of contact.

In an instant Lily found herself wrapped in her sister's hug while the preacher clapped Edward on the back and congratulated him.

Why was everyone so merry? They all knew she and Edward, given the choice, would never have married. Well, maybe the Dismukes didn't know that, but her family did.

Daisy held her hands and spoke, "We're taking Ellen home with us for the night." She gave a nod in the direction of the bench where Edward's niece still sat clinging to her handkerchief doll. Lily had never seen the child without that doll.

Lily watched as Edward accepted Tucker's welcome into their family. Lily hadn't thought about being alone with Edward. No, she needed Ellen to be at the cabin tonight. And every night.

"That's not necessary."

Daisy smiled and patted her hand. "We insist. I've already told her she can sleep in Rose's room."

"But…" Lily felt her life spinning like a toy top. She had to maintain some form of control.

Edward turned and met her gaze. He must have sensed her desperation, because he came to stand beside her. He was close enough for her to feel the warmth of him, but he didn't touch her. "Tucker just told me they've invited Ellen to their place."

"She can stay with us. There's no need." Better to face Ellen's reluctance than to face alone a husband she hadn't expected to have.

He leaned in to speak near her ear. His breath ran across her neck, leaving a chill with each word. "We've got a lot of things to sort out. I'd like to do it without Ellen's eager ears close by."

What did he want to sort out? She straightened her shoulders. There were a myriad of things. How they would handle finances, daily chores, the rebuilding of the workroom in her shop, and how to protect Ellen.

She agreed.

"Thank you, Daisy. That's very kind of you." Lily smiled at her sister but knew the smile didn't reach her eyes. Numbness was the only sensation she experienced at the moment, and she feared it would fade into regret.

Ellen plodded over to Edward. "Do I gotta go to the Barlows' farm?" Her bottom lip protruded, and the doll hung from her crossed arms.

He lifted the little girl's chin with one knuckle. "You know you love to go visit the Barlows. You can play with baby Rose." He smiled at her and patted her shoulder. "You'll have a good time, I promise. You can come say hello in the morning on your way into town for school."

Daisy moved to stand behind Ellen and put a hand on her shoulder. "Why don't we go by your cabin and get some clothes? Then we'll head out to the farm, and you can help John and James feed the animals."

Ellen's eyes aimed a dart of resentment at Lily before she agreed to Daisy's suggestion. "Bye, Uncle Edward."

"Goodbye, Ellen." As she started to tromp away, Edward called to her again. "Ellen, you forgot to tell your aunt Lily goodbye."

"Aunt Lily? I gotta call her 'aunt'?"

"You are permitted to call her Aunt Lily." He tilted his head to one side. "It's a privilege."

A long sigh came from her little body. "Bye, *Aunt* Lily."

"Goodbye, Ellen." She smiled at the girl, wondering how she must feel. Without warning, her home had changed today, and there was nothing she could do about it. In a way, Lily understood her childish frustration. She was almost tempted to cross her arms and pout, too.

Edward offered Lily his arm. She knew he was merely keeping up appearances. It was comforting and unsettling at the same time. Their marriage was the only way to remove themselves from the whirlwind of tortuous rumors they'd been caught up in for the past twenty-four hours.

Lily wanted to protect their good names. Individually. Hooking her hand on his arm and leaving the church felt as false as the lies Mrs. Croft had spread about them. Were they perpetrating one lie to negate the effects of another lie? Would God honor them for trying to save Ellen? She hoped so.

They rode in silence to her shop. Edward set the brake on the wagon.

"Do you need a few minutes to put your things together?" he asked.

Most of her clothes and personal belongings were still in trunks and crates. There would be little to pack.

She looked across the street to the cabin she would now share with Edward. Her husband.

Her husband? She had come here to escape a marriage to a man who only wanted a companion for his ailing mother. Now she sat in a wagon between the shop she was opening to start a new independent life and a cabin where her primary role would be to care for a young girl she'd only known a few days. A girl who'd made it plain that Lily was an intruder in her turbulent young life.

Lily had heard stories of people who disappeared in the night, leaving only a note for their loved ones, striking out on their own, hoping for a fresh start. She'd come here for that reason—with the blessing and help of her family. Had it only taken two days for her world to turn upside down?

Edward's touch on her sleeve drew her attention. "Are you all right?"

It was tempting to write a note and steal away in the night. But she could never leave her sisters and father like that. Not after all her father had done to give her a new life. Somehow she'd make this work. Edward had noble intentions, which was more than she could say for her former fiancé, Luther Aarens.

She shook off her thoughts and accepted her fate. "Fine, thank you."

Edward nodded toward her shop. "You'll want to get your clothes and such."

"Yes." She scooted to the edge of the wagon seat away from him and prepared to step down. "I'll need a little while to put some things back into the trunks."

"Wait a minute. I'll help you down." He climbed from the wagon and came around to assist her. With the briefest of contact, he lifted her and set her on the ground.

"You go in and take care of that. I'll make space in the cabin for you."

She looked at him when he spoke, but his gaze went over her shoulder. When he did focus on her, she turned away. "I won't need much space." She twisted her hands together.

"I remember you had a couple of pieces of large furniture upstairs." He pointed to the window of her front room above the shop. "From when I helped carry it in."

Awkward held new meaning as they stood talking about her things. Things she hadn't thought she'd share with anyone. Things she'd brought to make her comfortable in her new home. Nothing was turning out as she'd planned.

She remembered a verse in Proverbs. "In all thy ways acknowledge Him, and He shall direct thy paths." Her faith in God would have to sustain her now. There was no course except to move forward as she'd agreed.

"We can move those things another day. If you don't mind, we can just get my clothes and personal items today. Perhaps Tucker can help with the furniture later."

Edward shuffled from one foot to another. He must be as nervous as she was. "That's good." He dipped his head and looked over his shoulder at the cabin. "I'll just be on my way, then."

He turned and took a step. Not knowing she was going to do it before it happened, Lily reached for his arm. He stilled and turned back to her.

"I know this isn't what either of us thought we'd be doing today." When he looked at her hand on his arm, she dropped it. "I hope we can make this work without everything being uncomfortable or awkward."

His thin lips curled into a half smile. He really was a

giant of a man. Tall and broad with all the strength she imagined a blacksmith would need to do his job. But the softness of the smile and the way his almost-black eyes twinkled was a pleasant surprise. "No promises about not feeling awkward for a while. I haven't shared my home with another living soul until Ellen came to live with me a few months ago. I'm not quite sure you and I will see eye to eye on everything. It's a big adjustment to get to know someone new. I'm guessing we complicated it more than a little bit by getting married before we could do that."

She felt herself smiling in return. "That's a wise observation, Mr. Stone. I'm sure you're right."

"That's what I mean."

The smile faded and she asked, "What?"

"Mr. Stone? Really? Is that how you intend to address me?"

She gave a small chuckle. "I see. No. I don't think that will do any longer." She drew back her shoulders and took hold of her future with all her strength. "Edward, I'll be about a half hour preparing my things to move into our home. If you'd be so good as to meet me in the shop after you've finished preparing a space for me, I'll be most grateful."

She gave a little giggle. "How was that?"

He laughed in a deep tone. "That's just fine." He nodded. "Just fine, indeed."

When he headed for the cabin, she entered the shop. As she climbed the stairs to the home she'd only spent two nights in, she marveled that it would be the only two nights of her life spent as an independent woman.

Her dream of a shop wasn't dead. She wouldn't let it die. But her independence was over. She prayed for God to help her as she packed away the things she'd so carefully placed in her new home. When she'd asked for a new life, she wasn't prepared for this twist. God would have to light her path, because it was one she'd never dreamed would be hers.

In one major event, she'd gone from Lily Warren, milliner and shop owner, to Lily Stone, milliner, shop owner, wife and mother.

Chapter Four

Edward tossed his dirty clothes into a pile by the bedroom door. His cabin wasn't grand, but it wasn't small. If he'd built it himself, it would not have had two bedrooms, but the house was part of the deal when he'd bought his blacksmith shop from the previous owner. As soon as he was old enough, he'd moved out on his own to escape the stepmother his father had brought home shortly after his dear mother had died. She'd given no affection to him or Jane. Time and again he'd wished his father had never married her. Finding work as an apprentice to the town blacksmith had given him a purpose and place in life.

Eventually he'd nurtured a vague hope of one day having a family of his own. But over the years, he'd found it safer to retreat alone at night into the sanctuary of his home. His mistrust of women in general was based on years of watching his father's wife take advantage of his father. Her sweet facade had quickly faded after she'd convinced his father to marry her. She'd never truly loved him and had been horrid to Edward and Jane. Nothing they did was ever good enough for her. She'd settled into their home as mistress and ordered them about in her aloof manner, as though she felt them beneath her care or attention. Jane had been too young when she married, but until Wesley had whisked her away to Santa Fe, Edward had thought it was for the best.

Edward stripped the linens from the bed and added them to the pile by the door. A small crate from the back porch would suffice for his personal items. He put his shaving cup and brush in and then tossed in the small mirror from the top of his chest of drawers. He pulled a rag from his back pocket and took a swipe at the dust on top of the furniture.

Backing up in the doorway, he took a last look around. Not what he'd have done in normal circumstances for bringing home a wife, but it was the best he could manage in the half hour she'd allotted him. He stowed the small crate in a corner near the stove and gathered up the laundry. He tossed it onto the workbench on the back porch and headed back into the front room.

A light rapping sounded on the door, and his breath caught. He was doing this for Ellen. She needed a mother. Life might be upside down, but that little girl would always have a home with him.

He lifted the latch on the door and pulled it open. Lily stood in the street at the bottom of the porch steps. She must have knocked and backed as far away as she could.

He dragged his palms down the sides of his pants. "Hi."

Pink color soaked into Lily's cheeks. She really was a beautiful lady. At this moment, she must be just as nervous as he was. "Hello."

Edward stepped through the doorway. "Did you get everything packed?"

"Everything I'll need until we can move the furniture." She didn't look at him.

He reached inside the cabin and took his hat from the peg by the door. "Okay. I'll go get everything, then." He pushed the hat onto his head and walked down the porch steps.

She hesitated. "Would you mind if I took a look inside first?"

"Inside the cabin?"

"Yes. I want to see how much space there is, so I can decide what to bring and what to leave behind."

"Oh." He took the hat off again. "That makes sense." He shrugged his shoulders and lifted an arm to invite her up the steps. He heard a thump and turned to see the door of the livery open. Jim Robbins stood in front of his place and made no effort to hide his interest in the goings-on at Edward's house. Edward turned and looked up the street. Mrs. Winters was sweeping the sidewalk in front of the post office. He pivoted and saw Will Thomas in the doorway of the lumber mill.

Edward put his hat back on and took Lily by the elbow. "It seems we're being watched."

She followed his gaze and saw the obvious interest their neighbors were showing. She giggled like a schoolgirl. It was a light sound, like water over rocks in a stream in summertime. "You'd think there was a fire or something."

He chuckled. "One would think so."

"What should we do? Wave? Or ignore them."

He drew in a breath. "Do you trust me?"

"I believe I've proved that already. After all, I did marry you less than an hour ago."

Mr. Croft walked by on the street and tipped his hat.

He made a show of greeting Mr. Robbins when he arrived at the livery.

Edward leaned in close. "What goes on here will affect us all. How well your business does, and how well our marriage is accepted. All of it could have consequences for us and for Ellen."

Lily looked over his shoulder and nodded. "I'd say this town is very interested in us at the moment. I hope it will fade in time. Quickly, would be my preference."

"Then I say we do our part to keep the busybodies from having anything to talk about."

"How do you propose to do that?"

"By living the part of a normal married couple."

Lily's eyes grew wide.

He gave her elbow a slight squeeze. "What I meant to say is if we give every indication of being a normal married couple, when we're outside the cabin, no one looking will have any reason to question our relationship. The best way for them to concentrate on someone else is for there to be nothing to see here."

"I think I see what you mean." Her face relaxed.

"Good. So we're agreed?"

She nodded.

"Here we go, then." Edward leaned close and, with one hand behind her back and another behind her knees, he scooped her off her feet.

Caught unawares, she gave a tiny yelp and wrapped her arms around his neck. She whispered close to his ear. "What are you doing?"

"I'm carrying you across the threshold." He climbed the steps and walked into the cabin. He turned in the doorway and kicked the door closed with his foot.

Lily laughed. "I think I may have married a deranged man."

Edward laughed and set her on her feet. He put the distance of the room between them. "Not deranged." He closed the shutters across one of the front windows. "But never happy to be the center of attention." He closed the other shutters and dropped into a chair at the table.

Lily stepped to the cabinet next to the stove and looked out of the window that faced Main Street. "Then why did you make such a scene? Mr. Winters has joined his wife on the sidewalk, and they're talking to Mr. Croft. Mrs. Winters is smiling and looking in our direction."

"Close the shutters." Edward leaned back in the chair and stretched his legs out in front of him.

"It's the middle of the afternoon."

"I know. But if you don't want them walking by on this side of the street and trying to peek in the window, you'll close the shutters."

Lily swung the shutters closed. The dim interior of the room was lit only by the fire. He marveled again at how gracefully she moved.

He went to the stove and set the coffee to warm. "Why don't you sit by the fire? You've got to be bone tired."

A slight shrug of her shoulders was the only response.

"It's not the day either of us planned." He opened a tin of cookies Mrs. Dismuke had brought for Ellen. His niece might not want him to share her treats, but he'd deal with her later.

Lily sat on the edge of a chair facing the fire. "Nothing has gone like I planned for most of my life." He watched the back of her head as she shook it slowly back and forth. "I'd so hoped things would be different in Pine Haven."

Edward poured two cups of coffee. "Do you drink coffee?"

"Yes." She didn't turn away from the fire. Her shoulders slumped forward.

He brought a cup to her and set the tin of cookies on the table by her chair. "This might help you." He retrieved his cup and sat on the bench in front of the fire facing her.

She sipped the brew, and her face twisted. "Oh, my."

"Not to your taste?"

"Is it to yours?" She looked up at him.

"Not really. But it's the best I've been able to do."

She sat up straight and set the cup on the table. "Did you bake the cookies?" A wary eye told him she was being cautious when it came to his efforts at cooking.

"No. The preacher's wife brought them for Ellen. They're quite good."

"Do you think Ellen will be upset with you for sharing them with me?"

He grinned. She'd only been in town a couple of days, but she'd already figured out Ellen's personality. "Probably. So consider it her wedding gift to you."

She took a cookie and nibbled at it. Then she took another bite and picked up a second cookie.

"Have you eaten today, Lily?"

"I don't remember. Everything has happened so fast." She stared into the fire again. "I think I had some lunch."

"Eat another cookie, then, and we'll get some things figured out before we go get your trunks from the shop. I've got to take care of the wagon, too."

She put the half-eaten cookie down and stood. "I'm sorry. I forgot about the wagon."

"Relax." She was like a frightened colt, jumping at

every noise. "We need to wait a bit before we go outside again. If it's all the same to you, I'd like to talk for a few minutes."

She paced to the fireplace and back to the chair. "What are we doing?"

Edward stood and set his coffee on the table. "We're making life better. For you. And for Ellen."

Blue eyes looked up then. "We are, aren't we?" She seemed to calm a bit.

"Yes." He'd have to guard against those eyes. They were the kind of blue that could pull a man in against his will. Like a gorgeous sky that demanded attention. He took a step back. "Would you like to look around? Ellen's room is through that door." He gestured to the door closest to the fireplace. "I've cleared some space for you in my room." He pointed to the other door on the back wall of the room.

Lily stiffened. He didn't see it, but as soon as he said the words he knew it happened.

"Your room?"

"What I meant to say is, you'll have the other room." He nodded toward the fire. "I'll be sleeping out here."

"But I couldn't take your room."

"If you don't mind, I'd like to keep my clothes and such in there, but I brought out my shaving things and stripped the bed. I thought you might have fresh linens you'd like to put on it."

"Really, we can bring the settee from my rooms at the shop. I can sleep there." She wrung her hands. "You'd never fit on it." She lifted one hand to indicate his height. "You're much too tall." She pointed to the center of the room. "We could move the chairs back and…"

She was talking so fast he had to break in. "That

won't be necessary." He pointed to the floor. "This is where I slept when I came here as an apprentice. The former owner took me in."

"But now you're the owner, and a man ought to sleep in his own bed." Her voice became higher, and she was wringing her hands again.

He reached out and caught her hands in his. "Lily. Stop." He kept his tone calm. If she maintained this pace, she'd work herself into a frenzy. "It's going to be fine. I'll sleep out here. Ellen goes to bed early. She'll never know. You will take my bed. It's the best I could do with the time I had."

She withdrew her hands and put them to her cheeks. "It is all happening rather quickly, isn't it?" She lowered her hands and met his eye. "I'm sorry. I'm not usually the sort of person to panic."

"Anyone would be unsettled under the circumstances."

"You don't seem to be." She tilted her head to one side and drew her brows together. "Why is that?"

"I told you. I've been considering marriage for the sake of Ellen." He smiled at her. "Granted, I had thought to have more time for making the decision, but I was pondering it." He moved to the bedroom door and opened it. "If you'd like to take a look around, I'll see what I have that we could eat for supper."

"Thank you." She walked by him, and he went to see how much bread was left.

He had planned on making pancakes for Ellen and himself. It hardly seemed a fitting wedding supper. Even if they weren't in the throes of young love, they were married today. His bride deserved a fine meal.

Something banged on the floor in his bedroom.

Lily called out. "Sorry. I tripped on the broom."

He walked over and stood in the doorway of the room. "I shouldn't have left it there. It's usually on the back porch." He'd never hesitated about going into his own room before. But it wasn't just his anymore.

"Thank you for doing such a nice job of preparing for me." She stood in the center of his room with her hands clasped in front of her. "It's very nice."

"I'm sure it's not what you're accustomed to." He backed away from the door.

"Really, it's fine." She stepped into the front room again. "Let's go get my things. I'd like to close up the shop. There's a lot to do this evening." She had walked to the front door while she talked. "Did you find anything to eat?"

Edward grabbed his hat from its peg. "Nothing fit for a wedding supper." He opened the door. "I think we've earned a treat. Let's get your things and go to the hotel for supper."

Lily laid her hairbrush between the comb and mirror in the satin-lined box her father had given her for her last birthday and closed the lid. She ran her hand across the wooden box and marveled at its uniqueness. The beauty of the ornate dresser set made her smile every time she used it. It reminded her of her father's love.

Every woman deserved to feel special. She'd come to Pine Haven to bring beautiful things to the ladies in town. It was one thing she could do well. She knew what ladies liked and how the smallest treasure could brighten even the most menial life.

Now, three days into her new adventure and she was preparing for bed in a home she shared with a husband she just met.

Dinner had been delicious. The thick slices of ham served with the fluffiest potatoes were as fine as any she'd eaten. They'd dined at the hotel her father was buying and would run with her sister Jasmine, when he arrived in a few weeks' time. If it hadn't been her wedding supper, she knew she'd have been able to enjoy it more. Never had she dreamed her wedding would be a hasty affair orchestrated to prevent the demise of her good name in a town of strangers.

Lord, I don't know why all this happened. Help me to handle it in a way that pleases You. Please bless and protect Edward and Ellen.

She lowered the wick, and the lamp went out. Lying in bed and staring at the moonlight that shone around the shutters brought no calm to her rattled soul.

A rap at the door startled her. "Lily? Are you awake?"

Lily sat up in bed and pulled her mother's quilt under her chin. "Yes." Her voice was so low she wasn't sure Edward could hear her.

"I hate to disturb you, but I left my Bible by the bed."

"Just a minute." She climbed out of the bed and slid into her dressing gown. This time she cinched it securely. A loose robe would never happen to her again. Of course, the only time it mattered had already passed.

She barely opened the door. "Do you have a lamp? I put mine out and don't know where the matches are."

"Yes." Edward retrieved a lamp from the table by his chair near the fireplace and handed it to her. "I'm sorry to bother you. I'm having a bit of trouble getting to sleep. I usually read the Bible at night."

"I understand." She turned into the room and found the well-worn book. "I was just saying my prayers."

A smile lit his eyes. "I hope you said one for me."

Glad for the relative darkness, she passed the lamp back to him as her cheeks flamed warm. "I did. And for Ellen, too." She handed him the Bible and backed away from the door.

"Thank you."

"You're welcome." She looked over her shoulder into the room. "I guess I'll turn in now."

He nodded. "Well, good night, then. I'll see you in the morning. We've got a lot of work to do."

"Yes. I'll be ready." She closed the door and leaned against it. How would she ever get to sleep tonight? An exciting adventure into independence had turned into the journey that would last her lifetime. She prayed God would give her the strength to make it.

When she awoke the next morning, the cabin was quiet. She dressed without delay, grateful she'd thought to bring her pitcher and bowl with her. The privacy of Edward's bedroom shielded her from having to face her new life before she was alert. She opened the shutters over the window to be greeted by a sun much higher in the sky than she'd expected. How had she slept so late?

Opening the door into the front room, she braced for her first encounter with her husband. Her husband.

God, give me strength.

This was quickly becoming her constant prayer. God must be showing His sense of humor today, because Edward was nowhere to be seen. She took a peek into Ellen's room. Everything was just as it had been the night before.

Sunlight streamed through the windows in the front room. No time for breakfast now. She went back to her room and snatched up her hat and coat. This was no way to begin her new life. What would Edward think of her shirking her responsibilities on their first day of working to repair the shop?

Lily walked across the street without seeing anyone. She found the shop empty, too. Where was Edward? She hung her hat and coat on the hall tree and got to work. A full hour later the front door opened. Edward came in carrying a package wrapped in brown paper. He propped it in the windowsill and shrugged out of his coat.

"Oh, good. You're here." He hung his coat next to hers. "Did you sleep well?"

"Where were you?" Lily's stomach growled in hunger.

"Excuse me?" Edward went to the front door and started to remove the wooden trim from around the window he'd broken so he could get into the shop on the night of the fire.

"I've been here for over an hour. I thought we were going to work together this morning." Why didn't he look at her? Was he as uncomfortable as she was?

"I've been working for several hours, Lily." He dropped the trim pieces into a pile at his feet and scrubbed the end of the hammer along the edge of the frame to remove the remaining bits of broken glass.

"I wish you'd awakened me." Lily had established a comfortable working relationship with Edward as her landlord. But today he was also her husband. She didn't know how to behave toward him.

"I knocked on the door."

"I didn't hear you. You could have made certain I was awake."

He dropped the hammer into the small box of tools near his feet and turned to her. "Really?"

"Of course." She backed up a step from him. "I

wanted to be here early. I don't know when I've slept so late."

"How was I supposed to respect your privacy and wake you without coming into the room?"

Lily looked at her feet. "Oh. I see." She walked to the glass display case and picked up the rag she'd been using to wipe the soot from the furniture. Edward must be as off balance by their situation as she was.

She heard him tearing the paper from the package he'd brought with him.

"Will you hold this glass steady while I nail the trim work back into place?"

She dropped the rag and brushed her hands together. "Certainly."

Edward set the pane on the lip of the frame and held it steady. "Put your hands here and here."

Lily followed his instructions. He stooped to pick up the first piece of trim and slid it between her and the door. She stretched as far as possible to one side, so he could hammer without hitting her. He worked with several small nails between his lips. Each time he hammered one into place he retrieved another.

Talking around the nails, he admitted, "I knew you hadn't slept the night before. You needed the rest."

"I'm sorry." She shifted so he could put the next piece of trim on the opposite side of her, all while holding the pane of glass. "I wanted to help you."

"There was nothing you could do this morning. I was picking up the supplies we need." He tapped the last piece into place, and she backed away. It was difficult to be so close to him working, knowing neither of them had intended to be working together at all, much less as husband and wife.

"Well, all the same, I'd have been here if I were awake." Her stomach rumbled again.

"Let me guess." He picked up the box of tools and headed for the workroom. "You didn't eat breakfast."

She followed to retrieve the broom and dustpan. She might not have gone with him to buy the supplies, but she would clean up the mess. "No. I wasn't sure where you were. I was late enough as it was."

He dropped the box onto the workbench. "Lily, we need to establish some kind of expectations for our relationship and act accordingly."

She stilled, broom in hand, and leaned against the doorway between the shop and the workroom.

Edward exhaled as if he were gathering his nerve. "We were able to work together in a friendly manner before the fire. I'd like for us to continue to do that. We've both been on pins and needles since we decided to get married. We both did it for noble reasons. Do you think you can relax? I declare, the more nervous you are around me, the more nervous it makes me." He stopped and drew in a deep breath.

A rumbling laugh bubbled up in her throat. She tried to swallow it but couldn't. "You're so right. We're no different than we were two days ago."

His eyebrows shot up. "Maybe a little different."

She did laugh then. "Yes, but we're the same people. With the same goals."

"Some of the goals are different, too." He scrunched up his face a bit.

"You know what I mean." She stepped forward and put a hand on his arm. "I agree with you. Let's continue as the friends we were becoming before the fire."

"Good." He looked at her and then at her hand on his arm.

She dropped her hand. "I'm glad we got that settled." She turned to go back into the shop and sweep up the glass.

Edward followed her. "Would you like some lunch?"

"Yes, I would. As soon as I sweep up this mess, I'll go upstairs and put something together for us. All my food stores are still here."

"All right." He nodded toward the workroom. "Then I'll get to work in here."

"Okay, then." She swept up the glass, wondering what her life would be like now. Everything she'd envisioned was like the glass at her feet. Shattered. Beyond repair. Replaced by something new. The new glass served the same purpose, but the old glass would soon be forgotten. Could she forget her dreams of independence? Would her new life afford her the same fulfillment? Establishing her shop would make her financially independent. That would be a comfort to her as she watched the rest of her dreams disappear. Tonight Ellen would return, and Lily's new role as mother to the young girl would begin.

Lily knew opening a new business would be a great challenge. She was certain winning Ellen's trust would be greater.

Chapter Five

Edward stepped into the front of the shop and heard Lily cry, "Oh, no!"

She let out a yelp, and he was at the workroom door as she stumbled backward. The highest shelf in the storeroom was just beyond reach from her stool. She'd climbed onto the workbench, overreaching to push the extra hatboxes out of the way.

Seeing her arms flailing, he crossed the shop floor as she lost her struggle to right herself. The breath whooshed out of her as she landed against his chest.

"Wonderful." Edward set her to her feet. "I see you're still following Doc's orders."

Disapproval, not surprise, covered her face.

"I was just trying to make room to work." She brushed her hands together to remove the dust. "I'm perfectly fine."

"Just how fine would you be if I hadn't come along?"

"How do you know I wasn't startled by you coming into the shop unannounced?"

"Because I heard your screech while I was outside."

"Never you mind. I'm not hurt, and I've more work to do." Lily twirled and marched to the front of the shop.

"You're welcome." He followed her.

Lily hung her head but smirked. "Thank you so much for helping me catch my balance."

"Catch your balance? You'd be lying on the floor broken if I hadn't come in here when I did! You might want to be more careful if you intend to open your shop next week. Or at all."

"You're right. I have a tendency to lessen the intensity of things after the fact." She smiled. "Thank you for saving my life."

"Catching your balance? Saving your life?" Edward laughed. "Is there no middle ground with you, Lily?"

Her eyebrows shot up when he spoke her name. Would she be able to relax and accept a modicum of familiarity from him?

He grimaced and indicated the bell he'd dropped on the table when he'd rushed to help her. "I came to mount this."

She reached for the bell. "It's lovely." She studied his handiwork. It hadn't taken long to repair, but it was intricate work. He was glad she approved.

"I brought a new bracket to make sure it doesn't fall again." Their fingers brushed when she handed the bell to him. A tingling sensation caught him off guard. He didn't know if he was more surprised by how the touch of her fingers stirred his skin or how her words of kindness and approval brushed against his wary heart.

"Thank you. I've work to do in the back room. I'll leave you to it." Her quick steps confirmed her hurry to escape his presence. "If you need me, just give a shout." She darted a glance over her shoulder.

"It's a bit more likely you'll be calling out for help from me," Edward muttered as he turned to work on the bell.

"I heard that." She laughed. "You're probably right, but allow me the opportunity to think I might be safe on my own."

He'd replaced the burned shelves in the workroom by midafternoon, then left her to get her supplies set up as she pleased. That had given him time to go across the street to his shop and repair the bell. He hoped it was the last thing she'd need. After two days away from his shop, he was behind on his work.

Edward dropped the bell, and it clanged on the wooden floor.

"Are you all right out there, or do you need my help?" Lily's sarcasm danced into the room on her words.

"Got it." He inspected the bell for damage. "Thankfully, my foot broke its fall."

"Good thing it didn't hit you in the head. You'd have to make a new one." Lily snickered from the opening to the workroom.

He stood with his hands holding the bell above the door and angled his face to see her. Just as he suspected. A wide grin.

"Very funny." He chuckled before turning back to his work. He gave the nail one final rap and released the bell and bracket.

"Good as new." He started gathering his tools and putting them back in the box.

"Great."

He picked up his toolbox. "Is that everything?" He watched as she looked around the shop.

"I think so. The rest will be up to me. I've got to make new stock. I'm hoping it will only take a few days."

"Provided you don't sleep the mornings away?" He dipped his hat and stepped out the door. "I'll see you at home in a little while."

Edward heard her stamp her small foot on the floorboards as he closed the door, and a grin tugged at his mouth.

Standing on the steps of the building—his building— he marveled at the life one small creature could bring to a place. Not since his sister left town had he sparred with a woman. He found it invigorating.

A shudder ran up his back, and he tromped off the porch. That was not a healthy path to travel. Following the excitement of conversation with a young woman was not where he was headed in life. Not at all.

Their marriage was about Ellen. He'd serve himself well to remember that.

Edward opened the door to Ellen's room. "Come to the table, young lady. Aunt Lily called you several minutes ago."

His niece sat in the middle of the bed with her arms folded around the doll his sister had made for her. "I don't like carrots." Her bottom lip protruded.

He sat on the side of the bed. "You're saying you'd rather have pancakes again?" He tousled her hair, hoping to improve her disposition.

"I'm saying I don't like carrots." She kept her arms crossed, but lifted them and flopped them back down across her chest. "I don't know why you married her, anyway. First she took Momma's shop. Now she's taking you."

"She's not taking anything. She's cooked us a fine supper, and we are going to eat it with the gratitude she deserves."

"I don't like her."

Edward stood. "I don't like your attitude. Lily is here because I asked her to be. You will be kind to her." He moved to the door. "You've got two minutes to be at the table with a respectful attitude."

He closed the door and turned to see Lily standing at the table watching him.

"You heard?"

She nodded.

"She'll adjust."

Lily turned back to the stove and put food on a plate. She placed it on the table with two others. She took her seat at the foot of the table and folded her hands in her lap.

The clock on the mantel chimed seven times.

Edward sat at the head of the table.

Lily looked to Ellen's door. Nothing.

Edward bowed his head and said grace over the food. When he opened his eyes, Ellen was standing at his elbow.

"Take your seat and apologize to Aunt Lily for delaying the meal."

Ellen shuffled her feet and plopped into her chair. "Sorry."

"Ellen." He would not let her win what he was certain would be the first of many battles of wills.

The child narrowed her eyes at him and turned to Lily. The sugary sweetness of her words belied her true feelings. "I'm so sorry, Aunt Lily, for delaying this meal. I know it can't taste better if it gets cold."

He watched Lily draw in her bottom lip and chew it. How had he managed to find himself at the table with not one, but two reluctant females? Both would rather be anywhere than here with him.

Lord, I think I'm gonna need the wisdom of Solomon to bring these two together.

"You may find a cooling supper preferable to a chunk of bread and a cup of milk in your room before bed."

Edward wasn't sure who was more surprised by Lily's words. Ellen or him.

"You can't do that!" Ellen jumped up. "Uncle Edward won't let you!"

Lily looked at him. He had no doubt this moment would define how his new family would be from this night on.

"Sit down and be silent, Ellen. You may stay at the table only if you eat quietly. If you show any disrespect, you will do as your aunt has said."

Ellen opened her mouth, and he raised a finger in caution. She closed her mouth and looked at Lily and then him.

"Would anyone like a biscuit?" Lily passed the bowl of bread to Ellen, who took one and handed the bowl to him.

Ellen's attitude had degenerated to rudeness in the previous weeks, while they'd waited for word from her parents. He'd overlooked it because he was sorry for her. Watching Lily require good behavior or promise consequences confirmed he'd made the right choice for Ellen by marrying her.

He took a bite of the fluffy biscuit and closed his eyes. It was delicious.

"Well?" He opened his eyes at Lily's question.

"It's wonderful. I had no idea you were such a fine cook."

Lily spoke to Ellen. "Do you like it?"

Ellen looked to Edward for permission to speak. At his nod, she said, "Yes, ma'am."

Lily gave the child a small smile. "I'm glad. Now try your carrots. I think you'll find the brown sugar makes them taste a bit like candy."

By the end of the meal, Edward wondered if Lily was not just the right choice for Ellen but for him, as well.

Something was missing. On Friday after lunch, Lily stood in the middle of her shop and spun in a circle, taking in everything she'd arranged with such care. One hand came to her mouth, and she tapped a finger against her lips as she contemplated what it needed.

The clanging bell drew her attention. Edward's mouth lifted for a split second before settling into a bland expression. "I was passing by and saw you through the glass. How's everything coming along?"

She turned to the display case and back to the front windows.

"If you must know, something isn't right."

Edward took in the shop and shrugged his broad shoulders. "It all looks fine."

Lily drew her brows together. "Of course, it looks fine to you. You're a man."

His blank response caught her eye.

"That's not an insult, just an observation."

She spun again to the windows. "If I could just put my finger on what it is." She tapped one finger against her lips again.

"Not sure I can help you, but…"

"Aha! Oh, yes, you can! Wait right here." She dashed into the workroom and plundered through the crates she'd emptied. A lid fell to the floor, revealing what she searched for. "Eureka!"

She rushed back to the front room with a fashion magazine she'd received from Paris. Flipping through the pages, she found the picture she needed.

"Can you make this?" She pointed to a drawing of hat stands advertised for sale. They were different heights with a metal base anchoring a post that was capped with a metal cup inverted to hold a hat. They would be perfect in the front windows. She could order stands, but they wouldn't arrive before she opened.

"Of course, you can make these! You're an artist. The bell proves that." She was becoming overexcited, but this would set her apart from the other shops in town. The only other place that carried hats was the general store. Their hats were stored in boxes on a high shelf, and the owner had to open every one for any customer who showed an interest.

Edward studied the drawing. "Seems simple enough. How many do you want?"

"At least a dozen, in different heights and sizes." She pointed to the windows. "This was the best I could do, but stands will be so much better." She'd arranged small crates upside down and draped them with a length of fabric before placing the hats at various angles. Gloves hung over the edges of the boxes, and an open parasol was propped in the corner of one window.

"A dozen? Sure you need so many?"

"Yes. At least. I'll put some in the windows, a couple on the sideboard, and some on this table." She indicated the center of the room. "The hall tree has hooks, so I won't need any on that side of the room."

Lily smiled at the thought of the finished displays. "Can you have them by Monday?"

Edward chuckled. "Monday? You do realize this is Friday?"

"Yes. I'll pay for them. I really need them before I open." She looked out the front window into the street beyond. "As a matter of fact, I'm going to keep the shades down so the display will be a complete surprise when I open on Monday."

She pushed the magazine into his grip and started to dismantle the window display.

"I won't be able to finish by then." Edward came to stand close behind her.

Lily straightened to her full height. "Why ever not? They seem simple enough to me." She went back to her task, the matter settled in her mind.

"May I suggest you stick to making hats—" he waved a hand at the various displays "—and whatever else it is you do? Let me handle the blacksmith work."

She stopped her work as quickly as she'd started. "Hmm… I'm much too busy to argue with you today. And it would only serve to slow you down. Not a risk I'm willing to take." She pursed her mouth in a small show of triumph.

"I doubt you'd ever pass on an opportunity for a good argument, Lily."

She refused to give him the satisfaction of a retort. "Do as many as you can. I'll put them in the window and make do inside the shop until you finish the rest. I think six will be a good start."

At his lifted brow, she added, "You can have six for me, can't you?"

He stood without a word and watched her face. She didn't know what it was, but something made him decide to help her. In an instant his eyes shone with determination.

"I can do six, but I won't promise more."

Lily put a hand on his. "Thank you so much."

"They won't be ready until Monday morning. I'll bring them over first thing. You may have to delay the opening for a little while that morning to do your setup, but I can't do anything faster than that."

"Perfect." A new excitement filled her. She was going to make this work. Her days of toiling away in the background of her father's life were over. A bright future was in reach. And reach for it, she would.

Edward pulled his hand from hers.

"Oh, my. I did get a bit carried away. Sorry." She put a hand to her hair and pushed the blond curls behind her ears. Keeping the unruly tresses in a bun was a never-ending struggle.

"I'll be on my way, then." He slapped the magazine against the palm of his hand. "I just got a large order from a new customer. Mustn't keep her waiting." He gave a nod and slipped out the door. "But I won't accept payment for them."

"Why ever not?"

"You're my wife now. My responsibility is to provide for you."

Lily stiffened. "If you refuse payment, I'll rescind the order."

"Why? It's proper for a husband to provide for his wife."

"We both know this is not an ordinary marriage. You've done me a great favor by protecting my good name. The least I can do is make the most of this shop to help provide for our family and save this property."

She watched his eyes as he processed it all. "You may pay me for the materials. Nothing more."

"But your time. If you're making these, you won't be doing other projects that will pay for your time and materials."

Edward put up a hand. "I'll work in the evenings. That's my final word on the matter."

Lily knew pushing him further would insult his dignity as a man. She followed him onto the sidewalk. "Thank you, Edward."

"Uncle Edward? What are you doing?" Ellen sidled up next to Edward's far side. She tucked herself behind his leg and peered up at Lily. Her hair was mussed and her dress dirty.

He put a hand on the girl's shoulder. "I was checking on Aunt Lily."

"Hello," Lily said to Ellen.

"Uncle Edward told me you wouldn't take up his time."

"Ellen. Be kind." His cheeks flamed. Was that guilt in his eyes?

"Did he, now? Well, I'll let him get back to his work, then."

"You best. He's got lots of work to do and don't got time to waste on you."

Lily took a half step back. This was a strong-minded child. At only seven, she possessed the directness of someone much older without the wisdom to hold her tongue.

"Ellen, apologize this minute." Edward looked into the child's upturned face. She seemed to hold her own against her uncle. He dwarfed her in size but not spirit.

"Didn't say nothin' wrong."

"Ellen, say you're sorry."

A small foot scuffed the boards on the sidewalk. Ellen looked at Lily and then back at Edward in what appeared to be an effort to discern his seriousness.

"Sorry." Ellen's hands had been behind her back, but now she pulled the tattered and dirty handkerchief doll into the circle of the arms she folded across her chest.

"For?" Edward prompted his niece.

"For speaking when I should be quiet."

"I accept your apology."

"Can I go home now?" Ellen's words were quiet but resolute.

"Run on back to the shop. I'll be there in a bit." Edward gave Ellen a nudge and turned to Lily.

"I'm sorry. She can be difficult sometimes, but I'm doing the best I can."

God, forgive me for judging him so narrowly. Of course, there's more to this man than what I've seen in just a few days.

"I'm sure it's been hard for her since her parents left."

"No girl should be without her momma," Edward said.

Lily knew the pain of growing up without a mother. When hers passed away, she had been five years old. It was the hardest part of childhood. Her father had tried to fill the void of maternal nurturing in their home with a housekeeper. Beverly Norton had done her best. Lily and her sisters loved Beverly, but there was still something missing.

Lily had taken to mothering others in an effort to fill the hole in her young heart. First her doll, then her favorite dog and, finally, her father during his long illness. She'd been swallowed up in her efforts to replace her mother. Lily's Millinery and Finery was her attempt at finding herself again.

"I've been praying for them to return." It sounded feeble, but what else could she say?

He nodded his head with no outward sign of hope. "That's what we pray for. Every night. Can't say my hope isn't all but gone."

"Ellen is quite a handful."

He met her frank statement with a cold stare. "That's why I need your help."

"I didn't mean anything by that, Edward."

"Yes, you did, Lily. You might wish you didn't, but you did." He stepped off the sidewalk.

"Please, I wasn't trying to say you aren't doing a fine job with her."

Edward turned for a brief moment. "I'm doing my best. That's all my sister asked." He nodded his head in dismissal of further argument. "I'll be home late. Don't wait supper for me."

And he was gone, his shoulders not quite as square as before but still very much a man in charge of his world.

Would she ever learn to hold her tongue? There she stood moments ago thinking the child didn't know when to be silent, and she'd committed the same sin.

Lord, help me to be swift to hear and slow to speak. It's such a challenge for me.

"Duck." Edward stepped onto the porch of the general store with Ellen on his back. Tiny arms encircled his neck. She was getting so big he thought she might bump her head when he entered.

Giggles filled his ear when she leaned in close. "Can I have candy?" She asked the same question every Saturday morning.

He slid the child to stand on her feet. "Two pieces. Go pick out what you want, but wait until Mrs. Croft isn't busy to ask for it. I've got to get a few supplies." Little feet tapped a happy rhythm as they left him near the doorway.

Edward picked up a box of matches and went in search of shaving soap. He reached for the bar he usually bought and caught sight of Lily as she came through the front door. Moving behind a barrel of brooms, he was able to study her unnoticed. Her hat was set at an angle, her hair swept low over her forehead.

Lily looked in the opposite direction from where he stood. Her coat was buttoned against the gray morning, and she wore fine gloves. The hat was fancier than any he'd seen in Pine Haven. She was like a wave of beauty and all things fine coming into their midst.

Before he'd left the house, she'd told him she was going to change clothes and run errands. Then she planned to work in her shop afterward.

He still hadn't adjusted to having her in his life. The pancakes she'd made for breakfast had surpassed his meager cooking skills. Everything about her had improved his life.

She pivoted on the heel of a small boot and caught a glimpse of him. He feigned interest in a broom before acknowledging her with a tip of his hat. She came toward him with a purpose that pinned him to the spot.

"I didn't realize you'd be here." Her smile lit the dark corner of the store.

"Just needed a few things." He held up the box of matches.

Lily raised a delicate hand to touch her hair. "I need to replace some things that were damaged in the fire."

"I was about to speak to Mr. Croft about adding you to my account. You can charge your purchases."

Lily shook her head. "I told you I'm prepared to care for all of my needs. It was never my intent to be a burden on you."

Did she know how her words cut him? Or how he wished he could say he didn't need her money? How he hated the loan on the shop. If he'd never borrowed the money, he'd never have been in a position to need to have a tenant.

But then he might not have had reason to spend time with Lily. And she wouldn't have agreed to care for Ellen. Even with the good he saw in knowing her, he despised being beholden to her financially. One day he'd pay for everything she needed. He'd pay off the mortgage and free himself of that burden as quickly as possible. Then he'd be able to take care of his wife without the shame of needing her money.

She changed the subject. "How is my order coming along?" Directness was definitely one of her character traits. Not common in a young lady, but nice to see for a change.

"I'm making progress."

"Oh, I hoped seeing you out on the town meant you'd finished." Her pert response almost made him laugh. Until he realized she wasn't teasing.

"I have things to tend to. Your order will be ready

as, and when, promised." He tipped his hat to her and went to gather Ellen.

"Did you pick your candy?" His niece waited at the counter with her chin resting on fingers that clutched the edge of the glass case.

"Mrs. Croft made me wait while she helps another lady. Said I could wait till you were ready." The little face went from longing for the anticipated treat to scrunched with disapproval over being pushed aside.

Edward placed his items on the counter and gave her a wink. "Mr. Croft can help us." He lifted a hand to signal the owner. Mr. Croft added Lily to his account and tallied his purchases.

He couldn't help but notice Lily out of the corner of his eye as he paid. She held a blue fabric to the light in the front window. Without turning, he knew it matched her eyes perfectly—something he scolded himself for knowing. Mrs. Croft busied herself trying to convince Lily to make a purchase.

"Can we go to Mrs. Milly's today? I wanna play with Reilly." Ellen yanked on the end of his coat. "I hadn't got to go nowhere after school in too many days. All you do is work. I ain't havin' no fun."

"Lick that sugar off your lips, little missy." He watched the valiant effort to catch every speck of her weekly treat with her tongue. "You should know better than to complain when your mouth is full of candy."

A tiny hand went against her forehead. "I forgot. Thanks for the candy. Can I go play with Reilly now? He gots a new marble, and I wanna see it."

Edward put a hand on her shoulder and directed her to the door. "I don't see why not, since you asked so nice and all."

"Thanks for coming in, Mr. Stone," Liza Croft called to him as he opened the door.

Her next words were addressed to Lily but followed him for the rest of the day. "I'm surprised you and your husband aren't shopping together."

Lily's sharp intake of breath brought him to a stop in the open doorway.

"My husband is a very busy man. I don't think a woman should drain the life out of her husband by demanding his constant attention."

Edward walked out and let the door close behind him. A smile crossed his face at the thought of Lily's words of rebuke searing Mrs. Croft's nosy ears. In the time since he and Lily met, he'd learned she could stand her ground. They might not exactly be friends, but in this situation he knew they were allies.

Chapter Six

Sunday morning dawned clear and cool. After break-fast Lily dressed in her favorite blue dress, added a wool coat and walked the short distance to the church with Edward. Ellen had gone ahead to attend a children's class taught by Mrs. Winters before the service.

She cast a glance at Edward, who was stretching his neck to one side. "Did you sleep well?"

He straightened and said, "Yes."

"Really? And your neck isn't bothering you?"

"Just a little stiff."

"I'd feel better if you let me sleep on the settee and you took the bed. We could ask Tucker to come tomor-row and help you move my furniture from the rooms above the shop to your home." She paused, wondering what he would think of her next suggestion. "We could set up my bed in Ellen's room. There's ample space there. I could share with her."

Edward stopped, forcing her to wait on him. "We talked about this. Ellen needs things to be as normal as possible. That doesn't mean for her aunt to sleep in one room, while her uncle sleeps in another."

Lily tilted her head to one side and met his gaze. "That's exactly what we are doing."

"But Ellen doesn't know it." He started to walk again.

"Not yet, but the way you snore, it's only a matter of time."

"The way I snore?" He turned toward her. "I don't snore."

"Loud enough to wake me in the middle of the night." She laughed. "I thought a wild animal had gone under the house to keep warm and found itself caught."

"That can't be true."

"Oh, yes. Like wild dogs growling a warning to anyone who dares to come near."

"Well, if Ellen asks, I'll tell her I was disturbing you and moved to the front room so you could rest."

Lily's laughter ended. It wasn't right for him to work hard all day and sleep on the floor at night. There had to be a better solution. She'd think of something.

The muted sounds of singing reached her as they approached the church door. She closed her eyes in silent prayer.

Lord, please give me friends here. Help me make a good impression on the people of Pine Haven.

No sooner had she settled on the bench next to Edward than the door creaked open again and clanged to a close. Ellen clomped up the middle aisle to her uncle's side. Lily glimpsed his disapproval in the glance he shot the little girl. Ellen shrugged her shoulders and began to sing with utter joy.

Lily shook her head and smiled at the girl's oblivion to the distraction her entrance caused. The wet bodice of Ellen's dress suggested she'd been to the well for a drink of water. The braids Lily had carefully fashioned after much disagreement that morning were loose. She looked as though she'd been playing tag instead of attending a Bible lesson.

Lily spotted her sister, Daisy, a few rows in front of her. Daisy held baby Rose in her lap and sat between her sons. Tucker sat on the end of the bench. She wasn't jealous of Daisy. Not really. Lily had a family now. She'd chosen to marry Edward. But the fact that he didn't love her was clear from the start. She stuffed the dreams of having children of her own back into her heart and forced her attention on the service.

At least, that was her intention. Every time she shifted in the seat, she brushed against Edward's arm. She felt like a restless child trying, without success, to sit through the service without moving. The third time she bumped his shoulder, he looked down and captured her gaze with his. And there in that moment she stilled. The calm in his eyes poured peace into hers. At his discreet smile, she focused toward the front of the church and sedately took in the rest of the minister's sermon.

When the service ended, Lily and Edward were among the first of the congregation to make their way to the door. Reverend Dismuke shook her hand and welcomed her. His wife, Peggy, invited Lily to visit when she had time. Lily thanked them, complimented the minister on his message and descended the steps to stand in the churchyard while Edward excused himself to speak to someone about a job he was working on.

As the people came out of the small church, she looked down Main Street, taking in the sights of the new town that was now her home. Preparing the shop to open had kept her too busy to explore Pine Haven. During her first week, she'd only visited the doctor's office, the bank and the general store.

Of course, she'd been to the church and the hotel on her wedding day. Pleasure at the memory surprised her. Why would she smile at the thought of how her life had changed that day? Now her plans were gone. Replaced with their plans. Plans so vague they were yet to be made clear.

The vision of a handsome man in a leather apron manifested before her eyes. Only, instead of an apron, he wore his Sunday best.

Lily had been so lost in thought, she didn't notice Edward's approach. Even at midday the man cast a shadow over her small frame.

He tipped his hat. "Having pleasant thoughts?"

Her smile had betrayed her. "Just enjoying the day and surveying the town." Lily grabbed for any excuse to keep from letting him know her thoughts were of him. He couldn't know that. "It was a lovely service."

He smiled in agreement. This handsome churchgoer wasn't the same man who had carried her across the threshold. In midair, with strong arms. Against a broad chest. The man she'd seen this week was as strong as his stature. This Edward had a softness in his eyes.

Ellen stood beside him, holding his hand and frowning up at Lily.

"What did you learn in class today, Ellen?" Lily twisted the cords of her reticule around the fingers of her gloves as she spoke.

"Stuff about God."

Edward gave Ellen a telling look.

Lily tried again. "What exactly did you learn? About God's love? Or a particular Bible story?"

The girl pointed at Lily's reticule. "You tied your hands in a knot."

"Oh, my." Lily pulled the cords in vain. The knots grew tighter as she tugged.

"May I?" Edward reached a tentative hand toward her.

"No, thank you. I'll get it." She continued to struggle with the cords.

Ellen blurted out, "I want to go play."

"Do not interrupt, Ellen." Edward reached for Lily's hands. "Please."

She relented and held out her hands. The cords had tied her gloves together. "I do seem to be making it worse."

Dust flew up and scattered on Lily's shoes and skirt as Ellen kicked the ground at her feet.

"Ellen, be still. You'll soil Aunt Lily's dress." Edward didn't look up as he worked with the mass of tangles. His large hands made the heavy cords of the reticule seem tiny.

"There you go." He released the last of the knots and backed away, slipping his hands into the pockets of his trousers. He stared over her shoulder and asked, "Tell me. Did you get everything set up so you can open tomorrow?"

Was he as uncomfortable as she? When they worked together, they kept busy. This was the first occasion for them to be together as a family in the community. Their first day of rest and worship.

Ellen was clearly not enjoying herself. She stood close to Edward, arms folded, pouting while she waited for permission to leave them.

"I'm almost ready. There are a couple of things to do before you bring the hat stands in the morning." Lily studied Edward's profile. Today he was clean shaven. His brown hair curled behind his ears a bit. His shirt was not new, but it was clean. The brim of his well-worn hat shaded his face.

Daisy and Tucker approached them with their growing family. The twins asked to go run and play with the other children while the adults talked.

"Okay, boys, but don't go far. Your momma's got lunch ready for us at home." Tucker waved the boys away.

"We'll stay close!" James, the older twin, answered for both boys and tugged on his brother's arm. "Come on, John. They won't think we're coming if you don't hurry up." John took long, awkward strides to stay upright as James dragged him away.

"Can I go?" Ellen pulled on Edward's elbow.

"Just for a few minutes."

"Thanks!" She pivoted on one heel and lifted the other leg to run.

"Not so fast, young lady." Edward put a hand on her shoulder and turned her to face Lily. "You haven't answered the question about your Bible lesson."

"It was about family." Ellen jerked to look at him.

"What about family?" Edward's voice was deep and even.

Ellen twisted her face to Lily and drew in a deep sigh.

"Answer the question or go to the wagon without playing," Edward prodded.

"Okay, okay. Just let me think a minute." Ellen chewed her bottom lip and her eyebrows twisted toward one another. Lily could almost see the wheels of her mind turning.

In an instant Ellen's eyes opened wide, and she held

up one finger to touch the corner of her mouth. "It was about honoring your momma and papa. And since I don't get to see mine, I didn't want to hear it. I went outside and played by the water till it was time for church." A curt nod of her head, and Ellen flew away so fast Edward couldn't catch her.

Lily met Edward's unhappy gaze. "She's really hurting." She watched Ellen catch up to the boys.

"This is what I was afraid would happen. She's lashing out in pain because she doesn't know how to handle not knowing where her folks are."

"We'll get her through it." Lily put her left hand on his sleeve. Then she saw Daisy slip a thoughtful glance at Tucker. Oddly, Edward hadn't seemed to mind. He actually turned toward her when she put her hand on his sleeve. She jerked it away and held the offending reticule with both hands.

A smile turned up one corner of his thin lips. His dark eyes danced. She could see her embarrassment reflecting in their depths. He was enjoying her discomfort. Too much.

Daisy chimed in then. "Edward, will you and Ellen join us for the afternoon? Lily promised when she arrived on Monday that she'd spend her first Sunday with us at the farm. We'd love to have you."

"Thank you for the invite, but I think Ellen needs my attention today. It's been a busy week. That will probably explain part of her poor behavior earlier." He nodded at the group. "Y'all have a nice afternoon."

"Well, you and Ellen are welcome anytime. We'd love to have you out real soon." Daisy handed baby Rose to Tucker.

Tucker smiled at his daughter. "I'll bring Lily back to

town this evening, Edward." He put an arm around his wife, and they walked toward their wagon.

Lily had looked forward to spending time with Daisy and her family, but it didn't seem right to leave Edward to deal with Ellen alone. Not when that was their agreement.

"Are you certain? I can stay."

"You go. I'm going to try to help her come around to understanding our new arrangement. A little resistance at first was to be expected." He looked across the church yard to where the children played. "It's time for her to accept things now."

"Are you going to talk to her about her parents?" Lily knew it would be difficult.

Edward shook his head. "I won't tell her anything unless I know for certain it's true." He looked into her eyes. "Thank you for offering to stay with us. You go enjoy your family. Maybe Ellen will be in a better mood by the time you return."

"I'll pray for you. She's a strong-willed soul. It won't be easy for her to accept me as long as she's holding out hope for her parents to return."

"She'll adjust. It'll take time, but she will."

Lily watched him walk away with a heart heavy with thoughts of his sister. She wished she could do something to mend the pain he and Ellen shared. Braiding hair and cooking meals wasn't enough to make up for the loss the two of them were bearing. She prayed that somehow his sister and brother-in-law would return.

If they did, would Edward still want her to be his wife?

Edward sat on his porch and whittled. Ellen played with her handkerchief doll in the cabin behind him.

Through the barely open window, he could hear her cooing and pretending to coax the doll to sleep. She hummed the song her mother had sung to her as a babe.

The afternoon sun had settled low on the horizon when he saw Tucker's wagon coming up the road. At a distance he recognized Lily by the hat she'd worn to church.

He was glad she had family in the area. He couldn't fathom why her father had sent her to Pine Haven alone. Lily's reputation wouldn't have been compromised if her father had been here. But would he have been able to convince her to marry him and care for Ellen if she hadn't been concerned about what people thought of her?

Tucker slowed his wagon as he neared Edward's cabin. It was built to face a lane that ran beside his shop. The back of the cabin butted up close to the side of his shop, leaving just enough space to prevent the cabin from catching fire if there was ever an accident with the forge. The porch lined the front of the cabin and sat perpendicular to the main road. He enjoyed sitting outside in the evening after being closed in all day with the fire and metal of his work. It wasn't always possible in the winter, but sunshine had warmed the mild day.

"Evening, Tucker. Lily." Edward stood and dropped the small horse he was whittling onto the table by his chair. He stepped off the porch to help Lily from the wagon.

"Good evening to you." Tucker pulled the brake as the wagon came to a stop. "Not as cold as I thought it'd be. I need to get Mack shoed if you've got time this week."

"Be glad to. Just let me know when." Edward answered Tucker, but his gaze went beyond his friend to rest on Lily. She sat with her back straight. Her coat was buttoned all the way up, and she tugged at the wide ribbon of her hat. He smiled at how the color matched her eyes. He was certain it was intentional.

Tucker spoke and drew his attention. "I'm coming to town late tomorrow morning with Daisy. She wants to visit the shop on Lily's first day. Can I bring him by on the way in and leave him with you?"

"That'll be good." Edward watched as Lily continued to avoid looking at him. Was she uncomfortable with all men, or just him?

"First thing in the morning I've got some business to handle for Lily." He offered his hand to her as she moved to the edge of the wagon seat.

"Thank you." Lily gave him little more than a glance as she spoke. "I trust you were able to complete my order." Her eyes challenged him.

"Remember I promised you six stands tomorrow. The rest will be done by the end of the week." He released her hand, and they backed away from the wagon.

"Please don't be late. The windows will have to be dressed before I can open."

"I won't be. You just make sure you're ready. In my experience, it's not usually a woman waiting on a man, but rather the exact opposite." He tried not to grin at her, but the temptation to taunt her was irresistible. Her cheeks brightened at his words. He could almost see the wheels turning in her mind for something to say. No doubt, she'd thought of several things but was weighing the right choice.

"Perhaps your experiences have been with the wrong sort of woman."

Yes, she'd chosen well. Not the nicest statement, but

the one that brought the most reaction. Probably her first thought.

"I'm not in the habit of associating with the wrong sort of woman."

"So you do admit you are in the habit of associating with women." She was smirking now. How had she gotten the upper hand in a conversation about when he would deliver an order?

"Uncle Edward? Can you come inside? I need you." Ellen's voice broke into the conversation through the window.

"In a minute, honey," he said over his shoulder without looking back.

Ellen tugged the window until it opened wide. "It's important. I can't do it by myself." There was no real emergency, but a childish urgency in her words. He watched her stare at Lily. Did Lily threaten his niece's peace of mind? He'd hoped his talk with her after lunch would ease the tension between Ellen and Lily, but it seemed to have had the opposite effect.

"I'm coming, Ellen. Just as soon as I finish my business with Mr. Barlow."

The distant sound of hammering came from the direction of the main intersection in town.

Tucker indicated the noise with a nod of his head. "Have they been at that all afternoon?"

"Pretty much." Edward's distaste for working on Sunday was surpassed only by his disappointment that the town council was permitting a saloon to be built in the center of the growing town. "I wish they weren't building the place at all, much less working on the Lord's Day."

"Everything that comes to town because of the railroad isn't good for us." Tucker shook his head. "We'll have to pray for God to keep our community safe."

"That, and make sure Sheriff Collins stays on top of any riffraff who try to settle here," Edward agreed.

"Surely, the good people of Pine Haven will outnumber any new folks who try to change the community." Lily's pinched expression showed her reluctance to believe evil could find a home in her new town.

"We do now. But it'll take prayer and courage to keep the sort of evil that comes with a saloon from pollutin' the town." Edward wished he could be as naive as Lily. Life had taught him hard lessons. Sadly, they were lessons she, too, would learn in time.

"Uncle Edward? Are you coming?" Ellen's voice rang through the open window, her tone impatient.

"I'll see you in the morning, Edward." Tucker released the brake.

"If I'm not here, just leave Mack. I'll get right on it when I get back."

"Good night, Edward. Good night, Lily. Ellen." Tucker tipped his hat at the ladies.

"Bye, Mr. Barlow." Ellen stood framed in the open window, her hands on the sill. She sent a look to Lily that Edward was sure she hadn't intended for him to see.

Tucker steered the horses forward and pulled the wagon away from Edward's porch. Edward didn't move to go inside until Lily and the pretty hat disappeared through the front door. The last thing Ellen needed was to feel that he'd overlooked her by allowing himself to be distracted by Lily.

Lord, help me not to focus on what's not good for me. You know I get in more trouble than I can handle that way.

He pulled the front door open to find Ellen back at play with her doll, whatever assistance she'd needed earlier forgotten. Something about Lily didn't sit right with his niece. Over the past few months, he'd determined that nothing—and no one—would put Ellen at risk. She was his responsibility until her parents returned. No amount of curiosity or intrigue surrounding a petite blonde lady would move him to violate the promises he'd made to his sister and himself—not even if that lady was his wife.

Lily came into the front room, her hat and coat gone. "Have you two eaten supper?"

Ellen pretended she didn't hear the question, but Edward saw her cut her eyes at Lily. He put a hand on the girl's head and ruffled her hair. "No. We had a big lunch today. I was just about to see what I could round up for a light supper."

Lily was already tying on an apron. "How about some scrambled eggs and toast?"

"Sounds good to me." He turned to Ellen. "How about you, Ellen?"

She didn't look up. "I don't care." Her voice was rife with tension.

"Okay, then." Lily turned her back to them and put the cast iron skillet on the stove. "Eggs and toast for Edward, bread and milk in her room for Ellen." She pulled a bowl off the shelf and began to crack eggs into it.

Ellen's mouth dropped open. She looked at him and then at Lily. "But..."

"No buts." Lily didn't look away from her task. "We warned you that your manners would be polite or you would eat bread and milk in your room." She pulled the bread to her and began to slice thick pieces of toast.

"Uncle Edward." Ellen came to tug on his sleeve.

"Don't make me go to my room. It's too early. I want to play some more."

He could feel Lily's gaze on him when she retrieved the butter from the table. He couldn't risk siding with Ellen and undermining Lily's new authority. Parenting was hard. Being fair and wise wasn't easy. There weren't always absolute answers. He would do the best he could. "It's your choice, Ellen. You know the rules. If you are disrespectful, you choose to go to your room."

The little girl stood, palms up, eyes wide. "I can't believe this."

Lily turned then. "If you do not change your tone, you will have water with your bread. Disrespect for your elders will not be tolerated in our home."

Ellen stamped her foot. "It's not your home! It's my home!" She turned, ran into her room and slammed the door.

"Ellen, come back here." Edward called after her, but there was no response.

"I think we best give her time to calm down." Lily stood, wiping her hands on the apron. "Did something happen today that I'm unaware of?"

"I had a talk with her. I hoped it would make things better. She feels threatened by you." He shook his head. "I'm not sure what to think of it."

"Did she ask about her parents?" Lily's voice was barely more than a whisper.

"Yes. I tried to be vague, but she kept pressing."

The butter in the skillet started to crackle on the stove. Lily whipped the eggs with a fork and poured them into the pan. "How did you handle that?"

He came close to keep Ellen from overhearing their conversation. "I told her we have to pray for them, that they were sick and had been to the doctor. I didn't have the heart to tell her no one knows what happened after that."

"Poor child." She stirred the eggs. "If I'd known, I wouldn't have been so firm."

"You had no way to know. And, even so, she must be respectful."

"Yes, but we've got to show mercy in her situation. She'll never listen to me if she thinks I'm unkind."

"You were not unkind. You were trying to teach her."

"There's a time and place for everything. And when you're worried about your parents being far away and sick, it's not a time to go to bed with bread and water." Lily scooped the eggs out of the pan and onto a plate of toast.

"You go comfort her." Lily cracked more eggs and dropped them into the bowl. "I'll fix her something to eat. Tell her you'll read to her after supper. That always calmed me when I was a girl missing my mother."

He left her at the stove and went into Ellen's room, marveling that Lily would dismiss the poor treatment his niece had thrust on her and then cook a meal and offer comfort. Even so, he'd see that Ellen apologized before the meal.

Lily was exactly what Ellen needed. If only he could convince Ellen to let Lily care for her.

Chapter Seven

Lily admired the row of newly made hats lined up on her workbench. This might be Texas, a land known for hard work and strength, but Lily didn't believe there was a woman alive who didn't want to be feminine and look pretty. Even her sister Jasmine, who loved to ride the range and tend cattle, liked a fancy hat now and again. Lily would soon see if the women of Pine Haven would appreciate her offerings.

Concern for how to reach Ellen had combined with excitement over opening her shop and kept her from sleeping the night before. She'd awakened early and left breakfast for Edward and Ellen. She had to get everything just as she wanted in the shop. In her best dress she watched the hands of the clock creep slowly toward the hour of opening. Except for the windows—their shades pulled low waiting for Edward's arrival—she was ready.

No one coming today would see any evidence of last week's fire. Edward had worked quickly on the structure, and she'd worked long hours to make new stock.

Hoping the normalcy of the activity would calm her nerves, Lily decided to busy herself by creating another hat. She pinned two long feathers above the brim. Turning it from side to side, she decided to follow her first instincts and add a small tuft of silk net organza. She reached for her scissors just as the front bell announced a visitor.

"I'm coming." She set the hat on her workbench and brushed bits of thread and ribbon from her skirt. They floated to the floor to join the kaleidoscope of colors she'd used to make her inventory.

Lily stepped through the doorway into the front of the shop. "I thought you'd never get here." She stopped behind the glass case. With the windows covered, the dim room cast the face of her giant visitor in shadow.

"Hello to you, too." Edward approached her. He carried a display stand in one hand. He set it on the case and watched her face. "I finished."

Lily's mouth dropped open. She lifted a hand and traced the base of the delicate stand with her fingers. It was fashioned into a leaf. From the center of the leaf rose a stem. On each side of the stem, at different heights, additional leaves arched outward. Lily's hand followed the stem to touch the top of the stand. Thin metal curled to form a calla lily. The pistil in the center, perfectly shaped, completed the work of art.

"I can't believe it." The words came out like a soft breeze. "This is nothing like the picture I showed you."

"If you don't like it, you don't have to use them." Edward's response snapped Lily from her bewilderment.

"It's amazing! I've never seen anything so beautiful."

"Are you sure you like it?" Doubt played in his eyes.

"I'm positive. I just don't know what to say." Lily put up a hand to her cheek and felt the warmth of her blush. She was moved almost to tears by the beauty of his work. "I never imagined this. I don't know how to thank you." She moved her fingers to cover her lips and shook her head slowly back and forth. After several moments she tore her gaze from the beautiful display and lowered her hand.

"I was worried you wouldn't be able to finish."

"I had a slow couple of days." Edward backed up and nodded his head in the direction of the door. "Do you want to see the others?"

Lily eyed the stand again. "Of course." She crossed the boarded floor and went through the door he held open for her. They approached the back of his wagon, and he threw back the edge of a heavy canvas to reveal more of the beautiful stands, each nestled in the bed of straw. Varied heights and length of leaves, balanced on unique bases.

"I thought you might want the stands to reflect the concept of Lily's Millinery and Finery, even when you removed a hat to show a customer." Edward spoke from beside her as Lily took in the sight of his craftsmanship. "You can hang gloves or hankies on the leaves. I thought you might get more use of your shop space that way."

"What a wonderful idea." She was touched by his thoughtfulness. He may have been overworked and stressed to the limit by raising his niece alone, but his creativity wasn't diminished.

A sudden movement and high-pitched sneeze drew their attention to the far edge of the canvas near the seat of the wagon. The sound of metal snapping accompanied the sneeze.

"Ellen?" Edward spoke the child's name slowly and deliberately. His eyes narrowed in on the exact spot that now stirred beneath the canvas.

A whisper was his only answer. "Yes, Uncle Edward?"

He pulled the canvas from the wagon and exposed Ellen's hiding place behind his seat. "Get up, child."

"I'd rather not, if it's all the same to you." Ellen met his gaze without cowering. Lily could see the bravery to stand her ground was a show of spirit and not outright defiance.

"It's not the same to me." Edward lowered his chin and pinned her with his stare.

Lily watched the struggle between the two strong-minded people. Even though she'd only met them days before, she had seen firsthand the contest of wills that took place daily in their home. She was certain her marriage to Edward was the source of much of their recent conflict.

Ellen stood without moving from her spot. The hem of her calico dress almost hid the broken display stand at her feet. The edge of a leaf stuck through the hay that lined the wagon and hung on the lace of her small boot. She frowned at the offending leaf.

"It wouldn'a broke if you'd let me come with you in the first place." Her already full lower lip protruded farther.

"I didn't want you to come because I didn't want anything to get broken." Edward stepped around the lowered gate on the back of the wagon and retrieved the broken stand. He pulled the leaf free from her laces. "Tell Aunt Lily you're sorry."

Ellen jerked her head in Lily's direction. The pouting mouth became a snarl. "It ain't hers yet. She ain't paid for it. I'll tell *you* I'm sorry, but it ain't got nothin' to do with *her*."

Lily almost expected the child to spit as a way to punctuate her distaste at the idea.

"Ellen. Apologize this minute." Edward's voice brooked no argument, but Lily saw a challenge fly through Ellen's eyes before she turned back to Lily.

"I am so very sorry to have broken my uncle Edward's work." Ellen twisted up her mouth and cocked her head to one side. The saccharine in her voice spoke of bitterness Lily understood now. Having lost her own mother at the age of five, she had known the importance of her father's attention and the mounting jealousy from even a hint that someone would take it away. She imagined Ellen must feel the same way about her treasured uncle.

"I'm sure he can repair it, Ellen." Lily watched the girl's pride swell at Lily's words.

"You bet he can. He's the best blacksmith in Texas. Probably in the whole United States." Ellen gave a curt nod to emphasize her opinion. "I ain't never seen him turn down a job 'cause it was hard. He can make or fix anything."

"I imagine you're right." Lily smiled at the little girl standing like a statue in the back of the wagon. "These stands are beautiful and much fancier than what I ordered." Lily was beginning to realize Ellen's gruffness came from a place of deep pain. A pain Lily understood. "Would you like to come inside and have a look around?"

The little girl's brown eyes looked to Edward. "What do you think? Do you need help toting all this in?" There was an apparent reluctance to respond to Lily, but a child's curiosity about what was happening inside the shop must have prompted Ellen to stow away in the wagon in the first place.

"That depends on you, Ellen. Will you be careful?" Edward's tone warned that she would be held accountable for her actions.

"Yes, sir." Ellen's confidence and determination didn't waver. She stepped toward the edge of the wagon closest to Edward.

"You will help me repair this after school today." He held the pieces of the broken stand for Ellen to see, then put them under the seat to protect them from further damage.

"That'll be easy." Ellen grinned and wrapped her arms around his neck. "Now help me down, so I can see what she's done to Momma's shop."

Edward hoisted Ellen to the ground. "It's Aunt Lily's shop now."

"She's gonna have a hat store here, but it's still Momma's shop." A frown clouded her dark eyes. Ellen spoke to Edward but turned her head to Lily. "In my heart it always will be."

Recognizing the challenge, Lily said, "Your mother picked a wonderful building for a business. Come inside and see what I've done so far."

Edward called Ellen out of her reverie as she stood, hands on her hips, eyes drawn together, watching Lily's back disappear inside the shop.

"Take a stand with you. If you're going to help, you can start by helping me unload the wagon." He handed her one of the smaller stands and turned to pick up two of the largest ones. "And mind your manners. Lily has worked hard here, and we need to respect her efforts."

"She better not mess up Momma's shop. One day, Momma's coming back, and we're gonna open a bak-

ery here." Ellen stepped onto the porch. "That's all I got
to say about it."

"That's all you better say about it, or you'll be having
a long conversation with me later. Now go inside and
be nice." Edward winked at her to soften his words. He
took a deep breath and braced himself before they entered the shop together.

He had no idea what had just transpired at the wagon,
but he had a feeling Ellen may have met her match with
Lily. He was training Ellen to be strong. He wanted her
to stand up for what she believed in. He didn't want her
to be weak in any way. But, given her attitude toward
Lily, he needed to work on finding a balance to include
teaching her to be kind.

Edward and Ellen stopped just inside the door and
took in everything. Lily had arranged her wares with
care. A large round table stood in the center of the room.
The wood was polished down to the ornately carved
pedestal. Against one side wall stood a hall tree with a
large mirror. Lily had placed a chair in front of it. He
assumed she'd seat her guests there while they tried on
her hats. A long chest stood against the opposite wall.

Ellen broke the silence. "Where do you want me to
put this? It's kinda heavy."

"You can put them all on the floor by the windows.
I'll arrange them in a few minutes." Lily spread her arms
wide. "What do you think, Ellen?"

Ellen set the small stand down with a thud and went
to look in the mirror.

"Remember to be careful, Ellen." Edward set his load
near the opposite window.

"I didn't break nothin'." Ellen turned to Lily. "Why

you got such a big mirror? Don't you know what you look like?"

"Ellen." Edward sent her a warning glare.

"It's for my customers." Lily approached the mirror and met Ellen's gaze in the reflection. "Seeing how a new hat looks on you is important before you buy it. Sometimes a lady wants to see how the color looks with her eyes. Or she may want it to match her hair or dress."

"Can't see why you don't just put on something to keep your head warm in the winter and be done with it." Ellen stared at herself and tugged on the ribbons of her worn bonnet.

Lily seemed to hesitate a moment at Ellen's logic. Edward could see both of their faces in the mirror as he walked to the door to bring in more of the stands.

"You are right about a hat helping to keep you warm. But isn't it nice to have something to make you feel pretty, too?" Lily rested her hand on Ellen's shoulder.

"What good is pretty? Momma had lots of pretty hats, and she's gone."

"Ellen, let's not talk about that right now." Shocked by her outburst, Edward tried to silence her.

But Ellen's tirade wasn't finished. "If she hadn't been so worried about being pretty and having fancy things, maybe her and Pa could have stayed here and not left me." The girl dashed out of the door.

Lily stood with her hand over her mouth. She slowly turned to Edward. "I'm so sorry. I didn't mean to upset her." She lowered her hand to the base of her throat.

Edward silently scolded himself for noticing the delicate hand and the silkiness of golden hair draped across her shoulders. His niece had just run from the room after lashing out at Lily because she felt wounded anew by a reminder of the mother she felt had abandoned her.

Could he take away the hurt Ellen put in Lily's pain-filled eyes? That was a question he wasn't sure he wanted answered.

"I'm the one who should be apologizing. I'm sorry for Ellen's behavior." He looked through the window and watched as Ellen sat on the seat of the wagon and scrubbed tears from her cheeks with the back of her hand. He knew she hated to cry, especially in front of others.

He hoped he could explain. "You couldn't have known about my sister's dreams. When she was younger, all she wanted was to open a bakery. Cooking and serving others seemed to fulfill her. Then she married Wesley. Ellen was born the next year. Jane was so excited. She lived for Wesley and Ellen."

"She sounds like a lovely person."

"She was."

"I hope you aren't giving up on them." Lily's tone was almost pleading.

"I don't want to. I wish they'd never left."

"Why did they?"

Edward smirked a little at the memory. "Wesley wasn't the type to be content. Always wanted more. Got all dressed up in fancy clothes trying to impress people. At first, Jane didn't change. Then he had a small success with the hotel here in town. He convinced her they could make a real go of it in Santa Fe."

"Oh, my." Lily's voice was a faint whisper. "Poor Ellen." Pity filled her eyes.

He cleared his throat. As hard as he tried not to, he still choked up at the possibility that Jane might never come home. "I best get the rest of the stands off the wagon and get Ellen to school."

Lily gave him a sad smile, one that said she understood.

It took several trips to the wagon as he dug the stands out of the straw and brought them inside. Edward heard Lily moving around in the stockroom while he unloaded the wagon. He set the last stand on the floor and called out a goodbye. Because she'd insisted, he placed a bill on the glass case. Her soft voice caused him to stop as he reached the door.

Lily looked everywhere in the room but at him. "Please explain to Ellen that I didn't mean to bring up bad memories for her."

"I will. She'll be fine. She's learning to be tough. Life deals you a lot of hard things. It's best to learn that when you're young. Keeps you from being disappointed later in life."

"Not always, Edward. Not always." A depth of sadness seemed to rise from her heart and fill the rich blue eyes. Lily picked up his bill. "If you'll give me a moment, I'll pay you." She disappeared into the storeroom again.

When Lily returned, Edward took the bills she offered and stuffed them into his pocket without counting them as she backed away from him.

"I guess I'll see you at supper." He hated the distance he sensed between them. They both wanted the best for Ellen, yet at every turn the child tried her hardest to rebuff Lily's efforts.

"I may be late. It depends on how busy I am today."

"I'll try to have the rest of the stands by the end of the week."

"That'll be fine." She was already moving toward the

windows to arrange the hats in preparation for opening the shop.

He lifted his hat and opened the door. "And again, I'm sorry for Ellen's words. She was unkind."

"I understand." Lily stood still as he closed the door behind him.

Edward climbed into the wagon beside a silent Ellen. Lifting the reins, he released the brake and sent the horse forward.

Sad blue eyes threatened to haunt him for the rest of the day. As he and Ellen repaired the broken stand that afternoon, he saw visions of the gentle creature working in a shop, building a dream to succeed.

When Lily came home late that evening, Ellen was ready for bed. She had done her homework and chores and was playing quietly in her room.

"How was your day?" he asked when she closed the door.

"Long." He watched as she pulled off her gloves.

"Did you have a lot of trade?" He went to the stove and uncovered the bowl of soup he'd kept for her. He put it on a tray and added a cup of coffee.

"If you don't mind, I'm very tired. I'd like to go straight to bed." She looked toward Ellen's room. "Is there anything I can do to help with Ellen before I do?"

He wondered what had happened. This was not the response he expected after the excitement she'd shown over opening. "Ellen is ready for bed. Everything she needs is done."

She unbuttoned her coat, and he saw the slump of her shoulders.

"What about you, Lily? Is there anything I can do for you?" He indicated the tray. "I made some soup."

A tired smile did nothing to lift her face. "Thank you."

"You must be exhausted. Would you like me to carry the tray into the bedroom for you? I can put it on the table by the chair. You can relax and eat at your leisure."

"That would be perfect."

She stood in the center of the room while he took the tray to her room. When he came out again, he stopped in front of her. "You know you can tell me anything."

Lily put a hand on his arm. Its lightness reminded him that though she was a strong woman, she was also a delicate creature. "I just need to rest right now."

"I'll say good night, then." He backed away so she could walk into her room. "Ellen, come say good-night to Aunt Lily."

The little girl came to the doorway of her bedroom. "Good night."

Lily's smile was genuine this time. "Good night, Ellen. I pray you will sleep well tonight."

Ellen stared after her as Lily went into the room and closed the door. "What's wrong with her? She looks sad."

"She does, doesn't she?" Edward watched the door, wondering what happened today to bring this normally cheerful—if not fiery—woman to such a melancholy state. "Let's get you tucked into bed. You can say a prayer for her tonight, too."

He led Ellen to her room, promising himself that he'd spend extra time in prayer for both of them. He'd put wings on those prayers tomorrow and try to find out what had gone wrong today. Maybe it would be something he could remedy.

Chapter Eight

No customers yesterday didn't mean today wouldn't be good. Last night she'd felt guilty going to bed without telling Edward about the day, but she didn't have the heart to expose her failure to anyone, especially him. After all he'd done to assure her success, it didn't seem right to tell him no one had entered the shop except for her sister. Daisy had dropped in for a brief visit and promised to come again later in the week.

Lily heard the bell and slid off her stool in the storeroom. She was determined to be hopeful.

Lord, please let this be a customer. I can't make a success of this business without Your help.

"It's me." Ellen stood just inside the front door, holding the display stand she'd broken.

"Oh. Hello, Ellen." Lily came around the display case.

"Uncle Edward made me bring you this." She held out the smallest of the stands Edward had made. "He said you prob'ly need it."

Lily reached out to receive the stand. "Thank you. It looks wonderful. You can't even tell it was ever broken." Lily placed the stand in the center of one of the front windows. She had hoped to have the stand today but had set one of the hats and a pair of gloves in the spot just in case it wasn't finished until the other stands were ready. She picked up the hat and set it on the stand, tying the ribbon in a loose bow.

"What do you think?" Lily asked Ellen, who still stood by the door. The little girl's eyes missed nothing as she took in the shop. Like her uncle, she was observant.

"Not too bad," she finally answered, "if you like all this frilly stuff." Ellen's answer may have been meant as a rebuff, but Lily caught a glimpse of wonder in her face.

"Most ladies do like pretty things." Lily held the gloves she wanted to display with the hat. "Would you like to hang these on the leaf? Your uncle's idea to make these stands hold more than one item was wonderful."

"No, thanks." Ellen gave a cursory perusal of the shop and turned on her heel. "Uncle Edward sent me over as soon as I finished my chores. I've got to get to school."

"I'll be sure to thank him when I get home." Lily moved to the doorway as Ellen walked out.

"He's just doing his job. That's how he makes money to take care of me."

"I know you must be proud of him. He's a good uncle." Lily tried again to speak to Ellen without the tension that seeped into their conversations.

"The best. He only has time for me. Nobody else." A stubborn tilt to her head made Ellen cuter than she knew. The fierce protection was precious but unnecessary. Lily had no interest in taking Edward's time from her. Luther Aarens had made certain that Lily had no interest in a man. Their failed engagement, the way he'd treated her, was the reason she was determined to keep her heart as her own.

Perhaps there was a way to put the child at ease.

"I'm sure you're right. I felt the same way about my father after my mother died when I was a little girl."

"Your momma died?" The anger seemed to drain out of Ellen. She wilted before Lily's eyes.

In a soft voice, Lily answered. "She did. I was just a little younger than you are. I still miss her."

"You do?" Ellen whispered when she looked up at Lily.

Time stood still as a little girl and a grown woman shared the pain only someone in their situations could understand, each remembering a love made more dear by its loss. Death had stolen one mother. A lust for life had taken the other.

Lily nodded her head softly. "I do." She bent at the waist so she could be face-to-face with Ellen. "The love of your momma stays with you forever. It's the part of her that lives in your heart. I think it's a way God lets us keep them close."

"I do feel it." Ellen's eyes were filled with tears now. A smile pulled at one corner of her mouth. "Especially when I'm playing with the doll she made me." She reached into the pocket of her pinafore and pulled out the worn doll Lily had seen so many times. "Momma said if I practiced with my doll, then I'd learn how to be a good momma, too. She said her momma made her a doll like this, and that's how she knew how to take care of me." Sobs broke from the child, and Lily wrapped her in tender arms.

She murmured softly. "What a wonderful gift she gave you. She taught you how to love."

Ellen sniffed and backed away. "But she left me. I must not be the kind of girl a momma can love. I don't think I know how to love nobody now. Except Uncle Edward." She wiped her sleeve across her face to dry her eyes.

"I've seen how you protect your doll." Lily pushed Ellen's hair away from her face and cradled the small cheeks in her palms. "Protection is one way to show love."

"It is?" Scrunched eyebrows formed a disbelieving frown.

"It is. I'm sure your mother trusts your uncle Edward to protect you. She showed how much she loves you when she picked him to take care of you. His protection is the way he shows you he loves you. It's the way you love your doll." Lily gave her a smile and winked. "It's also how you love him. That's why you've been trying to protect him from me."

"How'd you know?" Ellen backed up, surprised.

"Because I did it to my papa when I was a little girl. If ever a lady got close to my papa, I'd get between them and make sure she knew my papa was busy taking care of me and my sisters. That he didn't want another lady because there was no lady like my momma."

"Did you get in trouble like I do?" Ellen's childlike honesty spoke without reservation.

"I did." Lily stood to her full height again but kept a comforting hand on Ellen's shoulder.

"Did another woman get your papa?" Wide eyes seemed to fear the answer to this question.

"No, Ellen. No other woman did."

"So you protected him from all of them?"

"After a while I learned Papa didn't need me to protect him. He's a big strong man who would never do anything to harm me or my sisters. He loved us so much that he would protect us."

"Uncle Edward is strong. He's big and strong." Pride burst from her young face.

"That he is. So don't you worry about protecting him, especially from me. I'm not going to try to take him from you. I understand how you feel. And I've learned enough about your uncle Edward to know he'll always protect you. You don't have to worry."

"But you married him. People get married 'cause they're in love. Uncle Edward must love you a lot more than me. He didn't even know you good, and he married you."

Did she dare to share the secret of her marriage with this child? "Your uncle did marry me for love. One of the reasons he married me was because he loves you."

The little face twisted in confusion. "I don't get it."

"He thought if he married me, you and I could be friends." She prayed she was helping by telling Ellen these things. "I was alone, and you have been missing your momma. He thought we could have each other while we wait to hear from your momma."

Lord, please bring Jane home. Don't let this be false hope I'm pouring into this little girl.

Ellen looked at the doll she clung to. Then she looked up at Lily. "I'm glad we talked."

"Me, too." Lily smiled.

"You're too pretty for me to stay mad at all the time. I was gettin' tired of having to say mean things to you."

"Thank you. I'm glad we got everything straight. Now we can be nice to each other." Lily stroked Ellen's hair, and her fingers caught in the knots that tangled the mass of brown waves. "You're very pretty, too, Ellen."

Pink tinted the girl's cheeks. "No, I'm not." She turned her face into one shoulder.

Lily reached under her chin and urged the child's small face to the front. "Yes. You are." The words were kind and soft-spoken. "I'm sure you're as pretty as your momma. You go home and ask your uncle." With another smile, Lily chucked Ellen under the chin and urged her on her way.

"Make sure and tell Uncle Edward thank you, if you see him before I do." She waved as Ellen bounced off the porch onto the dirt below.

"I will." She returned the wave and called over her shoulder. "See you later, Aunt Lily."

Aunt Lily? Without being prompted? Hmm. Lily smiled at the sound of that. Perhaps she and Ellen could be friends, after all. It was nice to think there would be no more incidents of taunting from the girl.

If only Ellen's uncle didn't set her nerves on edge. Maybe that would come in time.

Not that it mattered. Making a success of her shop before her father and Jasmine arrived demanded all of her attention. After the shop was established, she'd be so busy she wouldn't have time to remember Ellen's words. *Uncle Edward must love you a lot.* Ellen was too young to understand why Lily and Edward had married.

So why did the thought gnaw at her spirit? Did part of her still long to be truly loved? Her determination not to disappear into the background and be taken for granted had become a way to keep herself, and her heart, locked away from life.

Finding herself plunged into the middle of a new family had tilted her world on its axis. She had to be cautious to maintain her emotional equilibrium.

* * *

Edward nestled a small wooden horse in the straw-filled crate. He hadn't imagined his whittling would be an added source of income until Mrs. Croft had noticed one of the horses he'd carved for Ellen. Selling the toys to the general store kept him from feeling as though he was wasting the time he spent on his front porch. Time he used to think. The Lord knew he'd been doing a lot of that in recent days.

"Good morning, Stone." Edward turned to see Donald Croft in the open doorway.

"I was just on my way to see you." He put the last horse in the crate. "I got these done as quickly as I could. Thanks for letting me know you were running low."

Mr. Croft stepped into the blacksmith shop and picked up one of the horses. "Can't imagine how you do it. These are fast sellers. The kids love 'em." He moved the straw aside to survey the array of toys in the crate. "This oughta cover your tab and anything you may be needing for this week."

Liza Croft's shrill voice carried from the street outside. "Donald, where are you?"

"In here, Liza." The general store owner stepped nearer to the door and waved her inside.

"I declare, all I did was go into the bank for two minutes, and you disappeared." She came to stand beside her husband. "Well, aren't those the prettiest ones yet?" She picked up the smallest horse. "I'm going to put this one up for my niece. She'll love it."

With a swish of her ample skirt, she turned and went through the door into the street. She called over her shoulder. "Don't take too long, we're already late opening up today."

Mr. Croft shook his head. "It's a wonder I make a living at all. Some days she buys things faster than I can sell 'em."

Edward knew better than to comment. Mr. Croft might complain about his wife, but everyone in town knew it was a callous front to cover for the deep love he had for her.

Pulling the crate toward him, Mr. Croft spoke again. "I see your wife opened up shop yesterday."

Edward turned to look out the door at his building across the street. "I hope she's been busy."

Mr. Croft's face twisted into a frown. "I don't see how she can make a go of it with such a small selection. It's not like Milly Ledford's dress shop. Everybody wins in her case. I sell the fabric, and she makes the dresses. Hats and gloves don't seem to me to be a way to make a living." He looked out the doorway as a lady paused and looked at the hats in Lily's window before continuing on her way down the street. "See what I mean. I just don't think there's enough hat business in town to keep her open."

Edward straightened and took a step toward the door. "I hope she's successful. It's a help to me to have the place rented. And the town is growing."

Mr. Croft picked up Edward's crate. "Maybe. You never know. She'll need to offer a fine product is all I've got to say."

Edward grimaced inwardly. "Thanks for buying the horses."

"You're mighty welcome. Go ahead and work on some more carvings if you get the time. What about some kittens or puppies? The little girls might like those."

Edward nodded in agreement. "I'll see what I can do."

He walked to the front of the shop when Mr. Croft left and saw Mrs. Dismuke, the reverend's wife, look in the window of Lily's shop. He caught a glimpse of Lily watching hopefully through the window.

When Mrs. Dismuke walked away, Lily dropped her head and stepped to the rear of the store. She looked back and saw him watching her just before she went into the storeroom. A shadow of disappointment crossed her face. Edward was not pleased at the way it made him feel. Her business was her responsibility, not his.

But her success would benefit him. At least that's what he told himself as he headed across the street.

The bell on the front door rang when he entered the shop.

"I'm coming," Lily called out as she stepped from the storeroom into the shop. "Welcome to Lily's Millinery and…"

The greeting died on her lips when she saw him in the doorway. He closed the door against the chill of the day and turned toward her, hat in hand.

"Oh, it's you." Disappointment rang in her voice.

"Good morning to you, too." Edward smiled to tease her.

"I'm sorry. I didn't mean to be rude." She looked past him through the windows. "I thought you were a customer."

"No need to apologize." His gaze took in her efforts. "You've done a fine job in preparing your shop." He nodded toward the hats in the window. "Quite a variety of colors and styles you've got there."

"Thank you." She adjusted the ribbon on the hat taking center stage on the tallest stand he'd made. "The display stands are wonderful. I'm certain they'll be a big boost to the reputation my shop will build as people discover I'm open for business." She shifted the gloves on the leaf below the hat. "They are sure to be a topic of discussion."

"I'm glad you're pleased." He pulled at his collar and shifted his weight from one foot to the other. "So the customers like them, too?"

"No one has said anything yet." She looked to the street again.

"Oh." He moved to the glass case in the back of the store. "Have you had any customers yet?" Her answer could explain her sullen mood from the night before.

"Not yet, but it's early. I've seen several ladies looking in the windows." Lily talked faster than usual. "Ladies take a while to make decisions. They like to look and ponder before they decide if they're interested. I'm sure they'll be coming in soon."

"Have you placed an advertisement? Most folks in town read the paper. It comes out once a week."

"I have a notice coming out in tomorrow's edition." The small snort that followed the statement surprised him. What had he said to get her dander up so?

"Well, you don't have to get all snippy. I was only trying to help."

"I'm not snippy." Lily forced a delicate cough. "There's been so much dust to clean up. I still have a little tickle in my throat." Was she stretching the truth by trying to cover the fact that she'd snorted at him?

He reached a hand out to a small hat, then withdrew it before he touched the yellow ribbon.

"Do you like it?" Lily walked behind the counter and picked up the straw creation. "I made it to match this one." She gestured to the coordinating larger hat.

"I thought a mother and daughter might enjoy the pair." What was she thinking? Why would she speak to him about a mother and daughter wearing matching hats, when she knew he hadn't heard from his sister? He didn't need to be reminded of all that Ellen was missing.

Edward took a step back. "You're probably right."

"I'm sorry, Edward. I didn't mean to bring up a painful subject." Lily laid a hand on his arm.

"It's not a problem. I'm sure some little girl and her mother will love them." Another step back and her hand fell away from him. It just wouldn't be Jane and Ellen unless God brought his sister home safely.

He glanced over his shoulder to the street. "Well, I've got to get back to work."

"Please forgive me. I often speak without thinking. It's my worst trait. I really do try to control it." In all fairness, he knew she hadn't intended the words to hurt.

Edward held up a hand and interrupted her. "There's nothing to forgive, Lily. You're offering your wares to ladies who like this sort of thing." He moved toward the door and put his hat on, jamming it down a little farther than necessary. He wouldn't let himself react to Lily. He needed to bury his frustration over the disappearance of his sister.

Lily placed a hand on his arm again. He stared at her hand for a moment and then turned his face to hers.

He saw remorse in her eyes. "I really am sorry. I don't know why I always manage to say something that makes you uncomfortable."

He smiled a little then. "We'll get it sorted out." Over time they would resolve all the uncomfortable feelings. She'd grow accustomed to his ways, and he'd learn to understand her. What then? Eventually Ellen would grow up and start a life of her own. Would they be two friends sharing a home?

The sunlight coming through the windows dimmed, and he looked over his shoulder to see Mrs. Dismuke reaching for the door. Milly Ledford, the local dressmaker, stood behind her. Lily dropped her hand from Edward's arm and backed away.

Was she embarrassed to be seen close to him? Perhaps concerned they might misinterpret her hand on his arm as affection? Her face turned the slightest shade of pink.

Her next words to him confirmed his thoughts. "Thanks for stopping in." It was as though she were dealing with a customer or tradesman.

Edward chuckled and tipped his hat to the prospective customers. "Ladies." He turned back to Lily. "Lily." Unable to stop himself, he reached up and ran a finger down her warm cheek. "I'll see you at home later."

Lily lifted a hand to cover the trail of his finger on her face. What on earth had possessed him to do that? And why was she so pleased that he had?

She had no time to ponder his amusement. Her first customers had arrived. Lily ushered the ladies into the shop. The glances the two ladies exchanged were obvious. It seemed the topic of their sudden marriage had not been forgotten. She set her mind not to care what anyone thought, as long as they bought hats.

"Good morning, Mrs. Dismuke. Mrs. Ledford." She lifted an arm to indicate the interior of the fresh space. "Please take a moment to look around."

"Call me Milly." The dressmaker smiled a warm greeting. "I've been dying to get in here and see what you have."

"Me, too. And call me Peggy. Your sister and I are dear friends." The reverend's wife held up a package. "I looked in the window earlier, but wanted to pick up this dress Milly made for me first. Do you think you might have a hat to match the color?"

"Let's open it up and see." As she untied the string holding the brown paper together, the bell jangled on the front door. Two more ladies entered the shop. "Welcome to Lily's Millinery and Finery. If you'd like to take a look around, I'll be with you as soon as I can."

Lily's heart skipped a beat. In just a few short minutes, she'd gone from wondering if anyone would come to having more customers than she could help at one time. She glanced through the front window and caught sight of Edward as he tied on his apron. His eyes might be smiling, but the distance made it difficult to be sure.

"Oh, look, Milly. I think this one will be perfect." Peggy Dismuke's delighted voice brought Lily back to the moment.

Bustling through the rest of her busy day gave Lily no time to think about the handsome blacksmith. But when she flipped the sign to close the shop and pulled down the shade, his image seemed to float in the room behind her.

She turned to survey the space. The floors needed to be swept, and many of the items needed to be straightened. The sight of several empty display stands made her heart smile. With energy she hadn't known she possessed, Lily set to work pulling stock from the back room and arranging more of her original creations in the shop.

Lily forced herself to stop before she was finished. The shop would have to wait while she fulfilled her obligations to Edward and Ellen. There was supper to prepare and chores to do at home. She walked across the street, bundled against the brisk January evening.

"You're late." Edward sat at the table helping Ellen with her sums.

Not exactly a warm greeting. Lily shrugged out of her coat. "It was a busy afternoon. I've still got loads more work to do, but supper can't wait any longer."

Ellen dropped her pencil. "All done." She pushed her school things together in a stack and stood. "What's for supper?"

"I'm going to fry some slices of ham and boil some potatoes." Lily wrapped an apron around her skirt. "Would you like to help?"

"Sure!" Ellen carried her things to her room. "I'll be right back."

Edward watched Ellen leave. "What just happened?"

His surprise at Ellen's response almost made Lily laugh. "She's decided we can be friends."

"Oh, she did?" He added wood to the stove. "You'll have to tell me all about it."

Lily put a pot of water on to boil. "Not much to tell. We talked. Now she knows I understand her."

Ellen bounced back into the room. "What can I do? Fry the ham? Peel the potatoes?"

Lily chuckled at Ellen's eagerness. "Let's start with the basics and work up to knives and the stove on a night when I'm not in such a rush." Lily was peeling the potatoes. "You can set the table, and I'll let you pour the drinks. You can help me mix up the corn bread batter. I'll fry some small cakes on the stove."

The evening meal went without incident. It was refreshing to eat without wondering what might send Ellen into one of her moods. Lily admitted it was an added pleasure to watch Edward's disbelief at the change in the relationship between his niece and her.

"When we finish, I'll wash the dishes while you get ready for bed, Ellen." Lily needed to go back to the store for at least a couple of hours.

Edward pushed his chair away from the table. "That was a wonderful meal. Thank you, Lily." He tousled Ellen's hair. "And thank you, too, Ellen."

Ellen glowed under his praise. "I'm gonna learn real quick. I wanna be a good cook, so when Momma and Papa come to get me I can show them what a big girl I am now."

Edward stilled. The pain on his face showed how much he wanted Ellen to be able to do just that. "We'll keep praying, Ellen." He turned to Lily.

"I need to do a bit more work tonight." He picked up his hat.

"Um, I need to work tonight." She hadn't thought he wouldn't be around to get Ellen to bed.

"Why? You've been there all day. Can't it wait until morning?" He put the hat on and reached for his coat. He was talking to her, but he was preparing to walk out the door.

"What about me?" Ellen came out of her room in her nightgown. She still wore her braids and socks.

"Aunt Lily will be here with you." Edward shrugged his shoulders. "I'm sorry, Lily, but I didn't know you'd need the time, and I already promised a delivery first thing in the morning. I've got to finish."

Lily looked at him. "It's time for bed, Ellen." She opened the door. "I'll be in to read with you in a minute."

She stepped onto the porch, and Edward followed. "You promised that marrying you wouldn't keep me from running my shop." She folded her arms across her chest, not sure if it was because of the chill in the air or the stress between the two of them.

Edward was calm. He towered over her but didn't move to intimidate her. "And you promised to do all the things a mother would do for Ellen."

"I am." She swung her arms wide now. "I came to cook supper when I had more work to do."

"I'm sorry I didn't realize the kind of time you'd need in the evenings." He looked remorseful. "I need to get this order ready." He scuffed his boot against the boards of the porch. "If you'll watch her tonight, I'll make breakfast tomorrow, and you can go to the shop early."

She had a lot of work to do to be ready to open again tomorrow, but it wasn't wise to leave the child alone.

Ellen called from her room. "I'm ready to read now."

Edward waited for Lily's response.

"Oh, all right. I'll go in early tomorrow." She put a hand on the door. "But we need to iron out some details of how we're both supposed to get all our work done and take care of Ellen."

The child's voice rang out again. "Are you coming, Aunt Lily? I've got a storybook that Momma gave me."

"Thank you." Edward stepped off the porch. "Don't wait up. Just make sure the door isn't bolted, so I won't have to wake you."

He walked into the darkness without looking back. Lily wondered how hard the fight would be to maintain her independence. The promises were falling apart, and they'd only been married a week.

She'd take care of Ellen. But she'd take care of her business, too.

Chapter Nine

Edward stood in the bank at the teller's window on Wednesday morning. He sensed Lily's arrival before he turned away, cash in hand. He saw her before she saw him. A becoming touch of pink lit her cheeks. But he refused to concentrate on her beauty.

"I didn't expect to see you here this morning, Lily. I thought you'd be busy preparing for another busy day."

"I finished getting everything ready and had a couple of errands to run."

"Well, I'm glad you were able take care of everything this morning." He'd been sorry to keep her from working the night before, but he'd had no choice.

Her small hand shot out and grasped his arm. The white glove was trimmed with tiny pearl buttons. He silently scolded himself for noticing the minute details.

"I was wondering if you could come by the shop later today." Lily's face was fresh and open as she waited for his reply.

"What is it you need?" Edward took a step back, and her hand fell. He folded his money and stuffed it into his shirt pocket.

"I have an idea for a sign for the shop." The feather on her hat danced near her eyes. It swooped forward from its perch and swept across the edge of her forehead. As soft as the feather looked, he knew her hair would be softer. If he kept being distracted like this, she'd visit him in his dreams tonight. What was the matter with him?

"I'm very busy today." His voice sounded gruff, but he didn't want everyone listening to their conversation. He could see the bank owner, Lester Bennett, watching from his desk behind the half wall separating the lobby from the rest of the bank.

Both gloves wrung the reticule she held. "Okay." Her voice was small compared to the exuberance it had held a moment earlier. "At your convenience." She looked toward the teller window. "I'll just be off, then. I've got to deposit the receipts from yesterday. I still have another errand before I open today." She reached into the reticule and pulled out a handful of bills.

"Lily, you shouldn't keep that kind of cash on hand overnight." Worried someone might realize she was alone in the shop and try to rob her, he felt it important to caution her.

The now-familiar stiffness of her posture returned. "I seem to remember it was your suggestion that I take care of the hat business and you would take care of the blacksmithing." With a slight lift of her chin she added, "I am willing to abide by your original suggestion. I'm quite capable of taking care of my business." With a sharp turn, her tiny feet tapped across the wooden floor to the teller window.

Edward lifted his eyebrows and pushed his hat farther down on his brow. What a stubborn woman. She frustrated and intrigued him at the same time. Her lips set together in determination were beautiful.

He spun around and headed outside. He stepped off the boards and onto the dust of the street and lifted a silent prayer.

Lord, she's a mite stubborn, but it'd be a shame for her to be hurt over it. If she won't listen to me, I hope You send someone she will listen to.

He walked across to his shop and swung the big front doors wide. When he turned to go inside, he saw Lily step out of the bank into the morning sunshine. She tugged her glove on and fastened the pearl button at her wrist. Pivoting toward the post office, she stumbled and almost lost her balance. He was on the point of going to her aid when Winston Ledford came out of the bank and caught her by the elbow.

Seeing that man with his hand on Lily's arm sent a flash of anger through Edward's chest. He'd give him one second to let go.

Then Lily turned to Ledford and started a conversation. Edward wasn't close enough to hear their words. He stood speechless when she grasped the man's arm and nodded. She lifted the hem of her skirt with her other hand. Ledford took her hand from his arm and placed it on his shoulder before squatting at her feet. He reached toward her foot and paused.

What was she thinking? How dare she stand in the street with the saloon owner! And lift her skirt like that. She leaned on Ledford's shoulder for what seemed like an eternity, and then she backed away from him.

A smug look crossed the man's face as he stood and brushed his hands together. More words were exchanged, and Ledford dipped his head at Lily. Edward caught the moment Ledford saw him watching the scene.

Mr. Ledford eyed her, and the two continued talking.

Lily put up a gloved hand and touched the feather at her brow. Was she flirting with a saloon owner? What good could he do as her husband trying to guard her reputation if she insisted on this sort of behavior?

He heard Ledford laugh. A slight movement and Lily turned her attention across to the blacksmith shop. Edward couldn't prevent the scowl that crossed his face. She turned back to her conversation. He was fuming. Enough was enough. Just as he moved to step across the street, Ledford nodded his head at her and walked away.

Edward ignored the hand the man lifted in greeting to him. He slapped his work gloves against his thigh and turned to march into his shop. He wasn't sure what had just happened. But he was certain he'd speak to her about, so it wouldn't happen again.

Just as soon as he calmed down enough to be civil.

After lunch, Lily sat in the workroom making yet another hat suitable for a lovely spring dress. Yellow daisies circled the ribbon she'd woven through the straw at the base of the hat just above the brim. She reached for a length of white ribbon with one hand as she turned the hat first one way and then another. The front bell rang.

"Coming," Lily called out and slid from her stool. Two young ladies waited inside the front door. She took in their dresses, such as they were—bare shoulders, and necklines plunged to places no lady would consider proper. The fabrics were sheer in places, and bows pulled up the fabric at intervals to make the short skirts even shorter, revealing a hint of colorful petticoats. The dresses weren't identical but were so much alike Lily knew they'd come from the same place. They hadn't been purchased locally.

She quickly recovered her composure. "How may I help you, ladies?"

Her customers looked at each other and grinned. The younger of the two spoke first. "Winston sent us to see you. Said you might have some things we'd be interested in." While she spoke, the lady's eyes perused the hats on the hall tree against the side wall. Lily didn't think she could be more than twenty years old. Her painted cheeks and lips made it hard to be sure.

The other lady looked toward the back of the store and the glass display case where Lily kept her most expensive offerings. The materials were too delicate to risk putting them out where customers and their children could handle them.

"I think I see just the thing for my new yellow dress." This lady was a little older than the first, perhaps closer to thirty. Her makeup creased in the lines around her eyes. Lily decided life must have treated the woman unkindly.

"Winston?" Lily asked.

"Winston Ledford." The young lady spoke again. "Said he met you outside the bank this morning." She picked up a black parasol from the stand in the hall tree and opened it. With a slight spin of her wrist, the parasol twirled in the afternoon sunlight coming through the front windows.

Lily looked outside just in time to see Liza Croft turn from her display window and march across the street in the direction of the general store. She looked like a woman on a mission.

"Oh, Mr. Ledford." The rather distasteful encounter with the man came back to her. "He assisted me when my shoe became wedged in the sidewalk." Lily remembered him saying he'd send his girls by her shop.

He must have thought she wouldn't know how to handle these ladies. The smirk she'd seen in his eyes had been a challenge.

Lily walked behind the glass case and asked the older lady which hat she'd like to see.

"That one." She pointed to a hat Lily had made before her shop opened. It had turned out better than she'd imagined in the beginning. It was some of her best work, and she'd priced it accordingly. She pulled the white felt creation with organza and tiny roses from its place in the case. Several ladies had admired it, but no one had been willing to pay its price.

"Here you are." Lily smiled at the woman as she handed her the hat. "My name is Lily."

After a slight hesitation and a lifting of a brow, the lady responded. "I'm Virginia Jones. Most folks call me Ginger."

Lily adjusted a gilded mirror stand so Ginger could see her reflection. "Would you like to try it on?"

Ginger paused and leveled a frank stare at her. "You really want me to? Or are you just saying that because you're afraid to tell us to leave?"

Lily met the challenge from Ginger head-on. "Miss Jones, I'm in business to sell hats."

The young lady put down the parasol and laughed. "She's got you there, Ginger. I mean Miss Jones." She bowed in a mock curtsy.

"Be quiet, Lovey," Ginger snapped at her young companion. Then she turned back to Lily. "I think I would like to try this hat on, then." She reached up and removed the wisp of a hat she wore and set it on the case.

"If she's going to call you Miss Jones, I can be Lavinia Aiken, instead of Lovey. No sense in you being the only one treated like a lady." Lovey twisted her mouth in a smirk at Ginger.

"Of course, Miss Aiken. My goal is for all my customers to be treated well." Lily smiled at the younger woman before coming around the counter to help Ginger set the white hat on the crown of her head. "I have a splendid hat pin that would be perfect."

Ginger turned her head back and forth in front of the small mirror while holding the hat in place. "May as well do it up proper. Winston's buying today." She gave Lily a wink and spoke to Lovey. "You need to pick out something nice, too. No sense leaving empty-handed when we're being treated so well for a change."

Lily brought a cushion holding an array of hat pins from inside the case. She pulled one with a pearl-encrusted handle and laid it across her open palm to show Ginger. "What do you think?"

"It's right pretty. Is it expensive?" A smile crept into the dark eyes that had softened from cynicism to fun after Lily had made known her intention of selling her a hat.

Lily smiled back, enjoying the thought of Winston Ledford having to pay for his attempt at embarrassing her. "As a matter of fact, Miss Jones, it's one of my most expensive pieces."

"Then I think I'll just have to take it." Ginger accepted the pin and secured the hat to her head. She walked to the hall tree and took in her reflection from different angles. "What about you, Lovey? What has captured your fancy?"

Lily helped the two ladies choose several items. She followed them onto the sidewalk and thanked them for their patronage. "Please tell Mr. Ledford how much I appreciate him sending you by today." Ginger and Lovey laughed as they walked away, sharing the joke that, while Winston had attempted to intimidate Lily, all three ladies had benefited at his expense. The fancy hatboxes they carried were evidence of their success.

Turning to go back into her shop, Lily caught sight of Edward in the reflection of the display window. Liza Croft stood beside him wearing a deep frown. If Lily thought Edward looked unhappy this morning outside his shop, the expression he wore now would be considered thunderous. She stepped inside and closed the door, saying a prayer.

Lord, I don't know why some things happen, but thank You for the business. Please help Ginger and Lovey to know Your love and turn from the lives Mr. Ledford has made for them.

Lily set about straightening the merchandise that had been set in disarray by the two ladies. When the front bell rang, she put on a smile and turned to greet whoever was at the door.

Edward closed the door with unnecessary force and rounded to face her. "Just what do you think you're doing?"

Startled by his outburst, Lily didn't answer.

His brows came together in a deep crease that drew her into the depths of his brown eyes. It was like swimming in dark coffee. Hot and strong coffee. With a bite!

Edward pointed in the direction of the saloon without taking his eyes from her shocked face. "What are you doing entertaining those women?"

"Entertaining?" Lily fisted her hands and planted one on each hip. "Is that what you think I was doing?"

"I saw you laughing with them."

"We were laughing, but you have no idea what amused us, not that it's any of your business." Lily moved closer to him. She had to look up to see into his face. A storm lit her eyes. "I didn't come to Pine Haven to be bossed around by a man. If I'd wanted that, I could have stayed in East River and married Luther Aarens. At least he had better manners than to raise his voice to me."

"I heard you sending Mr. Ledford your thanks. That was quite a display you put on in front of the bank this morning, after my warning you to be careful. This town won't take kindly if you associate with the likes of the people from the saloon."

"Don't you come in here and tell me who I can and cannot associate with." Lily lifted a finger to poke his chest. He backed away as she stalked forward. "I opened this store to sell hats." Again she drove her finger into his chest. "I'll have you know those women spent enough money this afternoon to pay my rent to you for the next month." She took another step forward, and he was backed against the door. "And the laughter you heard was from three women who got the best of a man who tried to intimidate me."

"Intimidate you? How?" Edward couldn't move back, but she continued to move forward. She was straining her neck to look up at him now.

"Mr. Ledford told me this morning he'd send his girls around to my shop. Oh, he thought that was a fine joke. He had the nerve to laugh in my face. Sending them here was his way of provoking me."

"Why didn't you tell him no or send them on their way?" Edward reached up and captured her hand in his.

"Because I opened this shop to sell merchandise. They had money. His money. What better way to get back at him than to sell them my most expensive items?" She tried to tug her hand free, but he held it snugly. So she poked him again with the tip of her finger. "And what you saw this morning was me with my shoe stuck in the boards of the sidewalk. Mr. Ledford came out of the bank just in time to keep me from falling. He pulled my shoe loose from the planks. Nothing more." She suddenly deflated. Her head dropped, and her hand went limp in his.

Edward watched the color drain from her delicate face.

"Oh, no," she whispered. "If you think what you think…" Her voice trailed off to nothing. She raised her head to look at him. "What must everyone else think?"

Her eyes had turned violet with her temper. Now they swam in a blue sea of sorrow.

"I'm afraid they think what I thought." Edward released her hand. He didn't want to hurt her, but he couldn't send her a false message of support, either. This brave lady had come to town in a flourish of flowers and lace, but if she wasn't careful, her dream of success would die.

"I can't refuse to serve a customer because I don't agree with them. Those ladies were sent here to embarrass me. I thought I was being a good Christian to treat them with respect. If they don't see the value in themselves, shouldn't I show it to them by loving them? Jesus was always associating with people no one else would talk to."

"If you keep talking like that, Reverend Dismuke will want you to give a testimony in church come Sunday." He smiled at her and chuckled.

She giggled. "Do you think I should finish with the Scripture in Proverbs about the wealth of the sinner being laid up for the just, or do you think that would be too much?"

He laughed with her. "You might want to save that one for your second sermon."

Lily stopped and confessed, "I was pleased to take the wretched man's money."

He tried to ease her anxiety. "My concern is for your reputation. I know you're a good woman. Your father is a fine Christian man. But people in a small town can be unforgiving when they get the wrong impression."

"I couldn't help getting stuck in the sidewalk." Her back straightened, and her face regained some of its color.

Edward held up both hands in an attempt to prevent another stampede. He thought he might have a bruise from where she'd poked his chest. "I know that. But people only see bits and pieces. They don't know you."

"I've certainly done a fine job so far—parading through town in my nightclothes. Now I've been seen cavorting with the saloon owner and selling hats to his saloon girls. I'll be lucky to have a business at all by the end of the month." An exasperated, gushing sigh punctuated her words.

"It seems to me that none of it was your fault." Edward thought about each statement. It painted a bleak picture when she strung it all together like that. "'Cavorting' is too strong a word. I'd say something like, 'consorting.'" He tilted his head to one side, hoping she'd appreciate his attempt at humor.

She shook her head and gave a slight groan. "You're right. That sounds so much better." Her shoulders lifted as she took in a deep breath and lowered as she let it out. "There's not much I can do about it now."

"I'll try to help. I can make sure Reverend Dismuke knows why you welcomed those ladies into your shop. He can probably pass the word along to his wife, who can help by calming the fires of gossip started by Mrs. Croft."

Lily's eyes grew wide. "So that's where all this is coming from?"

Edward watched her, wondering what was in her mind. The emotions Lily had displayed in the past few minutes ranged from rage to sorrow to shame and back.

Resolve brought calm to her features. "Thank you for bringing these things to my attention. I assure you, I'll do everything in my power to make certain you are not embarrassed to have me as your wife."

"Lily, that's not what I meant." A new level of friendship had opened between them. Sharing spiritual truths and unpleasant facts, in an effort to come to a positive solution, was a difficult process for the best of friends. He thought they'd made progress by handling the events of the day. They'd ended the conversation with good humor, but in an instant she was all business again.

"But I saw you with Mrs. Croft before you came in here."

"Be reasonable, Lily." Edward captured her hand and turned it over in his. Today was the first day he'd noticed her hands without gloves. Calluses from the broom and pricks from her sewing needles and the tools of a milliner were scattered across her palm and fingers. He knew the other hand would be the same. This delicate-looking creature had an inner strength he hadn't seen until today. There was more to Lily Stone than the feminine surface she showed to the world. "Do you think I'd stand and talk to her without defending your honor?"

Her eyes were violet again, but he could see her fighting to believe him. She finally shook her head. "I guess not."

He dropped her hand and tipped his hat to her. "If you'll excuse me, Mrs. Stone, I have business with the reverend." He smiled at her, and the light that danced into her eyes ensured him of her gratitude.

"Thank you, Mr. Stone." She followed him outside. "Remember to come back when you have a few minutes so we can discuss the sign I want you to make."

The image foremost in his mind as he walked away was of her ashen face as she realized the situation she was in.

She was his wife now. It was his responsibility to protect her. He just hadn't known when he'd married her how often he'd have to protect her from herself.

Chapter Ten

Saturday dawned clear and cool. Lily dressed for the day with forced excitement for the first Saturday her business would be open. Surely she'd meet new people and have new customers today. Thursday and Friday had passed without a single sale. Oh, she'd seen several ladies on the sidewalk cast a look her way. In the end, they'd all gone away without stopping. Some had dared to come close enough to look in the window. She'd even heard one mother tell her young daughter they'd try to order her a hat from the general store because it wouldn't be right to shop at Lily's after what they'd heard.

Lily checked her reflection in the long mirror her father had given her on her sixteenth birthday. Edward had moved it over from her rooms a few days after their wedding.

She ran her hands down the front of her skirt to smooth the fabric. She wore blue again to match her eyes. The rich color always made her feel more feminine. After all, she was trying to sell stylish accessories to women who lived hard lives in the open country. Soft ruffles swooped up the side of the skirt and met in a large bow at the back of her dress. The bodice had small buttons and a lace collar. She knew just the hat she'd wear if she decided to venture out today. It was small with a tuft of blue organza nestled beneath a nose-gay of tiny berries. She pulled it from its box and put it on the bed.

First, she had to prepare breakfast. A few minutes later, Ellen came from her room rubbing her eyes and moaning about being tired.

"It's Saturday. You should be excited about a day with no school." Lily put a plate of scrambled eggs in front of the child. "You can play and even come visit me at the shop later if you'd like."

Edward opened the door and came in from the out-side. A cool wind whirled into the room before he could close the door. "It's a bit chilly this morning, ladies." He tousled Ellen's sleepy head and sat at the table.

"Here you go." Lily handed him a plate and joined them at the table.

Lily bowed her head while Edward gave thanks for their food. She prayed she'd have sales today that she could thank God for tonight.

Ellen perked up after a few bites of food. "Aunt Lily says I can go to the store today."

"She did?" Edward looked at Lily. "You can do that if you'd like." He grinned at Ellen. "Unless you want to help me with a special project."

"What?" Ellen was so excited she almost knocked over her milk when she waved her arms.

"Easy." He chuckled and moved the cup away from the edge of the table. "You'll have to choose without knowing." Lily watched the interaction between uncle and niece. The way he made little things fun for Ellen was sweet. He'd be a wonderful father.

Father? As his wife, if he had children, it would be with her. Lily choked on her biscuit. Edward thumped her on the back until she waved him off.

"Are you okay?" he asked.

"Fine." She sputtered again and took a drink of her coffee. "Thank you."

"What will it be, Ellen? A day in the hat shop or an adventure with me?"

"Hey!" Lily laughed. "Well, Ellen, do you want to try your hand at making a beautiful hat or work in a hot, smelly room and end up covered in soot?"

They all laughed then.

"I want to get dirty and smelly!" Ellen gave a strong nod of her head and speared another bite of eggs.

Edward smiled at Lily. "Nice try. But you just don't have my special touch for wooing her."

Lily stood and started to gather the dishes. "Next time I'll see about adding in a live toad or maybe a day of cleaning the stoves." Wrinkling her nose and scrunching her lips, she pulled a face at both of them. She still hadn't adjusted to sharing a house with the two of them. But on days like today, it didn't seem as difficult as she'd first thought it would be.

Everyone left the house in good spirits a few minutes later. Lily had just settled in to work on a new hat when the bell chimed. She bolted from the stool and stepped into the shop. "Good morning. Welcome to Lily's Millinery and Finery."

Daisy bustled into the shop. "Oh, Lily, how are you?" She hugged Lily.

Lily pulled away from her older sister without meeting

her eyes. "I'm fine. Thank you." She looked out the window toward the street. "Did you come to town alone?"

"No. The boys are with Tucker at the livery. Then they're coming around to pick up the supplies I got from the general store. I dropped by Peggy's earlier, and she wanted me to leave the baby with her while we shopped." Daisy made her way to the hall tree against the side wall. "This is lovely." She pulled the spring hat with yellow daisies Lily had made earlier in the week. "I must try this on."

"Sit down and let me help you." Lily removed Daisy's modest bonnet and straightened her hair. She reached for the hat. "This will be just right for you, I think. It's perfect for spring."

Daisy eyed her reflection in the large mirror. "I love it. I just bought a length of yellow gingham to make a new dress. This is exactly what I need for the spring picnic at church." She rubbed her abdomen and met Lily's gaze in the mirror. "I'll be needing some new clothes with more room around the middle by then." A smile creased her face.

"Daisy! How wonderful!" Lily hugged her sister. Daisy's face was aglow with joy for the life that grew inside her.

"Isn't it? Tucker's happy. The boys are beside themselves. They love Rose, but I think they want a brother this time."

"What about you?"

"I'll be thrilled with whatever God decides to bless us with. A healthy child is my only prayer." Daisy loosened the ribbon from the hat and pulled it from her head. "I'll take this, ma'am. Will you please wrap it up for me?" Her sober voice made Lily laugh.

"Yes, Mrs. Barlow. Is there anything else I can get for you today? Gloves, perhaps, or a parasol?" Lily wrapped the hat in tissue paper and put it in a hatbox.

"What do I owe you?"

Lily pushed the box across the glass case to her sister. "Not a thing. You and Tucker have been more help than I knew I would need. It's my gift to you."

Daisy frowned. "I can't accept it, Lily. I know what's going on." Her face grew serious.

"Whatever do you mean?"

"Peggy told me when I stopped at her house. What a horrid week it must have been for you." Daisy opened her reticule and pulled out some money.

"I won't take your money, Daisy. I did very well at the beginning of the week. Business will pick up. People just need to realize my shop is open." Lily nipped into the back room for a few seconds and returned with another hat. She went to the hall tree and put it in the spot that had held the hat Daisy had chosen.

"It's more than that, Lily." She came to stand near the hall tree. "Peggy said it didn't go well when she tried to talk to Mrs. Croft. She wasn't receptive to Peggy's explanations about your actions." At Lily's downcast look, she added, "I'm sorry. Because she's in the middle of town and most people do business at their store, she's developed a lot of influence. Which is sad, because most people know better than to hang on her every word."

Lily shrugged off her sister's sympathy. "Don't worry about it. People will see the truth. It may take time, but I came here to bring beauty to the ladies of this community. That's exactly what I'm going to do." She walked to the front display and watched two ladies come out of the post office next door. They looked in her window but scurried away when they saw her standing inside.

She turned back to Daisy. "When you and Peggy show up at church wearing my hats, ladies are going to want to come here, too. You're the prettiest way I know to drum up interest in my shop. So hurry up and make that pretty dress."

"I'm praying for you." Daisy hugged her tightly and retrieved her package.

"Thank you. I need it."

"How are you and Edward doing?"

"It's awkward, I guess." She pulled at the edge of her sleeve. "Ellen has decided to accept my presence. That's made things easier."

"But?"

"Daisy, you must know something of how I feel. You didn't expect to be married to Tucker when it happened."

"No, I didn't." Her sister put a hand on her arm. "It's not quite the same thing. I knew Tucker. We'd been dear friends."

Lily heaved a sigh. "Well, Edward wants to tell me what to do and how to run my business."

"Really? What has he said?"

She shrugged. "He thinks I should put my money in the bank every day when I close." It didn't sound horrible when she said it out loud. "He says I need to be careful who I choose to associate with."

Daisy made a small sound. "Hmm...that sounds like a husband trying to protect his wife." She gave Lily a serious look. "Try not to turn him away with your need for independence. God must have thought you two needed each other."

Lily shook her head. "I think God wanted Ellen to

be safe." She opened the door for Daisy and found Edward on the porch.

"Edward." Lily put her hand at the base of her throat. "You startled me." Her hand went up to touch the hair at the base of her neck.

"I'm sorry." He took off his hat and held it in both hands. "I came to check with you about making a sign."

Daisy cleared her throat behind Lily. "How do you do, Edward?"

"Daisy." Edward dipped his head in a greeting. "I'm fine, thank you. Just saw your husband coming out of the livery. He said he's on his way to pick you up at the general store, if you're finished with your shopping."

Lily backed up to allow Daisy to pass through the door.

"Thank you." Daisy went onto the porch and turned back to Lily. "Tucker and I want you all to come to lunch tomorrow."

Lily started to refuse, but Edward accepted. "We'd like that. It'll be good for Ellen. Thank you."

"Come right after church," Daisy said.

She stepped outside and waved as Daisy left. "I'm looking forward to it. An afternoon in the countryside will do us all some good."

Daisy made her way across the street, and Lily turned to Edward.

"If you'll give me a moment, I've made a rough drawing of what I have in mind. I'll get it and show you where I'd like the sign to be mounted." Lily wrung her hands together as she spoke.

They stepped inside. "Has it been any better today?" His gaze dared her to deny she knew what he meant.

"No." She motioned for him to follow her into the

workroom. "Peggy Dismuke came in and bought some handkerchiefs to send to her sister."

"It'll get better."

She opened her mouth to contradict him, but he held up a finger and tilted his head to one side. "I promise. Something else will happen. To someone else. And everyone will forget why you and I got married." He put the finger down and put his hat back on. "Now get your drawing, and let's see what you have in mind for a sign. Hopefully something to draw some positive attention in your direction." He smiled and leaned against the opening between the shop and the workroom.

A small smile caressed her lips and made its way to her eyes. Try as she might, she didn't understand how this man was such a comfort to her. He'd turned her life upside down.

She was grateful he was staying close by to help with the consequences of the upheaval.

On Sunday afternoon Edward entered Tucker and Daisy's cabin. Lily sat in the front room visiting with her sister. He and Tucker had been in the barn while the kids played outside after lunch.

"We need to load up and head back to town, Lily." He didn't like the looks of the sky.

"Surely you don't need to leave so soon?" Daisy put Rose back in her cradle and reached a hand to Tucker, who joined them.

Tucker put an arm around his wife and lifted a hand to point through the open door. "It seems there's a storm heading our way."

"Oh, my." Daisy went to the door and called to the kids to come quickly.

"How bad is it?" Lily moved to stand and Edward put a hand under her elbow to assist her from the chair. A trickle of heat trailed up the length of his arm. He saw she was not unaffected when she turned to him. He tried to focus on Ellen approaching with the twins.

"We better hurry, Uncle Edward. That looks like a mighty bad storm. I wanna get home now." Ellen's voice presented a brave front, but a slight tremble revealed her true anxiety.

Tucker closed the door against the growing wind. "You best hurry on."

"I want to be safe at home before the full force of this storm hits." Edward was concerned for his family. He wasn't accustomed to having a family to look after, but he wanted to do his best.

Lily turned back to him. "I hope the storm passes quickly so it won't hinder me from opening my shop tomorrow."

The quiet that met her words chilled more than the storm ever could. It was obvious no one here thought she'd have any customers tomorrow. He was doing everything he could think of to support her, but the fact was that people were avoiding her place.

"Oh, please, don't look at me like that." Lily implored Daisy to understand. "I simply must open. I can't let the gossip change me. Opening the store every day is the only way I know to combat the lies that have been spread about me."

"I don't think you'll have to worry about opening tomorrow." He didn't want to give her false hope.

"Why would you say that?" Lily grabbed her coat and rammed her arms into the sleeves. Try as he might, Edward couldn't match her speed. She was fastening the buttons before he could grasp the woolen collar to pull it straight. "How can I build a good name in Pine Haven if my own family and friends don't have faith in me?"

Daisy spoke up. "Lily, we have faith in you. I know your store will be a success. I heard more than one lady admire Peggy's new hat today. Rest assured she was singing your praises when they did."

Lily spun to look at him. "Why don't you think I need to worry about opening tomorrow, then?"

Edward put a hand on her shoulder. "It doesn't look to me like anyone will be going anywhere to shop tomorrow. This storm shows all the signs of keeping us tucked into our homes for several days."

Lily looked from one face to another. She lowered her head and reached for her reticule.

"Well, I need to be at home just in case." She peered through the window at the brooding gray sky. "Who knows? It may blow over without a whimper."

"Right. If you don't mind, I'd like to head on back just in case your optimism doesn't materialize." Edward shoved his hat down over his brow. "Ready, Ellen?"

"Yes, sir." The little girl tied her bonnet tight and pushed her hands deep into her pockets. "Bye, everybody!" Out the door she flew and clambered onto the wagon seat.

Edward offered his hand to Lily to help her into the wagon. In the rush to leave, she hadn't put on her ever-present gloves. When she put her hand in his, he felt the calluses on her palms he'd noticed once before. This woman he'd heard talking about frills and pampering wasn't taking the time to pamper herself. She appeared soft from a distance, but closer inspection showed the depth of strength and determination she possessed.

He walked around the front of the horses and checked the harnesses before he stepped up to join them. He passed a heavy blanket for Ellen and Lily to tuck around their legs.

"Ellen, move over and give Lily more room on the seat." Edward shifted to the far edge of the seat to allow Ellen to slide closer to him. He'd have to drive the team hard to get home before the storm broke. The last thing he needed was for Lily to bounce right off the wagon. "We'll be going home in a hurry. It's gonna be a bumpy ride." He released the brake and signaled his team to head for home.

"Do you think we'll get home before it storms?" Ellen had to raise her voice to be heard above the sounds of the horses and wagon. Each bump sent the three passengers jostling against each other.

"I'm trying my best." Edward held the reins firm and drove the team as hard as he dared on the rough terrain.

They hit a deep rut in the road, and Ellen's small frame lifted off the seat. Edward and Lily reached for her at the same time.

"You handle the team, and I'll hold her." Lily pulled Ellen close and wrapped her tightly with both arms.

The trip to town dragged on for what seemed like ages. Edward thought they just might make it home before the storm hit. No sooner had town come into view than sheets of sleet began to pelt the trio as they huddled together on the seat. He looked over at Lily's flimsy hat and knew it was already ruined. Ellen's bonnet would dry by the fire, but the feathers and ribbon Lily preferred were beyond repair. Another reminder that such things might please the eye but the troubles of life could wreak havoc on them without warning.

"Push Ellen under the seat and slide next to me." Edward was shouting now over the fierce wind.

"I don't want to!" Ellen clung to him.

"Now, child." Edward's voice brooked no argument. Lily helped her slide under the seat and moved next to him.

"Pull the blanket over our heads. I'm afraid this will get worse before it gets better."

Lily fought the wind and worsening sleet, but managed to pull the blanket around him and then tuck herself close with the blanket over their heads.

Her small frame fit against him, invoking a strong desire to protect her. He began to wonder if they would have been better off staying at Daisy's cabin. It was too late to turn back now. They'd have to press on for home.

Ellen was directly beneath them. Edward felt her small arms wrap around one boot. She hated storms. The week her parents left her with him, they'd had terrible rain for days. The continuous thunder and lightning had buried fright deep in the child's soul. Why hadn't he seen this one coming earlier? He should have had her safe at home. It was his duty to protect Lily as much as Ellen, even if Lily insisted she could take care of herself.

Blinding snow fell with the frozen rain, stinging his hands and arms. His hat protected his head, but he knew Lily would be getting the worst of it. Ellen was safe under the bench. There was no refuge between them and town. They had no choice but to struggle on through the storm.

He shouted at Lily. "Put your head down!"

"I can't! If I do, I won't be able to hold the blanket over your head."

"I've got the blanket. Come here!" He lifted his arm

and tucked her in close to his chest. He held the reins with one hand, snagged the far edge of the blanket with the other and pushed it into her hand. "Hang on to this!"

A streak of lightning lit the sky, and the team startled. It took all his strength to keep them from bolting. Ellen shrieked beneath the seat and tightened her hold on his boot. The echoing thunder rumbled low beneath the howling wind.

Edward narrowed his eyes, searching for the road that threatened to fade from view in the intensity of the storm. He pushed the horses as hard as he dared. "God, help us to get home safe."

"Amen!" Lily shouted from her cocoon beneath the edge of his elbow.

Edward didn't realize he'd prayed out loud. But right now they needed all the help they could get. He maneuvered the team around the last bend in the road before the edge of town and pulled on the reins. "Whoa, boys!"

He pulled the wagon to a stop under the roof that extended off the front of the livery. Icicles hung from the wagon. White puffs from the horses' nostrils floated up to be carried off by the wind.

"Make a run for the front porch." The sleet still pelted down. He had to raise his voice for Lily and Ellen to hear him. "I'm going to get the team inside the livery. Start the fire and get Ellen out of those wet clothes."

Chapter Eleven

"Let's go inside." Lily put a hand on Ellen's shoulder and urged her toward the front door of the cabin. The wind buffeted them on the porch.

"Don't!" The scream tore from Ellen. Her chin quivered, and she began to tremble. Melting snow dripped from her dress and coat. Black shoes pranced like a nervous horse in the middle of the frozen drift forming at her feet. Something just before terror emanated from the child's eyes.

Lily knelt before her and put a hand on each shoulder. "We're safe now, Ellen."

"Where's Uncle Edward? I want my uncle Edward!" The frightened voice rose to a fever pitch.

"He's putting the horses in the livery so they'll be safe, too." Lily spoke loud enough to be heard over the wind, but gently in an effort to calm the child.

"I want Uncle Edward." Sobs wrenched through Ellen. Lily pulled her close and pressed the child's wet face to her shoulder.

"He's coming, precious. Don't you worry. He's safe. He'll be right here." Lily swayed from side to side, rocking Ellen in her arms. "We're all safe." Lightning flashed and thunder followed before the light faded. The clap was deafening. Ellen and Lily both jumped and clutched each other more tightly. The child's scream was muffled by Lily's coat.

Edward ducked under the eave of the porch and knelt behind Ellen. "It's okay, baby girl. I'm here." He turned her to face him and wrapped his arms around her.

Lily immediately felt the chill of separation as Ellen's warmth pulled away from her. Snow blew onto the small porch with relentless force.

"I'll start the fire." She stood and skirted around the two as they clung to each other in the cold.

Lily searched in the dim cabin for matches near the hearth. Thankful he had laid the fire, she struck the match against the bricks and lit the kindling near the iron grate. She blew on the small flame, and the fire caught in earnest. She filled the kettle with water from a pitcher near the stove. Setting it to boil, she opened the front door again.

"Can you carry her in? The fire's going." Lily hoped Edward could hear her. The storm raged and blew its fury onto the porch, but the strength of it paled in comparison to the emotions she saw in the two shadowed figures. Ellen was curled against Edward, her tiny arms snaked around his neck. He held her close and spoke near her ear. Lily felt like an intruder in the scene. What tragedy racked their hearts and caused them to remain in a dangerous storm? Did the elements of nature dim in view of the heartache they nursed?

Edward rose at her words, lifting Ellen with him. He scooped her legs up and carried her like a baby in his arms. Lily backed into the room, holding the door wide for them to enter. He had to turn sideways to get through the doorway with Ellen.

Lily spread a blanket on the bench near the hearth, and Edward laid Ellen on it.

"Please get her some dry clothes and a towel."

She scurried to get the things he asked for, returning to find Ellen had stopped crying. Ellen sat on the bench facing the fire. Edward tugged at her coat and dropped it near his feet, in a wet heap with her shoes.

Lily pulled the shoes from the pile. "Edward, loosen the laces and put these on the hearth while I change her clothes." The kettle whistled. "Will you make tea?"

"Yes." He put the shoes down and went to the stove.

Minutes later Lily pulled a nightgown over Ellen's head and started to work on the long, thick hair with a towel.

Lily wrapped Ellen in a blanket and was pulling on her last sock when Edward handed Ellen the warm drink. "Be careful. It's very hot."

Lily smiled at the child, whose brown eyes reflected the flames.

"Thank you, Aunt Lily." Ellen's voice was a ragged whisper, her throat raw from crying in the storm.

Lily cupped her cheek in one hand. The fire had started to warm the tiny girl. "You're welcome, Ellen. Now let's see if I can find you something to eat."

"I'll take care of supper." Edward shrugged out of his coat. Water hit the floor, and rivulets traced the grain of the wood toward the fireplace. He hung the heavy garment on a hook near the fire's edge.

A smile teased Lily's face. "I'll do it."

"What about something simple and filling?" He sat on the hearth and tugged off his boots. Water spilled onto the floor at his feet. He rolled thick socks down his calves.

"You are making a mess." Lily picked up a bucket from the corner of the kitchen and rushed to put it in front of him. It was unusual to be this close to him. The awkwardness of the past weeks faded in the urgency of the moment.

He wrung the water from his socks into the bucket and laid them across the edge of the hearth near Ellen's. "I'd say it's a bit late to worry about how much melting snow and ice is in here." He pointed to direct her attention to the floor beneath her feet.

Lily looked down to see a growing puddle. Water ran from the front edge of her coat. Her dress swished with moisture, and her shoes were worse than Ellen's had been. Warmth filled her face when she looked back to Edward, and she giggled.

"I see your point." She removed her coat, hoping the rest of the water would be contained in one area. She hung it next to his on another iron hook. "These hooks are handy here."

"Jane insisted on them." He picked up Ellen's dress and wrung the water from it into the bucket at his feet. "She didn't want me soaking the floor when it rained."

"Momma doesn't like a mess." Ellen's fingers laced around her tea. The color was returning to her face. "You'd be in trouble today, Uncle Edward."

With an endearing gentleness, he ruffled Ellen's damp hair, his hand so large it dwarfed the child's head. "You are right."

Lily sensed she was an interloper in their world. She wanted to be at ease with Edward like she was now with Ellen.

Or did she?

"Sit here." Edward stood and indicated his place on the bench next to Ellen. "You need to get out of those wet shoes."

In the glow of the firelight, the cabin closed in on her. "I'm fine. Thanks." She would have backed away, but he caught her by the elbow and tugged her toward the seat.

"Don't be silly. You'll catch your death if you don't get out of those wet things."

Lily dropped onto the bench beside Ellen.

"Can you help me unlace my shoes, Ellen? My feet are a bit damp." She smiled at the girl and winked. "But don't you worry. I never get sick."

"Never?" Ellen slid off the bench and squatted at Lily's feet.

"Absolutely never." Lily shook her head in slow, exaggerated seriousness. "Why, once I had to walk all the way home from town in the pouring rain. It's about five miles from East River to my papa's ranch. I didn't even sneeze once."

Edward attempted to follow her lead. "So, five miles? That's a long walk for a lady. You must be pretty tough." He had moved to the kitchen.

Lily smiled at Edward and spoke to Ellen. "I'm tough all right. Just not real pretty."

"That's not true. You're pretty as can be." Ellen pulled the first wet shoe from Lily with a swoosh of effort. She landed on her seat on the hearth, and everyone laughed.

"Thank you, Ellen, but you're too kind. I'm tough because I was always taking care of whoever was sick at my house. Kinda made me strong." The second shoe came off without resistance. "Don't you worry about me catching anything. I'm much too slow at running," Lily teased Ellen, and gave her a quick embrace.

"Thank you, child." She set the shoes on the hearth to dry. "My toes are already starting to thaw." She moved near the bucket and looked at Edward. "If you'll turn the other way, sir, I'll take care of getting rid of some of the water in my skirt."

He stared for a moment as if he was lost. His eyes were on her stocking feet, watching her toes wiggle in their new freedom.

"Edward," Lily prompted. "Please." With one finger and a twist of her wrist, she made a swirling pattern.

"Oh. Of course." He walked behind the screen in the back corner.

"I think a quick twist will work wonders on this old skirt." Lily talked to Ellen as she wrung the water from her clothes into the bucket at her feet. She heard Edward washing his hands in the basin. "What do you think you want for supper?"

"Can I come out now?"

"Just a minute." She squeezed the last of the water her strength could wrench from the heavy skirt. "Now is fine." Lily dropped the hem to hang limp at her feet. The fabric might be ruined. She'd try her best to clean and restore the shape of the garment later.

He came out wiping his hands on a small towel. "I'll help. What about scrambled eggs? Maybe we could fry a few potatoes." He flipped the towel over one shoulder and moved to the stove. In quick fashion he had lit the burner and started cutting the potatoes.

"I'll make coffee." Lily poked at the pins holding her hair. "I'm about to dry out here."

"Ellen, you can slice the bread." Edward dropped

the potatoes into the hot grease in the cast iron skillet. Then he pulled out a bowl and began to crack open eggs to scramble.

"You surprise me. You know, before, I never would have pictured you as an efficient cook." Lily filled the coffeepot with water from the pitcher and set it on the back burner.

"Oh, he ain't much of a cook. Pancakes and eggs is about all we ever ate before you came." Ellen tore the bread in her haste to slice it.

"Don't talk bad about my cooking, or you'll have to do it." Edward pointed a fork at Ellen as he teased her.

Lily put a hand over the child's and guided her as she sliced the next piece. "Saw it slowly and gently. Back and forth. Then you'll have a nice piece to cover with butter." She released Ellen's hand and watched her cut the next piece. "Very nice.

"Do you want to learn more about how to cook, Ellen?" Lily thought it might be another way for her to bond with the child.

Ellen shrugged one shoulder and slid the plate of bread to the middle of the table. "Mrs. Dismuke tried to give me some lessons. She said I'm too young."

"I was your age when Mrs. Beverly started letting me help in the kitchen." Lily watched curiosity cross Ellen's face.

"Who's Mrs. Beverly?"

"She's my papa's housekeeper. She took care of us after my momma passed on."

"And she let you cook when you were seven?"

"Not by myself. She let me watch her at first. I could help stir and mix things together. I had to learn how to be careful before she let me near the stove."

"Did it take long?"

"Only a few lessons. Then I got to start helping with basic chores and cooking."

"Could you teach me?" Ellen's face was free of the shadows the storm had brought. She glowed in the light of the hurricane lamp on the table. "I could cook for Uncle Edward when you have to work late."

Lily had struck a chord with Ellen she hadn't known was there. This little girl's desire to care for her uncle mirrored her own at that age. "If it's okay with your uncle. If you promise you'll still do little-girl things, too." She rested a hand on Ellen's shoulder. "Sometimes we get in such a big hurry to grow up that we forget to be a kid." She chucked the tip of Ellen's chin with her finger. "You have to promise."

"I will! I promise!" Ellen jumped from her chair and flung herself around Edward's midsection. "Please, Uncle Edward, can I? Can I?"

He dropped his spatula and pushed Ellen's hair away from the stove. He picked her up and set her farther from the hot surface. "Not until I see you're ready to be cautious. You very nearly set your hair on fire." Lily knew the harshness in his voice was born of fear from having to protect Ellen from the hot stove.

Ellen slumped in his arms, and her bottom lip slid out. "I'm sorry. I didn't mean to." She looked up at his face. "Don't be mad. I'll be careful." The pleading broke the tension that surrounded him in the instant of danger.

"I know you didn't mean to get too close, Ellen, but that's how accidents happen." He was eye level with her now. "You're not mature enough to learn to cook yet."

"But Aunt Lily said…"

"The matter is not open for discussion. You finish

putting everything on the table now." Edward went back to the stove. Ellen put plates on the table, moping and murmuring under her breath.

"Mind your manners, Ellen." Edward kept his back to the room.

Did he think Lily would argue with him in front of his niece? Was he ashamed of his harsh reaction when Ellen got too close to the stove? Why did Edward marry her if he wasn't going to let her help with decisions like this for Ellen? Had he changed his mind?

Thunder sounded through the wind. Maybe the storm would blow over with the ferocity with which it arrived. Would they be able to navigate the changing climate of their lives? She wanted Edward to trust her with Ellen. She could make decisions that would help the little girl grow into a lovely young lady.

Would he learn to trust her to do that?

One could only hope.

"Ouch." Edward muttered under his breath when he nicked his hand for the second time. The small rabbit he was whittling would be stained with blood if he didn't slow down. He'd fussed at Ellen before supper for being careless, and now he was the one at risk.

Lily's soft voice floated across the room from behind him. She and Ellen had cleared away the dishes while he came to sit in front of the fire and whittle. Or escape. Lily's presence warmed the small cabin. The way she'd flittered across the space when they'd come home, helped get Ellen into dry clothes then scolded him for wetting the floor had made him smile.

If Ellen hadn't almost been hurt near the stove, he might still be in a pleasant mood. There was so much responsibility with the child. That's why he'd asked for Lily's help. And this evening, when she'd offered it, he'd turned her down. He couldn't explain why, even to himself.

Ellen's giggle joined Lily's airy laughter. He wouldn't look back again. The last time he dared to peek over his shoulder, Lily had caught him. Her smile told him she knew he wanted to be in the midst of the activity, but his pride prohibited it. The smell of burnt onions still hung in the damp air. He'd all but ruined their meal when he added onions to the frying potatoes and forgot to turn them in the skillet. He wouldn't stand around and risk the teasing he was sure he deserved.

Another stroke of his knife and the wooden rabbit's ear came off and landed in the pile of shavings at his feet. He threw the mangled animal into the fire and reached for a fresh piece of wood. Mr. Croft had asked him to create a variety of animals. The rabbit was his first attempt.

"Want some company?" Lily moved close to the fire and held her hands out to its warmth. He didn't look up at her. The tone in her voice warned him her cheeks would be rounded with a soft smile.

"Tired of being cooped up in here with the smell of burnt onions?" He chipped away large chunks of the wood to form the beginnings of a new rabbit.

"That could have happened to anyone. I daresay you wouldn't have done it if Ellen hadn't startled you so. Children can take away your focus quicker than anything else I know." She walked to the window near the front corner of the cabin and studied the sky. "The storm seems to have lost its fury. At least the sleeting has stopped."

Fresh shavings piled at his feet. He was being more deliberate. Cutting his hand again would only embarrass him further.

Edward turned the wood in his hand. "I expect the snow to end within the hour."

"Ellen is tired. I sent her to prepare for bed." Lily stood near the window with her back to him.

"I'll go in and say her prayers with her when she's done."

"I best be getting ready to turn in, too." Lily pushed away from the window and stepped close to the hearth. It was her habit to go into her room when Ellen went to bed. It had prevented them from being alone together. They were both adjusting to the lack of privacy their hasty marriage had imposed on them.

Maybe he could soothe over his mistakes earlier by encouraging her friendship now. "Why don't you sit up awhile?" He sliced away a large corner of the wood he held and turned it in his hand.

"Are you sure?" At his nod, she continued. "I think I will. I want to mend a couple of Ellen's dresses. I could do that while you work." Lily spoke softly. "I'll just go and tell her good-night first." Lily knocked on Ellen's door and entered at the girl's quiet invitation.

Edward lowered his head and saw the sad beginnings of a bunny. He couldn't concentrate on it. He stood and moved to lean against the mantel and stare into the flames. Rushing back to town this afternoon, he'd thought only of their safety as he'd tucked Lily close and covered her with his bulk. The effect she had on him had set him reeling. The memory of the scent of her damp hair filled him. Sweet and fresh.

He hadn't been close to a woman like that since he'd

danced with Eunice Hampton at the winter social just before Jane and Wesley left town. She'd been full of laughter and fun, but no emotion she stirred in him compared to the way he'd wanted to protect Lily today.

The door opened behind him. He didn't have to look to know it was Lily.

"Ellen said she's ready for you to come hear her prayers." Her heels clicked across the boards as she headed for his room.

He shook his head. He had to start thinking of it as *her* room.

When he came back into the front room, Lily sat snuggled in the corner of the settee she'd brought with her to Pine Haven. It was nicer than any furniture he had. It wasn't very big, so they'd been able to fit it into the room. There hadn't been room for everything she had, but they'd brought what they could to the cabin.

A small sewing basket stood open at her feet. She leaned into the corner of the settee so the light from the lamp on the table at her elbow spilled onto the dress she was mending.

He rocked his weight from one foot to the other. Never in his life had he entertained a lady in his home. He didn't count his sister. She'd entertained herself.

"Can I get you a cup of coffee?" He walked to the stove and poured a cup for himself.

"No, thank you." She tied a knot in the thread and used a small pair of scissors to cut it off close to the dress. "I don't want to risk spilling anything on Ellen's Sunday dress."

He set the pot back on the stove with a clink and sat in his chair by the fire. "Who taught you to sew?"

Lily must not have heard him. She looked up at him and said, "Hmm?"

He took a long drink of his coffee and set the cup on the hearth. "You told me your mother passed when you were a young girl. I was wondering who taught you to sew." He picked up the beginnings of the rabbit and started to whittle again. It would be easier to talk to her if he stayed busy. Maybe he wouldn't sound so nervous.

A smile crossed her face. "Mrs. Beverly, my father's housekeeper. She stepped in and did what she could with me and my sisters." She pulled a new length of thread through her needle and picked up another of Ellen's dresses. "I was the most interested in sewing and cooking. My oldest sister has been working the ranch for years, and Daisy moved here so long ago that I guess Mrs. Beverly had the most time to help me."

"I am indebted to her. As you can see from my attempts tonight, your cooking skills far surpass anything I could do."

She smiled at him. "Ellen told me your specialty is pancakes. Perhaps we should have them the next time you take over the cooking."

"The two of you seem to have come to some kind of agreement. How did you get her to stop being so defensive around you?" Ellen's animosity toward Lily had troubled him, but he didn't know what to do about it. He was relieved to see the drastic change in his niece's behavior. He picked up his cooling coffee and took a drink.

"She was worried I would steal your affections away from her."

He felt heat spill into his face as he sputtered and choked on the tepid liquid. "She thought that?"

"Yes, but you don't have to worry about Ellen imagining things that aren't happening. We talked about it, and she knows I'm not interested."

Not interested. What man wanted to hear his wife say she wasn't interested in his affections? In fairness, their marriage wasn't an affectionate arrangement, but her words stung nonetheless. He remembered her mentioning someone she'd planned to marry in East River.

"So, this Luther fellow still has your interest?"

Her mouth dropped open for just a moment. Then her face closed as all the progress they'd made in learning about each other disappeared. She rolled up the dress she was working on and stuffed it into the basket. She stood with an icy calm that was more powerful than the storm they'd endured on their way home.

"Wait, Lily." Edward stood. "I wasn't trying to imply anything."

"I heard no implication. I heard an accusation." She plucked up the basket and headed for her room. Now he could think of it as her room. She was using it to shut him out. He didn't know what else to think by her saying she wasn't interested in him.

Did he want her to be interested in him? He wanted her to be interested in Ellen. She'd done that. She'd built a bridge to his niece even after all the anger the child had aimed at her.

He slid between her and the bedroom door. "I didn't mean that." He put his hands on her arms. "Please forgive me."

She blew out a breath and squared her shoulders. "I am not interested in Luther Aarens. I haven't been since the moment I heard him tell his mother he only proposed to me so I could become a companion for her. That I was not someone he could ever love." No emotion accompanied her words. "I had been under the impression his attentions toward me were of a more personal nature. I was unaware he only wanted me for the service I could provide for his mother."

Edward didn't know what bothered him more—that her words were completely devoid of feeling, or the irony that after refusing to marry a man who wanted her to care for his mother, she'd married him to care for Ellen.

"I'm sorry." He didn't know what else to say.

"You've no need to be."

He didn't want to misunderstand her. "But you married me to care for Ellen." If she didn't want to care for Ellen, he needed to know now—before too much time passed. Ellen was beginning to show an attachment to Lily.

"You made no secret of the reasons for our marriage." She lifted her brows and let them fall again, her face a sad yet beautiful picture of resolve. "We can't always determine where we end up, can we, Edward? Or you wouldn't be a guardian to that precious girl, because you'd have kept her mother here. I would still be in East River happily married, but not to Luther Aarens. I might even have a child or two." She dropped her gaze to her hands. "Life isn't predictable. We have to stand up to whatever circumstances we're dealt and move forward."

"So you held no hope of romance or happiness when you came to Pine Haven?"

"I did not. I came here for independence and to start a life for myself."

"And I ruined that dream for you."

"I have a new life now. Just not the one I dreamed." Her words stung long after she stepped into the bedroom and closed the door.

Chapter Twelve

Ellen sneezed again. "Uncle Edward, I don't feel so good."

He pulled the skillet off the heat and bent down to look into her eyes. Glassy orbs in the depths of dark circles stared back at him. "Uh-oh." He put a hand to her forehead. The heat confirmed the suspicion of fever he got from her pink cheeks. "You go climb into bed. I'll bring some water before I go for the doc."

"I don't want Dr. Willis!" Panic struck her face.

He picked her up like a rag doll and carried her to her room. "You're going to be fine, pumpkin. I just want the doc to make sure you don't get any sicker." He pulled the quilt up to her chin and tucked it close around her. "I'll be right back with a cool drink of water."

When he returned, she sat up on top of the quilt he'd wrapped her in.

"Here you are." Edward held the cup for her.

Ellen drank deeply and lay back against the pillow. Her hair clung to the sides of her face in wet tendrils.

"You've got to stay covered up." He tucked the quilt around her again.

"It's too hot." She thrashed her head from one side to the other. "I don't want it."

"Leave the cover on. I'll be right back with the doc." He turned to peek at her before he closed her door. There was no way he'd wait to get help for her. Fever was a dangerous thing.

He grabbed his jacket from the peg by the door and tromped off the porch in the direction of the doctor's office. Lily came out of her shop as he rounded the corner. With a full head of steam, he couldn't stop.

Lily trotted to catch up to him. "What's wrong?"

"I need to get to the doc's office." He tried to sound calm, but the urgency of his mission came through in spite of his effort.

"Ellen?" Lily's face was serious in an instant.

"Yes. Fever. Sneezing. Achy." He picked up his pace.

"I'll stay with her until you get the doctor."

He pivoted on one heel. "I'll be there as fast as I can."

Lily stepped inside the cabin. When she'd left this morning, it had barely been light. Now the curtains were pulled back, and sunshine filled the room.

"Ellen?"

The sound of faint sobs came from the child's room. Lily tapped on the door and pushed it open a bit.

"I hear you're not feeling well." Lily smiled at the sliver of a girl hidden beneath the mound of a giant quilt.

"I'm so hot, Aunt Lily." Ellen didn't lift her head from the pillow, and her eyes barely opened.

"Let me help you." Lily pulled the cover back. She went to the small window and pushed it open slightly. A soft, cool breeze floated into the room.

"Uncle Edward said I had to stay under the quilt."

"My pa used to think that, too. Then we had a doctor who told us to cool him off when he had a fever." Lily picked up the cup by her bed. "I'll be right back with some water."

She dashed into the kitchen and poured water from the pitcher for the poor child.

"Drink this. Slowly." Lily slid her arm beneath Ellen's shoulders and lifted her enough to sip the cool liquid. Then Lily lowered Ellen to rest against the pillow.

Lily retrieved the washbowl from behind the screen in the main room and brought it with a cloth to Ellen's bedside. She wet the cloth and wrung it out gently over the bowl.

Rolling up the sleeves to Ellen's gown, Lily spoke soothing words to her while she wiped the girl's limbs, face and neck with the cool cloth. She dipped it into the water again and folded it to lie across Ellen's forehead.

"How's that? Better?" Lily stepped to the bedroom door at the sound of boots on the porch. "That'll be your uncle with the doctor."

"Ellen? Are you okay?" Edward came into the room.

An urgency raced across his features. He pulled the quilt over Ellen and banged the window shut. "I told you to stay under the quilt." He sat on the bedside and touched Ellen's face.

"Aunt Lily said it would help." Ellen spoke in a ragged whisper.

Edward turned to Lily. "I don't want her to catch a chill. That's how she got sick in the first place." He clutched Ellen's small hand in his.

Lily recognized the fear in his eyes. "We've got to get her fever down. When you bundle her up, it climbs."

"She made me feel better." Ellen coughed, her shoulders lifting from the pillow with the pain of exertion.

He pressed her gently onto the bed. "Try to take it easy. The doc said he'd be here as soon as he gets his bag."

Lily backed herself into a corner of Ellen's room. Her attempts to help the child had been seen as dangerous to her protective guardian. She hoped he wasn't right.

A knock sounded on the door, and Edward stood.

Lily held up a hand. "I'll let the doctor in. You can stay with Ellen."

She stepped out of the room and opened the front door for the doctor. "She's in the bedroom."

Dr. Willis wore a brown suit and carried a small black bag. "Thank you, Mrs. Stone." He moved at a brisk pace toward Ellen's room, never stopping as he spoke.

Lily put on some water to boil for broth. She went across the street and closed up her shop before coming back to help take care of Ellen.

Lord, please help this child. For all Edward's determination to be strong, he can't make her well. Let the fever break soon. Please.

Edward stepped out of the way so Dr. Willis could see Ellen.

"She got wet yesterday, Doc. We got caught in the storm on our way back to town. I got her home quick as I could. Warmed her up good by the fireplace and made her drink hot tea." He tried to keep the worry out of his tone.

"Did you go and get yourself sick, child?" The doctor laid a hand on her cheek. Then he lifted the cloth and touched her forehead.

"It was a good idea to put a cool cloth on her face." He dipped the cloth into the water and wrung it out again. "Does it make you feel better?" He folded the cloth and draped it across her forehead again.

Ellen whispered, "Yes, Aunt Lily did it." Several deep coughs wrenched her chest. "Said it would cool the fever." The words took all her strength, and she seemed to melt into the pillow.

"Let's get you cooled off. Edward, fold the quilt back while I open this window a bit." Dr. Willis tugged the window open and backed up so the breeze would reach the bed.

A small smile touched Ellen's face. "That's better, Uncle Edward."

Edward stood on the opposite side of the bed from the doctor. "Are you sure, Doc? Her momma always bundled her up against a chill." He took Ellen's small hand again.

"I'm sure." Dr. Willis set his bag on the side of the bed. He pulled out the pieces of his stethoscope and assembled it. "I'm going to listen to your chest now, Ellen." He put the ivory tips in his ears and listened to her breathe through the wooden bell-shaped chest piece.

He took several minutes to examine Ellen. "I'm going to give you some medicine for the cough. It tastes bitter, but most medicine does." The doctor made her swallow the first dose.

Dr. Willis handed a small bottle to Edward. "Give her a spoonful three times a day." He began to pack up his instruments. "And keep her room cool. Not damp, but cool. If the fever gets worse, wipe her down with a cool cloth." He picked up his bag. "If it starts to rain, close the window, but don't pile the cover on until the fever breaks."

"Dr. Willis?" Ellen tried to prop herself up on one elbow but fell back against the pillow.

"Yes, Ellen?"

"Am I gonna die?"

Edward's heart clinched. No matter how he tried to protect her, there were things in life a body couldn't foresee. They should never have gone to the Barlows' after church. He should have felt the storm coming. Like his ma used to in her bones.

"Not if I have anything to say about it." Doc Willis gave a wink and patted the side of the bed. "You'll be up running all over the place in a few days. Your aunt and uncle will probably be wishing for the quiet again. Just stay in bed. Rest and drink lots of water. It's the best way I know to put out the fire of a fever."

Relief washed over Edward at the doctor's words. A smile covered his face, and he kissed Ellen's brow. He nestled Ellen's doll in the crook of her arm. "I'm gonna see the doctor to the door. I'll be right back." He stepped into the front room and closed the bedroom door behind him.

Lily was at the stove. "How is she, Doctor?" He could hear the concern in her voice. "I'm making her some broth."

"That's just what she needs." The doctor put on his coat. "Edward will fill you in. I've got another patient coming to the office."

She thanked him and turned back to the stove. Edward could see her lips moving in silent prayer as he opened the front door.

"Doc, thank you for coming so quickly." The men stepped onto the porch so their conversation wouldn't disturb Ellen. "How much do I owe you?"

Dr. Willis rested his bag on the porch rail and buttoned his coat. "Can you put a couple of shoes on my horse?" He retrieved the bag.

"Bring her by, and I'll fix you right up." Edward clapped a hand on the doctor's shoulder. "Will she really be okay, Doc?" He had to ask, in case the doctor had put on a brave face for Ellen's sake.

"She'll be fine. Don't you worry. Good thing your wife was here to help cool her off. It's important to get the fever down quick. You were smart to snatch her up when you did. A woman like that doesn't come along every day."

"I don't rightly know how to let go and let her help me yet. I've been running my business and taking care of Ellen alone for so long."

"Just let her do what comes natural to her. She's a good woman. She proved today she's got good maternal instincts."

"I'll try."

"Remember to keep Ellen cool and make sure she takes her medicine."

Now the relief was real. "Thank you. I will. I don't care how it tastes."

The doctor chuckled. "When she starts to complain about the taste of the medicine, you'll know she's feeling better." He set a small derby on his head and left Edward on the porch. "She seems to like your wife. Maybe let her sit with the child and read, or whatever it is women do to keep young ones quiet while they heal."

When the doctor disappeared around the corner, Edward collapsed onto his chair on the porch and stared into nothing. Fear had clutched his heart when Ellen had come to him with such a high fever. He couldn't lose her.

Jane would never forgive him if something happened to her daughter while she was in his care.

Lord, please help Ellen. Thank You for the doctor's help and the medicine. Please take the fever from her. And bring Jane and Wesley home.

When Edward lifted his head, regret swamped him. He remembered the tone he'd used with Lily. He'd all but accused her of endangering Ellen.

But she'd been right.

Lord, I need Your help, too. And forgiveness. From You. And from Lily.

He went back into the cabin to find Lily at Ellen's bedside, feeding her broth. He sat on the opposite side of the bed holding Ellen's hand. "Does that make your throat feel better?"

Ellen nodded, and Lily gave her another spoonful of the warm liquid. "That's enough for now. You close your eyes. I promise one of us will be here when you wake up." Lily put a hand on Ellen's cheek. "Rest well."

When Ellen fell asleep, he slipped into the front room for a cup of coffee. Lily was putting on her coat. "If you'll stay with her until lunch, I'll come back for the afternoon."

"You don't have to do that. I know you want to keep your shop open as much as possible." He didn't want to hinder her from working. And he didn't know how upset she was with him about disagreeing over Ellen's care.

"It's best for Ellen if she knows we're both here for her."

"You're right. I'll take the first shift. If I have time, I'll make us some lunch while she rests."

Lily smiled a knowing smile. "Do you think that's a good idea? She might not need that much excitement today." With a wave of her hand, she was gone, laughing at his cooking skills. Or the lack of them.

She filled his thoughts while he sat by Ellen's bed. Doc Willis was right. Lily had proved herself today. Edward might not know why things happened as they did, but he was grateful to the Lord above for Lily's help. He needed to think of a way to show her.

Lily was surprised to see Ginger and Lavinia later that morning.

"I want a couple of your finest hankies," Ginger announced.

"I want a pair of gloves. Like a lady wears to church." Lavinia toyed with the lace on a white glove with pearl buttons.

"Those gloves would be perfect, Lavinia." Lily pulled the gloves from the display so the young woman could hold them.

Ginger was searching through an assortment of embroidered hankies from France. "She's got some idea she might want to go to church. Some fellow she met at the general store started up a conversation with her. Seems he's been looking for a wife but only wants a good church girl."

"I ain't wanting to get married yet, but he did make it seem like there might be more fellas in church than we've seen since we got to town." Lavinia handed the gloves back to Lily. "I might not have enough money for these. Mr. Winston said he won't pay for church gloves."

Lily smiled at Lavinia. "I'm running a special on church gloves today." She went to the glass display case and started to wrap the gloves for Lavinia. "Would you like a pair, too, Ginger?"

Ginger opened a colorful parasol and rested it on her shoulder. She tilted her head to one side while she studied her reflection in the hall tree mirror. "No, thank you, Mrs. Lily." She lowered the parasol. "My first husband was a churchgoing man. I've been in saloons too long to be accepted back in a church now."

"God never turns His back on someone returning to His house." Lily hoped the people at Pine Haven Church would welcome Ginger and Lavinia if they came.

Ginger's smile was doubtful. "You know it wouldn't be just God to face if I went back to church. His people aren't always as welcoming. From what I've heard, they aren't too happy with you for being friendly to us. I can't think they'd been any happier to see us in their church."

"You're always welcome as my guest." Lily folded the hankies Ginger had selected into a length of paper and tied it securely with string. "Never mind what people think."

"Keep telling yourself that, honey." Ginger took her package and tucked it into the bend of her arm. "Maybe after a while it'll be true. For now, I'll be at the saloon. Everyone's welcome there."

Lavinia followed Ginger out of the shop with a wave over her shoulder. "Bye, Mrs. Lily. I might see you at church. It depends on whether the saloon opens this week."

A second visit so soon from Ginger and Lavinia was unexpected. Hopefully, they'd surprise everyone in town by coming to church.

Lord, please let me reach these ladies for You. And let others love them with Your love.

The best surprise she could wish for was that the ladies would be treated well if they did show up for services.

* * *

Lily returned in the middle of the day. They shared sandwiches, and Lily stayed with Ellen while Edward went to work.

He tried to do a full day's work in a few hours, but he couldn't concentrate. His mind swung like a pendulum between concern for Ellen and thoughts of Lily. One a helpless child in certain need of his care, the other an independent woman who fought to cover any sign of weakness or need.

He finally gave up on work and came home. He went straight to Ellen's room to relieve Lily, who left him to watch over the sleeping child.

Edward jolted upright. He must have fallen asleep in the chair beside Ellen's bed. The afternoon had faded to evening.

He put a hand up to rub at the soreness in his neck. Ellen's breathing was raspy but even. He headed toward the front room to find Lily sitting at the table reading her Bible.

He ran a hand through his tousled hair and squinted to see her in the twilight. "I didn't mean to fall asleep."

"It's tiring to tend to the sick. I prepared supper." She stood and walked to the stove. "Is she better?"

"She's still sleeping."

Her eyes darted a glance over his shoulder to the open door to Ellen's room. "I want to make sure she has a good meal."

A moan came from Ellen's room, followed by a deep coughing spell. Edward rushed into the room and put an arm under Ellen's shoulders to help her sit up.

The child settled and sent a smile beyond him to the

doorway. "Lily." The whisper cost her another coughing spasm.

"Don't try to talk. You need to rest your voice." Lily's soft tone seemed to caress Ellen as she lay back against the pillow. Lily entered the room.

Edward offered her a chair. "Will you sit with Ellen while I dish up the food?" When she didn't move to answer, he reiterated, "Please? You must be tired, too."

"Okay. It will be good to sit a spell." Lily dipped her head in agreement.

From the front room Edward could hear Lily's hushed voice, but he couldn't make out the words. Once Ellen chuckled, only to end up coughing. He picked up the tray laden with fresh bread and stew and went back into Ellen's room.

"Ladies, you must take it easy for our patient to get well. No laughing or carrying on until the fever is gone." He hoped his lighthearted tone contradicted the seriousness of his words. Lily's presence was having a healing influence on Ellen. He could see it in the girl's face.

"We're being good. Aunt Lily was just telling me about one time when her papa was sick. He coughed and coughed until he tore his nightshirt. She had to sew it up again." Merriment played in Ellen's eyes.

Edward set the tray on the bed after Lily helped Ellen to sit up. He draped a napkin across the front of Ellen's nightdress and reached for the bowl of stew. "Want me to feed you?"

"I want Aunt Lily. She can tell me more stories."

Edward turned to look at Lily, his eyebrows raised. "Would you mind?" He offered her the bowl and spoon.

"I'd be glad to entertain the patient." She nodded toward the door. "You may take a break, if you'd like. We girls will be fine on our own for a bit."

Edward released the stew to her, careful not to brush her fingers with his. The heat of the bowl wouldn't move him like the warmth of her touch. He left the door ajar and headed for the stove.

He sat in front of the fire with a bowl of hearty stew. Dipping the bread into thick gravy, he savored Lily's cooking skills. She had spoiled them with her delicious meals.

From the sounds of giggling and laughter in the bedroom, it seemed she was also adept at nurturing children, despite his earlier belief to the contrary. Did she know she possessed so many talents? Her hats were beautiful, for sure, but the food and caring were natural. Care for her fellow man came easily to her.

That caring was the reason she wanted for customers. It was one thing to reach out to people. It was another thing entirely to do it to one's own detriment. Sacrificial caring was a strong Christian principle. He hated how it had marred her reputation among the good people of Pine Haven. When they got to know her as he and Ellen did, her true heart would be evident to all.

If only they'd give her time.

Deep in thought, he didn't hear Lily enter the room.

"She wants to rest now." Her voice drew him to its warmth. "It seems she's a little better. She was able to eat most of the stew."

A final swoop of his spoon around the inside of his bowl gathered the last bits of potatoes and gravy. He retraced the spoon's path with his last bite of bread and popped it into his mouth. He stood with the bowl in one hand and wiped his chin with the wrist of his sleeve.

"Who can blame her? This is the best stew we've had in this house in…well, in longer than I can remember." He set his bowl on the table and took Ellen's dishes from her. "Are you going to eat?"

"Yes." Lily ladled stew into a bowl and looked over her shoulder toward the bedroom. "Maybe we can get her to eat a little more after a while. She hasn't eaten much today."

"I'm glad she's been able to sleep." Edward stacked the bowls in the basin to wash later.

Lily examined her fingers, touching the nails, then turned her hands palm up and looked at him. "I'm sorry for upsetting you earlier."

Edward saw sorrow and hope in her eyes. "I wasn't upset with you." They stood with the table separating them. "I was worried about Ellen."

"I overstepped my bounds. I do that. I do or say something without thinking it through first." A nervous laugh bubbled in her throat. "Papa says it puts people off. He's forever scolding me for it."

Edward moved around the table. "You were right, you know." He reached a hand toward her, but the right to touch her wasn't his. He dropped it to his side. "Doc says cooling the fever was helpful. Thank you."

Blond waves framed her face, and relief turned her blue eyes to violet. Such beautiful eyes. This time she reached to rest a hand on his sleeve. It was as though a bird rested on his arm. The weight of it was so light he had to look to confirm its presence, but the wonder of it paralyzed him.

The air stilled. Peace settled between the two of them.

"I'm so glad. I don't think I could have stood it if

I'd caused Ellen more suffering. I know that was your concern."

He laid his hand over hers. "Thank you for understanding. Please forgive me for my harshness."

"If you'll forgive me."

A tug beneath his hand beckoned him to release her. A rightness in the comfort of her touch told him to resist. Sparks flew from the fireplace as a log crackled and shifted. He wrapped his fingers around her hand and rubbed his thumb across her knuckles. The violet eyes widened.

"Uncle Edward?"

Coughing and whimpers dragged him back to reality.

"Coming, Ellen." He released Lily's hand. "There's fresh coffee on the stove."

The violet faded to blue, and the moment was over. Had it really happened?

Lily picked up her bowl. "I'll see to the dishes after I eat."

"Thank you for the supper."

Lily waved off his thanks. "Let me know if I can help."

"I will."

More coughing made him realize it was time for Ellen's medicine. He went into her room to tend to her. While he soothed the child back to sleep, he wondered if he could soothe his heart back to its normal rhythm.

How could the touch of a callused hand bring comfort? Was it wise for him to allow himself to be comforted by her? He rubbed his sleeve at the memory of her hand under his.

The more he learned about his wife, the more he liked her. He'd have to be careful. She'd been faithful in her promise to help him with Ellen. He couldn't risk making Lily uncomfortable in their relationship by letting himself fall for her. She'd made it plain she wasn't interested in him. Ellen would suffer if he made Lily uneasy around him.

He didn't know who would suffer more. Ellen? Or him?

Chapter Thirteen

"What is that caterwauling?" Lily threw back the quilt, slid her feet into slippers and tied on her robe. "How's a body supposed to sleep with all that racket?" It had taken her hours to fall asleep. Thinking about her reaction to being so close to Edward had kept her awake. It wasn't only the closeness they'd felt, but the sudden backing away that had hindered her rest. This middle-of-the-night screeching was not a welcome sound.

She crept quietly through the front room of the cabin. Edward lay on his back, stretched out near the fire, snoring lightly.

The moon was high in the sky when she opened the front door to find a yowling kitten on the step. A tiny paw wedged between two boards was the apparent reason for its distress. She pulled the door closed behind her to keep from waking Edward or Ellen.

"You poor baby. No wonder you're crying so." She stooped to extricate the paw and landed on her seat on the porch when the freed animal launched itself at her.

"Oh, my. You are upset, aren't you, little one?" Lily pulled the kitten from its perch on her shoulder and cradled it in her hands. Tiny claws nipped at her flesh. Then a pink tongue dragged roughly across the knuckles on her thumbs. The crying turned to mews and nuzzling.

"You're trembling." Lily pulled the kitten into the lapel of her robe. She took the orange-and-black ball of fur to her room and wrapped it in a towel.

"I'm guessing you're just old enough to be away from your mother, but not quite confident." She rubbed the tiny head with the towel and promised her help to the lost animal.

By the time the sun came up, Lily had a plan. She hoped Edward would consent.

After breakfast, Lily and Edward assessed Ellen's improvement. They decided to leave her to rest. Edward would work and check in on her frequently. Lily would open the shop and come home for lunch.

Lily bundled the cat into a basket and covered it with a towel, praying it would be silent until she got it out of the cabin. She wanted to make sure it was healthy before telling Edward about it or giving it to Ellen.

She crossed the street and stepped onto the walk in front of her shop. She set the basket on the boardwalk and unlocked the door, humming a chipper tune at the thought of Ellen's reaction to her idea.

"Mrs. Stone." Winston Ledford's voice startled her when she reached to pick up the basket.

"Mr. Ledford." Lily's breath caught. She was forced to stop when he blocked her path.

"How is business?"

"Everything is well." She leaned to look beyond his shoulder.

"Looking for your Mr. Stone, are you?" Cold eyes awaited her reaction.

Lily stretched to her full height. "Not that it's any of your business, but I'm concerned about our niece. She's been ill."

"I'm sure you'll take good care of her." Cynicism dripped from every word. "I hear you've gone out of your way to be helpful to my girls."

"I make it my practice to be helpful to all my customers."

"Just be careful not to discourage my girls. I don't mind if you sell them hats and such, but I won't tolerate you interfering with their work." A serious weight filled his tone.

Lily caught sight of Edward opening the doors to his shop. He stopped to study her for a moment. She turned her attention back to the saloon owner.

"Mr. Ledford, any conversation I have with Mrs. Jones or Miss Aiken is entirely my business. I won't let you, or anyone else for that matter, tell me what to do." She hiked the basket up higher on her arm and took a step toward him. "So don't bother trying to threaten me again. I don't threaten."

He chuckled. What on earth could cause the man to chuckle when she was giving him such a solemn speech? She turned to follow his gaze toward the bank. Mrs. Croft was coming through the doorway, towing her reluctant husband by the sleeve. Exasperated, Lily pivoted in the direction of Edward's shop. His retreating back told her he'd seen and disapproved of her. Again.

"I think you may be correct, Mrs. Stone. I don't see you as a threat at all. I don't have to worry about you affecting my business. All I had to do was stand in the middle of town and engage you in conversation. You've affected your business by associating with me. I give it two weeks, at the most three, before you won't be an issue for anyone in Pine Haven." He touched the brim of his hat. "Good day to you."

The spiteful man left her standing on the sidewalk. Behind her was her shop, empty of customers for days on end, save for the preacher's wife and Mr. Ledford's employees. Behind her stood a nosy woman who chose to believe the worst of her without giving her an opportunity to prove her true Christian character. But the most painful of all was seeing the back of the husband she'd married to protect her name as he walked into his shop.

Why did it hurt so badly to be rejected? She'd come here to escape the confines of being at someone else's beck and call. To be on her own. But she was caught in the middle of a town in transition. She'd fooled herself to believe she could bridge the gaps between the old and new. She'd wanted to be left alone. Not to be alone.

A rumbling purr and the rustle of the towel covering the kitten drew her attention. Did Edward really believe she'd be consorting with the saloon owner? Had he opened the doors of his business a moment earlier, he'd have known it was a random encounter.

Why hadn't anyone been close enough to hear her rebuff him? If only she had a witness to her resistance to the man's attentions.

Lily stepped into her shop and closed the door. The little girl in bed with a fever needed the cheer a tiny kitten could bring. The cleaning and grooming of the small animal must be done before she approached Edward. She was certain the frightened animal would scratch and resist. But putting a smile on Ellen's pale face would make it worth the effort.

Edward may be angry with her, but surely he wouldn't refuse Ellen the joy of a warm, furry friend.

Edward tied on his leather apron. He refused to look at Lily standing in the open doorway of his shop. "Ellen is resting and I'm busy."

In spite of his frustration at her continued association with Winston Ledford, it took all his focus to keep from welcoming her. He wanted her here. He'd tried to help her. Her determined refusal to control her behavior in public was an obstacle not just to her business but to their relationship, as well.

A nagging voice in his head reminded him of her honorable goals. Of her caring nature. His angry mood silenced the voice. Seeing her on the street with the saloon owner rankled him for reasons he wasn't willing to explore.

He picked up a shovel and scooped coal into the forge in preparation for the morning's work.

"I've brought her something." She held the basket out for him to see.

Edward blew out a long sigh and turned to her. He had to put as much effort into this arrangement as he expected from her. He dropped the shovel back into the hopper, causing black dust to float in the air between them.

"I think God sent us a little help for her to pass the time while she has to rest." She took a step toward him.

The towel in the basket moved. Now he was curious. "What is it?"

"See for yourself." She held the basket closer.

A purring sound greeted him as he lifted the towel. The kitten looked to be about two months old. "Where did you get such a critter?" He dropped the towel back into the basket but left the cat uncovered. Button eyes of green watched his every move.

"He came to me in the middle of the night." The teasing chuckle in her throat chipped away at his ill humor.

"He did, did he?" Edward dropped the metal shank he'd need for his first project on the edge of the forge near the growing heat of the fire. "What did you do? Sleep with your window open?"

"No." Lily smiled at him in earnest. "He woke me from a sound sleep, crying because his paw was caught in the boards of the porch steps."

"You know, if you fed him, he'll never leave."

"Oh, I know. That's why I made sure to feed him right away."

Edward eyed the tiny creature. "How did you get him without me hearing you?"

She smiled, a slight lifting of the corner of her lips. "It might be hard for you to hear over your snoring."

"Well, you may as well give him a name, then. He's yours for life."

"I think Ellen will love him." She placed the basket on his workbench and lifted the tiny pet with her gloved hands.

Edward backed away from her. "I think he'll be a great cat for your shop."

Lily moved closer, petting the speckled fur with one hand while she cradled the kitten against her coat with the other. "But isn't he cute?"

"Not to me." A hand went up, palm out, to emphasize his disagreement with any notion that the cat should stay with Ellen.

"He's adorable. I know Ellen will think so."

"Nope. Not for one minute." He shook his head back and forth while she continued to pursue him with the animal.

She leaned in close and offered the cat to him, tripping over the corner of the coal hopper. The shovel slipped to the floor with a metallic crash.

Startled, the cat launched itself from Lily's hands to the front of his shirt. Lily stumbled backward and lost her balance. Flailing in an effort to stay on her feet was useless. She landed on her seat in the mound of coal. A cloud of dust rose around her. Before he could help, she pressed both hands on the sides of the hopper and pushed herself up.

Lily clapped her gloves together. A shower of powdered coal drifted to the ground, leaving a fine layer on the front of her pale blue skirt.

It didn't escape his notice that her clothes and hats complemented the color of her hair and eyes. Even covered in soot, she was as fine a lady as he'd ever seen.

"Are you all right?" Edward hoped she wasn't hurt. He extricated the tiny claws from his shirt and dropped the kitten into the basket.

"Perfectly fine, thank you." Without looking away from him, she rubbed her skirt smooth and tugged at the hem of her coat, leaving a streak of black wherever her ruined gloves touched.

He dared not laugh at her. The flash of light in her violet eyes warned him. But the rumble of humor bubbled in his chest as he fought back a grin.

She picked her chin up, stretching her spine to reach all of the height God had given her.

Certain the top of her head would nest pleasantly under his chin, he smiled.

"Is there something you find amusing?" Lily put a hand to her hair, and he chuckled. Her eyebrows shot up.

An unsuccessful attempt to compose himself was followed by outright laughter when she brushed a knuckle across the tip of her nose, leaving another streak of coal.

"Really, Edward, I do not see why you are so amused. You may be big and strong and handsome, but your manners are sorely lacking." Lily's eyes grew wide. "What I mean is…"

"I heard you. You don't need to explain." She'd called him handsome. Something in her voice when she said it made him wish it could be true.

"May I offer an apology for my lack of manners? It's not every day I see someone so prim and proper in such a state." He stepped to a bench on the far side of the shop and retrieved a clean rag. "There's some water in the rain barrel outside the front door. Feel free to freshen up, if you'd like." He held the rag out like a peace offering.

Lily reached for the rag and saw her sleeve. Then she peered down at the front of her skirt. "Oh, my. Is it everywhere?" She looked to him for the confirmation she knew was coming.

"Afraid it is." A smile threatened to crease his face.

"I must be a sight."

"I'd say you are." He grinned then. "Please forgive me. I didn't mean to laugh at your misfortune."

"Really?" She touched the rag to her nose and pulled it away. His face let her know she'd only made it worse. "I discern no end to your mirth at my expense."

"It's just amazing to me how you can manage to look so pretty all covered in soot like you are."

Lily felt her cheeks flame. He probably only called

her pretty because she'd foolishly said he was handsome. "Now you're just being silly. There is nothing pretty about my present state."

He stepped close and took the rag from her. With a gentle hand he dabbed at her nose and cheek. "That's better." His eyes locked on hers and dared her to breathe. "Just as I expected. Still as pretty as ever." One corner of his mouth lifted.

Lily's head reeled. He was too close…and tall…his muscular build imposing. Was she leaning toward him? Could she stop herself? Did she want to?

She'd been around strong men every day at her father's ranch, but this man was different. By not moving, without a word he asked her permission to stay near her. Was he asking to come nearer still? As her husband, did he think she should welcome his closeness?

The space of his workshop seemed to shrink. The heat from the fire in the forge seemed to grow hotter even though the bellows was still. She fought the urge to step back.

Dredging up new strength, she spoke. "Edward, I…" The whisper died in her throat.

"Uncle Edward?" Ellen's voice called from behind her. "How come I don't hear any hammerin'?" A disheveled head poked around the corner of the forge. She must have entered through a back door.

Lily took a step back. Edward pushed the end of the metal piece into the fire and pumped the bellows.

"Lily! I thought you were going to stay at your shop all morning." Ellen stepped toward Lily with outstretched arms.

Lily caught the child's arms before the anticipated hug. "I'm all dirty. Don't let it get on you."

"Why did you come here instead of to the house?" Curious eyes lifted to quiz her.

"I needed to see your uncle first."

"Why?" Ellen flung a glance over her shoulder at Edward. "He ain't sick."

"Speaking of sick, why are you out of bed?" Edward's face bore disapproval and compassion at the same time.

"I'm tired of being in bed. And my fever is better. You said so."

"You still have to stay in bed until you're completely recovered. Doc's orders."

Lily sought Edward's permission with her eyes to share the kitten. Surely he was too kind to deny the child this small comfort.

The kitten meowed in his basket on the bench.

Ellen's brows climbed her tiny forehead. "Uncle Edward?" She tucked her handkerchief doll into the pocket of her pinafore and reached for the cat.

"No, Ellen." Edward picked up his bellows and frowned at Lily.

"Oh, please." Ellen's voice was muffled as her nose nuzzled the fur of the tiny kitten. She lifted her pale face. "Has he got a name? Is he yours? Where did you get him?"

Lily chuckled at the string of questions. "He showed up on the porch steps last night. He doesn't have a name, and we were just discussing who will keep him." She gave a nod to Edward. "You'll have to ask him."

"Can I keep him, Uncle Edward?"

"No." Edward set the bellows aside and turned the metal in the fire.

"Please, Edward." She added her pleas to the little girl's.

"Can we call him Speckles? He's got so many speckles." The calico kitten licked at Ellen's hands.

"That's a wonderful name, Ellen." Lily was triumphant.

His shaking head marked the end of Edward's argument against the cat. "It appears I am outnumbered. But there will be conditions."

Lily laughed at his expression of mock defeat.

Ellen gave a weak laugh. "Can he take a nap with me? I'm supposed to stay in bed, but I get lonely."

"I think Speckles would like that very much." Lily touched the small animal's head.

"Aunt Lily, you're all speckled, too. Maybe I should call you Sparkles instead of Aunt Lily. You're all covered in shiny coal dust."

It was Edward's turn to laugh. "It sounds fitting to me."

"Very funny." She smiled at the two of them laughing and happy. It was a relief after the stress of Ellen's fever. "Ellen, I've got just enough time to tuck you back in bed before I have to go back to the shop."

"Thank you, Uncle Edward." Ellen snuggled the kitten close, and Lily retrieved the basket.

"Don't thank me. It was Aunt Lily's idea." He crouched in front of her. "It's only for while you're sick. Speckles goes back to her shop when you're well again."

The little girl put on a brave face and turned to Lily. "Can I come visit him there?"

"You certainly may."

"Back to bed with you, young lady." Edward dropped a kiss on Ellen's head as he stood. "I'll be over in a few minutes to give you your medicine."

"You go on ahead. I'll be right along in a minute."

Lily watched Ellen snuggle the kitten high into the curve of her neck. The little girl whispered to Speckles as she walked back the way she'd come.

"Edward?" A new idea formed in her active mind. Why hadn't she thought of this in the first place?

Edward pulled on thick gloves and picked up his hammer. "What is it now, Lily? I can see your mind churning away behind your eyes. I am certain this can't bode well for me." He checked the tip of the metal and pushed it back into the glowing coals.

"Actually…" She drew out the word, trying to decide the best way to broach this new subject.

"See. There it is. The plotting and planning I suspected." A smile pulled his lips into a thin line and dimples creased his cheeks.

"This idea would make it easier for you while Ellen is recovering. And it would keep her from being lonely."

"I thought Speckles was going to take care of that problem."

"He will, for the most part." Lily shifted from one foot to the other on her tiny heels. The hem of her skirt stirred the dust at her feet.

"I'm waiting." Edward's smile turned to a suspicious grin.

"What if Ellen stays with me through the day? I can make her a place in the workroom to rest. You can work without interruption, and she can keep me company."

The grin faded. "That's very kind of you, Lily, but she'll be fine at home."

"I know you're busy. You've got to shoe a horse for Dr. Willis, and you've still got to finish the other hat stands for me. And the sign."

"What about your work? Ellen needs her medicine,

and she'll have to eat. Not to mention the cat will have needs, too." He stood between the forge and the anvil shaking his head.

"I don't know why I didn't think of it before." Lily took a tentative step and placed a hand on his arm. The strength she drew from the touch was more for herself than to assure his attention. "I'm offering. And if we're being honest here, we both know I probably won't be very busy today." She tried to keep the disappointment from her voice.

Was it just a couple of weeks ago she hoped to be busy with customers, making new friends and living a life independent of the responsibility of tending the needs of others? How quickly Ellen had made her way into Lily's heart. The thought of the child alone in bed for the day was sad.

"Please let me do this. For Ellen. It's why you married me."

"I married you so she would have a motherly influence in her life."

"If she was my own flesh and blood, I'd want her close by while she is sick." She saw his resolve waver. "It's what we agreed to."

Chapter Fourteen

The January sun was setting, and a cool breeze had threatened from the west as he'd walked across the street to Lily's place. Without having to worry about Ellen, he'd been able to shoe Doc's horse and make good progress on the remaining stands for Lily. The drawing for the sign was complete, too.

The bell rang as he entered the shop. Lily must have seen him coming across the street. "We're in the workroom."

Ellen was perched in the middle of the makeshift cot Lily had made for her in the corner of the workroom, the kitten nestled asleep in her lap. "Uncle Edward, I was good today. I took a nap this morning and again after lunch." She rubbed the kitten's ears. "Two, if you count that short one before you came."

Lily stood near the cot. "I'd say she'll recover quicker than we first thought. Dr. Willis stopped in and was pleased with her progress. He thinks if we keep her quiet and restful for a few more days, she'll be as good as new."

"When he brought his horse by this morning, I told him she was here."

Edward had noticed the pristine shop when he arrived. The floors shone, and every hat was displayed with care. Lily must have worked while Ellen slept. Not one trace of a customer could be found.

"Are you ladies ready to go home?"

"I am." Ellen climbed off the cot and put the kitten in its basket.

"You two go ahead. I'll close up shop and be there in a few minutes." Lily bolted the back door and straightened the cot before following them into the front of the shop.

Edward lifted Ellen, and she wrapped her legs around his middle, the cat and basket hanging from her arm. "Don't be too long." He adjusted the child while Lily tucked a quilt around her small frame to keep her warm for the short trip across the street.

"Just a few minutes." She closed the door behind them.

By the time he had Ellen tucked into her bed with the kitten on the blanket, he heard Lily come into the cabin. He sat with Ellen, half listening to her ramble on about her day, never losing track of Lily's movements in the cabin. First she'd gone to her room and hung her coat in the wardrobe. Then she washed her hands in the bowl in her room. He strained to hear her light steps as she went to the stove to start their supper.

"I had fun with Speckles. He likes me. You really do need to let him stay with me all the time. He'll be lonely at night at Aunt Lily's shop." Ellen stopped petting the animal and looked up. "Are you listening to me, Uncle Edward?"

"Hmm?" He sat up in the chair and leaned his elbows on his knees. "Sure. You don't want the cat to be lonely."

"Yay!" She jumped from the bed and flung herself at him, kissing his cheek. "Thank you, Uncle Edward! Thank you!"

Lily came up behind him. How he heard her over the noise Ellen was making, he wasn't sure.

"What has happened in here?" Lily smiled and waited to hear what the commotion was all about.

"Uncle Edward said Speckles can stay here with me. Even after I'm well."

He didn't. "What?" He looked from Ellen to Lily. "I didn't say that."

"Yes, you did. You said 'sure.'"

Oh, no. He'd have to pay more attention, or these two would have his life turned upside down.

"I said, 'sure, I heard you,' not 'sure, you can have a cat.'"

"I'll leave you two to sort this out." Lily laughed. "I need to get the corn bread into the oven."

Upside down? It was too late. In the past few months, he'd gone from being a contented bachelor to full-time uncle, and now to guardian and husband. His world was more than upside down. It was topsy-turvy. Strangely, it wasn't as unsettling as he'd thought it might be.

When he tucked Ellen into bed later that night, she insisted on recounting her day to him, saying he wasn't paying attention before supper, so she'd tell it all again. She loved the hats Lily made. Did he think she could make pretty things when she grew up? On and on, she rattled about things Lily said and did. When she finally settled against the pillows after another dose of the dreaded medicine, she sighed and pulled the kitten into the circle of her arms.

"Uncle Edward?" Her words were whisper soft, weak with fatigue and the remains of the illness.

"Yes, sweetheart?" He touched her forehead and was glad to note her fever wasn't as high as it had been the previous day.

"Do you like Aunt Lily?"

Her eyes were closed. Could he save his answer in hopes she'd fall asleep?

Ellen turned onto her side and snuggled into the pillow. "Do you?" she asked again.

"Yes, I do." He straightened the blanket and extinguished the wick in the lamp on the bedside table. The shadows in her room danced in the glow of the moonbeams shimmering through the barren trees outside her window.

"Good. Me, too." Eyes closed, a yawn settled Ellen deeper into the night. "I know she's pretty. But I think she's strong, too."

"I think you're right, little one." He kissed her forehead.

"Thank you for letting me keep Speckles." Her words were barely a whisper as slumber pulled at her.

"You rest now. I love you." He turned in the doorway and took one last look at her sleeping form. She was right. Lily was pretty and strong. Unlike any woman he'd ever known. She was grounded in her faith, even when putting it into practice put her reputation at risk. She was beautiful. There was no denying that. In fact, Lily was disproving a lot of his long-held beliefs about women. And life in general.

If only he could shake the image of her engaged in

conversation with the saloon owner. Why did she continue to jeopardize her standing in the community by associating with Winston Ledford?

He closed the door to Ellen's room and turned to see Lily on the settee, one of Ellen's dresses in her lap and her sewing basket at her feet.

"Is she all settled in?" Lily concentrated on the needle she was threading.

Edward looked over his shoulder. "Yes. She was asleep before I left the room." He went to the stove and poured himself a cup of coffee. "Can I get you a cup?"

Lily looked up from her mending with a small smile and a shake of her head. "No, thank you."

She was the picture of solace. How had this woman never married before she came to Pine Haven? Were the men in her hometown daft? Lily should be sitting in a home full of love and children of her own, not in front of his fire, mending Ellen's clothes after having cooked them a meal. She deserved to be loved. Just like Ellen deserved her mother and father.

Then Winston Ledford's face came back to him, smiling at Lily in the street. Had Lily allowed her charitable heart to cast her in a negative light in her home community, too? People could be persnickety creatures when it came to what they considered appropriate behavior of a young lady.

He drank a large gulp of his coffee and strangled on its heat. He sputtered and lowered himself into his chair near the fire.

"Are you okay?" Lily looked up again.

"Fine. Just drank it too fast."

"You better be careful." She spoke absentmindedly, but it was just the opening he needed.

"Speaking of being careful." He paused and considered his next words. "There's something I need to say."

"You sound serious." Her hands stilled. "What is it?"

"I saw you this morning." He cleared his throat. "Talking to Winston Ledford again."

The slow intake of breath and slight rise in her head warned of her dismay. "Again?" Her even tone was taut with tension and the effort to control it.

"Well, you have talked to him before."

"I have." She wasn't making this easy.

"It's just that I married you to protect your reputation, and..."

The calm left her. "And what? Do you honestly think I'd risk my reputation after paying so dearly to restore it? You aren't the only one who gave up something for this marriage."

She was right. He was benefiting from her relationship with Ellen. Her world had turned upside down in a much shorter time than his. She was probably reeling from the spin of it.

He started over. "What I mean to say is, I think it would be easier to protect yourself in the future if you avoid the likes of Winston Ledford. He can only hurt you."

"He came up to me on the street. What was I to do? Short of being rude, I had to at least speak to the man." She tilted her neck back and looked at the ceiling. "And the irony of it all is that he's as upset by my kindness to Mrs. Jones and Miss Aiken as everyone else in town."

"He's upset? Was he unkind to you?" He was out of his chair before he realized it. It was one thing for him to caution Lily, but another thing entirely for that snake of a man to treat his wife in a manner unbecoming of a gentleman.

"He warned me not to upset his girls, as he calls them."

"Did he threaten you?" He sat on the settee beside her and reached for her hand. It trembled in his. "What did he say?" If he harmed Lily in any way... He forced himself to listen to her answer rather than marching out the front door and into the saloon to confront the man.

"Not exactly. He just told me not to discourage them. He doesn't want them to be tempted away from the life he's offered them." She sighed. "In the end he said he didn't have to do anything to me. He said I'd destroy myself just by being kind to them." She looked up into Edward's eyes. "And to him." She shook her head. "But I wasn't kind to him. I told him not to threaten me. I told him he couldn't tell me who to talk to and not talk to."

Edward put his other hand over hers and held it snug until the trembling stopped. "I'm sorry."

She squinted her pretty blue eyes at him. "You're sorry? You didn't do anything."

"I did exactly what Winston Ledford did. I tried to tell you what to do and who to associate yourself with."

"But you're trying to protect me." Her eyes softened when she said the words. "And he was trying to protect himself."

"I'm not that good with explaining myself, but I really do want to protect you."

Lily laid her other hand on top of his. Its warmth and gentleness were welcome.

"You know, Edward, we want the same things. I want my business to succeed for me, but also for Ellen and for you. I don't want to do anything to put that at risk."

"I realize that. I knew it before, but Winston Ledford has a knack for infuriating me."

"Are you jealous?" She started to smirk. Then, as if she heard the words after she said them, she pulled her hands away. Her voice lost all its mirth. "There's no need to be."

He tugged her hands back into his. "I know." He gave her hands a light squeeze and released them before going to stoke the fire.

They had reached a new understanding of one another tonight. He knew it would help them as they cared for Ellen. But he was beginning to wonder how much they could help each other.

Before they turned in for the night, Lily convinced him to let Ellen spend the day with her again tomorrow and every day until Doc said she could return to school.

Morning would bring a new day. Filled with what, he did not know. But he was eager to find out.

"You need to stay on the cot. I promised your uncle Edward."

"I just want to go outside for a minute." Ellen juggled the kitten and her doll in her small hands.

"It's time to rest. You've been up a bit more today. I don't want you to overdo it and relapse."

"What's relasp?" Ellen squinted at Lily and dropped her doll. Speckles wriggled free and swatted at the edges of the doll's hem.

"Relapse." Lily picked up the doll. "It means to go backward. The time you've spent resting has made you stronger. If you try to do too much too soon, you'll get worse instead of better." The doll was worn and dirty. She unfurled the wrinkled edges of its dress.

"I don't want to get sicker." Ellen harrumphed and leaned back against the pillows. She pulled at the kitten's ears. "But I'm tired of resting. I thought all this resting was gonna make me not be tired."

Lily laughed. "It will. It just takes time. Remember, Dr. Willis said the hard part would be resting when you started to feel better."

"Well, this must be the hard part then. 'Cause I'm ready to get up."

"I think I know something we can do that won't tire you."

Hope stirred in Ellen's eyes. The fever had left her sockets sunken and dull. The color had started to come back into her cheeks, but fatigue washed it away again in a matter of minutes if she exerted herself.

"What can we do?"

"I can get a basin of warm water and some soap. You can give your doll a bath."

"It won't hurt her?"

"No, of course not, silly girl. No more than it hurts when you take a bath." Lily chucked Ellen under the chin and gave her the doll.

"Sometimes, Momma had to scrub mighty hard behind my ears and under my fingernails." Ellen giggled.

Lily set the basin on her workbench and helped the child onto her stool.

Together they worked to clean the doll. Endless play had soiled the handkerchief but not beyond repair. When they set the doll on the bench to dry, Ellen went back to her cot without argument.

"Do you think my momma misses me as much as I miss her?" Ellen lay back and pulled Speckles close.

Lily didn't want to give Ellen false hope about the return of her parents, but she didn't think Edward wanted her to make the child think they were never coming back. She answered the only way she knew how. "I'm sure she does." Lily pulled a quilt over the child. "Didn't she tell you so in her letters?"

"The letters stopped coming." A tear slid down one cheek, and Lily sat down to draw Ellen into her arms.

"Oh, honey, they were too sick to write." They rocked back and forth, Ellen sobbing and Lily crying in silence. Lily remembered the pain of realizing her mother was gone.

"I wish they'd come back." Ellen lifted her head and gulped in air, then collapsed against Lily and wailed.

"Hush, baby. It's okay." There were no words to ease the pain in Ellen's heart. Lily knew she wasn't qualified to help her, but Edward wouldn't be back for hours. "Don't wear yourself out with crying."

"I can't stop. My heart hurts. And I want my momma!" Her voice climbed in hopeless desperation with each word.

Lily tried her best to comfort Ellen. What did one say to a child who didn't know if her parents were coming back for her? The weeping spell and Lily's rocking motion lulled the sad girl to sleep. She was gently snoring when Lily went into the front of the shop.

One look out the window confirmed that hers was the only shop void of business again today. How long could she stay open without regular customers? If it weren't for the trickle of lady passengers who stopped in while the train took on water, she wouldn't have sold more than two hats this week. Thankfully, those ladies were generally pleasant and happy to spend their money.

Maybe she should write a letter to her father and let

him know what was happening in Pine Haven. She didn't want him to be taken by surprise by her lack of steady business when he came to town.

The train whistle blew, announcing the arrival of new passengers.

She could write tomorrow. If no one came today. Or maybe next week. Maybe this lull would blow over and she'd never have to share her struggles with him. It would be enough to convince him she was content in her marriage—failing as a shop owner was something she hoped to avoid.

"How was your afternoon?" Edward ruffled Ellen's hair and scratched the cat behind the ears. He'd had a long day's work and was looking forward to a good meal. Lily keeping Ellen with her for the day had allowed him to catch up on several small projects.

"Better than the morning," Lily said. "The trade from the train was better than yesterday afternoon."

"What have you two been up to?" He took off his jacket and hung it on a peg by the door.

"I helped with the corn bread." Ellen was excited. She was still a bit pale, but he was glad to see her feeling better.

"She worked hard." Lily put plates on the table. "As hard as someone can when they're resting."

Again Lily had helped Ellen and made her feel special. He was tired from having lost sleep while Ellen was so ill. Tonight nothing would make him happier than sitting around the table with this beautiful woman who gave so freely of herself without expectation of reward.

"It smells delicious." Edward looked at Ellen. "You

better make sure there's plenty of butter on the table for me."

"Yes, sir!" A happy girl put the butter on the table and went to her room.

"Thank you for all you've done for her." He caught Lily's hand in his when she turned back to the stove. It was delicate and warm. Soft and strong at the same time. "You've really made her life better."

"She wanted to learn." Lily didn't look at him.

"She's wanted a lot of things I couldn't give her." He hoped he wasn't making her uncomfortable, but he couldn't resist reaching out to her. "You're the first person who's taken the time with her."

"Ellen is a delightful child. Anyone would be blessed by spending time with her."

A chuckle escaped his chest. "We both know she did her best to run you off in the beginning."

"Only because she was afraid." Her quick response was serious. He had to lean in to hear Lily's whispered words. "Afraid I'd take you away from her."

He gave her hand a slight squeeze. Lily tugged to pull her hand away.

Edward didn't release her. "Instead, she brought us together." He didn't blink for fear he'd miss her reaction to his words.

She slid her hand from beneath his. "She knows she'll never have to worry about you leaving her."

Ellen's voice interrupted them. "Are you coming? It'll all be cold if you don't come now." She slid into her chair at the table and put her doll on the seat by her.

Lily untied her apron and hung it by the back door. She smoothed the front of her dress and came to the table. He watched her every move from his seat opposite her. She unfolded her napkin and laid it in her lap before reaching for Ellen's hand and bowing her head so he could say grace. Everything about this woman was refined and beautiful.

As he thanked God for the meal, he wondered what she must think of him. Or if she thought of him at all.

In true Texas fashion, Sunday morning the wind howled outside his window. Last Sunday's snowstorm had blown in with a fury and was gone in hours. Most of the week had been sunny with mild weather. Today promised to be another blast of winter.

Edward was grateful he didn't live where the weather stayed cold and brutal for months on end. Enduring the scattered days of cold was enough for him.

"I'm ready." Ellen came from her room.

"The wind is a mite rough. We could stay home today." He touched the glass on the window with the back of his hand to gauge the outside temperature.

"Uncle Edward, I'm well. Doc Willis said so when he came by yesterday." She pulled her new hat to adjust the angle.

"He said your fever is gone. He didn't say for you to go out in the wind." Why must everything be an argument with this child?

Lily came out of her room wearing her blue coat and pulling on her gloves. "Why, Ellen, you look fetching today."

Lily was fetching, too. The blue of her coat matched her eyes. Her golden hair glimmered in the morning light spilling through the windows.

"Thank you, Aunt Lily." Ellen tugged at the ribbon. "I did the bow like you showed me." Lily had given Ellen the hat on Friday after supper. It was stouter than anything she owned, but very pretty at the same time. The new hat seemed to make Ellen glow. He fought back his sadness at the thought of what her parents were missing by not being part of her life.

Edward forced his attention back to deciding whether or not Ellen should go out today. "She wants to go to church, but I'm not sure about the weather."

"I promise to bundle up and stay warm. I won't even ask to play outside."

Lily asked Ellen, "Are you certain you'll be able to sit still while everyone else is playing?"

A solemn expression accompanied the child's response. "I will." She turned to Edward. "Please, can I go? Aunt Lily said she made my new hat so even bad, cold weather couldn't hurt me." She swiveled back and forth without moving her feet. The bottom edges of her coat caught on the motion and swished like the church bell he heard ringing in the distance.

"I don't know." He opened the door to gauge the wind.

"Please, Uncle Edward. I miss my friends. You already made me miss Bible class."

Lily added, "I think she'll be okay."

"Well, if you promise no argument about dawdling outside in the weather, I guess we can risk it."

"Oh, boy!" Ellen skipped to the front door.

"Whoa, there. No running and getting all excited. I don't want you to overdo it."

"I won't. I don't want to relasp." Ellen grabbed his hand and tugged him out the door. Lily followed them down the steps. "Let's hurry so I don't get cold."

Edward laughed and caught her up to put her on the wagon seat. "Cover up with that blanket."

Lily took his hand, and he helped her into the wagon.

"Thank you, Edward." Her voice was quiet as she tucked the blanket close around her legs. He climbed aboard, and they made their way to the church.

"I'm afraid we might be in for some more cold weather, the way the wind's blowing."

"As long as it doesn't snow and storm like it did last week, I'll be fine." Lily put her arm around Ellen and pulled the child close.

"I just hope it holds off till after the service. The thought of being caught out like that again doesn't appeal to me." Edward pulled up close to the church door and set the brake. He swung his weight off the side of the wagon, boots stirring up the dirt as he landed.

"Ellen." He took his niece by the waist and set her down. He turned back to the wagon. "Lily."

"Thank you." Lily held out her hand to him.

Instead of taking her hand, he encircled Lily's waist with his hands and lowered her to the ground. Heat spilled into her cheeks as he released her.

"Hold a seat for me." He gave her a wink and climbed back into the wagon. "I'll be right in." He didn't know why he had the sudden urge to flirt with his wife like a schoolboy, but he did.

Lily stood frozen on the spot where he had set her down. Had he winked at her? Her eyes saw it, but her mind wasn't sure.

Ellen called from the church doorway. "Come on, Aunt Lily."

Just inside the front door, Lavinia Aiken stood wringing her hands and making a valiant effort to blend into the wall. Mrs. Croft entered and gave a small snort as she made her way to her customary seat.

"Lavinia, you came." Relief at Lavinia's presence pushed all thoughts for herself from Lily's mind. "Do you see the gentleman who invited you?"

"No. Mr. Ledford was right. I don't belong here." She probably would have backed away, but Lily took her by the hand.

"You do, too. Church is for everyone." Lily smiled. "I see you wore the gloves."

A smile turned to a smirk. "Ginger told me it wouldn't matter. Said I could dress like a lady, but I wouldn't be welcome here."

Lily faced the front of the church and tucked Lavinia's hand inside her elbow. "Yes, you are. Come sit with me." The drag against her progress as she headed toward an open bench made her wonder if she'd be able to convince Lavinia to stay.

A small gust of cool air stirred the hair at the nape of Lily's neck as the door opened and closed behind her. In an instant Edward was at Lavinia's other side. "Good morning. Welcome to Pine Haven Church."

Lily could have kissed him for his kindness. She released Lavinia and introduced them. "Edward, this is Lavinia Aiken. Miss Aiken, Edward Stone, my husband." She didn't know how long before she'd grow accustomed to referring to him in such a way.

Edward said, "Pleased to meet you, Miss Aiken." A slight smile lifted Lavinia's face.

"Uncle Edward, sit here." Ellen pulled Edward's hand, and he slid onto the bench beside her. "Is she your friend, Aunt Lily?"

"Yes, Ellen. This is Miss Aiken. Miss Aiken, this is Ellen Sanford, my niece."

"I like your gloves. Did you get 'em at Aunt Lily's shop? That's where I got my hat." Ellen tugged at the bow.

"Yes, thank you." The quiver in Lavinia's voice diminished with each passing minute. "Your hat is quite lovely."

Reverend Dismuke stepped up to the lectern, drawing everyone's attention to the front of the church.

"Please sit with us." Lily indicated the seat beside Edward and Ellen. She stepped in next to Edward. Lavinia sat on the end of the bench.

Joy at having Lavinia in church beside her filled Lily's heart. She could forget all the empty days in her shop and the gossip she'd endured. She'd shared the love God had for her, and Lavinia had responded to it. Nothing else mattered.

The deep voice that sang beside her during the opening hymn held a higher place of esteem to her. Edward had shown kindness, not just to her but to Lavinia, as well. He was a respected member of the community and the church. His acceptance of someone new in their midst would carry a lot of weight.

Lily treasured his acceptance of her as his friend and not just someone to help with Ellen. All the more so, as she learned his character. Living in the same home with Edward and Ellen had given her the opportunity to see how genuine his goodness was. This close to him in church, where every time he shifted in the seat he bumped her shoulder, was proving to be a serious distraction. She might have to spend extra time in Bible study this week to make up for missing most of the sermon.

Somehow they were making this arrangement work. The only time she'd seen him upset or angry was when there was danger, like the night of the fire, or a potential problem, like trying to protect her reputation.

She had grown to love Ellen. And now she was beginning to enjoy Edward's company. If his actions and demeanor today were an indication of his feelings, he wasn't unhappy, either.

Did she dare to hope they were building a lasting relationship?

Chapter Fifteen

Immediately after the closing prayer, Lily found herself pulled into a hug by Daisy. "Good morning, little sister."

"Hello, Daisy. This is my friend, Lavinia Aiken."

"I'm Daisy Barlow. It's so nice to meet you."

Certain Daisy knew who Lavinia was and why she'd come to Pine Haven, Lily appreciated the enthusiastic greeting.

"Won't you join us for lunch?" Daisy asked.

"Oh, I couldn't possibly." Lavinia was shying away.

"I'm concerned about the weather." Lily turned to Lavinia. "Why don't you come to lunch at our home? I prepared a stew this morning. The cold creeping through the walls last night made me want something hearty today." She leaned in close and lowered her voice. "I even made a cake. Just because it's Sunday, of course."

Edward buttoned his coat. "You ladies make your plans. I'm going to get Ellen wrapped up in the wagon. I'm ready for some of that stew. I hope you'll join us, Miss Aiken."

Daisy patted Lily on the arm. "Well, maybe next week the weather won't be so chilly. I hope you will make plans to attend the Winter Social. It's only a couple of weeks away."

Lily nodded her agreement. "I'm looking forward to the opportunity to get to know more of the ladies in town."

"Harold and Minnie Willis have offered their barn for the event. It's one of the biggest in the county and close to town. You should come, too, Miss Aiken. It'll be great fun." Daisy smiled and said her goodbyes.

When lunch was over, Ellen was sent to bed for a nap. Edward excused himself to work in his shop. Lily knew he was going to whittle and only left the house to give her time to visit with Lavinia. His thoughtfulness pleased her, but it was no longer a surprise. If she stopped to think on it, he was always doing something for someone else.

Lily pulled her fork across the plate, gathering the last of the crumbs and icing. "Thank you for staying for dessert, Lavinia. A cake always makes it feel more like Sunday to me."

"I haven't had a meal like this since I came to Pine Haven." Lavinia took a sip of hot tea.

"Did you enjoy the church service this morning?" Lily had waited to broach the subject, not sure Lavinia would want to talk about it.

"To be honest, I was a little surprised."

"How so?" She hoped it was a good surprise.

"Everyone was so nice." Lavinia stared into the fire. "Well, almost everyone."

Lily knew she was referring to Mrs. Croft. "The church is a haven for everyone in a community. A place where you can be loved and helped. Most everyone tries to live up to that purpose."

Lavinia turned to her. "Do you think they would accept me every week?" Wariness caused her voice to wobble.

"I'm sure of it."

Lavinia looked back into the flames. "The part where the preacher man talked about all things being new..." Her voice trailed into silence.

"That's one of my favorite verses in the Bible. I love knowing God will help me start over." Lily spoke softly. She was hoping to encourage Lavinia, but the words were true for her, too. The new start God had given her in Pine Haven came at a time when she needed hope.

Please give me the right words, Lord. Help Lavinia to see how much You love her.

"Is that for anybody, or just people in the church?" Lavinia's questions were sincere.

"It's for anyone. God gives us all the opportunity to start our lives over with His care and direction. He removes the effect our past has on our future. He gives us new direction and purpose."

"I'd like that." Moisture filled Lavinia's eyes as she looked back at Lily. "Ever since I got to Pine Haven I've felt I was disappointing my family. None of them ever worked in a saloon. They were all honest, God-fearing folks." She hung her head. "I think they'd be ashamed of me."

Lily chose her words with care. "Sometimes in life we find ourselves in difficult circumstances. We don't always see the choices God has put before us. We can choose what looks like the only path and discover later our true purpose is in a much different direction." Lily paused.

That's what she'd done when she agreed to marry

Luther. How grateful she was that God revealed a new choice by allowing her to come to Pine Haven. She couldn't imagine going back to a life where she didn't count. Where all that mattered was what she did for someone else, and no one saw her for who she was and the value she had as a person.

Finding herself married to Edward, a virtual stranger when they'd pledged themselves to each other, had changed her life. In her heart she realized God had given her a better future with Edward and Ellen than she'd have had with Luther. She was beginning to think it was better than her plan to be alone, too.

"Is it too late for me to change paths?" Lavinia's breath caught on a sigh. "The more I think about spending every night of the week dancing with strange men, the more scared I get. I don't want to be someone men only see as a way to forget their troubles and have a good time."

"It's never too late." Lily leaned back in her chair. "I'm proof of that."

"You?"

"Yes, me." It was her turn to stare into the fire. "I spent years caring for my sick father, while all my friends married and started families of their own. After a while, people stopped seeing me as Lily, and I became Mr. Warren's daughter. I was the girl who served the punch at social events, never the one who got asked to dance."

"But you're so pretty. How could anyone overlook you?"

"My duties to my father kept me busy. Over time, I grew comfortable. Then I withdrew from any opportunity. The withdrawal threatened to become bitterness.

I began to feel trapped, but I knew a good daughter wouldn't abandon her father in his time of need."

The memories of Luther's first attempts to woo her flooded her mind. In hindsight she saw his unabashed efforts to pawn her off on his mother. She remembered the evenings she talked with the older lady over coffee while Luther begged off to work in his office. How had she been so blind?

"It was so bad that when my father regained his health, I jumped at the first—and only—suitor who presented himself. I came to my senses the night I heard him telling his mother he'd never really love me, but I would be a good companion. For both of them."

"No wonder you wanted to come here. I'd rather work on my own than have a heartless man take care of me." Lavinia gasped. Her eyes widened as the weight of her words sank in.

"We aren't so different after all. In my situation, it was a suitor. In your case, it's Winston Ledford." Lily smiled at her. "At least you've realized it before you're as old as I am."

"But you had your faith in God. What can I do? I've come all this way because I didn't have anyone or anything left at home."

"God has given us all a measure of faith. All we have to do is believe."

Lavinia thought for a few moments. "I'd like to change paths like the preacher said today. I don't want the old things in my life to continue. I want a new life, but I don't know how."

"It's simple. Like Reverend Dismuke said, just pray and ask God to guide you. He will."

"Will you pray with me?"

"Gladly." Lily took Lavinia's hand and prayed for her new friend. She thanked God for their friendship and prayed for God to show Lavinia the path He had for her life—and for Lavinia to have the strength and determination to follow it.

"Thank you." A new light of hope shone in her eyes when Lavinia spoke again. "I know I don't want to be a part of the saloon. But I don't know what kind of work I can get in Pine Haven. The saloon was my only means of support. Mr. Ledford won't take kindly to me deciding I don't want to work for him."

"We'll think of something." Lily was so pleased Lavinia wouldn't be working at the saloon when it opened in a few weeks—so glad she spoke without thinking. "In the meantime, you can stay in the rooms above my shop."

Shock covered Lavinia's face. "I can? Won't the landlord mind if you take in a boarder?"

It was more important for her friend to be away from the saloon than for Edward to give his permission first. "I'll settle everything with my husband." Another thought came to Lily. "And I'll write a letter to my father to see if he can make a place for you at the hotel."

"Oh, Lily, I don't have money to stay in the hotel." Worry drew her brows together.

"Not as a patron. To work there. My father is buying the hotel in town. He and my sister and his housekeeper are moving to Pine Haven soon."

"Really? A respectable job?" Surprise lit Lavinia's features. "I'll do anything. Scrub floors, wash clothes, cook. Whatever they need."

Lily laughed at her giddiness. "It's settled, then. You can stay over the shop until we hear from my father or you find another job and a place of your own."

Edward came in the front door, a cold wind blowing behind him.

Lily rose from her place on the settee. "I need to step over to the shop with Lavinia. We may be a while." She decided it would be best to talk to Edward about Lavinia's plans when the two of them were alone.

He stood in front of the fire warming his hands. "That's fine. If you're late, I'll give Ellen a light supper and turn in. I've got a busy week ahead."

Lily and Lavinia worked in the rooms above the shop to prepare it for Lavinia. With no extra room in the cabin, Lily had left her bed when she moved into Edward's home.

By the time Lily got home, Edward was stretched out before the fire asleep. Watching the moonlight as the wind howled outside her window that night, she pondered the best way to approach Edward. Would he care that Lavinia was staying over the shop? Surely not, if it was just a short stay.

She smiled at the peace that had flooded Lavinia after they prayed. Lily's Millinery and Finery might not be doing as well as she hoped, but it was worth every penny she'd lost in business to see a young woman choose a better life.

Lord, keep her safe and help her find a job.

It was easier to pray for Lavinia than it was to deal with her own situation. Would her business continue to suffer? How would people view her now that Lavinia was staying in her rooms?

Tomorrow they would set the place in proper order for Lavinia's stay. Rearranging her former home was the easy part.

A cloud danced across the face of the moon. She'd have to talk to Edward in the morning.

Edward awoke with a start. He had a busy day and would need to drive Ellen to school to keep her out of the cold. He could hear Lily moving around in her room.

He rapped on her door.

Lily called softly. "Just a minute."

He spoke through the door. "I just wanted to let you know I'm going to get the wagon. I've got deliveries to make today and want to drive Ellen to school."

Her muffled voice came to him. "Okay, but I need to talk to you."

"Can it wait? I need to load the wagon, too."

"Sure. I'll wake Ellen and make some breakfast."

Loading the orders took longer than he anticipated. When he came back inside, Lily was on her way out the door. "I've got to run. Can you come by the shop today to talk?"

"I'll try, but I can't promise today."

"I left breakfast on the table for you."

"Thank you." He closed the door against the brisk morning.

He turned to see Ellen almost ready. "Let's get going so you're not late."

He dropped Ellen at school and headed to make his first delivery. As he crossed the intersection in the middle of town, he looked to see if the road was clear. He was dumbfounded to see Lily follow Miss Aiken into the saloon.

What was she thinking? Had she given up on ever having a successful business? She had promised him that she understood why he wanted her to avoid Winston Ledford.

"Whoa!" Edward pulled the reins and made a hard left turn. He set the brake and jumped from the wagon in front of the saloon. Disbelief that he was about to push open the swinging doors of a saloon caused him to shudder. He'd vowed never to darken the door of this establishment. Why did this woman have the power to draw him into situations? Could he save her from herself? Did she want to be saved?

"We're not open." Winston Ledford stood at the end of a magnificent hand-carved bar. A crate of whiskey being unpacked by a man behind the counter evidenced the future ugliness that would, no doubt, take place in the room.

"I'm not here for business. I've come for my wife." Come to get her. And to leave. All as quickly as possible.

A smirk stretched across Winston's face. "The ladies in the saloon are not available for gentlemen until we open next month."

Edward clenched his fists at his side, willing himself to stay calm. This man was as slick as any snake he'd ever seen. "My wife is not one of your ladies."

"You saw her come in here, didn't you?" The smirk became a grin.

A door opened near the top of the stairs running along the wall opposite the bar. Both men turned at the sound.

"Edward, what are you doing here?" Lily started down the steps, a valise in one hand. Lavinia followed her, carrying another bag.

"We'll talk about that outside." He met her at the foot of the steps. "Let me take that." He took both valises and followed the ladies to the front door.

"Come back anytime." Winston leaned against the bar, arms folded across his chest. His suit was pressed and clean, the tailoring exact, the very picture of arrogance. "You're always welcome."

The ladies left without acknowledging his words.

Edward leveled a glare at the man. "You'll be doing yourself a favor if you stay away from my wife."

"I'll do as I please, Stone. I always do."

"Don't say I didn't warn you." The saloon doors swung wildly behind him.

He dropped the valises into the back of the wagon.

"Would you care to tell me what's going on here?" He struggled to control the grit in his tone. He looked from Miss Aiken to Lily.

Lily smiled and laid a gloved hand on his sleeve. "It's awfully cold. Can we tell you after we get back to the shop?"

Edward extended a hand to help them into the wagon. It took all his restraint to remain quiet as he climbed aboard and turned the wagon around for the short drive to Lily's shop.

Once the ladies were inside and he'd unloaded the valises, Edward closed the door against the wind.

"Now, if you don't mind, I'd like to know exactly what you were thinking going into a saloon. Especially after all that has happened since you've been in Pine Haven." Try as he did to prevent it, his words rang with acidity. Miss Aiken was in the background when he directed his indignation at Lily.

"You were asleep last night when I got home. I tried to talk to you this morning, but you didn't have time. That's why I asked you to come by the shop today." She had the audacity to look hurt. "Surely you know me well

enough by now not to question my actions or motives."
Pain filled her voice.

He'd hurt her again. Would he ever get it right with
this woman?

*Lord, You know she gets the better of me. Give me
wisdom.*

"Please don't be angry with Lily. It was my fault."
Lavinia took a step toward him. "She was helping me
get my things." She pointed to the valises at his feet.

He'd carried the bags for them. Blinded by his anger,
he'd gone through the motions of helping them without
considering the implications of the heavy bags. And how
quickly they must have packed them.

Edward turned to Lily.

She finished Miss Aiken's explanation. "Lavinia has
decided she doesn't want to work or live in the saloon."
Her eyes begged him to understand.

Miss Aiken spoke again. "Lily offered to help me. I
didn't think about how it would look for her to go with
me, or I'd have gone alone."

Lily broke in, "I didn't want to risk Winston Ledford
trying to manipulate her or force her to stay."

"I see." He pulled his hat off and spun it in his hands.
The anger was replaced with regret. "Will you forgive
me, Lily?" Once again he'd misjudged her. She was always helping someone. And it seemed all she got for it
was grief. From him and everyone else.

"I shouldn't." One side of her mouth pulled up.
"You've got to learn to trust me."

"You're right. Again." Lost in the blue depths of her
eyes, he found himself swimming in emotions unfamiliar to him. A sensation of falling caught him off balance.
So much so, he had to adjust his footing.

"I'm so sorry for causing this misunderstanding." Miss Aiken's voice came to him.

He cleared his throat. "It's not your fault."

"Since you're here, I have some business I'd like to discuss with you." Lily's straightforward manner effectively closed the subject.

"If you'll both excuse me, I'll head upstairs." Miss Aiken eyed her valises before disappearing into the workroom.

The stairs creaked with her ascent before Lily spoke again.

"There's more to tell you about Lavinia."

"What?" The hair on his arms and neck bristled. If Winston Ledford had harmed that poor girl, he'd be paying another visit to the saloon. Twice in one day, after a pledge to never go, would be unavoidable.

"Oh, Edward, it's the most wonderful news." She reached her gloved hand to his sleeve. It was a habit of hers that gave him pleasure.

Lily lowered her voice and leaned close to him. The scent of honeysuckle filled his next breath. "After lunch yesterday, Lavinia talked to me about the sermon. She's prayed and asked God to redirect her life according to His plan." Beautiful blue eyes turned to violet as he watched joy overwhelm her.

"That is wonderful news."

"It complicates matters to a certain degree."

"How do you mean?"

"Now she doesn't have a job or anywhere to stay. If it's not a problem for you, I've offered for her to stay here in the rooms over the shop."

Edward saw her big heart expanding to include another person in need. Since he'd met her, she'd married him for Ellen's sake, offered friendship to ladies who were shunned by everyone else in town and now she was willing to take in someone with nowhere to go. Was there no end to her generosity? Did she see the potential for continued harm to her business if she followed through with this plan? "Are you sure this is a good idea?"

Hopeful eyes pleaded with him. "As the landlord, you have final say."

"Have you considered what people will think?" He hated the words, but they had to be said.

Lily smiled. "Edward, don't you see? Now people will see how important it is to reach out in love to others."

"Some may, but others will gossip. What if Miss Aiken changes her mind and wants to return to the saloon?"

"Without a safe place to start a new life, that's exactly what could happen. I know with friends and time, she can make a go of it."

"I wish everyone had your optimism." He huffed out a sigh. "If you really want to do this, I have no objection as the landlord."

"Thank you, Edward!" Lily stepped up on her toes and brushed her lips across his cheek.

The air stilled, and she froze in place, pink staining her face. Their eyes locked as she lowered herself onto her heels, hand still resting on his arm. Surprise at her kiss turned to pleasure. He put a hand over hers. "You're most welcome, Lily. I'm glad I can do something to make you happy." The gravel in his voice was beyond his control. "Very happy."

Her other hand went up to cover her mouth. He took a step back and set his hat low over his brow. With a smile he said, "Let me know if you need my help arranging the furniture upstairs."

He sat on the seat of his wagon, knowing he had a full day's work ahead of him. No amount of work would take his mind off the wife he'd left rescuing a friend.

God, help me to understand her motives and see her heart before I jump to protect her. I want to be a good husband.

He lifted the reins and let them fall to signal his team it was time to go. What would it be like to be Lily's true husband? Not just her protector and friend, but the person she turned to for comfort and support—because she loved him. He left town behind and headed to a nearby ranch to make his first delivery, the memory of her kiss fresh on his mind. Could they build a true marriage on a foundation of convenience?

"What have you done?" Lily spoke to herself.

Lavinia appeared in the doorway to the workroom. "Do I need to find somewhere else to go?"

Watching Edward leave without a backward glance, Lily soaked in the stupidity of her actions. How could she kiss him? Their marriage wasn't one of love or affection. They'd both agreed to that before the ceremony.

But his eyes—the surprise she'd seen in them. Was it filled with pleasure? Or was she completely out of her mind? How could she face him tonight?

She turned to answer Lavinia, but her mind was on the blacksmith. Tonight couldn't come soon enough. Nor could she dread its coming more.

That evening, when Lily walked into the cabin, Ellen met her at the door wearing her Sunday best.

"Uncle Edward is taking us to the hotel for supper.

He says it's time we had a treat." Her young face glowed with anticipation.

"He did, did he?" Lily removed her hat.

"Yep, and I can eat dessert, too."

Edward came out of her bedroom. "I'm guessing Ellen has shared the news." He was also wearing clothes he usually reserved for church services. They'd agreed to keep his things in her room for Ellen's sake. Careful scheduling allowed them to change clothes without raising suspicions in the child's mind about their marriage. Ellen was always in bed before them, and Edward rose in the mornings before she awoke.

"Yes, she seems to be excited about a special dinner."

"I hope you don't mind. I thought you'd enjoy a rest from cooking." He paused before adding, "You work so hard all day, and then in the evenings, too."

She smiled, pleased at the kind gesture. "I look forward to it."

At the restaurant, Lily sat in the chair Edward held for her. "This is lovely. No wonder Papa is so happy with his purchase." She put the linen napkin in her lap and took in the beauty of her surroundings. They sat at a table near the fireplace. Sconces glowed against the floral wallpaper.

"My momma picked the colors." Ellen wiggled in her chair. "She said eating in a pretty room makes the food taste better."

"Did she now?" Edward winked at his niece. "Did she also tell you that little girls in pretty rooms must be still?"

Ellen drew in a fanciful breath, inhaling the atmosphere. "I know. It's just been such a long time since we

came here." She stilled and dropped both hands into her
lap. "It kinda makes me miss Momma and Pa."

"I think being in this lovely room your mother decorated should make you feel close to her." Lily put a hand
under Ellen's chin. "It's okay to be happy and remember happy times."

A strong sniff preceded agreement. "I'll try."

Edward used the leather-bound menu to hide much of
his face, but she knew he was fighting the same memories Ellen fought.

"We don't have to eat here. I have plenty of ham for
sandwiches at home. I can bake a batch of cookies while
we eat them." She reached for her reticule.

The menu lowered slowly, and Edward caught Ellen's
eye. "Do you wish to leave?"

"No, Uncle Edward. I'm starting to like it. We just
didn't come for such a long time. I forgot how it makes
me think of Momma."

"It's settled, then." He turned to Lily and gave her a
dimpled smile. "You've cooked for us every night. Tonight we would like to treat you. This is the best place
we know to do that."

"If you're certain." Lily placed her reticule back on
the corner of the table and picked up a menu. "The smell
of fresh bread has given me an appetite."

"If I'd tried to cook for you at home, the only smell
would be bacon frying to go with flapjacks." Edward
chuckled. "Or maybe some burning onions."

"I love the smell of bacon." She laughed with him.

"Me, too," Ellen chimed in and laughed with them.
"But I want fried chicken tonight." She looked at Lily.
"Uncle Edward can't fry chicken. He tried one time.
There was a fire!"

Edward's face turned red. "It was a small grease fire. Contained in the skillet. No one was hurt." The volume of his voice lowered with each defensive word as though he recognized their futility.

Lily smiled at his protest and thought of the fire that brought them together. The smile faded. That fire hadn't been contained. Only the future would tell if anyone would be hurt by the consequences of that night.

They ordered their food and sat talking while they waited for it to come.

"Miss Aiken seems to be happier." Edward took a long drink from his water glass.

Was he as nervous as she was? The way he tugged at the collar of his best shirt made her think so. Was he remembering how she had kissed him?

Thinking it best to keep the conversation on safe topics, she answered, "She is. It's as if the weight of the world has lifted from her shoulders. I've written to my father inquiring about the possibility of her working for him."

"You've been a true friend to her."

"We all need friends." She couldn't stop the smile from covering her face. "I'm grateful for you and Ellen."

He raised his glass. "We are the ones who are grateful for you."

The food arrived. Ellen's hearty appetite overrode her manners, and Edward cautioned her to eat slowly.

The meal was delicious, and Lily found herself relaxing in Edward's company. Ellen's childish banter made them both laugh. Could they settle into being a friendly family that shared in special occasions and enjoyed being together?

Edward took a roll from the bowl in the center of the

table and buttered it. "You've certainly had a hand in spoiling her to good food."

"Aunt Lily, could you teach Uncle Edward to make biscuits like yours?" Ellen spoke around a mouthful of potatoes. "That way, when you have to work late, he can make supper."

Edward raised an eyebrow and waited for her answer. Could she work in close proximity to a man who set her on edge? Would she make a complete fool of herself by falling at his feet or spilling flour all over the kitchen?

"I'm not much of a teacher, Ellen."

"You taught me stuff." The child reached for her glass of milk and drank deeply.

"Children are easier." No, she didn't think she could teach Edward. The way his eyes penetrated hers. Searching. What would he find there?

A few weeks ago it would have been a lonely woman no longer seeking companionship, someone convinced she'd rather be alone than used or taken for granted again.

Tonight he would find someone who surprised even her. The days and weeks in Pine Haven had brought a myriad of changes to her life. For the first time she had lived alone. That hadn't gone as she'd anticipated. The rejection she faced and the likelihood her shop would fail before her father arrived had surprised her. The confidence that dared her to try this adventure had shifted. Her marriage to Edward, finding herself as a wife and substitute mother, had shifted her heart.

Living in Pine Haven was not about being her own person anymore. It was about finding peace. Knowing she was living her life in a way that pleased God. Knowing Lavinia was waiting for her at the shop was more important than a hat sale or a shipment of parasols.

In seeking a place to belong, Lily had found a new person inside herself. Someone who was willing to risk everything if it meant another human being would be better for the effort.

Sitting in this hotel, having supper with two people she'd grown very fond of, Lily realized the seeking was over. She'd found what was missing from her life. Acceptance.

Chapter Sixteen

Edward put his silverware on his empty plate. He watched Lily savor the food and thought about the night he'd brought her here after their wedding.

He put up a hand and pulled at his collar. The strangling sensation was something he remembered from being a lad trying to work up the nerve to speak to a girl at school. "Have you decided if you want to go to the church social?"

"That would be such fun!" Ellen pushed the last of her roll into her already full mouth.

"Ellen, remember your manners."

"Yes, sir." The little girl speared green beans and waited.

The interruption had kept Lily from answering him. "I'd like to take you."

"I think we should all go." Lily smiled at Ellen but didn't look at him.

Edward leaned forward. "Ellen will be there."

Lily turned to him.

"I'm asking if you'd consider letting me take you to

the Winter Social like a social call." There, he'd said it. Now he could breathe.

Well, maybe after she answered.

Pink lit Lily's cheeks, and she worried her bottom lip with her teeth. Then he saw it. A glimmer of light. Replaced in an instant by caution. Had her sudden kiss given him false hope? Part of him wanted a real marriage. Would Lily be willing to try to build that with him? Was courting her after they were married the right way to approach her?

"I'd be honored to accompany you."

"But…" He waited for the withdrawal of her reluctant consent.

"What about Lavinia? I can't leave her on her own so soon. It's important for her to feel she's part of the church family."

Swoosh. Air filled his eager lungs. "She may come along with us."

"Are you sure?"

"As long as you are saying yes, I'm sure." An excitement bubbled inside his chest. For a minute he imagined himself not unlike Ellen. So happy he couldn't be still.

"That's settled, then." Lily's smile was demure. And beautiful. Her voice soft. "Now, Ellen, tell me. How is Speckles doing today?"

Lily's blue eyes lingered on his face while she listened to the latest adventures of the mischievous kitten.

This would be the best Winter Social in years. He was certain of it.

Edward flipped the last pancake onto a plate and set it on the table just as Lily opened the bedroom door. "Good morning."

"Good morning to you, Edward. What has you up and about so early?" She came to the stove and poured a cup of coffee. The skirt of her dress brushed against his leg. It was a dress he hadn't seen. The ruffles on the cuffs were white against the pale green of the sleeves. Everything she wore was feminine and beautiful. Just like her.

But this morning he had a different young lady on his mind. "I wanted to talk to you for a few minutes before Ellen wakes." He indicated the table, and they both sat down. Ellen's reaction to the hotel dining room had him concerned about how the child was handling her parents' absence.

"This looks wonderful. Two meals in a row where I didn't have to cook?" Lily thanked him for cooking and said grace over the food. "What do you want to talk to me about?"

"What did you think about Ellen's mood last night at the hotel?" He speared a piece of ham and added it to the pancakes on his plate. "I think she's trying very hard to be patient about Jane and Wesley not being here, but I don't know if it's time we started planting the seed in her mind that they may not return."

Lily put her fork down. "Do you think that's necessary? Is there no hope?"

"I wish I knew. I've contacted the town doctor again and the sheriff. Neither of them has heard anything more than they were able to tell me before we married." He looked toward Ellen's room. "I just don't want her to have false hope and be crushed later."

"That's one way to look at it." Lily focused on some unseen place. "What would you tell her?"

"At this point, just that we can't find them." He shook his head, hating that he was in the position of breaking his niece's heart. "She might take it better if we tell her what we know in stages."

Lily dropped her voice to almost a whisper. "I remember when my mother passed, how I felt. I don't know how hard it would have been to not know what happened. It was tragic to know my mother was gone from this life, but to wonder if she was sick and couldn't get to me... I don't know how I'd have felt about that. Especially at Ellen's age. She's too young to have so much put on her."

"That's what I'm afraid of. If we don't tell her anything, will she go on talking of Jane and Wesley as if they'll be home in a few weeks? If we start to hint at the possibility that they might not return, it may help ease the blow."

"I'd like to give her hope." Lily's blue eyes darkened with sorrow.

"She's going to have to adjust to the idea that we may be her parents from this time forward."

"I think having an uncle and aunt who love her is keeping her from feeling abandoned."

"I do, too, but I won't give her false hope. I can't pretend, when the sheriff and the doctor have all but said they're gone."

"But they haven't said it." She reached across the table and put her hand on his. "If you won't give it more time, at least give her hope."

A thump from Ellen's room let them know she was awake. "I'll give it two weeks. I'll contact the sheriff again." He lowered his voice. "Then we'll have to tell her."

"I pray you hear good news." Lily pulled her hand back as Ellen opened her door.

Edward couldn't help but notice the extra care Lily

showered on Ellen during breakfast, coaxing a smile more than once with her antics. Ellen's doll was transformed by their imagination into a lovely princess dining in a palace by the time he got up from the table. He stood behind Ellen's chair and mouthed *Thank you* to Lily.

Lily had been good for Ellen. No matter what happened, he knew he'd done the right thing by marrying her.

Only God knew who would benefit more from having her in their lives—Ellen or Edward.

"You haven't been here two weeks, and you've learned more about making hats than I did in three months under the milliner at home in East River." Lily put one of Lavinia's creations on a stand in the front window.

"Do you really think it's good enough to put in the window?"

Lavinia's timidity was surprising. How did this sweet young girl ever imagine herself as a saloon girl? And why did Winston Ledford think she was up for the job? Once again, Lily offered a silent prayer of thanks that Lavinia had responded to God's love for her.

"I do." Lily tied the ribbon and turned the angle just so. "It's a good thing Edward finished these extra stands and brought them. We've been busier in the last week than I was the first week I opened."

Lavinia dropped her head. "I feel so badly for causing you all that trouble."

Lily dismissed her concern with a heartfelt smile. "The trouble was all but forgotten when you walked away from the saloon. I told you the church folks and people in town would see the change in your life."

"I'm glad people have realized your kindness and

friendship to me was the reason I was brave enough to turn to God for a new life." She dabbed at a tear threatening to fall from her lashes. "I can't imagine if I had to be at the saloon when they open tomorrow evening."

"Thankfully, you'll never have to worry about that again." Lily handed her a feather duster. "If you'll dust in here, I'll bring out the other hats we made last night."

"Yes, ma'am." Lavinia gave a playful bow and took the duster. She became serious when she straightened. "Thank you again for letting me help you here until your father arrives. I know my room and board are costing you."

"The sales of the hats you've made are more than covering the costs. I think Ginger must be telling people to come here, too." Lily reached into the cash box and pulled out an envelope. "As a matter of fact, I've got something for you. Here is your commission on the things you've sold."

"Lily, you can't pay me. We agreed I would help out."

"That was before you revealed your God-given talents." She pressed the envelope into Lavinia's hand. "After you finish the dusting, why don't you see if Mrs. Croft has a ready-made dress you can purchase to wear to the Winter Social on Sunday?"

The clothes Mr. Ledford had purchased for Lavinia had been left at the saloon. She wore the few things she'd brought with her when she'd moved to Pine Haven. Lily knew she needed more.

"Are you sure she wants to see the likes of me in her store?"

"Yes. She spoke to me after Bible study on Wednesday evening." Lily put her hands on Lavinia's shoulders. "Nothing too flowery, mind you, but kindly just the same. Something about noticing what a good worker you are."

They both laughed.

"I guess seeing me sweep the sidewalk every morning when she goes to the bank and post office has made us friends of a sort." Lavinia tucked the envelope in her skirt pocket. "Thank you. I'll go as long as we aren't busy."

Lily went to look out the front window. The Winter Social was in two days. Since their supper at the hotel, Edward had been kind and attentive. They'd even shared a cooking lesson. She noticed he laughed more readily. She made it a habit to sit in front of the fire after Ellen went to bed at night. They'd talked about everything from their childhood to their favorite Bible verses.

He made one excuse after another to come to her shop. He'd made two trips with her orders—first the additional stands, then the sign. Yesterday he'd come back to mount the sign on its hinges in the window sill. She pulled at the loose tendrils hanging at the base of her neck and looked through the glass, wondering if he'd come again today. A smile betrayed her hopes to anyone who might see.

Lost in thought, she didn't notice Winston Ledford until he stood facing her on the opposite side of the glass. She started and backed away. He opened the door and entered.

"Ladies." He removed his hat.

"Mr. Ledford." Lily noticed Lavinia backing into the workroom and stepped to block his line of sight. "What can I do for you?"

"You've done more than enough, Mrs. Stone." He peered over her shoulder.

"If you're not interested in making a purchase, I'm rather busy." She refused to be frightened of this man or his threats.

"I warned you not to interfere in my business."

"I have not." God had successfully drawn Lavinia away from his business. She trusted the Lord to protect her from Winston's anger.

"Lovey's presence here speaks to the fact that you have, indeed."

"Miss Aiken is not your business."

"She is the reason I am short on workers for my new establishment. I've come to speak with her."

"She does not wish to speak with you." Lily had known he wouldn't settle so easily when Lavinia left. They'd discussed how they would handle any attempts he might make to contact her.

Ignoring Lily, he called out, "Lovey, come here."

Lily heard the rustling of Lavinia's skirts. "There's no need, Miss Aiken. I'll take care of this." She opened the door and gestured for him to leave.

Taking advantage of her leaving a clear path, Winston stepped toward the workroom.

"I believe my wife has asked you to vacate the premises, Ledford." Edward's voice resonated from behind her. With her back to the door she hadn't seen him approach, but she'd never been more glad to see him. "As her landlord—and husband—I'm going to insist you comply with her wishes at once."

Lily could see the wheels of the saloon owner's mind turning, deciding how likely it would be for him to come out ahead in a confrontation with Edward. Wisely, he opted to leave.

"This is not over, Lovey. You can't hide in this hat

shop forever." Winston turned to Lily. "You leave me little choice today, but whether you like it or not, I am a merchant in this town now. I will make a success of it. And I will not allow you, or anyone else, to get in my way."

"Careful, Ledford. I'm restraining myself. If anything were to happen to these little ladies, or if they became concerned something might happen to them, I'd be forced to protect them. You don't want to be the cause for that concern," Edward said.

"You misunderstand, Stone. My purpose is to offer viable employment to ladies in this town. Making more money in a month than this hat shop will see in six." He was tall enough to look down on Edward as he passed him to leave.

Unintimidated, Edward turned to fill the doorway. "Your presence isn't welcome here. Remember that."

He closed the door and turned to Lily. "Are you all right?"

"We're fine. Thank you for showing up when you did."

Lavinia came from the workroom. "I'm so sorry. I can find another place to stay. Do you think there's a possibility I could start working at the hotel before your father arrives?"

"It's not your fault, Miss Aiken." Edward watched out the window as Mr. Ledford walked toward the center of town.

Lily gave her a brief hug. "You're not going anywhere. I've grown accustomed to having you here."

"I can't believe he came here looking for me. I told him when I left that I wouldn't be back." Lavinia began to dust the shop.

"Try to stay out of his way as much as you can. He'll get the point soon enough." Edward turned to Lily. "I'll be watching him. If either of you feels threatened at any time, let me know."

She was determined not to be intimidated. "Thank you, Edward. I pray it doesn't come to that."

Lavinia moved to the other side of the shop with the duster, and Edward leaned closer to Lily.

"Are we still on for the Winter Social?"

She smiled at him. "Yes. Ellen asked when she brought Speckles to visit this morning. She said he would be lonely while she was in school." She indicated the basket in the corner. "Poor little thing had been crying before she got here. It might have something to do with an incident she said involved an ash bin at the edge of the hearth." Lily giggled at the thought of Edward cleaning up after a kitten he hadn't wanted in the first place.

"That cat should be grateful to be inside." A mock snarl crossed his face. "I've spent more time cleaning up after the little rascal than I can spare. Be warned. He's not as cute as he looks."

"Like you?" She giggled until she heard Lavinia excuse herself from the room.

"Looks like you've gone and said it now." Edward gave her a wink.

"Oh, my. I'll have to be more careful. You might go getting the wrong idea." Enjoyment in his presence filled her with satisfaction. Taunting him was one of her new favorite things to do. That strong masculine face turning pink pleased her to no end.

"I best be going." Edward opened the door, ducked his head a bit and walked onto the sidewalk.

"I'm glad you came." She wiggled her fingers at him and held her breath until the door closed.

The Winter Social couldn't come soon enough. For the first time in her adult life, she was excited about attending a social event. No one would expect her to serve the punch or wash up when everything was over. She would go as Edward's wife and enjoy the afternoon and evening.

Yes, this new life suited her just fine. New friends, a successful business—now that everyone realized the positive results of her association with Lavinia and Ginger—and a husband who winked at her when he came to her rescue.

Rescue? Did she really need Edward to rescue her from Winston?

No.

Was it nice to know he was there if she did?

Absolutely.

Edward laughed and picked his hat up off the ground. He beat it against his leg to remove the layer of dust it had collected when it was knocked off the table by his worthy opponent in the final arm-wrestling match. It was the one event at the Winter Social all the men enjoyed.

Doc Willis clapped him on the back. "Wouldn'a thought I could beat a man who swings a hammer all day long."

"To be honest, that's probably how you won. I didn't think you could, either." Edward laughed and turned to look for Ellen. He found her among the children eating cookies in the corner. The barn had been set up with sections for each activity. A smaller place than the Willis ranch couldn't hold a crowd this size. The food was along one wall, the games for kids were in one corner, and the men were testing one another's strength in the opposite corner. The ladies were gathered at the tables visiting, the meal long since passed.

"If I can have everyone's attention…" Reverend Dismuke stepped onto a makeshift platform fashioned of hay bales with planks of wood across the top. "It's time for the pie auction."

The men cheered and gathered around the preacher. Someone off to one side held up the first pie.

"Remember, you'll be sharing the pie with the baker, so bid carefully. This pie was made by my wife. I thought we best auction it first, so there's no fighting over it at the end." Several people chuckled, and Reverend Dismuke smiled at Peggy. Not wanting to miss out on the excitement, the ladies had come to stand behind the men. "You all know the money we raise tonight goes to help fund the school for the rest of the year, so bid like the providers you are."

A sporting round of bids followed as several pies were sold to the husbands of the women who baked them. Laughter and teasing filled the atmosphere as the bids went higher and higher.

"This next pie is from a newcomer." Lavinia's pie was held in the air. "It smells mighty fine. You can't see it from where you're standing, but these look like some of the finest pecans of the crop. Miss Aiken, where are you?"

Lavinia tried to hide her face, but Lily pointed her out.

"Who'll start the bidding for this pie?" For a few seconds Lily was afraid no one would bid. She watched Lavinia withdraw into herself. Her arms folded across her chest, and her head hung as she clinched her jaw.

Then a quiet voice came from the opposite side of the barn with a substantial bid. Lily tried to see the bidder, but she was too short. Lavinia peeked up at her.

"Do you know the bidder?" Lily could see her friend's face brighten with relief.

"It's the young man from the general store who invited me to church." Lavinia spoke in hushed tones. "I've seen him in service a couple of times since I started attending, but he hasn't spoken to me."

The reverend called for more bids. After a short round of back and forth, Lavinia's pie sold for a good sum. She put her hand over her mouth to catch a bubbling giggle that threatened to draw attention to her.

Lily smiled and hugged her friend. "You've done it, Lavinia. You've made a place for yourself among the good people of Pine Haven."

"Thank you, Lily. I couldn't have dreamed it without your friendship and encouragement."

A shy cowhand approached holding his newly purchased pie. "Miss Aiken, would you please join me for some pie?"

The two walked toward the tables where everyone had eaten the meal earlier.

"You should be very pleased with yourself." Edward's voice came from behind Lily. "That young lady's life is forever changed for the better because of you."

"God made the difference for her." Lily dashed a happy tear from her lashes. "I just got to be a witness to the transformation."

Edward threw one hand into the air and called out a price. Lily turned to see her pie was up for bids.

An ominous bid came from a spot near the back of the barn. Unnoticed until this moment, Winston Ledford had entered the barn. Lily's mouth dropped open. Several ladies gasped. A low rumble from some of the men signaled their agreement with the ladies.

Lily heard Mrs. Croft's voice above the others. "The nerve of that man! What is he doing here?"

Edward looked at Winston. He held his hand up and topped Winston's bid.

Winston doubled Edward's bid.

The crowd no longer masked their curiosity.

Edward did not look away from Winston. He raised his price again.

Winston countered with another doubling of the offer.

Lily knew it was more than anyone had paid for a pie that night. Not even the wealthiest of ranchers had offered so much money. She leaned in close to Edward and whispered. "It's too much money. He's trying to provoke you."

Edward turned to Reverend Dismuke. "I will pay three times his offer."

"Going, going, gone! Sold to Edward Stone. Thank you for your contribution to the school fund." The crowd applauded. Lily knew it wasn't just for the amount of money raised, but the show of wills they'd witnessed between the two men.

Without hesitation, the preacher asked for the next pie, and everyone's attention moved to the bidding.

"Edward, you didn't have to do that. It's so much money." Lily put her hand on his arm.

He covered it with one of his own and lowered his head so their eyes were level. "There was no way I would let that man buy your pie. You are not for sale." He gave her hand a squeeze. "Would you care to join me for dessert?"

A smile of relief and gratitude crossed her face. "I'd like that. May I ask Ellen to share it with us?"

"You may." Edward released her and went to collect his pie. "I'll be right with you."

Lily saw him head in the direction of Winston Ledford. Somehow she imagined the saloon owner wasn't accustomed to anyone getting the better of him. To see her husband win their contest of wills pleased her immensely. Pleased and excited her. For the first time in her life she hadn't been at the punch bowl. She'd been at the center of attention.

The attention hadn't been fun for her. But the victory Edward claimed meant she was no longer a wallflower. And the sweetness of the pie wouldn't be the only memory her mind would savor when the night ended.

After he confirmed that some of the men were watching Winston Ledford leave the property, Edward started to relax. He paid his bid and collected his pie. Lily and Ellen sat with punch cups when he came to the table.

"Aunt Lily's pie is the best one ever!" Ellen picked up her fork while he cut wedges for everyone.

"Looks like it to me. I've never seen such a fancy crust." He winked at his niece and gave her the first piece.

The three of them laughed and ate their treat in relative privacy, nestled as they were in the corner of a barn filled with people.

Edward had reached for a second slice when Ellen's demeanor started to change.

"Did you eat too fast, Ellen?" Lily must have noticed it, too.

"No." Ellen sniffed, and her eyes swam in fresh tears.

In an instant Edward was beside her, squatting to be level with his niece as she sat on the bench. He touched her forehead with the back of his hand. No fever. "Do you hurt somewhere?"

"Here." She pulled her doll from her pocket and held it to her chest. She sniffled, and the tears fell onto her cheeks.

"Does your tummy hurt? Or has someone hurt your feelings?" Lily asked softly.

"I miss Momma and Papa." She sobbed in earnest now. "Momma loves the socials." Ellen buried her head in his shoulder. "And Papa always buys her pie."

He folded her into his arms and rocked her. Tears soaked his shirt. "Honey, I know. I miss them, too."

Lily reached a hand to rub Ellen's back while he held the child close.

He put his hands on Ellen's shoulders and pushed her back just enough to see her reddened face. "Let's get you home." He'd been afraid this was coming. The child couldn't continue to wonder and wait on her parents. He had to tell her what he knew.

The background noise of others eating pie and laughing had faded away when Ellen started to cry. Now it crashed into his mind like a maddening wave of chaos. He had to get Ellen home. To console her. To protect her. To tell her the truth.

Edward stood, bringing Ellen into his arms like a babe cradled against its mother. "Please see to a ride for Miss Aiken while I get Ellen to the wagon."

He carried Ellen into the night and wrapped her in a blanket on the front seat of the wagon.

Lily joined them, and he leaned to speak softly in her ear. "We need to tell her."

Lily exhaled and her soft, warm breath teased his neck above the collar of his shirt. Her whisper was more faint than his. "Must we? Now?"

He took her hand and gave it a reassuring squeeze. "She'll only get more distraught later if we don't face this."

He felt the answering pressure of her gloved hand in his as she said, "May God give us the words." He turned to Ellen, where she sat on the edge of the seat.

"Ellen, we need to talk about your momma and papa." He held the child's hands in his and looked up into her tearstained face.

"I don't want to, Uncle Edward." She sniffed big and stuck out her bottom lip. "You don't look happy. I don't want to hear anything about them that's not happy."

Lily moved in close beside him and put a hand over his on Ellen's. "Uncle Edward wants to help you understand."

Ellen swallowed a gulp of air. "I'm afraid you're gonna tell me Momma won't come back. Her or Papa."

Edward cleared his throat. "They've been gone a long time, Ellen. Sometimes things happen that can't be helped. If your momma and papa could be here, you know they would."

"They're coming back for me!" Ellen's voice rose in desperation.

Suddenly, Edward couldn't believe his ears.

"I'm here, baby girl."

Ellen squealed and threw her arms wide. Edward

caught her as she lunged from the wagon. He set her down, and she ran into her mother's open arms.

Edward was speechless. Jane was crying and kissing Ellen's face. He put an arm around Jane, thrilled at the sight of his sister. And worried by Wesley's absence.

"How? When?" Surprise at her sudden appearance left him befuddled.

Jane laughed through her tears and spoke to him over the top of Ellen's head. The child had become lodged in her embrace. "I just arrived. I came by wagon with friends. I'll explain it all to you."

He leaned close and asked quietly, hoping Ellen wouldn't hear, "Where's Wesley?"

Ellen leaned back and looked up into her mother's face. "Where's Papa?"

Jane squatted in front of Ellen and put a hand on each of the girl's shoulders. "Honey, Papa wanted so much to come home to you."

"Where is he?" Ellen looked around, searching the shadows of the moonlit night.

Edward's heart broke at the pain he saw on his sister's face. He could only imagine what she'd been through. He put a hand on her shoulder to reassure her.

Jane looked up at Edward and then back to Ellen. "I got very sick. That's why my letters stopped. I was too sick to write, but Papa took good care of me."

"He's a good papa." Ellen's lips trembled. Edward knew her mind was trying to prepare her for what her heart didn't want to hear.

Jane continued, "Yes, he was. No one could have loved you or me more than he did." She took a deep breath. "That's why he never left me while I was sick. But then he got sick, too."

A tear slid down his sister's face. He'd do anything to take from her the sorrow he saw in her eyes.

"Your papa was sicker than I was. He helped me get better, but…" Her words halted. Finally she was able to finish. "Papa couldn't get better. He was just too sick. I'm so sorry, Ellen, but he passed. Last week."

Ellen cried, "No, Momma!" The little girl fell against her mother's shoulder and wailed.

Edward went down on one knee and wrapped the two of them in a hug. He held them while they wept. He sensed Lily behind him and knew she was praying for them. Had it only been minutes before that he'd tried to find the words to prepare Ellen for this possibility?

When Jane was able to calm Ellen to a point that he felt it was best to go home, Edward helped his sister and niece into the back of the wagon. Jane's friends had their wagon nearby, and he arranged for them to bring Jane's things by his home the next day.

He covered Jane and Ellen with a blanket and helped Lily onto the seat beside him. Ellen, worn-out from her tears, fell asleep with her head in her mother's lap.

Lily hadn't said a word since Jane had come upon them while they talked to Ellen. He knew she'd worried over Ellen's reaction, should anything have happened to her parents. Now, they were facing it.

Chapter Seventeen

Edward carried Ellen into the cabin and laid her on her bed. When he came back into the front room, Jane and Lily were introducing themselves.

"His wife?" Jane turned when he came into the room. "I thought you were never getting married."

He looked from his sister to his wife. "A lot happened while you were gone."

"I can see that," Jane said. "It's lovely to meet you, Lily. I wish I'd been here for your wedding."

Lily began, "If you'd been here—"

"I wish you could have been here, too," Edward interrupted. He'd come to stand by Jane and tried to shake his head without Jane noticing. "It was a simple church ceremony. Just after the first of the year." He didn't want Lily to tell Jane the circumstances of their marriage. He didn't want Lily to seem less than a real wife to his sister. Where the need to protect her came from, he couldn't say. Over the time they'd been together, it had just become part of who he was.

Jane looked to Lily. "I'm glad to have a sister."

Lily acknowledged her words with a forced smile.

Edward didn't know what was going on in Lily's mind, but he could see the storm brewing in her violet eyes.

Their whole world had changed tonight. Again.

Having Jane home was a blessing he'd begun to think would never happen. Losing Wesley was a burden he hated for his sister and niece to bear.

Lily finally spoke. "Have you eaten?"

Jane tugged her gloves off. "Not since breakfast, but you don't have to bother. I can grab some bread and a slice of cheese."

"It's no bother. You must be famished from traveling so far." Lily tied on her apron. Edward watched her now-familiar movements as she broke eggs into a bowl.

He took Jane's coat and hung it by the door. "Come sit at the table. I'll get you a cup of coffee, and you can tell me everything."

Sadness filled Jane's face. She sat in Ellen's chair at the table and told them all that had happened since she and Wesley had left Pine Haven. They'd established their business and had hopes of doing well. They made preparation to come for Ellen just before they took ill.

"But the sickness…that was the worst of all." She hung her head. "So many people. Most of our neighbors. It struck our area of the city, and in a matter of days people were sick and dying. The doctor was overwhelmed, though I guess it wasn't as bad as it could have been. They were able to keep people from coming into our part of town. In a matter of weeks, it had died away. It hit the young and old worst. The doctor said because Wesley tended me so long, he was weaker when he got sick." A tear dropped from her lashes. "He died because he was taking care of me."

Edward's heart broke for her. As displeased as he'd

been by their decision to leave Ellen behind, he now realized that to take her would have put her at risk of death. He thanked the Lord for letting her be safe with him.

"I'm so sorry for the loss of your husband." Lily put a plate of scrambled eggs and toast in front of Jane. "He must have loved you dearly."

Jane smiled up at Lily. "He did. The doctor tried to get him to send me to the hospital, but he didn't want me to get worse. He thought being around others would make me sicker. The hospital in our area filled up with patients. In the end, we had to be taken to another hospital."

"How did you have the strength to come after all of that? Why didn't you wire? I would have come for you." Edward hated the thought of her suffering alone.

"I know. That's why I didn't send a telegram." She asked Lily, "Isn't that just like our Edward? He'd drop everything and dash off to help someone else."

Lily turned to him. Her eyes were solemn. "That's one of the first things I learned about him."

Jane continued, "By the time Wesley passed, we'd spent all our money on hospital bills. Wesley had borrowed against the business. I sold it to have the money to pay the undertaker and settle the mortgage."

"Jane, I'm so sorry about Wesley, but don't you worry about you and Ellen." He didn't know what else to say. His sister had gone away dreaming of a better life only to find herself back in the same place, but without her husband and practically without funds.

"We'll get through this." He put a hand on her shoulder. "We always do."

Lily listened to Jane's heart-wrenching story. Watching Edward's compassion for her grief, Lily remembered how kind he'd been to her the night of the fire. He'd rushed into a burning building to save her. And after risking his life for her, he'd pledged himself to her to protect her reputation—and for the sake of his niece. She'd never known anyone more selfless.

He sat at the table listening to his sister's plight, and Lily knew he'd never leave Jane or Ellen without his support and care. Without Wesley to provide for Jane and Ellen, he would take responsibility for them.

Would Jane want to open the bakery now? If she did, what was to become of Lily's Millinery and Finery? There were a couple of vacant buildings in town, but until her father arrived, Lily had no way of securing another location.

Jane and Ellen could sleep in Ellen's room tonight, but that would never do for a permanent arrangement. And Edward couldn't continue to sleep on the floor in front of the fire. He deserved a bed and the privacy of a bedroom in a cabin filled with women.

There were so many questions. And no answers.

Lily's mind swirled with it all. "If you don't mind, I'm going to turn in for the night."

"Thank you for cooking for me, Lily. You'll have to let me return the favor." Jane was a picture of kindness, a woman anyone would love for a sister-in-law.

"She's an amazing cook, Jane. You're in for a real treat." Edward beamed as if he was proud of her. Was he?

"Jane, if you'd like, I think I have something you could use to sleep in for the night." Lily stepped into her room. She pulled a nightgown and robe from her wardrobe. Jane was a bit taller than her, but it would do for a night. When she turned around, Jane was at the bedroom door.

"This is so thoughtful." She accepted the clothes. "I'm sorry for barging into your home like this."

Edward came to stand behind Jane. "You're always welcome in my home."

My home. Did he not consider it to be her home, too? Lily watched them and wondered what her role in his life would be after tonight. Nothing was happening like either of them expected.

Edward asked, "Jane, why don't you sleep with Ellen? We'll figure out something more permanent over the next few days."

"Thank you, Edward. I knew I could count on you." Jane turned and slipped into Ellen's bedroom, closing the door quietly behind her.

"I think I'll say good-night." Lily moved to close the door.

Edward put a hand on the door. "Would you mind sitting up a bit? There's a lot to talk about." He grinned at her. "Please."

This was the playful expression he'd begun to wear over the past few days. He seemed to be inviting her out of her shell and into his life. But all that had changed now.

"For a little while." She went to the stove and poured them each a cup of coffee. They sat at the table, and she cut him another piece of the pie he'd won at the auction. She cringed when she thought of the price he'd paid. "Was it only a few hours ago that we were at a pie auction?"

He used the side of his fork to cut a large bite. "It seems like days instead of hours."

Lily ate a bite of her pie while he polished off most of his piece.

She put her fork on the plate. "What will you do about caring for Jane and Ellen?"

"I guess it depends on what Jane wants to do." He took a drink of coffee. "I'll talk to her about that in the morning."

"It's all so sudden for her. Losing her husband and having a child to raise without a father. It's a lot for any woman."

"I'll be there to help her. She won't be alone like a lot of widows." He pushed his plate toward the center of the table.

"You're very reliable. That must be why she trusted you to care for Ellen while they were gone." She couldn't bring herself to look at him but stared into her coffee. "I'm so heartbroken for that dear child over the loss of her father, but so relieved that her mother is home to care for her."

"Because we thought they were both gone, it is a blessing for Jane to be back."

"I'll help you do whatever you decide is best." He no longer needed her. With Jane home, Ellen had her mother. And with her husband dead, Edward had the added burden of Jane on him. It wasn't fair for him to have to care for her, as well.

"Thank you. You've been a tremendous help with Ellen." He went to put his plate and cup in the basin. "She'll need us all now to help her adjust to her pa being gone."

"I'll pray for her. God knew what He was doing by establishing such a strong relationship between you and Ellen. She'll turn to you more now than ever before." She put her dishes in the basin. "If you don't mind, I'd like to turn in."

He reached for her hand. Had he reached for her this afternoon, she'd have expected a warmth and tenderness at his touch. Tonight, her heart was cold with confusion. Her future once again lay before her, clouded by situations beyond her control.

"The pie was delicious. Worth every penny." He touched her cheek with the back of his other hand, the knuckles rough from hard work. Work he'd have to increase to keep up with his new responsibilities.

Lily had forgotten all about Winston Ledford and his challenge. The music in the barn and the sounds of laughter had faded from her mind. Tonight she heard the echo of her heart as it cried out to be loved by a man who had only married her to care for a child who no longer needed her.

She loved him. More than anyone or anything she'd ever loved in her life. In a way she'd never loved before. Why did her heart spill this truth to her now? When the one she needed didn't need her anymore.

Tomorrow might hold unwelcome changes in her life. She wouldn't let her heart lead her this time. Luther had tempted her with the idea of love. A love he never had for her. Edward had never offered her love. Only his name in exchange for nurturing Ellen.

She stepped out of his reach. "I'm glad you liked the pie. It was for a good cause. The school is important to the community."

Edward put his hand in his pocket. "I see. So you think I bought the pie for the school?"

"No." She twisted her hands together in front of her. She didn't want to hurt him, but if she opened herself to him, only to be rejected later, she didn't think she'd have the courage to move beyond it. "I know you bought the pie to protect me. The same way you married me to protect me."

The grin he'd used to entice her into sharing pie with him moments before was gone.

She finished her thought before she lost her courage. "It's the same way you'll protect Jane and Ellen." She fought back tears. "You're a good man, Edward Stone."

"Lily, are you upset with me? Have I done something wrong?"

"No. You've done everything right." She couldn't bear it if she broke down in front of him. Realizing she loved him had tilted her world on its axis. She needed time to sort it all out. Before she said or did anything to make herself look foolish or needy. The last thing she wanted was for him to take care of her because he had to.

Why didn't she see it before?

All that time when she'd resisted helping others because she faded into the background of life, she'd wanted to be appreciated for who she was—not what she did for others.

She'd done the same thing to Edward. Unknowingly. She couldn't use him. It would make her no different than Luther. Was that how he saw her? Did she look to him like someone who had only accepted his offer of marriage for what she would benefit from it?

Her love for him poured over every thought she had. Nothing was the same anymore. Not the way she felt about him. Not even the way he looked to her was the same. He'd always been handsome. Through the filter of love she saw him for who he really was. Inside. A loving champion. A brave protector.

Used by everyone who could benefit from him.

She wouldn't do that to him. Not anymore. She needed time alone to pray and think.

"I need to go to bed. Please forgive me. I'll do the dishes in the morning." She opened the door and looked back at him. "Good night, Edward."

He stood silent, perplexed by her retreat.

Inside her room, she leaned against the closed door, eyes lifted in prayer.

Lord, help me. I never thought to love him, but I do. What do I do? If he still needed me, we might be able to make something of our marriage. As it is, I can't risk destroying our friendship by letting him know how I feel.

If Jane and Ellen moved out, their marriage would change. Hiding her newly discovered feelings without Ellen acting as a buffer between them would make their marriage more challenging. She could move into Ellen's room and treat him like the friend he had become. Could her heart bear it?

Lily was up early the next morning. Spending the night in anxious prayer had yielded no answers. The only positive thought was Ellen in the arms of her mother. In the end that was the thing that mattered most.

Hoping to avoid questions from Jane, Lily dressed quickly and went to wake Edward. His reaction to Jane's questions about their sudden marriage let her know he didn't want his sister to know the details of their relationship.

She knelt to lean over his sleeping form and wished he loved her. He lay on his back. The steady rise and fall of his chest, coupled with the peaceful expression, made her want to let him rest. Unable to help herself, she reached to move a wisp of hair that fell across his forehead. He stirred, and she snatched her hand away.

"Good morning, Edward," she whispered and put a hand on his shoulder to nudge him a bit. "I thought you'd want to be up before Jane wakes."

He drew in a deep breath and opened his eyes. The cloud of sleep in them cleared to a smile like none he'd ever given her. Light shone in their depths. Without the guard of wakefulness, did he harbor feelings for her, too? "Lily." He lifted his hand and caressed her cheek.

The door to Ellen's room opened, and Jane came into the room. Lily jerked to her feet. Edward leaned up on one elbow.

Jane spoke first. "I'm sorry, I didn't mean to interrupt…" She left the rest of her thought to hang in the tense air.

"You've no need to apologize." Lily tried to think of something else to say. What would her sister-in-law think of her? Edward sleeping on the floor, and his wife sneaking around in the early morning to wake him didn't portray an image of a happy newlywed couple.

Edward lumbered to his feet. "You're not interrupting, Jane." He folded the quilt and tossed it onto the settee. "Lily was just…"

He looked to her for help, but she didn't know what to say. "I was just deciding what to make for breakfast." She hurried to the stove. "How about oatmeal? It's a chilly morning."

The three of them set about their morning routine. No one mentioned the awkwardness of Jane discovering Edward in the front room. Ellen woke while Lily cooked. She came to the table without brushing her hair. Her doll hung over from the crook in her elbow.

Lily tousled her hair. "You need to brush your hair."

"Momma does it for me." Ellen backed away from her touch.

Jane turned from stoking the fire. "Ellen, did Aunt Lily teach you to brush your hair?"

Ellen shot a glance from Lily to her mother. "She did, but you always did it before. I like it when you do it."

Lily turned back to the stove and ladled oatmeal into bowls. Edward didn't need her help with Ellen now that Jane was back. It appeared Ellen didn't need her, either.

Jane spoke to Ellen. "I'll brush your hair tonight before bed as a treat. This morning you will do as your aunt Lily said." Ellen tromped into the bedroom and closed the door. Jane smiled at Lily. "She has always been a mite stubborn. Thank you for teaching her. She has such thick hair, I always found it quicker to do it myself. You've saved me much work in the future."

"Ellen is a sweet child. She likes to have her own way, but she is a dear."

"What a gracious description of my little one." Jane chuckled and came to pour milk for Ellen and coffee for the adults.

Lily liked Jane. She admired the way she spoke to Ellen. She appreciated that Jane hadn't belabored the situation this morning by insisting on knowing why Edward wasn't in the bedroom with his new wife. Jane was considerate, someone Lily would choose for a friend. She hoped Jane wouldn't think less of her if she found out that Edward hadn't wanted to marry her.

Edward came in the front door carrying an armload of firewood. He put the wood on the hearth. "I hope you two are getting to know one another." He brushed his gloves together and pulled them off.

"We are, brother dear." Jane set the platter of ham

Lily had cooked on the table. "You've married quite a nice person. Ellen told me Lily has even taught her to brush her own hair."

He came to the table. "Lily has taught us all a lot. Even taught me and Ellen a bit about cooking." He caught Lily's attention and winked at her again. If he didn't stop this open flirtation, how was she to rein in her heart?

Ellen came out of her room dressed for school with her hair neatly brushed. Jane pulled her into a hug.

"Momma, do I gotta go to school today?" Ellen's eyes were filled with hope for a day at home. She dropped into her seat at the table.

"Not today, moppet. I want to spend every minute of today with you." Jane sat beside her daughter.

Edward prayed and the food was passed around the table. "Jane, we need to make some arrangements for your future."

A pall settled over the table. "I've been thinking about that all the way home from Santa Fe." Jane put her fork down and looked at Ellen. "How would you like to help me open the bakery and run it? We're going to need to earn money, and I could use a good helper."

Ellen swallowed big. "Do you mean it? I can help?" Her eyes filled with tears as her young heart tried again to digest the loss of her father. "But how will we do it without Papa?" She dashed the back of her hand across her eyes. "And Lily has her shop in the bakery now."

Jane looked at Edward and then back to Ellen. "You let the adults work out the details. You just be ready to become a baker." Jane put a hand on Ellen's on the table. "Without Papa here, we'll have to take care of ourselves." Sadness washed over Ellen at the words.

Edward cleared his throat. "I'm going to make certain you're both taken care of."

Lily listened like a stranger in the place she'd come to think of as home. She'd allowed herself to become the mistress of this house, and now she sat listening to Edward pledge himself as provider to his sister and her daughter. Where would she fit in the scheme of things? Did she?

As soon as she could, Lily excused herself and headed to the shop, leaving Edward and his family to plan a future that might not include her. She couldn't sit and listen. Edward would have to tell her later. If Jane was going to take over the building, Lily didn't know what would happen to her business.

With a deep love for Edward filling her heart and mind, she knew the shop wasn't important. Not when her marriage was on the brink. Would he want her out of his life, the same way his sister was about to say she wanted Lily out of her building?

Edward and Jane walked into Lily's shop to the sound of the clanging bell. He rubbed his hands together in the warmth of the room.

Jane looked everywhere at once and spoke softly to herself, "Oh, my. This is lovely."

Lily came through the doorway that led to the workroom. "Good after...noon..." The words died on her lips when she saw him and Jane. Her face was pale, and her eyes were the lightest blue he'd ever seen them.

"We wanted to come by and let you know what we've worked out." He hoped Lily would be as pleased with their decision as he and Jane were.

Lily stopped beside the glass display case that held

her most valuable merchandise and put a steadying hand on the heavy piece of furniture. "I'm ready." She looked as if she was braced for bad news.

Jane burst out with their plans. "I'm going to open my bakery!" She looked around the shop with a smile as big as Texas. He'd wanted Jane to do this before. Watching her excitement confirmed his belief that her own bakery would go a long way toward making her happy again.

Lily balled the hand that held the side of the display case into a fist. Her knuckles grew white. "I'm very happy for you. You deserve a fresh start after all you've been through."

Edward grinned at Lily. "I knew you'd agree. That's what I think, too. It will be something positive that she and Ellen can do together. It's not the life we all hoped they'd have." He put a hand on Jane's shoulder. She smiled in acknowledgment of his sympathy. "But I think it's the best way to move on with their lives."

Lily wrung her hands in front of her skirt. "When do you plan to open?"

Jane had moved to the front window. "Almost immediately. Ellen and I will move in this afternoon."

"That soon?" Lily looked surprised.

"I don't want to put you and Edward out any more than I already have. You've been so gracious to care for Ellen, but I think the sooner she and I get settled into our new life, the sooner she'll accept her father's passing and begin to heal."

Lily paled. "Do you think she's ready for such a big adjustment so soon?"

Edward answered her. "I think it will give her something to keep her mind on. Give her hope." He added,

"Plus, she's been telling her mother about the things you've taught her."

"Where is she?" Lily looked through the front glass as if expecting to see Ellen outside the shop window.

"She's packing her things. She promised to have everything together before Edward and I return, so she can scurry on over," Jane answered. "Edward was kind enough to come along so I could satisfy my curiosity about what you've done with this place. Everything is lovely. Much nicer than I'd imagined it could be."

"I did my best." Lily's voice wavered. "It's a lovely building."

Jane nodded. "The windows were what caught my eye. Beautiful displays are so important for drawing the customers in."

The door opened with a flourish, and the bell announced Ellen's arrival. She flung her arms around her mother. "I'm all finished." She gave Lily a giant smile. "Isn't it wonderful, Aunt Lily? Me and Momma are going to open the bakery at last. She's even gonna let me help name it." She took a deep breath and asked her mother, "Can I start bringing my stuff across the street? It's not too heavy."

Edward laughed. "I'll carry everything over this afternoon." Seeing these three ladies safe and happy was more than he'd dared to dream. His heart still contracted a bit when he looked at Jane with Ellen. He was so grateful God had seen fit to spare Jane. Ellen wouldn't grow up without her loving mother in her life. Edward would do everything he could as her uncle to make up for the void left by her father's passing.

"I'm very happy for you, Ellen." Lily's love for his niece was apparent. "You'll have to let me know which name you decide on. I want to be one of your first customers." Lily looked at him then. He saw the brewing storm in her eyes as they darkened.

He wanted to speak to Lily alone. "Now that you've shared your news, Ellen, why don't you and your mother have lunch at the hotel? I imagine she might even let you have dessert today."

"Can we, Momma? Just the two of us?" Ellen tugged on Jane's hand.

Jane laughed at her daughter's excitement. "If you promise to be on your best manners." She put a hand on Edward's sleeve. "Thank you for all your help. I don't know what I'd have done without you at the bank today. And thank you, Lily, for being so kind. I know my arrival has unsettled your world. I'm grateful for all you've done for Ellen and Edward."

"It has been my joy to spend time with Ellen."

Ellen left her mother's side and went to hug Lily. "I had fun with you, too, Aunt Lily." She released her and went with Jane out of the shop.

Edward watched them go and turned to see Lily wipe a finger under one eye. "Are you crying?" He went to her side.

"I'm fine." She took a step back. "If you'll excuse me, I've quite a lot to think about." She pivoted to go into the workroom. He put a hand on her elbow.

"Lily, tell me what's wrong. I know the news about Wesley isn't what we'd hoped for, but it's almost like a miracle that Jane is home with Ellen."

She kept her back to him. "God was merciful. I know that my father was a rock to me and my sisters after our mother passed. Jane and Ellen will help each other heal. It's good they have the bakery to give them something to look forward to." Her voice caught, and he tugged her elbow until she turned to him.

"What's wrong then?"

"Don't you know?" Lily spread her hands out and spun to the left and right. "All of this. How am I supposed to close my shop in one afternoon? Where will I store everything until I can figure out what to do? And there's the question of Lavinia. Where will she go?" She almost didn't breathe for talking so fast. "I guess she could sleep in Ellen's room tonight, but she can't stay there. I'm sure you'll want me to move my things in there." She stopped and looked at him, despair in her eyes. "Or do you want me to do that this afternoon?" She gasped and choked back a sob. "Or do you want me there at all?"

Her words spun in his ears like a twister. Where had the torrent come from? "Why would you close your shop? And why can't Lavinia stay here?"

"There isn't room upstairs for three people. It's just big enough for Jane and Ellen. And if she wants to open the bakery immediately, I'll have to have my merchandise out of the way." She sighed and looked over his shoulder. "And the sign." Tears filled her eyes, but she didn't let them fall. "It fits so perfectly in this window. I don't know if I can find somewhere new and use it. It's exactly what I wanted. You captured the heart of my designs when you made it." She turned to him. "Do you think you could alter it?" She sniffled on the last words.

"Alter it?" He reached for her hands. "It's fine right where it is."

"But it's going to be a bakery now." Her frown was full of sorrow, not anger.

"Oh, Lily, did you think Jane was going to come in here and run you out?"

"She said she wanted to move in this afternoon. She talked about the display windows and Ellen said she could carry her things across the street."

"All of that is true. Jane loved those windows from the first time we looked at this building. And she is moving this afternoon."

"That's why I've got to figure out what I'm going to do with everything." She stopped crying and stared at him. The strength she'd shown in every situation came to the fore again. "Lavinia will help me." She pulled her hands, but he didn't let her go. He would never let her go.

"Lily, Jane is buying the building between the post office and the bank. I went with her to the bank to arrange a loan to help her until your father arrives and buys the hotel."

A cloud crossed her face. "Two doors down from here?" Her voice was very soft, wary even.

"Yes. It was actually built by the same man who built this place." He leaned close to her. "It has the same display windows."

"It does?" Confusion still filled her face.

"It does." He put a hand on her cheek. "So you don't need to close your shop. Jane is going to start fresh in a new location. She'll still be across the street from me, so I can keep an eye on her and Ellen."

"But what about us?" There was a plea in her words that gave his heart hope. Hope he never thought he'd experience. After a lifetime of working and doing good for others, he'd given up hope of having something wonderful for himself. Somewhere along the way, he'd become content to muddle through life without thinking about all he was missing by being alone.

Since he'd married Lily for the sake of Ellen, he thought this was just a new chapter in the story of his life—with the same ending. He'd solve someone else's problem with little to no thought or benefit for himself.

But his life had changed forever the day he'd married her. When he'd brushed that kiss across her gentle cheek after Reverend Dismuke had spoken the ceremonial words over them, his heart had awakened. Like a new morning with just a twinge of light breaking through the darkness of a long night, the changes had been gradual. The darkness gave way to shadows that were banished in the full light of a new day. Today. The day he knew he loved Lily with every part of who he was.

God, please don't let her dash my hope. I never dreamed You'd bring someone as amazing as Lily into my life. Please let her love me as much as I love her. If not, please let her stay long enough for me to show her how I feel.

Lily didn't know what to think. Or how to feel. She'd gone from contentment with Edward and Ellen the day before to realizing she loved him. Then his sister, a woman who truly needed him, had come into their lives and turned everything upside down.

That wasn't fair. Lily's life had turned upside down when Edward swept her into his arms the night of the fire. No matter how she'd dismissed his kindnesses and attention, he'd won her heart. But did he want it?

Edward squeezed her hands in his. "What about us?" His handsome face crinkled into a smile. "You and me?" The smile grew.

She couldn't hide her biggest fear. "You don't need me anymore."

He pulled her hands together and pressed his lips to her knuckles. "You don't think I need you?"

Her head spun. She couldn't think straight if he kissed her. And those eyes. They drew her into the brown depths. She could see her reflection in the dark center. "You married me for Ellen."

He grew serious. "I did."

Lily didn't realize she was holding her breath. "You didn't lie to me about why you wanted us to marry, but I've grown to believe you would be a part of my life forever. And now you don't need me anymore."

A twinkle danced in his eyes. "What do you intend to do?" He released her hands.

"I guess I could move into Ellen's room, unless you want me to move here with Lavinia." She hadn't had time to think.

"I don't want you to do that."

"But with Jane here, you don't need me." She braced herself for his response. How could she survive without him? He'd gotten inside her thoughts. Her prayers. Her dreams.

Edward leaned back a bit. "Do I need you? Will I be able to take my next breath without you?"

Lily stumbled a step away from him. Catching one hand in his, he righted her. She didn't speak.

"I will. But I can guarantee you, that breath won't be as sweet. I'll get hungry tomorrow, and I'll eat. But I won't be satisfied."

He tugged on her hand. "I can still see, but without you, nothing is as beautiful."

Lily's mind reeled with a dance she never thought

she'd dance when she'd watched life pass her by from behind a punch bowl in East River. She seemed to melt in front of him. An aching, slow dissolving of the fear of his rejection.

He took advantage of this rare moment of her silence. "When you offered friendship to Miss Aiken and Mrs. Jones, I thought you were taking too much of a risk." His smile was so distracting. The words tumbled from his lips. She must concentrate. In the space of just a few minutes, her world spun around. The nuances still unclear, she forced her focus on his words.

"You proved me wrong." He smiled and dropped his hand to her waist. "When you didn't want to tell Ellen that her parents were probably not coming back, I thought you were refusing to face reality and trying to protect Ellen from the inevitable truth. To be honest, I'd given up hope of Jane coming home again. The letters had stopped. Then the telegraph came saying they'd been gravely ill and couldn't be found."

She wanted to stanch the flow. His heart had been evident from the first day they met, from the minute she felt it beating in his chest when he carried her out of the fire. Only a selfless man would care like he did. For Ellen. For the church. Even for Mrs. Croft in all her orneriness.

"Edward."

He shook his head to silence her. "I didn't think they were coming back. Over and again you've shown hope and faith." He released her and stepped back.

She tried to breathe. To take in every word. To embrace the hope he was talking about. Hope she'd relinquished in the dark of last night.

He took her hand and stared into her eyes. "You

taught me by example. So much so, I'm going to take a big step for me." He reached to tuck a strand of hair behind her ear, the touch gentle and full of caring. "I'm going to have faith you'll be willing to risk your happiness with someone who's settled with contentment for too long. I don't just need you. I love you." He pulled her hand back to his lips and brushed the knuckles with a promise.

She found her voice. "I was so weary of helping others all the time. That's why I made the needlework of the verse in the workroom. I had to remember to care for others more than I care for myself. I got lost taking care of others before." She put her other hand in his and pulled them together between the two of them as she leaned closer. "But I've learned that when I help others, I'm becoming a better person. You've shown me the joy of helping others. You sacrificed your life to take care of Ellen—and then to marry me and save my reputation in this town. When I took care of my father, I was happy to do it, but I got tired. Taking care of Ellen was a joy. Taking care of you will be my life's delight. I love you."

She leaned away from him and warned, "I'm never going to be able to avoid controversy. If I see someone in need, it doesn't matter to me what people will think if I help them."

Edward gathered her into his arms. He kissed her temple. "That's one of my favorite things about you."

All the breath swooshed from her when he dropped to one knee, taking both her hands in his. "Will you stay married to me, so we can spend our days loving and caring for each other?"

His eyebrows wrinkled his forehead as he waited.

"On one condition." Lily couldn't believe this was

happening. How did the loneliest woman in East River become the happiest woman in Pine Haven?

"What would that condition be?" Dimples came into view, teasing her for an answer.

"Only if you promise to catch me when I fall."

"I promise." And he proved his word by pulling her off balance into his waiting arms.

Epilogue

March 1881

The day was finally here. The morning train would arrive soon.

Edward reached to help Lily from the wagon. The feel of her waist in his hands as he set her to the ground never grew old. How had he managed to snare such a lovely woman?

"You can let go now." Lily tapped him on the shoulder.

"I don't want to." He winked and grinned.

Ellen ran up the sidewalk with Speckles in his basket. The kitten dug his claws into the wicker, seemingly accustomed to her boisterous ways. Ellen had convinced her mother that Speckles should live with them.

"I can't wait to meet your papa." The child gave Lily a hug. "Uncle Edward says he's real nice."

Laughter bubbled in Lily's throat. "He is. I think your uncle Edward might be just a bit nervous to meet him again today."

"He might be nervous, but Uncle Edward ain't never

scared." Ellen skipped over to a nearby bench and sat playing with Speckles.

Edward covered the hand Lily tucked into his elbow with one of his own. "I know God brought you here. The letters your father and I have exchanged since our marriage have been pleasant. I see no reason to be nervous." Funny how tight his collar felt as he said the words. Mr. Warren had agreed for them to marry, but it was the first time he'd meet the man as his son-in-law.

Winston Ledford stepped through the door of the depot onto the platform.

"Ledford." Edward greeted the man, trying to follow Lily's example of being hopeful that people could change.

Edward felt Lily's reassuring squeeze on his arm. "Hello, Mr. Ledford."

"Stone, Mrs. Stone." Winston touched the brim of his hat with two fingers.

"I hear you two are the guests of honor at a big shindig today."

"We are," Lily answered for them. "My father is hosting a celebration of our marriage. You're welcome to come. We want to share how God has blessed us with all our friends and neighbors."

"No, thank you, Mrs. Stone. You may have won Lovey over to your Bible ways, but not me."

"You'll be in our prayers," Lily countered in her true Christian fashion, loving people who didn't know they needed to be loved.

"Don't know as I can stop you from praying, but don't expect to see me in your church." Winston Ledford made his way to the edge of the building and disappeared around the corner.

"Some people take longer than others to realize God loves them." Edward pulled her close. "Don't give up. You won me over."

"You didn't need winning over." She smiled at him. "You just needed to remember how big God's love is."

Jane joined them on the platform. "Ellen insisted we be here for your reunion with your family." His sister embraced Lily. "I think reunions are wonderful." She smiled at Ellen as she bounded up to them.

"I'm especially pleased to meet the man who made it possible for me to stay in Pine Haven. Because of his purchase of the hotel, I had the funds to open the bakery." She kissed Ellen on the top of her head.

"Momma lets me work in the bakery, too. Momma's Bakery will be mine when I grow up."

Lily smiled at Ellen. "Tell me again how you chose the name for the bakery." She knew her niece loved to share the story.

"I always called it Momma's Bakery. She makes the best bread and cakes I ever ate, and everybody loves her cooking. Your store has your name on it, so Momma should have her name on the bakery."

Edward rubbed Speckles behind the ears. "I'm relieved to have you back in town, Jane, and to know you're staying. Don't know what I'd do without Ellen to make me smile."

Lily added, "I'm glad you found a good location. My shop is doing so well, with Lavinia's promise to stay on and help, I'm able to keep up. I wasn't sure how I'd handle having to move."

A whistle blew in the distance. The train would arrive in minutes.

Edward pulled Lily aside.

"I love you." He whispered the words to her. "Are you ready?"

The violet of her eyes told him she was. "Yes." She lifted a gloved hand to touch the side of his face. "Lavinia is closing the shop now. Daisy and her family will meet us at the hotel. They thought Papa would want a moment to greet his new son-in-law before the celebration. Daisy can hardly wait to tell him and Jasmine about their coming addition. She didn't want to take away from our moment. So much joy for Papa in one day."

He put an arm around her shoulders. The sweet scent of her hair filled his senses. "I've been thinking about something."

She turned to look at him, their faces almost touching. "What would that be?"

"With Jane and Ellen moving into their new home over the bakery, it's been awfully quiet at our house."

"It has been." She leaned against his shoulder, and he put his other arm around her.

"Maybe we need to give Ellen a cousin or two." She jerked her face to his. Pink flooded her cheeks.

"I'd like that very much." She stepped up to kiss his cheek.

"Is that so?" He grinned at her. "Before I met you, I thought I'd spend the rest of my days alone or with Ellen."

Lily took a step back and stumbled. He caught her by the elbows and settled her onto her feet.

"God always puts someone in your life to love you." The softness of her answer pulled him in. "And someone for you to love."

* * * * *

Dear Reader,

I hope you enjoyed *The Marriage Bargain*. Lily's need to be valued for more than what she could do for others, and Edward's determination to protect his young niece, are both reasonable objectives. Motivation is important for any goal to be valuable.

Corrupt motives can tempt anyone. We see Mrs. Croft's motivation as, at best, a curious soul, at worst, a nosy and interfering neighbor. Jane and Wesley were driven to succeed. Lily was motivated to take Winston Ledford's money in response to the way he treated her.

God often reminds me to question my personal motives for things. Even when they are pure, my methods can be faulty. Lily learned this when she determined to start a new life and wanted to protect herself from becoming lost in another person's needs.

I pray the characters in *The Marriage Bargain* will remind you to love even when it costs you, to reserve judgment on situations you only see from the outside, to pursue the dreams God has given you and to recognize the people God has put in your life to love you—and to be loved by you.

Visit angelmoorebooks.com for the latest news and to connect with me on social media.

God bless you.
Angel Moore

REQUEST YOUR FREE BOOKS!

2 FREE INSPIRATIONAL NOVELS
PLUS 2 *FREE* MYSTERY GIFTS

Love Inspired® HISTORICAL

YES! Please send me 2 FREE Love Inspired® Historical novels and my 2 FREE
mystery gifts (gifts are worth about $10). After receiving them, if I don't wish to receive
any more books, I can return the shipping statement marked "cancel." If I don't cancel,
I will receive 4 brand-new novels every month and be billed just $4.99 per book in the
U.S. or $5.49 per book in Canada. That's a saving of at least 17% off the cover price.
It's quite a bargain! Shipping and handling is just 50¢ per book in the U.S. and 75¢ per
book in Canada.* I understand that accepting the 2 free books and gifts places me under
no obligation to buy anything. I can always return a shipment and cancel at any time.
Even if I never buy another book, the two free books and gifts are mine to keep forever.

102/302 IDN GH6Z

Name	(PLEASE PRINT)	
Address		Apt. #
City	State/Prov.	Zip/Postal Code

Signature (if under 18, a parent or guardian must sign)

Mail to the **Reader Service**:
IN U.S.A.: P.O. Box 1867, Buffalo, NY 14240-1867
IN CANADA: P.O. Box 609, Fort Erie, Ontario L2A 5X3

Want to try two free books from another series?
Call 1-800-873-8635 or visit www.ReaderService.com.

---

* Terms and prices subject to change without notice. Prices do not include applicable
taxes. Sales tax applicable in N.Y. Canadian residents will be charged applicable taxes.
Offer not valid in Quebec. This offer is limited to one order per household. Not valid
for current subscribers to Love Inspired Historical books. All orders subject to credit
approval. Credit or debit balances in a customer's account(s) may be offset by any other
outstanding balance owed by or to the customer. Please allow 4 to 6 weeks for delivery.
Offer available while quantities last.

Your Privacy—The Reader Service is committed to protecting your privacy. Our
Privacy Policy is available online at www.ReaderService.com or upon request from
the Reader Service.

We make a portion of our mailing list available to reputable third parties that offer
products we believe may interest you. If you prefer that we not exchange your name with
third parties, or if you wish to clarify or modify your communication preferences, please
visit us at www.ReaderService.com/consumerschoice or write to us at Reader Service
Preference Service, P.O. Box 9062, Buffalo, NY 14240-9062. Include your complete
name and address.

LIH15

SPECIAL EXCERPT FROM

Love Inspired HISTORICAL

Booming Cowboy Creek has everything a man could need—except for women. But when a group of mail-order brides arrive, town founder Daniel Gardner is shocked to see Leah Swann, the girl he used to love. She's a widow now, needing a husband to care for her... and for the baby she has on the way.

Read on for a sneak preview of
Cheryl St.John's WANT AD WEDDING,
the exciting first book in the new miniseries
COWBOY CREEK,
available April 2016 from Love Inspired Historical.

"Gentlemen, please make a path and escort our brides forward!"

A smattering of applause followed his request, and from the outer edge of the platform, the crowd parted unevenly, allowing three figures in ruffles and flower-bedecked hats to make their way through the gathering to the stack of crates. Daniel jumped down beside Will and they stood on either side of the group of ladies.

Daniel removed his hat, and every cowboy doffed his own. "Welcome to Cowboy Creek." He glanced aside. "We're still missing someone."

"Mrs. Swann was with us a moment ago," the petite young woman beside him said. "She must have become lost in the crowd somewhere."

"Let the lady through!" Daniel called, standing as tall as he could manage and peering above the crowd. He was thinking that perhaps he would need to get back on the stack of crates, when he spotted a blue feathered hat on a pale gold head of hair. "There she is. Mrs. Swann! Let her through."

The poor woman steadied her wisp of a hat atop her head with one white-gloved hand and turned this way and that, speaking to men as she choreographed her way through the crowd. Disengaging herself from the attentions of an overeager cowboy, she nearly stumbled forward. Daniel caught her elbow to steady her.

"Oh! Thank you. This is quite a reception!" She glanced up. Cornflower blue eyes rimmed with dark lashes opened wide in surprise. The world stood still for a moment. The crowd noise faded into the void. "Daniel?"

Daniel's gut felt as though he'd been standing right on the tracks and stopped the locomotive with his body. "Leah Robinson?"

She was as pretty as ever. Prettier maybe, her face having lost the roundness of girlhood and her skin and bone structure having smoothed into a gentle comeliness.

Mrs. Swann was Leah Robinson, one of his best friends before the war. Will had once shown him a wedding announcement from a Chicago newspaper, and all these years Daniel had pictured her just as she had been back then, full of youth and vitality, and married to the army officer she'd chosen. That had been a lifetime ago. So what was she doing traveling to Cowboy Creek with their mail-order brides?

Don't miss WANT AD WEDDING
by Cheryl St.John, available April 2016 wherever
Love Inspired® Historical books and ebooks are sold.

www.LoveInspired.com

LIHEXP0316